# ETHICS
## Theory and Practice

*Edited by*

**Manuel Velasquez**

*and*

**Cynthia Rostankowski**

PRENTICE HALL, Englewood Cliffs, New Jersey 07632

*Library of Congress Cataloging in Publication Data*

Main entry under title:

Ethics, theory and practice.

Includes bibliographical references.
1. Ethics—Addresses, essays, lectures.   2. Social
ethics—Addresses, essays, lectures.   I. Velasquez,
Manuel G.   II. Rostankowski, Cynthia
BJ1012.E896   1985      170      84–15945
ISBN 0–13–290487–X

Cover design: Wanda Lubelska/Filip Pagowski
Manufacturing buyer: Harry P. Baisley

 © 1985 by Prentice-Hall, Inc.
A Paramount Communications Company
Englewood Cliffs, New Jersey 07632

Printed in the United States of America

20 19 18 17 16

ISBN 0-13-290487-X

Prentice-Hall International (UK) Limited, *London*
Prentice-Hall of Australia Pty. Limited, *Sydney*
Prentice-Hall Canada Inc., *Toronto*
Prentice-Hall Hispanoamericana, S. A., *Mexico*
Prentice-Hall of India Private Limited, *New Delhi*
Prentice-Hall of Japan, Inc., *Tokyo*
Simon & Schuster Asia Pte. Ltd., *Singapore*
Editora Prentice-Hall do Brasil, Ltda., *Rio de Janeiro*

*This book is dedicated to Manuel E. Velasquez, Manuel Velasquez's father, and Allen Leinwand, Cynthia Rostankowski's spouse.*

# CONTENTS

# PREFACE

Most general ethics texts do one of two things: Some provide an introduction to ethical theory by treating various normative theories in depth (such as utilitarianism, natural law, and so on) but provide little or no practical application. Others focus on discussions of current moral controversies (such as abortion, euthanasia, and so on) but lack a thorough treatment of the ethical theories that underlie these discussions. This text remedies both of these defects by combining a thorough development of theoretical normative ethics with an extensive survey of current moral issues that shows how normative theory is applied in practice.

We have divided the text into two parts. The first is a section on ethical theory in which four theories—natural law, Kantian theory, utilitarianism, and social contract theory—are treated in separate chapters. Each chapter in this first part contains a classical reading as well as a contemporary one, and each chapter is introduced by a case study that serves to illustrate relevant features of the theory under consideration. Using the case as background, each chapter provides an introductory explanation of the normative theory.

The second part of the text is comprised of readings on ten ethical issues: torture, nuclear war, suicide, abortion, euthanasia, sexual ethics, aid for the needy, sexism and racism, capital punishment, and the environment. Each of the chapters in this part treats a single issue, and each is introduced by a case study and a discussion of the significant ethical concerns involved in the case. The readings in each of these chapters have been selected to illustrate the applications of the four theories introduced in the first part. Thus the student not only comes to understand ethics theoretically, but also becomes familiar with practical applications of the theories in terms of specific issues and actual cases.

Chapters One and Six serve as introductions to the materials that follow them. Chapter One considers the general nature of ethical reasoning. Ethical relativism and emotivism are examined in this chapter in order to highlight the role of reason and argument in ethical decision making. In Chapter Six, by means of the ethical issue of torture, the student is led through applications of the various approaches to ethical decision making provided by the ethical theories that the text has presented. Once the student has become familiar with the process of applying theory to practice, he or she is then ready to proceed through other issues and to develop expertise in applying ethical theory, as well as in analyzing relevant ethical issues and understanding what follows from the consistent application of theory to practice.

We have edited the readings substantially to make them relevant to the issues that are treated. For this reason, some important but tangential arguments have been omitted. Also, we have left out most footnotes, retaining only those that are important for understanding an argument or for a bibliographical citation. By eliminating everything that is not essential to the issues being discussed, we hope to avoid confusing the beginning student.

It should be clear from the above that this text is intended for the entry-level college student. No sophistication in the study of ethics is presumed, although an understanding of and familiarity with the issues themselves are expected. We see the reader as a young adult of the last quarter of the twentieth century, one who is aware of the moral controversies of the world in which we live, but who may be puzzled and confused about how best to approach them.

During the last few years we have found that most students come to college and enroll in courses because they are looking for answers. This presents a particular problem for those of us who teach philosophy, because our subject does not lend itself to providing answers but rather to raising thought-provoking questions and to examining in a critical manner various reasoned approaches to the questions. This dichotomy between the goal of the student and the nature of philosophy helped prompt us to write this book.

The student's search for answers can be met in at least two ways: First, the student can be given *facts*—for example, *that* Mercury is the planet nearest the sun, or *that* the United States ranks only twelfth with respect to the prevention of infant mortality. Second, the student can be provided with an understanding of *method*—for example, *how* to solve problems in mathematics, or *how* to proceed correctly in carrying out a chemistry experiment. Now there are answers of the first sort to be had in philosophy: Kant said *this*, Mill said *that*. But these are not the substance of philosophizing. Knowing that Kant or Mill said this or that is important only insofar as one knows and *understands* the significance of the statement as a jumping-off point for thought. However, the study of philosophy can provide the student with meaningful answers of the second sort: It provides the student with knowledge of how to reason, how to assess, how to criticize, and how to arrive at his or her own rational decisions. And what application of rational decision making can be more relevant than morality?

Morality has to do with actions freely performed that significantly harm or benefit ourselves or others. Every person is fundamentally concerned with his or her well-being and usually with the well-being of others. Since ethics is the philosophical study of that which is of fundamental interest to every normal human, and since ethics, conceived of as providing reasoned methods of moral decision making, can be acutely relevant to today's college student, we feel that ethics is a particularly apt discipline for introducing the college student to philosophy.

No textbook, nor the best instruction in the world, can teach a student to be ethical, but a teacher can aspire to remove some of the confusion that confronts today's student. This text is an outgrowth of that aspiration. If clarity and understanding are achieved, then the text does what it was intended to do.

We are grateful to many people for their generous assistance in this endeavor. Special thanks go to the Jesuit community of the University of Santa Clara, which provided continuing support to Manuel Velasquez; also to Allen Leinwand, Cynthia Rostankowski's spouse, for moral and practical support and for much useful advice on the preparation and content of the text. Also, we appreciate the comments and criticisms of Leon Hooper and William Spohn, both of whom read versions of the entire text and provided many valuable insights. We extend our gratitude also to the anonymous reviewers from Prentice-Hall, whose objectivity and candor put us in touch with our idiosyncrasies and assisted us in either overcoming or selecting among them. Thanks also go to our ever-patient department secretary, Mrs. Shiela Speciale, who assisted in every phase of the preparation of the manuscript. And last but by no means least, we wish to thank the many students in our classes who were the "test subjects," who read and responded to the several versions of the manuscript as it evolved. All the people mentioned above caught many of our mistakes and corrected them for us, and set us on the path of truth when they caught us going astray. The errors that remain are our responsibility. If nothing else, preparing an ethics text has made us understand the meaning of responsibility.

# CHAPTER ONE
# THE NATURE OF ETHICS

Tobias Schneebaum was born and raised in New York City. In 1955 he traveled to Peru on a Fulbright grant and there, while exploring the jungle, he met a primitive tribe of natives who took him in and made him one of their own:

> It was the fourth day and I was walking along munching on fried bits of yucca that I had soaked in a stream to soften. . . . I made out a group of men, their bodies variously painted in black and red, looking tiny against the gigantic backdrop of the jungle that stretched so high above them. No one moved; no one turned his eyes away or looked anywhere but straight at me. . . . This was the beginning of my meeting with the Akaramas, and now, living within their lives, I have become what I have always been and it has taken a lifetime, all of my own life, to reach this point, where it is as if I know finally that I am alive. . . . His name was Yoreitone, he said. He was the chief and he had come to me now to tell me how happy he was at my arrival. . . . "You have come a long way and you will rest with us. . . . We are content that you have come and you will remain." . . . Now I can answer, "I have come a long way and I am happy to rest with you."[1]

Schneebaum lived among the Akaramas for a long period of time, adopting their dress, food, habits, and way of life. He became so deeply

1. Tobias Schneebaum, *Keep the River On Your Right* (New York: Grove Press, 1969), pp. 65, 66, 71. Reprinted by permission of Grove Press, Inc., and Don Congdon Associates, Inc. Copyright © 1969 by Tobias Schneebaum.

enmeshed in their world that he eventually came to feel that only among the Akaramas had his life ever had any real meaning and happiness:

> And coming upon my people, now my lovers, my friends, I shed my past as I did my clothes. . . . I absorbed them through my flesh, an osmosis whereby they came into me, inside me, ran along with my bloodstream, became white and red corpuscles, the air that entered me, the food of my gullet and stomach, crept along my dermis like a second skin. They entered into my pores. . . . I continue and will forever love them. . . . In that past life of mine . . . I set myself apart, seeing no pleasure in the marriage covenant, or in a TV set or bridge or in owning any kind of car. And then I came out here and for the first time joined a real community; . . . always before my coming here I had searched for some filling, as if there had been within me such a vast emptiness that my whole being, my whole physical self and my soul, were together in search of some region then not known to me.[2]

Schneebaum had so much affection for the Akaramas that he eagerly accepted all their customs and practices. Then one day the tribesmen took him on a raid of a neighboring village:

> The smell of smoke drifted toward us and I heard the muffled sounds of a village, not our own. My companions, twenty-three of them, went on in single file, and then broke into groups as the forest opened into a clearing, each group moving toward one of the several huts. . . . Great cries of EEEE-eeee!! hit the air and ears as we ran into a fire-lit hut and animal arrows in front of my eyes were used as spears, and axes split into skulls. I stood and watched, no word or sound from me, but shaking, trembling with cold, my breathing coming in gasps. No time was passing, but seven men lay there dead, bellies and chests open, still pouring out hot blood, heads crushed and dripping brain, while women huddled far in a corner, chanting in deep moans and holding the fright-filled faces of their children into the red paint of their breasts. . . .
> We did not sleep that night, but walked on until the early morning [carrying the dead men back with us]. When we reached our river . . . we washed, and then we rested. In the light of day, in the thoughts that ran through me, I could not sleep, but rested my head on [my friend] Michii's chest, with [my other friend] Darinimbiak's legs woven with mine. It was evening, and I had dozed at times before I felt Michii move out from under me and we three got up and crossed with all the others to where fires were burning in the open and the human flesh [of the dead men] was already roasting. . . . Four got up, one picked a heart from the embers, and they walked into the forest. Small groups of others rose, selected a piece of meat, and disappeared in other directions. . . . Michii [took a heart,] looked up at the moon and showed it to the heart. He bit into it as if it were an apple, taking a large bite, almost half of the heart, and chewed down several times, spit it into a hand, separated the meat into six sections and placed some into the mouths of each of us. We chewed and swallowed. He did the same with the other half of the heart. He turned Darinimbiak onto his stomach, lifted his hips so that he crouched on all fours. Darinimbiak growled. Mayaarii-ha! Michii growled. Mayaarii-ha!, [he repeated, and] bent down to lay himself upon Darinimbiak's back and entered him. . . .
> I am a cannibal.[3]

2. Ibid., pp. 69, 70, 110, 111, 180.
3. Ibid., pp. 102, 103, 105, 106, 107, 110.

The wanton killing of the innocent villagers, the cannibalism, and the ritual homosexuality that Schneebaum encountered among the Akaramas are obvious examples of activities that violate our own morality. That is, they violate the beliefs most Americans have about what is morally right and wrong and morally good and evil. Ethics, the subject of this book, can be defined as the study of morality in this sense. It is a systematic inquiry into the beliefs we have and the judgments we make about what is morally right and wrong and morally good and evil. It is an inquiry that attempts to answer the questions, "What kinds of conduct are morally right or wrong?" and "What things are good and what are evil?"[4]

How did Schneebaum perceive the morality of the killings and cannibalism among the Akaramas? The question is difficult to answer. He clearly felt extreme discomfort and confusion. Yet he joined them and ate roasted human flesh when it was offered to him. Why? Perhaps because, as he himself tells us, he had come to feel a deep love for the tribe and wanted desperately to be a part of their community. His decision, in other words, was apparently based on emotion: on his feelings for the Akaramas, on his desire for acceptance by them, and on his willingness to go along with the norms of this group.

Reliance on emotions and on group norms is one way of settling moral issues.[5] But it is a method that contrasts sharply with the approach used in ethics. For in saying that ethics is a systematic inquiry into right and wrong, we are saying that it is an inquiry that proceeds through the rational and critical examination of the reasons, arguments, and theories that can be given to show that one type of behavior is morally right or that another is morally wrong. In short, ethics tries to answer moral questions by appealing to rational considerations and not to emotions or to the norms of this or that group.

## THE CLASSICAL VIEW OF ETHICS:
### Plato's *Crito*

The attempt to settle moral questions by the use of rational methods has a long history. Twenty-three hundred years ago, the Greek philosopher Socrates, whom Plato describes in his "dialogues," argued that before acting, a person ought to consider the arguments for and against various alternatives and, disregarding "the opinions of the many," he should be "guided by reason." In the selection from Plato's dialogue, *Crito*, which is the first reading in this chapter, Socrates is awaiting execution for crimes against the state, of which he is innocent. His friends have devised a plan to help him escape and Socrates considers reasons for and against going

---

4. For an excellent and readable discussion on the subject of ethics see William K. Frankena, *Ethics*, 2nd ed. (Englewood Cliffs, N.J.: Prentice-Hall, 1973).

5. For a psychological study of the adequacy of following group norms see L. Kohlberg, "The Claim to Moral Adequacy of a Highest Stage of Moral Judgment," *Journal of Philosophy*, vol. 70 (1973), pp. 630–46; Kohlberg's approach to moral psychology may be more fully studied in T. Lickona, ed., *Moral Development and Behavior* (New York: Holt, Rinehart & Winston, 1976).

along with their scheme. Although the state is wrong in condemning him, Socrates points out that to do wrong in order to save oneself from a wrongful deed is itself a wrongful deed, and one ought never knowingly do wrong regardless of what "the many" believe. Further, by escaping, Socrates would be disobeying the laws of the state and, if the laws could speak, they would point out that such disobedience would be wrong for three reasons: "first, because in disobeying us he is disobeying his parents; secondly, because we are the authors of his education; thirdly, because he has made an agreement with us that he will duly obey our commands." It is clear from the dialogue that Plato has three arguments in mind here: (1) The laws of the state are like a parent to Socrates since they provided the marriage and family laws that made it possible for him to be born; since parents ought to be obeyed, the laws ought to be obeyed. (2) Socrates benefited and took advantage of the education and other goods the laws of the state had to offer; in fairness, he ought now to do his part by rendering obedience to those laws. (3) By freely choosing to remain in the state, Socrates tacitly agreed to obey its laws; since agreements ought to be kept, Socrates now ought to obey the law that condemns him to death. Socrates concludes, therefore, that to save himself would be wrong, as shown by these arguments.[6]

Thus, Socrates provides a classical example of the rational methods ethics uses. When faced with a moral question about what one ought to do (for example, "Ought I obey the law?"), one lines up the rational arguments relevant to the issue (for example, "Everyone ought to do what they agree to do; citizens tacitly agree to obey the law; therefore, citizens ought to obey the law"), and then impartially accepts the conclusion supported by the strongest arguments (for example, "I ought to obey the law even if it has condemned me to death").

Regardless of what we might think of the strengths and weaknesses of the arguments that convince Socrates, it is clear that for him and Plato moral questions must be settled by rational methods. They do not rely on emotion or on conventional group norms (or, as Socrates says, on "the opinions of the many") when determining what one ought to do. Instead they rely on rational argumentation.

## A CONTEMPORARY VIEW OF ETHICS:
### Edward Westermarck's "Ethical Relativity"

The classical view that ethics can be a rational enterprise is frequently criticized. One of the main arguments against it is the objection that moral right and wrong depend not on reason, but on one's culture. Consider the Akaramas' raid of the neighboring village, and the killings, cannibalism,

---

6. Plato's views on morality are more fully discussed in Terence Irwin, *Plato's Moral Theory: The Early and Middle Dialogues* (Oxford: Oxford University Press, 1977). Plato's *Crito* is analyzed in R. E. Allen, *Socrates and Legal Obligation* (Minneapolis: University of Minnesota Press, 1980) and A. D. Woozley, *Law and Obedience: The Arguments of Plato's "Crito"* (Chapel Hill, N.C.: University of North Carolina Press, 1979).

and homosexuality that Schneebaum witnessed and in some of which he participated. Were these actions morally wrong or morally right? Although in our culture most people see them as wrong, it is clear that the Akaramas did not. Is morality, then, relative to a person's culture? Do right and wrong, and good and evil, depend on the culture in which one happens to live?

In thinking about these questions, many people accept the sociological theory known as "cultural relativism," the view that different cultures have completely different beliefs about morality. The Akaramas' culture, for example, clearly has different beliefs from ours about killing innocent villagers and cannibalizing their remains.

Some people then go on to adopt the more radical and more controversial philosophical theory known as "ethical relativism," which holds that since different cultures have diverse moral beliefs, there is no way to decide whether an action is morally right or wrong other than by asking whether the people of this or that culture believe it is morally right or wrong. That is, ethical relativism is the view that if the members of a culture believe a certain sort of action is morally right, then it really is morally right to perform that kind of action in that culture. By the same token, if the members of another culture believe the same sort of action is morally wrong, then it really is morally wrong to perform it in that other culture. Thus, although cannibalism and killing of the innocent is wrong in America, there is nothing wrong with it if it is done in Peru. Consequently, according to this theory, to the extent that Tobias Schneebaum had become part of the Akaramas' culture, it was not really wrong for him to participate in these activities.[7]

Ethical relativism should not be confused with cultural relativism. The former is a highly controversial philosophical theory, while the latter is a widely accepted sociological description of some important differences between cultures. While ethical relativism tries to give an answer to the ethical question, "What actions are really morally right?" cultural relativism only gives an answer to the question, "What actions do different cultures believe are morally right?"

The selection by Edward Westermarck entitled "Ethical Relativity" is taken from his book of the same title and is an attempt to show that ethical relativism is true. Westermarck, a sociologist and philosopher, begins by pointing out that moral judgments vary from culture to culture. Some of these variations seem to be the result of variations in the "external conditions of life" that different societies face. Variations that depend on external conditions of life (including killing of the aged and infanticide), Westermarck argues, do not show that "there is no objective standard of morality." Two different societies may both adhere to the same

---

7. For an anthology of articles on ethical relativism, see John Ladd, ed., *Ethical Relativism* (Belmont, Calif.: Wadsworth, 1973). For a readable discussion of the problems surrounding the issue of ethical relativism, see Richard Brandt, *Ethical Theory* (Englewood Cliffs, N.J.: Prentice-Hall, 1959), ch. 11.; see also Paul W. Taylor, "Four Types of Ethical Relativism," *Philosophical Review*, vol. 62 (1954), pp. 500–16, and Carl Wellman, "The Ethical Implications of Cultural Relativity," *Journal of Philosophy*, vol. 60 (1963), pp. 169–84.

standards of morality, but external circumstances may force one society to pursue these standards through one set of customs while the other society pursues them through a different set. For example, two societies may both hold that survival of the community is a moral standard that should be pursued. But short food supplies may force one society to pursue community survival by adopting the custom of abandoning the aged during times of hardship, while adequate food supplies may allow the other society to pursue community survival through customs that do not allow such acts. Thus, although these two societies have different customs about the permissibility of abandoning the aged, they are both pursuing the same underlying moral standard: community survival. The fact that these two societies make different moral judgments about abandoning the aged does not show that there is no objective moral standard that both societies must follow.

Similarly, Westermarck argues, one cannot show that there are no objective moral standards by pointing to the different moral opinions societies have if those differences arise from different religious beliefs. (Westermarck argues that the different moral opinions societies have about suicide, human sacrifice, and homosexuality have arisen from the different religious beliefs of these societies.) Here again, two societies may both be pursuing the same moral standard, but their different religious beliefs may lead them to pursue it through different customs.

Westermarck claims, however, that many cultures differ in the extent to which it is believed to be wrong to injure members of other cultures, or the extent to which it is believed to be wrong to injure animals. Cultural differences of this sort, in Westermarck's view, cannot be explained except on the assumption that morality rests on emotion and that moral judgments have no "objective validity." Westermarck concludes, therefore, that cultural differences of this sort prove that moral right and wrong are always relative to the feelings of the members of a given culture. Thus, Westermarck believes that ethical relativism is true, apparently because he believes that cultural relativism is true.[8]

## A SECOND CONTEMPORARY VIEW OF ETHICS:
## A. J. Ayer's "Emotivism"

During the first half of this century, several philosophers proposed a second objection to the classical view that ethics is based on reason. These philosophers held that ethical statements are really expressions of emotion designed to influence people's behavior. Thus, when we Americans say "Cannibalism is morally wrong," we are merely expressing the negative feelings we have toward cannibalism and thereby trying to get people to stay away from cannibalism.

The view that ethical statements merely express emotions or that they are merely devices for influencing people's behavior is called "emo-

---

8. For another attempt to argue from cultural relativism to ethical relativism, see Ruth Benedict, *Patterns of Culture* (New York: Pelican Books, 1946), ch. 7.

tivism"or, sometimes,"noncognitivism."[9]This view is proposed in the reading by A. J. Ayer, a well-known British philosopher, entitled "Emotivism." The reading is drawn from his book *Language, Truth, and Logic,* in which Ayer proposes that we accept what he calls the "verification principle." According to this principle, a statement is meaningful if it is possible to prove that it is true or false by pointing to some observation that we could make by using our senses. If a statement cannot be proven or disproven on the basis of some such "sense-experience"—and if it is not a tautology (like "A chair is a chair")—then Ayer claims we must conclude that the statement "is neither true nor false but literally senseless." According to Ayer, all "scientific" statements are "significant" or "meaningful" because they express facts and so can be proven or disproven by using our senses to determine what the facts are. However, moral judgments are nonscientific statements that merely express emotions; we cannot prove or disprove them on the basis of any sense observations. Consequently, Ayer argues, moral judgments are not literally meaningful and "they have no objective validity whatsoever."

If emotivism were true, of course, then ethics could not be based on reason, since ethical statements could not be evaluated as true or false. Like other exclamations (such as "Ouch!" or "Wow!") moral judgments would not state true or false propositions, so no reasons or arguments could be given showing they were true or false. Thus, emotivism poses a real challenge to the classical view that ethics is based on reason.

## A CONTEMPORARY VERSION OF THE CLASSICAL VIEW:
### James Rachels' "Can Ethics Provide Answers?"

Although ethical relativism and emotivism may seem plausible upon initial consideration, both involve significant difficulties that have led many of today's philosophers to reject them.[10] In the fourth reading, which is taken from James Rachels' essay, "Can Ethics Provide Answers?" some of the main arguments against relativism and emotivism are reviewed.

Rachels accounts for popular misgivings concerning clear-cut answers to questions about morality in terms of (1) the past association of morality with religion, (2) various sociological discoveries that pointed to an apparent relativity of values among different cultures, and (3) the emotivist theory. Rachels points out that the apparent differences among cultures concerning beliefs about right and wrong might not be as fundamental as they sometimes appear. Differing circumstances and differing beliefs about matters of fact may result in differing evaluations of actions

9. Another influential version of emotivism is Charles Stevenson, *Ethics and Language* (New Haven, Conn.: Yale University Press, 1944). For a discussion of emotivism, the reader should consult J. O. Urmson, *The Emotive Theory of Ethics* (New York: Oxford University Press, 1969).

10. Other criticisms of ethical relativism may be found in Solomon Asch, *Social Psychology* (Englewood Cliffs, N.J.: Prentice-Hall, 1952), ch. 13, and W. T. Stace, *The Concept of Morals* (New York: Macmillan, 1937). For criticisms of emotivism, see W. D. Hudson, *Modern Moral Philosophy* (New York: Doubleday, 1970), pp. 107–54.

in two cultures, even though the fundamental values of both may be the same. Moreover, even though two groups may have different moral beliefs relating to the same issue, it does not follow that both sets of beliefs must be equally true. Although some people accept the view that the earth is flat and others that the earth is spherical, both views are not equally true. The same holds for contradictory beliefs about matters of moral concern: cultural differences do not show that ethical relativism is correct.

Rachels also points out that emotivism cannot account for the way in which moral views are rationally criticized. If emotivism were true, no rational arguments could be given for or against any moral view. Since rational arguments clearly play an essential role in moral criticism, emotivism must be mistaken.

Ultimately, Rachels, like Plato and Socrates, argues that moral judgments must be based on reason, and that such reason can be examined and criticized for its accuracy and logical consistency. It is only by appealing to these kinds of rational arguments that we can determine whether we or the Akaramas are correct in our views on killing, cannibalism, or homosexuality.

# CRITO

*Plato*

SCENE:—*The Prison of Socrates*

*Socrates.* Why have you come at this hour, Crito? It must be quite early?

*Crito.* Yes, certainly.

*Soc.* What is the exact time?

*Cr.* The dawn is breaking.

*Soc.* I wonder that the keeper of the prison would let you in.

*Cr.* He knows me, because I often come, Socrates; moreover, I have done him a kindness.

*Soc.* And are you only just arrived?

*Cr.* No, I came some time ago.

*Soc.* Then why did you sit and say nothing, instead of at once awakening me?

*Cr.* I should not have liked myself, Socrates, to be in such great

From *The Dialogues of Plato,* 3rd ed., vol. 2, trans. Benjamin Jowett (London: Oxford University Press, 1892), pp. 143, 144, 145, 146, 147, 148, 149, 150, 151, 152, 153, 154, 155, 156.

trouble and unrest as you are—indeed I should not: I have been watching with amazement your peaceful slumbers; and for that reason I did not awake you, because I wished to minimize the pain. I have always thought you to be of a happy disposition; but never did I see anything like the easy, tranquil manner in which you bear this calamity.

*Soc.* Why, Crito, when a man has reached my age he ought not to be repining at the approach of death.

*Cr.* And yet other old men find themselves in similar misfortunes, and age does not prevent them from repining.

*Soc.* That is true. But you have not told me why you come at this early hour.

*Cr.* . . . Socrates, let me entreat you once more to take my advice and escape. For if you die I shall not only lose a friend who can never be replaced, but there is another evil: people who do not know you and me will believe that I might have saved you if I had been willing to give money, but that I did not care. Now, can there be a worse disgrace than this—that I should be thought to value money more than the life of a friend? For the many will not be persuaded that I wanted you to escape, and that you refused.

*Soc.* But why, my dear Crito, should we care about the opinion of the many? Good men, and they are the only persons who are worth considering, will think of these things truly as they occurred.

*Cr.* But you see, Socrates, that the opinion of the many must be regarded, for what is now happening shows that they can do the greatest evil to any one who has lost their good opinion. . . .

*Soc.* Dear Crito, your zeal is invaluable, if a right one; but if wrong, the greater the zeal the greater the danger; and therefore we ought to consider whether I shall or shall not do as you say. For I am and always have been one of those natures who must be guided by reason, whatever the reason may be which upon reflection appears to me to be the best; and now that this chance has befallen me, I cannot repudiate my own words: the principles which I have hitherto honoured and revered I still honour, and unless we can at once find other and better principles, I am certain not to agree with you; no, not even if the power of the multitude could inflict many more imprisonments, confiscations, deaths, frightening us like children with hobgoblin terrors. What will be the fairest way of considering the question? Shall I return to your old argument about the opinions of men?—we were saying that some of them are to be regarded, and others not. . . . In questions of just and unjust, fair and foul, good and evil, which are the subjects of our present consultation, ought we to follow the opinion of the many and to fear them; or the opinion of the one man who has understanding? ought we not to fear and reverence him more than all the rest of the world: and if we desert him shall we not destroy and injure that principle in us which may be assumed to be improved by justice and deteriorated by injustice;—there is such a principle?

*Cr.* Certainly there is, Socrates.

*Soc.* Take a parallel instance:—if, acting under the advice of those who have no understanding, we destroy that which is improved by health and is deteriorated by disease, would life be worth having? And that which has been destroyed is—the body?

*Cr.* Yes.

*Soc.* Could we live, having an evil and corrupted body?

*Cr.* Certainly not.

*Soc.* And will life be worth having, if that higher part of man be destroyed, which is improved by justice and depraved by injustice? Do we suppose that principle, whatever it may be in man, which has to do with justice and injustice, to be inferior to the body?

*Cr.* Certainly not.

*Soc.* More honourable than the body?

*Cr.* Far more.

*Soc.* Then, my friend, we must not regard what the many say of us: but what he, the one man who has understanding of just and unjust, will say, and what the truth will say. And therefore you begin in error when you advise that we should regard the opinion of the many about just and unjust, good and evil, honourable and dishonourable.—'Well,' some one will say, 'but the many can kill us.'

*Cr.* Yes, Socrates; that will clearly be the answer.

*Soc.* And it is true: but still I find with surprise that the old argument is unshaken as ever. And I should like to know whether I may say the same of another proposition—that not life, but a good life, is to be chiefly valued?

*Cr.* Yes, that also remains unshaken.

*Soc.* And a good life is equivalent to a just and honourable one—that holds also?

*Cr.* Yes, it does.

*Soc.* From these premises I proceed to argue the question whether I ought or ought not to try and escape without the consent of the Athenians: and if I am clearly right in escaping, then I will make the attempt; but if not, I will abstain.

Let us consider the matter together, and do you either refute me if you can, and I will be convinced; or else cease, my dear friend, from repeating to me that I ought to escape against the wishes of the Athenians: for I highly value your attempts to persuade me to do so, but I may not be persuaded against my own better judgment. And now please to consider my first position, and try how you can best answer me.

*Cr.* I will.

*Soc.* Are we to say that we are never intentionally to do wrong, or that in one way we ought and in another we ought not to do wrong, or is doing wrong always evil and dishonourable, as I was just now saying, and as has been already acknowledged by us? Are all our former admissions which were made within a few days to be thrown away? And have we, at our age, been earnestly discoursing with one another all our life long only to discover that we are no better than children? Or, in spite of the opinion of the many, and in spite of consequences whether better or worse, shall we insist on the truth of what was then said, that injustice is always an evil and dishonour to him who acts unjustly? Shall we say so or not?

*Cr.* Yes.

*Soc.* Then we must do no wrong?

*Cr.* Certainly not.

*Soc.* Nor when injured injure in return, as the many imagine; for we must injure no one at all?

*Cr.* Clearly not.

*Soc.* Again, Crito, may we do evil?

*Cr.* Surely not, Socrates.

*Soc.* And what of doing evil in return for evil, which is the morality of the many—is that just or not?

*Cr.* Not just.

*Soc.* For doing evil to another is the same as injuring him?

*Cr.* Very true.

*Soc.* Then we ought not to retaliate or render evil for evil to any one, whatever evil we may have suffered from him.

*Cr.* You may proceed, for I have not changed my mind.

*Soc.* Then I will go on to the next point, which may be put in the form of a question:—Ought a man to do what he admits to be right, or ought he to betray the right?

*Cr.* He ought to do what he thinks right.

*Soc.* But if this is true, what is the application? In leaving the prison against the will of the Athenians, do I wrong any? or rather do I not wrong those whom I ought least to wrong? Do I not desert the principles which were acknowledged by us to be just—what do you say?

*Cr.* I cannot tell, Socrates; for I do not know.

*Soc.* Then consider the matter in this way:—Imagine that I am about to play truant (you may call the proceeding by any name which you like), and the laws and the government come and interrogate me: 'Tell us, Socrates,' they say; 'what are you about? Are you not going by an act of yours to overturn us—the laws, and the whole state, as far as in you lies? Do you imagine that a state can subsist and not be overthrown, in which the decisions of law have no power, but are set aside and trampled upon by individuals?' What will be our answer, Crito, to these and the like words? Any one, and especially a rhetorician, will have a good deal to say on behalf of the law which requires a sentence to be carried out. He will argue that this law should not be set aside; and shall we reply, 'Yes; but the state has injured us and given an unjust sentence.' Suppose I say that?

*Cr.* Very good, Socrates.

*Soc.* 'And was that our agreement with you?' the law would answer; 'or were you to abide by the sentence of the state?' And if I were to express my astonishment at their words, the law would probably add: 'Answer, Socrates, instead of opening your eyes—you are in the habit of asking and answering questions. Tell us,—What complaint have you to make against us which justifies you in attempting to destroy us and the state? In the first place did we not bring you into existence? Your father married your mother by our aid and begat you. Say whether you have any objection to urge against those of us who regulate marriage?' None, I should reply. 'Or against those of us who after birth regulate the nurture and education of children, in which you also were trained? Were not the laws, which have the charge of education, right in commanding your

*[handwritten marginal note: counter-argument]*

father to train you in music and gymnastic?' Right, I should reply. 'Well then, since you were brought into the world and nurtured and educated by us, can you deny in the first place that you are our child and slave, as your fathers were before you? And if this is true you are not on equal terms with us; nor can you think that you have a right to do to us what we are doing to you. Would you have any right to strike or revile or do any other evil to your father or your master, if you had one, because you have been struck or reviled by him, or received some other evil at his hands?—you would not say this? And because we think right to destroy you, do you think that you have any right to destroy us in return, and your country as far as in you lies? Will you, O professor of true virtue, pretend that you are justified in this? Has a philosopher like you failed to discover that our country is more to be valued and higher and holier far than mother or father or any ancestor, and more to be regarded in the eyes of the gods and of men of understanding? Also to be soothed, and gently and reverently entreated when angry, even more than a father, and either to be persuaded, or if not persuaded, to be obeyed? And when we are punished by her, whether with imprisonment or stripes, the punishment is to be endured in silence; and if she leads us to wounds or death in battle, thither we follow as is right; neither may any one yield or retreat or leave his rank, but whether in battle or in a court of law, or in any other place, he must do what his city and his country order him; or he must change their view of what is just: and if he may do no violence to his father or mother, much less may he do violence to his country.' What answer shall we make to this, Crito? Do the laws speak truly, or do they not?

*Cr.* I think that they do.

*Soc.* Then the laws will say, 'Consider, Socrates, if we are speaking truly that in your present attempt you are going to do us an injury. For, having brought you into the world, and nurtured and educated you, and given you and every other citizen a share in every good which we had to give, we further proclaim to any Athenian by the liberty which we allow him, that if he does not like us when he has become of age and has seen the ways of the city, and made our acquaintance, he may go where he pleases and take his goods with him. None of us laws will forbid him or interfere with him. Any one who does not like us and the city, and who wants to emigrate to a colony or to any other city, may go where he likes, retaining his property. But he who has experience of the manner in which we order justice and administer the state, and still remains, has entered into an implied contract that he will do as we command him. And he who disobeys us is, as we maintain, thrice wrong; first, because in disobeying us he is disobeying his parents; secondly, because we are the authors of his education; thirdly, because he has made an agreement with us that he will duly obey our commands; and he neither obeys them nor convinces us that our commands are unjust; and we do not rudely impose them, but give him the alternative of obeying or convincing us;—that is what we offer, and he does neither. . . . Are we right in saying that you agreed to be governed according to us in deed, and not in word only? Is that true or not?' How shall we answer, Crito? Must we not assent?

*Cr.* We cannot help it, Socrates.

*Soc.* Then will they not say: 'You, Socrates, are breaking the covenants and agreements which you made with us at your leisure, not in any haste or under any compulsion or deception, but after you have had seventy years to think of them, during which time you were at liberty to leave the city, if we were not to your mind [i.e., if you disagreed with us], or if our covenants appeared to you to be unfair. You had your choice, and might have gone either to Lacedaemon or Crete, both which states are often praised by you for their good government, or to some other Hellenic or foreign state. Whereas you, above all other Athenians, seemed to be so fond of the state, or, in other words, of us her laws (and who would care about a state which has no laws?), that you never stirred out of her; the halt, the blind, the maimed were not more stationary in her than you were. And now you run away and forsake your agreements. Not so, Socrates, if you will take our advice; do not make yourself ridiculous by escaping out of the city. . . .

'Listen, then, Socrates, to us who have brought you up. Think not of life and children first, and of justice afterwards, but of justice first, that you may be justified before the princes of the world below. For neither will you nor any that belong to you be happier or holier or juster in this life, or happier in another, if you do as Crito bids.

This, dear Crito, is the voice which I seem to hear murmuring in my ears, like the sound of the flute in the ears of the mystic; that voice, I say, is humming in my ears, and prevents me from hearing any other. And I know that anything more which you may say will be vain. Yet speak, if you have anything to say.

*Cr.* I have nothing to say, Socrates.

*Soc.* Leave me then, Crito, to fulfil the will of God, and to follow whither he leads.

# ETHICAL RELATIVITY

*Edward Westermarck*

### [1. Ethical Relativity Is the Denial of the Objectivity of Moral Judgments.]

Ethical relativity implies that there is no objective standard of morality, and objectivity presupposes universality. As truth is one it has to be the same for any one who knows it, and if morality is a matter of truth

From Edward Westermarck, *Ethical Relativity* (London: Routledge and Kegan Paul PLC, 1932), pp. 183–85, 187–88, 189, 191, 192, 194–95, 196–97, 208, 209, 210–11, 213, and 216–17.

and falsity, in the normative sense of the terms, the same must be the case with moral truth. If a certain course of conduct *is* good or bad, right or wrong, it is so universally, and cannot be both good and bad, right and wrong. The universality of truth does not mean, of course, that everybody knows what is true and false. It has constantly been argued against ethical subjectivism that the variety of moral judgments no more justifies the denial of moral objectivity than the diversity in judgments about the course of things disproves the objectivity of truth. The validity or fallacy of this argument depends in the first place upon the causes to which the variability of moral judgments is due. . . .

### [2. The Denial of the Objectivity of Moral Judgments Is Not Established by Diverse Moral Opinions that Arise from Different External Conditions of Life.]

[T]he variability of moral valuation depends in a very large measure upon . . . different ideas relating to the objective nature of similar modes of conduct and their consequences. Such differences of ideas may arise from different situations and external conditions of life, which consequently influence moral opinion. We find, for instance, among many peoples the custom of killing or abandoning parents worn out with age or disease. It prevails among a large number of savage tribes and occurred formerly among many Asiatic and European nations, including the Vedic people and peoples of Teutonic extraction; there is an old English tradition of "the Holy Mawle, which they fancy hung behind the church door, which when the father was seaventie, the sonne might fetch to knock his father in the head, as effete and of no more use." This custom is particularly common among nomadic hunting tribes, owing to the hardships of life and the inability of decrepit persons to keep up in the march. In times when the food-supply is insufficient to support all the members of a community it also seems more reasonable that the old and useless should have to perish than the young and vigorous. And among peoples who have reached a certain degree of wealth and comfort, the practice of killing the old folks, though no longer justified by necessity, may still go on, partly through survival of a custom inherited from harder times, and partly from the humane intent of putting an end to lingering misery. What appears to most of us as an atrocious practice may really be an act of kindness, and is commonly approved of, or even insisted upon, by the old people themselves.

Or take the widespread custom of infanticide. Among the lower races custom often decides how many children are to be reared in each family, and not infrequently the majority of infants are destroyed. This wholesale infanticide is also mainly due to the hardships of savage life. The helpless infant may be a great burden to the parents both in times of peace and in times of war. It may prevent the mother from following her husband about on his wanderings or otherwise encumber her in her work. Moreover, a little forethought tells the parents that their child before long will become a consumer of provisions perhaps already too scanty for the family. Savages, who often suffer greatly from want of food, may have to choose between destroying their offspring or famishing themselves. . . .

### [3. The Denial of the Objectivity of Moral Judgments Is Not Established by Diverse Moral Opinions that Arise from Different Religious Beliefs.]

The variability of moral judgments largely originates in different measures of knowledge, based on experience of the consequences of conduct, and in different beliefs. In almost every branch of conduct we notice the influence which the belief in supernatural forces or beings or in a future state has exercised upon the moral ideas of mankind, and the great diversity of this influence. Religion or superstition has on the one hand stigmatized murder and suicide, on the other hand it has commended human sacrifice and certain cases of voluntary self-destruction. . . .

Hardly any pagan practice has been more revolting to the moral feelings of Christians than that of human sacrifice, which is found not only among many savages, but occurred in early times among all Indo-European peoples, the Semites, and the Japanese, and in the New World among the Mayas and the Aztecs, who practised it on an enormous scale. The gods were supposed to be gratified by such offerings—because they had an appetite for human flesh or blood, or because they required attendants, or because they were angry and could only be appeased by the death of him or those who aroused their anger or some representative of the offending community, or who could exactly tell why? The chief thing is that people know or believe that on some certain occasion they are in danger of losing their lives; they attribute this to the designs of a supernatural being; and, by sacrificing a man, they hope to gratify that being's craving for human life and thereby avert the danger from themselves. That this principle mainly underlies the practice of human sacrifice appears from the circumstances in which it generally occurs. Human victims are often offered in war, before a battle, or during a seige; for the purpose of stopping or preventing epidemics; as a method of putting an end to a devastating famine or drought; or with a view to averting perils arising from the sea or from rivers. In these cases the offering of human sacrifices is mostly a matter of public concern, a method of ensuring the lives of many by the death of one or a few. But human life is also sacrificed, by way of substitution, for the purpose of preventing the death of some particular person, especially a chief or a king, from sickness, old age, or other circumstances. I do not say that the practice of human sacrifice is in every case based on the idea of substitution, but I think there is sufficient evidence to prove that it is as a rule a method of life-insurance—absurd, no doubt, according to our ideas, but not an act of wanton cruelty.

Whilst human sacrifice has shocked the feelings of Christians, there are other cases in which Christian morals and legislation have treated as most horrible crimes acts which most peoples have looked upon with considerable moral indifference, if not as altogether blameless. One such case is suicide. It is not often that savages are reported to attach any stigma to it; if they deny self-murderers the ordinary funeral rites or bury them in a separate place, they do so for fear of having anything to do with them or in order to prevent them from mixing with the other dead, because their ghosts are looked upon as dangerous. In China and Japan suicide is in many circumstances regarded as an honourable act. Among the Hindus it has always been considered one of the most acceptable rites that can be offered to their deities. . . .

According to the Christian doctrine, as formulated by Thomas Aquinas, suicide is unlawful for three reasons. It is against a natural inclination and contrary to the charity which a man ought to bear towards himself; by killing himself a person does an injury to the community of which he is a part; and he usurps the office of judge on a point not referred to him, because the judgment of life and death belongs to God alone. The second of these arguments is borrowed from Aristotle, and is entirely foreign to the spirit of early Christianity with its enthusiastic commendation of the hermit life. But the other two are deeply rooted in some of the fundamental doctrines of Christianity—in the sacredness of human life, in the duty of absolute submission to the will of God, and in the extreme importance attached to the moment of death. The earthly life is a preparation for eternity, sufferings which are sent by God are not to be evaded but to be endured. The man who takes away the life given him by the Creator displays the utmost disregard for the will and authority of his Master; and, worst of all, he does so in the very last minute of his life, when his doom is sealed for ever. . . .

Another case in which the difference of moral opinion between Christians and pagans has been equally radical is the attitude towards homosexual practices. . . .

. . . Among uncivilized peoples such practices are generally taken little notice of; they may be a subject for derision or contemptuous remarks wounding the vanity of the delinquent by the implication that he must be unable to procure the full natural enjoyment of his impulse if he has to resort to such substitutes. The laws of the ancient Scandinavians ignored homosexuality, though passive pederasts were much despised by them, being identified with cowards and regarded as sorcerers. Chinese law makes little distinction between unnatural and other sexual offences; but as a matter of fact the former are regarded by the Chinese as less hurtful to the community than ordinary immorality, and pederasty is not looked down upon. In Japan there was no law against homosexual intercourse till the revolution of 1868, and we are told that in the period of Japanese chivalry it was considered more heroic if a man loved a person of his own sex than if he loved a woman. Mohammed forbade sodomy, and the general theory of his followers is that it should be punished like fornication; but in the Mohammedan world it is practically regarded, at most, as a mere peccadillo.

In a very different light was it looked upon by the Hebrews. Unnatural sins are not allowed to defile the land of the Lord: whosoever shall commit such abominations shall be put to death. The enormous abhorrence of them expressed in this law had a very specific reason, namely, the Hebrews' hatred of a foreign cult. Unnatural vice was the sin of a people who was not the Lord's people, the Canaanites, who thereby polluted their land, so that he visited their guilt and the land spued out its inhabitants. We know that sodomy entered as an element into their religion: besides female prostitutes there were male prostitutes, or *qedēshīm*, attached to their temples. The sodomitic acts committed with the latter seem, like the connections with the female temple prostitutes, to have had in view to transfer blessings to the worshippers; in Morocco supernatural benefits are to this day expected not only from heterosexual, but also from homosexual intercourse with a holy person. The *qedēshīm* are frequently alluded to in the Old Testament, especially in the period of the monarchy, when rites of a foreign origin made their way into both Israel and Judah. And it is natural that the Yahveh worshippers should regard their practice with the utmost horror as forming part of an idolatrous cult.

The Hebrew conception of homosexuality passed into Christianity. The notion that sodomy is a form of sacrilege was here strengthened by the habits of the gentiles, among whom St. Paul found the abominations of Sodom rampant. During the Middle Ages heretics were accused of unnatural vice as a matter of course. Indeed, so closely was sodomy associated with heresy that the same name was applied to both. Thus the French *bougre* (from the Latin *Bulgarus,* Bulgarian), as also its English synonym, was originally a name given to a sect of heretics who came from Bulgaria in the eleventh century and was afterwards applied to other heretics, but at the same time it became the regular expression for a person guilty of unnatural intercourse. In mediaeval laws sodomy was also repeatedly mentioned together with heresy, and the punishment was the same for both. It thus remained a religious offence of the first order. And in this fact and its connection with Hebrew ideas we find the answer to the problem we set out to solve. Like suicide, the kind of sexual perversion of which I have now spoken has been stigmatized as a crime of the greatest magnitude on account of its relation to specific religious beliefs. . . .

In so far as differences of moral opinion depend on . . . specific religious or superstitious beliefs . . . or on different conditions of life or other external circumstances, they do not clash with that universality which is implied in the notion of the objective validity of moral judgments. We shall now examine whether the same is the case with other differences that, at least apparently, are not due to purely cognitive causes.

**[4. The Denial of the Objectivity of Moral Judgments Is Established by Diverse Moral Opinions that Arise from Differences in the Altruistic Sentiments Felt Toward Strangers and Animals. Moral Opinions Are Based on Emotions.]**

When we study the moral rules laid down by the customs of savage peoples we find that they in a very large measure resemble the rules of civilized nations. In every savage community homicide is prohibited by custom, and so is theft. Savages also regard charity as a duty and praise generosity as a virtue, indeed their customs relating to mutual aid are often much more exacting than our own; and many of them are conspicuous for their avoidance of telling lies. But in spite of the great similarity of moral commandments, there is at the same time a difference between the regard for life, property, truth, and the general well-being of a neighbour which displays itself in savage rules of morality and that which is found among ourselves: it has, broadly speaking, only reference to members of the same community or tribe. Primitive peoples carefully distinguish between an act of homicide committed within their own community and one where the victim is a stranger: while the former is in ordinary circumstances disapproved of, the latter is in most cases allowed and often considered worthy of praise. And the same holds true of theft and lying and the infliction of other injuries. Apart from the privileges granted to guests, which are always of very short duration, a stranger is in early society devoid of all rights. And the same is the case not only among savages but among nations of archaic culture as well.

When we pass from the lower races to peoples more advanced in civilization we find that the social unit has grown larger, that the nation has taken the place of the tribe, and that the circle within which the infliction of injuries is prohibited has been extended accordingly. . . .

It would be in vain to deny that the old distinction between a tribesman or fellow-countryman and a foreigner is dead among ourselves. The prevailing attitude towards war, the readiness with which wars are waged, and the notions as to what is allowed in warfare indicate the survival in modern civilization of the ancient feeling that the life, property and general well-being of a foreigner are not on a par with those of a compatriot. In times of peace this feeling may disclose itself in the form of national aggressiveness, under the flag of patriotism, or perhaps in the behaviour towards the aborigines of some distant country. But both law and public opinion certainly show a very great advance in humanity with regard to the treatment of foreigners. And if we pass to the rules laid down by moralists and professedly accepted by a large portion of civilized humanity, the change from the savage attitude has been enormous. . . .

It is obvious that the expansion of the moral rules has been a consequence of the expansion of the social unit and of increased intercourse between different societies, and if, as I maintain, the range of the moral emotions varies with the range of the altruistic sentiment, there is every reason to assume that an immediate cause of the greater comprehensiveness of the moral rules has been a corresponding widening of that sentiment. . . .

The variations of the altruistic sentiment in range and strength are also responsible for other differences of moral opinion. Even among ourselves there is no unanimity as to the dictates of duty in cases where a person's own interests collide with those of his fellow-men. . . . In some men the altruistic sentiment is stronger than in others and, consequently, more apt to influence their consciences with regard to their own conduct and their judgments on other people's conduct. And while everybody will no doubt agree that some amount of self-sacrifice is a duty in certain circumstances, the amount and the circumstances can hardly be fixed in general rules, and on the whole, in cases of conflicting interests the judgment must to a large extent remain a matter of private opinion.

There is further the variety of moral opinion relating to men's conduct towards the lower animals. . . .

Indifference to animal suffering has been a characteristic of public opinion in European countries up to quite modern times. . . . Till the end of the eighteenth century and even later cock-fighting was a very general amusement among the English and Scotch, entering into the occupations of both the old and young. Other pastimes indulged in were dog-fighting, bull-baiting, and badger-baiting. . . .

. . . In the course of the nineteenth century humanity to animals, from being conspicuous in a few individuals only, became the keynote of a movement gradually increasing in strength. . . .

Yet though greater intellectual discrimination may lessen the divergencies of moral opinion on the subject, nothing like unanimity may be expected, for the simple reason that humanity to animals is ultimately based on the altruistic sentiment, and sympathy with the animal world is a feeling which varies greatly in different individuals. . . .

. . . This is just what may be expected if moral opinions are based on emotions. The moral emotions depend upon cognitions, but the same cognitions may give rise to emotions that differ, in quality or intensity, in different persons or in the same person on different occasions, and then there is nothing that could make the emotions uniform. Certain cognitions inspire fear into nearly every breast, but there are brave men and cowards in the world, independently of the accuracy with which they realize impending danger. Some cases of suffering can hardly fail to call forth compassion in the most pitiless heart; but men's disposition to feel pity varies greatly, both in regard to the beings for whom it is felt and as to the intensity of the emotion. The same holds true of the moral emotions. To a large extent, as we have seen, their differences depend upon the presence of different cognitions, but very frequently the emotions also differ though the cognitions are the same. The variations of the former kind do not interfere with the belief in the universality of moral judgments, but when the variations of the moral emotions may be traced to different persons' tendencies to feel differently in similar circumstances on account of the particular nature of their altruistic sentiments, the supposed universality of moral judgments is a delusion.

# EMOTIVISM

*A. J. Ayer*

## PREFACE

. . . I divide all genuine propositions into two classes: those which, in this terminology, concern "relations of ideas," and those which concern "matters of fact." The former class comprises the *a priori* propositions of logic and pure mathematics, and these I allow to be necessary and certain only because they are analytic. That is, I maintain that the reason why these propositions cannot be confuted in experience is that they do not make any assertion about the empirical world, but simply record our determination to use symbols in a certain fashion. Propositions concerning empirical matters of fact, on the other hand, I hold to be hypotheses, which can be probable but never certain. And in giving an account of the method of their validation I claim also to have explained the nature of truth.

To test whether a sentence expresses a genuine empirical hypothesis, I adopt what may be called a modified verification principle. For I require of an empirical hypothesis, not indeed that it should be conclusively verifiable, but that some possible sense-experience should be relevant to the determination of its truth or falsehood. If a putative proposition fails to satisfy this principle, and is not a tautology, then I hold that it is metaphysical, and that, being metaphysical, it is neither true nor false but literally senseless. It will be found that much of what ordinarily passes for philosophy is metaphysical according to this criterion, and, in particular, that it can not be significantly asserted that there is a non-empirical world of values. . . .

## CRITIQUE OF ETHICS

[I]t is our business to give an account of "judgements of value" which is both satisfactory in itself and consistent with our general empiricist principles. We shall set ourselves to show that in so far as statements of value are significant, they are ordinary "scientific" statements; and that in so far as they are not scientific, they are not in the literal sense significant, but are simply expressions of emotion which can be neither true nor false. . . .

We begin by admitting that the fundamental ethical concepts are unanalysable, inasmuch as there is no criterion by which one can test the validity of the judgements in which they occur. . . . We say that the reason why they are unanalysable is that they are mere pseudo-concepts. The

From A. J. Ayer, *Language, Truth and Logic* (New York: Dover Publications, Inc., 1952), pp. 31, 102–103, 107–109. Copyright © 1946 A. J. Ayer.

presence of an ethical symbol in a proposition adds nothing to its factual content. Thus if I say to someone, "You acted wrongly in stealing that money," I am not stating anything more than if I had simply said, "You stole that money." In adding that this action is wrong I am not making any further statement about it. I am simply evincing my moral disapproval of it. It is as if I had said, "You stole that money," in a peculiar tone of horror, or written it with the addition of some special exclamation marks. The tone, or the exclamation marks, adds nothing to the literal meaning of the sentence. It merely serves to show that the expression of it is attended by certain feelings in the speaker.

If now I generalise my previous statement and say, "Stealing money is wrong," I produce a sentence which has no factual meaning—that is, expresses no proposition which can be either true or false. It is as if I had written "Stealing money!!"—where the shape and thickness of the exclamation marks show, by a suitable convention, that a special sort of moral disapproval is the feeling which is being expressed. It is clear that there is nothing said here which can be true or false. Another man may disagree with me about the wrongness of stealing, in the sense that he may not have the same feelings about stealing as I have, and he may quarrel with me on account of my moral sentiments. But he cannot, strictly speaking, contradict me. For in saying that a certain type of action is right or wrong, I am not making any factual statement, not even a statement about my own state of mind. I am merely expressing certain moral sentiments. And the man who is ostensibly contradicting me is merely expressing his moral sentiments. So that there is plainly no sense in asking which of us is in the right. For neither of us is asserting a genuine proposition.

What we have just been saying about the symbol "wrong" applies to all normative ethical symbols. Sometimes they occur in sentences which record ordinary empirical facts besides expressing ethical feeling about those facts: sometimes they occur in sentences which simply express ethical feeling about a certain type of action, or situation, without making any statement of fact. But in every case in which one would commonly be said to be making an ethical judgement, the function of the relevant ethical word is purely "emotive." It is used to express feeling about certain objects, but not to make any assertion about them.

It is worth mentioning that ethical terms do not serve only to express feeling. They are calculated also to arouse feeling, and so to stimulate action. Indeed some of them are used in such a way as to give the sentences in which they occur the effect of commands. Thus the sentence "It is your duty to tell the truth" may be regarded both as the expression of a certain sort of ethical feeling about truthfulness and as the expression of the command "Tell the truth." The sentence "You ought to tell the truth" also involves the command "Tell the truth," but here the tone of the command is less emphatic. In the sentence "It is good to tell the truth" the command has become little more than a suggestion. And thus the "meaning" of the word "good," in its ethical usage, is differentiated from that of the word "duty" or the word "ought." In fact we may define the meaning of the various ethical words in terms both of the different feelings they are ordinarily taken to express, and also the different responses which they are calculated to provoke.

We can now see why it is impossible to find a criterion for determining the validity of ethical judgements. It is not because they have an "absolute" validity which is mysteriously independent of ordinary sense-experience, but because they have no objective validity whatsoever. If a sentence makes no statement at all, there is obviously no sense in asking whether what it says is true or false. And we have seen that sentences which simply express moral judgements do not say anything. They are pure expressions of feeling and as such do not come under the category of truth and falsehood. They are unverifiable for the same reason as a cry of pain or a word of command is unverifiable—because they do not express genuine propositions.

# CAN ETHICS PROVIDE ANSWERS?

*James Rachels*

. . . A great many people, including many philosophers, believe that there are no "answers" in ethics. It is a remarkable situation: people make judgments every day about what should or should not be done; they feel strongly about those views, and sometimes they become angry and indignant with those who disagree. Yet, when they reflect on what they are doing, they profess that their judgments are no more "true" than the contrary ones they reject so vehemently. The explanation of this puzzling situation goes deep into our history, and into our understanding of the world and our place in it.

Throughout most of western history there was thought to be a close connection between ethics and religion. In Plato's [Dialogues] Socrates offered powerful arguments for separating the two, but this point of view did not prevail. (Socrates, it will be remembered, was tried and convicted of impiety.) Right and wrong continued to be defined by reference to God's will, and human life came to be regarded as meaningful only because of its place in God's plan. The church, therefore, was the guardian of the moral community and its main authority.

By the eighteenth century these ideas had begun to lose their grip on people's minds, largely because of changes that had taken place in the

From James Rachels, "Can Ethics Provide Answers?" *The Hastings Center Report,* vol. 10, no. 3 (June 1980), pp. 33–39. Reproduced by permission of *The Hastings Center Report.* Copyright © 1980 Institute of Society, Ethics and the Life Sciences, 360 Broadway, Hastings-on-Hudson, New York 10706.

conception of the physical world. The physical sciences had successfully challenged the ancient belief that the earth is the center of the cosmos; instead, it was recognized to be a relatively insignificant speck. The next step would be the realization that, from a cosmic point of view, human beings are themselves insignificant. In his famous essay on suicide, published posthumously in 1783, Hume took that step, declaring that "The life of a man is of no greater importance to the universe than that of an oyster."[1] The aim of this essay was to defend the permissibility of suicide; in doing that, Hume was particularly eager to separate religious from moral notions, and to dispel the idea that human life is a gift from God that can rightly be taken only by God. This belief he considered to be a compound of "superstition and false religion," and he held that the purpose of our thinking should be to replace superstition and false religion with reason and understanding. The truth, in his view, is that *we* care about human life, because we are human, and that is all there is to it. Our lives have no more, and no less, importance than that. If he had lived to see it, Hume would no doubt have felt vindicated by the second great modern change in our conception of the world and our place in it that came from the biological sciences. The thought that we are the products of an evolutionary history much like that of all the other animals has further eroded confidence about any special place for humanity in the scheme of things.

In our own time, however, it has been the social sciences that have presented the greatest challenge to traditional ideas about human beings. The sociologists have impressed upon us that moral standards differ from culture to culture; what the "natural light of reason" reveals to one people may be radically different from what seems obvious to another. This, of course, has been known for a long time. Herodotus made the point very clearly in the fifth century B.C.:

> Darius, after he had got the Kingdom, called into his presence certain Greeks who were at hand, and asked—"What he should pay them to eat the bodies of their fathers when they died?" To which they answered, that there was no sum that would tempt them to do such a thing. He then sent for certain Indians, of the race called Callatians, men who eat their fathers, and asked them, while the Greeks stood by, and knew by the help of an interpreter all that was said—"What he should give them to burn the bodies of their fathers at their decease?"
>
> The Indians exclaimed aloud, and bade him forbear such language. Such is men's wont herein; and Pindar was right, in my judgment, when he said, "Custom is the king o'er all."[2]

---

1. The essay on suicide, together with other relevant works, is conveniently reprinted in *Hume's Ethical Writings*, edited by Alasdair MacIntyre (New York: Collier, 1965). Of the many commentaries on Hume, Rachel Kydd's *Reason and Conduct in Hume's Treatise* (New York: Russell & Russell, 1964) is especially recommended.

2. *The History of Herodotus*, translated by George Rawlinson, adapted by John Ladd in *Ethical Relativism* (Belmont, Cal.: Wadsworth, 1973), p. 12. *Ethical Relativism* is a good collection of articles on the relation of ethics to culture.

Today any educated person could list countless other examples: the Eskimos allow first-born daughters to die of exposure; the Moslems practice polygamy; the Jains will not eat meat. With the communications media providing constant contact with other parts of the world, it may now seem simply naive to think that our moral views are anything more than one particular cultural product. . . .

Thus, in many people's minds, . . . [e]thics can no longer exist as a subject having as its aim the discovery of what is right and what is wrong; for this supposes, naively, that there *is* a right and wrong independent of what people already happen to believe. And that is precisely what has been brought into doubt. Ethics as a subject must disappear, to be replaced, perhaps, by something like "values clarification." We can try to become clearer about what our values are, and about the possible alternatives. But we can no longer ask questions about the truth of our convictions.

With such impressive intellectual forces behind it, it is not surprising that this way of thinking about ethics has been tremendously influential. However, most contemporary philosophers have, with good reason, taken a dim view of these arguments. In the first place, the fact that different societies have different moral codes proves nothing. There is also disagreement from society to society about scientific matters: in some cultures it is believed that the earth is flat, and that disease is caused by evil spirits. We do not on that account conclude that there is no truth in geography or in medicine. Instead, we conclude that in some cultures people are better informed than in others. Similarly, disagreement in ethics might signal nothing more than that some people are less enlightened than others. At the very least, the fact of disagreement does not, by itself, *entail* that truth does not exist. Why should we assume that, if ethical truth exists, everyone must know it?

Moreover, it may be that some values are merely relative to culture, while others are not. Herodotus was probably right in thinking that the treatment of the dead—whether to eat or to burn them—is not a matter governed by objectively true standards. It may be simply a matter of convention that respect is shown in one way rather than another. If so, the Callatians and the Greeks were equally naive to be horrified at each other's customs. Alternative sexual customs—another favorite example of relativists—might also be equally acceptable. But this does not mean that there are *no* practices that are objectively wrong: torture, slavery, and lying, for example, could still be wrong, independently of cultural standards, even if those other types of behavior are not. It is a mistake to think that because some standards are relative to culture, all must be.

While contemporary philosophers have not been impressed by the social scientific arguments concerning ethics, they have nevertheless found certain other arguments against ethics to be plausible. Those arguments go back to Hume, who maintained that belief in the very possibility of an objectively correct ethical system is part of the old "superstition and false religion." Stripped of false theology, Hume said, we should come to see our morality as nothing more than the expression of our feelings.

In our own time Hume's thoughts have been adapted to support a theory according to which moral judgments are not really judgments at all, but disguised imperatives. According to this theory, known as emotivism, when one makes a moral judgment such as,

> It is wrong to make someone the subject of an experiment without his permission,

one is actually saying no more than,

> *Don't* make someone the subject of an experiment without his permission.

Alternately, as it was sometimes said, one is doing nothing more in making these judgments than expressing one's attitude, and urging others to adopt that attitude. Even though they may be sincere or insincere, imperatives and expressions of attitude are neither true nor false—and so, moral judgments are neither true nor false.[3]

If *this* is what moral judgments are, then once again ethics has lost its status as a subject. There are no truths for it to investigate. It cannot even be a branch of psychology, for although psychology is concerned with attitudes, it is only concerned with nonmoral truths *about* attitudes, which, unlike expressions *of* attitude, are true or false.

There is now an extensive philosophical literature cataloguing the deficiencies of emotivism. One of the main problems with the theory was its failure to account for the place of reason in ethics. It is a point of logic that moral judgments, if they are to be acceptable, must be founded on good reasons: if I tell you that such-and-such action is wrong, you are entitled to ask *why* it is wrong; and if I have no adequate reply, you may reject the advice as unwarranted. The emotivists were able to give only the most anemic account of the relation between moral judgments and the reasons that support them. Moral reasoning, on this theory, turned out to be indistinguishable from propaganda. If moral judgments are merely expressions of attitude, then reasons are merely considerations that influence attitudes. It was a natural outcome of the theory that *any* fact that influences attitudes counts as a reason for the attitude produced; thus, if the thought that Jones is black causes you to think badly of him, then "Jones is black" becomes a reason in support of your judgment that he is a bad man.

Obviously, something had gone wrong. Not just any fact can count as a reason in support of just any judgment. For one thing, the fact must be relevant to the judgment, and psychological influence does not necessarily bring relevance with it. But this is only the tip of an iceberg. Arguments in support of moral judgments can be criticized, and found adequate or inadequate, on any number of other grounds. Once this is realized, however, we have taken a big step away from emotivism, and

---

3. The classic defense of emotivism is Charles L. Stevenson, *Ethics and Language* (New Haven: Yale University Press, 1944). J. O. Urmson, *The Emotive Theory of Ethics* (London: Hutchinson, 1968), provides a critical assessment.

all the other trends of thought I have been describing, toward the recognition of ethics as an autonomous subject.

## ETHICS AND RATIONALITY

Ultimately the case against ethics can be answered only by demonstrating how moral problems are amenable to solution by rational methods. In any particular case the right course of action is the one that is backed by the best reasons. Consider, for example, euthanasia. We may determine whether mercy-killing is right or wrong by formulating and assessing the arguments that can be given for and against it.[4] This is at bottom what is wrong with . . . cultural relativism: if we can produce good reasons for thinking that this practice is wrong, and show that the arguments in its support are unsound, then we have proven it wrong regardless of what . . . one's cultural code might say. And emotivism runs afoul of the same fact: if a stronger case can be made for euthanasia than against it, then mercy-killing *is* permissible, no matter what one's attitude might be.

The first and most obvious way that a moral argument can go wrong is by misrepresenting the facts. A rational case for or against a course of conduct must rest on some understanding of the facts of the case—minimally, facts about the nature of the action, the circumstances in which it would be done, and its likely consequences. Even the most skeptical thinkers agree that reason has this role to play in moral judgment: reason establishes the facts. Unfortunately, however, attaining a rational view of the facts is not always a simple matter. In the first place, we often need to know what the consequences of a course of action will be, and this may be impossible to determine with any precision or certainty. Opponents of euthanasia sometimes claim that, if mercy-killing were legalized, it would lead to a diminished respect for life throughout the society, and we would end up caring less about the elderly, the mentally retarded, and so forth. Defenders of euthanasia, on the other hand, heatedly deny this. What separates the two camps is a disagreement about "the facts," but we cannot settle the issue in the same easy way we could settle an argument about what would happen if Coca-Cola were boiled. We seem to be stuck with different estimates of what would happen if euthanasia were legalized, which may be more or less reasonable, but which we cannot definitively adjudicate.

Moreover, it is often difficult to determine the facts because the facts are distressingly complex. Take, for example, the question of whether the government of South Vietnam, which the United States supported during the late war, was democratic. This question figured prominently in some of the debates of the time. I take it to be primarily a matter of fact, but it was not a *simple* matter of fact. In order to decide the matter, one had to

---

4. A survey of the relevant arguments may be found in James Rachels, "Euthanasia," in *Matters of Life and Death,* edited by Tom Regan (New York: Random House, 1980) p. 28–66.

fit together into a pattern all sorts of other facts about the operation of that government and its relation to its citizens. That the government was, or was not, democratic was a kind of conclusion resting on those other facts; it was a matter of what the simpler facts added up to.

Suppose, though, that we have a clear view of the relevant facts, so that our arguments cannot be faulted on that ground. Is there any other test of rationality that the arguments must pass? Hume's official view was that, at this point, reason has done all it can do, and the rest is up to our "sentiments." Reason sets out the facts; then sentiment takes over and the choice is made. This is a tempting idea, but it only illustrates a common trap that people fall into. Philosophical theses may seduce with their beautiful simplicity; an idea may be accepted because of its appeal at a high level of generality, even though it does not conform to what we know to be the case at a lower level. In fact, when Hume was considering concrete ethical issues, and not busy overemphasizing the role of sentiment, he knew very well that appeals to reason are often decisive in other ways. In the essay on suicide to which I have already referred, he produced a number of powerful arguments in support of his view that a person has the right to take his own life, for example, when he is suffering without hope from a painful illness. Hume specifically opposed the traditional religious view that, since life is a gift from God, only God has the right to decide when it shall end. About this he made the simple but devastating observation that we "play God" as much when we save life as when we take it. Each time a doctor treats an illness, and thereby prolongs a life, he has decreed that the patient's life shall not end *now*. Thus if we take seriously that only God may determine the length of a life, we would have to renounce not only killing but saving life as well.

This point has force because of the general requirement that our arguments be consistent, and consistency, of course, is the prime requirement of rationality. Hume did *not* argue that the religious opponent of suicide has got his facts wrong—he did not insist that there is no God, or that God's will had been misunderstood. If Hume's objection were no more than that, then no religious person need be bothered by it. Hume's objection was much stronger, for he was pointing out that we may appeal to a general principle (such as "Only God has the right to decide when a life shall end") only if we are willing to accept *all* its consequences. If we accept some of them (the prohibition of suicide and euthanasia), but not others (the abandonment of medicine), then we are inconsistent. This point, which has fundamental importance, will be missed if we are blinded by overly simple doctrines like "Reason establishes the facts; sentiment makes the choice."

Let me mention one other way in which the requirement of consistency can force a change in one's moral views. I have been emphasizing that a moral judgment, if it is to be acceptable, must be backed by reasons. Consistency requires, then, that if there are exactly the *same* reasons in support of one course of conduct as there are supporting another, those actions are equally right, or equally wrong. We cannot say that $X$ is right, but that $Y$ is wrong, unless there is a *relevant difference* between $X$ and $Y$.

This is a familiar principle in many contexts: it cannot be right for a teacher to give students different grades unless there is a relevant difference in the work that they have done; it cannot be right to pay workers different wages unless there is some relevant difference between the jobs they do; and so on. This principle underlies the social ideal of equality.

It has recently been noticed that this principle has even more radical implications than egalitarians have realized, for if applied consistently it would require that we rethink our treatment of animals. We routinely perform experiments on chimpanzees that we would never perform on humans—but what is the difference between chimps and humans that justifies this difference in treatment? One answer might be that humans are far more intelligent and sensitive than chimpanzees; but this only invites a further query: suppose the humans are mentally retarded, so that they are *less* intelligent than chimps? Would we then be willing to experiment on retarded humans in the same way? And if not, why not? What is the difference between the individuals in question, which makes it all right to experiment on one but not the other? At this point the defender of the status quo may be reduced to asserting that, after all, the humans are *human,* and that's what makes the difference. This, however, is uncomfortably like asserting that, after all, women are *women,* or blacks are *black,* and that's why *they* may be treated differently. It is the announcement of a prejudice, and nothing more.[5]

## THE LIMITS OF RATIONALITY

The preceding discussion will not have dispelled all the nagging doubts about ethics. Rational methods can be used to expose factual error and inconsistency, in the ways I have described, but is that enough to save ethics from the charge that, at bottom, there is no "truth" in its domain? Couldn't two people who are equally rational—who have all the relevant facts, whose principles are consistent, and so on—still disagree? And if "reason" were inadequate to resolve the disagreement, wouldn't this show that, in the end, ethics really is only a matter of opinion? These questions will not go away.

There is a limit to what rational methods can achieve, which Hume described perfectly in the first appendix to his *Inquiry Concerning the Principles of Morals* (1752):

> Ask a man *why he uses exercise;* he will answer, *because he desires to keep his health.* If you then inquire *why he desires health,* he will readily reply, *because sickness is painful.* If you push your inquiries further and desire a reason *why he hates pain,* it is impossible he can ever give any. This is an ultimate end, and is never referred to any other object.
>
> Perhaps to your second question, *why he desires health,* he may also reply that *it is necessary for the exercise of his calling.* If you ask *why he is anxious on that*

---

5. These arguments are advanced with great vigor by Peter Singer in his book *Animal Liberation* (New York: New York Review/Random House, 1975).

*head,* he will answer, *because he desires to get money.* If you demand, *Why? It is the instrument of pleasure,* says he. And beyond this, it is an absurdity to ask for a reason. It is impossible there can be a progress *in infinitum,* and that one thing can always be a reason why another is desired. Something must be desirable on its own account, and because of its immediate accord or agreement with human sentiment and affection.[6]

The impossibility of an infinite regress of reasons is not peculiar to ethics: it applies in all areas. Mathematical reasoning eventually ends with axioms that are not themselves justified, and reasoning in science ultimately depends on assumptions that are not proven. At some point reasoning must always come to an end, no matter what the subject.

The *difference* between ethics and other subjects is in the involvement of the emotions. In order for anything to count as an ultimate reason for or against a course of conduct, one must *care* about that thing in some way. In the absence of any emotional involvement, there are no reasons for action. The fact that the building is on fire is a reason for me to leave only if I care about not being burned; the fact that children are starving is a reason for me to do something only if I care about their plight. (On this point the emotivists were right, whatever defects their overall theory might have had.) It is the possibility that people might care about different things, and so accept different ultimate principles between which "reason" cannot adjudicate, which continues to undermine confidence in the subject itself.

Now let us return to the question of ethical disagreement. When disagreement occurs, two explanations are possible. There could be some failure of rationality on the part of one or the other person, or they could simply be different, in that they care about different things. In practice, when important matters are at issue, we always proceed on the first hypothesis. We present arguments on the assumption that those who disagree have missed something: they are ignorant of relevant facts, they have not thought through what they know, they are not consistent, and so on. We do not credit the idea that they are "different."

Is this procedure reasonable? Are there any real-life examples of ethical disagreement where the explanation is that the people who disagree, while being rational enough, simply care about different things? If there are, they are notoriously hard to find. The familiar examples of the cultural anthropologists turn out upon analysis to have other explanations. The Eskimos who allow their first-born daughters to die of exposure, and who abandon feeble old people to a similar fate, do not have less respect for life than other peoples who reject such practices. They live in different circumstances, under threat of starvation in a hostile environment, and the survival of the community requires policies which otherwise they would happily renounce. The Ik, an apparently crude and callous people indifferent even to the welfare of their own children, took on those characteristics only after a prolonged period of near-starvation, which virtually destroyed their tribal culture. There may be some dis-

6. Hume's *Ethical Writings,* p. 131.

agreements which reflect cultural variables—I have already mentioned Herodotus' Greeks and Callatians, for example—but beyond that, and barring the kind of disaster that reduced the Iks, it is plausible to think that people are enough alike to make ethical agreement possible, if only full rationality were possible.

The fact that rationality has limits does not subvert the objectivity of ethics, but it does suggest a certain modesty in what can be claimed for it. Ethics provides answers about what we ought to do, given that we are the kinds of creatures we are, caring about the things we will care about when we are as reasonable as we can be, living in the sort of circumstances in which we live. This is not as much as we might want, but it is a lot. It is as much as we can hope for in a subject that must incorporate not only our beliefs but our ideals as well.

# CHAPTER TWO
# NATURAL LAW ETHICS

On the afternoon of November 12, 1948, Hideki Tojo stood silently in a hushed Japanese courtroom before his judges. The night before, he had written a short haiku poem:

> Gazing upward,
> I hear reverently
> The voice of God
> Calling me
> From the pure and boundless sky.[1]

The poem was a premonition. For on that November afternoon the voice of the presiding judge rang out clearly in the quiet courtroom: "Accused Hideki Tojo, the International Military Tribunal for the Far East sentences you to death by hanging."

Hideki Tojo was tried and hanged by the United States and its allies for his part in leading Japan into World War II. Tojo was minister of war and premier of Japan from the beginning of the war until its end and was instrumental in its conduct. According to his judges, Tojo, together with other Japanese leaders, had "participated in . . . a conspiracy" whose ob-

---

1. Robert J. C. Butow, *Tojo and the Coming of the War* (Stanford: Stanford University Press, 1961), p. 522.

ject was "that Japan should secure the . . . domination of East Asia and of the Pacific."[2] Speaking for the court, one of the judges declared:

> That object, . . . [to] secure Japan's domination by preparing and waging a war of aggression, was a criminal object. Indeed, no more grave crimes can be conceived of than a conspiracy to wage a war of aggression, for . . . the inevitable result of its execution is that death and suffering will be inflicted on countless human beings. . . . From the opening of the war in China until the surrender of Japan in August 1945, torture, murder, rape and other cruelties of the most inhumane and barbarous character [were] freely practiced by the Japanese Army. . . . Atrocities [were] committed in all theaters of war on a scale so vast, yet following so common a pattern . . . that only one conclusion [is] possible—the atrocities [were] either secretly ordered or willfully permitted by the Japanese Government or individual members thereof. . . . [These atrocities included] ruthless killing of prisoners by shooting, decapitation, drowning, and other methods; death marches in which prisoners, including the sick, were forced to march long distances under conditions which not even well-conditioned troops could stand, many of those dropping out being shot or bayonetted by the guards; forced labor in tropical heat without protection from the sun; complete lack of housing and medical supplies, in many cases resulting in thousands of deaths from disease; beatings and torture of all kinds to extract information or confessions or for minor offences; killing without trial of recaptured prisoners after escape; killing without trial of captured aviators.[3]

Tojo was only one of several Japanese "war criminals" tried and sentenced by the United States and its allies for launching the "illegal" war of aggression that became World War II and for treating prisoners and enemy civilians inhumanely. Twenty-four other Japanese officials were tried and punished along with him. And in Nuremberg, Germany, dozens of Nazi officials were tried and sentenced to death and imprisonment for their part in the "illegally" conducted war and for the systematic slaughter of millions of European Jews.

But the trials of these Japanese and Germans all took place under a cloud. None of the defendants had broken the laws of their own countries since all of their actions had been sanctioned by the legal systems of their own nations. And since they were not American citizens they were not subject to American law. Moreover, prior to the trials, respected legal scholars had pointed out that international law did not hold individuals criminally liable for conducting wars.[4] How then could it be held that the Japanese and German defendants had committed any crimes, that is, that they knowingly and deliberately had broken a criminal law? Expressing the feelings of all the Japanese and German leaders, Tojo testified: "Never at any time did I conceive that the waging of this war could be challenged as an international crime, or that regularly constituted officials

2. Richard Minear, *Victors' Justice* (Princeton, N.J.: Princeton University Press, 1971), p. 193.

3. Quoted in Butow, op. cit., pp. 509–10.

4. Hans Kelsen, "Will the Judgment in the Nuremberg Trial Constitute a Precedent in International Law?" *International Law Quarterly* (Summer 1947), pp. 167–71.

of the vanquished nations could be charged individually as criminals under any recognized international law."[5] What law had these German and Japanese leaders actually broken? Would they have to be set free in spite of having committed such inhumane acts?

The law that had been broken was identified at Tojo's trial. In a lengthy opinion, Justice Henri Bernard wrote:

> There is no doubt in my mind that such a war of aggression is and always has been a crime in the eyes of reason and universal conscience—expressions of natural law upon which an international tribunal can and must base itself to judge the conduct of the accused tendered to it. . . . [The natural law] is the law shared by all individuals and all nations. . . . It exists outside and above nations. Although opinions differ as to its nature, its existence is not seriously contested or contestable.[6]

In referring to the "existence" of a "natural law" that is "not seriously contested," Justice Bernard was suggesting that in the conscience of every person there exists a basic knowledge of right and wrong. In other words, that there is a moral law that is so much a part of human nature that everyone is aware of it. This law exists above nations in the sense that every citizen of every nation must obey it, no matter what his own laws say. The officials who had started World War II were criminals because they had knowingly violated this fundamental natural law that is part of the conscience of every person. Thus, although technically these men had not broken any written or human laws, they had knowingly broken the natural law of morality and they were tried and sentenced accordingly.

As Justice Bernard pointed out, opinions differ about what the natural law requires. However, there are some basic features that all views on natural law ethics share. First, a natural law view of morality holds that there are certain fundamental principles of right and wrong that bind human beings of every nationality. For example, Justice Bernard was suggesting that when they began a war that was certain to impose innumerable deaths and great suffering on innocent human beings, the Japanese and German leaders had violated a moral principle that all human beings must follow: the principle that it is wrong to destroy innocent human lives. Second, a natural law view of morality holds that these fundamental principles are based on our human nature: we human beings are made in such a way that we cannot help but value the good these principles protect. For example, human beings cannot help but instinctively see that human life is valuable, and the principle that it is wrong to destroy innocent human life protects these lives on which our natural instincts place such a high value. Third, a natural law theory of morality

5. Courtney Browne, *Tojo: The Last Banzai* (New York: Holt, Rinehart and Winston, 1967), pp. 230–31.
6. International Military Tribunal for the Far East, *Trial of Japanese War Criminals*, Transcript and Documents, Judgment of the International Military Tribunal for the Far East, vol. 4, Dissenting Opinion of Justice Henri Bernard, pp. 10 and 18; quoted in John Appleman, *Military Tribunals and International Crimes* (Indianapolis: Bobbs-Merrill, 1954), p. 261.

holds that all human beings are aware of these fundamental moral principles because all normal adults come to know them through the use of their natural reasoning abilities. Once they start thinking about the value of human life, all human beings realize that it is wrong to destroy the lives of innocent people.

Natural law theories have had a profound and lasting influence in ethics. From the time of the Greeks and on down to the present day, natural law has provided the basis for explaining why certain actions are right or wrong, regardless of what "human laws" might say.[7] In our own century, natural law ethics has been at the center of controversies over the punishment of war crimes, the morality of nuclear war, the morality of abortion, the practice of homosexuality, and the legalization of euthanasia. It is difficult, if not impossible, to understand these controversies and make up one's mind about them unless one understands the principles on which they depend.

In this chapter we will look at two important versions of natural law ethics. The first is taken from Saint Thomas Aquinas' *Treatise On Law*, a short work that was written during the thirteenth century. This is a classical explanation of natural law and most twentieth-century versions have been deeply influenced by it.[8] We will then jump forward seven centuries to look at a contemporary version of natural law theory in the writings of philosopher Germain Grisez. Grisez's work is particularly important because many other modern philosophers follow his approach.

## THE CLASSICAL VERSION OF NATURAL LAW ETHICS:
### Aquinas' Treatises on Law and Justice

Aquinas' *Treatise on Law* is taken from a longer work entitled the *Summa Theologica*. Like the rest of the *Summa*, Aquinas' *Treatise on Law* is divided into short chapters called "questions." Each question is a separate inquiry that is further subdivided into articles. In each of the latter, Aquinas

---

7. The ancient Greeks, five centuries before Christ, held that there was an unwritten law of justice to which the laws of man must conform. (See Sophocles, *Antigone*, and Aristotle, *Nicomachean Ethics*, bk. 5.) The early Christians also held that there was an unwritten law of natural right and wrong, one whose transgression God wrathfully punished (Romans 1:26, 27; 2:14, 15). Throughout the Middle Ages, philosophers held that there was a law of nature to which everyone must conform (Saint Augustine, *On Free Choice of the Will*, bk. 1; Saint Thomas Aquinas, *Summa Theologica*, q. 94, a. 2). The American Declaration of Independence held that the colonies were justified in freeing themselves from British rule because the laws of nature entitled them to do so. And in our own century, several philosophers and lawyers have developed their own theories to explain the requirements of the natural law of morality (see, for example, John Finnis, *Natural Law and Natural Rights* [Oxford: Clarendon Press, 1980] and A. P. D'Entreves, *Natural Law* [London, 1951]).

8. Readers who would like to read more extensive commentaries on Aquinas' natural law theory of ethics should consult one of the following: D. J. O'Connor, *Aquinas and Natural Law* (London: Macmillan, 1967); Vernon J. Bourke, *Ethics* (New York: Sheed and Ward, 1951); F. C. Copleston, *Aquinas* (New York: Penguin Books, 1955); Anthony Kenny, ed., *Aquinas* (Garden City, N.Y.: Doubleday, 1969).

states his own view on the various questions he poses and tries to answer the major objections to it.

The *Treatise on Law* begins with a discussion in Question 90 of the *Summa Theologicae* of the qualities that all laws must have. Aquinas argues first that all laws must be determined by reason. That is, laws cannot be senselessly arbitrary. Laws are made in order to achieve some end, and only by using our reason can we determine how we can achieve those ends. Thus, reason must enter into the making of all laws. Second, Aquinas argues that all laws must be designed to achieve the common good of the whole society. We make laws in order to secure our happiness, but we can do so only if society as a whole is functioning well. It stands to reason, then, that if we are to achieve happiness, we must design our laws so that they will benefit the whole society. Third, Aquinas claims that only the people as a whole—or someone who is concerned with the good of the whole society—has the right to make laws. Laws must be designed to achieve the good of the whole society, so they must be made by someone who has this good in mind. But only the people as a whole or a representative acting on their behalf will keep the good of all society in mind. Fourth, Aquinas concludes that laws must be promulgated. In other words, they must be made known to those who are to obey them. Otherwise, they will have no influence on our actions. So, Aquinas concludes, a rule can be counted as a true law only if (1) it is reasonable, (2) it is aimed at the good of the whole society, (3) it is made by the people as a whole or someone concerned with their good, and (4) it is enacted openly and not in secret.

We can clarify what Aquinas means by a true law if we look briefly at what was going on in Germany during World War II. When Hitler came to power, he declared that any decree or order he issued automatically became the law of Germany; subsequently he issued orders that began the war and secretly ordered the systematic killing of Jews. These orders often contradicted the German constitution, they were inconsistent with each other, and they violated basic judicial rights established by other laws.[9] Thus, to the extent that Hitler's decrees were inconsistent, they were irrational: they did not have their source in reason but were simply the expression of his arbitrary will. Consequently, it is clear, first, that these decrees were not reasonable. Second, Hitler's decrees obviously were not aimed at the good of the whole society: they were designed to satisfy his own personal desires and those of his fellow Nazis. Third, these decrees were not made by a person concerned with the good of the whole society: they were made by a man dedicated only to the interests of a small group. And fourth, these decrees were not openly promulgated: they were so inhumane that many of them had to be enacted and carried out in secret. Hitler's decrees, then, did not have any of the characteristics of what Aquinas means by a true law. Thus, when the German leaders were brought before their judges after the armistice and tried as war

9. Marsh, "Some Aspects of the German Legal System Under National Socialism," *Law Quarterly Review*, vol. 62 (October 1946), pp. 366–74.

criminals, they could not hold that in following Hitler's orders they were merely obeying the law. Aquinas would say they so clearly contradict our basic notions of what law is that they could not be counted as such.

But what, exactly, is the "good of society" toward which all law must aim? In the succeeding questions Aquinas tried to clarify this issue. He begins in the first article of Question 91 by pointing out that there is an obvious order in the universe. In every creature there are certain "natural forces and inclinations" that move it toward certain ends and enable it to act in certain ways. If a person believes in God (as Aquinas did), this order will be seen as one that God imposes on the universe when He instills in each creature whatever tendencies it has. For the believer, this order thus existed in the mind of God from all eternity, and as such it may be said to be the eternal law that governs the universe. The eternal law, is, there· fore, the order of the universe as it would exist in the mind of God, and it is an order that is realized in creatures through the natural forces and inclinations that are part of their natures. The existence of this order, of course, does not depend on one's personal beliefs about God, in fact, the nonbeliever will attribute it to other causes.

In the second article of Question 91, Aquinas points out that human beings are also part of the order of the universe. They too have certain natural inclinations that move them toward certain ends and that enable them to carry out certain physical and mental activities. But human beings are ordered toward their proper ends and activities in a way that is radically different from other creatures. Human beings have reason, and by using their reason they must discover for themselves what they must do to achieve their ends. The natural law, according to Aquinas, consists of the way our minds operate when we are reasoning about what we will do to achieve our ends. Our minds generally follow certain principles of reasoning, and these impose an order on our thinking that is analogous to the order that nature imposes on the activities of all living things. These principles of reasoning are what Aquinas means by the natural law. Thus, the natural law is the eternal law as it is realized in human beings.

What exactly are these principles of reasoning that constitute the natural law? Aquinas begins to explain their nature in the third article of Question 91. There he argues that these principles by themselves do not provide us with detailed human laws by which we must organize our societies. Aquinas here distinguishes between practical reason and theoretical reason. The former involves our mental ability to reason to a decision about what we will do, the latter our ability to reach a conclusion about the nature of reality. According to Aquinas, whether we are dealing with practical matters or theoretical matters, we must follow certain principles if our reasoning is to be correct. He reasons as follows.

We are not born with an innate knowledge of what reality is like (we do not have, for example, an innate knowledge of scientific theories). But we are naturally endowed with a knowledge of the principles of logic that enable us to discover the nature of reality through theoretical reasoning (and thereby we discover the conclusions that make up the sciences). Similarly, we are not born with an innate knowledge of the human laws by which our society must be organized if it is to achieve our ends. But we are naturally endowed with a knowledge of certain principles of practical reasoning (which comprise the natural law) that enable us to figure out the social arrangements by which we can achieve our ends. Consequently, Aquinas concludes, it is necessary for us to use our reason to decide on the human laws by which we will organize our society. In the United States, for example, we protect human life by passing certain criminal laws, but in other societies the same end is achieved by the passage of different laws. Natural law does not provide us with detailed civil laws by which we must organize society; it only provides the principles of practical reasoning by which each society can determine its own human laws.

In Question 94, Aquinas provides an explanation of the basic principles or rules of the natural law. It is here that he finally describes the moral values that true laws must protect if they are to achieve the good of everyone in society. He begins by suggesting that the principles that make up the natural law are self-evident. That is, to anyone who knows what these principles mean, it will be obvious that they are true. But to show why these principles are self-evident, Aquinas must first explain what he means by self-evident. In his view, it comes down to this: a proposition is self-evident when its predicate tells us what we already knew was part of the meaning of its subject. For example, the proposition "Bachelors are unmarried" is self-evident since we already know that "unmarried" is part of the meaning of "bachelor." Similarly, "Whatever is a triangle is three-sided" is also self-evident because by definition part of the meaning of "triangle" is "three-sided figure."

Aquinas next draws a parallel between the principles that govern theoretical reasoning and the principles that comprise the natural law. A theoretical principle is a rule we follow when we are reasoning correctly about the nature of reality, i.e., about theoretical matters. A principle of theoretical reasoning may thus be seen as a principle of logic that theoretical reason employs. The example of such a principle that Aquinas proposes is the rule of consistency, which says, "What is real cannot be said to be and not to be at the same time." Obviously, we must follow this rule in all our theoretical reasoning processes or we would end up contradicting ourselves. Moreover, Aquinas implies that this principle of theoretical reasoning is self-evident because part of the meaning of "real" is "what cannot both be and not be."

Just as there are self-evident rules of logic that we follow when we are reasoning about theoretical matters, Aquinas suggests that there are also self-evident rules we must follow when we are reasoning about practical matters, that is, when we are reasoning about what we should do. In particular, when we are reasoning correctly about what we should do, we follow the basic rule, "What is good ought to be pursued in action." Aquinas is suggesting here that whenever we reason about what we ought to do, we always move from the thought that something is good, and the thought that it can be attained through a certain action, to the conclusion that we ought to carry out that action. For example, if I come to the conclusion that I ought to study, it is because there is something I think is good (such as high grades), and I think that the action of studying will attain that good. This basic rule is, according to Aquinas, self-evident because part of the meaning of "good" is "what ought to be pursued."

Thus, Aquinas concludes that the basic natural law is the self-evident principle "What is good ought to be pursued," and its contrary, "What is evil ought to be avoided." This basic natural law is a rule that governs all practical reasoning. But what things are good for us? Aquinas suggests that something is good for us if we are drawn to it by those inclinations that are part of every human being's nature. And there are, he suggests, three basic goods to which human nature is naturally inclined: first, the good of life; second, the good of family life; and third, the good of knowledge and of an orderly social life. Consequently, the pursuit of these basic goods is also part of the natural law. That is, all men and women recognize that life, family, knowledge, and an orderly social life ought to be pursued and never destroyed. All true laws, then, must seek to maintain these values or they will fail to achieve the good of the whole society. If Aquinas had known about the laws of the Nazis, he would certainly have condemned them as immoral.

Article four argues that all people recognize the same basic goods, and that it is self-evident to everyone that these goods ought to be preserved. However, it cautions that we cannot conclude that people everywhere must have the same moral beliefs. Different societies may use the principles of practical reason to come to different conclusions about how the basic goods are to be attained. Theoretical reasoning thus differs in an important way from practical reasoning.

In a piece of theoretical reasoning, several incompatible conclusions cannot follow from the same premises. But since practical reasoning is concerned with finding means to an end, and since often there are several different incompatible means for achieving the same end, it follows that there may be several different correct but incompatible conclusions about the means by which an end will be attained. In the modern world, for example, we use a system of private property as a means for maintaining an orderly social life. Consequently, in our world, theft of property is wrong. But in some primitive tribal cultures all property is owned in common, so the social order is not necessarily destroyed when people make off with things. In these primitive cultures, theft of property is not wrong. Thus, although people everywhere have the same basic moral values, they may still differ in the particular moral rules they adopt to achieve those values.

In Question 95 and Question 96, Aquinas explains the relationship between natural law and human law in more detail. First, he argues that an ordinance is not a valid human law unless it conforms to the natural law. In other words, a valid law is a law that imposes the obligations of justice upon us, and only the principles of the natural law can impose such moral obligations. Aquinas further explains that when human laws are unjust or immoral we have no obligation to obey them. Human laws are unjust, he notes, when they violate the rights of human beings and the rights of God.

In a later treatise, the *Treatise on Justice,* Aquinas applies his views on natural law to the problem of killing and in doing so he adds an important qualification to his views. He points out, first, that it is always wrong to kill oneself because suicide destroys the basic value of life, and the natural law says that this value must be preserved.

But is it wrong, say, to kill in self-defense? It depends, Aquinas claims, on one's intentions. Sometimes our actions can have double effects. My act of self-defense, for example, may have the effect of preserving my life and the effect of killing the person who is attacking me. When an action has two effects like these, it is not immoral if I intended only the good effect (saving my life) and did not inflict more harm than was necessary to achieve this good effect. But it would be wrong for me intentionally to seek the death of the person who is attacking me. After all, the natural law says that life must be preserved, so it is wrong to take life intentionally.

## A CONTEMPORARY VERSION OF NATURAL LAW ETHICS:
### Germain Grisez's "Ethical Arguments"

In many respects, Germain Grisez's views are much like those of Aquinas, although Grisez develops his by setting them against a popular contemporary approach to ethics: utilitarianism (which will be discussed more fully in Chapter Four). Grisez points out that utilitarianism holds it is possible to add together the good effects of an action and subtract its bad effects. However, Grisez argues, it is not possible to add and subtract the values produced by an action because values are incommensurable. Trying to add up and subtract different values from each other is like trying to add up and subtract apples and oranges. Instead, Grisez claims, we must acknowledge that there are several different kinds of values or goods, and that these values cannot be weighed "one against another, as if there were comparable goods and a common measure."

Grisez goes on to argue that there are in fact eight basic goods that all human beings instinctively recognize. This is so because everything we do is done in pursuit of one or more of them. The basic goods are these: (1) life, (2) activities engaged in for their own sake, (3) experiences sought for their own sake, (4) knowledge, (5) integrity, (6) genuineness, (7) justice and friendship, and (8) worship and holiness.

Moral good and evil, Grisez argues, depend on the attitude with which we choose to pursue particular instances of these goods. Morally evil choices are choices that pursue a certain instance or realization of a basic good but with the narrow attitude that the other goods are not worth pursuing or that the goods other people pursue are not worthwhile. Consequently, a morally evil choice will pursue a particular instance of one good by directly destroying a particular instance of another good or by not helping other people pursue particular instances of the basic goods. In contrast, morally right choices pursue particular instances of these goods with an open attitude that respects all of them equally. Thus, a morally right choice will not seek to destroy directly a particular instance of any of the basic goods and will help other people pursue particular instances of these goods.

What does Grisez mean by "directly destroy" a particular instance of a basic good (or "act directly against the realization of a basic good")? He argues that a person "directly destroys" a particular instance of a basic good when the person intentionally sets about destroying a particular instance of that good as a means of achieving a particular instance of some other good. For example, if I intentionally kill someone as a means to my pleasure, I have "directly destroyed" an instance of the basic good of life.

However, as Grisez points out, sometimes an act that is not itself evil may have two effects: an act might produce an instance of a basic good while also destroying an instance of another basic good. Such actions, Grisez tells us, have often been dealt with by applying the principle of double effect, a principle whose adequacy he questions. The modern understanding of this principle holds that actions with such double effects are not wrong if: (1) the action itself is morally indifferent, (2) the person intends only to achieve the good effect, (3) the destruction of an instance of a good is not the means by which the person intends to achieve an instance of another good, and (4) there is a "proportionately grave reason" for allowing the destruction of that instance of a good. For example, by spending my time studying I am gaining knowledge (a good effect), but I am also prevented from doing anything to help starving people in India stay alive (the bad effect). However, I can see there is nothing wrong in doing this if I apply the four considerations mentioned above: (1) Studying is in itself a morally indifferent act. Moreover, (2) I am studying only with the intention of gaining knowledge. (3) I am not studying in order to kill people in India. And (4) I have a "proportionately grave reason" for studying since I will need knowledge to preserve my own life in the future. Consequently, it is not wrong for me to study, although an unintended and unavoidable side effect of this is that I am prevented from helping the people of India preserve their lives.

Grisez claims that if the principle of double effect is properly understood it can be compatible with his own views. However, he argues that some people interpret the third condition in a manner that is too restrictive. They hold that the third condition means that the evil effect must always occur after the good effect. Instead, according to Grisez, we should hold that the third condition means only that the bad effect must be indivisible from the good effect.

Thus Grisez, like Aquinas, holds that there are some basic human goods that all of us ought to pursue, no matter what our nationality. In his view, our human nature is such that even the Japanese and German leaders during World War II could not help but instinctively see these goods as values that should not directly be destroyed. Like Aquinas, Grisez would have held that the crimes against humanity of which the Japanese and Germans were accused were essentially crimes against the natural law, a law of which all men and women are aware. Moreover, like Aquinas, Grisez believes that when an action has a double effect, a crucial factor in determining the morality of the act is the intention with which it was done.

Grisez's views have developed considerably since the excerpts presented here were originally published (especially his views on double effect). We are reprinting them because for many who are concerned with ethics, they are a classic exposition of the theory of modern natural law. Readers who want a fuller and more recent picture of Grisez's views should consult his later works.[10]

*[handwritten: a systematic argument in writing a including a methodical discussion of the facts & principles involved and conclusion reached.]*

# TREATISES ON LAW AND JUSTICE

*Saint Thomas Aquinas*

## Treatise on Law

We must now consider the basic influences on human actions. . . . We will discuss law here first. Our discussion of law will be divided into two main parts: First we will discuss the nature of law in general (we do this in Questions 90 to 92); Second, we will discuss each particular kind of law (we do this in Questions 93 to 108). In our discussion of the general nature of law, we must address these questions: First, what are the essential characteristics of law (Question 90)? Second, what are the different kinds of laws (Question 91)? . . .

### QUESTION 90: WHAT ARE THE ESSENTIAL CHARACTERISTICS OF LAW?

We will divide this question into four subsidiary issues or "articles." In Article 1 we will ask whether reason is the source of all law; in Article 2 we will ask what the general purpose of law is; in Article 3 we will ask

10. See, for example, Germain Grisez and Joseph M. Boyle, Jr., *Life and Death with Liberty and Justice: A Contribution to the Euthanasia Debate* (Notre Dame and London: University of Notre Dame Press, 1979), esp. pp. 336–407; Germain Grisez and Russell Shaw, *Beyond the New Morality: The Responsibilities of Freedom*, rev. ed. (Notre Dame and London: University of Notre Dame Press, 1980); Germain Grisez, *The Way of the Lord Jesus*, vol. 1, *Christian Moral Principles* (Chicago: Franciscan Herald Press, 1983).

*[handwritten margin notes: "to make by declaration / known by proclaim; : proclaim a law); to put into action or force / codify / everyone should know"]*

who in general makes the law, and in Article 4 we will ask whether every kind of law must be promulgated. [In each article, we will proceed by first stating the main objections against our view, then we will state our view, and provide replies to each of the main objections.]

### Article 1: Is Reason the Source of All Law?

*First objection:*   It would seem that not all law has its source in reason. For Saint Paul himself says: "I see a law in my bodily parts that is at war with the law my reason gives" (Romans 7:23). Now our reason has nothing to do with how our bodily parts function since reason is not a physical thing. Consequently, the [biological] laws according to which our bodily parts function do not have their source in reason.

*Second objection:*   Moreover, if law had its source in reason, it would have to reside in our reason and would then have to be one of three things: it would have to be part of the power of reason itself, or it would have to be a skill that reason has, or it would have to be an activity of reason. But a law is not itself the power by which we reason. Nor is a law a reasoning skill like the intellectual skills we discussed in an earlier treatise. Nor is a law a kind of reasoning activity, for then it would stop existing as soon as we stopped reasoning, as we do when we fall asleep. Consequently, law does not have its source in reason.

*Third objection:*   Moreover, a law moves its subjects to act. But strictly speaking it is the will that always moves us toward this action or that one. Consequently, law need not have its source in reason, it need only arise from the will. This accords with the view of that philosopher of law who said: "Law is nothing more than what pleases the sovereign."

BUT IN SUPPORT OF MY OWN VIEW there is the fact that law is a prescription or a prohibition. But only reason can determine prescriptions or prohibitions. So law must have its source in reason.

I STATE MY OWN VIEW AS FOLLOWS: A law is a kind of guide and standard for one's actions; it obligates one to do certain things and prohibits one from doing others. (In fact, the word "law" is derived from the Latin word *ligando,* which means "obligating," since the law obligates us to certain acts.) Now only reason can provide guides and standards for human actions [i.e., actions that are deliberate and intentional] since we ultimately determine all of our human actions by using our reason. For only by using reason can we determine what we ought to do if we are to attain our ends, and we determine all of our actions on the basis of whether or not they will attain our ends. Now the power that ultimately determines what a certain thing ought to do is the power that determines all guides and standards for that thing. . . . We are therefore left with the conclusion that all laws must be determined by the power of reason.

*Reply to the first objection:*   Since a law is a kind of guide and standard, it can be said to be "in" things in two ways. First, it is in a sense present "in" the mind that is doing the guiding and setting the standards. In this primary sense, law is present only "in" reason. Second, a law can be said to be "in" the thing whose actions are guided and evaluated by the standards of the law. In this second sense we say that a certain law is present "in" any creature that possesses natural drives and forces that lead it to act in a law-like manner. The regularities that arise from such natural forces and inclinations can be called "laws" in a secondary sense. They are the result of laws that, in the primary sense, are "in" the mind of their Creator. Now the "law of our bodily parts" that Saint Paul refers to is a law merely in this secondary sense since he is referring to the natural forces and drives that constitute the [biological] functions of our physical parts.

*Reply to the second objection:*   We often distinguish between the activity of doing something and what the activity produces; for example, we distinguish between the activity of building and the building that is produced. Similarly, we should distinguish between the activities of reason (i.e., coming to understand and reasoning things out), and what those mental activities produce. The activities of reason produce definitions, from these they produce propositions, and from these they produce syllogisms or arguments. Now practical reason [i.e., our ability to reason to a decision about what we will do] also uses a kind of syllogism when reaching decisions about what action to perform. So we can expect that just as theoretical reason [i.e., our ability to reason to a conclusion about the nature of reality] in its syllogisms draws conclusions from certain propositions, so also practical reason will use general propositions to reach decisions about what is to be done. These general propositions on which practical reason bases its decisions are laws. Laws, therefore, can exist in the mind as propositions that we are actually thinking about or as propositions that we know but are not presently thinking about.

*Reply to the third objection:*   It is true that the will provides the motive that moves the reason. For it is only when one wills an end that reason moves to determine the act that will attain the end. But if the will of a sovereign passes a law that commands some action by which he hopes to achieve his ends, his will by that very fact is submitting itself to what reason has determined [to be the correct action for achieving those ends]. This must be kept in mind when interpreting the slogan that "law is nothing more than what pleases the sovereign." For otherwise, the will of the sovereign would make for lawlessness instead of law.

### Article 2: Is All Law Aimed at the Good of the Whole Society?

*First objection:*   It would seem that not all law is intended to achieve the good of the whole society. For specific orders or prohibitions can also be laws. But such orders are aimed at achieving particular goods. So laws are not always intended to achieve the good of the whole society.

*Second objection:* Moreover, law directs men to act in certain ways. But the actions of men are always concerned with their own particular affairs. Therefore laws are also always concerned with the good of individuals. . . .

BUT IN SUPPORT OF MY OWN VIEW there is the maxim attributed to Saint Isidore that says: "Law is not enacted for the private benefit of any individual, but must serve the whole body of citizens."

I STATE MY OWN VIEW AS FOLLOWS: Law is a guide and standard for one's actions. Consequently, as we have seen, law must have its source in that power that determines all actions. Since all actions are determined by reason, law too must be determined by reason. Now, ultimately, reason determines the actions we are to perform by determining whether they attain that end that we are ultimately seeking in all that we do. That end is our well-being or happiness for, as we argued earlier, in all the activities of our lives we are seeking happiness. Consequently, when reason makes law, it must be concerned above all with establishing a [social] order that will attain our happiness or well-being.

Moreover, the kind of well-being or happiness with which the law is properly concerned must be the well-being of the whole society. For the complete well-being of the part depends on the well-being of the whole. Now an individual human being is a part of a whole social system. So if the law is to achieve the individual's complete well-being or happiness, it must aim at the well-being or happiness of the whole society. That is why the philosopher Aristotle had to define "legal" in terms of the well-being of a whole political society. Thus, in the fifth part of his book, *Ethics,* he wrote, "We say actions are 'legally just' when they produce and maintain the well-being of a political society in all its parts," and such a civic society, he points out in his *Politics,* is a complete social system. . . . Thus the orderly arrangements imposed by the law are all intended to achieve the good of the whole society, that is, they are intended to achieve the "common good."

*Reply to the first objection:* Orders and prohibitions are really acts of applying the law to matters that the law regulates. For if the law is to achieve the good of the whole society, it must set ends for each particular part. This is why orders and prohibitions concerning particular matters must be given, even though the law is intended to achieve the good of the whole society.

*Reply to the second objection:* It is true that action is always concerned with particulars. This does not mean, however, that actions are not aimed at the good of the whole society. For I am not saying that a particular action commanded by the law is an instance (or exemplification) of the concept of the good of the whole society; I am claiming, rather, that the particular actions commanded by the law have the good of the whole society as their end.

### Article 3: Can Any Individual Determine What the Law Will Be?

• • •

I STATE MY OWN VIEW AS FOLLOWS: As we have seen, the law is principally and primarily intended to achieve the good of the whole society. Now how the good of the whole is to be achieved is up to the people as a whole or to the person who acts on behalf of them all. For here, as in all other matters, determining the means is the right of him who seeks the end [and since the law is a means for achieving the good of society as a whole, society as a whole has the right to determine the law]. Consequently, law is to be determined only by the people as a whole or by a public official who is charged with securing the good of the whole society.

• • •

### Article 4: Is Promulgation Essential to the Law?

*First objection:* It would seem that promulgation is not essential to all law. For natural law (which we will discuss below) is law in the fullest sense of the word, yet it needs no promulgation. Therefore, promulgation is not essential to all law. . . .

I STATE MY OWN VIEW AS FOLLOWS: As we have seen, law is essentially a guide and standard imposed on actions. Now a rule can be a guide and standard only to the extent that it is effectively inculcated on those for whom it is supposed to serve as a guide and standard. This necessary inculcation is provided when the rule is brought to their attention by being promulgated among them. Thus, a rule can become a law, that is, a guide and standard, only if it is promulgated.

We can now formulate a definition of law by drawing together the conclusions of the last four articles. A law is something that meets these four conditions: (1) it is an orderly arrangement determined by reason, (2) that is intended to achieve the good of the whole society, (3) that is enacted by the person who is charged with caring for that whole society, and (4) that is promulgated among that society's members.

*Reply to the first objection:* Even natural law is promulgated. It was promulgated in that very act by which God made man's mind in such a way that he would know it by the use of his natural powers of understanding (as we will explain below).

## QUESTION 91: WHAT TYPES OF LAWS ARE THERE?

Next we must consider the different types of laws there are. We will divide this question into the following subsidiary issues or "articles": in Article 1 we will ask whether there are laws that are eternal; in Article 2 we will ask whether there are natural laws; in Article 3 we will ask whether there are human laws. . . .

### Article 1: Are There Laws that Are Eternal?

• • •

I STATE MY OWN VIEW AS FOLLOWS: As we saw [in Question 90, Article 3], a law is an order determined by the practical reason of a ruler who governs a complete social system. Now it is clear that the universe is a complete system [that has an orderly arrangement]. If we believe there is a God who governs the universe through His provident direction, then the order of the universe must be imposed by God's reason. Consequently, the order imposed on the universe can be said to consist of a set of laws. These laws originally exist as ideas in the reason of God, who is the ruler of the universe. And since these ideas could not have been formed in God's reason at a particular moment in time [for God does not change], they must have existed in His reason from all eternity. Consequently, the laws that govern the universe are in fact eternal.

• • •

### Article 2: Are There Laws that Are in Us as Part of Our Nature?

*First objection:*  It would seem that there are no laws that are in us as part of our nature. For the eternal law orders all of our actions, since, as Augustine points out, "The eternal law justly and completely orders all things." It would be superfluous for our nature to provide laws that would put order into actions of ours that are already ordered. And nature does not generate superfluous things.

*Second objection:*  As we saw in Question 90, Article 2, laws are guides that men follow to attain their ends. But nature does not govern creatures by providing them with guides they can follow or not as they choose. For the laws of nature govern nonrational creatures through natural forces and instincts that blindly carry them toward their appointed ends. This is not the way human beings are guided since they use their reason and will to decide for themselves how they will attain their ends. So there cannot be a law that governs our actions like a law of nature would.

BUT IN SUPPORT OF MY OWN VIEW there is the interpretation given to that Biblical text, "The Gentiles, who do not have the Judaic law, know by nature what that law requires." The standard interpretation of this text is as follows: Although the Gentiles do not have the written law of the Jews, yet they have the natural law, which everyone is aware of and through which everyone becomes conscious within himself of what is right and what is wrong.

I STATE MY OWN VIEW AS FOLLOWS: A law is a guide and standard for action. Consequently, as we saw in Question 90, Article 1, law can be said to be "in" things in two ways. First, it is present "in" the mind that guides and sets standards for its subjects and, second, it can be said to be "in" the subjects whose actions are guided and evaluated by those standards. For the guides and standards by which the activities of a subject are evaluated derive from the guides and standards in the reason of the person who determines those activities.

Now it is clear from the preceding article that the eternal law is the guide and standard for everything that is subject to God's provident direction. Obviously, therefore, the activities of all things are equally determined by the eternal law. Their activities are determined by the natural forces and inclinations that were made part of their natures when they were created. These natural forces and inclinations cause creatures to engage in their appropriate activities and attain their appropriate ends.

Now rational creatures are also subject to God's provident direction, but in a way that makes them more like God than all other creatures. For God directs rational creatures by instilling in them certain natural inclinations and capacities that enable them to direct themselves as well as other creatures. Thus human beings also are subject to the eternal law and they too derive from that law certain natural inclinations to seek their proper end and proper activity. These inclinations of our nature constitute what we call the natural law; they are the effects of the eternal law imprinted "in" our nature.

Thus, even the Scripture suggests that our natural ability to reason (by which we distinguish right from wrong) in which the natural law resides, is nothing more than the image of God's own reason imprinted on us. For Psalm Four asks, "Who will show us what is right?" and it answers, "The light of Thy Mind, O Lord, which has been imprinted upon us."

*Reply to the first objection:*   This objection would be correct if the natural law were separate from the eternal law. But as we have just said, the natural law is derived from the eternal law.

*Reply to the second objection:*   All the activities of our reason and will are based on laws that are in us as part of our nature. For all of our reasoning activities are based on certain principles of reasoning and knowledge of these principles is part of our nature. Likewise, any desire our will has for this or that particular thing is ultimately based on our desire for happiness, and our awareness of this basic desire for happiness is part of our nature. Thus, it must be granted that natural laws lie at the basis of the way we [use our reason and will to] decide how we will attain our ends.

### Article 3: Is Human Law Necessary?

*First objection:*   It would seem that it is not necessary for there to be laws made by humans. For as Augustine pointed out, "The eternal law completely orders all things,  and the laws that are part of our nature constitute the eternal law as it applies to us. Consequently, the laws that are part of our nature would be sufficient to order all of our affairs. So it is not necessary for humans to make additional laws.

• • •

I STATE MY OWN VIEW AS FOLLOWS: As we have said, laws are determined by practical reason. Now if one examines the matter, he will discover that reason follows the same procedure whether it is engaged in practical reasoning or in theoretical reasoning. For as we have pointed out, in both cases reason proceeds by drawing conclusions on the basis of certain principles. When it is engaged with theoretical matters, reason follows certain principles of reasoning that are indemonstrable, the knowledge of which is part of our nature. By relying on these principles of reasoning, we are able to derive the theories of the different sciences. Knowledge of these theories is not part of our nature, but is the result of our reasoning efforts.

In the same way, when our practical reason must come to some conclusion about more specific social arrangements, its reasoning is based on the rules that consitute the natural law. These rules are like principles of reasoning that are indemonstrable and that everyone knows. The specific social arrangements that are thus determined by our reason are what we call human laws, provided, of course, that they meet the four conditions we laid down in our definition of law.

*Reply to the first objection:*    Our reason cannot grasp what is in God's mind down to the last detail; we must arrive at the details in our own imperfect way. Thus, for example, God does not impart his scientific knowledge to us by implanting in us a detailed knowledge of all truths. Instead, he implants in our nature a knowledge of the basic principles of reasoning [and by following these we discover new truths].

In the same way, all the particular detailed directives of the eternal law are not implanted in us. Instead, there are certain basic principles that God has made part of our nature and that practical reasoning uses [to determine more detailed directives]. Thus, our reason must go beyond these principles in order to arrive at the detailed enactments of the law.

• • •

We will next examine more closely each of the various kinds of law. We will begin by first examining the eternal law in Question 93. Second, we will examine the natural law in Question 94.

## QUESTION 93: WHAT IS THE ETERNAL LAW?

### Article 1: Is the Eternal Law the Governing Plan in God's Mind?

• • •

I STATE MY OWN VIEW AS FOLLOWS: Before any craftsman makes something, he must have in his mind an idea of what he will make. Similarly, before a ruler governs his subjects, he must have in his mind some idea of what his subjects are to do. The craftsman's idea of what he will make constitutes a plan of the object to be made (it is also part of what we call his skill). And the ruler's idea of what his subjects are to do constitutes a kind of law (provided it meets the four conditions laid down in our definition of law).

Now since God is the wise creator of the universe, He is like the craftsman who makes something. And He is also like the ruler since He governs every act and motion of every single creature. Consequently, the idea in God's wise mind, according to which everything was created, can be called a plan (or an ideal, or even a part of God's skill); and since everything is also governed according to this same idea, it can also be called a law. So the eternal law is nothing more than a plan in God's mind, in accordance with which every act and motion is directed.

• • •

## QUESTION 94: WHAT IS THE NATURAL LAW?

• • •

### Article 2: Does the Natural Law Consist of One Rule or of Several?

• • •

I STATE MY OWN VIEW AS FOLLOWS: The natural law consists of rules that guide practical reason much like the principles of logical reasoning guide theoretical reason. These guides are alike because both are self-evident propositions. We should note, however, that we use the word "self-evident" in two ways: *either true or false*

First, we sometimes say a proposition is self-evident without adding any qualification to our statement. [When we say without qualification that a proposition is self-evident, we mean that the truth of the proposition is immediately evident to anyone who knows what the proposition means.] In a self-evident proposition, the predicate is part of the meaning of the subject. For example, "Man is a rational animal" is self-evident because "rational animal" is part of the definition of "man." *meaning contained in*

Second, we sometimes say a proposition is self-evident only *to* certain people. We say a proposition is self-evident only *to* certain people when we mean to indicate that it is not immediately evident to everyone that the proposition is true. This happens when [the predicate of a proposition is part of the meaning of its subject but] some people are ignorant of what the predicate or the subject means. For example, "Man is a rational animal" is not self-evident to the person who is ignorant of the fact that man by definition is a rational animal.

Thus (as the philosopher Boethius pointed out) when a self-evident proposition contains terms whose meaning we all know, the proposition will be self-evident to everyone. [That is, it will be self-evident to everyone that the proposition is true.] But when a self-evident proposition contains technical terms whose meaning is known only to experts, it will be self-evident only to those experts. . . .

Let us return now to our main discussion. Study shows that human beings acquire knowledge in stages. The first and earliest notion we grasp is the notion of what it is for something to be real. For everything else we learn about the real world presupposes we know what reality is. [Consequently, everyone knows the meaning of "real."] Now there is a fundamental proposition that is based on the meaning of "real." This is the proposition that "What is real cannot be said to be and not to be at the same time." [And since everyone knows the meaning of "real" it is self-evident to everyone that this proposition is true.] Moreover, this proposition is a principle of reasoning on which all the rest of our reasoning about reality is based.

Now something analogous happens in practical reasoning. Just as the notion of "reality" is the first and earliest notion we grasp [in all our reasoning], so also the notion of "goodness" is the first and earliest notion we grasp in our practical reasoning (i.e., when we reason about the acts we ought to perform). For all of our acts are done in pursuit of some end, and "being an end" carries the meaning of "being good." [Consequently, everyone knows the meaning of "good."] Now there is a fundamental proposition that is based on the meaning of "good." This is the proposition that "What is good ought to be pursued in our actions; what is evil ought to be avoided." [And since everyone knows the meaning of "good," it is self-evident to everyone that this proposition is true.] Moreover, this proposition is a basic principle for practical reasoning.

Thus, the basic natural law is this fundamental rule of practical reasoning [that is self-evident to everyone]. All other rules of the natural law are based on it. For when our practical reason perceives that certain kinds of things are good for our human nature, practical reason will [follow this basic rule and] draw the conclusion that those kinds of things ought to be pursued in our actions. [Such derivative conclusions are also rules and they too are part of the natural law.]

[But what kinds of things does practical reason perceive as good for our human nature?] A thing is good if it is an end that we have a natural inclination to desire; it is evil if it is destructive of what our nature is inclined to desire. Consequently, those kinds of things that our nature is inclined to desire are perceived by practical reason as good for our human nature. And [in accordance with the basic rule] practical reason will conclude that those kinds of things ought to be pursued in our actions. But if practical reason sees a certain type of thing as destructive of what human nature is inclined to desire, it will conclude that that type of thing ought to be avoided.

It is possible, therefore, to enumerate the derivative rules of the natural law by enumerating, in order, the kinds of things that our nature is inclined to desire. First, like every other nature, human nature is inclined to desire its own survival. Consequently, it is a natural law that we ought to preserve human life and avoid what is destructive of life.

Second, like every other animal nature, human nature is inclined to desire those things that nature teaches all animals to desire by instinct. For example, all animals have an instinctive desire to come together in a union of male and female, and an instinctive desire to care for their

the basic Goods

young. [Consequently, it is a natural law that we ought to make the fulfillment of these desires possible.]

Third, human nature is inclined to desire those goods that fulfill reason. This aspect of our nature is found only in human beings. Thus, human nature is inclined to desire knowledge (for example, to know the truth about God) and to desire an orderly social life. Consequently, it is a natural law that we ought to dispel ignorance and avoid harming those among whom we live.

[Thus, there is only one basic natural law, but there are these three kinds of derivative natural laws that flow from it.]

• • •

### Article 4: Do the Same Natural Laws Hold True for All Men?

• • •

I STATE MY OWN VIEW AS FOLLOWS: . . . Theoretical reasoning and practical reasoning both proceed from general premises to particular conclusions. However, they differ in an important respect. For if the premises in a piece of theoretical reasoning are known with certainty to be true, the truth of a certain conclusion will necessarily follow. But practical reasoning is concerned with what our actions can bring about and such things can be brought about in more than one way. Consequently, even though we may be certain about the general premises of a piece of practical reasoning, the more particular the conclusions we try to derive, the more possibilities there are for going wrong.

Thus, in theoretical reasoning all men may *correctly* draw only *one* true conclusion from those general premises that everyone accepts as true (although not everyone may *know* that the conclusion follows). But in practical reasoning different men may *correctly* draw *different* conclusions from the same general premises; and even when there is only one correct conclusion, not everyone may *know* what it is.

Thus, it is clear that in both theoretical reasoning and practical reasoning, the same basic general principles will hold true for everyone and will be equally known to everyone. And the particular conclusions drawn by *theoretical* reasoning will also hold true for everyone although they will not be known to everyone. For example: [in geometry theoretical reason at one point draws] the conclusion that the three angles of a triangle are together equal to two right angles. This conclusion is obviously true for everyone. But not everyone knows it is true [especially if they have not studied geometry].

However, the *particular* conclusions drawn by *practical* reasoning may not hold true for everyone and may not be known to everyone. For example, everyone knows and it is always true that we should act in accordance with our general rational principles [such as the general principle that we should seek an orderly social life]. From these general principles it is possible to draw the particular conclusion that borrowed property should be returned to its owner [for the sake of an orderly social life]. But although this particular conclusion holds true in most cases, nonetheless situations can arise in which it does not hold true. Suppose, for instance, that someone planned to kill his fellow citizens with a knife of his that I borrowed from him. Then for me to return the borrowed knife to him would actually violate the general principle [that we must seek an orderly social life]. . . . Moreover, due to passion, bad habits, or perverse natures, some people may not even know that it is wrong to take property from its owner and keep it. Julius Caesar wrote, for example, that among the Germanic barbarian tribes theft was not considered wrong.

We can summarize our discussion as follows: The general principles of the natural law hold true for everyone and are known by everyone. But different people may sometimes correctly draw different conclusions from these principles, and even when there is only one correct conclusion various people may be ignorant of it. . . .

### QUESTION 95: WHAT IS THE NATURE OF HUMAN LAWS?

• • •

#### Article 2: Are All Human Laws Based on the Natural Law?

• • •

I STATE MY OWN VIEW AS FOLLOWS: As Saint Augustine says, "that which is not just seems to be no law at all." Consequently, an ordinance is a valid law only to the extent that it is just. Now we say that something is just when it conforms to rational [moral] principles. And as we saw [in Question 94, Article 2], the basic [moral] principles of our reason constitute the natural law. So an ordinance enacted by humans is a valid law only to the extent that it conforms to the natural law. If an ordinance contradicts the natural law then it is not a valid law but a corruption of law.

• • •

### QUESTION 96: WHAT AUTHORITY DO HUMAN LAWS HAVE?

• • •

#### Article 4: Are We Morally Obligated to Obey Human Laws?

• • •

I STATE MY OWN VIEW AS FOLLOWS: The ordinances human beings enact may be just or unjust. If they are just then we have a moral obligation to obey them since they ultimately derive from the eternal law of God. . . .

An ordinance may be unjust for one of two reasons: first, it may be contrary to the rights of humanity; and second, it may be contrary to the rights of God. A law can be contrary to the rights of humanity in any of three ways. First, the law might not be aimed at achieving the common good. This would be the case, for example, if a ruler passed a law that imposed heavy taxes that merely fed the ruler's greed and pride and had no communal benefits. Second, the law might not have been enacted by a legitimate authority. This would be the case, for example, if someone tried to pass a law although he was not delegated the power to do so. Third, the law might distribute burdens unequally. This would be the case, for example, if a law were aimed at achieving the common good, but the burdens involved in achieving that good were distributed unfairly among the citizens. Ordinances that are contrary to the rights of humanity in any of these three ways are not valid laws but acts of violence. . . . We have no moral obligation to obey such ordinances except perhaps to avoid giving bad example or to prevent social disorder. . . .

A law will also be unjust when it is contrary to the rights of God. This would be the case, for example, if a tyrant were to pass a law requiring the worship of idols or any act that is against divine law. It is utterly wrong to obey such laws. . . .

## Treatise on Justice

### QUESTION 64: IS ALL KILLING WRONG?

• • •

#### Article 5: Is It Always Wrong to Kill Oneself?

• • •

I STATE MY OWN VIEW AS FOLLOWS: It is always wrong to kill oneself. . . . For everything by nature loves its own existence, and by nature seeks to keep itself alive and to resist its destruction so far as it can. Consequently, suicide is contrary to this natural inclination. . . . Hence, suicide violates the natural law and is therefore always wrong. . . .

• • •

#### Article 7: Is It Wrong to Kill a Man in Self-Defense?

• • •

I STATE MY OWN VIEW AS FOLLOWS: It is possible for a person's action to have two effects, one of which he intended to bring about while the other was not part of his intention. When this happens, we evaluate the morality of the person's action by what he intended and not by what he did not intend. For when a person does something without intending to do it, we say he did it accidentally [and so he is not to blame].

Now when a person acts in self-defense, his action might have two effects: his action may have the effect of saving his life, but it may also have the effect of killing his attacker. When an act of self-defense has two effects like these, it is not wrong so long as the person intended only the effect of saving his own life, and so long as the person did not use more force than was necessary to save his own life. For the natural law requires a person to preserve his own life. So it is not wrong to intentionally act for this end so long as one's action is not out of proportion to the end.

But it would be wrong for a person to kill an attacker in self-defense if the person deliberately intended to kill the attacker. For taking life is against the natural law, so it is wrong for anyone to intentionally act for this end. The exception to this is the public authority who is acting for the good of the whole society and not out of private animosity.

# ETHICAL ARGUMENTS

*Germain Grisez*

Utilitarianism holds that the moral good or evil of human acts is determined by the results of the acts. If an act has good consequences then that act will be good; if it has bad consequences, it will be bad. Of course, most acts have consequences that are partly good and partly bad. Therefore, utilitarianism holds that the morally good act will be the one that on the whole gives the best results. Whenever we act there are alternatives, including not acting or delaying action. If we can add up the good results expected from each alternative and subtract in each case the expected bad results from the good, then according to utilitarian ethics we should choose the act that carries the prospect of the *greatest net good*. Only that act will be a morally good and right one to choose. Other possibilities will be more or less immoral depending upon how far their net value falls short of the single morally good act. . . .

[But there] simply is no way to determine the "greatest net good" if we take into account . . . *all* the probable good and bad consequences of all the alternatives concretely possible. For the possible alternatives open to us at any given moment are unlimited until we assume a certain definite good. And the humanly significant consequences of any act can be endlessly pursued into the ever more complex and remote and uncertain future. Moreover, diverse goods—even diverse forms of classical utilitarianism's pleasure—are incommensurable with one another. There is no least common denominator, and so there can be no scale for weighing goods against one another.

Many a couple has decided to have another car rather than another child, but such a choice has never been made merely by rational calculation. The two are not commensurable. A decision was reached only when the good of having another car was accepted as the standard by which to judge the merits of having another baby. It is precisely because goods are incommensurable that we are able to determine our course of action freely; if utilitarian calculation were possible, the conclusions of such calculations would impose themselves on us just as unavoidably as do the conclusions of arithmetic problems. . . .

Actual moral decisions are never so simple. But there are judgments that can be made in this way. In technology, engineering, industry, crafts, and arts judgments about how to proceed are necessary. In making such judgments, it is taken for granted that the desired result is good. The only relevant alternatives are the various ways of producing it. These alternatives are judged by their efficiency. The manner of proceeding that is decided on will be considered a good one if it succeeds—that is, if it gets the results one wants.

Moral judgment is not like this because it is not concerned with some particular, limited, definite goal that is produced by an action that has a meaning only from that goal. No. Moral judgment is concerned with the good of the person acting himself and with the good of other persons. This good is not achieved by any particular action, but rather *in* as well as *through* the whole of human life. Man is not a product; what he is to be is not fixed, but constantly expanding.

The peculiarity of persons, in comparison with things, is that persons are not limited by what they are. For a person is a capacity to reflect, and reflection allows the self to stand back from itself and so to go beyond itself. Utilitarianism, far from being an antidote to modern depersonalization, is a consequence of it. If human life itself has to be judged good or bad by its utility, then man is no better than a machine. And this is precisely the outcome of utilitarianism, for it seeks to judge the moral value of human action by its consequences. But in truth human action is considered from a moral point of view precisely to the extent that it is seen not as leading to particular ends but as going to make up the whole which is a person's life itself. . . .

[U]tilitarianism goes wrong by ignoring this fact: that there is no "greatest net good," since goods are incomparable. Utilitarianism logically must presuppose that the choice is already made, the value-perspective already settled, that there is no self-determination. But in this assumption utilitarianism violates the facts of everyday experience, for we constantly find ourselves having to determine ourselves to realize one possibility rather than another. And we do this not by weighing one against another, as if there were comparable goods and a common measure, but by accepting one way of being good rather than the other as the standard by which we shall proceed in this case.

Our problem in choosing is like that of a person who is asked which is worth more, a dollar bill or a copper cent. So long as the credit of the government is good, the bill will be worth more *as money*. But if one desperately needs a bit of copper to bridge a gap in an electrical circuit, the penny would be worth something and the paper bill worth nothing. So it is whenever we choose: we must settle which of two or more possible "betters" will be realized by us.

Thus we determine ourselves by taking as a measure of good the standard by which one alternative will appear decisively better. And once we have chosen, the rejected alternatives seem to pale in attractiveness; no longer impartially considering all possibilities from the perspective of each in turn, we view the whole set of possibilities from the single viewpoint of the good proper to the one to which we have committed ourselves. . . .

The source of the meaning or purpose of what we do is revealed when we ask: "Why did I choose *that*?" The answer must be given in terms of the good we saw in the possibility we chose. Although that good was not compelling to the exclusion of alternative possibilities which carried their own incommensurable goods, the good proper to the alternative we chose was a necessary condition for our choice of it and was a sufficient reason to make that choice intelligible (even if immoral). Thus the freedom of self-determination is not irrational, as if we could act with no reason at all. Rather, freedom is possible because each alternative that is open to us presents itself with a reason adequate to render its selection intelligible.

The immediate reason why we choose in a particular case often is subordinate to an ulterior motive. If we ask a laborer why he is working, he may answer: "To make money." If we ask why he wants to make money, he may reply: "To feed myself and my family, because we get hungry, and to get other necessaries to stay alive." If we try to press the inquiry beyond this point, we may find ourselves none too gently rebuffed, not because the person we are questioning is ignorant of a motive beyond the one stated, but because there is no further purpose. To attempt to question the self-sufficiency of a purpose that is in fact ultimate will seem to a simple person evidence that we are ridiculing him.

Considering the ultimate motives for which we act from a psychological point of view, we discern various categories of basic human needs. These are broader than the specific objects of physiological drives which in other animals are satisfied by instinctive behavior. We are interested, for example, not only in satisfying hunger and thirst, in avoiding immediate physical threats, and so on, but in preserving our lives, maintaining physical and mental health, and attaining a condition of safety and security.

If we consider the basic human needs in this broad fashion, we will find the categories of good for which we can act. For we can act only for that which engages our interest, and nothing engages our interest unless it corresponds to some fundamental inclination within ourselves or to an interest derived from such an inclination. The objects of such inclinations are what we mean by basic human needs, understood broadly as explained above.

The technique of questioning, both by reflection on our own purposes and by discussion with others, can be joined to a survey of psychological literature and a comparison with the categories of human activity found by anthropologists to be useful to interpret the facts of life in any culture.

Each of these approaches has its own limitations. The question technique sometimes terminates not in any objective basic need, but rather in an emotional motivation that reflects an unarticulated need only in its impact on feeling. For example, a child may say he plays ball "for fun"; he does not articulate his interest in terms of the value he achieves in the performance itself. The psychologists emphasize physiology and hence they distinguish drives—e.g., hunger and thirst—which subserve a unified intelligible motive—e.g., the preservation of life and health. The anthropologists sometimes include categories of activity which correspond not to basic needs, but to intermediate goods which are only means to more basic needs—e.g., warfare, property, and the form of economy.

A thorough, critical study of all of these approaches would be desirable; however, it would be a major undertaking in itself. I think that such a study would lend empirical support to the following list of fundamental human goods:

1.  Life itself, including physical and mental health and safety.
2.  Activities engaged in for their own sake (e.g., games and hobbies) including those which *also* serve an ulterior purpose (e.g., work performed as self-expression and self-fulfillment, which also has a useful and economically significant result).
3.  Experiences sought for their own sake (e.g., esthetic experiences and watching professional athletic competitions).
4.  Knowledge pursued for its own sake (e.g., theoretical science and speculative philosophy).
5.  Interior integrity—harmony or peace among the various components of the self.
6.  Genuineness—conformity between one's inner self and his outward behavior.
7.  Justice and friendship—peace and cooperation among men.
8.  Worship and holiness—the reconciliation of mankind to God.

The first four of these groups of goods are understandable without introducing the notion of self-determination in their very meanings. Their achievement depends on human action but their meaning does not. The latter four, by contrast, cannot be understood without including the idea of self-determination. The first four embrace the perfections of a human being according to his specific nature: the exercise of natural functions, physical activity, psychic receptivity, and cognitive reflection. The latter four embrace the perfections of human beings according to their capacity to reflect and to live self-conscious lives: unity achieved by reflection and self-determination at each level on which alienation is experienced or believed to exist.

These categories of goods easily can be defined in such a way that the division is logically exhaustive. However, that procedure would only raise a question concerning the adequacy of the description of each member of the division. A more convincing test of the adequacy of this classification is to try to find basic human goods that cannot be located in it. I think that if the considerations mentioned above in respect to the limitations of various approaches are borne in mind, no purpose of human action that is really final will be found in addition to those listed.

In any case, it will be sufficient for our present purpose to note that any list of basic human goods would have to include life itself. Many people spend the greatest part of their time and effort for no other purpose, and simply staying alive generally is regarded as a good even when other goods cannot be achieved.

We are conscious of these basic goods in two distinct ways. By experience, we are aware of our own inclinations and of what satisfies them; our own longings and delights are facts of our conscious life that we discover as we discover other facts. At the same time, by understanding we interpret these facts in a special way; our intelligence is not merely a spectator of the dynamics of our own action, but becomes involved as a molder and director. Understanding grasps in our inclinations the possibilities toward which they point and understanding becomes practical by proposing these possibilities as goals toward which we might act.

Thus we understand, prior to any choice or reasoning effort, that the basic human goods are possible purposes for our action. To the extent that any action requires some purpose, the basic goods present themselves as purposes-to-be-realized, not merely as objective possibilities. We understand the preservation of our own lives, the pursuit of knowledge, the cultivation of friendship, and the rest as goods-to-be-sought by us. . . .

But it is clear that choice is necessary and it is absurd to say that every choice is necessarily evil simply because it is a choice. Clearly, then, the appeal of the goods cannot be taken as the direct determinant of moral obligation. Everything we can do becomes possible only in virtue of these goods; no human act, good or evil, fails to respond to one or more of them, or succeeds in responding in every possible way to all of them. If the basic human goods, which are principles of practical reason, clarify the possibility of every choice, they cannot of themselves determine why some choices are morally good and others morally evil.

What does make this difference? What divides moral good from moral evil? The answer is that moral goodness and evil depend upon the attitude with which we choose. Not that any and every choice would be good if only it were made with the proper attitude, for some choices cannot be made with the right attitude. But if we have the right attitude, we make good choices; if we have the wrong attitude, we make evil ones.

But what is the right attitude? It is realistic, in the sense that it conforms fully with reality. To choose a particular good with an appreciation of its genuine but limited possibility and its objectively human character is to choose it with an attitude of realism. Such choice does not attempt to transform and belittle the goodness of what is not chosen, but only to realize what is chosen.

The attitude which leads to immoral choices, by contrast, narrows the good to the possibilities one chooses to realize. The good is not appreciated in its objectively human character, simply as a good, but as *this* good of *such* a sort to be achieved *by me*. Instead of conforming to the real amplitude of human possibility, such an attitude transforms that possibility by restriction. Immoral choice forecloses possibilities merely because they are not chosen; rather than merely realizing some goods while leaving others unrealized, such choice presumes to negate what it does not embrace in order to exalt what it chooses. Goods equally ultimate are reduced to the status of mere means for maximizing preferred possibilities; principles of practical reason as fundamental as those that make the choice possible are brushed aside as if they wholly lacked validity.

No single good, nothing that can be embraced in the object of any single choice, is sufficient to exhaust human good, to fulfill all of the possibilities open before man. If we choose with an attitude of openness to goods not chosen, the good is not restricted. We respect the possibility we cannot realize through this choice. But if we restrict our perspective by redefining what is good according to our particular choice, we are attempting to negate the meaningfulness of what we reject and to absolutize what we prefer.

A proper attitude respects equally all of the basic goods and listens equally to all of the appeals they express through principles of practical reason. Because of the incompatibility of actual alternatives, a choice is necessary. But a right attitude does not seek to subvert some principles of practical reason by an appeal to others. An immoral attitude involves such irrationality, for while the evil choice depends upon the principles of practical reason, it seeks to invalidate the claims of those principles which would have grounded an alternate choice.

If the principle that distinguishes moral good from evil is an attitude such as we have just described, still two serious questions must be considered. First, is not moral evil something more interpersonal than the unrealistic and narrow attitude just described? Does not moral evil involve the violation of the good of others? From a religious viewpoint, must it not be seen as alienation from God—a rejection of his love? Second, how does an open attitude such as we have described shape itself into concrete moral obligations to do or avoid specific acts?

The answer to the first question is easy. The principle of moral evil can be located in the unrealistic attitude described, but the impact or significance of such evil is by no means limited to oneself.

If I choose with the attitude that my commitment defines and delimits the good, I shall lack the detachment to appreciate the possibilities of others' lives, which could complement my own by realizing the values I cannot. Their good, which I do not choose, will become for me at best a non-good, something to which I shall remain indifferent. Egoism can decrease only to the extent that I am open to the embrace of all goods, those as well as these, yours as well as mine. The attitude of immorality is an irrational attempt to reorganize the moral universe, so that the center is not the whole range of human possibilities in which we can all share, but the goods I can actually pursue through my actions. Instead of community, immorality generates alienation, and the conflict of competing immoralities is reflected by incompatible personal rationalizations and social ideologies, each of which seeks to remake the entire moral universe in conformity with its own fundamental bias. . . .

The second question—how a morally right attitude can shape itself into specific obligations—is extremely important for ethical theory. . . .

. . . We must ask what our moral judgments would be if we were perfectly integrated in accord with a right moral attitude.

First, if we were open to all of the goods, we would at least take them into account in our deliberations. We would never make a choice by which one of the goods was seriously affected without considering our action in that light. Thus, we would never choose to act in a way that caused anyone's death without being aware of the impact of what we were doing. In this respect, Protestant situationism reveals moral sensitivity that seems missing from some utilitarian theories.

Second, if we had a right moral attitude we would avoid ways of acting that inhibit the realization of any one of the goods and prefer ways of acting that contribute to each one, other things being equal. One who has a positive attitude toward human life certainly makes a presumption in its favor and does not gratuitously negate this good (or any other).

Third, if we had a truly realistic appreciation of the entire ambit of human goods, we would not hesitate to contribute our effort to their realization in others, when our help is needed urgently, merely because no particular benefit accrued to ourselves. True enough, we have primary obligations to realize human goods in ourselves and in those near us, for we can do in ourselves what no one else can. But we should be more interested in *the good* than in *our* good. Therefore, we reveal an immoral attitude if we prefer our own good merely because it is ours, when our help is urgently needed by others. For this reason, one who had a morally right attitude certainly would prefer another's life to his own comfort, or to other goods to which he would prefer his own life.

Fourth, if we had a right moral attitude, we would fulfill our role in any cooperative venture into which we enter not only to the extent necessary to get out of it what we seek for ourselves but to the full extent needed to achieve the good whose concrete possibility depends on the common effort. This principle does not preclude the criticism of institutions or the reformation of structures, but it does rule out attempts to revise social relationships simply to make them more favorable to ourselves, even at the expense of the common good. Thus we cannot rightly seek to preserve and protect our own lives by institutions, such as criminal law, which we refuse to apply equally to the rights of others. Equality before the law is a moral principle as well as a legal one.

Fifth, if we were fully integrated toward the goods, we would carry out our engagements with them. As our life progresses, we make commitments, such as choice of career, which preclude the pursuit of many other possibilities. If these commitments are made in view of the real good we can achieve, we will not set them aside merely because we encounter difficulties. A genuine respect for the goods we do not choose to pursue will make us doubly dedicated to the realization of those on which we concentrate our efforts.

The teacher who is cynical about education, the corrupt politician, the careless physician, the slipshod craftsman—all show a lack of faithful dedication to what they have chosen as their own share of man's effort to achieve the goods open to us. Parents and physicians both are especially engaged in the good of human life in the helpless and dependent. Therefore, failure on their part to protect and promote this good is an abdication of responsibility that reveals an improper moral attitude.

All of the preceding ways in which concrete moral obligations take shape reveal something about the reason why human life, which is one of the basic goods, must be respected. Yet none of these forms of obligation would require an unexceptionable respect for life. Not even the parent and physician need always act to preserve and promote life, for sometimes other goods also are very pressing. A proper moral attitude is compatible with the omission of action that would realize a good, provided that omission itself is essential to realize another good (or the same generic good in another instance).

However, there is still another mode of moral obligation which binds us with greater strictness. If we had a right moral attitude, which means a truly realistic appreciation of each human good, we would never act directly against the realization of any basic good and we would never act in a way directly destructive of a realization of any of the basic goods. To act directly against a good is to subordinate that good to whatever leads us to choose such a course of action. We treat an end as if it were a mere means; we treat an aspect of the person as if it were an object of measurable and calculable worth. Yet each of the principles of practical reason is as basic as the others and each of them must be respected by us equally if we are not to narrow and foreshorten human goodness to conform to our choices.

Of course, each of the basic human goods may be inhibited or interfered with when we act for any good. But it is one thing for inhibition or interference with other goods to occur as unsought but unavoidable side-effects of an effort to pursue a good, and it is quite another thing directly to choose to inhibit or destroy a realization of a basic human good. To reluctantly accept the adverse aspects of one's action is one thing; to purposely determine ourselves to an action that is of its very character against a basic good is quite another matter.

It is only possible for us to do this insofar as a direct attack on a good can be useful to some ulterior good consequence—the end rationalizes the means. But, against utilitarian theories, I think we must maintain that the end which rationalizes the means cannot justify the means when the means in question involves turning against a good equally basic, equally an end, equally a principle of rational action as the good consequence sought to be achieved.

Here, I believe, we arrive at the reason why we consider actions which kill human beings to be generally immoral. Human life is a basic good and it is intrinsic to the person, not extrinsic as property is. To choose directly to destroy a human life is to turn against this fundamental human good. We can make such a choice only by regarding life as a measurable value, one that can be compared to other values and calculated to be of less worth. To attempt such a rationalization is to reduce an end to the status of mere means. Whatever good is achieved by such a means could not have been chosen except by a pretense that the good of the life which is destroyed is not really an irreplaceable human possibility. Undoubtedly, it is for this reason that those who seek to justify direct abortion and other direct attacks on human life strive to deny the humanity and/or personality of the intended victims. . . .

Yet there remain conflict cases such as those in which most moral systems have admitted the justifiability of killing human beings. To such cases we must now turn our attention.

## THE JUSTIFIABLE DOING OF THE DEADLY DEED

• • •

The history of the development of . . . [the principle of double effect] which has interesting applications in many problems besides those involving human life, has been traced in more detail by others. Here it will suffice to recapitulate the principle as it is currently understood.

One may perform an act having two effects, one good and the other bad, if four conditions are fulfilled simultaneously.

1. The act must not be wrong in itself, even apart from consideration of the bad effects. (Thus one does not use the principle to deal with the good and bad effects of an act that is admittedly murder.)
2. The agent's intention must be right. (Thus if one aims precisely at death, the deadly deed cannot be justified by the principle.)
3. The evil effect must not be the means to the good effect, for then evil will fall within the scope of one's intention, and evil may not be intended even for the sake of an ulterior good purpose. (Thus it is certainly wrong to kill someone in order to inherit his wealth.)
4. There must be a proportionately grave reason for doing such an act, since there is a general obligation to avoid evil so far as possible. (Thus one may not use poison deadly to children to kill rodents in a public park.)

The last condition can easily become a field for a covert, although limited, utilitarianism. However, that is not necessary. Though human good is not calculable and though diverse modes of human good are incommensurable, the basic human goods do require protection when possible. Human life may not be destroyed frivolously or gratuitously, as in the example cited, where safer methods of achieving desirable objectives are readily available.

The four conditions of the principle of double effect can be illustrated by a relevant example in the area of our concern. If a woman suffering from invasive carcinoma of the cervix also is pregnant, treatment of the disease is likely to result in the fetus' death. Yet such treatment can be justified. For (1) the treatment would not be wrong apart from its deadly effect on the fetus; (2) neither the mother nor the physician need include the fetus' death within the scope of intention—which might be indicated by the fact that they would proceed in the same way if there were a similar problem without pregnancy and, on the other hand, would use a treatment that would save the fetus if such a method were available; (3) the fetus' death does not produce the desired cure, but is truly incidental to the procedure; and (4) the mother's life and health are of fundamental importance, and may not be able to be safeguarded in a way harmless to the fetus. If the four conditions are actually fulfilled, the deadly deed is compatible with a right moral attitude; it will not involve turning directly against the basic good of human life.

I think that the principle of double effect in this formulation is compatible with the theory of moral good and evil outlined above. That is, I do not think that it permits what ought not to be permitted, provided it is properly understood and applied. My question is whether the principle is more restrictive than it needs to be. The third condition generally is interpreted in a way that excludes the justification of any action in which in the order of objective causality the good effect depends on the evil one. The other three conditions could be fulfilled in cases where abortion seems genuinely necessary to save the mother's life, but the third condition obviously is usually violated in such cases. . . .

[It] seems to me that the principle of double effect in its modern formulation is too restrictive insofar as it demands that even in the order of physical causality the evil aspect of the act not precede the good. The critics are right, I believe, in their insistence that the behavioral aspect of the act is not morally determinate apart from the meaning that shapes the human act. In this respect, Aquinas' formulation seems to me to have been more accurate, for he did not make an issue of which effect (aspect of the act) is prior in physical causality, but he did insist that when a single human act has a good and a bad aspect the latter could not rightly fall within the scope of intention, even as a means to a good end.

From the point of view of human moral activity, the initiation of an indivisible process through one's own causality renders all that is involved in that process equally immediate. So long as no other human act intervenes or could intervene, the meaning (intention) of the behavior which initiates such a process is no less immediate to what is, from the point of view of physical causality, a proximate effect or a secondary or remote consequence. For on the hypothesis that no other human act intervenes or could intervene, the moral agent who posits a natural cause *simultaneously* (morally speaking) posits its foreseen effects. The fact that not everything in the behavior which is relevant to basic human goods equally affects the agent's moral standing arises not from the diverse physical dispositions of the elements of the behavioral aspect of the act, but from the diverse dispositions of the agent's intention with regard to the intelligible aspects of the act.

But it is the intelligible aspects of the indivisible human act that count, not purposes sought and values hoped for in ulterior human acts, whether of the agent himself or of another. For otherwise the end will justify the means, and some sort of utilitarianism or inadequate consistency-criterion will replace the true standard of moral value.

Moreover, even if the particular process initiated by one's behavior is in fact indivisible, he obviously does not escape full moral responsibility for significant aspects of it that could have been avoided by the choice of an alternative behavior having the same determining intention but a diverse mode of accomplishment. Then too, if the unity of the process is merely *de facto*, arising from the agent's failure to divide and limit his behavior, then the act is not truly indivisible and the determining intention will not exclude moral responsibility for aspects of the act that could have been excluded, but were not.

This theoretical formulation will be considerably clarified by application to some examples. . . .

The modified principle of double effect would not justify committing adultery to save one's children from a concentration camp, because the saving effect would not be present in the adulterous act, but in a subsequent human act—that of the person who releases them. Therefore, adultery is intended as a means to an ulterior good end. On the other hand, a mother who saves her child by purposely interposing her body as a shield against an attacking animal is justified, since the very performance which is self-destructive also is protective.

Transplantation of organs which deprives the donor or life or health cannot be justified, because the good effect to the recipient is in a subsequent human act, at least potentially. That is, although the surgical procedures form a continuous whole and can be chosen in a single human act, the two phases of the operation are not necessarily united and the first can be chosen without the second—as is evident since the surgeon may decide not to carry out the implant after the organ has been removed from the donor. If transplantation of organs does not deprive the donor of life and health, it is not contrary to this basic good and so may be justified as an act of giving, just as is the case in blood donations.

# CHAPTER THREE
# KANTIAN ETHICS

In 1961 an experimental psychologist named Stanley Milgram advertised for volunteers to serve as teachers in what he told them were "experiments in memory and learning."[1] The procedure was simple. The volunteer teachers were to sit at the controls of an electric "shock generator" with thirty switches marked from 15 volts to 450 volts. Every fourth switch was labeled with a description such as "Slight Shock," "Moderate Shock," "Strong Shock," "Very Strong Shock," "Intense Shock," "Extreme Intensity Shock," "Danger: Severe Shock," and, on the last switch, "X X X." The teachers were introduced to a person who would serve as the learner for the purposes of the experiment and whose task was to memorize lists of words that each teacher would read to him. The learner was strapped to a chair with electrodes on his wrists and the teachers were instructed that they were to administer gradually increasing shocks to the learner every time he gave a wrong answer.

As the experiment proceeded, the learner failed to memorize many of the words and each time this happened the teachers were told to administer more intense shocks. As the shocks rose in voltage, the learner began to grunt in pain, then started to protest with growing vehemence. At 150 volts he was crying out and begging that the experiment be discon-

---

1. A full account of this experiment may be found in Stanley Milgram, *Obedience to Authority: An Experimental View* (New York: Harper & Row, 1974).

tinued. At 270 volts he began screaming in agony. Shortly thereafter he lapsed into complete silence.

When the volunteer teachers heard the learner's first protests, they turned to the experimenter and asked whether they should stop. Each time the experimenter insisted that it was essential for them to continue, saying there was no danger of any damage and that he took complete responsibility. Under his direction, sixty percent of the volunteer teachers, although shaken and agitated, continued to administer shocks to the screaming learner until the most severe voltage was reached and the learner had apparently fainted or expired.

But the sufferings of the learner were only apparent, for he was merely an actor feigning pain. The entire experiment was really an elaborate deception designed to see how the volunteer teachers would respond when a trusted authority (the experimenter) ordered them to impose pain on another person. The effects on the distressed volunteer teachers were clinically described in Milgram's report:

> The procedure created extreme levels of nervous tension in some subjects. Profuse sweating, trembling and stuttering were typical expressions of this emotional disturbance. One unexpected sign of tension—yet to be explained—was the regular occurrence of nervous laughter, which in some subjects developed into uncontrollable seizures. The variety of interesting behavioral dynamics observed in the experiment . . . point to the fruitfulness of further study. . . . Subjects were observed to sweat, tremble, stutter, bite their lips, groan, and dig their fingernails into their flesh. These were characteristic rather than exceptional responses to the experiment. . . . [One experimenter] observed a mature and initially poised businessman enter the laboratory smiling and confident. Within 20 minutes, he was reduced to a twitching, stuttering wreck, who was rapidly approaching the point of nervous collapse.[2]

Milgram defended his experiment by pointing to the socially beneficial consequences it had produced: it was learned that almost two out of three people will inflict apparent pain on another person if required to do so by a trusted authority who continually reassures them there is no danger. Thus, the experiment shed light on the nature of authority and showed that most people will obey an authority even when the authority orders them to harm others. Several critics, however, claimed that Milgram's elaborate hoax had simply used people as a means to further his own research and that he had manipulated and duped them into feeling extreme guilt and a loss of self-esteem by publicly revealing something embarrassing and shameful about themselves.[3] The critics charged that Milgram had treated his volunteers in ways that no human being should

---

2. Stanley Milgram, "Behavioral Study of Obedience," *Journal of Abnormal and Social Psychology*, vol. 67, no. 4 (1963), pp. 371, 375, 377.

3. See Diana Baumrind, "Some Thoughts on Ethics of Research: After Reading Milgram's 'Behavioral Study of Obedience,'" *American Psychologist*, vol. 19, no. 6 (1964), pp. 421–23; see also the articles collected in Tom L. Beauchamp, Ruth R. Faden, R. Jay Wallace, Jr., and LeRoy Walters, eds., *Ethical Issues in Social Science Research* (Baltimore: Johns Hopkins University Press, 1982).

treat another; in ways, in fact, that we would not want to see universally (i.e., always) practiced by psychologists, no matter what the benefits.

In arguing that it is wrong to use people as a means or to treat them in ways we would not want to see universalized, Milgram's critics were appealing to moral principles that the German philosopher Immanuel Kant developed in the eighteenth century. Kant claimed that our basic moral duties are summed up in a principle he called the categorical imperative: "I am never to act unless I am acting on a maxim that I can will to become a universal law." A second way of expressing this categorical imperative, Kant claimed, is as follows: "Always treat humanity, whether in your own person or in the person of any other, never simply as a means, but always also as an end." The categorical imperative, Kant argued, requires that we show respect for the humanity and dignity of all persons and that we treat each other in accordance with those principles that express the kind of conduct we think should be universally practiced. Moreover, Kant held, these requirements of the categorical imperative must be adhered to regardless of any desires that might be satisfied by violating them. Thus, the Kantian critics of Milgram were arguing that his experiments were immoral because they violated Kant's categorical imperative.

The first reading in this chapter is taken from Kant's *Foundations of the Metaphysics of Morals*. In this work, Kant puts forth his major arguments in support of the categorical imperative. As the reader will see, Kant's arguments are rather difficult, so we have provided a fairly detailed analysis of the reading. Despite their difficulty, Kant's arguments are worth studying since they provide a powerful alternative to moral views (such as utilitarianism, which is discussed in Chapter Four) that hold that any behavior (including deception, manipulation, torture, and so on) is morally permissible so long as it produces more social benefits than anything else one could do. Moreover, Kant's views have profoundly influenced contemporary moral philosophers, many of whom have developed more or less modified versions of his principles. Foremost among these is Richard M. Hare, a moral philosopher who currently teaches at Oxford University in England. In spite of some important differences, Hare's views on "universalizability" in ethics are in many ways similar to those of Kant. The second reading in this chapter is an excerpt from Hare's book, *Freedom and Reason*, in which he claims that we should act only on those moral prescriptions that we would be willing to "universalize."

## THE CLASSICAL VERSION OF KANTIAN ETHICS:
### Kant's *Foundations of Metaphysics of Morals*[4]

Kant opens the first section of his work with the dramatic declaration that nothing in the world is "good without qualification except a good will." By

4. There are a number of fine commentaries on Kant's *Foundations of the Metaphysics of Morals*. The reader who wishes to examine them might try one or more of the following: Bruce Aune, *Kant's Theory of Morals* (Princeton: Princeton University Press, 1979); Brendan

"will" Kant means that part of a person that reasons about and decides what he will do. Here Kant is claiming that when a person's will is morally good, it is good under all conditions: its goodness does not depend upon anything outside of itself. All other personal characteristics (intellectual talents, character traits, and even qualities that help the good will) have value to the extent that they aid us in doing what is right, but they become evil when they are used for evil ends. They are, therefore, "qualified" goods: their goodness depends on how they are used; that is, their goodness depends on the goodness of the will of the person who uses them. Similarly, gifts of fortune are seen as good only if they come to the person with a good will. If an evil person achieves these gifts through evil means, we commonly feel that the person does not deserve the gift and that it is bad for the person to have it.

But what constitutes a good will? When do we say that a person's will is good? According to Kant we do not say a person has a good will merely because the person performs certain external actions. For a person can have a good will and may try to do what is right, but may be prevented from doing it by physical circumstances—such as paralysis. Instead, Kant claims, we determine whether a person has a good will by looking only at the person's "willing," that is, by looking at the reasons on which the person bases his decisions concerning what he will do.

What sorts of reasons or motives, then, characterize the actions of the good-willed person? We can answer this question, Kant suggests, if we look at the sort of reasons a person might have for doing what is morally right, that is, for doing his moral duty. There are, Kant claims, three types of reasons one might have for doing one's duty. First, a person may do his duty out of self-interest, as when he does what is right not because he enjoys doing it but because it will get him something he wants. A grocer may be honest, for example, because it is in his self-interest to appear honest to his customers. Second, a person may carry out his duty motivated by direct inclination, that is, by the immediate satisfaction or pleasure it gives him. A person may be kind to others, for example, because showing kindness makes the person feel good. Third, a person may do something simply because he believes it is the morally correct thing to do. Kant refers to this third kind of motivation as acting from duty. A person would be acting only from duty if, for example, he did what was right simply because he thought it was right and not because he believed it to be in his own self-interest or because it was immediately satisfying to him.

Which of these sorts of reasons must a person have in order to have a good will? Clearly, if a person does the right thing, but does it motivated only by self-interest, we would not say that the person has a good will (for self-interest is also the motive of the crook). And, according to Kant, the person who does the right thing motivated only by direct inclination is

E. A. Liddell, *Kant on the Foundation of Morality* (Bloomington, Ind.: Indiana University Press, 1970); Onora Nell, *Acting on Principle: An Essay on Kantian Ethics* (New York: Columbia University Press, 1975); H. J. Paton, *The Categorical Imperative* (London: Hutchinson, 1947); Robert Paul Wolff, *The Autonomy of Reason* (New York: Harper & Row, 1973).

also not necessarily a person of good will. Consider, for example, a person who preserves his life or helps others only because of the enjoyable feelings connected with living or with the activity of helping others—a person, that is, who would not continue to do these things if those enjoyable feelings were no longer present. The man who preserves his life or who helps others only because it makes him feel good, Kant points out, really does not have a different motivation from the man who does evil because evil makes him feel good: such a person would engage in any activity he found enjoyable, whether or not it was evil. Kant concludes that direct inclinations do not provide the type of reasons that enable us to say that a person has a good will. But now imagine a person who refrains from suicide, or who helps others, simply because he believes it is right to do so, even though he will get absolutely nothing out of it. In both of these cases, Kant claims, the person would have a good will: such a person's actions, done from duty, are based on the sort of reasons that alone characterize the person of good will. Kant concludes, therefore, that a person's conduct has true moral value only to the extent that it is done from duty.

What does it mean to say that a person is motivated by duty and not by self-interest or direct inclination? According to Kant, if we analyze the motive of acting from duty, we will see that at bottom it involves feeling respect for nothing more than universal law, that is, for moral principles that we think all human beings ought to live up to, even if they have no desire to do so. (A principle in this context is a rule, such as one of the Ten Commandments, that requires us to behave in a certain way.) For example, when we keep our promises because we believe that doing so is a moral duty, we feel respect for the principle that people ought to keep their promises. Further, we feel that everyone, including ourselves, should try to live up to this principle, even when we are not inclined to do so. Therefore, Kant concludes, a person is acting from duty to the extent that he does things because he feels it is required by moral principles that everyone always ought to follow. As Kant puts it: "That is, I am never to act unless I am acting on a maxim that I can will to become a universal law." Here, a maxim is seen as the principle on which a person is acting and a universal law as a rule stating that everyone should act on that principle. So, in different terminology, Kant is saying this: "I am never to act on a principle that I could not be willing to have everyone act upon." This is Kant's basic version of the categorical imperative, and he illustrates it with the example of the duty to keep one's promises.

What, then, would Kant say about the Milgram experiments? According to Kant, in order to determine whether it was morally right for Milgram to carry out these experiments, we must ask whether Milgram would have been willing to have everyone act on those principles on which he was acting when he decided to perform the experiments. We do not know exactly what these principles were, but let us suppose that one of them was the following: "One may deceive whomever one wants if doing so will produce knowledge that one thinks is worth having." Now Kant would ask whether we could possibly choose to live in a world in which people went around deceiving each other whenever they felt it would produce knowledge they felt was worth having. The answer to this question, Kant would hold, will give you the answer to the question, "Was it ethical for Milgram to carry out these experiments?"

In the second section of his work, Kant offers a second, more philosophical account of the categorical imperative based on an analysis of what he calls "imperatives." An imperative is a statement or principle that expresses what a person ought to do. For example, "You ought to be honest," is an imperative in Kant's sense. Kant divides all imperatives into two groups: categorical imperatives (not to be confused with the basic principle he calls *the* categorical imperative) and hypothetical imperatives. Categorical imperatives are principles that require every person to perform a certain action (or refrain from performing a certain action) regardless of the ends that person happens to desire. For example, the unqualified principle, "You should not kill harmless children" is a categorical imperative. Hypothetical imperatives, on the other hand, are principles which require a person to do something only if he or she happens to desire a certain end. For example, "You should put on a coat if you want to be warmer" is a hypothetical imperative.

Kant indicates that there are two main kinds of hypothetical imperatives: First, imperatives of skill that indicate what one ought to do if one wants to achieve some specific goal and, second, imperatives of prudence that indicate what one ought to do if one wants to be happy. Categorical imperatives, however, all consist of a third kind of principle: moral principles. All true moral principles are categorical imperatives because all persons should do what true moral principles require no matter what desires they happen to have. Consequently, Kant argues, in order to determine whether I am acting on true moral principles, I need only ask myself whether I am acting on principles that could be categorical and not hypothetical; that is, principles that I could be willing to have everyone act on regardless of what they happen to desire. Thus Kant again reaches the conclusion he labels the single principle of the categorical imperative: "Act only on that maxim which you can will to be a universal requirement, that is, a universal law." (It is the *single* principle of the categorical imperative because all other categorical imperatives are based on this one fundamental principle.)

Almost immediately, Kant announces that this basic categorical imperative can be expressed in a slightly different version: "Act as if the maxims you choose to follow always became universal laws of nature." This is the first alternative version that Kant gives of the single categorical imperative. What Kant means by this is that in order to see whether I am acting on a principle that I could be willing to have everyone act on, I should imagine what the world would be like if that principle became part of everyone's nature. Then I must ask whether I would want to live in such a world.

Kant goes on to illustrate this first version of the categorical imperative by giving four examples of how it should be applied. These examples suggest that a person should ask himself two questions about any principle he is thinking of following: (1) Can I conceive of a world in which everyone follows this principle? and (2) Would I be willing to live in such a world? Kant points out that sometimes we cannot even conceive of a world in which everyone follows a certain principle because there is some contradiction in thinking that human beings could all act in accordance with that principle; in such cases we have a "perfect" or absolute duty not to act on that principle. (A perfect duty is a duty that commands an act that it would be morally wrong to omit.) Sometimes, it is possible for us to conceive of a world in which everyone follows a certain principle, but we would not be willing to live in such a world; in such cases we have an "imperfect" duty not to act on that principle. (An imperfect duty is a duty that commands an act that would be meritorious or good for us to perform but which it would not be morally wrong to omit.)

Kant claims next that there is a second way of expressing the basic categorical imperative and to explain this, he distinguishes between subjective ends and objective ends. A subjective end is some object that I personally happen to desire and for which I am acting. If I work, for example, because I happen to desire money, then money is a subjective end for me: it is an end I personally desire and for which I am working. An objective end, on the other hand, is some being for whose sake everyone believes they should act, no matter what desires we personally happen to have. An objective end is an end for whose sake everyone recognizes they should act.

Kant now states that if the categorical imperative is really binding on everyone (as it must be if it is valid) then everyone must be motivated to follow it no matter what desires they happen to have. In other words, there must be something that can motivate everyone to follow it in spite of their particular desires. But a subjective end cannot motivate everyone to follow the categorical imperative. A subjective end, such as money, will motivate only those who happen to have a desire for that particular subjective end. Since not everyone sees money as a valuable thing, not everyone can be motivated by it. It is clear, then, that only some objective end could provide the universally recognized motive that the categorical imperative requires. Thus if the categorical imperative is valid, there must be some objective end for whose sake everyone knows they should act and for whose sake everyone is acting when they follow the categorical imperative.

But is there any such objective end? According to Kant, there is only one: persons. Persons are rational beings whose existence everyone recognizes should be promoted. When we humans do something, we usually do it for the sake of a person for whom we recognize it is worth doing things—ourselves. And just as we each recognize that we ourselves are beings for whose sake we should act, so also we must each recognize that since others are like ourselves we should also act for their sake as well. Thus all persons (and only persons) are objective ends, beings for whose sake everyone knows they should act no matter what personal desires they happen to have. So persons must be the objective end for whose sake we are acting when we follow the categorical imperative. (Another way of putting this point is as follows: the basic categorical imperative requires us to act on principles that treat everyone the same. Why should we treat everyone the same? Because we recognize that all persons are intrinsically valuable. Thus to say that we should act only on those principles that we are willing to have everyone follow is to say that we should treat all persons as having an equal intrinsic value.) Thus, if it is true that we all should follow the categorical imperative, then it is also true that we should all treat persons as objective ends: beings for whose sake we should act no matter what personal desires we happen to have.

Kant points out that this necessitates that persons never be turned into mere "means" (that is, into instrumental "things") for satisfying our personal desires.[5] In other words, I should never do something to a person in order to get something I desire unless I am also doing it for the sake of that person. Or, as Kant expresses it in the second version of the basic categorical imperative: "So act as to treat humanity, whether in your own person or in that of another, always as an [objective] end and never *merely* as a means." To treat a person as a means is to treat the person as a thing that is to be used to satisfy someone's desires. To treat a person as an end is to treat the person as a being whose existence as a free rational person is intrinsically valuable.

To explain in more detail what he means by treating people as ends and not merely as means, Kant again provides four examples that illustrate the second version of the basic categorical imperative. These suggest that to treat a person as an end and not merely as a means, I must do two things: (1) I must not use the person as a thing whose only function is to satisfy desires; instead I must always also give the person the opportunity to freely and rationally choose whether or not to go along with my action, and (2) I must promote the person's capacity to engage in free rational choices and must promote those choices. Thus, for Kant, to treat a person as an end is basically to respect and promote that person's free rational choices. Kant claims that some actions treat persons as things whose only function is to satisfy desires and whose free consent need not be sought; such actions go against the first precept listed above and are violations of perfect duties. Some actions do not treat people as things (perhaps because they are omissions in which we are not really acting on or doing anything to anyone) but they still fail to promote people's free choices; these actions go against the second precept listed above and are violations of imperfect duties.

Kant's meaning here may become clearer if we apply these notions to the Milgram experiments. First, since Milgram's plan relied on deceiving his subjects, it is clear that they were not given an opportunity to give or

5. Notice that Kant is suggesting here that the distinction between a subjective end and an objective end is between the things that we desire and pursue (subjective ends) and the persons for whom we desire and pursue these things (objective ends). For example, if I desire money for myself, then money is my subjective end and I myself am my objective end; if I desire money for you, then money is again my subjective end but you are now my objective end. On this point see Alan Donagan, *The Theory of Morality* (Chicago: University of Chicago Press, 1977), pp. 63–64.

withhold their free consent. Second, it is clear that Milgram was not carrying on the experiments in order to help his subjects develop their ability to make free and rational choices. Thus it would seem that Milgram was in fact using his subjects merely as means and not respecting them as ends in themselves.

At the end of the second section of his work, Kant provides yet a third version of the categorical imperative. He expresses it in these words: "According to this [third] principle a maxim must be rejected if it is inconsistent with the idea that the will is itself the maker of its universal laws." Essentially, Kant is saying that I should act only on those universal moral principles that I have freely and rationally chosen for myself, independent of my personal desires or the personal desires of anyone else. Kant calls this the principle of autonomy because it expresses the idea that a human being is moral only to the extent that he is able to free himself from blindly following his own desires or the desires of others (parents, peers, Church, and so on). Kant argues that the principle of autonomy is really implicit in the meanings of the first and second versions of the categorical imperative. For the first version implies that a person should follow universal moral principles, and the second that in following these principles a person should not turn himself into a means for satisfying anyone's desires. Thus together these first two versions imply that a person should live only by those universal moral principles that he has chosen for himself independent of anyone's personal desires, including his own.

But is it really possible for human beings to free themselves from the forces of desire? That is, is it really possible for human beings to act autonomously—or is such a morality beyond our reach? Kant believes this is a critically important question, but he waits until the third section of his work to answer it.

Kant begins this section by pointing out that having a free will and having a will that should follow the moral law is really one and the same thing. (After all, as we saw at the end of the second section, to say that one should follow universal moral principles is to say that one must make one's choices free of the forces of desire.) Kant then presents an argument to show that the will is free from a practical point of view. He argues that every rational being (like ourselves) who thinks he can act on the world must regard himself as free. For if we think the actions we are performing are really our own actions (that is, actions for which we are responsible), then they must be actions that issue from our own free choices. Actions that issue from forces (like our desires) over which we have no control are not really actions we ourselves choose to carry out, but are instead actions for which those forces are responsible. For practical purposes, then, we must assume we are free since we think we are responsible for at least some of our actions. In particular, Kant points out, when we make a rational judgment about some matter, we assume that we are free and that we are not being forced to make the judgment by forces out of our control. Thus we must assume that we are free when we make judgments concerning the principles we will follow.

But even if, for practical purposes, we must assume we are free, this still does not solve a major theoretical objection: Isn't it clear that everything we see in the world around us is causally determined by physical forces? If so, then our own actions must be determined and we are not really free, but merely think we are. Kant next turns to trying to answer this major theoretical objection.

There are, Kant claims, two ways of looking at ourselves. First, we can look at ourselves simply as creatures of sensation, and then we must think of ourselves as passively acted upon by the forces of nature. If we look at ourselves in this way we do not appear to be free. Second, we can look at ourselves as creatures of reason and understanding (as rational beings) and then we know that just as our reason is free to spontaneously act by thinking up ideas for itself, so also it is free to act by choosing for itself. If we look at ourselves in this second way, we must assume that we are free. As human beings, Kant points out, we cannot help but look at ourselves in both ways and so we see ourselves now apparently pulled by the forces of desire and now free to choose independent of desire. That is, since we belong both to the world of sense and to the world of reason, we feel ourselves pressured by our desires to go against the moral law that reason sets before us. Thus, although it is true that from one point of view we are determined by the forces of desire, this does not contradict the fact that we are also free. For in claiming we are free, we are simply looking at ourselves from a different point of view. Moreover, Kant claims, the first way of looking at ourselves (as creatures of sensation) is merely an appearance and the second way of looking at ourselves (as creatures of reason) gets at the reality underlying appearances or at the way things really are in themselves.

Kant ends his work by pointing out that there is really no way of explaining the freedom that we have. All we can do is refute those who claim that freedom and morality are impossible. And that, he thinks, is precisely what he has done.

## A CONTEMPORARY VERSION OF KANTIAN ETHICS:
### R. M. Hare's "Moral Reasoning"

Richard M. Hare is acknowledged to be one of the best moral philosophers alive today. In *Freedom and Reason,* the book from which the reading "Moral Reasoning" is taken, Hare argues against "naturalist" theories of ethics, which claim that moral concepts can be defined in nonmoral or "natural" terms. For example, the theory "X is immoral means that X is disapproved of by most people" is a naturalist theory of ethics. Hare claims that such naturalist theories assume that moral reasoning is deductive. That is, they assume that one deduces the morality of an act from nonmoral or natural premises. Instead, in Hare's view, we must recognize that moral reasoning is much more like the testing of hypotheses that goes on in scientific inquiry, where one looks "for hypotheses which will stand up to the test of experiment." In moral reasoning, Hare states, we proceed by testing our moral judgments to see whether we can accept their consequences. If we cannot, then the moral judgments are also not acceptable.

But how does moral reasoning generate consequences from our moral judgments and how are these tested? Hare claims that it is the "meanings and functions" of moral language that enable us to derive certain consequences from our moral judgments and test them for acceptability. According to Hare, the meaning and function of moral language is such that acceptable moral judgments must be both "prescriptive" and "universalizable." An acceptable moral judgment must be prescriptive in the sense that we must be willing to accept whatever it implies. And a moral judgment is universalizable (as Kant suggested) in the sense that it logically implies some universal moral principle. For example, the judgment "John ought to return the money he owes" implies the universal principle "Anyone in circumstances like John's ought to return the money he owes." In general, the judgment that it is morally right (or wrong) for a certain person to perform a certain act in certain circumstances implies the universal principle that it would be morally right (or morally wrong) for all persons to perform the same act if they were in the same circumstances. Hare points out that prescriptivity and universalizability together imply that a moral judgment is acceptable only if we would be willing to accept having everyone else follow the universal moral principle that our judgment implies. And this in turn implies that we must be willing to have others treat us in accordance with these universal moral principles. If I am not willing to have all others treat me (even in hypothetical situations) in accordance with the moral principles implied by my judgment, then it is not an acceptable moral judgment for me to act on. Hare uses the Biblical parable of the two debtors to illustrate his theory of how moral reasoning proceeds.

What would Hare say about the Milgram experiments? He would probably state that in order to determine whether it was ethical for Milgram to carry them out, we must ask whether Milgram would accept the universal principle "It is morally right for anyone to do to others what I did to my experimental subjects." And to see whether this universal principle is acceptable to him, we must ask whether Milgram would be willing to accept having others do to him what he did to his experimental subjects. In short, would Milgram be willing to be treated in the way he treated others? As Hare suggests, this would amount to applying the "golden rule."

# FOUNDATIONS OF THE METAPHYSICS OF MORALS

*Immanuel Kant*

### FIRST SECTION: TRANSITION FROM OUR ORDINARY RATIONAL KNOWLEDGE OF MORALITY TO PHILOSOPHICAL UNDERSTANDING

#### [Only A Good Will Is Good Without Qualification]

It is impossible to think of anything in the universe—or even beyond it—that is good without qualification, except a good will. Intellectual talents such as intelligence, cleverness, and good judgment are undoubtedly good and desirable in many respects; so also are character traits such as courage, determination, and perseverence. But these gifts of nature can become quite evil and harmful when they are at the service of a will that is not good. It is the same with gifts of fortune such as power, wealth, honor, and even health and that general well-being and contentment we call happiness. These will produce pride and conceit unless the person has a good will, which can correct the influence these have on the mind and ensure that it is adapted to its proper end. Moreover, an impartial rational spectator would not feel any pleasure at seeing a person without a good will enjoying continuous happiness. Thus it seems that having a good will is a necessary condition for even deserving happiness.

Not even those qualities that help the good will in its action can be said to have an unqualified value. The value of such qualities always depends on the goodness of the will. This is why the esteem that we justly have for them is qualified and why we do not regard them as absolutely good. For example, moderation, self-control, and thoughtfulness are good in many respects and they even seem to be part of what makes a person good. Yet they do not deserve to be called good without qualification (although they were unconditionally praised by ancient philosophers). For without a good will, they may become extremely bad. Cool self-control in a criminal, for example, not only makes him far more dangerous but also makes him more hateful than he would have been without it.

#### [The Good Will and External Actions]

A good will is good not because of the actions it carries out or the effects it brings about. Nor does its goodness depend on how fit it is to achieve certain goals. A good will is good simply in virtue of its willing—

that is, it is good in itself. By itself it has greater value than any object it could produce merely in order to satisfy an inclination, nay even to satisfy the sum total of all inclinations. To see this, suppose that because of bad luck or because of a natural handicap, a certain good will was unable to carry out its intentions. Suppose that even though it tried its best it was not able to achieve anything at all. Nevertheless, so long as it remained a good will (not merely wishing to do good, but trying with all the means in its power) it would still shine by its own light like a jewel that has its whole value in itself. Its usefulness or productivity can neither add nor subtract anything from this value. Its usefulness would be merely like a setting that enables us to deal with it more easily in our ordinary affairs and that makes it more attractive to those who are not yet expert judges. But its usefulness would not be what recommends it to the expert, nor what determines its value. . . .

### [The Good Will and the Three Types of Motivations]

Thus, we will have to analyze the concept of a will that is good in itself. . . . We will do this by examining the idea of acting *from duty*. The concept of acting from duty includes the concept of a good will, but as subject to certain temptations and obstacles. However, these obstacles do not hide or obscure the good will; instead, they make it shine all the more brightly by contrast.

We will begin our investigation by simply setting aside all those actions in which a person does what he knows is wrong in order to achieve some purpose. For with such actions the question whether they are done *from duty* cannot arise at all, since they are actually opposed to duty.

We can next set aside those actions which conform to duty and which a person does out of self-interest, although he may not have a *direct inclination* toward doing the action. For we can easily see that since such actions are done from *self-interest*, they are not done *from duty*.

However, it is harder to tell whether a person's action is done *from duty* when his action conforms with duty and the person also has a *direct inclination* toward the action. [Some examples may help us to distinguish *duty* from *self-interest* and *direct inclination,* and may help us see what *duty* involves.] Consider, as a first example, that every grocer has a duty not to overcharge his inexperienced customers. And when he has a lot of competition, the smart grocer will conform with this duty and never overcharge, so that children as well as adults will buy from him. The grocer is thus being *honest* with people. But we would not say that such a grocer was acting *from duty* or from principles of honesty. Rather his actions conformed with duty only because his own interests required him to act as he did. We also would not say that such a grocer was acting from *direct inclination,* that is, out of a kind of love that he felt for his customers. Thus, in this case, it is easy enough to see that the action was done merely from self-interest and not from duty or from direct inclination. [Clearly such an action has no moral worth.]

Consider, next, the duty everyone has to preserve his own life. Obviously, everyone also feels a *direct inclination* to do this. But for this very reason the anxious care that most people take to stay alive has no intrinsic value, and their maxim has no moral significance. They preserve their life as duty requires, but not *because* duty requires it. But imagine a man who has suffered so much misfortune and despair that he no longer enjoys life. Suppose that he is a strong-minded individual and that instead of becoming sad or dejected, he is angry at his fate and would like to commit suicide. If such a man continues to preserve his life even though he does not love it; and if he preserves it not from inclination or fear, but from duty, then his maxim has a moral value.

Consider another example: we all have a duty to help others when we can. Now there are some people who are so sympathetic that they feel pleasure when they spread joy around them and are delighted when they can make others happy. But I maintain that the benevolent actions of such people, however proper and likable they may be, do not have true moral value. They do not have true moral value because acting for the sake of the pleasure or delight one derives from an action is on a level with acting on any other inclination, such as the inclination to be honored. If, acting out of desire for honor, one happens to do something that is beneficial, right, and deserving of honor, then one deserves praise and encouragement but not moral admiration. Such actions are carried out for reasons that have no moral content; to have moral content they must be done *from duty*, not for the sake of some *direct inclination*. But now suppose that this kind man was overwhelmed with some tragedy of his own and that as a result he no longer felt the same sympathetic pleasure when he did good to others. Imagine, further, that he still has the power to help others although he is not touched by their troubles because he has so many of his own. Now suppose that he arouses himself from this dead insensibility and helps others without any inclination to do so, but simply from duty. Then, at that point, his action has genuine moral value.

Or take a man who is otherwise upright, but whom nature has made unsympathetic to the sufferings of others. Perhaps he is blessed with exceptional endurance and fortitude about his own troubles and he assumes that others are the same—and such a man would certainly not be the most deficient human being nature ever produced. But although nature has not made it easy for him to reach out to help others, could he not still find in himself a source from which he can draw a far higher value than from a good-natured temperament? Unquestionably. His character will have the highest kind of moral value when he helps others from duty and not merely from inclination. . . .

There remains, then, in this, as in all other cases, this [proposition]: namely, that a man should . . . [act] not merely from inclination but from duty, and by doing this his action first acquires true moral value. . . .

Our second proposition is this: That an action done from duty derives its moral value not from the purpose that is to be attained by it but from the maxim on which it is based. Moral value, therefore, does not depend on achieving the objective for which we are acting; instead, moral value depends on the principle on which the will chooses to act, regardless of its desires. It is clear from what we have said that the objects we may desire to achieve by our actions (that is, the effects of our actions but regarded as ends which move the will) cannot give to actions any unqualified or moral value. In what, then, can their value lie if it is not to lie in the will and in its motive for seeking the object? The moral value of our actions must lie in the principle that guides the will without regard to the ends that can be attained by the actions. For the will stands between its *a priori* principle, which is formal, and its *a posteriori* desire, which is material, as between two roads it must choose. Now the will must choose for the sake of something. As we have seen, when the will acts from duty it does not act for the sake of satisfying any material desire. The will that acts from duty must therefore act for the sake of a formal principle.

## [Duty and Respect for Universal Moral Law]

Our third proposition follows from our first two propositions. The third proposition can be put this way: Duty is the necessity of acting from respect for the [moral] law. I can feel an *inclination* toward a thing I make or bring about. But I cannot have *respect* for such a thing precisely because it is something I control through my willing and it is not the willing itself. Similarly, I cannot have respect for an inclination, whether it is my own or someone else's. At most, I can choose to approve the inclinations I have; and I can perhaps love the inclinations others have when they are favorable to my own interests. But I can have respect for something only if it is a principle to which my will must submit and is not something that my will can make or bring about as it chooses. That is, I can have respect for something only if it does not serve my inclinations, but rules over them, or at least disregards them when I make a choice. In other words only a [moral] law can be an object of respect, and hence a command. Now an action done only from duty must wholly exclude the influence of inclination and of every object of desire. Thus [when acting only from duty] nothing can determine the will except objectively the [fact that this is a requirement of the moral] *law* and subjectively *pure respect* for this law of action; thus we have the maxim[1] that I should follow such a law even when it is contrary to all my inclinations.[2] . . .

1. A "maxim" is a principle on which a particular subject (i.e., a particular rational being) in fact acts; I call this a "subjective principle." The objective principle (i.e., the principle that would also serve as a subjective principle for all rational beings if reason had full sway over the faculty of desire) is a *law* of action.

2. It might be objected that by using the word *respect* I am appealing to an obscure feeling instead of supplying a precise concept of reason. But although respect is a feeling, it is not a feeling aroused by an outside influence, but is self-induced by one's own rational concepts. It can, therefore, be precisely distinguished from all feelings of the former kind, which may be the result either of inclination or fear. What I recognize immediately as a [moral] law for me, I recognize with respect. So "respect" refers to the consciousness that my will is subordinate to a law, without any influence from my senses. That is, "respect" refers to my awareness that the [moral] law is something to which my will must submit itself. "Respect" is thus something that the [moral] law arouses in me; it is not something that causes the law to come into existence. Respect is actually the awareness of a value to which even my self-love must give way. Respect is not really a kind of inclination or a kind of fear, although it has similarities to both. The only thing that can be the object of respect is the

### [I Should Act Only on Maxims I Can Will to Be Universal]

But what sort of law can this be that mere awareness of it is enough to make the absolutely good will choose to follow it regardless of the results? Since I have ruled out every motive based on the desirable results of obeying any particular law, no other motive is left for the good will to act on except the motive of obeying the [moral] law simply because it is a universal law. That is, *I am never to act unless I am acting on a maxim that I can will to become a universal law.*

Thus, the basic principle that the will must follow is the principle of conforming to universal law (as distinct from a law that would require a particular action). Only this principle can prevent duty from becoming a vain delusion and a mythical notion. The ordinary reason of humanity in its practical judgments agrees perfectly with this, and always has in view the principle here suggested. For example, suppose that I ask myself: Would it be morally permissible for me to make a promise I do not intend to keep when I am in trouble? . . . The shortest and most unerring way for me to discover whether a lying promise is consistent with duty is to ask myself: Would I be willing to have my maxim (that is, the principle: "I will get out of my difficulties with false promises") be a universal law, for myself as well as for others; and would I be able to say to myself, "Everyone may make a false promise when he finds himself in a difficulty that he cannot escape in any other way"? As soon as I ask myself these questions, I become aware that although I might desire to lie, I am certainly not willing to have lying become a universal law. For if lying promises became the rule, there would soon be no promises at all. There would be no promises because people would stop believing each other when they said that they intended to keep their promises; and if one person over-hastily accepted the lying promise of another, that person would soon learn to do the same thing to others. So as soon as my maxim became a universal law, it would destroy itself.

I do not, therefore, need any great genius to see what I have to do so that my will can be morally good. Even if I have very little experience of the world, even if I cannot prepare for all contingencies ahead of time, all I have to ask myself is this: Could you will to have your maxim become a universal law? If not, then you should not act on that maxim. You should not act on it, not because it is not in your self-interest and not because it is not in the interest of others. You should not act on it simply because it cannot be a universal law. That is, it cannot become the kind of law that reason tells me I must immediately respect. Of course, we have

---

[moral] law; that is, the law we impose on ourselves and yet are aware of as something that imposes itself on us. It imposes itself on us in the sense that it must be followed without consulting self-love; we impose it on ourselves in the sense that our will freely chooses whether or not to follow it. In the former aspect, it is like fear; in the latter aspect, it is like inclination. Respect for a person is really only respect for the law (of honesty, and so forth) that he exemplifies in his actions. For example, when we feel respect for a person who has worked at developing his abilities, it is because we believe we all have a duty to improve our abilities. And, properly speaking, we really feel respect for this law (viz., that we should all work at developing our abilities). Thus, all our moral appraisals are really based on respect for the [moral] law.

not yet uncovered the foundations on which this respect is based (this is a philosopher's inquiry). But we at least now see that to have respect for something is to see it as having a value that far outweighs the value of any object of desire. It is also clear that the necessity of acting from pure respect for the practical law is what constitutes duty, to which every other motive must yield because it is what makes a will good in itself, and the value of such a will is above everything.

Thus, by restricting ourselves to a study of the ordinary moral knowledge that every human reason has, we have found the basic principle of morality. . . .

## SECOND SECTION: TRANSITION FROM POPULAR MORAL PHILOSOPHY TO THE METAPHYSICS OF MORALS

In the first section we advanced by natural steps from our ordinary moral judgments (which are certainly worth our respect) to a philosophical analysis. But now we want to move from this popular philosophy to a "metaphysics" of morals. The popular philosophical analysis of the last section established its conclusions by appealing to examples and went no further. In a "metaphysical" investigation, however, we are not limited to empirical examples but examine even ideal concepts that have no empirical examples, since metaphysics includes the study of everything we know. In order to reach a metaphysics of morals we will have to examine and describe clearly how practical reason derives the notion of duty from the general rules it follows.

### [Imperatives and the Will]

Everything in nature acts according to laws. But only rational beings have the ability to act according to their own idea of a law, that is, the ability to follow their own principles. To have this ability is to have a will. Since the ability to use principles in deciding what one will do requires reason, the will is nothing but practical reason. Now if there were a being whose reason infallibly determined his will, he would always do whatever his reason recognized to be objectively right. His will would be free from the influence of desire and so it would choose only what reason decided was objectively necessary for him to do, that is, only what his reason recognized as good. But this is not the case with beings like us, whose will is not completely determined by reason. Our wills are exposed to the influence of subjective desires that sometimes oppose what reason sees is objectively right. Since our wills are not in complete harmony with reason, we do not always choose what reason recognizes is objectively right. Because our will is subject to desires that oppose reason, we experience the objective laws of reason as constraints. That is, the relationship between our wills (which are not completely good) and the objective law is conceived as a relationship in which these principles of reason are imposed on the will of a rational being who, because of his nature, does not necessarily follow these principles.

When the idea of an objective principle imposes an obligation that constrains such a will it is called a "command of reason"; and a statement of this command is called an "imperative."

All imperatives are expressed by the word "ought." By this word, imperatives indicate the relation between an objective law of reason (an obligation) and a will that does not necessarily follow the law because of its nature. As we have said, this relation is experienced as a constraint. Imperatives say that something would be good to do or to forbear, but they say it to a will like ours that does not always do what it knows to be good. . . .

### [The Main Types of Imperatives]

Now all imperatives command either *hypothetically* or *categorically*. Hypothetical imperatives indicate that it is necessary to perform a certain action because the action is a means to something else that the will seeks (or that it could seek). A categorical imperative is one that indicates that it is necessary to perform a certain action whether or not the action achieves any further ends; that is, a categorical imperative indicates that a certain action is objectively necessary for us to perform. . . .

Accordingly, a hypothetical imperative only says that an action is good as a means to some goal, either a goal one could seek or a goal one is actually seeking. In the former case, the imperative would be a "problematic" imperative; in the latter, it would be an "assertorial" imperative. A categorical imperative that declares an action to be objectively necessary in itself, without reference to any goal or end, is an "apodictic" imperative.

Anything a rational being can bring about can serve as a goal for some will. Consequently, there are an infinite number of hypothetical principles indicating the actions that are the necessary means to the goals people might have. There are, first, the principles of the practical sciences, which propose certain ends and provide directions about how those ends may be attained. These imperatives may therefore be called imperatives of *skill*. Here the question is not whether the end is rational and good, but only what one must do in order to attain it. The prescriptions used by the physician to make his patient healthy and those used by a poisoner to kill are of equal value so long as we are concerned only with the best way to achieve the end. Since in early youth it cannot be known what ends we are likely to seek during our lifetime, our parents seek to teach us a great many of the skills needed to choose the best means for attaining all sorts of goals. Parents cannot know what goals their children will seek, so they teach them the means to whatever goals they might seek. Their anxiety about teaching the means is so great that they commonly neglect to teach the child how to judge the value of his ends.

Second, there are those hypothetical imperatives that are concerned with a certain end that all rational beings pursue (so far as imperatives apply to them, viz., as dependent beings). This is an end that rational beings not merely *may* pursue but that we can rest assured they all *actually* pursue by a natural necessity. This end is happiness. A hypothetical imperative that indicates that it is necessary to perform a certain action as a means to attaining happiness may be called an "assertorial" imperative. Such imperatives do not present the action as necessary for some goal we *might* have, but for a goal we know for sure and *a priori* that everyone has. Everyone has it because it is part of their nature. The skill of choosing the means to one's own happiness may be called *prudence,* in the narrowest sense of the term. This kind of imperative, that is, imperatives of prudence, which indicate the means by which one can attain happiness, are all hypothetical imperatives since they command an action not absolutely, but only as a means to an end.

There is a third kind of imperative that commands certain actions directly and not as a means to some end. Imperatives of this kind are *categorical* and not *hypothetical.* They are not concerned with the material goals of the action or with its intended results; instead they are concerned only with the form of the action and the principle that requires it. The goodness of such an action essentially depends on whether the agent's mental intention is to make his action conform to the principle; the goodness of such an action does not depend on whether the action achieves certain results the agent wanted to achieve. Imperatives of this kind are the imperatives of *morality.* . . .

### [The Basic Principle of the Categorical Imperative]

Merely knowing what a hypothetical imperative says does not tell me what I ought to do unless I want the end for which it indicates the means. But merely knowing what a categorical imperative says immediately tells me what I must do. For a categorical imperative states only the required action and the necessity that my maxim[1] conform to that requirement. Since there are no conditions attached to the requirement, the categorical imperative states only that my maxim should conform to a requirement that is universal. And it is this conformity alone that the imperative properly asserts to be necessary.

There is therefore but a single basic principle of the categorical imperative, namely, this: *Act only on that maxim that you can at the same time will to be a universal requirement, that is, a universal law.*

Now if all imperatives of duty can be derived from this basic imperative, then we can at least show what we mean by duty, even if we have not yet shown that there are or can be actions done from duty.

### [The First Version of the Categorical Imperative]

We can express the basic principle of the categorical imperative in different words if we first note that the universal laws of cause and effect that govern the world are what we properly mean by "nature" in the most

---

1. A "maxim" is a subjective principle of action, and must be distinguished from an objective principle, namely, a practical law [i.e., a law of action]. A maxim is a principle that a particular person rationally adopts, but as influenced by that person's particular characteristics (such as the person's ignorance or desires). Thus a maxim is the principle on which a person *in fact acts.* But a practical law is an objective principle on which a person *ought to act,* that is, an imperative. For a practical law is an objective principle that binds every rational being.

general sense of the word (these laws give nature its form). For nature is the existence of things insofar as they are structured by general laws. Consequently, the basic principle of the categorical imperative can also be expressed in the following version: *Act as if the maxims you choose to follow always became universal laws of nature.*

We will now enumerate a few of the duties that follow from this first version of the categorical imperative. We will adopt the usual practice of classifying duties into perfect and imperfect duties and subclassifying each of these into duties to ourselves and duties to others.

*1. Perfect duty to oneself.* Imagine a man who has been reduced to despair by a series of misfortunes. Suppose he feels tired of living, but is still able to ask himself whether it would be contrary to duty to take his own life. So he asks whether the maxim of his action could become a universal law of nature. His maxim is this: "Out of self-love I will adopt the principle that I will end my life once it contains more evils than satisfactions." Our man can then ask himself whether this principle, which is based on the feeling of self-love, can become a universal law of nature. He will see at once that a system of nature that contained a law that destroyed life by means of the very feeling whose function it is to sustain life would contradict itself. Therefore, such a law could not be part of a system of nature. Consequently, his maxim cannot become a universal law of nature so it violates the basic principle of morality.

*2. Perfect duty to others.* Imagine another person who finds himself forced to borrow some money. He knows that he will not be able to repay it, but he also knows that nobody will lend him anything unless he promises to repay it. So he is tempted to make such a promise. But he asks himself: Would such a promise be consistent with duty? If he were to make such a promise the maxim of his action would be this: "When I need money, I will borrow it and promise to repay it even if I know that I will never do so." Now I personally might be able to live according to this principle of self-interest. But the question is: Is it right? So I ask myself: What if my maxim were to become a universal law? Then I see at once that it could never even become a universal law of nature since it would contradict itself. For suppose it became a general rule that everyone started making promises he never intended to keep. Then promises themselves would become impossible as well as the purposes one might want to achieve by promising. For no one would ever believe that anything was promised to him, but would mock all "promises" as empty deceptions.

*3. Imperfect duty to oneself.* Imagine a third man who has a useful natural ability that he could develop through practice and exercise. However, he is comfortably situated and would rather indulge in pleasure than make the effort needed to develop and improve himself. But he asks himself whether his maxim of neglecting his natural gifts as he is tempted to do is consistent with his duty. He sees then that a system of nature could conceivably exist with such a universal law, even if everyone (like the South Sea islanders) were to let his talents rust and devoted his life to idleness, amusement, and sex—in a word, to pleasure. But although his maxim *could* be conceived as a universal law of nature, he could not *will* it to be a universal law of nature; that is, he could not will such a law to be implanted in us like a natural instinct. For our natural abilities enable us to achieve whatever goals we might have, so every rational person who has any goals whatever necessarily wills to have his abilities develop.

### 4. Imperfect duty to others.

Imagine a fourth man who is prosperous, while he sees that others have to put up with great wretchedness. Suppose he could help them, but he asks himself: What concern is it of mine? Let everyone have whatever happiness God or his own efforts can give him. For my part I will not steal from people or envy their fortune. But I do not want to add to their well-being or help them when they are in need! Undoubtedly, if such a way of thinking became universal, the human race could continue to exist; it might even be better off than if everyone were to talk about sympathy and good will and occasionally practiced it, but generally continued to cheat whenever they could and betrayed and violated the rights of others. However, although that maxim *could* be a universal law of nature, one could not *will* it to be a universal law of nature without having one's will come into conflict with itself. For we know that many situations will arise in which one will need the love and concern of others. So if one were to will such a law of nature, one would be depriving himself of that aid he knows he will need.

These are a few of the duties that can be derived from the principle we have laid down. They fall into two classes. The basic rule for evaluating the morality of our actions is this: We must be *able to will* that the maxim of our action should be a universal law. One class of duties (the perfect duties) consists of actions whose maxim cannot even be consistently *conceived* as a universal law of nature, much less could we *will* such maxims to be universal laws of nature. The second class of duties (the imperfect duties) consists of actions whose maxims *could* become universal laws of nature, but it is impossible for us to *will* that their maxims should be universal laws since such a will would be in conflict with itself. It is easy enough to see that the first class of actions violate our strict duties, while the second class violate only what it would be meritorious for us to do. Thus these four examples cover the main kinds of duties and show that even the strictness of the obligation can be determined by this one principle and not by reference to the purpose of the action.

We have thus established at least this much—that if duty is a meaningful concept that validly imposes authoritative laws on our actions, it can only be expressed in categorical, and not in hypothetical, imperatives. We have also clearly and distinctly shown what the categorical imperative will require in a complete classification of duties. This is a very important matter since the categorical imperative must be the basis of all our duties if it is correct. We have not yet, however, proven *a priori* that this imperative is in fact valid; that is, we have not yet shown that there is a true practical law that commands us absolutely and without any other motive and that to follow such a law is to do our duty.

### [Subjective Ends and Objective Ends]

We think of the will as the power to choose our own actions according to the idea we have of certain laws. Such a power can be found only in rational beings. Now we call something an *end* if the will chooses its actions for the sake of that thing (if an end were presented by reason alone it would have to hold for all rational beings). On the other hand, we call a thing a *means* if it is something we can use in the actions by which we pursue the end we seek.

The subjective basis that gives rise to a desire is some kind of *stimulus*, while the objective basis on which the will acts is some kind of *motive for acting*. Consequently, we can distinguish between *subjective ends,* which arise from stimuli, and *objective ends,* which arise from motives for acting that are valid for every rational being. The principles on which we act are *formal* if they do not make any reference to subjective ends; they are *material* if they refer to subjective ends and if they consequently are based on the presence of some particular stimulus.

The material ends that a rational individual happens to want to produce through his actions all have only a relative value since they are valuable only in relation to the particular desires that this individual happens to have. Such relative values cannot be the basis for principles that universally and necessarily bind all rational beings and all choices; that is, they cannot be the basis for a practical law. These relative ends can give rise only to hypothetical imperatives.

Suppose, however, that there were something whose very existence had an absolute value, something which, being an end in itself, could be the basis for specific laws. Then such an end could serve as the basis for a categorical imperative, that is, for a practical law.

### [The Second Version of the Categorical Imperative]

Now I say that man and generally any rational being exists as an end in himself. In all his actions, whether they concern himself or other rational beings, a man must always be regarded as an end and not merely as a means to be arbitrarily used by this or that will.

All objects of desire have only a conditional value. For such objects would have no value if our appetites and the desires that arise from them did not exist. Moreover, the appetites that give rise to our desires also do not have an absolute value that makes them intrinsically desirable; on the contrary, every rational being would like to be wholly free of these appetites. Thus the value of any object that can be produced by our action is always conditional.

Similarly, the nonrational creatures that are produced by nature also have only a relative value: they are means and so we call them *things*. Rational beings, on the other hand, are called *persons* because their very nature makes them ends in themselves who must not be used merely as means. Thus, their nature imposes limits on what we are free to do to them and it commands our respect. Persons, therefore, are not merely subjective ends whose value depends on our actions. They are, rather, objective ends, that is, beings whose existence is an end in itself. Persons are ends who should not be turned into means to some other end we put in their place. For if we turn persons into means then nothing whatever will have absolute value. And if all value is relative and contingent, then there can be no supreme practical principle of reason.

So if there is a valid supreme practical principle, that is, a categorical imperative for the human will, it must be based on the idea of something that is an end for everyone precisely because it is an end in itself. A practical principle that is based on such a concept would be an objective principle for the will and would therefore be a universal practical law. Now such a principle can be based on this idea: that rational nature exists as an end in itself. For each one of us necessarily conceives his own existence as an end in itself, and to this extent such a principle is a *subjective* principle, that is, a principle on which we in fact base our actions. But every other rational being regards its existence in the same way, based on the same rational principle that holds for me. Consequently, the principle is also an *objective* principle that can serve as a supreme practical law from which all laws of the will can be derived. Accordingly [a second version of] the categorical imperative can be formulated as follows: *So act as to treat humanity, whether in your own person or in that of any other, always also as an end and never merely as a means.* We will now inquire whether this version can be applied in practice.

We will again consider our previous four examples:

*1. Necessary (or strict) duty to oneself.*    A person who is thinking of committing suicide should ask himself whether his action is consistent with the idea that humanity is an end in itself. If he kills himself to escape his suffering, he is using a person (himself) merely as a means to maintain a tolerable existence. But a person is not a thing. That is to say, a person cannot be used merely as a means, but must always be respected as an end in himself. I cannot, therefore, dispose of my own person by mutilating, despoiling, or killing myself. (It belongs to ethics proper to define this principle more precisely, so as to avoid all misunderstanding. For example: can I amputate my limbs in order to save my life, or can I expose my life to danger with a view to defending myself? These questions cannot be discussed here.)

*2. Necessary (or strict) duty to others.*    A man who is thinking of making a lying promise will realize that he would be using others merely as means because he would not be letting them participate in the goal of the actions in which he involves them. For the people I would thus be using for my own purposes would not have consented to be treated in this way and to that extent they would not have participated in the goals to be attained by the action. Such violations of the principle that our humanity must be respected as an end in itself are even clearer if we take examples of attacks on the freedom and property of others. It is obvious that the person who violates such rights is using people merely as means without considering that as rational beings they should be esteemed also as ends;

that is, as beings who must be able to participate in the goals of the actions in which they are involved with him.

*3. Contingent (or meritorious) duty to oneself.*  We should not only refrain from violating our own humanity as an end in itself, but we should also try to make our actions harmonize with the fact that our humanity is such an end. Now humanity has certain abilities that we can perfect to a greater or lesser extent. These abilities are meant to serve whatever purposes nature might have intended our humanity to achieve. When we neglect to develop these abilities we are not doing something that is destructive of humanity as an end in itself. But such neglect clearly does not advance humanity as an end in itself.

*4. Contingent (or meritorious) duty to others.*  All men by nature want to be happy. Now humanity probably could survive even if people never helped each other achieve their happiness, but merely refrained from deliberately harming one another. But this would only be a negative way of making our actions harmonize with the idea that humanity is an end in itself. The positive way of harmonizing with this idea would be for everyone to help others achieve their goals so far as he can. The goals of every person who is an end in himself should also be my goals if my actions are really to be in full harmony with the idea that that person's humanity is an end in itself.

The principle we have been discussing (that humanity and generally every rational nature is an end in itself) is the supreme restriction imposed on every man's freedom of action. It is not drawn from our factual experience. For, first of all, the principle is universal in the sense that it applies to all rational beings and we cannot have experience of all possible rational beings. Second, the principle does not say that all men in fact adopt humanity as a subjective end; the principle says, rather, that humanity is an objective end that must, as a requirement, override any subjective end we might happen to have. For these reasons, the principle must be derived from pure reason.

### [Autonomy and the Third Version of the Categorical Imperative]

Now, according to the first version of the categorical imperative, the objective basis for adopting a practical law is to be found in the rule and its form of universality, that is, the extent to which it can be a law, such as a law of nature. However, the *subjective* basis for adopting a practical law is the *end*. And according to the second version of the categorical imperative, every rational being is an end for every person (including himself) because a rational being is an end in itself. From these two versions we may now derive a third practical principle for the will, a principle that expresses the basic condition that must be met if the will is to conform with universal practical reason. This third principle is based on this idea: that the will of every rational being is a will that makes its own universal law.

According to this principle: _a maxim must be rejected if it is inconsistent with the idea that the will is itself the maker of the universal laws it follows_. Thus the will is not merely subject to the law, but is subject in a special way: it must be regarded as giving the law to itself and consequently it is subject to a law of which it knows it is the author.

The first version of the categorical imperative was based on the idea that our actions must conform to universal laws as if they were laws of nature. The second version was based on the universal supremacy of rational beings as ends in themselves. Neither of these versions based their authority on an appeal to some desire that might move us to act because these two versions could be categorical only if they were not based on this or that person's particular desires. However, we have merely *assumed* that these imperatives are categorically binding, because such an assumption is necessary to explain what duty is. But we have not yet been able to give an independent proof showing that the practical propositions that impose such categorical commands are valid. And we will not be able to provide such a proof within this section.

There is one thing, however, that we have been able to do within this section. And that is to make explicit in an exact statement of the categorical imperative the criterion that distinguishes categorical imperatives from hypothetical imperatives. What distinguishes a categorical imperative is the fact that in willing an action from duty we must not be influenced by our own interests. This distinguishing characteristic is made explicit in the third version of the categorical imperative, namely, in the idea that the will of every rational being must be seen as a will that makes universal law.

It is true that a will that is subject to laws may be motivated to follow the law by its own interests. But a will that is itself the ultimate source of all the universal laws it follows cannot possibly be motivated to follow these laws because of its own interests. For then the will would need another law that required it to take into account only those personal interests that could motivate universal laws, and then it would not be the ultimate source of all its laws.

Consequently, if we can prove it is valid, the principle that every human will makes universal law from its maxims is a fitting statement of the categorical imperative. It is fitting in this respect: that precisely because it focuses on the idea of making universal law, it is clearly not based on personal interest. Thus, unlike all other kinds of imperatives, it is clearly unconditional. Or, better yet, to put it in different words: if there is a valid categorical imperative (that is, a law that truly binds the will of every rational being), then it must command us never to act on a maxim unless the maxim is one that we can conceive as a universal law that we are giving to ourselves. Only if it commands this will the practical principle and the imperative that we follow be unconditional; for only then will it necessarily rule out all personal interests.

We need not wonder why all earlier attempts to discover the basic principle of morality have thus far failed. Philosophers saw that man was bound to laws by duty, but they did not see that the laws to which he is subject are only those that he himself makes, though at the same time they are universal. Nor did they see that he is only required to act in conformity with what his own will determines—a will, however, that is designed by nature to give itself universal laws. For when earlier philosophers conceived man as subject to a moral law (no matter what it might be), the law they proposed had to appeal to some interest, either to attract men to follow it or to constrain them from violating it. Since such a law did not originate in man's own will, something else had to oblige the will to act according to the law. Now this inevitable conclusion means that all the labor they spent in finding a supreme principle of duty was wasted. For they never appealed to duty, but only to the necessity of acting from a certain interest. Whether this interest was personal or otherwise, the imperatives they proposed as moral laws were in fact only hypothetical and could not provide a moral command. I will therefore call my third version the principle of *autonomy* of the will, that is, the principle of self-imposed law. By contrast, the principles of other philosophers I classify under the term *heteronomy*, that is, externally imposed law. . . .

### [These Analytical Methods Do Not Prove the Categorical Imperative]

The will's autonomy consists in its capacity to be its own law without being influenced by the objects of choice. The principle of autonomy then is this: Always choose to act in such a way that your choice is based on a maxim that is also a universal law. This rule of action is an imperative, that is, it necessarily binds the will of every rational being. But we cannot prove that it is binding on every will by simply analyzing the meaning of the term "will" and showing that part of the meaning of "will" is "bound by universal law." For this rule of action is not based simply on the meanings of the words. To prove that this categorical imperative really binds every will, we must move beyond the objects we experience and advance to a critical investigation of our subject, that is, of pure practical reason. For this rule of action, which is based on something other than the meanings of the words it contains, imposes a command that is supposed to be necessarily binding. And such necessary propositions must be capable of being established wholly *a priori*, that is, independent of the objects we experience. This investigation, however, does not belong in the present section.

On the other hand, we have shown that the principle of autonomy is the principle of morality by simply analyzing the meanings of the terms that are involved. For we have made such an analysis and we have found that "moral principle" means "categorical imperative," and that "categorical imperative" means "an imperative that commands autonomy" as we have been discussing. . . .

### [But Is Autonomy Possible?]

However, we have not yet shown that it is necessary or even possible for us to obey this practical *a priori* proposition that is not based on the meanings of words and that commands us to act autonomously without being influenced by our personal interests. In this section we have limited ourselves to developing a metaphysics of morals and so we have not yet proved that this command is a valid command for us. We have merely analyzed the meaning of our ordinary concept of "morality" and have shown that autonomy of the will is part of this meaning, in fact, that it is the essential meaning of "morality." (This section, then, like the first, was based merely on an analysis of certain concepts.) Consequently, if someone believes that morality is not a mythical false idea, but that it is a valid reality, then he must also believe that this principle of autonomy is valid. If morality is not to be a mere creation of our minds, then we must prove that the categorical imperative and autonomy of the will are valid, that is, that they are true *a priori* principles that are absolutely necessary for us to follow.

Of course, we will be able to prove that these principles are valid only if it is possible for pure practical reason to establish principles that cannot be established by a mere analysis of concepts. But we cannot venture to establish such principles until we have provided a critical investigation of the power of reason itself. In the third section we will describe some of the main conclusions that such a critical investigation would establish, at least as far as is necessary for our present purposes.

## THIRD SECTION: TRANSITION FROM THE METAPHYSICS OF MORALS TO A CRITIQUE OF PURE PRACTICAL REASON

### The Concept of Freedom Is the Key that Explains the Autonomy of the Will

The will is a causal power that living beings have if they are rational. We say such a causal power has *freedom* if its acts are not determined by causal influences other than itself. The causal powers of nonrational beings, however, are ruled by *physical necessity* since their acts are determined by the causal influences of other things.

Now the preceding definition of freedom is negative and it does not help us understand the essence of freedom. But it points us to a positive idea of freedom that is more helpful.

Notice that causal powers always act according to laws, that is, laws that lay down that when a certain "cause" obtains, a certain other thing called an "effect" must be produced. Consequently, although a free will is not determined by physical laws, it must nevertheless act according to some kind of law. In fact, a free will must be a causal power that acts according to a special kind of immutable law. Otherwise the idea of a free will would be incoherent.

Now physical necessity is a causality that is heteronomous, that is, everything in the physical world happens through externally imposed causes. What else then can freedom of the will be but a kind of autonomy? That is, freedom of the will is the ability of the will to act in accordance with laws it imposes on itself. But the proposition "The will in every action gives its laws to itself" only expresses the principle of acting on no other maxims except those in which the will gives itself a universal law. Now this is precisely the [third] formula of the categorical imperative, the essential principle of morality. Thus "free will" and "a will subject to moral laws" really mean the same thing.

Thus, if we were to assume the will is free, then by merely analyzing the meaning of "free will" we could conclude that the will is subject to the categorical imperative. Nevertheless, the categorical imperative would not thereby be proven to be true (it would be based on an unproven assumption, viz., the assumption that the will is free). . . . Further argument is required before we can show that it is legitimate to believe that freedom is possible and thereby show that it is possible to be subject to the categorical imperative.

### Freedom Must Be Presupposed as a Property of the Will of All Rational Beings

If we are to establish the possibility of acting morally, it is not enough to point to some grounds for believing that my own will is free unless I can also provide grounds for believing that the wills of all rational beings are free. For since morality is a requirement on us only because we are rational beings, it must also be a requirement on all rational beings. Consequently, if we are to show that morality is binding on us because we are free, we have to show that all rational beings are free. It is not enough, then, to try to prove that I must be free by pointing to some alleged experiences I have of freedom (which indeed is quite impossible since freedom can only be proven through an *a priori* argument). Instead, we have to provide an argument that will show that freedom belongs to the activity of all rational beings who have a will.

My argument will be based on this idea: any being who must attribute freedom to himself when he acts is for that very reason really free from a practical point of view. That is to say, all moral laws that are connected with freedom are as binding on him as if his will had been shown to be free by a conclusive theoretical proof. Now my argument is this: every rational being who has a will also has the idea of freedom and assumes he is free when he acts. For to have a will is to have practical reason, that is, reason that can act causally on other objects. Now we cannot possibly conceive of a reason that consciously believes its judgments are being made for it by forces other than itself. For reason would attribute such judgments not to itself but to those other forces. Thus reason must regard itself as the source of its principles, and cannot attribute them to outside influences. We may conclude, then, that practical reason—that is, the will—must regard itself as free. That is to say, the will of a rational being can attribute its willing to itself only if it assumes it is free. From a practical point of view, therefore, freedom must be attributed to every rational being.

## [The Two Theoretical Points of View]

. . . Consider, next, whether we might be looking at ourselves from one point of view when, relying on *a priori* arguments, we think of ourselves as acting freely, but then look at ourselves from another point of view when, relying on our senses, we perceive our actions as causally determined.

What I am suggesting is something that even the most ordinary intelligence can understand and might already suspect in some obscure way. I am referring to the fact that all knowledge acquired through our senses is based completely on the way the objects in our world affect our senses, and apart from these impressions we know nothing about what the objects in themselves are really like. Consequently, no matter how much we might sharpen and improve our observations, the knowledge we acquire through our senses tells us only how objects *appear* to us, not about how objects are *in themselves*. Thus, underlying the appearances that things present to our senses, there must be a reality—namely, things as they are in themselves—that we never see. So we must distinguish between the *world of the senses* (things as they appear to us), which appears differently to different observers, and that *world of understanding* (things as we understand them really to be) that is the one underlying reality presenting these different appearances.

Now this distinction also applies to ourselves. We cannot know our real nature, not even through introspection. For we did not make ourselves and have no knowledge of ourselves other than what we can gather through observation. So we know ourselves only as we appear to our senses, including the introspective senses through which we observe our inner life. And yet we know that behind these appearances, this collection of inner impressions, there must lie a reality, namely the real self as it is in itself. Thus, insofar as we are passive recipients of the impressions presented to our senses we belong to the world of the senses. But we must also count ourselves as members of the underlying world of understanding, especially insofar as we know that we are active and independent of the senses. . . .

Now there is in fact a power in man that sets him apart from everything else, even from himself insofar as he is passively affected by sense objects. That power is reason. The activity of reason is wholly spontaneous, unlike our sense powers, which are passive since they merely respond to being affected by things. . . . Reason, however, engages in a pure spontaneous activity. This is especially clear in the case of what I call its "pure ideas" [such as the idea of God or of an infinite universe], since in thinking of these reason goes beyond anything that the senses could present. . . .

As a result, when a rational being thinks of himself *as an intelligence* he must regard himself as an active member of the world of understanding; when he thinks of himself in terms of his sense powers he regards himself as a passive part of the world of sense. Consequently, a rational being has two points of view from which he can regard himself, and consequently he must recognize two kinds of laws governing his powers and all his actions. First, insofar as he belongs to the world of sense, he finds himself subject to laws of the forces of nature (heteronomy); second, in belonging to the intelligible world he is subject to laws that, being independent of the forces of nature, have their foundation not in sense experience but in reason alone.

As a rational being who belongs to the world of intelligence, man will necessarily see his own will as free. For freedom is nothing more than being able to act independently of the causal forces of the world of sense, and this is the kind of freedom that reason will necessarily attribute to itself.

... We see now that when we think of ourselves as free we are thinking of ourselves as members of the world of understanding and we then recognize that the will is autonomous and consequently that morality is possible. But when we feel as if we are being restrained by an obligation, we become aware that we are not merely members of the world of pure thought but that we are also creatures of sensation. . . .

### Why Acting on the Categorical Imperative Is Possible

When he thinks of himself as an *intelligence,* every rational being sees himself as a member of the world of understanding, and when he exercises his causal powers in that world he calls his causality a "will." But he also sees himself as part of the world of sense, the world in which the actions produced by his will seem to appear. Yet we cannot help but view all actions that occur in the world of sense as events that are caused by other forces in that world, namely by desires and appetites. Consequently, if I were a member only of the world of understanding, then all of my actions would actually possess the autonomy that would belong to a pure will; in other words, I would freely act on the supreme moral principle. And if I were a member only of the world of sense, then my actions would be wholly determined by those laws of nature that govern my desires and appetites; in other words, I would have to follow an externally imposed law of nature that would make me seek happiness. However, the world of understanding contains the basic reality that lies behind the world of sense and its laws; and that world of understanding also directly governs my will. It follows that, although on the one side I must see myself as belonging to the world of sense, yet, on the other side, I must also see myself as belonging to the world of understanding where I am directly subject to the law of reason, that is, to autonomy. Since I belong to both worlds, I end by looking upon the laws of the world of understanding as imperatives that constrain me, and the actions they require appear to me to be "duties."

And thus what makes categorical imperatives possible is this: that because I have the idea of freedom I am able to think of myself as a member of the world of understanding. If I were a member of only this world, all my actions would invariably conform to autonomy of the will. But since at the same time I see myself as a member of the world of sense, I am aware of my actions as constrained by the rule that they "ought" to conform to autonomy of the will. And my awareness of this categorical "ought" implies a proposition that is not based on experience or an analysis of the meanings of words, namely the proposition that my will is affected by sense desires and yet it is also a pure, self-directing member of the world of understanding. This world of understanding contains the supreme law that my will must follow even though it is affected by sense desires.

We have come now to the source of that logical conflict of reason we noticed earlier: the freedom we attribute to the will seemed incompatible with the causal determination of nature. . . . It would indeed be an inescapable contradiction if when we thought of man as free, we were thinking of "man" in the same sense as when we think of man as causally determined. But the task of philosophy is to show that this seeming contradiction is an illusion. For no contradiction arises if we realize that when we say "man is free" we are using the term "man" in one sense, but when we say "man is determined" we are referring to man insofar as he is part of the world of nature and determined by its laws. And, as we have seen, both of these aspects of man can and must be combined in one and the same individual. . . .

However, reason would pass beyond its limits if it tried to explain how pure reason can be practical, that is, if it tried to explain how freedom is possible. For in order to explain anything, we must appeal to some law of our sense experience. But freedom is a mere idea; we cannot explain it by appealing to some law of nature or to some possible experience. No example or analogy can make freedom fully comprehensible to us. . . . We can only defend freedom by refuting the arguments of those who claim it is impossible.

# MORAL REASONING

## R. M. Hare

And as ye would that men should do to you, do ye also to them likewise.

St. Luke, VI, 31

**6.1.** Historically, one of the chief incentives to the study of ethics has been the hope that its findings might be of help to those faced with difficult moral problems. That this is still a principal incentive for many people is shown by the fact that modern philosophers are often reproached for failing to make ethics relevant to morals.[1] This is because one of the main

---

1. I have tried to fill in some of the historical background of these reproaches, and to assess the justification for them, in my article in *The Philosophy of C. D. Broad,* ed. P. Schilpp.

tenets of many recent moral philosophers has been that the most popular method by which it was sought to bring ethics to bear on moral problems was not feasible—namely the method followed by the group of theories loosely known as 'naturalist'.

The method of naturalism is so to characterize the *meanings* of the key moral terms that, given certain factual premises, not themselves moral judgements, moral conclusions can be deduced from them. If this could be done, it was thought that it would be of great assistance to us in making moral decisions; we should only have to find out the non-moral facts, and the moral conclusion as to what we ought to do would follow. Those who say that it cannot be done leave themselves the task of giving an alternative account of moral reasoning.

Naturalism seeks to make the findings of ethics *relevant* to moral decisions by making the former not morally *neutral*. It is a very natural assumption that if a statement of ethics is relevant to morals, then it cannot be neutral as between different moral judgements; and naturalism is a tempting view for those who make this assumption. Naturalistic definitions are not morally neutral, because with their aid we could show that statements of non-moral facts *entailed* moral conclusions. And some have thought that unless such an entailment can be shown to hold, the moral philosopher has not made moral reasoning possible.

One way of escaping this conclusion is to say that the relation linking a set of non-moral premises with a moral conclusion is not one of entailment, but that some other logical relation, peculiar to morals, justifies the inference. This is the view put forward, for example, by Mr. Toulmin.[2] Since I have argued elsewhere against this approach, I shall not discuss it here. Its advocates have, however, hit upon an important insight: that moral reasoning does not necessarily proceed by way of *deduction* of moral conclusions from non-moral premises. Their further suggestion, that therefore it makes this transition by means of some other, peculiar, non-deductive kind of inference, is not the only possibility. It may be that moral reasoning is not, typically, any kind of 'straight-line' or 'linear' reasoning from premises to conclusion.

**6.2.** A parallel from the philosophy of science will perhaps make this point clear. It is natural to suppose that what the scientist does is to reason from premises, which are the data of observation, to conclusions, which are his 'scientific laws', by means of a special sort of inference called 'inductive'. Against this view, Professor Popper has forcibly argued that in science there are no inferences other than deductive; the typical procedure of scientists is to propound hypotheses, and then look for ways of testing them—i.e. experiments which, if they are false, will show them to be so. A hypothesis which, try as we may, we fail to falsify, we accept provisionally, though ready to abandon it if, after all, further experiment refutes it; and of those that are so accepted we rate highest the ones which say most, and which would, therefore, be most likely to have been falsified if they were false. The only inferences which occur in this process

2. S. E. Toulmin, *The Place of Reason in Ethics*, esp. pp. 38-60. See my review in *Philosophical Quarterly*, i (1950/I), 372, and *LM* 3.4.

are deductive ones, from the truth of certain observations to the falsity of a hypothesis. There is no reasoning which proceeds from the data of observation to the *truth* of a hypothesis. Scientific inquiry is rather a kind of *exploration*, or looking for hypotheses which will stand up to the test of experiment.[3]

We must ask whether moral reasoning exhibits any similar features. I want to suggest that it too is a kind of exploration, and not a kind of linear inference, and that the only inferences which take place in it are deductive. What we are doing in moral reasoning is to look for moral judgements and moral principles which, when we have considered their logical consequences and the facts of the case, we can still accept. As we shall see, this approach to the problem enables us to reject the assumption, which seemed so natural, that ethics cannot be relevant to moral decisions without ceasing to be neutral. This is because we are not going to demand any inferences in our reasoning other than deductive ones, and because none of these deductive inferences rely for their validity upon naturalistic definitions of moral terms.

Two further parallels may help to make clear the sense in which ethics is morally neutral. In the kind of scientific reasoning just described, mathematics plays a major part, for many of the deductive inferences that occur are mathematical in character. So we are bound to admit that mathematics is relevant to scientific inquiry. Nevertheless, it is also neutral, in the sense that no discoveries about matters of physical fact can be made with the aid of mathematics alone, and that no mathematical inference can have a conclusion which says more, in the way of prediction of observations, than its premises implicitly do.

An even simpler parallel is provided by the rules of games. The rules of a game are neutral as between the players, in the sense that they do not, by themselves, determine which player is going to win. In order to decide who wins, the players have to play the game in accordance with the rules, which involves their making, themselves, a great many individual decisions. On the other hand, the 'neutrality' of the rules of a game does not turn it into a game of chance, in which the bad player is as likely to win as the good.

Ethical theory, which determines the meanings and functions of the moral words, and thus the 'rules' of the moral 'game', provides only a clarification of the conceptual framework within which moral reasoning takes place; it is therefore, in the required sense, neutral as between different moral opinions. But it is highly relevant to moral reasoning because, as with the rules of a game, there could be no such thing as moral reasoning without this framework, and the framework dictates the form of the reasoning. It follows that naturalism is not the only way of providing for the possibility of moral reasoning; and this may, perhaps, induce those who have espoused naturalism as a way of making moral thought a rational activity to consider other possibilities.

The rules of moral reasoning are, basically, two, corresponding to

---

3. K. R. Popper, *The Logic of Scientific Discovery* (esp. pp. 32 f.). See also his article in C. A. Mace (ed.), *British Philosophy in the Mid-Century*, p. 155.

the two features of moral judgements which I argued for in the first half of this book, prescriptivity and universalizability. When we are trying, in a concrete case, to decide what we ought to do, what we are looking for (as I have already said) is an action to which we can commit ourselves (prescriptivity) but which we are at the same time prepared to accept as exemplifying a principle of action to be prescribed for others in like circumstances (universalizability). If, when we consider some proposed action, we find that, when universalized, it yields prescriptions which we cannot accept, we reject this action as a solution to our moral problem—if we cannot universalize the prescription, it cannot become an 'ought'.

It is to be noticed that, troublesome as was the problem of moral weakness when we were dealing theoretically with the logical character of the moral concepts, it cannot trouble us here. For if a person is going to reason seriously at all about a moral question, he has to presuppose that the moral concepts are going, in his reasoning, to be used prescriptively. One cannot start a moral argument about a certain proposal on the basis that, whatever the conclusion of it, it makes no difference to what anybody is to do. When one has arrived at a conclusion, one may then be too weak to put it into practice. But *in arguing* one has to discount this possibility; for, as we shall see, to abandon the prescriptivity of one's moral judgements is to unscrew an essential part of the logical mechanism on which such arguments rely. This is why, if a person were to say 'Let's have an argument about this grave moral question which faces us, but let's not think of any conclusion we may come to as requiring anybody to *do* one thing rather than another', we should be likely to accuse him of flippancy, or worse.

**6.3.** I will now try to exhibit the bare bones of the theory of moral reasoning that I wish to advocate by considering a very simple (indeed over-simplified) example. As we shall see, even this very simple case generates the most baffling complexities; and so we may be pardoned for not attempting anything more difficult to start with.

The example is adapted from a well-known parable.[4] A owes money to B, and B owes money to C, and it is the law that creditors may exact their debts by putting their debtors into prison. B asks himself, 'Can I say that I ought to take this measure against A in order to make him pay?' He is no doubt *inclined* to do this, or *wants* to do it. Therefore, if there were no question of universalizing his prescriptions, he would assent readily to the *singular* prescription 'Let me put A into prison'. But when he seeks to turn this prescription into a moral judgement, and say 'I *ought* to put A into prison because he will not pay me what he owes', he reflects that this would involve accepting the principle 'Anyone who is in my position ought to put his debtor into prison if he does not pay'. But then he reflects that C is in the same position of unpaid creditor with regard to himself (B), and that the cases are otherwise identical; and that if anyone in this position ought to put his debtors into prison, then so ought C to put him (B) into prison. And to accept the moral prescription 'C ought to put me into prison' would commit him (since, as we have seen, he must be

4. Matthew xviii. 23.

using the word 'ought' prescriptively) to accepting the singular prescription 'Let *C* put me into prison'; and this he is not ready to accept. But if he is not, then neither can he accept the original judgement that he (*B*) ought to put *A* into prison for debt. Notice that the whole of this argument would break down if 'ought' were not being used both universalizably *and prescriptively;* for if it were not being used prescriptively, the step from '*C* ought to put me into prison' to 'Let *C* put me into prison' would not be valid.

The structure and ingredients of this argument must now be examined. We must first notice an analogy between it and the Popperian theory of scientific method. What has happened is that a provisional or suggested moral principle has been rejected because one of its particular consequences proved unacceptable. But an important difference between the two kinds of reasoning must also be noted; it is what we should expect, given that the data of scientific observation are recorded in descriptive statements, whereas we are here dealing with prescriptions. What knocks out a suggested hypothesis, on Popper's theory, is a singular statement of fact: the hypothesis has the consequence that *p;* but not-*p*. Here the logic is just the same, except that in place of the observation-statements '*p*' and 'not-*p*' we have the singular *prescriptions* 'Let *C* put *B* into prison for debt' and its contradictory. Nevertheless, given that *B* is disposed to reject the first of these prescriptions, the argument against him is just as cogent as in the scientific case.

We may carry the parallel further. Just as science, seriously pursued, is the search for hypotheses and the testing of them by the attempt to falsify their particular consequences, so morals, as a serious endeavour, consists in the search for principles and the testing of them against particular cases. Any rational activity has its discipline, and this is the discipline of moral thought: to test the moral principles that suggest themselves to us by following out their consequences and seeing whether we can accept *them*.

No argument, however, starts from nothing. We must therefore ask what we have to have before moral arguments of the sort of which I have given a simple example can proceed. The first requisite is that the facts of the case should be given; for all moral discussion is about some particular set of facts, whether actual or supposed. Secondly we have the logical framework provided by the meaning of the word 'ought' (i.e. prescriptivity and universalizability, both of which we saw to be necessary). Because moral judgements have to be universalizable, *B* cannot say that he ought to put *A* into prison for debt without committing himself to the view that *C*, who is *ex hypothesi* in the same position *vis-à-vis* himself, ought to put *him* into prison; and because moral judgements are prescriptive, this would be, in effect, prescribing to *C* to put him into prison; and this he is unwilling to do, since he has a strong inclination not to go to prison. This inclination gives us the third necessary ingredient in the argument: if *B* were a completely apathetic person, who literally did not mind what happened to himself or to anybody else, the argument would not touch him. The three necessary ingredients which we have noticed, then, are (1) facts; (2) logic; (3) inclinations. These ingredients enable us, not indeed to arrive at an evaluative conclusion, but to *reject* an evaluative proposition. We shall see later that these are not, in all cases, the only necessary ingredients.

6.4. In the example which we have been using, the position was deliberately made simpler by supposing that B actually stood to some other person in exactly the same relation as A does to him. Such cases are unlikely to arise in practice. But it is not necessary for the force of the argument that B should *in fact* stand in this relation to anyone; it is sufficient that he should consider hypothetically such a case, and see what would be the consequences in it of those moral principles between whose acceptance and rejection he has to decide. Here we have an important point of difference from the parallel scientific argument, in that the crucial case which leads to rejection of the principle can itself be a supposed, not an observed, one. That hypothetical cases will do as well as actual ones is important, since it enables us to guard against a possible misinterpretation of the argument which I have outlined. It might be thought that what moves B is the *fear* that C will actually do to him as he does to A—as happens in the gospel parable. But this fear is not only irrelevant to the moral argument; it does not even provide a particularly strong non-moral motive unless the circumstances are somewhat exceptional. C may, after all, not find out what B has done to A; or C's moral principles may be different from B's, and independent of them, so that what moral principle B accepts makes no difference to the moral principles on which C acts.

Even, therefore, if C did not exist, it would be no answer to the argument for B to say 'But in my case there is no fear that anybody will ever be in a position to do to me what I am proposing to do to A'. For the argument does not rest on any such fear. All that is essential to it is that B should disregard the fact that he plays the particular role in the situation which he does, without disregarding the inclinations which people have in situations of this sort. In other words, he must be prepared to give weight to A's inclinations and interests as if they were his own. This is what turns selfish prudential reasoning into moral reasoning. It is much easier, psychologically, for B to do this if he is actually placed in a situation like A's *vis-à-vis* somebody else; but this is not necessary, provided that he has sufficient imagination to envisage what it is like to be A. For our first example, a case was deliberately chosen in which little imagination was necessary; but in most normal cases a certain power of imagination and readiness to use it is a fourth necessary ingredient in moral arguments, alongside those already mentioned, viz. logic (in the shape of universalizability and prescriptivity), the facts, and the inclinations or interests of the people concerned.

It must be pointed out that the absence of even one of these ingredients may render the rest ineffective. For example, impartiality by itself is not enough. If, in becoming impartial, B became also completely dispassionate and apathetic, and moved as little by other people's interests as by his own, then, as we have seen, there would be nothing to make him accept or reject one moral principle rather than another. That is why those who, like Adam Smith and Professor Kneale, advocate what have been called 'Ideal Observer Theories' of ethics, sometimes postulate as their imaginary ideal observer not merely an impartial spectator, but an impartially *sympathetic* spectator.[5] To take another example, if the person who faces the moral decision has no imagination, then even the fact that someone can do the very same thing to him may pass him by. If, again, he lacks the readiness to universalize, then the vivid imagination of the sufferings which he is inflicting on others may only spur him on to intensify them, to increase his own vindictive enjoyment. And if he is ignorant of the material facts (for example about what is likely to happen to a person if one takes out a writ against him), then there is nothing to tie the moral argument to particular choices.

• • •

**6.9.** It is necessary, in order to avoid misunderstanding, to add two notes to the forgoing discussion. The misunderstanding arises through a too literal interpretation of the common forms of expression—which constantly recur in arguments of this type—'How would you like it if . . . ?' and 'Do as you would be done by'. Though I shall later, for convenience, refer to the type of arguments here discussed as 'golden-rule' arguments, we must not be misled by these forms of expression.

First of all, we shall make the nature of the argument clearer if, when we are asking *B* to imagine himself in the position of his victim, we phrase our question, never in the form 'What *would* you say, or feel, or think, or how *would* you like it, if you were he?', but always in the form 'What *do* you say (*in propria persona*) about a hypothetical case in which you are in your victim's position?' The importance of this way of phrasing the question is that, if the question were put in the first way, *B* might reply, 'Well, of course, if anybody did this to me I should resent it very much and make all sorts of adverse moral judgements about the act; but this has absolutely no bearing on the validity of the moral opinion which I am *now* expressing'. To involve him in contradiction, we have to show that he *now* holds an opinion about the hypothetical case which is inconsistent with his opinion about the actual case.

The second thing which has to be noticed is that the argument, as set out, does not involve any sort of deduction of a moral judgement, or even of the negation of a moral judgement, from a factual statement about people's inclinations, interests, &c. We are not saying to *B* 'You are as a matter of fact averse to this being done to you in a hypothetical case; and from this it follows logically that you ought not to do it to another'. Such a

5. It will be plain that there are affinities, though there are also differences, between this type of theory and my own. For such theories see W. C. Kneale, *Philosophy*, xxv (1950), 162; R. Firth and R. B. Brandt, *Philosophy and Phenomenological Research*, xii (1951/2), 317, and xv (1954/5), 407, 414, 422; and J. Harrison, *Aristotelian Society*, supp. vol. xxviii (1954), 132. Firth, unlike Kneale, says that the observer must be 'dispassionate', but see Brandt, op. cit., p. 411 n. For a shorter discussion see Brandt, *Ethical Theory*, p. 173. Since for many Christians God occupies the role of 'ideal observer', the moral judgements which they make may be expected to coincide with those arrived at by the method of reasoning which I am advocating.

deduction would be a breach of Hume's Law ('No "ought" from an "is" '), to which I have repeatedly declared my adherence. The point is, rather, that because of his aversion to its being done to him in the hypothetical case, he cannot accept the singular *prescription* that in the hypothetical case it should be done to him; and this, because of the logic of 'ought', precludes him from accepting the moral judgement that he ought to do likewise to another in the actual case. It is not a question of a factual statement about a person's inclinations being inconsistent with a moral judgement; rather, his inclinations being what they are, he cannot assent sincerely to a certain singular prescription, and if he cannot do this, he cannot assent to a certain universal prescription which entails it, when conjoined with factual statements about the circumstances whose truth he admits. Because of this entailment, if he assented to the factual statements and to the universal prescription, but refused (as he must, his inclinations being what they are) to assent to the singular prescription, he would be guilty of a logical inconsistency.

# CHAPTER FOUR
# UTILITARIAN ETHICS

By 1940, Hitler's armies had succeeded in overrunning most of Europe and stood ready to launch an invasion of England. England was in serious peril, not only because of the strength and skill of the German forces, but because their swift and surprising tactics made it difficult to guess their plans. However, by sheer luck and determination, British intelligence succeeded in breaking the code the Germans used to communicate among themselves. Through a secret intelligence operation code-named "Ultra," the English were able to intercept and decipher radioed German messages and gain crucial information. Ultra was a highly significant strategic advantage for the British, who went to great lengths to ensure its secrecy. So long as the Germans did not realize their code had been broken, the British had free access to all their plans. British chances of defeating Germany in fact depended heavily on being able to maintain the secret of Ultra's ability to decode German communications. By the middle of 1940, moreover, Ultra had saved thousands of lives and it was clear that it would save many thousands more if it could continue its operations.

On November 14, 1940, Ultra decoded plans for a German air raid on the city of Coventry. Situated about ninety miles northwest of London, Coventry is in a heavily populated area, important for historical, architectural, and industrial reasons. The decoded message posed a terrible dilemma, for if the families living in Coventry were warned or evacuated, the Germans would immediately realize the British had intercepted their message and broken their code. Yet if the people of Coventry were not warned, then hundreds, even thousands, would be killed or maimed. Captain F. W. Winterbotham, who was in charge of Ultra, knew at once that the British prime minister, Winston Churchill, would have to be the one to decide whether or not to warn the families of Coventry. Winterbotham later described what took place:

> At about 3 pm on November the fourteenth . . . a city with the . . . name Coventry was spelt out [by the Ultra decoding team]. . . . Churchill was at a meeting so I spoke direct to his personal secretary and told him what had happened. . . . I had little doubt that [the decoded message would be referred] to the Prime Minister for a decision as to what to do and it would be an agonizing decision to have to make. There were, perhaps, four or five hours before the attack would arrive. It was a longish flight north and the enemy aircraft would not cross the coast before dark. I asked the personal secretary if he would be good enough to ring me back when the decision had been taken, because if Churchill decided to evacuate Coventry, the press, and indeed everybody, would know we had pre-knowledge of the raid . . . [and our] source . . . would obviously become suspect. . . . I imagine that the Prime Minister must have consulted a number of people before making up his mind. . . . This is the sort of terrible decision that sometimes has to be made on the highest levels in war. . . . I am glad it was not I who had to take it.[1]

Churchill chose not to warn the citizens of Coventry. He ordered that only the usual wartime alerts should be issued to fire-fighting services and ambulances, a customary procedure for British cities in that area. The German bombers arrived as scheduled that night and in the devastation that followed four hundred people died and thousands of others were left injured and homeless.

Churchill's decision to sacrifice the lives of the people of Coventry in order to preserve the secret that would later save thousands of other lives, and ultimately help win the war, is a classic example of the kind of moral reasoning advocated by utilitarianism. Utilitarianism is based upon the principle that an action is morally right if it produces a greater quantity of

1. From F. W. Winterbotham, *The Ultra Secret* (New York: Harper and Row, 1974; London: George Weidenfeld and Nicolson Limited, 1974), pp. 60–61. Copyright © 1974 by F. W. Winterbotham. Reprinted by permission of the publishers. Various historians have challenged the accuracy of Winterbotham's account of the Coventry incident. In a letter to the authors of this text, Winterbotham wrote: "It may interest you to know a bit more about the raid on Coventry which was given to me privately after my book was published. 1) Professor Jones, my scientific assistant who claims no one had prior knowledge of the raid . . . was not informed for security reasons. 2) Churchill was having his daily sleep 2–3 pm and was not told until he awoke. Meantime the Royal Air Force had confirmed the target by locating the coordinates of the bombing beams set up by the Germans. Now by 3 pm it was finally decided only to take the usual anti-raid precautions used for all targets, i.e., alert the A.A. batteries and put the Fire and Ambulance Services on full alert without disclosing the precise target. . . . 3) The signal which came to me in London from the 'code crackers' gave 'Coventry' in clear. I was to discover much later that this was a deduction from the coordinates of the beam in the Ultra Signal and that the Germans had only given the code name 'Korn.' Historians have accused me of inaccuracy, [but] the official historians many years later did not have *my* message, only the German signal."

good or happiness than any other possible action.[2] Winston Churchill seems to have decided that greater good, or happiness, would be produced by keeping the Ultra operation secret—and thus saving future lives, winning the war, and securing peace—than would be produced by protecting the city of Coventry. In reaching this decision, Churchill may have guessed at the number of lives that would probably be saved by keeping Ultra secret and the number of lives that such secrecy would probably cost. Similarly, he may have estimated the number of lives that would be saved by warning the inhabitants of Coventry and subtracted the future lives that would probably be lost as a result of not having access to German secrets. He may then have decided that more lives would be saved by keeping Ultra secret, and concluded that secrecy was the morally proper course of action.

Utilitarianism is thus a moral theory that requires one to look at the end results or consequences of one's actions to determine their morality. It is therefore sometimes called a "teleological" theory (from the Greek word *telos*, which means "end" or "result") or a "consequentialist" theory of morality.

All utilitarian theories claim that the morality of an action depends on the amount of goodness the action produces, although utilitarians hold considerably different views concerning what goodness consists of. Some, like John Stuart Mill, hold that pleasure or happiness (or satisfaction or some other pleasant state of consciousness) is the only basic good; others hold that there are many things besides pleasant states of mind that are intrinsically good, such as friendship, knowledge, love, courage, health, beauty, and so on.[3] During the Coventry incident, Winston Churchill may have assumed that human lives were the basic values in terms of which his decision should be made. Regardless of their views on what constitutes goodness, utilitarians all agree that only intrinsic or ultimate goods should be taken into account when evaluating the morality of our actions. Intrinsic goods are things we value for themselves, and not merely because of what they will get us.

Utilitarians also agree that in order to determine the morality of an act, one must measure the amount of good the act will produce, and subtract from this the amount of evil it will also produce. The net result is

2. Utilitarianism has a long history. Classical accounts of utilitarian theory can be found in Jeremy Bentham, *The Principles of Morals and Legislation* (Oxford, 1789); John Stuart Mill, *Utilitarianism* (London, 1861); Henry Sidgwick, *Outlines of the History of Ethics*, 5th ed. (London, 1902). Some modern expositions of utilitarian thought may be found in Michael D. Bayles, ed., *Contemporary Utilitarianism* (Garden City, N.Y.: Doubleday, 1968); and J. J. C. Smart and Bernard Williams, *Utilitarianism: For and Against* (London: Cambridge University Press, 1973). A lively and very readable account of utilitarianism and its implications is Peter Singer, *Practical Ethics* (London: Cambridge University Press, 1979). Critical accounts of utilitarianism may be found in David Lyons, *The Forms and Limits of Utilitarianism* (London: Oxford University Press, 1965) and D. H. Hodgson, *Consequences of Utilitarianism* (London: Oxford University Press, 1967).

3. The view that there are goods other than states of consciousness is suggested by G. E. Moore, *Principia Ethics* (London: Cambridge University Press, 1903) and William K. Frankena, *Ethics*, 2nd ed. (Englewood Cliffs, N.J.: Prentice-Hall, 1973).

the "utility" of the act.[4] The morally correct act is the one that is likely to produce the greatest amount of utility. For example, in making his decision concerning the fate of Coventry, Churchill may have estimated the number of lives that would be saved if he warned the people of Coventry, and weighed these against the many more lives that would be saved by keeping the Ultra project secret. Ultimately, he may have reasoned, the greater good would be produced by keeping the Ultra project secret.

The readings in this chapter are concerned with utilitarianism. The first, by John Stuart Mill, is taken from his classic work entitled, aptly enough, *Utilitarianism*. The second, by Richard Brandt, describes a contemporary variant of utilitarian theory called rule utilitarianism.

## THE CLASSICAL VERSION OF UTILITARIAN ETHICS:
### John Stuart Mill's *Utilitarianism*

Mill published *Utilitarianism* in 1861 as an attempt to correct what he felt were some important misunderstandings about utilitarian morality.[5] Mill begins by pointing out in Chapter One that it is not possible to give a logical proof that utilitarianism is correct. Utilitarianism holds that everyone should seek happiness. Now ordinarily one proves that one should seek a certain object by showing that that object will get one something else that one desires. But happiness is an ultimate end, that is, it is desired for its own sake and not because it will get us something else that we want. So there is no way of proving that one should seek happiness. All one can do, Mill says, is present considerations that can sway the reader's intellect, and this he attempts to do in the chapters excerpted here.

Mill's definition of utilitarianism is summed up in Chapter Two in what he calls the greatest happiness principle:

> Actions are right in proportion as they tend to promote happiness; wrong as they tend to produce the reverse of happiness. By happiness is intended pleasure and the absence of pain; by unhappiness, pain and the privation of pleasure.

4. Obviously, there are many problems involved in trying to measure or even estimate the quantity of good mental states such as pleasure or satisfaction, and many more problems in trying to subtract from them the quantity of bad mental states such as pain or dissatisfaction. These measurement problems multiply when one attempts to add together the good mental states of different people or subtract the bad mental states of one set of people from the good mental states of others; the problem of trying to add or subtract different people's mental states is today referred to as the problem of "interpersonal comparison of utilities." For a compact discussion of these issues, see A. K. Sen, *Collective Choice and Social Welfare* (San Francisco: Holden-Day, 1970). Measurement problems are discussed in Alastair MacIntyre, "Utilitarianism and Cost-Benefit Analysis: An Essay on the Relevance of Moral Philosophy to Bureaucratic Theory," in *Values in the Electric Power Industry*, ed. Kenneth Syre (Notre Dame, Ind.: University of Notre Dame Press, 1977), and Tom L. Beauchamp, "Utilitarianism and Cost-Benefit Analysis: A Reply to MacIntyre," in *Ethical Theory and Business*, eds. Tom L. Beauchamp and Norman E. Bowie (Englewood Cliffs, N.J.: Prentice-Hall, 1979).

5. Readers interested in more extensive accounts of Mill's utilitarianism can consult J. P. Plamenatz, *The English Utilitarians* (London: Oxford University Press, 1949) and Karl Britton, *John Stuart Mill* (London, 1953).

Mill claims that this utilitarian principle is based on a certain theory of life (that is, a certain view of human nature), namely that in all their actions people are only seeking pleasure (or happiness) or fleeing pain. But many critics, Mill points out, think this theory of life is "mean and groveling . . . worthy only of swine." For it seems to imply that humans are motivated by desires for pleasures that are no different from those that motivate swine! Mill answers this criticism by arguing that human beings experience mental pleasures that are qualitatively different from those bodily pleasures animals experience.

But how are pleasures and pains measured and compared to each other when they are qualitatively different from each other? Mill answers this question by proposing a simple test: "Of two pleasures, if there be one to which all or almost all who have experience of both give a decided preference . . . that is the more desirable pleasure." Thus, if people who are acquainted with both mental and bodily pleasures prefer the mental pleasures, then mental pleasures are to be counted as having more value than bodily pleasures. And, Mill claims, human beings clearly prefer the mental pleasures to the bodily pleasures animals experience, as is proved by the fact that "few human creatures would consent to be changed into any of the lower animals for a promise of the fullest allowance of a beast's pleasures."

But why should we accept the utilitarian principle? Mill tries to answer this question in Chapter Four. There he reminds us that he has already shown (in Chapter One) that "questions of ultimate ends do not admit of proof." Instead, Mill proposes a strange (many people would say a fallacious) consideration in support of his view that we ought to seek everyone's happiness:

> No reason can be given why the general happiness is desirable, except that each person, so far as he believes it to be attainable, desires his own happiness. This, however, being a fact, we have not only all the proof which the case admits of, but all which it is possible to require, that happiness is a good, that each person's happiness is a good to that person, and the general happiness, therefore, a good to the aggregate of all persons.

Here Mill seems to be pointing out that each of us clearly desires his own happiness. This is proof enough that everyone recognizes that one's own happiness is a good, that is, that one's own happiness is intrinsically valuable and ought to be pursued. But if each of us recognizes that our own happiness is intrinsically valuable, Mill seems to conclude, then each of us must also recognize that everyone else's happiness has a similar value. (Mill may here be assuming that whatever makes our happiness intrinsically valuable must also make the happiness of others intrinsically valuable.) And so, Mill claims, we all ought to pursue the general happiness, that is, the happiness of everyone, including ourselves. Interpreted in this way, Mill's argument is certainly sound, although one could question whether the fact that we each desire happiness is proof enough that we attribute intrinsic value to happiness. However, Mill could also be interpreted as saying something like the following.

He might be arguing that each of us clearly desires his own happiness and that since we each desire our own happiness, we must all desire the happiness of everyone. Interpreted in this second way, Mill's argument would clearly be fallacious because from the fact that I desire my own happiness it does not follow that I (along with everyone else) desire everyone's happiness. Probably it is best to reject this second interpretation, although many philosophers today hold that it is the correct one. It is best to see Mill as arguing that since we each attribute an intrinsic value to our own happiness (as evidenced by the fact that we act for the sake of our happiness) and since the happiness of others does not differ from ours in a relevant way, we must (if we are to be consistent) each attribute an intrinsic value to the happiness of everyone. Consequently, we must all recognize that the happiness of everyone is intrinsically valuable and ought to be pursued.

But aren't there other things besides human happiness that we desire and seek as valuable? Mill claims that if people desire other things—such as virtue, money, power, or fame—it is because these are means to happiness and are consequently associated with happiness. Desire for these things, according to Mill, "is not a different thing from the desire of happiness." Thus Mill is claiming that only happiness is intrinsically valuable. When it seems that people attribute intrinsic value to other experiences (such as the experience of being virtuous or the experience of having money or power) it is because these other experiences are, for them, part of the experience of being happy. Thus, in the end, only the mental experience of being happy is ever given an intrinsic value. Mill concludes that "happiness is the sole end of human action, and the promotion of it the test by which to judge of all conduct; from whence it necessarily follows that it must be the criterion of morality." That is, since we attribute an intrinsic value to happiness and only to happiness (as is evidenced by an analysis of our pursuits and desires), it follows that in all of our actions we ought to be pursuing happiness (our own and that of others) and only happiness.

It should be clear from this brief account that Mill's version of utilitarianism is a bit different from the version that we surmised Winston Churchill could have used in making the Coventry decision. We suggested that Churchill may have assumed that human lives were the ultimate values in terms of which one's decisions should be made. For Mill and for many twentieth-century utilitarians, however, the basic value is pleasure or satisfaction. Thus, if Mill had been responsible for the Coventry decision, he would not have asked himself how many lives his decision would lose or save. Instead, he would have asked himself how much pleasure or satisfaction or happiness his decision would ultimately produce. In the end, Mill probably would have come to the same decision as Churchill since the more lives one saves, the greater the opportunities there are for satisfaction or happiness. But sometimes Mill's method would come to a conclusion quite different from that of the method we have attributed to Churchill. If a person, for example, had nothing to look forward to but a life filled with pain and empty pleasure, Mill's utilitarianism would imply that the person's life should not continue. But if one thought that life itself was an ultimate value, as we are supposing that Churchill did, then one might come to the conclusion that putting a person to death is wrong even if that person's life was filled with pain. Thus there are different forms of utilitarianism and these different forms can come to distinctly different conclusions.

## A CONTEMPORARY VERSION OF UTILITARIAN ETHICS:
### Richard Brandt's "Toward a Credible Form of Utilitarianism"

In classical utilitarianism, the principle of utility is applied to particular actions and is therefore called "act utilitarianism." Churchill's decision to allow Coventry to be destroyed to save the secret of Ultra is an example of an act utilitarian approach. By contrast, "rule utilitarianism" is a contemporary type of utilitarianism that emphasizes the importance of rules for moral action.[6] Rule utilitarians hold that we should act only according to those rules we think will promote the greatest happiness. Thus, the principle of utility is seen as a guide for deciding what rules we should follow, rather than for deciding what particular actions we should perform.

Some contemporary philosophers have espoused the rule utilitarianism view because they believe it does not have the same problems act utilitarianism does. As the Coventry case shows, act utilitarianism can sometimes lead to decisions that leave us uneasy. If Churchill had used a form of rule utilitarianism, he perhaps might have reasoned as follows: The greatest happiness will be achieved if everyone sticks to the rule, "Innocent lives should never be put at risk"; since that rule promotes the greatest happiness, I must follow it and protect the people of Coventry.

Richard Brandt reasons along these lines in the selection that follows. In order to avoid some of the difficulties act utilitarianism may encounter, Brandt formulates a version of rule utilitarianism that stresses the importance of a learnable set of rules that everyone should follow. According to Brandt, the rules we should follow are those that satisfy two main criteria: (1) Will everyone be better off by recognizing these rules instead of other rules? and (2) Can people be expected to follow these rules? Brandt is not saying that we should follow whatever moral rules our society already recognizes. He is saying, rather, that we should follow those ideal rules that would produce the most utility for everyone in society. Brandt's account is interesting because it suggests that morality is a way of life and not merely a series of separate actions performed in particular circumstances. Readers who would like to examine Brandt's views in greater detail should consult his later writings.[7]

6. Accounts of rule utilitarianism may be found in the following: J. O. Urmson, "The Interpretation of the philosophy of J. S. Mill," *Philosophical Quarterly*, vol. 3 (1953), pp. 33–39; Stephen Toulmin, *An Examination of the Place of Reason in Ethics* (London: Cambridge University Press, 1950); Marcus G. Singer, *Generalization in Ethics* (New York: Knopf, 1961); R. B. Brandt, "Some Merits of One Form of Rule Utilitarianism," in Philippa Foot, ed., *Theories of Ethics* (London: Oxford University Press, 1967).

7. See Richard B. Brandt, *A Theory of the Good and the Right* (New York: Oxford University Press, 1979).

# UTILITARIANISM

*J. S. Mill*

## CHAPTER I. GENERAL REMARKS

. . . On the present occasion, I shall, without further discussion of the other theories, attempt to contribute something toward the understanding and appreciation of the "utilitarian" or "happiness" theory, and toward such proof as it is susceptible of. It is evident that this cannot be proof in the ordinary and popular meaning of the term. Questions of ultimate ends are not amenable to direct proof. Whatever can be proved to be good must be so by being shown to be a means to something admitted to be good without proof. The medical art is proved to be good by its conducing to health; but how is it possible to prove that health is good? The art of music is good, for the reason, among others, that it produces pleasure; but what proof is it possible to give that pleasure is good? If, then, it is asserted that there is a comprehensive formula, including all things which are in themselves good, and that whatever else is good is not so as an end but as a means, the formula may be accepted or rejected, but is not a subject of what is commonly understood by proof. We are not, however, to infer that its acceptance or rejection must depend on blind impulse or arbitrary choice. There is a larger meaning of the word proof, in which this question is as amenable to it as any other of the disputed questions of philosophy. The subject is within the cognizance of the rational faculty; and neither does that faculty deal with it solely in the way of intuition. Considerations may be presented capable of determining the intellect either to give or withhold its assent to the doctrine; and this is equivalent to proof.

We shall examine presently of what nature are these considerations; in what manner they apply to the case, and what rational grounds, therefore, can be given for accepting or rejecting the utilitarian formula. But it is a preliminary condition of rational acceptance or rejection that the formula should be correctly understood. . . . Before, therefore, I attempt to enter into the philosophical grounds which can be given for assenting to the utilitarian standard, I shall offer some illustrations of the doctrine itself, with the view of showing more clearly what it is, distinguishing it from what it is not, and disposing of such of the practical objections to it as either originate in, or are closely connected with, mistaken interpretations of its meaning. . . .

From John Stuart Mill, *Utilitarianism*, in *Dissertations and Discussions: Political, Philosophical and Historical*, vol. III (New York: Henry Holt and Company, 1874), pp. 300–91. Selections are from pp. 305–6, 308–13, 314–15, 323–24, 348–54.

## CHAPTER II. WHAT UTILITARIANISM IS

. . . The creed which accepts as the foundation of morals "utility" or the "greatest happiness principle" holds that actions are right in proportion as they tend to promote happiness; wrong as they tend to produce the reverse of happiness. By happiness is intended pleasure and the absence of pain; by unhappiness, pain and the privation of pleasure. To give a clear view of the moral standard set up by the theory, much more requires to be said; in particular, what things it includes in the ideas of pain and pleasure, and to what extent this is left an open question. But these supplementary explanations do not affect the theory of life on which this theory of morality is grounded—namely, that pleasure and freedom from pain are the only things desirable as ends; and that all desirable things (which are as numerous in the utilitarian as in any other scheme) are desirable either for pleasure inherent in themselves or as means to the promotion of pleasure and the prevention of pain.

Now such a theory of life excites in many minds, and among them in some of the most estimable in feeling and purpose, inveterate dislike. To suppose that life has (as they express it) no higher end than pleasure—no better and nobler object of desire and pursuit—they designate as utterly mean and groveling, as a doctrine worthy only of swine, to whom the followers of Epicurus were, at a very early period, contemptuously likened; and modern holders of the doctrine are occasionally made the subject of equally polite comparisons by its German, French, and English assailants.

When thus attacked, the Epicureans have always answered that it is not they, but their accusers, who represent human nature in a degrading light, since the accusation supposes human beings to be capable of no pleasures except those of which swine are capable. If this supposition were true, the charge could not be gainsaid, but would then be no longer an imputation; for if the sources of pleasure were precisely the same to human beings and to swine, the rule of life which is good enough for the one would be good enough for the other. The comparison of the Epicurean life to that of beasts is felt as degrading, precisely because a beast's pleasures do not satisfy a human being's conceptions of happiness. Human beings have faculties more elevated than the animal appetites and, when once made conscious of them, do not regard anything as happiness which does not include their gratification. I do not, indeed, consider the Epicureans to have been by any means faultless in drawing out their scheme of consequences from the utilitarian principle. To do this in any sufficient manner, many Stoic, as well as Christian, elements require to be included. But there is no known Epicurean theory of life which does not assign to the pleasures of the intellect, of the feelings and imagination, and of the moral sentiments a much higher value as pleasures than to those of mere sensation. It must be admitted, however, that utilitarian writers in general have placed the superiority of mental over bodily pleasures chiefly in the greater permanency, safety, uncostliness, etc., of the *contextual?*

former—that is, in their circumstantial advantages rather than in their intrinsic nature. And on all these points utilitarians have fully proved their case; but they might have taken the other and, as it may be called, higher ground with entire consistency. It is quite compatible with the principle of utility to recognize the fact that some kinds of pleasure are more desirable and more valuable than others. It would be absurd that, while in estimating all other things quality is considered as well as quantity, the estimation of pleasure should be supposed to depend on quantity alone.

If I am asked what I mean by difference of quality in pleasures, or what makes one pleasure more valuable than another, merely as a pleasure, except its being greater in amount, there is but one possible answer. Of two pleasures, if there be one to which all or almost all who have experience of both give a decided preference, irrespective of any feeling of moral obligation to prefer it, that is the more desirable pleasure. If one of the two is, by those who are competently acquainted with both, placed so far above the other that they prefer it, even though knowing it to be attended with a greater amount of discontent, and would not resign it for any quantity of the other pleasure which their nature is capable of, we are justified in ascribing to the preferred enjoyment a superiority in quality so far outweighing quantity as to render it, in comparison, of small account.

Now it is an unquestionable fact that those who are equally acquainted with and equally capable of appreciating and enjoying both do give a most marked preference to the manner of existence which employs their higher faculties. Few human creatures would consent to be changed into any of the lower animals for a promise of the fullest allowance of a beast's pleasures; no intelligent human being would consent to be a fool, no instructed person would be an ignoramus, no person of feeling and conscience would be selfish and base, even though they should be persuaded that the fool, the dunce, or the rascal is better satisfied with his lot than they are with theirs. They would not resign what they possess more than he for the most complete satisfaction of all the desires which they have in common with him. If they ever fancy they would, it is only in cases of unhappiness so extreme that to escape from it they would exchange their lot for almost any other, however undesirable in their own eyes. A being of higher faculties requires more to make him happy, is capable probably of more acute suffering, and certainly accessible to it at more points, than one of an inferior type; but in spite of these liabilities, he can never really wish to sink into what he feels to be a lower grade of existence. We may give what explanation we please of this unwillingness; we may attribute it to pride, a name which is given indiscriminately to some of the most and to some of the least estimable feelings of which mankind are capable; we may refer it to the love of liberty and personal independence, an appeal to which was with the Stoics one of the most effective means for the inculcation of it; to the love of power or to the love of excitement, both of which do really enter into and contribute to it; but its most appropriate appellation is a sense of dignity, which all human beings possess in one form or other, and in some, though by no means in exact, proportion to their higher faculties, and which is so essential a part of the happiness of those in whom it is strong that nothing which conflicts with it could be otherwise than momentarily an object of desire to them. Whoever supposes that this preference takes place at a sacrifice of happiness—that the superior being, in anything like equal circumstances, is not happier than the inferior—confounds the two very different ideas of happiness and content. It is indisputable that the being whose capacities of enjoyment are low has the greatest chance of having them fully satisfied; and a highly endowed being will always feel that any happiness which he can look for, as the world is constituted, is imperfect. But he can learn to bear its imperfections, if they are at all bearable; and they will not make him envy the being who is indeed unconscious of the imperfections, but only because he feels not at all the good which those imperfections qualify. It is better to be a human being dissatisfied than a pig satisfied; better to be Socrates dissatisfied than a fool satisfied. And if the fool, or the pig, are of a different opinion, it is because they only know their own side of the question. The other party to the comparison knows both sides. . . .

From this verdict of the only competent judges, I apprehend there can be no appeal. On a question which is the best worth having of two pleasures, or which of two modes of existence is the most grateful to the feelings, apart from its moral attributes and from its consequences, the judgment of those who are qualified by knowledge of both, or, if they differ, that of the majority among them, must be admitted as final. And there needs be the less hesitation to accept this judgment respecting the quality of pleasures, since there is no other tribunal to be referred to even on the question of quantity. What means are there of determining which is the acutest of two pains, or the intensest of two pleasurable sensations, except the general suffrage of those who are familiar with both? Neither pains nor pleasures are homogeneous, and pain is always heterogeneous with pleasure. What is there to decide whether a particular pleasure is worth purchasing at the cost of a particular pain, except the feelings and judgment of the experienced? When, therefore, those feelings and judgment declare the pleasures derived from the higher faculties to be preferable *in kind,* apart from the question of intensity, to those of which the animal nature, disjoined from the higher faculties, is susceptible, they are entitled on this subject to the same regard. . . .

I must again repeat what the assailants of utilitarianism seldom have the justice to acknowledge, that the happiness which forms the utilitarian standard of what is right in conduct is not the agent's own happiness but that of all concerned. As between his own happiness and that of others, utilitarianism requires him to be as strictly impartial as a disinterested and benevolent spectator. In the golden rule of Jesus of Nazareth, we read the complete spirit of the ethics of utility. "To do as you would be done by," and "to love your neighbor as yourself," constitute the ideal perfection of utilitarian morality. As the means of making the nearest approach to this ideal, utility would enjoin, first, that laws and social arrangements should place the happiness or (as, speaking practically, it may be called) the interest of every individual as nearly as possible in harmony with the interest of the whole; and, secondly, that education and opinion, which have so vast a power over human character, should so use that power as to establish in the mind of every individual an indissoluble association between his own happiness and the good of the whole, especially between his own happiness and the practice of such modes of conduct, negative and positive, as regard for the universal happiness prescribes; so that not only he may be unable to conceive the possibility of happiness to himself, consistently with conduct opposed to the general good, but also that a direct impulse to promote the general good may be in every individual one of the habitual motives of action, and the sentiments connected therewith may fill a large and prominent place in every human being's sentient existence. If the impugners of the utilitarian morality represented it to their own minds in this its true character, I know not what recommendation possessed by any other morality they could possibly affirm to be wanting to it; what more beautiful or more exalted developments of human nature any other ethical system can be supposed to foster, or what springs of action, not accessible to the utilitarian, such systems rely on for giving effect to their mandates. . . .

• • •

## CHAPTER IV. OF WHAT SORT OF PROOF THE PRINCIPLE OF UTILITY IS SUSCEPTIBLE

It has already been remarked that questions of ultimate ends do not admit of proof, in the ordinary acceptation of the term. To be incapable of proof by reasoning is common to all first principles, to the first premises of our knowledge, as well as to those of our conduct. But the former, being matters of fact, may be the subject of a direct appeal to the faculties which judge of fact—namely, our senses and our internal consciousness. Can an appeal be made to the same faculties on questions of practical ends? Or by what other faculty is cognizance taken of them?

Questions about ends are, in other words, questions [about] what things are desirable. The utilitarian doctrine is that happiness is desirable, and the only thing desirable, as an end; all other things being only desirable as means to that end. What ought to be required of this doctrine, what conditions is it requisite that the doctrine should fulfill—to make good its claim to be believed?

The only proof capable of being given that an object is visible is that people actually see it. The only proof that a sound is audible is that people hear it; and so of the other sources of our experience. In like manner, I apprehend, the sole evidence it is possible to produce that anything is desirable is that people do actually desire it. If the end which the utilitarian doctrine proposes to itself were not, in theory and in practice, acknowledged to be an end, nothing could ever convince any person that it was so. No reason can be given why the general happiness is desirable, except that each person, so far as he believes it to be attainable, desires his own happiness. This, however, being a fact, we have not only all the proof which the case admits of, but all which it is possible to require, that happiness is a good, that each person's happiness is a good to that person, and the general happiness, therefore, a good to the aggregate of all persons. Happiness has made out its title as *one* of the ends of conduct and, consequently, one of the criteria of morality.

But it has not, by this alone, proved itself to be the sole criterion. To do that, it would seem, by the same rule, necessary to show, not only that people desire happiness, but that they never desire anything else. Now it is palpable that they do desire things which, in common language, are decidedly distinguished from happiness. They desire, for example, virtue and the absence of vice no less really than pleasure and the absence of pain. The desire of virtue is not as universal, but it is as authentic a fact as the desire of happiness. And hence the opponents of the utilitarian standard deem that they have a right to infer that there are other ends of human action besides happiness, and that happiness is not the standard of approbation and disapprobation.

But does the utilitarian doctrine deny that people desire virtue, or maintain that virtue is not a thing to be desired? The very reverse. It maintains not only that virtue is to be desired, but that it is to be desired disinterestedly, for itself. Whatever may be the opinion of utilitarian moralists as to the original conditions by which virtue is made virtue, however they may believe (as they do) that actions and dispositions are only virtuous because they promote another end than virtue, yet this being granted, and it having been decided, from considerations of this description, what *is* virtuous, they not only place virtue at the very head of the things which are good as means to the ultimate end, but they also recognize as a psychological fact the possibility of its being, to the individual, a good in itself, without looking to any end beyond it; and hold that the mind is not in a right state, not in a state conformable to utility, not in the state most conducive to the general happiness, unless it does love virtue in this manner—as a thing desirable in itself, even although, in the individual instance, it should not produce those other desirable consequences which it tends to produce, and on account of which it is held to be virtue. This opinion is not, in the smallest degree, a departure from the happiness principle. The ingredients of happiness are very various, and each of them is desirable in itself, and not merely when considered as swelling an aggregate. The principle of utility does not mean that any given pleasure, as music, for instance, or any given exemption from pain, as for example health, is to be looked upon as a means to a collective something termed happiness, and to be desired on that account. They are desired and desirable in and for themselves; besides being means, they are a part of the end. Virtue, according to the utilitarian doctrine, is not naturally and originally part of the end, but it is capable of becoming so; and in those who love it disinterestedly it has become so, and is desired and cherished, not as a means to happiness, but as a part of their happiness.

To illustrate this further, we may remember that virtue is not the only thing originally a means, and which if it were not a means to anything else would be and remain indifferent, but which by association with what it is a means to comes to be desired for itself, and that too with the utmost intensity. What, for example, shall we say of the love of money? There is nothing originally more desirable about money than about any heap of glittering pebbles. Its worth is solely that of the things which it will buy; the desires for other things than itself, which it is a means of gratifying. Yet the love of money is not only one of the strongest moving forces of human life, but money is, in many cases, desired in and for itself; the desire to possess it is often stronger than the desire to use it, and goes on increasing when all the desires which point to ends beyond it, to be compassed by it, are falling off. It may, then, be said truly that money is desired not for the sake of an end, but as part of the end. From being a means to happiness, it has come to be itself a principal ingredient of the individual's conception of happiness. The same may be said of the majority of the great objects of human life: power, for example, or fame, except that to each of these there is a certain amount of immediate pleasure annexed, which has at least the semblance of being naturally inherent in them—a thing which cannot be said of money. Still, however, the strongest natural attraction, both of power and of fame, is the immense aid they give to the attainment of our other wishes; and it is the strong association thus generated between them and all our objects of desire which gives to the direct desire of them the intensity it often assumes, so as in some characters to surpass in strength all other desires. In these cases the means have become a part of the end, and a more important part of it than any of the things which they are means to. What was once desired as an instrument for the attainment of happiness has come to be desired for its own sake. In being desired for its own sake it is, however, desired as *part* of happiness. The person is made, or thinks he would be made, happy by its mere possession; and is made unhappy by failure to obtain it. The desire of it is not a different thing from the desire of happiness any more than the love of music or the desire of health. They are included in happiness. They are some of the elements of which the desire of happiness is made up. Happiness is not an abstract idea but a concrete whole; and these are some of its parts. And the utilitarian standard sanctions and approves their being so. Life would be a poor thing, very ill provided with sources of happiness, if there were not this provision of nature by which things originally indifferent, but conducive to, or otherwise associated with, the satisfaction of our primitive desires, become in themselves sources of pleasure more valuable than the primitive pleasures, both in permanency, in the space of human existence that they are capable of covering, and even in intensity.

Virtue, according to the utilitarian conception, is a good of this description. There was no original desire of it, or motive to it, save its conduciveness to pleasure, and especially to protection from pain. But through the association thus formed it may be felt a good in itself, and desired as such with as great intensity as any other good; and with this difference between it and the love of money, of power, or of fame—that all of these may, and often do, render the individual noxious to the other members of the society to which he belongs, whereas there is nothing which makes him so much a blessing to them as the cultivation of the disinterested love of virtue. And consequently, the utilitarian standard, while it tolerates and approves those other acquired desires, up to the point beyond which they would be more injurious to the general happiness than promotive of it, enjoins and requires the cultivation of the love of virtue up to the greatest strength possible, as being above all things important to the general happiness.

It results from the preceding considerations that there is in reality nothing desired except happiness. Whatever is desired otherwise than as a means to some end beyond itself, and ultimately to happiness, is desired as itself a part of happiness, and is not desired for itself until it has become so. Those who desire virtue for its own sake desire it either because the consciousness of it is a pleasure, or because the consciousness of being without it is a pain, or for both reasons united; as in truth the pleasure and pain seldom exist separately, but almost always together— the same person feeling pleasure in the degree of virtue attained, and pain in not having attained more. If one of these gave him no pleasure, and the other no pain, he would not love or desire virtue, or would desire it only for the other benefits which it might produce to himself or to persons whom he cared for.

We have now, then, an answer to the question, of what sort of proof the principle of utility is susceptible. If the opinion which I have now stated is psychologically true—if human nature is so constituted as to desire nothing which is not either a part of happiness or a means of happiness—we can have no other proof, and we require no other, that these are the only things desirable. If so, happiness is the sole end of human action, and the promotion of it the test by which to judge of all human conduct; from whence it necessarily follows that it must be the criterion of morality, since a part is included in the whole.

# TOWARD A CREDIBLE FORM
# OF UTILITARIANISM

*Richard B. Brandt*

## INTRODUCTION

. . . The view to be discussed is a form of "rule-utilitarianism." This terminology must be explained. I call a utilitarianism "act-utilitarianism" if it
holds that the rightness of an act is fixed by the utility of *its* consequences,
as compared with those of other acts the agent might perform instead.
Act-utilitarianism is hence an atomistic theory: the value of the effects of a
single act on the world is decisive for its rightness. "Rule-utilitarianism,"
in contrast, applies to views according to which the rightness of an act is
not fixed by *its* relative utility, but by conformity with general rules or
principles; the utilitarian feature of these theories consists in the fact that
the correctness of these rules or principles is fixed in some way by the
utility of their general acceptance. In contrast with the atomism of act-
utilitarianism, rule-utilitarianism is in a sense an organic theory: the rightness of individual acts can be ascertained only by assessing a whole social
policy.

Neither form of utilitarianism is necessarily committed on the subject of what counts as "utility": not on the meaning or function of such
phrases as "maximize intrinsic good," and not on the identity of intrinsic
goods—whether enjoyments, or states of persons, or states of affairs,
such as equality of distribution.

In recent years, types of rule-utilitarianism have been the object of
much interest. And for good reason. Act-utilitarianism, at least given the
assumptions about what is valuable which utilitarians commonly make,
has implications which it is difficult to accept. It implies that if you have
employed a boy to mow your lawn and he has finished the job and asks
for his pay, you should pay him what you promised only if you cannot
find a better use for your money. It implies that when you bring home
your monthly pay-check you should use it to support your family and
yourself only if it cannot be used more effectively to supply the needs of
others. It implies that if your father is ill and has no prospect of good in
his life, and maintaining him is a drain on the energy and enjoyments of
others, then, if you can end his life without provoking any public scandal
or setting a bad example, it is your positive duty to take matters into your
own hands and bring his life to a close. A virtue of rule-utilitarianism, in
at least some of its forms, is that it avoids at least some of such objectionable implications.

From Richard B. Brandt, "Toward a Credible Form of Utilitarianism," in *Morality and the
Language of Conduct,* Hector-Neri Castaneda and George Nakhnikian, eds. (Detroit: Wayne
State University Press, 1963), pp. 109–10, 115, 118, 123–25. Reprinted by permission of the
Wayne State University Press. Copyright © 1963 Wayne State University Press.

In the present paper I wish to arrive at a more precise formulation of a rule-utilitarian type of theory which is different from act-utilitarianism and which is not subject to obvious and catastrophic difficulties. To this end I shall, after an important preliminary discussion, begin by considering two formulations, both supported by distinguished philosophers, which, as I shall show, lead us in the wrong direction. This discussion will lead to a new formulation devised to avoid the consequences of the first theories. . . .

## ACCEPTED RULES VS. JUSTIFIABLE RULES AS THE TEST OF RIGHTNESS

It is convenient to begin by taking as our text some statements drawn from an interesting article by J. O. Urmson.[1] In this paper, Urmson suggested that John Stuart Mill should be interpreted as a rule-utilitarian; and Urmson's opinion was that Mill's view would be more plausible if he were so interpreted. Urmson summarized the possible rule-utilitarian interpretation of Mill in four propositions, of which I quote the first two:

A.  A particular action is justified as being right [in the sense of being morally obligatory] by showing that it is in accord with [is required by] some moral rule. It is shown to be wrong by showing that it transgresses some moral rule.
B.  A moral rule is shown to be correct by showing that the recognition of that rule promotes the ultimate end.

Urmson's first proposition could be taken in either of two ways. When it speaks of a "moral rule," it may refer to an *accepted* moral rule, presumably one accepted in the society of the agent. Alternatively, it may refer to a *correct* moral rule, presumably one the recognition of which promotes the ultimate end. If we ask in which way the proposed theory should be taken, in order to arrive at a defensible theory, part of the answer is that qualifications are going to be required, whichever way we take it. I think it more worthwhile and promising, however, to try to develop it in the second interpretation. . . .

For a start, we might summarize the gist of Urmson's proposal, construed in the second way, as follows: "An act is right if and only if it conforms with that set of moral rules, the recognition of which would have significantly desirable consequences." A somewhat modified version of this is what I shall be urging.

One minor amendment I wish to make immediately. I think we should replace the second clause by the expression, "the recognition of which would have the *best* consequences." . . .

But why insist on the amendment? The reason is that the original, as I stated it (but not necessarily as Urmson intended it), is insufficiently comparative in form. The implication is that a rule is acceptable so long as

1. J. O. Urmson, "The Interpretation of the Moral Philosophy of J. S. Mill," in *The Philosophical Quarterly*, vol. 3 (January 1953), pp. 33–39.

it is significantly better than no regulation at all. But the effect of this is tolerantly to accept a great many rules which we should hardly regard as morally acceptable. Consider promises. There are various possible rules about when promises must be kept. One such possible rule is to require keeping *all* promises, absolutely irrespective of unforeseeable and uncontemplated hardships on the promisee. Recognition of this rule might have good consequences as compared with no rule at all. Therefore it seems to satisfy the unamended formula. Many similar rules would satisfy it. But we know of another rule—the one we recognize—with specifications about allowable exceptions, which would have much better consequences. If we are utilitarian in spirit, we shall want to endorse such a rule but not both of these rules; and the second one is much closer to our view about what our obligations are. The amendment in general endorses as correct many rules which command our support for parallel reasons, and refuses to endorse many others which we reject for parallel reasons. . . .

## RULE-UTILITARIANISM: A SECOND APPROXIMATION

[T]he formulation we have suggested is itself open to interpretations that may lead to problems. How may we construe Urmson's proposal, so that it is both unambiguous and credible? Of course we do not wish to go to the opposite extreme and take "recognition of" to mean merely "doffing the hat to" without attempt to practice. But how shall we take it?

I suggest the following as a second approximation.

First, let us speak of a set of moral rules as being "learnable" if people of ordinary intelligence are able to learn or absorb its provisions, so as to believe the moral propositions in question in the ordinary sense of "believe" for such contexts. Next, let us speak of "the adoption" of a moral code by a person as meaning "the learning and belief of its provisions (in the above sense) and conformity of behavior to these to the extent we may expect people of ordinary conscientiousness to conform their behavior to rules they believe are principles about right or obligatory behavior." Finally, let us, purely arbitrarily and for the sake of brevity, use the phrase "maximizes intrinsic value" to mean "would produce at least as much intrinsic good as would be produced by any relevant alternative action." With these stipulations, we can now propose, as a somewhat more precise formulation of Urmson's proposal, the following rule-utilitarian thesis: "An act is right if and only if it conforms with that learnable set of rules, the adoption of which by everyone would maximize intrinsic value."

This principle does not at all imply that the rightness or wrongness of an act is contingent upon the agent's having *thought about* all the complex business of the identity of a set of ideal moral rules; it asserts, rather, that an act is right if and only if it *conforms* to such a set of rules, regardless of what the agent may think. Therefore the principle is not disqualified from being a correct principle about what is objectively right or wrong, in Moore's sense; for it makes rightness and wrongness a matter of the facts, and totally independent of what the agent thinks is right, or of what the agent thinks about the facts, or of the evidence the agent may have, or of what is probably the case on the basis of this evidence.

An obvious merit of this principle is that it gives expression to at least part of our practice or procedure in trying to find out what is right or wrong. For when we are in doubt about such matters, we often try to think out how it would work in practice to have a moral code which prohibited or permitted various actions we are considering. We do not, of course, ordinarily do anything as complicated as try to think out the *complete* ideal moral code; we are content with considering whether certain specific injunctions relevant to the problem we are considering might be included in a good and workable code. Nevertheless, we are prepared to admit that the whole ideal code is relevant. For if someone shows us that a specific injunction which we think would be an acceptable part of a moral code clearly would not work out in view of other provisions necessary to an ideal code, we should agree that a telling point had been made and revise our thinking accordingly.

In order to get a clearer idea of the kind of "set of rules" (with which right actions must conform) which could satisfy the conditions this rule-utilitarian principle lays down, let us note some general features such a set presumably would have. First, it would contain rules giving directions for recurrent situations which involve conflicts of human interests. Presumably, then, it would contain rules rather similar to W. D. Ross's list of prima facie obligations: rules about the keeping of promises and contracts, rules about debts of gratitude such as we may owe to our parents, and, of course, rules about not injuring other persons and about promoting the welfare of others where this does not work a comparable hardship on us. Second, such a set of rules would not include petty restrictions; nor, at least for the most part, would it contain purely prudential rules. Third, the rules would not be very numerous; an upper limit on quantity is set by the ability of ordinary people to learn them. Fourth, such a set of rules would not include unbearable demands; for their inclusion would only serve to bring moral obligation into discredit. Fifth, the set of rules adoption of which would have the best consequences could not leave too much to discretion. It would make concessions to the fact that ordinary people are not capable of perfectly fine discriminations, and to the fact that, not being morally perfect, people of ordinary conscientiousness will have a tendency to abuse a moral rule where it suits their interest. We must remember that a college dormitory rule like "Don't play music at such times or in such a way as to disturb the study or sleep of others" would be ideally flexible if people were perfect; since they aren't, we have to settle for a rule like "No music after 10 P.M." The same thing is true for a moral code. The best moral code has to allow for the fact that people are what they are; it has to be less flexible and less efficient than a moral code that was to be adopted by perfectly wise and perfectly conscientious people could be.

# CHAPTER FIVE
# SOCIAL CONTRACT
# ETHICS

The American ship *William Brown* sailed from Liverpool, England, on March 13, 1841, headed for Philadelphia. Thirty-seven days later, as it neared Newfoundland, the ship struck an iceberg and sank. Thirty-two passengers and nine of the crewmen crowded into a leaky lifeboat and escaped across the stormy ice-cold sea. Most of these terrified people were eventually rescued, but the crewmen were later brought to trial for the desperate steps they took to save the floundering lifeboat. At the trial of Mr. Holmes, one of the accused, the court record summarized what happened:

> As soon as she was launched, the lifeboat began to leak. The passengers had buckets and tins and, by bailing, were able to reduce the water. The plug came out more than once, and finally, got lost; but its place was supplied by different expedients. The lifeboat and all on board were in great jeopardy. The edge was 5 to 12 inches above the water. Even without a leak she would not have supported one-half her company had there been a moderate wind. She would have swamped very quickly. The people were half naked, and were all crowded together like sheep in a pen. Loaded as the lifeboat was on Tuesday morning, the chances of living were much against her.
>
> Notwithstanding all this, the lifeboat, loaded as she was, did survive throughout the night of Monday. Tuesday morning it began to rain. Tuesday night the wind began to rise, the sea grew heavier, and once, or oftener, the waves splashed over the boat's bow so as to wet, all over, the passengers who were seated there. Pieces of ice were floating around and during the

day icebergs had been seen. About 10 o'clock Tuesday night, it being then dark, the rain falling rather heavily, the sea somewhat freshening, and the boat having considerable water in it, the first mate, who had been bailing for some time gave it up. Earlier he had said it might be "necessary to throw some overboard." Now he exclaimed: "This work won't do. Help me, God. Men: go to work." Holmes and the crew did not proceed upon this order. After a little while, the mate exclaimed again: "Men, you must go to work, or we shall all perish." They then went to work and began to throw over some of the passengers. Holmes was one of the persons who assisted in throwing the passengers over. The first man thrown over was one Riley, who Holmes and the others told to stand up, which he did. Then they threw him over, and afterwards Duffy, who, in vain, besought them to spare him, for the sake of his wife and children who were on shore. Coming to Charles Conlin, the man exclaimed: "Holmes, dear, sure you won't put me out?" "Yes, Charley," said Holmes, "you must go, too." And so he was thrown over. Next was an Irish youth, Francis Askin, who offered Holmes five sovereigns to spare his life till morning, "when," he said, "if God don't send us some help, we'll draw lots, and if the lot falls on me, I'll go over like a man." Holmes said, "I don't want your money, Frank," and put him overboard. When Askin was put out, he had struggled violently. Next one McAvoy was seized who asked for five minutes to say his prayers and was allowed to say them before he was cast overboard. Two men, very stiff with cold, who had hidden themselves, were thrown over after daylight.

On Wednesday morning, the weather cleared, and early in the morning the lifeboat was picked up by the ship "Crescent." All the persons who had not been thrown overboard were thus saved.[1]

During Holmes' trial, the prosecution argued that the defendant had a duty to look after the well-being of the passengers because by becoming a member of the crew he had agreed to serve and protect them. In other words, Holmes should have spared their lives even if it meant sacrificing his own.

Holmes responded with an unusual argument in his own defense. He conceded that so long as we live in a safe and secure society we must live up to the moral duties we have toward others. However, he argued, when the passengers and crew of the ship were thrown into the sea, they were in effect ripped out of society and put into a "natural" or wild state where each person had to depend on his own wits to save his life. In this desperate situation, everyone had to fend for himself and no one could be expected to adhere to moral duty at the expense of his life. According to the court records, Holmes argued that:

in a state of imminent and deadly peril, all men are reduced to a "state of nature," and that there is, then, no distinction between the rights of sailor and passenger. He insisted largely upon the existence of the state of nature, as distinguished from the social state, and contended that to this state of nature the persons in the lifeboat had become reduced on Tuesday night, at 10 o'clock, when the passengers were thrown over.[2]

1. *United States v. Holmes,* 26 Fed. Cas. 360 (No. 15385), (C.C.E.D. Pa. 1842).
2. Ibid.

Essentially, Holmes was arguing that so long as we live in society we can legitimately expect people to live up to their duties because we know there is a government that will keep us all safe while we go about our lives. However, if we are taken out of society and put into a wild state of nature in which there is no government and in which each person has to fight with others for his life, no one can be expected to live up to his moral duties.

In distinguishing between the social state and the state of nature, Holmes was appealing to what is called social contract theory. Classical social contract theory is based on four premises:

1.  There are several morally significant differences between living in an orderly governed society and living in a state of nature.

2.  In an orderly governed society, people have generally agreed to adhere to moral norms in their relationships with each other and these moral norms are enforced by society. Consequently, a person in society knows that others will usually behave morally toward himself and that it is safe for him to behave morally toward others. In such a lawfully ordered society, it is legitimate to expect people to live up to their moral obligations.

3.  The state of nature is the uncivilized state or wild condition of people who have not yet come together to form an orderly society. Because there is nothing to keep people from harming and killing each other in this lawless state of nature, everyone knows that if a person tries to adhere to moral norms others will probably take advantage of him. Since it is dangerous to put oneself at a disadvantage by acting morally in the state of nature, no one can be expected to act morally. Thus, there is no morality in the state of nature: everyone legitimately can and will do whatever is necessary to preserve his own life.

4.  People move out of the state of nature and into a social state by agreeing to adhere to certain moral norms and to enforce these norms through appropriate sanctions. This agreement is the social contract that holds society together. If this agreement ever breaks down (during a war or a revolution, for example) and people are once again reduced to fighting for their lives with each other, they have returned to the state of nature and can no longer be expected to act morally. In other words, morality makes sense only so long as there is a social contract that forms a basis for orderly human relationships.

In his defense, then, Holmes was arguing that when the crew and passengers cast out on the stormy sea in the overcrowded lifeboat they left behind the safely governed and orderly social state in which morality makes sense. On the wild waves of the ocean, they were all thrown back into the state of nature since each person knew that he would die unless someone else was thrown overboard to lighten the lifeboat. Lawlessness thus took over and no one could any longer be expected to adhere to morality since doing so would probably cost one's life. The moral duties that make sense when people live in a well-governed social state became meaningless and for this reason, Holmes argued, he did not violate his moral duties to the passengers, since these duties no longer existed. According to his position, there can be no morality in the state of nature, where the agreements that establish an orderly society no longer exist.

The social contract theory on which Holmes based his defense has had a long history.[3] Since the time of Plato, many people have held that morality arises out of the agreements people make with each other when they establish orderly social relationships; i.e., morality is based on a social contract. Although Plato himself did not hold this view, he described the social contract theories of some of his fellow philosophers as follows:

> These philosophers say that by nature it is beneficial to be unjust to others, but it is harmful to bear the injustices of others. And the harm of suffering the injustices of others outweighs the benefits of being able to be unjust to others. So when men have had a taste of living in a world in which everyone acts unjustly toward each other and in which no one is able to gain the benefits of injustice without being harmed by others, they all come to this opinion: that it is better for everyone if they each mutually agree neither to harm others nor be harmed by others. Then they will begin to establish laws and contracts with each other and "justice" is whatever these laws require. This, then, is the origin of justice.[4]

Since Plato's day, several different kinds of social contract theories have been developed.[5] One type of social contract theory holds that governments are formed by a social contract: governments are instituted when citizens come together and agree to set up a form of organization that can enforce law and order among themselves and can protect them from foreign invasion. Other types of social contract theory hold that moral norms are formed by a social contract. These are established when people mutually agree to adhere to certain norms and to enforce these norms among themselves. This is the kind of social contract theory that Holmes appealed to in his defense and that Plato describes in the passage just cited. Still other types of social contract theories hold that both moral norms and governments are established by a social contract. As we shall see in the first reading, this is the view of Thomas Hobbes.

Social contract theories also differ in their views on when people make a social contract. One type holds that sometime in the distant past the founding members of each society had to come together to form a social contract. This, as we shall see, is Hobbes' view. A second type of social contract theory holds that each member of society implicitly enters a

---

3. A historical survey of social contract theories may be found in J. W. Gough, *The Social Contract*, 2nd ed. (Oxford: Clarendon Press, 1957); see also Otto Gierke, *Natural Law and the Theory of Society*, trans. Ernest Barker (Cambridge: Cambridge University Press, 1934).

4. Plato, *Republic*, bk. 2.

5. Other classical social contract theories may be found in Ernest Barker, ed., *Social Contract* (New York: Oxford University Press, 1962). For contemporary versions of social contract theories, see G. R. Grice, *The Grounds of Moral Judgment* (Cambridge: Cambridge University Press, 1967); Michael Walzer, *Obligations: Essays on Disobedience, War, and Citizenship* (Cambridge, Mass: Harvard University Press, 1970); Joseph Tussman, *Obligation and the Body Politic* (New York: Oxford University Press, 1960). Criticisms of social contract theories may be found in J. P. Plamenatz, *Consent, Freedom, and Political Obligation*, 2nd ed. (London: Oxford University Press, 1968).

social contract with the other members of society when he or she chooses today to continue living in society. A third type of social contract theory holds that people never actually make a social contract with each other, but that we should each live up to those moral norms we would agree to if we were to make a social contract with each other. As we will see, this last position is that of John Rawls, the most prominent social contract philosopher living today.

## A CLASSICAL VERSION OF SOCIAL CONTRACT ETHICS:
### Thomas Hobbes' *Leviathan*

Thomas Hobbes was born in 1588 in Malmesbury, England. He entered Oxford University at the age of fourteen and graduated in 1608 with a bachelor's degree. The selections that follow are taken from his greatest work, *Leviathan* (1651), in which Hobbes sets forth his social contract view of morality.[6]

Hobbes argues that human beings have two main characteristics. First, people are by and large "equal in . . . body and mind." No one person is so physically strong or so mentally superior that that person can force everyone else to do what he wants. And second, all human beings are driven by a desire for "gain," "safety," and "reputation." Because we are by and large equal, and because we are driven by these desires, we would be constantly fighting with each other if there were no political force to keep us at peace. If human beings were in a state of nature in which there was no common power (that is, no public force capable of enforcing legal and moral rules), then they would be, Hobbes writes, in a continual "war, and such a War as is of every man against every man."

In such a state of nature, Hobbes claims, our lives would be "solitary, poor, nasty, brutish, and short." Morever, in such circumstances nothing could be said to be morally right or morally wrong because right and wrong cannot exist unless everyone is living according to the same rules (or laws), and no one will live according to the same rules unless there is someone (an individual or a group) capable of enforcing those rules. Where moral rules are not enforced, there can be no morality. Nor can there be any such thing as private property, since by definition private property is property that it is morally wrong for other people to invade.

The state of nature is so dangerous, uncomfortable, and unpredictable that when people are in it they will look for ways of leaving it in order to save their lives. In the state of nature, Hobbes believes, human

---

6. The reader interested in pursuing Hobbes' thought in more detail might consult one of the following: David Gauthier, *The Logic of the Leviathan* (London: Oxford University Press, 1964); M. M. Goldsmith, *The Political Philosophy of Hobbes: The Rationale of the Sovereign State* (New York: Columbia University Press, 1966); Richard Peters, *Hobbes* (London: Penguin Books, 1956); Howard Warrender, *The Political Philosophy of Hobbes: His Theory of Obligation* (Oxford: Oxford University Press, 1957). For articles on Hobbes, see K. C. Brown, ed., *Hobbes Studies* (London: Oxford University Press, 1965) and Maurice Cranston and Richard S. Peters, *Hobbes and Rousseau* (Garden City, N.Y.: Doubleday, 1972).

reason will come to certain conclusions about what must be done to preserve one's life. Hobbes calls these conclusions natural laws, although he is referring to something rather different from what Aquinas meant by the same term. For Hobbes, a natural law is a conclusion that human reason comes to concerning what people must do if they are to preserve their lives in the state of nature.

There are, for Hobbes, several natural laws. The first and most basic is the conclusion that if people are to preserve their lives they will either have to find some way of living peacefully with each other or they will have to retain the freedom to fight others in self-defense. That is, they will have to find some way of getting everybody to stop fighting or they will have to assert their freedom to fight.

The second natural law is the conclusion that since no one will stop fighting unless everyone else stops fighting, each person will have to agree to give up his freedom to fight when everyone else agrees to do the same. Clearly, unless everyone agrees to stop fighting, people will remain in the perilous state of nature and their lives will remain in danger.

The third natural law is that everyone will have to live up to the agreements he makes. Obviously, if people do not keep the agreement to stop fighting, they will continue to exist in the state of nature. Hobbes also points out that people will not keep their agreements in the state of nature so long as there is no "force sufficient to compel" everyone to keep their agreements. How, then, can people in a state of nature make an effective agreement to stop fighting? It would seem that any agreement they make would be doomed to failure because without a force capable of upholding this agreement no one could be sure that other people would keep it. And if no one is sure that other people would keep the agreement, they would be foolish to keep it themselves. So it would seem that agreements in the state of nature would always be doomed to fail.

Hobbes argues, however, that there is a type of agreement that will succeed in the state of nature. This occurs when the people making the agreement simultaneously give someone (or some group) the power to enforce it. Hobbes claims, then, that people in the state of nature would eventually enter into a social contract in which each person agrees to give up his freedom to fight and further agrees to form a force powerful enough to compel everyone to live up to the agreement. This law-keeping force, which Hobbes calls the sovereign, is in fact the government. Thus, according to Hobbes, a government is formed when people in the state of nature agree "to confer all their power and strength upon one man, or upon one assembly of men" who "shall act . . . in those things which concern the common peace and safety." By agreeing to form such a political force, people simultaneously create the power that enforces their agreement.

Once a governing force has been created, Hobbes claims, the terms "right" and "wrong," "good" and "evil," and the rules of private property can all acquire a meaning. Moral right and wrong will be based on the rules the sovereign enforces. And because there is now a sovereign that can force everyone to live up to moral rules, people in an orderly society can live by these rules without fear that by doing so they will be leaving themselves open to attack by others.

It should be clear from this short summary that the English sailor, Holmes, based his courtroom defense on the kind of social contract theory that Hobbes proposes. Hobbes would have agreed with Holmes that when people are reduced to a situation in which there is no effective sovereign they can no longer be expected to live up to any moral norms. In such a situation, the so-called "law of the jungle" takes over, and men and women may do whatever they need to preserve their own lives.

## A CONTEMPORARY VERSION OF SOCIAL CONTRACT ETHICS: John Rawls' *A Theory of Justice*

John Rawls, a contemporary philosopher who teaches at Harvard University, is the author of *A Theory of Justice,* from which the next selection is taken.[7] Unlike Hobbes, Rawls does not hold that people ever lived in a state of nature, nor does he believe that our ancestors once joined together in an agreement to enforce the rules necessary for an orderly society. Instead, in Rawls' view, the best way of discovering the moral rules by which we should live is by imagining that a group of rational people once joined together and agreed to choose the moral rules by which they would live. Thus, for Rawls, the social contract is not a historical reality but an imaginary device that we can use to discover our moral principles.

Rawls suggests that we should ask ourselves this question: What principles would a group of rational, self-interested people agree to live by if they knew they would have to live together in a society governed by those principles but did not yet know what each of those principles would turn out to be like? For example, would such a group of rational, self-interested people agree to live in a society governed by a principle that allowed discrimination against blacks if none of them knew whether he would turn out to be a black person in that society? Clearly, rational people would reject such a racist principle, so it cannot be morally acceptable. Thus Rawls claims that a principle is morally justified if and only if it would be agreed to by a group of rational, self-interested people who know they will live in a society governed by the principles to which they agree but who do not yet know what sex, race, abilities, religion, desires, social position, income, or other particular characteristics each of them will possess in that future society.

Rawls refers to the situation of such an imaginary group of rational persons as the "original position," and he describes their ignorance of any particulars about themselves as the "veil of ignorance." Because the

7. For more materials on Rawls, see Brian Barry, *The Liberal Theory of Justice: A Critical Examination of the Principal Doctrines in "A Theory of Justice" by John Rawls* (Oxford: Clarendon Press, 1973); Normal Daniels, ed., *Reading Rawls: Critical Studies of "A Theory of Justice"* (New York: Basic Books, 1974); Robert Paul Wolf, *Understanding Rawls: A Reconstruction and Critique of "A Theory of Justice"* (Princeton, N.J.: Princeton University Press, 1977).

parties to the original position do not know any particular facts about themselves, they will be forced to be fair and impartial and cannot show any favoritism toward any special group. Clearly, the original position in Rawls is the imaginary equivalent of the state of nature in Hobbes.

According to Rawls, such an imaginary group of rational persons would reject the principle of utilitarianism. Instead, he argues, they would agree to live by two principles of justice:

> First: each person is to have an equal right to the most extensive basic liberty compatible with a similar liberty for others.
>
> Second: social and economic inequalities are to be arranged so that they are both (a) to the greatest benefit of the least advantaged and (b) attached to offices and positions of fair equality of opportunity.

Rawls goes on to explain that the first principle means that each person's freedoms must be protected from invasion by others and must be equal to the freedoms of all other persons. The second principle has two parts. The first, which Rawls calls the "difference principle," asserts that society must improve as far as possible the position of its most needy members, such as the sick and the disabled. The second part, which Rawls calls the "principle of fair equality of opportunity," says that everyone should have an equal opportunity to qualify for the more privileged positions in society; in other words, morality prohibits discrimination.

But why would the parties to the original position agree to these two principles? Rawls spends a good deal of time explaining exactly what the parties to the original position are like and why they would accept his two principles instead of, say, utilitarian principles. He points out, first, that we are to imagine that the parties to the original position want as many "primary social goods" as possible. (Primary social goods are things that a person can use to satisfy his desires, whatever they might turn out to be.) Second, Rawls says, the parties to the original position know they are to live in a society in which they must cooperate with each other, although there will be conflicts among themselves. Third, they will be behind a "veil of ignorance" so that no one knows what social status, abilities, strength, intelligence, and other characteristics each one will have. Fourth, they will be rational insofar as each person will agree only to those principles that will result in a society in which he will be able to have the greatest amount of primary social goods.

In the original position, Rawls then argues, the parties would first accept a principle of equality. Thus they would agree to his first principle of justice, which requires equal freedoms for everyone. Second, he claims that the parties to the original position would also agree to allow social and economic inequalities if such "inequalities set up various incentives which succeed in eliciting more productive efforts." That is, the parties to the original position would allow some people to have more than others if this situation served to spur those people on to produce more goods and thereby leave everyone better off. However, the parties to the original position will all want to have an equal chance at these more lucrative jobs, so they will insist on the principle of fair equality of opportunity. Finally, Rawls argues that the parties to the original position will want to protect themselves in case they turn out to be among the "least advantaged" members of society. Because of this, they will agree to the difference principle, which directs that society improve the lot of the needy. Thus, Rawls concludes that "the balance of reasons clearly favors the two principles of justice."

But what would Rawls say about the case of the sailor, Holmes? Clearly, because Rawls does not think that the social contract is a historical event, he does not think that our ancestors ever came together to make a social contract. Nor does he think that people today can come in and out of the state of nature (except in their imaginations). For Rawls, the social contract is an imaginary construct that enables us to discover morality; it does not create morality, nor is it necessary for morality. Rawls would probably therefore disagree with Holmes' claim that morality did not exist in the lifeboat situation. In Rawls' scheme of things, morality did not cease to exist when the ship's passengers found themselves on the stormy sea, nor did morality cease to exist when it became clear that some of them would have to leave the lifeboat if anyone was to survive. Rawls might claim, in fact, that Holmes should have asked himself: What does morality require of people in our situation? And to answer this question, Holmes could have used the device of the "original position." That is, Holmes could have discovered his moral duties by asking himself: What principles concerning lifeboat situations would a group of rational, self-interested people agree to if they knew they might someday find themselves in a floundering lifeboat but they did not know who they might turn out to be in that lifeboat?

The reader might well ask himself how this question should be answered.

# LEVIATHAN

*Thomas Hobbes*

## OF THE NATURAL CONDITION OF MANKIND AS CONCERNING THEIR FELICITY, AND MISERY

Nature hath made men so equal, in the faculties of the body, and mind; as that though there be found one man sometimes manifestly stronger in body, or of quicker mind than another; yet when all is reckoned together, the difference between man, and man, is not so considerable, as that one

From *The English Works of Thomas Hobbes of Malmesbury*, vol. III, William Molesworth, ed. (London: John Bohn, 1839), pp. 110–13, 115–18, 120–21, 124–25, 130–31, 153, 157–59, 165.

man can thereupon claim to himself any benefit, to which another may not pretend, as well as he. For as to the strength of body, the weakest has strength enough to kill the strongest, either by secret machination, or by confederacy with others, that are in the same danger with himself.

And as to the faculties of the mind, . . . I find yet a greater equality amongst men, than that of strength. . . . For such is the nature of men, that howsoever they may acknowledge many others to be more witty, or more eloquent, or more learned; yet they will hardly believe there be many so wise as themselves; for they see their own wit at hand, and other men's at a distance. But this proveth rather that men are in that point equal, than unequal. For there is not ordinarily a greater sign of the equal distribution of any thing, than that every man is contented with his share.

From this equality of ability, ariseth equality of hope in the attaining of our ends. And therefore if any two men desire the same thing, which nevertheless they cannot both enjoy, they become enemies; and in the way to their end, which is principally their own conservation, and sometimes their delectation only, endeavour to destroy, or subdue one another. And from hence it comes to pass, that where an invader hath no more to fear, than another man's single power; if one plant, sow, build, or possess a convenient seat, others may probably be expected to come prepared with forces united, to dispossess, and deprive him, not only of the fruit of his labour, but also of his life, or liberty. And the invader again is in the like danger of another.

And from this diffidence of one another, there is no way for any man to secure himself, so reasonable, as anticipation; that is, by force, or wiles, to master the persons of all men he can, so long, till he see no other power great enough to endanger him: and this is no more than his own conservation requireth, and is generally allowed. Also because there be some, that taking pleasure in contemplating their own power in the acts of conquest, which they pursue farther than their security requires; if others, that otherwise would be glad to be at ease within modest bounds, should not by invasion increase their power, they would not be able, long time, by standing only on their defence, to subsist. And by consequence, such augmentation of dominion over men being necessary to a man's conservation, it ought to be allowed him.

Again, men have no pleasure, but on the contrary a great deal of grief, in keeping company, where there is no power to over-awe them all. For every man looketh that his companion should value him, at the same rate he sets upon himself: and upon all signs of contempt, or undervaluing, naturally endeavours, as far as he dares, (which amongst them that have no common power to keep them in quiet, is far enough to make them destroy each other), to extort a greater value from his contemners, by damage; and from others, by the example.

So that in the nature of man, we find three principal causes of quarrel. First, competition; secondly, diffidence; thirdly, glory.

The first, maketh men invade for gain; the second, for safety; and the third, for reputation. The first use violence, to make themselves masters of other men's persons, wives, children, and cattle; the second, to defend them; the third, for trifles, as a word, a smile, a different opinion, and any other sign of undervalue, either direct in their persons, or by reflection in their kindred, their friends, their nation, their profession, or their name.

Hereby it is manifest; that during the time men live without a common power to keep them all in awe, they are in that condition which is called war; and such a war, as is of every man, against every man. . . .

In such condition, there is no place for industry; because the fruit thereof is uncertain: and consequently no culture of the earth; no navigation, nor use of the commodities that may be imported by sea; no commodious building; no instruments of moving, and removing, such things as require much force; no knowledge of the face of the earth; no account of time; no arts; no letters; no society; and which is worst of all, continual fear, and danger of violent death; and the life of man, solitary, poor, nasty, brutish, and short. . . .

To this war of every man, against every man, this also is consequent; that nothing can be unjust. The notions of right and wrong, justices and injustice have there no place. Where there is no common power, there is no law: where no law, no injustice. Force, and fraud, are in war the two cardinal virtues. Justice, and injustice are none of the faculties neither of the body, nor mind. If they were, they might be in a man that were alone in the world, as well as his senses, and passions. They are qualities, that relate to men in society, not in solitude. It is consequent also to the same condition, that there be no property, no dominion, no *mine* and *thine* distinct; but only that to be every man's, that he can get; and for so long, as he can keep it. And thus much for the ill condition, which man by mere nature is actually placed in; though with a possibility to come out of it, consisting partly in the passions, partly in his reason.

The passions that incline men to peace, are fear of death; desire of such things as are necessary to commodious living; and a hope by their industry to obtain them. And reason suggesteth convenient articles of peace, upon which men may be drawn to agreement. These articles, are they, which otherwise are called the Laws of Nature. . . .

## OF THE FIRST AND SECOND NATURAL LAWS, AND OF CONTRACTS

A law of nature, *lex naturalis,* is a precept or general rule, found out by reason, by which a man is forbidden to do that, which is destructive of his life, or taketh away the means of preserving the same; and to omit that, by which he thinketh it may be best preserved. . . .

And because the condition of man, as hath been declared in the precedent chapter, is a condition of war of every one against every one: in which case every one is governed by his own reason; and there is nothing he can make use of, that may not be a help unto him, in preserving his life against his enemies; it followeth, that in such a condition, every man has a right to every thing; even to one another's body. And therefore, as long as this natural right of every man to every thing endureth, there can be no security to any man, how strong or wise soever he be, of living out the time, which nature ordinarily alloweth men to live. And consequently it is a precept, or general rule of reason, *that every man, ought to endeavour peace, as far as he has hope of obtaining it; and when he cannot obtain it, that he may seek, and use, all helps, and advantages of war.* The first branch of which rule, containeth the first, and fundamental law of nature; which is, *to seek peace, and follow it.* The second, the sum of the right of nature; which is, *by all means we can, to defend ourselves.*

From this fundamental law of nature, by which men are commanded to endeavour peace, is derived the second law; *that a man be willing, when others are so too, as far-forth, as for peace, and defence of himself he shall think it necessary, to lay down this right to all things; and be contented with so much liberty against other men, as he would allow other men against himself.* For as long as every man holdeth the right, of doing any thing he liketh; so long are all men in the condition of war. But if other men will not lay down their right, as well as he; then there is no reason for any one, to divest himself of his: for that were to expose himself to prey, which no man is bound to, rather than to dispose himself to peace. . . .

Right is laid aside, either by simply renouncing it; or by transferring it to another. . . .

The mutual transferring of right, is that which men call CONTRACT. . . .

Again, one of the contractors, may deliver the thing contracted for on his part, and leave the other to perform his part at some determinate time after, and in the mean time be trusted; and then the contract on his part, is called PACT, OR COVENANT. . . .

If a covenant be made, wherein neither of the parties perform presently, but trust one another; in the condition of mere nature, which is a condition of war of every man against every man, upon any reasonable suspicion, it is void: but if there be a common power set over them both, with right and force sufficient to compel performance, it is not void. For he that performeth first, has no assurance the other will perform after; because the bonds of words are too weak to bridle men's ambition, avarice, anger, and other passions, without the fear of some coercive power; which in the condition of mere nature, where all men are equal, and judges of the justness of their own fears, cannot possibly be supposed. And therefore he which performeth first, does but betray himself to his enemy; contrary to the right, he can never abandon, of defending his life, and means of living.

But in a civil estate, where there is a power set up to constrain those that would otherwise violate their faith, that fear is no more reasonable; and for that cause, he which by the covenant is to perform first, is obliged so to do. . . .

## OF OTHER LAWS OF NATURE

From that law of nature, by which we are obliged to transfer to another, such rights, as being retained, hinder the peace of mankind, there followeth a third; which is this, *that men perform their covenants made:* without which, covenants are in vain, and but empty words; and the right of all men to all things remaining, we are still in the condition of war.

And in this law of nature, consisteth the fountain and origin of JUSTICE. For where no covenant hath preceded, there hath no right been transferred, and every man has right to every thing; and consequently, no action can be unjust. But when a covenant is made, then to break it is *unjust:* and the definition of INJUSTICE, is no other than *the not performance of covenant.* And whatsoever is not unjust, is *just.*

But because covenants of mutual trust, where there is a fear of not performance on either part, as hath been said in the former chapter, are invalid; though the original of justice be the making of covenants; yet injustice actually there can be none, till the cause of such fear be taken away; which while men are in the natural condition of war, cannot be done. Therefore before the names of just, and unjust can have place, there must be some coercive power, to compel men equally to the performance of their covenants, by the terror of some punishment, greater than the benefit they expect by the breach of their covenant; and to make good that property, which by mutual contract men acquire, in recompense of the universal right they abandon: and such power there is none before the erection of a commonwealth. And this is also to be gathered out of the ordinary definition of justice in the Schools: for they say, that *justice is the constant will of giving to every man his own.* And therefore where there is no *own,* that is no property, there is no injustice; and where there is no coercive power erected, that is, where there is no commonwealth, there is no property; all men having right to all things: therefore where there is no commonwealth, there nothing is unjust. So that the nature of justice, consisteth in keeping of valid covenants: but the validity of covenants begins not but with the constitution of a civil power, sufficient to compel men to keep them: and then it is also that property begins. . . .

## OF THE CAUSES, GENERATION, AND DEFINITION
## OF A COMMONWEALTH

The final cause, end, or design of men, who naturally love liberty, and dominion over others, in the introduction of that restraint upon themselves, in which we see them live in commonwealths, is the foresight of their own preservation, and of a more contented life thereby; that is to say, of getting themselves out from that miserable condition of war, which is necessarily consequent, as hath been shown . . . , to the natural passions of men, when there is no visible power to keep them in awe, and tie them by fear of punishment to the performance of their covenants, and observation of those laws of nature set down [above]. . . .

The only way to erect such a common power, as may be able to defend them from the invasion of foreigners, and the injuries of one another, and thereby to secure them is such sort, as that by their own industry, and by the fruits of the earth, they may nourish themselves and live contentedly; is, to confer all their power and strength upon one man, or upon one assembly of men, that may reduce all their wills, by plurality of voices, unto one will: which is as much as to say, to appoint one man, or assembly of men, to bear their person; and every one to own, and acknowledge himself to be author of whatsoever he that so beareth their person, shall act, or cause to be acted, in those things which concern the common peace and safety; and therein to submit their wills, every one to his will, and their judgments, to his judgment. This is more than consent, or concord; it is a real unity of them all, in one and the same person, made by covenant of every man with every man, in such manner, as if every man should say to every man, *I authorise and give up my right of governing myself, to this man, or to this assembly of men, on this condition, that thou give up thy right to him, and authorize all his actions in like manner.* This done, the multitude so united in one person, is called a COMMON-WEALTH, in Latin CIVITAS. This is the generation of that great LEVIATHAN, or rather, to speak more reverently, of that *mortal god,* to which we owe under the *immortal God,* our peace and defence. For by this authority, given him by every particular man in the commonwealth, he hath the use of so much power and strength conferred on him, that by terror thereof, he is enabled to perform the wills of them all, to peace at home, and mutual aid against their enemies abroad. And in him consisteth the essence of the commonwealth; which, to define it, is *one person, of whose acts a great multitude, by mutual covenants one with another have made themselves every one the author, to the end he may use the strength and means of them all, as he shall think expedient, for their peace and common defence."*

And he that carrieth this person, is called SOVEREIGN, and said to have *sovereign power;* and every one besides, his SUBJECT. . . .

## OF THE RIGHTS OF SOVEREIGNS BY INSTITUTION

A *commonwealth* is said to be *instituted,* when a *multitude* of men do agree, and *covenant, every one, with every one,* that to whatsoever *man,* or *assembly of men,* shall be given by the major part, the *right* to *present* the person of them all, that is to say, to be their *representative;* every one, as well he that *voted for it,* as he that *voted against it,* shall *authorize* all the actions and judgments, of that man, or assembly of men, in the same manner, as if they were his own, to the end, to live peaceably amongst themselves, and be protected against other men. . . .

. . . To the sovereignty, is annexed the whole power of prescribing the rules, whereby every man may know, what goods he may enjoy, and what actions he may do, without being molested by any of his fellow-subjects; and this is it men call *property.* For before constitution of sovereign power, as hath already been shown, all men had right to all things; which necessarily causeth war: and therefore this property, being necessary to peace, and depending on sovereign power, is the act of that power, in order to the public peace. These rules of property, or *meum* and *tuum,* and of *good, evil, lawful,* and *unlawful* in the actions of subjects, are the civil laws; that is to say, the laws of each commonwealth in particular.

# A THEORY OF JUSTICE

*John Rawls*

### 3.    THE MAIN IDEA OF THE THEORY OF JUSTICE

My aim is to present a conception of justice which generalizes and carries to a higher level of abstraction the familiar theory of the social contract as found, say, in Locke. . . . In order to do this we are not to think of the original contract as one to enter a particular society or to set up a particular form of government. Rather, the guiding idea is that the principles of justice for the basic structure of society are the object of the original agreement. They are the principles that free and rational persons concerned to further their own interests would accept in an initial position of equality as defining the fundamental terms of their association. These principles are to regulate all further agreements; they specify the kinds of social cooperation that can be entered into and the forms of government that can be established. This way of regarding the principles of justice I shall call justice as fairness.

Thus we are to imagine that those who engage in social cooperation choose together, in one joint act, the principles which are to assign basic rights and duties and to determine the division of social benefits. Men are to decide in advance how they are to regulate their claims against one another and what is to be the foundation charter of their society. Just as each person must decide by rational reflection what constitutes his good, that is, the system of ends which it is rational for him to pursue, so a group of persons must decide once and for all what is to count among them as just and unjust. The choice which rational men would make in this hypothetical situation of equal liberty, assuming for the present that this choice problem has a solution, determines the principles of justice.

In justice as fairness the original position of equality corresponds to the state of nature in the traditional theory of the social contract. This original position is not, of course, thought of as an actual historical state of affairs, much less as a primitive condition of culture. It is understood as a purely hypothetical situation characterized so as to lead to a certain conception of justice. Among the essential features of this situation is that no one knows his place in society, his class position or social status, nor does any one know his fortune in the distribution of natural assets and abilities, his intelligence, strength, and the like. I shall even assume that the parties do not know their conceptions of the good or their special psychological propensities. The principles of justice are chosen behind a veil of ignorance. This ensures that no one is advantaged or disadvantaged in the choice of principles by the outcome of natural chance or the contingency of social circumstances. Since all are similarly situated and no one is able to design principles to favor his particular condition, the principles of justice are the result of a fair agreement or bargain. For given the circumstances of the original position, the symmetry of everyone's relations to each other, this initial situation is fair between individuals as moral persons, that is, as rational beings with their own ends and capable, I shall assume, of a sense of justice. The original position is, one might say, the appropriate initial status quo, and thus the fundamental agreements reached in it are fair. This explains the propriety of the name "justice as fairness": it conveys the idea that the principles of justice are agreed to in an initial situation that is fair. The name does not mean that the concepts of justice and fairness are the same, any more than the phrase "poetry as metaphor" means that the concepts of poetry and metaphor are the same.

Justice as fairness begins, as I have said, with one of the most general of all choices which persons might make together, namely, with the choice of the first principles of a conception of justice which is to regulate all subsequent criticism and reform of institutions. Then, having chosen a conception of justice, we can suppose that they are to choose a constitution and a legislature to enact laws, and so on, all in accordance with the principles of justice initially agreed upon. Our social situation is just if it is such that by this sequence of hypothetical agreements we would have contracted into the general system of rules which defines it. Moreover, assuming that the original position does determine a set of principles (that is, that a particular conception of justice would be chosen), it will then be true that whenever social institutions satisfy these principles those engaged in them can say to one another that they are cooperating on terms to which they would agree if they were free and equal persons whose relations with respect to one another were fair. They could all view their arrangements as meeting the stipulations which they would acknowledge in an initial situation that embodies widely accepted and reasonable constraints on the choice of principles. The general recognition of this fact would provide the basis for a public acceptance of the corresponding principles of justice. No society can, of course, be a scheme of cooperation which men enter voluntarily in a literal sense; each person finds himself placed at birth in some particular position in some particular society, and the nature of this position materially affects his life prospects. Yet a society satisfying the principles of justice as fairness comes as close as a society can to being a voluntary scheme, for it meets the principles which free and equal persons would assent to under circumstances that are fair. In this sense its members are autonomous and the obligations they recognize self-imposed.

One feature of justice as fairness is to think of the parties in the initial situation as rational and mutually disinterested. This does not mean that the parties are egoists, that is, individuals with only certain kinds of interests, say in wealth, prestige, and domination. But they are conceived as not taking an interest in one another's interests. They are to presume that even their spiritual aims may be opposed, in the way that the aims of those of different religions may be opposed. Moreover, the concept of rationality must be interpreted as far as possible in the narrow sense, standard in economic theory, of taking the most effective means to given ends. I shall modify this concept to some extent, as explained later, but one must try to avoid introducing into it any controversial ethical elements. The initial situation must be characterized by stipulations that are widely accepted.

In working out the conception of justice as fairness one main task clearly is to determine which principles of justice would be chosen in the original position. To do this we must describe this situation in some detail and formulate with care the problem of choice which it presents. These matters I shall take up in the immediately succeeding chapters. It may be observed, however, that once the principles of justice are thought of as arising from an original agreement in a situation of equality, it is an open question whether the principle of utility would be acknowledged. Offhand it hardly seems likely that persons who view themselves as equals, entitled to press their claims upon one another, would agree to a principle which may require lesser life prospects for some simply for the sake of a greater sum of advantages enjoyed by others. Since each desires to protect his interests, his capacity to advance his conception of the good, no one has a reason to acquiesce in an enduring loss for himself in order to bring about a greater net balance of satisfaction. In the absence of strong and lasting benevolent impulses, a rational man would not accept a basic structure merely because it maximized the algebraic sum of advantages irrespective of its permanent effects on his own basic rights and interests. Thus it seems that the principle of utility is incompatible with the conception of social cooperation among equals for mutual advantage. It appears to be inconsistent with the idea of reciprocity implicit in the notion of a well-ordered society. Or, at any rate, so I shall argue.

I shall maintain instead that the persons in the initial situation would choose two rather different principles: the first requires equality in the assignment of basic rights and duties, while the second holds that social and economic inequalities, for example inequalities of wealth and authority, are just only if they result in compensating benefits for everyone, and in particular for the least advantaged members of society. These principles rule out justifying institutions on the grounds that the hardships of some are offset by a greater good in the aggregate. It may be expedient but it is not just that some should have less in order that others may prosper. But there is no injustice in the greater benefits earned by a few provided that the situation of persons not so fortunate is thereby improved. The intuitive idea is that since everyone's well-being depends upon a scheme of cooperation without which no one could have a satisfactory life, the division of advantages should be such as to draw forth the willing cooperation of everyone taking part in it, including those less well situated. Yet this can be expected only if reasonable terms are proposed. The two principles mentioned seem to be a fair agreement on the basis of which those better endowed, or more fortunate in their social position, neither of which we can be said to deserve, could expect the willing cooperation of others when some workable scheme is a necessary condition of the welfare of all. Once we decide to look for a conception of justice that nullifies the accidents of natural endowment and the contingencies of social circumstance as counters in quest for political and economic advantage, we are led to these principles. They express the result of leaving aside those aspects of the social world that seem arbitrary from a moral point of view.

• • •

## 11. TWO PRINCIPLES OF JUSTICE

I shall now state in a provisional form the two principles of justice that I believe would be chosen in the original position. In this section I wish to make only the most general comments, and therefore the first formulation of these principles is tentative. As we go on I shall run through several formulations and approximate step by step the final statement to be given much later. I believe that doing this allows the exposition to proceed in a natural way.

The first statement of the two principles reads as follows.

> First: each person is to have an equal right to the most extensive basic liberty compatible with a similar liberty for others.
>
> Second: social and economic inequalities are to be arranged so that they are both (a) reasonably expected to be to everyone's advantage, and (b) attached to positions and offices open to all.

There are two ambiguous phrases in the second principle, namely "everyone's advantage" and "open to all." Determining their sense more exactly will lead to a second formulation of the principle. . . .

By way of general comment, these principles primarily apply, as I have said, to the basic structure of society. They are to govern the assignment of rights and duties and to regulate the distribution of social and economic advantages. As their formulation suggests, these principles presuppose that the social structure can be divided into two more or less distinct parts, the first principle applying to the one, the second to the other. They distinguish between those aspects of the social system that define and secure the equal liberties of citizenship and those that specify and establish social and economic inequalities. The basic liberties of citizens are, roughly speaking, political liberty (the right to vote and to be eligible for public office) together with freedom of speech and assembly; liberty of conscience and freedom of thought; freedom of the person along with the right to hold (personal) property; and freedom from arbitrary arrest and seizure as defined by the concept of the rule of law. These liberties are all required to be equal by the first principle, since citizens of a just society are to have the same basic rights.

The second principle applies, in the first approximation, to the distribution of income and wealth and to the design of organizations that make use of differences in authority and responsibility, or chains of command. While the distribution of wealth and income need not be equal, it must be to everyone's advantage, and at the same time, positions of authority and offices of command must be accessible to all. One applies the second principle by holding positions open, and then, subject to this constraint, arranges social and economic inequalities so that everyone benefits.

These principles are to be arranged in a serial order with the first principle prior to the second. This ordering means that a departure from the institutions of equal liberty required by the first principle cannot be justified by, or compensated for, by greater social and economic advantages. The distribution of wealth and income, and the hierarchies of authority, must be consistent with both the liberties of equal citizenship and equality of opportunity. . . .

[At this point Rawls gives a "more exact" statement of the second principle to remove "two ambiguous phrases . . . namely 'everyone's advantage' and 'open to all.' " The "more exact" statement of the second principle is this: "Social and economic inequalities are to be arranged so that they are both (a) to the greatest benefit of the least advantaged and (b) attached to offices and positions open to all under conditions of fair equality of opportunity." Part (a) of this principle he calls "the difference principle" and part (b) he calls the principle of "fair equality of opportunity." The "more exact" statement of the principle is repeated below.]

• • •

### 13. . . . THE DIFFERENCE PRINCIPLE

• • •

To illustrate the difference principle, consider the distribution of income among social classes. Let us suppose that the various income groups correlate with represenative individuals by reference to whose expectations we can judge the distribution. Now those starting out as members of the entrepreneurial class in property-owning democracy, say, have a better prospect than those who begin in the class of unskilled laborers. It seems likely that this will be true even when the social injustices which now exist are removed. What, then, can possibly justify this kind of initial inequality in life prospects? According to the difference principle, it is justifiable only if the difference in expectation is to the advantage of the representative man who is worse off, in this case the representative unskilled worker. The inequality in expectation is permissible only if lowering it would make the working class even more worse off. Supposedly, given the rider in the second principle concerning open positions, and the principle of liberty generally, the greater expectations allowed to entrepreneurs encourages them to do things which raise the long-term prospects of [the] laboring class. Their better prospects act as incentives so that the economic process is more efficient, innovation proceeds at a faster pace, and so on. Eventually the resulting material benefits spread throughout the system and to the least advantaged. I shall not consider how far these things are true. The point is that something of this kind must be argued if these inequalities are to be just by the difference principle. . . .

. . . And therefore, as the outcome of the last several sections, the second principle is to read as follows.

Social and economic inequalities are to be arranged so that they are both (a) to the greatest benefit of the least advantaged and (b) attached to offices and positions open to all under conditions of fair equality of opportunity. . . .

## 14. FAIR EQUALITY OF OPPORTUNITY
## AND PURE PROCEDURAL JUSTICE

I should now like to comment upon the second part of the second principle, henceforth to be understood as the liberal principle of fair equality of opportunity. . . .

. . . I should note that the reasons for requiring open positions are not solely, or even primarily, those of efficiency. I have not maintained that offices must be open if in fact everyone is to benefit from an arrangement. For it may be possible to improve everyone's situation by assigning certain powers and benefits to positions despite the fact that certain groups are excluded from them. Although access is restricted, perhaps these offices can still attract superior talent and encourage better performance. But the principle of open positions forbids this. It expresses the conviction that if some places were not open on a basis fair to all, those kept out would be right in feeling unjustly treated even though they benefited from the greater efforts of those who were allowed to hold them. They would be justified in their complaint not only because they were excluded from certain external rewards of office such as wealth and privilege, but because they were debarred from experiencing the realization of self which comes from a skillful and devoted exercise of social duties. They would be deprived of one of the main forms of human good. . . .

## 15. PRIMARY SOCIAL GOODS AS
## THE BASIS OF EXPECTATIONS

. . .Now primary goods, as I have already remarked, are things which it is supposed a rational man wants whatever else he wants. Regardless of what an individual's rational plans are in detail, it is assumed that there are various things which he would prefer more of rather than less. With more of these goods men can generally be assured of greater success in carrying out their intentions and in advancing their ends, whatever these ends may be.

• • •

## 20. THE NATURE OF THE ARGUMENT
## FOR CONCEPTIONS OF JUSTICE

The intuitive idea of justice as fairness is to think of the first principles of justice as themselves the object of an original agreement in a suitably defined initial situation. These principles are those which rational persons concerned to advance their interests would accept in this position of equality to settle the basic terms of their association. It must be shown, then, that the two principles of justice are the solution for the problem of choice presented by the original position. In order to do this, one must establish that, given the circumstances of the parties, and their knowledge, beliefs, and interests, an agreement on these principles is the best way for each person to secure his ends in view of the alternatives available.

Now obviously no one can obtain everything he wants; the mere existence of other persons prevents this. The absolutely best for any man is that everyone else should join with him in furthering his conception of the good whatever it turns out to be. Or failing this, that all others are required to act justly but that he is authorized to exempt himself as he pleases. Since other persons will never agree to such terms of association these forms of egoism would be rejected. The two principles of justice, however, seem to be a reasonable proposal. In fact, I should like to show that these principles are everyone's best reply, so to speak, to the corresponding demands of the others. In this sense, the choice of this conception of justice is the unique solution to the problem set by the original position.

By arguing in this way one follows a procedure familiar in social theory. That is, a simplified situation is described in which rational individuals with certain ends and related to each other in certain ways are to choose among various courses of action in view of their knowledge of the circumstances. What these individuals will do is then derived by strictly deductive reasoning from these assumptions about their beliefs and interests, their situation and the options open to them. . . .

. . . I shall consider for the most part the choice between the two principles of justice and two forms of the principle of utility (the classical and the average principle).

• • •

## 22. THE CIRCUMSTANCES OF JUSTICE

The circumstances of justice may be described as the normal conditions under which human cooperation is both possible and necessary. Thus, as I noted at the outset, although a society is a cooperative venture for mutual advantage, it is typically marked by a conflict as well as an identity of interests. There is an identity of interests since social cooperation makes possible a better life for all than any would have if each were to try to live solely by his own efforts. There is a conflict of interests since men are not indifferent as to how the greater benefits produced by their collaboration are distributed, for in order to pursue their ends they each prefer a larger to a lesser share. Thus principles are needed for choosing among the various social arrangements which determine this division of advantages and for underwriting an agreement on the proper distributive shares. These requirements define the role of justice. The background conditions that give rise to these necessities are the circumstances of justice.

• • •

## 24. THE VEIL OF IGNORANCE

The idea of the original position is to set up a fair procedure so that any principles agreed to will be just. The aim is to use the notion of pure procedural justice as a basis of theory. Somehow we must nullify the effects of specific contingencies which put men at odds and tempt them to exploit social and natural circumstances to their own advantage. Now in order to do this I assume that the parties are situated behind a veil of ignorance. They do not know how the various alternatives will affect their own particular case and they are obliged to evaluate principles solely on the basis of general considerations.

It is assumed, then, that the parties do not know certain kinds of particular facts. First of all, no one knows his place in society, his class position or social status; nor does he know his fortune in the distribution of natural assets and abilities, his intelligence and strength, and the like. Nor, again, does anyone know his conception of the good, the particulars of his rational plan of life, or even the special features of his psychology such as his aversion to risk or liability to optimism or pessimism. More than this, I assume that the parties do not know the particular circumstances of their own society. That is, they do not know its economic or political situation, or the level of civilization and culture it has been able to achieve. The persons in the original position have no information as to which generation they belong. . . .

As far as possible, then, the only particular facts which the parties know is that their society is subject to the circumstances of justice and whatever this implies. It is taken for granted, however, that they know the general facts about human society. They understand political affairs and the principles of economic theory; they know the basis of social organization and the laws of human psychology. Indeed, the parties are presumed to know whatever general facts affect the choice of the principles of justice. There are no limitations on general information, that is, on general laws and theories, since conceptions of justice must be adjusted to the characteristics of the systems of social cooperation which they are to regulate, and there is no reason to rule out these facts. It is, for example, a consideration against a conception of justice that, in view of laws of moral psychology, men would not acquire a desire to act upon it even when the institutions of their society satisfied it. For in this case there would be difficulty in securing the stability of social cooperation. It is an important feature of a conception of justice that it should generate its own support. That is, its principles should be such that when they are embodied in the basic structure of society men tend to acquire the corresponding sense of justice. Given the principles of moral learning, men develop a desire to act in accordance with its principles. In this case a conception of justice is stable. This kind of general information is admissible in the original position. . . .

## 25. THE RATIONALITY OF THE PARTIES

I have assumed throughout that the persons in the original position are rational. In choosing between principles each tries as best he can to advance his interests. But I have also assumed that the parties do not know their conception of the good. This means that while they know that they have some rational plan of life, they do not know the details of this plan, the particular ends and interests which it is calculated to promote. How, then, can they decide which conceptions of justice are most to their advantage? Or must we suppose that they are reduced to mere guessing? To meet this difficulty, I postulate that they accept the account of the good touched upon in the preceding chapter: they assume that they would prefer more primary social goods rather than less. Of course, it may turn out, once the veil of ignorance is removed, that some of them for religious or other reasons may not, in fact, want more of these goods. But from the standpoint of the original position, it is rational for the parties to suppose that they do want a larger share, since in any case they are not compelled to accept more if they do not wish to, nor does a person suffer from a greater liberty. Thus even though the parties are deprived of information about their particular ends, they have enough knowledge to rank the alternatives. They know that in general they must try to protect their liberties, widen their opportunities, and enlarge their means for promoting their aims whatever these are. Guided by the theory of the good and the general facts of moral psychology, their deliberations are no longer guesswork. They can make a rational decision in the ordinary sense. . . .

The assumption of mutually disinterested rationality, then, comes to this: the persons in the original position try to acknowledge principles which advance their system of ends as far as possible. They do this by attempting to win for themselves the highest index of primary social goods, since this enables them to promote their conception of the good most effectively whatever it turns out to be. The parties do not seek to confer benefits or to impose injuries on one another; they are not moved by affection or rancor. Nor do they try to gain relative to each other; they are not envious or vain. Put in terms of a game, we might say: they strive for as high an absolute score as possible. . . .

## 26. THE REASONING LEADING TO THE TWO
## PRINCIPLES OF JUSTICE

In this and the next two sections I take up the choice between the two principles of justice and the principle of average utility. Determining the rational preference between these two options is perhaps the central problem in developing the conception of justice as fairness as a viable alternative to the utilitarian tradition. I shall begin in this section by presenting some intuitive remarks favoring the two principles. I shall also discuss briefly the qualitative structure of the argument that needs to be made if the case for these principles is to be conclusive.

It will be recalled that the general conception of justice as fairness requires that all primary social goods be distributed equally unless an unequal distribution would be to everyone's advantage. No restrictions are placed on exchanges of these goods and therefore a lesser liberty can be compensated for by greater social and economic benefits. Now looking at the situation from the standpoint of one person selected arbitrarily, there is no way for him to win special advantages for himself. Nor, on the other hand, are there grounds for his acquiescing in special disadvantages. Since it is not reasonable for him to expect more than an equal share in the division of social goods, and since it is not rational for him to agree to less, the sensible thing for him to do is to acknowledge as the first principle of justice one requiring an equal distribution. Indeed, this principle is so obvious that we would expect it to occur to anyone immediately.

Thus, the parties start with a principle establishing equal liberty for all, including equality of opportunity, as well as an equal distribution of income and wealth. But there is no reason why this acknowledgment should be final. If there are inequalities in the basic structure that work to make everyone better off in comparison with the benchmark of initial equality, why not permit them? The immediate gain which a greater equality might allow can be regarded as intelligently invested in view of its future return. If, for example, these inequalities set up various incentives which succeed in eliciting more productive efforts, a person in the original position may look upon them as necessary to cover the costs of training and to encourage effective performance. One might think that ideally individuals should want to serve one another. But since the parties are assumed not to take an interest in one another's interests, their acceptance of these inequalities is only the acceptance of the relations in which men stand in the circumstances of justice. They have no grounds for complaining of one another's motives. A person in the original position would, therefore, concede the justice of these inequalities. Indeed, it would be shortsighted of him not to do so. He would hesitate to agree to these regularities only if he would be dejected by the bare knowledge or perception that others were better situated; and I have assumed that the parties decide as if they are not moved by envy. In order to make the principle regulating inequalities determinate, one looks at the system from the standpoint of the least advantaged representative man. Inequalities are permissible when they maximize, or at least all contribute to, the long-term expectations of the least fortunate group in society

. . .

## 29. SOME MAIN GROUNDS FOR THE TWO PRINCIPLES OF JUSTICE

In this section my aim is to use the conditions of publicity and finality to give some of the main arguments for the two principles of justice. I shall rely upon the fact that for an agreement to be valid, the parties must be able to honor it under all relevant and foreseeable circumstances. There must be a rational assurance that one can carry through. The arguments I shall adduce fit under the heuristic schema suggested by the reasons for following the maxi-min rule. That is, they help to show that the two principles are an adequate minimum conception of justice in a situation of great uncertainty. Any further advantages that might be won by the principle of utility, or whatever, are highly problematical, whereas the hardship[s] if things turn out badly are intolerable. It is at this point that the concept of a contract has a definite role: it suggests the condition of publicity and sets limits upon what can be agreed to. Thus justice as fairness uses the concept of contract to a greater extent than the discussion so far might suggest.

The first confirming ground for the two principles can be explained in terms of what I earlier referred to as the strains of commitment. I said . . . that the parties have a capacity for justice in the sense that they can be assured that their undertaking is not in vain. Assuming that they have taken everything into account, including the general facts of moral psychology, they can rely on one another to adhere to the principles adopted. Thus they consider the strains of commitment. They cannot enter into agreements that may have consequences they cannot accept. They will avoid those that they can adhere to only with great difficulty. Since the original agreement is final and made in perpetuity, there is no second chance. In view of the serious nature of the possible consequences, the question of the burden of commitment is especially acute. A person is choosing once and for all the standards which are to govern his life prospects. Moreover, when we enter an agreement we must be able to honor it even should the worst possibilities prove to be the case. Otherwise we have not acted in good faith. Thus the parties must weigh with care whether they will be able to stick by their commitment in all circumstances. Of course, in answering this question they have only a general knowledge of human psychology to go on. But this information is enough to tell which conception of justice involves the greater stress.

In this respect the two principles of justice have a definite advantage. Not only do the parties protect their basic rights but they insure themselves against the worst eventualities. They run no chance of having to acquiesce in a loss of freedom over the course of their life for the sake of a greater good enjoyed by others, an undertaking that in actual circumstances they might not be able to keep. Indeed, we might wonder whether such an agreement can be made in good faith at all. Compacts of this sort exceed the capacity of human nature. How can the parties possibly know, or be sufficiently sure, that they can keep such an agreement? Certainly they cannot base their confidence on a general knowledge of moral psychology. To be sure, any principle chosen in the original position may require a large sacrifice for some. The beneficiaries of clearly unjust institutions (those founded on principles which have no claim to acceptance) may find it hard to reconcile themselves to the changes that will have to made. But in this case they will know that they could not have maintained their position anyway. Yet should a person gamble with his liberties and substantive interests hoping that the application of the principle of utility might secure him a greater well-being, he may have difficulty abiding by his undertaking. He is bound to remind himself that he had the two principles of justice as an alternative. If the only possible candidates all involved similar risks, the problem of the strains of commitment would have to be waived. This is not the case, and judged in this light the two principles seem distinctly superior.

A second consideration invokes the condition of publicity as well as that of the constraints on agreements. I shall present the argument in terms of the question of psychological stability. Earlier I stated that a strong point in favor of a conception of justice is that it generates its own support. When the basic structure of society is publicly known to satisfy its principles for an extended period of time, those subject to these arrangements tend to develop a desire to act in accordance with these principles and to do their part in institutions which exemplify them. A conception of justice is stable when the public recognition of its realization by the social system tends to bring about the corresponding sense of justice. Now whether this happens depends, of course, on the laws of moral psychology and the availability of human motives. I shall discuss these matters later on. . . . At the moment we may observe that the principle of utility seems to require a greater identification with the interests of others than the two principles of justice. Thus the latter will be a more stable conception to the extent that this identification is difficult to achieve. When the two principles are satisfied, each person's liberties are secured and there is a sense defined by the difference principle in which everyone is benefited by social cooperation. Therefore we can explain the acceptance of the social system and the principles it satisfies by the psychological law that persons tend to love, cherish, and support whatever affirms their own good. Since everyone's good is affirmed, all acquire inclinations to uphold the scheme.

When the principle of utility is satisfied, however, there is no such assurance that everyone benefits. Allegiance to the social system may demand that some should forgo advantages for the sake of the greater good of the whole. Thus the scheme will not be stable unless those who must make sacrifices strongly identify with interests broader than their own. But this is not easy to bring about. The sacrifices in question are not those asked in times of social emergency when all or some must pitch in for the common good. The principles of justice apply to the basic structure of the social system and to the determination of life prospects. What the principle of utility asks is precisely a sacrifice of these prospects. We are to accept the greater advantages of others as a sufficient reason for lower expectations over the whole course of our life. This is surely an extreme demand. In fact, when society is conceived as a system of cooperation designed to advance the good of its members, it seems quite incredible that some citizens should be expected, on the basis of political principles, to accept lower prospects of life for the sake of others. It is evident then why utilitarians should stress the role of sympathy in moral learning and the central place of benevolence among the moral virtues. Their conception of justice is threatened with instability unless sympathy and benevolence can be widely and intensely cultivated. Looking at the question from the standpoint of the original position, the parties recognize that it would be highly unwise if not irrational to choose principles which may have consequences so extreme that they could not accept them in practice. They would reject the principle of utility and adopt the more realistic idea of designing the social order on a principle of reciprocal advantage. We need not suppose, of course, that persons never make substantial sacrifices for one another, since moved by affection and ties of sentiment they often do. But such actions are not demanded as a matter of justice by the basic structure of society.

Furthermore, the public recognition of the two principles gives greater support to men's self-respect and this in turn increases the effectiveness of social cooperation. Both effects are reasons for choosing these principles. It is clearly rational for men to secure their self-respect. A sense of their own worth is necessary if they are to pursue their conception of the good with zest and to delight in its fulfillment. Self-respect is not so much a part of any rational plan of life as the sense that one's plan is worth carrying out. Now our self-respect normally depends upon the respect of others. Unless we feel that our endeavors are honored by them, it is difficult if not impossible for us to maintain the conviction that our ends are worth advancing. . . . Hence for this reason the parties would accept the natural duty of mutual respect which asks them to treat one another civilly and to be willing to explain the grounds of their actions, especially when the claims of others are overruled. . . . Moreover, one may assume that those who respect themselves are more likely to respect each other and conversely. Self-contempt leads to contempt of others and threatens their good as much as envy does. Self-respect is reciprocally self-supporting.

Thus a desirable feature of a conception of justice is that it should publicly express men's respect for one another. In this way they insure a sense of their own value. Now the two principles achieve this end. For when society follows these principles, everyone's good is included in a scheme of mutual benefit and this public affirmation in institutions of each man's endeavors supports men's self-esteem. The establishment of equal liberty and the operation of the difference principle are bound to have this effect. The two principles are equivalent, as I have remarked, to an undertaking to regard the distribution of natural abilities as a collective asset so that the more fortunate are to benefit only in ways that help those who have lost out. I do not say that the parties are moved by the ethical propriety of this idea. But there are reasons for them to accept this principle. For by arranging inequalities for reciprocal advantage and by abstaining from the exploitation of the contingencies of nature and social circumstance within a framework of equal liberty, persons express their respect for one another in the very constitution of their society. In this way they insure their self-esteem as it is rational for them to do. . . .

The tentative conclusion, then, is that the balance of reasons clearly favors the two principles of justice over the principle of average utility, and assuming transitivity, over the classical doctrine as well. Insofar as the conception of the original position is used in the justification of principles in everyday life, the claim that one would agree to the two principles of justice is perfectly credible.

# CHAPTER SIX
# APPLYING MORAL THEORY: THE ISSUE OF TORTURE

In the first part of this book, the reader was introduced to several important approaches to moral issues: natural law ethics, Kantian ethics, utilitarian ethics, and social contract ethics. In the chapters that follow, we will see how these approaches are used in coming to moral judgments about various questions that face us today. Thus we will examine how moral principles are applied to contemporary problems such as abortion, euthanasia, capital punishment, war, aid to the needy, and so on.

In this chapter, we will discuss the moral questions surrounding the use of torture by governments, applying the principles we have just studied. In particular, we will see how two ethicians use utilitarian, Kantian, and social contract principles to come to rather different conclusions about this issue.

Contemporary Western culture typically regards torture as unacceptable and inhumane. Nonetheless, it is still widely practiced in many parts of the world. According to Amnesty International's twentieth anniversary report, published in 1981, allegations of torture have been leveled at sixty member countries of the United Nations since 1976. Some of these allegations are being documented by a Canadian medical study:

> Toronto has become one of the few places in the world where torture is under study as a medical phenomenon. . . . The Canadian documentation, said Dr. Philip Berger, one of the researchers in Toronto, "has convinced a

lot of people who live on another planet psychologically that this goes on . . ."

In all, according to Genevieve Cowgill of Amnesty International, doctors have seen 500 torture victims in Toronto since 1977. Canada's liberal immigration policies have brought in political refugees from many areas . . . and the Canadian doctors have examined torture victims from Turkey, Somalia, South Africa, El Salvador and other countries. . . .

Ricardo, according to his story, was a teenager when four naval officers came to his home in Chile in 1975 and shot and killed his uncle. Ricardo was so angry that he threw stones at their car. The officers took him away. He was held for three days, handcuffed, slapped and hit on the back of the head with a wet rubber truncheon before he was released.

The authorities arrested him again in 1978 after he delivered a church sermon with political overtones. He said he was punched in the face 50 times when arrested, then taken to a military camp that housed 800 political prisoners.

The torture was varied, he said. He reported that his tormentors tied him naked to a table and beat him with a truncheon and punctured his tongue with a needle. During one three-hour period, he said, they applied electricity to his genitals six times.

"The pain is impossible to describe," he told Berger. . . . "I felt like I would blow up." Between electric shocks, he said, he was punched. He said he was forced to watch the executions of eight other prisoners, five by firing squad, three by hanging.

After eight months, the Chilean military authorities released Ricardo and he left for Toronto. He described himself to Berger as "one of the lucky ones."

When Berger examined him a few weeks later, Ricardo was suffering from headaches, nervousness and discharge from the ears. He told Berger that he felt tense when people watched him, and his hands were wet all the time. In the physical examination, Berger found 17 areas of scars. . . .

Berger believes that an anti-torture center might have helped Ricardo. . . . Berger said, "He just got depressed and killed himself."[1]

Torture is a unqualified horror. It is difficult to read the account of the atrocities the Chilean government inflicted on Ricardo and continue to think such practices could ever be justified. Yet, as the news story just cited makes clear, many governments look upon torture as a justifiable instrument of politics. What might lead people to hold this belief? Are there social benefits so great that sanctioning torture would be permissible in order to achieve them—or evils so terrible that torture would be justified in order to avoid them?

Torture is generally carried out by a government for political purposes. By torturing Ricardo, for example, the Chilean government was attempting to discharge political dissension that it may have felt was harmful to the long-term welfare of the nation. With this in mind, some philosophers have argued on utilitarian principles that although torture is generally wrong, it may be morally right when it is used to secure national interests whose importance clearly outweighs the harm that torture

1. *Los Angeles Times*, September 13, 1982.

causes. Where the welfare of the nation is at stake, these philosophers argue, we will be served best if governments and officials take whatever steps are necessary to secure it—even if this means inflicting torture. Thus, although it generally might be wrong for a private individual to torture another (because the good an individual might derive from torture generally would not outweigh its evils), nevertheless it is legitimate and perhaps even obligatory for governments to inflict torture for reasons of national security or to protect other public interests that are clearly beneficial enough to outweigh the evils of such a practice. The pain caused by torture, for example, might be outweighed by the pain that would result from a violent national revolution brought about by unchecked dissension. Arguing along these lines, someone might claim that although the Chilean government might have been mistaken in its belief that Ricardo posed a threat to Chile, nevertheless it was doing what it believed would bring about the greatest balance of good over evil for the Chilean nation and to that extent its actions were justified from a utilitarian point of view.

Some authors have also argued that if a person commits a major crime or engages in terrorism that significantly injures others, that person forfeits his human rights. The criminal or terrorist, in this view, puts himself outside the ring of civilized moral standards we all recognize and enters into a sort of Hobbesian state of nature. Having refused to accept the moral obligations that civilized society imposes on all its members, the criminal or terrorist must also forfeit the moral protections that civilized society offers.

Is it permissible to torture such a person? Some authors have claimed that in some cases the torture of such criminals or terrorists could be justified. In support of their position, these authors have appealed to a modified social contract view that holds that moral rights apply only to those who have accepted the obligations of civilized society. Suppose that Ricardo was an active member of a group of political dissenters that was engaged in acts of sabotage and violence. And suppose that large numbers of Chileans were being injured and killed by these acts. Would it have been wrong to inflict torture on Ricardo in an attempt to force him to reveal the names of those involved so that the violence and killings could be brought to an end? Many people believe that torture would be justified in such circumstances precisely because Ricardo would have put himself beyond the reach of civilized moral standards and thereby would have forfeited their protection.

The first essay in this chapter, "The Case for Torture" by Michael Levin, adopts a position similar to the views we have been discussing. Levin argues, apparently on utilitarian grounds, that torture is sometimes justified since "the decision to use torture as a matter of balancing innocent lives against the means needed to save them." In Levin's view, the evil of inflicting torture on one person must in some cases be balanced against the evil of allowing many innocent persons to die, and in such cases the greater evil would be the latter. Moreover, Levin argues, the terrorist "renounces civilized standards, and he can have no complaint if civilization tries to thwart him by whatever means necessary." Thus, Levin can be interpreted as appealing also to something like a social contract view of morality. He claims that moral protections can be renounced and that the restrictions of morality are voluntarily assumed by law-abiding citizens.

Even if one were to decide that torture is sometimes justified, this would still leave many troubling questions unanswered. When a government uses torture in the pursuit of obviously immoral ends who is morally responsible? Do the citizens of the country bear the responsibility for all the acts of torture of a government or is it the torturers alone? Are the government officials to be held accountable or is it the nation as a whole? And who is to decide whether or not torture is justified in pursuit of a specific political objective? From what we know about Ricardo's case, the government was not protecting any significant national interest when it decided to torture him. Moreover, when wrongful torture results in death, as it did in the case of Ricardo, who is to be held responsible? In fact, should we even say that death is a greater evil than the pain of torture? For many people, torture arouses more outrage than the imposition of a legally instituted death penalty. Why is this so? Could it be that inflicting death is less evil than inflicting torture?

Reflecting on these questions, many individuals have decided that torture is always unjustified. It is unjustified, first, because as a practical matter it is not possible to ensure that a government restrict itself in the use of torture. Once a government is allowed to employ torture, it will use this method not merely to pursue the public interest but also to pursue the private and venal aims of corruptible officials. Second, and more important, torture is unjustified because it violates the dignity and respect that is owed to every human being, no matter what that human being has done. To inflict torture upon a person for the sake of any political or public end is to use him as a means and to fail to treat him as an end. Thus, by appealing to a Kantian view of morality, some philosophers have stated that torture is immoral under all circumstances, no matter what benefits it might generate.

Henry Shue argues along these lines in the second article in this chapter, entitled "Torture." Shue does not believe that torture is ever justified, no matter what the reason for its use or the sort of person it is used upon. Shue first examines the argument that since torture is a lesser evil than killing, and since killing is morally permissible in a "just war," it must follow that torture is morally permissible in the course of a "just war" or "just combat." To this argument, Shue replies that killing in war is morally permissible only when the war is a "fair fight" in which the victim can defend himself. But torture is inflicted against a defenseless person who "is entirely at the torturer's mercy" and it is wrong to attack a defenseless person. Shue then argues that "terroristic torture" (torture inflicted to intimidate others, thereby discouraging them from doing what the victim did) is always immoral because it violates "the Kantian principle that no person may be used *only* as a means." Shue also argues that "interrogational torture" (torture inflicted to extract information from the victim) is also immoral because in practice the victim would not be able to defend himself against the torturers even by providing the information they wanted.

It should be clear that in determining whether torture is morally justified, the principles of Kantian, utilitarian, and social contract ethics all come into play. But what exactly is their role? To answer this question, we will have to recall some of the topics that were discussed in Chapter One. (The reader may find it helpful to review James Rachels' article, "Can Ethics Provide Answers?") Let us begin by noticing that when a person judges a certain kind of activity to be morally right or wrong, that person's judgment must be based on some sort of reasons. Obviously, there are various kinds of reasons that can be offered in support of a moral judgment. First, one might claim that a certain kind of action is wrong on the basis of nothing more than personal emotional reaction or personal tastes. Thus, for example, a person might say, "Torture makes me feel terrible, so it must be wrong." Second, one might claim that torture is wrong on the basis of the opinions held by other members of one's country or social group. A person might say, for example, "Everyone I know thinks that torture is wrong, so it must be wrong."

Neither of these kinds of reasons is an adequate basis for a moral judgment. Personal emotional reactions or personal tastes will not suffice for the simple reason that my tastes and my feelings do not make an action morally right or wrong. For example, the fact that I have a strong emotional reaction against men wearing chartreuse shoes does not make it immoral for men to wear chartreuse shoes. Similarly, the fact that I have a strong emotional reaction against certain sexual activities does not make it immoral for people to engage in those activities. Personal tastes and personal emotional reactions provide good reasons for judgments that describe my own personal likes or dislikes, but they do not provide adequate reasons for judgments about the morality of an action in general. If a certain kind of action is wrong, there must be something about the act itself that makes it wrong, something more than the feelings or emotions I happen to have about it.

In the same way, the opinions of a group do not by themselves provide adequate reasons for a moral judgment. Again the reason is simple: the fact that other people believe something is immoral does not make it immoral. In general, as the saying goes, "Believing doesn't make it so." For example, the fact that other people believe the earth is flat does not make it flat. Similarly, the mere fact that other people believe something is wrong does not make it wrong. In other words, there must be something about the activity itself that makes it wrong, aside from the beliefs certain people happen to have about it.

In order to provide an adequate support for a moral judgment, one must identify some fact or feature of the matter being judged that can be shown to be morally relevant by an appeal to rationally defensible moral principles. This does not mean, however, that when a person makes a moral judgment he must be able to formulate or defend the principles on which that judgment is based. Rather, it means that when making a moral judgment the person's decision must be based on features that could be shown to be morally relevant by an appeal to a plausible or rationally defensible moral principle. For example, in the first reading Levin defends his judgment that torture is sometimes justified by appealing to the fact that torture could sometimes save lives. Thus, it is a fact about torture itself (and not about his feelings or beliefs of others) that Levin points to his argument. How would one show that this fact is morally relevant? By appealing to the utilitarian principle that an action is morally correct when it produces more social benefits than any other alternative. Although Levin does not explicitly appeal to this principle, nevertheless he assumes it. Moreover, as we have seen, this utilitarian principle is plausible and it can be rationally defended. In the second reading, Shue makes his assumptions more explicit in that he actually appeals to Kantian principles to justify his reasons for thinking that torture is immoral. Such Kantian principles can also be rationally defended.

Thus, the principles that were studied in the first part of this text play an important—in fact, an essential—part in justifying our moral judgments. Each of the four kinds of principles we studied identifies certain critical features of our lives and activities, and provides a rationally justifiable way of showing that these features are morally relevant. Natural law ethics provides rational grounds for thinking that there are certain basic goods and that it is morally wrong directly to destroy these goods. Utilitarianism provides rational grounds for thinking that the social benefits and harms resulting from an action should be weighed and that the moral action is the one that will provide the greatest net balance of benefits (or the least net harm). Kantian ethics provides rational grounds for thinking that if our actions are to be moral we must be willing to universalize the principles on which they are based and that our actions must not treat anyone as a mere means but always also as an end. And social contract ethics provides rational grounds for thinking that morally correct behavior should conform to those social practices and principles that the members of society have freely and rationally consented to accept (either tacitly or explicitly) or which they would accept if they were able to give their free and rational consent. Thus, each of the four kinds of principles identifies certain factors as relevant to judging whether an activity is morally right or wrong, and each of the four approaches provides rational grounds for thinking that those kinds of factors are relevant to our moral judgments.

Moral principles are applied, then, by examining those features of our activities that these principles identify as relevant and coming to a judgment about the morality of the activities by appealing to those features. As the disagreement between Levin and Shue indicates, the application of moral principles will sometimes lead to conflicting judgments. According to one principle, an action such as torture might always be wrong, while other principles might indicate that it is sometimes permissible. What are we to do in case of such a conflict?

First, it is important to note that different moral principles do not always lead to conflicting judgments. In fact, moral principles tend to converge on the same judgments in most of those matters that form the core of our morality. For example, whether one appeals to utilitarianism, natural law, the categorical imperative, or Rawls' principles of justice, it will turn out that lying, rape, enslavement, murder, theft, child abuse, assault, slander, fraud, and so on are generally morally wrong, whereas honesty, kindness, mutual aid, and keeping one's promises are generally morally right. Where, then, do different moral principles lead us in different directions?

Moral principles seem to diverge, first, in those matters that are currently feeling the impact of large technological or institutional change. For example, Levin claims that modern technology has created a new form of terrorism and that torture is permissible when this new form of terrorism is involved. Similarly, many people have argued that birth control, medical technology, new weapons, and new methods of production have raised new and controversial questions in sexual ethics, medical ethics, the ethics of warfare, and environmental ethics. Because these changes are very recent, we have not yet reached any settled judgments about them, and so the application of our principles tend to diverge.

Second, moral principles may also diverge where there is a question about whether particular kinds of circumstances change the way those principles should be applied. For example, we might agree that in general it is wrong to torture people; but is it wrong to torture people in the particular kinds of circumstances that Levin describes? Similarly, we might agree that in general it is wrong to kill people; but is it wrong to kill a terminally ill cancer patient who is in terrible pain and who wants to die? Because we may not have considered certain particular circumstances when formulating a general moral principle, we may be forced to change our views when we face these new circumstances and it is natural to expect that there will be a great deal of disagreement in the process.

Third, moral principles often diverge when people hold different views about the factual issues involved in a certain question. For example, Levin seems to hold that it is possible for governments to restrain themselves in the use of torture. Shue, however, believes that once governments are allowed to use torture they will not adhere to any restraints in its use. Here Levin and Shue are not disagreeing about a moral issue but about a factual matter. Similarly, some people hold that it is possible to permit euthanasia and limit it to those cases where the terminally ill freely consent to die; others believe that once euthanasia is allowed it will be used to force the aged to accept death. Here again we have a factual, not a moral disagreement. It is only natural to expect that there will be disagreement about the application of moral principles to those matters about which there is a great deal of factual disagreement.

Fourth, there are some cases in which it appears that people's disagreement derives wholly from a disagreement over their moral principles. Levin does not seem to think that terrorists must be treated "as ends" while Shue obviously holds that all persons must be respected as "ends." Here the disagreement is at a basic moral level insofar as one person holds that certain features are not morally relevant, while the other person holds the opposite opinion.

Thus, although the core of our morality might be relatively uncontroversial, there are many important areas in which, for a variety of reasons, our moral principles seem to lead to conflicting judgments. In fact, most of the issues dealt with in the remainder of this book are those about which there is a great deal of controversy. What is one to do in such cases? When faced with conflicting moral judgments about a certain matter, one has no choice but to examine the various arguments proposed by different ethicians and make up one's own mind about which arguments are the strongest. When embarking on this process, there are certain questions one should consider.

First, one must ask whether the arguments are logical. That is, are they consistent or do they contradict themselves at various points? Do the arguments follow the rules of logic or do they commit fallacies of some sort? Do the arguments present logically sound reasons for their conclusions or do they rely on rhetorical devices, bias, prejudice, emotionalism, rationalization, or other appeals to irrelevant matters? Do the arguments make assumptions that are inconsistent with other views the author holds? For example, Levin seems to rely on both a utilitarian and a social contract view of morality in his discussion of torture. Is there any inconsistency between these views? Does Shue present a logical argument for his position, or does he at some points rely on rhetorical appeals?

Second, when faced with conflicting moral arguments, one must ask whether the arguments are based on correct and adequate factual information. For example, Shue claims that governments will not adhere to any restraints once torture is allowed. Is this true? Is there any factual evidence for this claim? Is the evidence adequate? Does it meet the minimal standards of acceptable evidence?

Third, when authors exhibit a basic disagreement over the proper moral principles that should be applied to a certain issue, one should ask oneself which of these moral principles is more acceptable or which has a greater weight in this issue. For example, should we give greater weight to the utilitarian principles to which Levin seems to subscribe or should we give greater weight to the Kantian principles to which Shue appeals? Which of these two types of principles does the reader judge to be more acceptable?

Fourth, when faced with conflicting moral arguments, one should ask which argument involves assumptions, factual beliefs, and moral principles that are consistent with other assumptions, beliefs, and principles one holds and that, for good reasons, one is not willing to change. For example, if I believe that in other matters governments do not willingly restrain their actions, then it would be inconsistent for me to accept Levin's view that governments can be expected to apply torture in a restrained manner. On the other hand, if I have reasoned that utilitarian principles make more sense than Kantian principles, it would be inconsistent for me to accept Shue's Kantian argument over Levin's utilitarian one. Thus, in making a moral judgment about one matter, I must be consistent with the views I hold on other matters if I have good reasons not to change those other views. It is inconsistent to make a moral judgment on the basis of arguments that contradict other views I hold if I am so convinced of the reasonableness of those views that I cannot change them. Of course, I might decide to accept a certain argument and change certain conflicting views I previously held. For example, I might previously have thought that utilitarian principles were more reasonable than Kantian principles. But after reading and reflecting on Levin's and Shue's essays on torture, I might come to the conclusion that Kantian principles are more reasonable and I might then change my views about the acceptability of utilitarian principles. Thus, we must be ready to change our moral views if after rational reflection we decide that our earlier views were inadequate. Indeed, moral maturity is in part constituted by one's willingness to examine and rationally revise the moral views one uncritically accepted from one's family, peers, nation, or culture. But if an argument contradicts certain views that we cannot change even after we have rationally reflected on them, then the argument cannot be accepted.

The reader, then, must be willing to make some hard moral judgments in reflecting on the application of moral principles in the essays that follow. For the most part, the essays focus on questions that fall outside the core of "settled" issues that constitute most of our ordinary morality. They focus instead on issues that are controversial because of rapid technological or social change, baffling special circumstances, uncertainty over factual matters, or disagreements over basic moral principles. In studying these essays, the reader will have to decide for himself where the truth lies and will have to be ready to adjust his moral views when this seems necessary.

One final matter must be pointed out: not all of the articles that follow are directly concerned with the application of moral principles. Some merely clarify an important moral concept that is involved in the discussion of a particular issue. For example, a number of the essays on euthanasia are devoted to clarifying the distinction between "passive" and "active" euthanasia. Similarly, some of the articles on abortion set out to clarify the meaning of the term "person," while several of the readings on the environment deal with the meaning of moral "rights." We have also included articles on suicide that discuss what "suicide" actually involves, as well as articles on sexual morality that are wholly devoted to clarifying the concept of a "sexual perversion." Although these readings do not focus on the application of moral principles as such, they are nevertheless essential if one is to have an adequate understanding of the issues.

# THE CASE FOR TORTURE

*Michael Levin*

It is generally assumed that torture is impermissible, a throwback to a more brutal age. Enlightened societies reject it outright, and regimes suspected of using it risk the wrath of the United States.

I believe this attitude is unwise. There are situations in which torture is not merely permissible but morally mandatory. Moreover, these situations are moving from the realm of imagination to fact.

*Death:* Suppose a terrorist has hidden an atomic bomb on Manhattan Island which will detonate at noon on July 4 unless . . . (here follow the usual demands for money and release of his friends from jail). Suppose, further, that he is caught at 10 a.m. of the fateful day, but—preferring death to failure—won't disclose where the bomb is. What do we do? If we follow due process—wait for his lawyer, arraign him—millions of people will die. If the only way to save those lives is to subject the terrorist to the most excruciating possible pain, what grounds can there be for not doing so? I suggest there are none. In any case, I ask you to face the question with an open mind.

Torturing the terrorist is unconstitutional? Probably. But millions of lives surely outweigh constitutionality. Torture is barbaric? Mass murder is far more barbaric. Indeed, letting millions of innocents die in deference to one who flaunts his guilt is moral cowardice, an unwillingness to dirty one's hands. If *you* caught the terrorist, could you sleep nights knowing that millions died because you couldn't bring yourself to apply the electrodes?

Once you concede that torture is justified in extreme cases, you have admitted that the decision to use torture is a matter of balancing innocent lives against the means needed to save them. You must now face more realistic cases involving more modest numbers. Someone plants a bomb on a jumbo jet. He alone can disarm it, and his demands cannot be met (or if they can, we refuse to set a precedent by yielding to his threats). Surely we can, we must, do anything to the extortionist to save the passengers. How can we tell 300, or 100, or 10 people who never asked to be put in danger, "I'm sorry, you'll have to die in agony, we just couldn't bring ourselves to . . ."

Here are the results of an informal poll about a third, hypothetical, case. Suppose a terrorist group kidnapped a newborn baby from a hospital. I asked four mothers if they would approve of torturing kidnappers if that were necessary to get their own newborns back. All said yes, the most "liberal" adding that she would like to administer it herself.

I am not advocating torture as punishment. Punishment is addressed to deeds irrevocably past. Rather, I am advocating torture as an acceptable measure for preventing future evils. So understood, it is far less objectionable than many extant punishments. Opponents of the death penalty, for example, are forever insisting that executing a murderer will not bring back his victim (as if the purpose of capital punishment were supposed to be resurrection, not deterrence or retribution). But torture, in the cases described, is intended not to bring anyone back but to keep innocents from being dispatched. The most powerful argument against using torture as a punishment or to secure confessions is that such practices disregard the rights of the individual. Well, if the individual is all that important—and he is—it is correspondingly important to protect the rights of individuals threatened by terrorists. If life is so valuable that it must never be taken, the lives of the innocents must be saved even at the price of hurting the one who endangers them.

Better precedents for torture are assassination and pre-emptive attack. No Allied leader would have flinched at assassinating Hitler, had that been possible. (The Allies did assassinate Heydrich.) Americans would be angered to learn that Roosevelt could have had Hitler killed in 1943—thereby shortening the war and saving millions of lives—but refused on moral grounds. Similarly, if nation A learns that nation B is about to launch an unprovoked attack, A has a right to save itself by destroying B's military capability first. In the same way, if the police can by torture save those who would otherwise die at the hands of kidnappers or terrorists, they must.


*Idealism:* There is an important difference between terrorists and their victims that should mute talk of the terrorists' "rights." The terrorist's victims are at risk unintentionally, not having asked to be endangered. But the terrorist knowingly initiated his actions. Unlike his victims, he volunteered for the risks of his deed. By threatening to kill for profit or idealism, he renounces civilized standards, and he can have no complaint if civilization tries to thwart him by whatever means necessary.

Just as torture is justified only to save lives (not extort confessions or recantations), it is justifiably administered only to those *known* to hold innocent lives in their hands. Ah, but how can the authorities ever be sure they have the right malefactor? Isn't there a danger of error and abuse? Won't We turn into Them?

Questions like these are disingenuous in a world in which terrorists proclaim themselves and perform for television. The name of their game is public recognition. After all, you can't very well intimidate a government into releasing your freedom fighters unless you announce that it is your group that has seized its embassy. "Clear guilt" is difficult to define, but when 40 million people see a group of masked gunmen seize an airplane on the evening news, there is not much question about who the perpetrators are. There will be hard cases where the situation is murkier. Nonetheless, a line demarcating the legitimate use of torture can be drawn. Torture only the obviously guilty, and only for the sake of saving innocents, and the line between Us and Them will remain clear.

There is little danger that the Western democracies will lose their way if they choose to inflict pain as one way of preserving order. Paralysis in the face of evil is the greater danger. Some day soon a terrorist will threaten tens of thousands of lives, and torture will be the only way to save them. We had better start thinking about this.

# TORTURE

*Henry Shue*

Whatever one might have to say about torture, there appear to be moral reasons for not saying it. Obviously I am not persuaded by these reasons, but they deserve some mention. Mostly, they add up to a sort of Pandora's Box objection: if practically everyone is opposed to all torture, why bring it up, start people thinking about it, and risk weakening the inhibitions against what is clearly a terrible business?

Torture is indeed contrary to every relevant international law, including the laws of war. No other practice except slavery is so universally and unanimously condemned in law and human convention. Yet, unlike slavery, which is still most definitely practiced but affects relatively few people, torture is widespread and growing. According to Amnesty International, scores of governments are now using some torture—including governments which are widely viewed as fairly civilized—and a number of governments are heavily dependent upon torture for their very survival.

So, to cut discussion of this objection short, Pandora's Box is open. Although virtually everyone continues ritualistically to condemn all torture publicly, the deep conviction, as reflected in actual policy, is in many cases not behind the strong language. In addition, partial justifications for some of the torture continue to circulate.

One of the general contentions that keeps coming to the surface is: since killing is worse than torture, and killing is sometimes permitted, especially in war, we ought sometimes to permit torture, especially when the situation consists of a protracted, if undeclared, war between a government and its enemies. I shall try first to show the weakness of this argument. To establish that one argument for permitting some torture is unsuccessful is, of course, not to establish that no torture is to be permitted. But in the remainder of the essay I shall also try to show, far more interestingly, that a comparison between some types of killing in combat

From Henry Shue, "Torture," in *Philosophy and Public Affairs,* vol. 7, no. 2 (Winter 1978), pp. 124–27, 129–37. Copyright © 1978 by Princeton University Press. Excerpts reprinted by permission of Princeton University Press.

and some types of torture actually provides an insight into an important respect in which much torture is morally worse. This respect is the degree of satisfaction of the primitive moral prohibition against assault upon the defenseless. Comprehending how torture violates this prohibition helps to explain—and justify—the peculiar disgust which torture normally arouses.

The general idea of the defense of at least some torture can be explained more fully, using "just-combat killing" to refer to killing done in accord with all relevant requirements for the conduct of warfare. The defense has two stages.

A.  Since  (1) just-combat killing is total destruction of a person,
            (2) torture is—usually—only partial destruction or temporary inca-
                pacitation of a person, and
            (3) the total destruction of a person is a greater harm than the partial
                destruction of a person is,
    then    (4) just-combat killing is a greater harm than torture usually is;
B.  since   (4) just-combat killing is a greater harm than torture usually is, and
            (5) just-combat killing is sometimes morally permissible,
    then    (6) torture is sometimes morally permissible.

To state the argument one step at a time is to reveal its main weakness. Stage B tacitly assumes that if a greater harm is sometimes permissible, then a lesser harm is too, at least sometimes. The mistake is to assume that the only consideration relevant to moral permissibility is the amount of harm done. Even if one grants that killing someone in combat is doing him or her a greater harm than torturing him or her (Stage A), it by no means follows that there could not be a justification for the greater harm that was not applicable to the lesser harm. Specifically, it would matter if some killing could satisfy other moral constraints (besides the constraint of minimizing harm) which no torture could satisfy.[1]

A defender of at least some torture could, however, readily modify the last step of the argument to deal with the point that one cannot simply weigh amounts of "harm" against each other but must consider other relevant standards as well by adding a final qualification:

(6')  torture is sometimes morally permissible, provided that it meets whichever
      standards are satisfied by just-combat killing.

If we do not challenge the judgment that just-combat killing is a greater harm than torture usually is, the question to raise is: Can torture meet the

---

1. Obviously one could also challenge other elements of the argument—most notably, perhaps, premise (3). Torture is usually humiliating and degrading—the pain is normally experienced naked and amidst filth. But while killing destroys life, it need not destroy dignity. Which is worse, an honorable death or a degraded existence? While I am not unsympathetic with this line of attack, I do not want to try to use it. It suffers from being an attempt somehow just to intuit the relative degrees of evil attached respectively to death and degradation. Such judgments should probably be the outcome, rather than the starting point, of an argument. The rest of the essay bears directly on them.

standards satisfied by just-combat killing? If so, that might be one reason in favor of allowing such torture. If not, torture will have been reaffirmed to be an activity of an extremely low moral order.

## ASSAULT UPON THE DEFENSELESS

The laws of war include an elaborate, and for the most part long-established, code for what might be described as the proper conduct of the killing of other people. Like most codes, the laws of war have been constructed piecemeal and different bits of the code serve different functions. It would almost certainly be impossible to specify any one unifying purpose served by the laws of warfare as a whole. Surely major portions of the law serve to keep warfare within one sort of principle of efficiency by requiring that the minimum destruction necessary to the attainment of legitimate objectives be used.

However, not all the basic principles incorporated in the laws of war could be justified as serving the purpose of minimizing destruction. One of the most basic principles for the conduct of war (*jus in bello*) rests on the distinction between combatants and noncombatants and requires that insofar as possible, violence not be directed at noncombatants. . . . One fundamental function of the distinction between combatants and noncombatants is to try to make a terrible combat fair, and the killing involved can seem morally tolerable to nonpacifists in large part because it is the outcome of what is conceived as a fair procedure. To the extent that the distinction between combatants and noncombatants is observed, those who are killed will be those who were directly engaged in trying to kill their killers. The fairness may be perceived to lie in this fact: that those who are killed had a reasonable chance to survive by killing instead. It was kill or be killed for both parties, and each had his or her opportunity to survive. No doubt the opportunities may not have been anywhere near equal—it would be impossible to restrict wars to equally matched opponents. But at least none of the parties to the combat were defenseless.

Now this obviously invokes a simplified, if not romanticized, portrait of warfare. And at least some aspects of the laws of warfare can legitimately be criticized for relying too heavily for their justification on a core notion that modern warfare retains aspects of a knightly joust, or a duel, which have long since vanished, if ever they were present. But the point now is not to attack or defend the efficacy of the principle of warfare that combat is more acceptable morally if restricted to official combatants, but to notice one of its moral bases, which, I am suggesting, is that it allows for a "fair fight" by means of protecting the utterly defenseless from assault. The resulting picture of war—accurate or not—is not of victim and perpetrator (or, of mutual victims) but of a winner and a loser, each of whom might have enjoyed, or suffered, the fate of the other. Of course, the satisfaction of the requirement of providing for a "fair fight" would not by itself make a conflict morally acceptable overall. An unprovoked and otherwise unjustified invasion does not become morally acceptable just because attacks upon noncombatants, use of prohibited weapons, and so on are avoided.

At least part of the peculiar disgust which torture evokes may be derived from its apparent failure to satisfy even this weak constraint of being a "fair fight." The supreme reason, of course, is that torture begins only after the fight is—for the victim—finished. Only losers are tortured. A "fair fight" may even in fact already have occurred and led to the capture of the person who is to be tortured. But now that the torture victim has exhausted all means of defense and is powerless before the victors, a fresh assault begins. The surrender is followed by new attacks upon the defeated by the now unrestrained conquerors. In this respect torture is indeed not analogous to the killing in battle of a healthy and well-armed foe; it is a cruel assault upon the defenseless. In combat the other person one kills is still a threat when killed and is killed in part for the sake of one's own survival. The torturer inflicts pain and damage upon another person who, by virtue of now being within his or her power, is no longer a threat and is entirely at the torturer's mercy.

It is in this respect of violating the prohibition against assault upon the defenseless, then, that the manner in which torture is conducted is morally more reprehensible than the manner in which killing would occur if the laws of war were honored. In this respect torture sinks below even the well-regulated mutual slaughter of a justly fought war.

## TORTURE WITHIN CONSTRAINTS?

But is all torture indeed an assault upon the defenseless? For, it could be argued in support of some torture that in many cases there is something beyond the initial surrender which the torturer wants from the victim and that in such cases the victim could comply and provide the torturer with whatever is wanted. To refuse to comply with the further demand would then be to maintain a second line of defense. The victim would, in a sense, not have surrendered—at least not fully surrendered—but instead only retreated. The victim is not, on this view, utterly helpless in the face of unrestrainable asault as long as he or she holds in reserve an act of compliance which would satisfy the torturer and bring the torture to an end.

It might be proposed, then, that there could be at least one type of morally less unacceptable torture. Obviously the torture victim must remain defenseless in the literal sense, because it cannot be expected that his or her captors would provide means of defense against themselves. But an alternative to a capability for a literal defense is an effective capability for surrender, that is, a form of surrender which will in fact bring an end to attacks. In the case of torture, the relevant form of surrender might seem to be a compliance with the wishes of the torturer that provides an escape from further torture.

Accordingly, the constraint on the torture that would, on this view, make it less objectionable would be this: the victim of torture must have available an act of compliance which, if performed, will end the torture. In other words, the purpose of the torture must be known to the victim, the purpose must be the performance of some action within the victim's power to perform, and the victim's performance of the desired action must produce the permanent cessation of the torture. I shall refer to torture that provides for such an act of compliance as torture that satisfies the constraint of possible compliance. As soon becomes clear, it makes a great difference what kind of act is presented as the act of compliance. And a person with an iron will, a great sense of honor, or an overwhelming commitment to a cause may choose not to accept voluntarily cessation of the torture on the terms offered. But the basic point would be merely that there should be some terms understood so that the victim retains one last portion of control over his or her fate. Escape is not defense, but it is a manner of protecting oneself. A practice of torture that allows for escape through compliance might seem immune to the charge of engaging in assault upon the defenseless. Such is the proposal.

One type of contemporary torture, however, is clearly incapable of satisfying the constraint of possible compliance. The extraction of information from the victim, which perhaps—whatever the deepest motivations of torturers may have been—has historically been a dominant explicit purpose of torture is now, in world practice, overshadowed by the goal of the intimidation of people other than the victim. Torture is in many countries used primarily to intimidate potential opponents of the government from actively expressing their opposition in any form considered objectional by the regime. Prohibited forms of expression range, among various regimes, from participation in terroristic guerrilla movements to the publication of accurate news accounts. The extent of the suffering inflicted upon the victims of the torture is proportioned, not according to the responses of the victim, but according to the expected impact of news of the torture upon other people over whom the torture victim normally has no control. The function of general intimidation of others, or deterrence of dissent, is radically different from the function of extracting specific information under the control of the victim of torture, in respects which are central to the assessment of such torture. This is naturally not to deny that any given instance of torture may serve, to varying degrees, both purposes—and, indeed, other purposes still.

*Terroristic torture,* as we may call this dominant type, cannot satisfy the constraint of possible compliance, because its purpose (intimidation of persons other than the victim of the torture) cannot be accomplished and may not even be capable of being influenced by the victim of the torture. The victim's suffering—indeed, the victim—is being used entirely as a means to an end over which the victim has no control. Terroristic torture is a pure case—the purest possible case—of the violation of the Kantian principle that no person may be used *only* as a means. The victim is simply a site at which great pain occurs so that others may know about it and be frightened by the prospect. The torturers have no particular reason not to make the suffering as great and as extended as possible. Quite possibly the more terrible the torture, the more intimidating it will be—this is certainly likely to be believed to be so.

Accordingly, one ought to expect extensions into the sorts of "experimentation" and other barbarities documented recently in the cases of, for example, the Pinochet government in Chile and the Amin government in Uganda. Terroristic torturers have no particular reason not to carry the torture through to the murder of the victim, provided the victim's family or friends can be expected to spread the word about the price of any conduct compatible with disloyalty. Therefore, terroristic torture clearly cannot satisfy even the extremely mild constraint of providing for the possibility of compliance by its victim.[2]

The degree of need for assaults upon the defenseless initially appears to be quite different in the case of torture for the purpose of extracting information, which we may call *interrogational torture.*[3] This type of torture needs separate examination because, however condemnable we ought in the end to consider it overall, its purpose of gaining information appears to be consistent with the observation of some constraint on the part of any torturer genuinely pursuing that purpose alone. Interrogational torture does have a built-in end-point: when the information has been obtained, the torture has accomplished its purpose and need not be continued. Thus, satisfaction of the constraint of possible compliance seems to be quite compatible with the explicit end of interrogational torture, which could be terminated upon the victim's compliance in providing the information sought. In a fairly obvious fashion the torturer could consider himself or herself to have completed the assigned task—or probably more hopefully, any superiors who were supervising the process at some emotional distance could consider the task to be finished and put a stop to it. A pure case of interrogational torture, then, appears able to satisfy the constraint of possible compliance, since it offers an escape, in the form of providing the information wanted by the torturers, which affords some protection against further assault.

Two kinds of difficulties arise for the suggestion that even largely interrogational torture could escape the charge that it includes assaults upon the defenseless. It is hardly necessary to point out that very few

2. A further source of arbitrariness is the fact that there is, in addition, no natural limit on the "appropriate" targets of terroristic torture, since the victim does not need to possess any specific information, or to have done anything in particular, except possibly to have acted "suspiciously." Even the latter is not necessary if the judgment is made, as it apparently was by the Nazis, that random terror will be the most effective.

It has been suggested that there might be a category of "deserved" terroristic torture, conducted only after a fair trial had established the guilt of the torture victim for some heinous crime. A fair procedure for determining who is to be tortured would transform the torture into a form of deterrent punishment—doubtless a cruel and unusual one.

Such torture would stand only with a general deterrent theory of punishment according to which *who* is punished depends upon guilt, but *how much* he or she is punished depends upon supposed deterrent effects. I would think that any finding that terroristic torture could be fitted within a deterrent theory of punishment (provided the torture was preceded by a fair trial) could cut either way and would be at least as plausible a reason for rejecting the general theory as it would be for accepting the particular case of terroristic torture. But I will not pursue this because I am not aware of any current practice of reserving torture as the sentence for people after they are convicted by a trial with the usual safeguards. Torture customarily precedes any semblance of a trial. One can, of course, imagine various sorts of torture other than the two common kinds discussed here.

3. These two categories of torture are not intended to be, and are not, exhaustive. See previous note.

actual instances of torture are likely to fall entirely within the category of interrogational torture. Torture intended primarily to obtain information is by no means always in practice held to some minimum necessary amount. To the extent that the torturer's motivation is sadistic or otherwise brutal, he or she will be strongly inclined to exceed any rational calculations about what is sufficient for the stated purpose. In view of the strength and nature of a torturer's likely passions—of, for example, hate and self-hate, disgust and self-disgust, horror and fascination, subservience toward superiors and aggression toward victims—no constraint is to be counted upon in practice.

Still, it is of at least theoretical interest to ask whether torturers with a genuine will to do so could conduct interrogational torture in a manner which would satisfy the constraint of possible compliance. In order to tell, it is essential to grasp specifically what compliance would normally involve. Almost all torture is "political" in the sense that it is inflicted by the government in power upon people who are, seem to be, or might be opposed to the government. Some torture is also inflicted by opponents of a government upon people who are, seem to be, or might be supporting the government. Possible victims of torture fall into three broad categories: the ready collaborator, the innocent bystander, and the dedicated enemy.

First, the torturers may happen upon someone who is involved with the other side but is not dedicated to such a degree that cooperation with the torturers would, from the victim's perspective, constitute a betrayal of anything highly valued. For such a person a betrayal of cause and allies might indeed serve as a form of genuine escape.

The second possibility is the capture of someone who is passive toward both sides and essentially uninvolved. If such a bystander should happen to know the relevant information—which is very unlikely—and to be willing to provide it, no torture would be called for. But what if the victim would be perfectly willing to provide the information sought in order to escape the torture but does not have the information? Systems of torture are notoriously incompetent. The usual situation is captured with icy accuracy by the reputed informal motto of the Saigon police, "If they are not guilty, beat them until they are." The victims of torture need an escape not only from beatings for what they know but also from beatings for what they do not know. In short, the victim has no convincing way of demonstrating that he or she cannot comply, even when compliance is impossible. (Compare the reputed dunking test for witches: if the woman sank, she was an ordinary mortal.)

Even a torturer who would be willing to stop after learning all that could be learned, which is nothing at all if the "wrong" person is being tortured, would have difficulty discriminating among pleas. Any keeping of the tacit bargain to stop when compliance has been as complete as possible would likely be undercut by uncertainty about when the fullest possible compliance had occurred. The difficulty of demonstrating that one had collaborated as much as one could might in fact haunt the collaborator as well as the innocent, especially if his or her collaboration had struck the torturers as being of little real value.

Finally, when the torturers succeed in torturing someone genuinely committed to the other side, compliance means, in a word, betrayal; betrayal of one's ideals and one's comrades. The possibility of betrayal cannot be counted as an escape. Undoubtedly some ideals are vicious and some friends are partners in crime—this can be true of either the government, the opposition, or both. Nevertheless, a betrayal is no escape for a dedicated member of either a government or its opposition, who cannot collaborate without denying his or her highest values.

For any genuine escape must be something better than settling for the lesser of two evils. One can always try to minimize one's losses—even in dilemmas from which there is no real escape. But if accepting the lesser of two evils always counted as an escape, there would be no situations from which there was no escape, except perhaps those in which all alternatives happened to be equally evil. On such a loose notion of escape, all conscripts would become volunteers, since they could always desert. And all assaults containing any alternatives would then be acceptable. An alternative which is legitimately to count as an escape must not only be preferable but also itself satisfy some minimum standard of moral acceptability. A denial of one's self does not count.

Therefore, on the whole, the apparent possibility of escape through compliance tends to melt away upon examination. The ready collaborator and the innocent bystander have some hope of an acceptable escape, but only provided that the torturers both (a) are persuaded that the victim has kept his or her part of the bargain by telling all there is to tell and (b) choose to keep their side of the bargain in a situation in which agreements cannot be enforced upon them and they have nothing to lose by continuing the torture if they please. If one is treated as if one is a dedicated enemy, as seems likely to be the standard procedure, the fact that one actually belongs in another category has no effect. On the other hand, the dedicated enemies of the torturers, who presumably tend to know more and consequently are the primary intended targets of the torture, are provided with nothing which can be considered an escape and can only protect themselves, as torture victims always have, by pretending to be collaborators or innocents, and thereby imperiling the members of these two categories.

# CHAPTER SEVEN
# THE ETHICS OF NUCLEAR WAR

In Hiroshima, Japan, the morning of August 6, 1945, was a clear one. Shortly after eight o'clock, people on their way to work heard an airplane flying overhead and many paused to watch it. These people later said they saw something drop from the aircraft. What they saw was an atomic bomb, which exploded over Hiroshima a few seconds later. Seventy thousand people died instantly; fifty thousand others were later killed by the firestorms that raged through the city and by the radiation that rained down on them. The survivors left gruesome accounts of that terrible day:

> As I looked up at the sky from the backyard of my house, I heard the faint buzzing of a B-29 but the plane was not visible. The sun was glaring in the cloudless summer sky. Suddenly, I saw a strange thing. There was a fireball like a baseball growing larger . . . and then something fell on my head. I was 14 years old. How many seconds or minutes had passed, I could not tell, but regaining consciousness I found myself lying on the ground covered with pieces of wood. When I stood up in a frantic effort to look around there was darkness. Terribly frightened, I thought I was alone in a world of death. . . . When the darkness began to fade I found that there was nothing around me. My house, the next-door neighbor's house, and the next had all vanished. . . . I found my mother . . . and my mother began to shout madly for my sister. . . . Children were calling their parents' names, and parents were calling the names of their children. Suddenly mother cried. . . . Four or five meters away my sister's head was sticking out. . . . She was crushed under the collapsed house. . . . Mother and I . . . pulled her out. . . . Night came

and I could hear many voices crying and groaning with pain and begging for water. Someone cried, "Damn it! War tortures so many people who are innocent!" The sky was red with flames. . . .[1]

A girl was standing in the middle of the road staring vacantly. . . . She was eight years old. The wound on her head looked like a cracked pomegranate. Silently I carried her on my back. . . . Then I heard a girl's voice clearly from behind a tree, "Help me, please." Her back was completely burned and the skin peeled off and was hanging down from her hips. . . .[2]

Most of the A-bomb survivors were burned all over their bodies. They were not only naked, but also their skin came off. Suffering from the severe pain of the burns, they were wandering around looking for their parents, husbands, wives, and children.[3]

I was walking along the Hijiyama Bridge. . . . A woman, who looked like an expectant mother, was dead. At her side, a girl of about three years of age brought some water in an empty can she had found. She was trying to let her mother drink from it. . . .[4]

A high school student asked me to give him some water. I heard that if people who had been exposed to the A-bomb drank water, they would die. So I would not give him water. The next day when I passed by the place, he was lying on the ground dead. I wished then that I had let him drink some water, even if he would have died sooner. . . .[5]

We were walking along the streetcar line. Wherever we went we saw dead horses and bodies. . . . When I crossed Miyuki Bridge I saw Professor Takenaka standing at the foot of the bridge. He was almost naked, wearing nothing but shorts and he had a rice ball in his right hand. Beyond, the northern area was covered by red fire burning against the sky. Far away, Ote-machi was also a sea of fire. That day Professor Takenaka had not gone to Hiroshima University and the A-bomb exploded when he was at home. He tried to rescue his wife who was trapped under a roofbeam but all his efforts were in vain. The fire was threatening him also. His wife pleaded, "Run away, dear!" He was forced to desert his wife and escape from the fire. So he was now at the foot of Miyuki Bridge. But I wonder how he came to hold that rice ball in his hand? His naked figure, standing there before the flames with that rice ball looked to me as a symbol of the modest hope of human beings.[6]

The decision to drop the bomb on the people of Hiroshima was made while the United States was at war with Japan. It was based on a moral theory: utilitarianism. Henry L. Stimson, the American secretary of war, later wrote:

1. From *Unforgettable Fire: Pictures Drawn by Atomic Bomb Survivors*, edited by the Japan Broadcasting Association (New York: Pantheon Books, 1977), pp. 43–44. Copyright © 1977 by NHK. Reprinted by permission of Pantheon Books, a division of Random House, Inc.
2. Ibid., p. 13.
3. Ibid., p. 69.
4. Ibid., p. 75.
5. Ibid., p. 68.
6. Ibid., p. 46.

The ultimate responsibility for the recommendation to the President [concerning the A-bomb] rested upon me, and I have no desire to veil it. . . . I felt that to extract a genuine surrender from the [Japanese] Emperor and his military advisers, they must be administered a tremendous shock which would carry convincing proof of our power to destroy the Empire. Such an effective shock would save many times the number of lives, both American and Japanese, that it would cost. . . . Our enemy, Japan, commanded forces of somewhat over 5,000,000 armed men. Men of these armies had already inflicted upon us . . . over 300,000 battle casualties. [They] . . . had the strength to cost us a million more. . . . Additional large losses might be expected among our allies and . . . enemy casualties would be much larger than our own. . . . My chief purpose was to end the war in victory with the least possible cost in lives. . . . The face of war is the face of death; death is an inevitable part of every order that a wartime leader gives. The decision to use the atomic bomb was a decision that brought death to over a hundred thousand Japanese . . . But this deliberate, premeditated destruction was our least abhorrent choice.[7]

The testimony of the Hiroshima survivors and the rationalizations of Secretary Stimson bring into sharp relief the basic moral issue in modern war: Are we morally justified in using the terribly destructive nuclear weapons we now have at our disposal when, as one of the Hiroshima survivors says, doing so "tortures so many people who are innocent"? Secretary Stimson held that although "the face of war is the face of death," nonetheless, using nuclear weapons to kill massive numbers of civilians is permissible if such killing results in the saving of a greater number of lives. Many critics have questioned this utilitarian justification; others have raised questions concerning the morality of even producing and stockpiling nuclear weapons, which in their view only adds to the risk of inflicting more Hiroshimas on humanity. Yet others have claimed that nuclear weapons are necessary if we are to "deter" our enemies from attacking our interests. The articles that follow examine the major issues raised by these debates.[8]

Contemporary arguments on the morality of nuclear weapons have generally focused on two major issues: (1) the morality of using nuclear weapons in the course of a war or other international conflict, and (2) the morality of stockpiling nuclear weapons for the purpose of deterring others from using nuclear arms against us or from engaging in some other major military confrontation with us. The readings in this chapter are organized around these two major issues. The first three articles pri-

7. Henry L. Stimson, "The Decision to Use the Atomic Bomb," *Harper's Magazine,* vol. 194, no. 1161 (February 1947), pp. 101, 102, 106, 107.
8. There are now several anthologies of articles on the moral issues raised by nuclear weapons and their use in war: John C. Bennett, ed., *Nuclear Weapons and the Conflict of Conscience* (New York: Scribner's, 1962); Richard A. Wasserstrom, *War and Morality* (Belmont, Calif.: Wadsworth, 1970); William J. Nagle, ed., *Morality and Modern Warfare* (Baltimore: Helicon Press, 1960); Thomas A. Shannon, ed., *War or Peace* (Maryknoll, N.Y.: Obis Books, 1982); Walter Stein, ed., *Nuclear Weapons: A Catholic Response* (New York: Sheed and Ward, 1961). For a more extended discussion of many of these issues, see Michael Walzer, *Just and Unjust Wars* (New York: Basic Books, 1977) and Paul Ramsey, *The Just War: Force and Political Responsibility* (New York: Scribner's, 1968).

marily address the morality of using nuclear weapons in war, while the three succeeding articles are concerned with the morality of nuclear deterrence.

Discussions concerning the morality of using nuclear weapons in wartime often proceed by appealing to the "just war theory," which lays out the conditions under which a nation is morally justified in fighting a war. The assumption behind this theory is that although war is always bad, nevertheless a nation is sometimes morally justified in using war to defend itself against the injustice of another nation or to help others defend themselves against injustice. The just war theory was developed during the early Middle Ages and was eventually incorporated into the ethics of natural law. Saint Thomas Aquinas, for example, held that a war was just only if three conditions obtained:

1.  The war must be legally declared by a public authority who is legitimately authorized to commit a people to war; the war must not be declared by a private individual or group that has not been entrusted with the care of the common good or by someone without the legal authority to declare war.

2.  The war must be pursued for a morally just cause, such as self-defense or to take back what was unjustly seized; it is wrong to engage in a war against a nation that has done nothing to deserve it.

3.  Those who are engaged in fighting the war must have a rightful intention, that is, they must intend only to achieve the just end and must not be motivated, for example, by a desire to inflict injury out of sheer cruelty or revenge.

Since the Middle Ages, the just war theory has been elaborated in various different ways. Today, those who use it to evaluate the morality of war and of the weapons of war often add the following conditions to those of Aquinas:

4.  The war must be fought only as a last resort; it is wrong to engage in a war if there are other means of achieving one's just ends.

5.  There must be a reasonable probability of achieving the end for which the war is fought; it is wrong to commit a nation to a war that is hopeless or futile.

6.  The war must be aimed at achieving a good that is proportional to the injuries that the war will probably inflict; it is wrong to engage in a war that will produce more harm than good.

7.  The war must be fought without using any means that are themselves immoral; that is, it is wrong to use methods of warfare that inflict more injuries or deaths than are truely necessary to achieve one's ends or methods that are designed intentionally to kill innocent civilians.

The just war theory has been highly influential in contemporary discussions of the morality of using nuclear weapons because it contains two important conditions that are said to be crucial to such debates: the requirement that the injuries inflicted by a war must be "proportional" to the good that will be achieved (condition 6), and the requirement that the war must not use immoral methods of warfare that inflict more injuries than necessary or that intentionally kill innocent civilians (condition 7). Some people have argued that nuclear weapons cannot be used without violating both these conditions.

First, it is sometimes argued that once nations begin using nuclear weapons their use will escalate and many millions, perhaps billions, of people will lose their lives. Some have even argued that a nuclear war would totally annihilate all human life on earth. There is no military or political objective, some ethicians claim, whose pursuit can justify the risk of losing that many lives. Thus, the use of nuclear weapons will inflict an evil that cannot be proportional to any good one might want to achieve. Second, some people have argued that nuclear weapons are an immoral means of waging war because they inevitably inflict more injuries than are necessary for achieving our ends and because they will inevitably slaughter innocent civilians. As the recollections of the Hiroshima survivors suggest, nuclear weapons kill and maim civilian men, women, and children who are innocent of any responsibility for the military actions of their leaders. It is never morally justified, some ethicians claim, to use weapons that are certain to kill indiscriminately such innocent civilians when there are other weapons that can achieve our ends without inflicting such massive injuries.

Not everyone agrees, however, that using nuclear weapons is immoral, and those who defend their use often also take a stand on the just war theory. These people argue that it is morally permissible to use nuclear weapons in a war so long as the war is being fought for a just cause, such as self-defense, and so long as the weapons are used in a "limited" fashion against only military targets. Some ethicians claim that since it is morally just for a nation to use war as a last resort to defend itself against an attacking military force it can probably beat, it is also morally permissible to use nuclear weapons in such a war, so long as their destructiveness is limited to defeating the attacker and so long as care is taken to ensure that no civilians are intentionally killed. People who hold this view have then argued that it is possible to use nuclear weapons in a "controlled" manner so that their impact is limited to destroying only attacking military forces, with no innocent civilians deliberately killed. Moreover, others have argued that it would not necessarily be wrong to kill the civilian citizens of an attacking enemy nation. In this view, modern wars are "total" in the sense that everyone in a particular country bears a responsibility for the war. Thus there are no innocent civilians in a modern war. Still others have argued that morality does not apply to the relations between nations; in particular, morality does not apply when nations are at war. Consequently, it is not immoral to use weapons that have the capacity to kill the civilian citizens of an enemy nation.

The second major moral issue raised by nuclear weapons concerns the question of whether nuclear deterrence is a moral strategy for preventing other nations from using their own weapons against us. One view is that only the threat of mutual nuclear annihilation can restrain modern world powers from beginning a nuclear war, and this fact alone is sufficient to justify stockpiling nuclear weapons and using them as a threat to deter potential aggressors. At the other extreme is the view that since nuclear deterrence poses such grave risks for humanity—and since it involves an immoral intent to kill millions of innocent civilians—it is an immoral strategy and, consequently, nuclear powers should unilaterally disarm. Somewhere in between is the view of those who believe that although nuclear deterrence is an evil that calls for bilateral disarmament, nevertheless it is an evil that is presently necessary to avoid the greater evil of nuclear war, so long as bilateral disarmament is not possible.

The articles that follow cross back and forth over the many questions raised by the various positions that have been sketched above. The first three are concerned primarily with the morality of using nuclear weapons. The recurring issue in these is the question of whether it is moral to kill innocent civilians in war, as was done in the bombing of Hiroshima. In "Morality of Nuclear Armament," John Connery adopts a version of the natural law theory of the just war, although he does not explicitly refer to such a theory. Connery argues that under certain conditions (those indicated by the just war theory) it is morally permissible to engage in a defensive war, so long as the violence is "in proportion to the aggression" and so long as "the noncombatant [is] not the direct target of any destructive weapon." He then argues that nuclear weapons could be used within these constraints so long as they are aimed only at military targets and so long as any loss of civilian life is "balanced by a proportionate good to the defender." If the atomic bomb is used in this way, any loss of civilian lives would be an indirect and unintended effect of a morally legitimate act.

In the next article, entitled "The Hydrogen Bombing of Cities," John Ford argues against the position advocated by Connery. Ford also assumes the framework of natural law and the just war theory when he assumes that "it is never permitted to kill directly noncombatants in wartime" and that the evils of war must be proportionate to the good that is to be achieved. Ford argues that the use of nuclear weapons in practice would involve a direct intention to kill the innocent, that such an intention could not be avoided, and that there could be no "proportionate justifying reason" for allowing the millions of deaths that the use of nuclear weapons would inflict.

In the third article, "The Morality of Using Nuclear Weapons," Manuel Velasquez, a Kantian, argues that utilitarian, natural law, and Hobbesian approaches to the morality of using nuclear weapons are all inadequate. Instead, he claims that we must ask whether nuclear weapons violate the traditional rule that noncombatants may not be killed during a war. Velasquez argues that "counter-value," "counter-force," and "limited" nuclear strikes must all violate noncombatant immunity. The combatant/noncombatant distinction, he states, is based on the Kantian principle that people must be treated as ends and not merely as means. Velasquez closes by considering several objections to his views.

The last two articles are concerned with using the threat of nuclear weapons as a strategic deterrent to war. In "Ethics and Nuclear Deterrence," Douglas Lackey argues on utilitarian grounds that the strategy of trying to prevent war by using the threat of nuclear annihilation is immoral because the costs are too large, thus outweighing the benefits. He then argues that nuclear deterrence is also wrong on deontological grounds. (A deontological approach to morality is any approach other than utilitarianism; here it is a view, such as natural law, which holds that directly killing the innocent is wrong.) Nuclear deterrence is immoral, Lackey argues, because it involves an immoral threat against the lives of innocent persons.

The final article, "The Ethics of Nuclear Deterrence: A Contractarian Account," by Christopher W. Morris, is based on a modified version of Hobbes' social contract approach to morality. Morris argues that although the direct killing of the innocent is ordinarily morally wrong, it is not immoral to kill the innocent (or to threaten to kill the innocent) when retaliating against (or deterring) an enemy nuclear attack. Morris first argues that "countervalue" strategies aimed at civilians have a better chance of avoiding war than "counterforce" strategies aimed solely at military targets. But is it moral directly to kill or threaten to kill innocent persons? Morris argues that the "absolutist" natural law view that it is always wrong directly to kill the innocent is mistaken. Also mistaken, in his opinion, is the utilitarian view that the greater good sometimes overrides the principle that it is wrong to kill the innocent. Instead, Morris argues that we must accept the basic moral principle that the innocent may not be killed directly. However, basic moral principles only apply between parties that are interacting in a cooperative and mutually beneficial manner. During a nuclear war such cooperation is no longer possible so such basic moral principles no longer apply. Thus, it is not immoral for a warring nation to kill the innocent civilians of its opponent. Consequently, it is also not immoral to threaten to kill another nation's innocent population during a nuclear war. However, it would still be wrong to kill innocent members of third-party nations with whom we are not at war.

# MORALITY OF NUCLEAR ARMAMENT

*John R. Connery*

The truly Christian conscience with its sincere regard for the dignity of the human person is shocked at any violence directed against human beings. Even when associated with legitimate self-defense, the need for violence evokes feelings of deep regret, especially when it results in the loss of human life. This is as it should be. A moral conscience sensitive to violence is our best safeguard against any excess in this direction.

From John R. Connery, "Morality of Nuclear Armament," *Theology Digest,* vol. 5, no. 1 (Winter 1957), pp. 9–12. Reprinted by permission of the publisher.

But regret over the need for violence in repelling unjust aggression is in itself no reflection on the morality of the defense itself. However distasteful, the use of violence may be perfectly legitimate, and although the regret and distaste may increase with the degree of violence demanded by the situation, neither the intensity of the distress nor the measure of the violence resorted to can be used as independent moral yardsticks. The morality of the violence will depend on its proportion to the aggression. One will not rout a burglar with an atomic bomb. The moral conscience will allow for adequate defense, but it will not tolerate unnecessary or disproportionate violence.

When the aggression is on an individual level, the moral problem of defense may be simple enough. It is relatively easy to accommodate defense measures to an individual act of aggression. But when the aggression takes place on a national level, the problem of defense assumes a much more complex character. The concept of "total war" has been advanced in recent times, but moralists are still generally agreed that, although more people are actually involved in warfare today than in former times, a distinction between combatant and noncombatant must still prevail. This distinction makes defense against an aggressor nation a much more delicate problem than defense against an individual aggressor. How can one defend oneself adequately against an aggressor nation and still maintain a distinction between combatant and noncombatant?

It is in this connection that the quantitative aspect of defense measures takes on a greater moral significance. And it is precisely in this area that nuclear warfare creates a serious moral problem. The greater the destructive potential of the weapon, the less discriminating is the warfare likely to be. It would seem that present nuclear weapons, such as the H-bomb, either have been, or at least can be, developed far beyond the demands of any single known military target. The use of such weapons, then, carries with it the necessary destruction of noncombatants or at least nonmilitary objects.

It is with these large-sized nuclear weapons that we are concerned. Must there be some limit to the size and the number of such weapons in our armament program? That such limitation is a desirable goal for world peace conferences no one will deny. But it is difficult to say whether even limited disarmament on a world-wide scale can be hoped for in the present world situation. Even if agreements could be arrived at, it is not clear just how reliable they would be. For practical purposes, then, it is necessary to consider the prospect of limitation of nuclear weapons on a unilateral basis. Would such a unilateral limitation of armaments be dictated by moral considerations of an imperative nature? Or to put the question more concretely: Is the use of destructive weapons of megatonic or multimegatonic proportions an absolutely unjustifiable war measure?

## INDISCRIMINATE WARFARE

Given an isolated military target of such proportions that nuclear destructive forces would be required to eliminate it effectively, all moralists would agree that the use of such weapons would be justified. But this would seem to be a purely theoretical case, hardly realized in modern warfare. The actual situation in the modern world is that the war potential of nations is concentrated in heavily populated areas. The use of megatonic destructive forces on such targets would necessarily carry with it tremendous civilian losses. Would this necessarily be classified as indiscriminate warfare?

Moralists agree that the noncombatant may not be the direct target of any destructive weapon, large or small. This means that one may neither deliberately aim his attack at noncombatants nor drop bombs without distinction on combatants and noncombatants alike. Such bombing would be contrary to sound moral principles, even if resorted to only in retaliation.

It would be equally immoral to direct even at a military target a weapon whose destructive power would go far beyond the demands of the defense, especially if it were uncontrollable. Such an attack could hardly be interpreted as other than indiscriminate and irresponsible warfare.

But granted a sufficiently important military target which could not be safely eliminated by any less drastic means, nuclear bombing would be morally justified, even if it involved the resultant loss of a large segment of the civilian population. It is presumed, of course, that the good to be achieved is at least equal to the expected damages.

## PERENNIAL PROBLEM

The unavoidable loss of civilian life consequent upon a legitimate attack on a military target is not a moral problem peculiar to nuclear warfare. It has always been a problem of warfare. And moralists have always recognized that this indirect loss of civilian life was allowable, if the alternative was an equivalent loss to the defender. But there is a vast difference from the moral standpoint between attacking noncombatants and allowing their death incident to a legitimate attack on combatants. The latter is an unwanted and unavoidable adjunct to a legitimate moral defense.

But to be justified, the loss of civilian life must be unavoidable and balanced by a proportionate good to the defender. Thus, if precision bombing of individual industrial plants in enemy territory would achieve the same result with less loss of civilian life than nuclear bombing of a whole industrial area, the latter would not be justified. But if precision bombing would mean losses to the defender equivalent to the civilian losses resulting to the enemy from nuclear bombing, the latter could legitimately be employed.

To illustrate, let us suppose that in a city in enemy territory there are two war plants which I want to eliminate. They are in the same area of that city but separated by a small residential section. I can knock out these plants by precision bombing; or I can knock them out by one superbomb, but with concomitant destruction of the civilian area between them. If I can achieve my goal with precision bombing of the individual plants, I would not be allowed to bomb the whole industrial area. But if precision bombing would be very costly to me both in money and in the lives of my own men, so that I could honestly say that my losses in such bombing would be proportionate to the loss of civilian life in bombing the industrial area, the use of the superbomb would be morally justified.

Now, whether the case concerns two industrial plants in the same area, or two industrial areas in the same city, or even two industrial cities in the same region, though the application is more appalling, the principle remains the same.

## SUFFICIENT REASON

An important consideration, of course, in deciding between precision bombing and large-scale bombing of an industrial area is the military strength of the enemy. Thus, for instance, if my enemy were in possession of nuclear bombs which I had good reason to believe he would use, it would be suicidal for me to choose the more leisurely precision bombing. His possession of such weapons would never justify a direct attack on his civilian population but it would give me the sufficient reason to knock out his war potential as quickly and as effectively as possible, even with a tremendous loss of civilian life. The only alternative to a quick and fatal blow at his war machine would be the destruction of my own population—which is certainly a sufficient reason for allowing the incidental, though perhaps staggering, losses to the enemy.

These are awe-inspiring, and even terrifying, reflections. They point up the critical need of effective agreements among nations to limit armaments. But they also bring out, I believe, the fact that in the absence of such agreements moral considerations will not force conscientious nations into a position of military inferiority.

## THE MORALIST'S ROLE

A moralist does not feel qualified as a moralist to pass judgment on the adequacy of our present nuclear weapons to deal with the modern unjust aggressor. He can only set up the moral framework for the licit use of such weapons. It is up to the scientist and the military expert to decide when the weapons we have at our disposal are adequate to a defense within that framework. Certainly, if we have at our disposal nuclear weapons adequate to a legitimate defense against any foreseeable aggression, one could hardly justify the production of more destructive weapons. The possession of such weapons would be tantamount to an invitation to unnecessary and irresponsible destruction. Moreover, if present nuclear weapons carry with them large-scale civilian losses and damage, moral considerations would demand that some effort be made to eliminate the destruction not essential to the military effort. And if, for instance, some bomb could be developed with all the explosive power of the H-bomb but without subsequent contamination of civilian areas, the use of the H-bomb could hardly be justified. But any other move in the direction of unilateral limitation of armaments or even disarmament would be on a voluntary rather than an obligatory basis.

Whether a voluntary move toward unilateral disarmament would ease the world situation without at the same time weakening our own position is matter for a prudential decision on the part of those who are in possession of all the facts of the case. It may be that in a situation where agreements among nations cannot be reached or trusted the best guarantee against the use of the bomb will be the fact that both parties are in possession of it. In support of this position one might advance the experience with mustard gas during World War II. A somewhat embarrassing examination of conscience regarding the use of the A-bomb at Hiroshima and Nagasaki might lead to the same conclusion. Would we have used the bomb if we were not sure that the enemy was in no position to retaliate in kind? These experiences are not in themselves decisive but they should certainly be taken into consideration in any decision relating to unilateral disarmament.

# THE HYDROGEN BOMBING OF CITIES

*John C. Ford*

Instead of thinking of Moscow as the target of an all-out multimegaton H-bomb attack, let us imagine a more familiar scene: the New York-Newark area, with its ten million inhabitants and important military targets. Would it be permissible, in order to win a just war, to wipe out such an area with death or grave injury, resulting indiscriminately, to the majority of its ten million inhabitants?

In my opinion the answer must be in the negative. If I assert that it is wrong to kill a million schoolchildren, I do not have to prove my assertion. It is those who assert the contrary who have the burden of the proof. . . .

[It] is never permitted to kill directly noncombatants in wartime. Why? Because they are innocent. That is, they are innocent of the violent and destructive action of war, or of any close participation in the violent and destructive action of war. It is such participation *alone* that would make them legitimate targets of violent repression themselves.

From John C. Ford, "The Hydrogen Bombing of Cities," *Theology Digest*, vol. 5, no. 1 (Winter 1957), pp. 6–9. Reprinted by permission of the publisher.

## TOTAL WAR

It is the fashion to say: "But today war is different. War is total. Everybody, or almost everybody, in the enemy country contributes to the war effort. Everybody is more or less a combatant." This is fallacious.

It is true that the wearing of a uniform is no longer the criterion of combatant status. It is true that to a great extent civilian participation has increased. But even if it were ten times what it used to be, that increase is comparatively insignificant. The real, significant difference between war three hundred years ago and war today is that man has increased his destructive attacking power not ten but ten thousand times, and has learned to carry that destructive power hundreds of times faster to the very heart of every civilian population on earth. Air power and nuclear weapons have done it.

That is the only true sense in which modern war is total. It is total because the total civilian population can be subjected to total violent attack and totally annihilated by it. Modern war is not total in the sense that all the civilians, or almost all of them, or anywhere near the majority of them, are waging it, that is, prosecuting it by violent action, or by cooperating closely in its violent prosecution. Contributing to the war effort does not make a person a combatant. A ten-year-old girl saves bottle caps for the scrap steel drive. She contributes to the war effort. In fact, she helps to make munitions. May I shoot her down on the theory that she is a combatant, an unjust aggressor, and therefore a legitimate target for total violent repression? No. . . .

The New York-Newark area is one of the most highly industrialized areas on earth. But, stretching the term "combatant" to the very limit and beyond all reasonable limits, and including in it all the employees of all manufacturing industries of every kind, and all those engaged in public utilities, in transportation, in communications, and in contract construction in that whole area . . . , they would all together constitute less than 25 per cent of the total ten million inhabitants. Three-quarters of that population, seven and one-half million people, are innocent human beings, innocent of the one thing which in our theology would make them legitimate targets of direct violence, namely violent war-making, or sufficiently close cooperation in violent war-making.

## DIRECT INTENTION

But it may be urged that the hydrogen bombing of cities could be justified because there would be no *direct* intention of killing the innocent—that the death or maiming of millions of innocent people would not be intentional. It would merely be the reluctantly permitted side effect of a good action, the destruction of military targets. It is my contention that the civil and military leaders who would plan and execute the dropping of a series of high megaton H-bombs on an area like Moscow or New York: 1) *would not* in practice avoid the direct intention of violence to the innocent; 2) *could not* avoid such an intention even if they would; and 3) even if they would and could avoid it, would have no *proportionate justifying* reason for permitting the evils which this type of all-out nuclear warfare would let loose.

In the first place it is unreal to imagine that policy makers and military leaders will restrict their intention to the destruction of military targets and combatant personnel. In the last war when we really wanted to hit only military targets, as in the bombing of Rome, we made sure that was all we hit. When we wanted to "destroy enemy morale" we bombed out whole areas of densely populated cities. The *United States Strategic Bomber Survey* declared that area bombing was "intended primarily to destroy morale, particularly that of the industrial worker." An official Army Air Force publication, *Target: Germany,* made it clear that the purpose of the bombing was "terror and devastation carried to the core of the warring nation." Terror bombing means killing and maiming innocent noncombatants in order to frighten the resistance out of those who survive. We did this in Germany. If we do not intend to do it again, why are we stock-piling large quantities of high-megaton H-bombs? The military targets for such bombs are few and far between. If we are really intending to hit only military targets, why do we not concentrate on the smaller nuclear weapons which can be honestly aimed at military objectives? It is academic and unreal to talk about the principle of the double effect where it is clear that the actual intent will be to win the war by wiping out everything in sight.

In the second place, they could not avoid the direct intent even if they would. If I saw a black widow spider crawling across the shiny bald pate of my neighbor, could I take a sledge hammer and swing it down full on the spider, intending directly only the death of the spider? Could I honestly say I had no direct intention of killing the man? Especially if there were a flyswatter handy? Notice the question is not whether it would be permissible to act this way. No one would permit it. The question is whether it is psychologically and honestly possible to avoid the direct intent of killing which seems to be implicit in my choice of the sledge hammer in those circumstances.

## INCIDENTAL EFFECT

There comes a point where the immediate evil effect of a given action is so overwhelmingly large in its physical extent, in its mere bulk, by comparison with the immediate good effect, that it no longer makes sense to say that it is merely incidental, not directly intended, but reluctantly permitted. It is not a question of the physical inevitability of the evil effect. It is a question of its incidentality. I can see how a bombardier could drop a hydrogen bomb on an enemy fleet at sea, intending directly only the destruction of the fleet, while permitting reluctantly the inevitable deaths of some innocent women and children by chance aboard. But I doubt that the man with the sledge-hammer can intend to kill only the poisonous spider and call the death of his neighbor merely incidental. And I doubt that the air-strategist can drop his H-bombs on New York-Newark and call the resultant deaths of millions of innocent people merely incidental.

Given the size and power of the destructive weapon chosen, given the size and character of the area aimed at, and given the immense extent of the human carnage involved, it does not seem possible any longer to say: "I am making an attack on certain precise and quite limited military targets; all the rest I reluctantly permit as incidental to this military attack." Especially when I have at hand smaller weapons capable of destroying these precise military targets without the mass human carnage.

To my mind common sense repudiates this interpretation of what is happening. Common sense indicates rather that the destruction of the targets is incidental to the destruction of the area; that in choosing the H-bomb as my weapon in these circumstances I am choosing the death of the innocent millions. Merely telling myself that I do not intend this directly will not change the actual state of affairs. I can no longer believe myself.

## PROPORTIONATE REASON

In the third place, even if the policy makers and military leaders would and could avoid the direct intention of killing millions of innocent people, there cannot be any proportionate reason to justify the evils which this type of all-out nuclear warfare would let loose on the world.

It is illegitimate to appeal to the principle of the double effect when the alleged justifying cause is speculative, future, and problematical, while the evil effect is definite, enormous, certain, and immediate. The hoped-for good effect, in the H-bombing of Moscow, for instance, would presumably be self-preservation from Russia's physical attack and the preservation of our country from the threat of materialistic socialism. But would it work? We do not know. Physically the attack might boomerang. As for the atheistic communism, the extermination of Moscow and the Muscovites might or might not preserve us from it. Ideas have a way of surviving bombardments, but the millions of innocent do not survive. Their wholesale slaughter is immediate, certain, irrevocable.

Furthermore, if this kind of warfare were once conceded by moralists to be legitimate, it would mean the practical abandonment of any distinction between innocent noncombatants and guilty aggressors. . . . We would be adopting, in practice at least, the immorality of total war.

## SURVIVAL OF THE RACE

Worst of all, it seems entirely probable that once a world-wide war got started, once the high-megaton H-bombs began to fall across the world, there would be at stake, not the survival of this nation or that, but the survival of civilization and even of the human race itself. Einstein said he did not know what weapons would be used in the next war, but in the war after that it would be stone clubs. To H-bomb Moscow would be to embrace the serious risk of such an all-out nuclear war. The probable outcome for the human race? Extinction. No proportionate reason can be assigned for "permitting" the extinction of the human race.

The threat of . . . communism presents us with terrifying problems. But I think these problems are entirely oversimplified when reduced to the stark dilemma: either wipe them out or be wiped out yourselves.

# THE MORALITY OF USING NUCLEAR WEAPONS

*Manuel Velasquez*

I want to advance the discussion of the claim that nuclear weapons are immoral because they cannot distinguish between civilian and military targets. Up to this point, such discussions have left a good deal to be desired. First, they have failed to show why the morality of war should be approached through an analysis of the distinction between civilian and military targets and not through other popular approaches. Second, they have failed to justify the claim that nuclear weapons cannot distinguish between civilian and military targets. And third, and most important, they have failed to demonstrate the moral significance of the distinction between civilian and military targets. In this essay, I hope to make up for these deficiencies. In the first section, I will argue that other popular approaches to the morality of nuclear war are inadequate. In the second section, I will justify the claim that nuclear weapons must violate the traditional immunity of civilian noncombatants. In the third section, I will show that the distinction between civilian and military targets is morally significant. And in the fourth section, I will respond to several possible objections.

## I. ALTERNATIVE APPROACHES: UTILITARIANISM, NATURAL LAW PROPORTIONALISM, AND REALISM

Discussions of the morality of nuclear war often take one of two approaches. The first, and undoubtedly the most popular, is one that is common to both utilitarian and natural law "proportionalist" treatments of the morality of war. It proceeds by asking whether the evils of using nuclear weapons are outweighed by or are proportional to the political objectives that such uses might achieve. If the evil of killing the many people that would die in a nuclear holocaust is greater than the good that would be achieved, then it would be wrong to use nuclear weapons. Utilitarians usually talk about weighing the evils of using nuclear weapons against the good that such uses might achieve. If more good than evil would result, and if no other alternative will produce a greater balance of good over evil, then it is moral to use such weapons; otherwise it would be immoral. Natural law proponents of "just war" theories usually talk about the proportionality of the goods and evils that would result from using nuclear weapons: the lives and other basic goods that nuclear weapons would destroy indirectly must be proportional to the basic goods that would be achieved directly.

Arguments of this sort have taken two conflicting forms. Some have claimed that the evils of waging a nuclear war are so great that they cannot possibly be worth the achievement of any political objective, no matter how desirable. Others, interestingly, have argued that some political objectives are so important that they outweigh even the risks of waging a nuclear war. Those who take the first position commonly focus on the massive numbers of people that nuclear weapons might kill and on the large economic, social, and environmental damage that nuclear weapons could inflict. If the use of these weapons escalates into a major war between the United States and Russia, for example, several hundred million people would be killed, the natural environment might suffer irreversible damage, and the economic and social systems of both nations might collapse. On the other hand, those who claim that some political objectives are important enough to risk even such massive losses often focus on values such as liberty, democracy, equality, culture, happiness, and so on. They argue that these values are so important that it is worth risking even nuclear death in order not to lose them. In other words, "better dead than red." This view holds that the quality of certain forms of life are so undesirable that it is better to die than to see humanity subjected to them.

These disagreements concerning the relative value of the evils of nuclear war are instructive because they are not accidental features of utilitarian or proportionalist approaches to the morality of using nuclear weapons in an international conflict. Rather, they are inherent to all such approaches to war in general and to nuclear war in particular. Utilitarian or proportionalist approaches must proceed by asking whether the potential losses inflicted by using nuclear weapons are worth the potential gains. But there is no objective way of determining the answer to the question. For to answer this question we must assume that there is some objective way of measuring and comparing the costs and benefits of waging war when in fact there is no objective scale on which the usual costs and benefits of war can be measured and compared. Wars today (and certainly any nuclear war of the future) are commonly fought for a variety of intangible, controverted, and incommensurable values such as lives, liberties, equalities, legal systems, forms of government, cultures, technologies, land, dominance, power, stability, honor, happiness, revenge, and so on. And the value of each of these goods differs radically in the estimations of different people. Some people prefer death to a life without liberty (like the patriot who exclaimed, "Give me liberty or give me death!"), much like the advocates of euthanasia who prefer death to a life of pain. Others obviously prefer to live unfree than not to live at all. Consequently, any claim to the effect that a certain objective of a war is worth more or less than the costs of waging that war must be based on the subjective preferences of the person or persons making such a claim. Thus, there is no objective way of answering the utilitarian or proportionalist question: Will the losses inflicted by using nuclear weapons be worth the potential gains? Any answer given to this question may appear to be objective, but it will necessarily be based on the subjective preferences of the person or persons who determined the scale on which the losses and gains are to be measured and compared. For this reason, both the utilitarian and the natural law proportionalist approaches to evaluating the morality of nuclear war must be rejected.

A second, and more despairing, approach that is often taken when considering the morality of nuclear war is that of the moral nihilist, an approach that is unfortunately sometimes referred to as the "realist" approach. The so-called "realist" holds that the use of nuclear weapons in war is not immoral because morality does not apply to the conduct of war. The most important form of this argument is based on the idea that nuclear wars are fought between nations and that nations exist in a Hobbesian state of nature. That is, nations exist in a world in which there is no force powerful enough to guarantee that they act morally toward each other. In the absence of such a guarantee, no nation can expect that other nations will temper their actions by moral restraints and any nation that does restrain itself by morality will be at a disadvantage. Thus, in a world in which other nations disregard moral constraints and take any means to advance their self-interest, no nation can be expected or required to put itself at a disadvantage by imposing on itself the restraints of morality. Since no nation can be required to adhere to moral principles, it follows that it is meaningless to evaluate their actions—including their nuclear wars—according to whether or not they adhere to these principles.

Three points can be made against this objection. First, even if I am in a situation in which other agents do not adhere to any moral restraints, it does not logically follow that in that situation my actions (or theirs, for that matter) are no longer subject to moral principles. All that follows is that since such a situation is different from the situations in which we normally act, the moral requirements placed on me are different from the moral requirements that obtain in more normal circumstances. For example, morality requires that in normal circumstances I am not to attack or kill my fellow citizens. But when one of these citizens is attacking me on a dark street, morality allows me to defend myself by counterattacking or even killing that citizen. What moral principles require in one set of circumstances, then, is different from what they require in other circumstances. Thus, if a country is in constant danger of an unjust nuclear attack from others, it may be morally justified in taking measures to defend itself that would not be morally justified in different circumstances. This by no means implies, however, that moral principles no longer apply in such a hostile situation. On the contrary, our recognition of the moral legitimacy of defensive measures in hostile situations shows that we can and do evaluate such measures from a moral point of view.

Second, the objection is mistaken in claiming that we exist in a world in which there are no forces to ensure that nations will act morally. For just as people, are motivated to act morally in part by an understanding of the extent to which they depend on each other, in part by social pressures, and in part by the belief that the costs of hostility generally outweigh its benefits, so also nations are motivated to act morally in part by a recognition of their mutual dependencies, in part by the pressure of world opinion, and in part by the expectation that they have more to lose from aggression than they have to gain. International conflicts are common enough, to be sure, but it is false to claim that we are constantly at war with each other or that weak nations are unrelentingly attacked by the strong.

Third, when we evaluate the acts of a nation, we are evaluating them as something brought about by human beings. And human beings clearly do not exist in a Hobbesian state of nature. There are strong psychological and social forces operating upon human beings that ensure that they will generally adhere to morality. Consequently, human beings are subject to morality and therefore so are the acts of the nations they knowingly and intentionally bring about, including their wars. Thus, the realist approach to evaluating the morality of war is inadequate.

If utilitarian, proportionalist, and realist approaches are rejected, then one must seek other alternatives. The most promising is the view that nuclear weapons, like other weapons, are moral only if they are used in such a way as to respect the traditional rules concerning just and unjust methods of pursuing a war. Foremost among these rules is the one that rests on the distinction between killing combatants and killing noncombatants. Military tradition has always held that in any war, even a war of self-defense, it is morally permissible to kill combatants, but morally impermissible to kill noncombatants. Can nuclear weapons be used in such a way as to respect this traditional distinction? I will turn now to an examination of this question.

## II. NUCLEAR WEAPONS AND NONCOMBATANT DEATHS

I will discuss the definition of a noncombatant at some length in the third part of this essay. At this point, it is enough to say that a noncombatant is a civilian who is not actively engaged in the military pursuit of a war. Obviously, nuclear weapons could be used in many different ways, some of which would not necessarily injure civilian noncombatants. For example, if an attacking naval convoy was annihilated with a nuclear bomb in the middle of an ocean, it is possible and even likely that no civilians would be killed. But such imaginary examples are a far cry from the scenarios realistically contemplated in our military policies.

Our own strategists foresee the use of nuclear weapons in three rather different ways. First, if we are attacked by the nuclear forces of the Soviet Union or another nation we intend to retaliate with a "counter-value" strike, that is, a nuclear strike intended to inflict "unacceptable damage" by destroying a certain portion of what the attacking nation most values—its population and its property. In 1965, Secretary of Defense Robert McNamara defined "unacceptable damage" as 25 percent of the population of the U.S.S.R. and 70 percent of its industry; in 1979, another secretary of defense, Harold Brown, revised this definition to mean 34 percent of the Soviets' population and 62 percent of their industry. Obviously, such counter-value strikes will necessarily kill civilian non-combatants and will not be limited to purely military targets, for they are not intended to deflect incoming missiles, nor are they intended to destroy the enemy's military ability to deliver a killing blow. They are not even intended to eliminate the military or political leaders who launched the nuclear attack in the first place. In fact, the only purpose of a counter-value strike is to kill the civilian friends, relatives, and countrymen of the persons responsible for the attack. It is as if we were to revenge ourselves on a murderer by killing his wife and children. In other words, nuclear deterrence is based on the idea that just as we can prevent a potential criminal from breaking the law by threatening to kill his wife and children, so we can also prevent our enemies from launching their missiles by threatening to kill an "unacceptable" percentage of their relatives and countrymen. A counter-value strike is simply the means by which such a threat would be carried out. Clearly, then, counter-value strikes are unavoidably intended to kill innocent noncombatants.

The second major contemplated use of nuclear weapons is in a "counter-force" strike, that is, a nuclear strike intended to destroy the military forces of another nation. A counter-force strike could be used to disable the nuclear forces of an enemy before it used them, or to destroy its remaining nuclear weapons after it had launched an initial attack. At one extreme, a counter-force strike might consist of a "full-scale" attack on ten or more ICBM silos or bomber bases; at the other extreme, it might be a "limited" attack consisting of a single bomb detonated over a single, isolated ICBM silo. I will set aside such limited attacks for now, since they will be discussed more fully later on.

What is the probability that a full-scale counter-force strike would kill civilians? It is virtually certain that the deadly destructiveness would spill out beyond the boundaries of any military targets. In fact, four types of spill-over effects are inevitable. First, the nuclear blast of bombs intended to destroy military bases or missile silos would extend beyond the perimeters of the target and kill civilians. This would be due partly to the inaccuracy of missile technology, partly to the sheer size and rapidity of nuclear blasts, and partly to the fact that military installations are usually located near civilian centers. Second, radioactive fallout from nuclear detonations would drift beyond target areas and kill civilians several hundred miles away. For example, the fallout from a nuclear bomb intended to destroy an ICBM silo in Cheyenne, Wyoming, would be carried eastward by prevailing winds and would kill 50 percent of the population of Omaha, Des Moines, Chicago, and Detroit. Third, the effects of radiation would spill over to unborn generations who were not part of the intended military target. These survivors would suffer the effects of genetically transmitted diseases and would contract cancer from residual radioactivity. And fourth, if detonated in the numbers contemplated in a full-scale counter-force strike, nuclear explosions could produce catastrophic and irreversible effects on the world's ecological and social systems. Not only is there a slim although unlikely chance that the ozone layer would be depleted, there is also a more likely possibility that the wholesale destruction of plants, animals, and industries would alter the balance on which the production of our food depends and would bring about a collapse of our economic and social systems. This would inflict starvation and severe deprivation on populations far from the intended military targets, and do so for many generations to come. Thus, it is virtually certain that a full-scale counter-force attack would kill innumerable noncombatant civilians.

The third main contemplated use of nuclear weapons has already been mentioned: so-called "limited" strikes brought against specific military targets. Two types of limited strikes are mentioned in our military policies: (1) a limited counter-force strike consisting of a single large nuclear warhead (or a very few warheads) used strategically to disable an enemy nuclear installation, and (2) a limited tactical strike consisting of relatively small nuclear weapons used on a battlefield during a continuing military operation. Will such limited nuclear strikes kill civilians? It is highly probable, and perhaps inevitable.

There are three arguments that lead one to think that limited nuclear strikes will escalate into full-scale nuclear exchanges. Our military strategists contemplate the use of limited tactical weapons in a European theater (where we presently have several thousand deployed) or in some other arena of confrontation with the Soviet Union. The first reason for thinking that such uses of nuclear weapons must escalate is connected to the tactics that emerge on these and other battlefields.

Since the early 1960s, NATO has held several mock nuclear battles in European countries. Each time, two things happened, and very quickly. Once commanders realized that nuclear weapons might be used, they deployed their troops thinly over several hundred square miles so that each nuclear warhead would strike as few men as possible. As a result, each side then began to throw a large number of warheads over the battleground in order to destroy the thinly spread forces of the other side. Not surprisingly, communications quickly broke down between the widely scattered troops. The second thing that happened was related to the fact that nuclear weapons, especially on an exposed battlefield, are highly vulnerable. Consequently, if one side starts throwing nuclear warheads on a battlefield, the other side must immediately launch its own warheads or watch them be blown up on the ground. In every NATO exercise, all commanders in the field chose to launch their warheads immediately rather than wait to have them destroyed. It is not hard to guess the results of the combined effects of widely spread military targets, weapons vulnerability, and communications breakdowns. In a matter of hours, all semblance of battlefield order and control disintegrated and uncontrolled launchings of nuclear bombs over Europe escalated. Hypothetical civilian casualties were estimated to be between 5 and 20 million dead. In addition, each side had killed tens of thousands of its own troops with its own nuclear weapons. We can expect that the interactions that emerged on a mock battlefield in Europe would be replicated worldwide once the two superpowers began to use nuclear weapons.

The second reason why limited nuclear exchanges would probably escalate relates to a technical characteristic of nuclear weapons that conventional weapons do not possess. Conventional bombs become less efficient as their explosive force increases, while nuclear weapons become more efficient. Increasing the explosive force of a conventional bomb requires inserting additional tonnage of explosives that makes the bomb increasingly cumbersome and difficult to launch. But multiplying the explosive force of a nuclear bomb requires adding only a few more pounds of explosives to its weight, thus making the bomb negligibly heavier while increasing its force by several magnitudes. In a military conflict, strategic considerations pressure each party into using bombs of larger rather than smaller explosive force. This is true for two reasons: first, the larger the blast area, the more targets a single bomb can destroy; and, second, the larger the blast area, the less chance there is of missing the target. If only conventional weapons are used in a conflict, their decreasing efficiency eventually slows, then halts this drive toward larger bombs. But if nuclear weapons are used, no such limiting technological factor exists. On the contrary, the greater efficiency of larger nuclear bombs fuels the drive toward bombs of ever greater explosive force.

The third reason why limited nuclear engagements would probably escalate has to do with the nature of the conventions that alone can keep a confrontation from escalating. In a military conflict in which both sides have nuclear bombs, each has the capacity to impose a virtually unlimited amount of damage on the other. Consequently, if there are to be any limits to these damages, the limits must be voluntarily assumed by each side. But if the parties to a military conflict are to limit voluntarily the (potentially limitless) destruction that each can inflict on the other, two conditions must obtain: (1) there must be some mutually recognized and clear limit that each party knows the other side is aware of, and (2) each side must have some assurance that the other will not transgress that clear and mutually recognized limit. In the absence of either of these conditions, neither side will put itself at a disadvantage by accepting a limit that might not be clear or that its opponent might not respect. At present, the line between conventional weapons and nuclear bombs provides the basis for such a limit. Each side knows the other is aware of this limit and it will be immediately clear if one side chooses to go beyond it. Moreover, it is a limit that both sides know the other respects because of the possibly devastating consequences of its violation. However, once the line separating conventional and nuclear weapons has been crossed, there is no other threshold that can provide the basis for the same kind of limit during an international confrontation. The pressures toward escalation could not then be contained.

Taken together, the three considerations sketched above imply that once nuclear weapons begin to be used in a limited manner against purely military targets, the exchange of bombs will escalate to the point where noncombatant civilians will certainly be killed. It is clear, then, that the major ways in which we contemplate using nuclear weapons all fail to respect the traditional moral principle that in war it is permissible to attack combatants but impermissible to attack noncombatants.

But why should it matter that innocent people are killed? Are not the lives of soldiers worth as much as the lives of civilians? Why then should it be immoral to kill civilian noncombatants but not military personnel? What is the moral significance of the traditional distinction between combatants and noncombatants? We must turn next to answering these questions.

## III. THE MORAL BASIS OF THE COMBATANT/ NONCOMBATANT DISTINCTION

Since the time of the ancient Greeks and Romans, on through the early and late medieval Christian eras, and even up to the twentieth century, when international military rules of war were formally codified and ratified, the principle of the immunity of noncombatants has been emphatically and repeatedly affirmed. The principle is simple: In war, it is morally permissible to attack and kill enemy combatants, but it is wrong deliberately to kill noncombatants.

The basic difficulty in appealing to this traditional principle, however, is that it is not clear why the distinction between combatants and noncombatants should be morally important. One could maintain that death is equally evil whether one is a combatant or a noncombatant and that, consequently, it is irrelevant whether it is combatants or noncombatants who get killed in a nuclear attack. What matters are (1) the numbers of people that are killed, and (2) whether killing that many people is worth the objectives for which the war is fought. The problem with maintaining this view is that, as I argued earlier, there is no objective way of determining whether a given quantity of deaths is worth the objectives for which wars are usually fought. Having rejected such utilitarian and proportionalist weighings as nothing more than personal or group preferences, we must attempt to clarify the moral significance of the combatant/ noncombatant distinction.

What, then, is the basis of this distinction and why does it matter? The difference between a combatant and a noncombatant is rooted in the difference between an assailant who is attacking my life and a bystander who does not pose such a threat. Imagine, for example, that one afternoon an enemy of mine begins shooting at me on a street that is completely deserted except for a woman carrying a child. In this situation, the right to self-defense justifies my killing the assailant if this is the only way I can stop him from killing me. But I am not justified in killing the innocent woman and her child since neither of them pose a threat to my life.

But appealing to the principle of self-defense simply shifts the problem to another area. For now we must ask: What is the basis of the moral distinction that the principle of self-defense makes between an assailant and a bystander? Why do I have a moral right to take the life of someone who is attacking me but not of the innocent bystander? It would appear that if it is evil to kill a person in the first place, then it is just as evil to kill the attacker. Thus we must answer this question: What is it about the assailant that renders him morally liable to my attack and what is it about the bystander that renders her morally immune from my attack?

The moral distinction between the assailant and the bystander that is built into the principle of self-defense can be explained by appealing to the Kantian principle that persons must be treated as ends and never merely as means. To treat a person merely as a means is to treat the person in a manner intentionally designed to achieve my own purposes without any regard for the person's own rational choices. To treat a person as an end is to treat the person as he has freely and rationally consented to be treated. Now the deathly attack of my assailant violates Kant's principle insofar as my assailant, in attempting to achieve his own purposes, treats me as I have not consented to be treated. When I repulse his attack, however, I do not violate the Kantian principle because in attacking me the assailant knew that I might attempt to defend myself and nonetheless he consented to enter the attack. My assailant, therefore, may be taken to have consented to a situation in which he would be making himself subject to a counterattack. I do not wrong him, therefore, when I attack him, for I then treat him as he has consented to be treated. The innocent bystander and her child, however, have not given any similar consent. If I should kill either of them, I would be attempting to achieve my own purposes without regard for their freedom of choice. I would therefore be using them merely as means and would be violating the Kantian principle.

This interpretation of the right of self-defense is, I believe, the intuition that underlies the combatant/noncombatant distinction. The combatant, like the assailant, has implicitly consented to bear the brunt of the counterattacks of the enemy. However, the noncombatant cannot be taken to have given a similar consent. To kill the former in war, therefore, does not violate the Kantian principle, while killing the latter does.

If the analysis above is correct, and if my interpretation of the Kantian principle is acceptable, then we can see why it has always been a traditional rule of war that it is immoral indiscriminately to kill noncombatants. And since we know that the major ways in which we contemplate using nuclear weapons will inevitably result in the mass killing of civilian noncombatants, such uses are immoral. But they are immoral not because the numbers killed are not worth the objectives we hope to gain; rather, they are immoral because in using weapons in this way we are killing those we have no right to kill—bystanders who are innocent of any attack against us.

## IV. OBJECTIONS AND REPLIES

There are four important objections that might be raised against my argument on the morality of using nuclear weapons. The first concerns the correlation I make between being a combatant and giving consent. Contrary to what I imply, someone may want to claim that combatants do not always consent to war, nor do noncombatants always withhold their consent. Young soldiers may be drafted, for example, and thereby forced to be combatants against their will. In the same way, being a civilian does not preclude one from consenting to and actively participating in a military attack.

This objection can be easily answered. It assumes that I equate being a soldier with giving consent to a war. However, all I claim is that being a soldier (as traditionally defined, i.e., wearing a uniform, carrying a gun, and being subject to military authority) is *prima facie* evidence that one has consented to fight in a war, while being a civilian merely implies the absence of such *prima facie* evidence. Although consent should be construed as one defining characteristic (along with active participation) of a combatant, a person's military status should be treated as merely *prima facie* evidence of such consent. Of course, this leaves unanswered several questions about how we are to identify those who have consented to a war and separate them precisely from those who have not. But such questions are irrelevant to my argument. For it is clear that however you choose to draw the lines between those who consent (perhaps the reader might want to count all those who voted for the present government or those who work in military industries as "consenting combatants") and those who do not consent (idiots and small children clearly do not consent), our contemplated uses of nuclear weapons will certainly kill and injure members of the nonconsenting groups. At the very least, nuclear weapons will kill children, idiots, pacifists, future generations, foreign nationals, and others who have clearly not consented.

A second objection that might be brought against my argument is that it ignores the citizen's responsibility for the acts of his government. All the members of a nation, my critic may claim, are collectively responsible for the acts of that nation's government. And in virtue of this collective responsibility, each citizen must share in the burdens of the government's actions, just as each shares in its benefits. Thus, when the nation's government declares a war, all the members of that nation are morally responsible for the act and must therefore share in its consequences, including becoming liable to attack. To this way of thinking, there are no innocent noncombatants when the modern nation is involved in a war since all citizens share the responsibility and therefore none are immune from attack.

A fundamental difficulty on which this criticism must founder, however, is that its major premise is highly questionable. Why should membership in a nation make me morally responsible for the acts of its government? There are three ways in which a critic might attempt to argue for this premise, all of which prove to be unsatisfactory.

First, one might adopt a so-called "organic theory" of the state and claim that a nation is just like a living organism, with its citizens the constituent parts of the organism. Just as we attribute to a whole organism what each of its parts does, so also can we attribute the acts of the government to the citizenry as a whole. But surely no one today will find this organic theory of the state acceptable. The citizens of a nation are autonomous: they can think, live, and choose independently of the nation in a way that is utterly different from the parts of an organism. Thus, the organic analogy on which the theory depends is so deficient that one wonders why anyone could ever have taken it seriously.

Second, one might adopt a social contract theory of the state and hold that by becoming members of it all citizens agree to accept responsibility for the acts of the government in return for the services the government performs. But this argument is also based on an unacceptable fiction since most citizens never made such a voluntary agreement. Citizenship is usually acquired by birth and the citizen makes no agreements at that time.

Third, one might propose an argument based on a presumed "principle of fairness": since all citizens accept the benefits provided by the state, in fairness they must also accept its burdens, including responsibility for its wars. But this argument too is obviously false. The mere fact that I accept a benefit from a group in no way makes me morally responsible for the acts of that group or its leaders. If a university gives me a scholarship, for example, I do not become morally responsible for the criminal acts of its administrators, nor may I take credit for their wise activities.

But the main problem with all these theories is that they misconstrue the notion of moral responsibility. One is morally responsible only for one's own intentional or negligent actions and omissions, and for what one knowingly or negligently brings about or helps to bring about or fails to prevent through one's own intentional actions and omissions. I am not morally responsible for the evil you do so long as I had no hand in your doing it (in other words, if I did not encourage you or aid you) and so long as I did not stand idly by when I knew I could prevent you from doing it. To the extent, therefore, that a citizen has no hand in the government's decision to wage war (he did not vote for the government or agree with its decision), and no hand in its execution (the citizen is not knowingly working for the military or for a war-related industry), and did not stand idly by when he could have helped to prevent the war, to that extent the citizen is not morally responsible for the war and may not be treated as a combatant who has consented to the war. It is clear that in any nation there are many people (such as children, idiots, pacifists, and so on) who are precisely in that position. They are in no way morally responsible for the war undertaken by their government and may not be knowingly killed or attacked.

The third objection that can be raised against my argument is that if my view is correct we would have a moral obligation unilaterally to disarm, and unilateral disarmament would simply increase the risk of war so long as the Soviets do not disarm. Why would a critic think my view implies that we have an obligation unilaterally to disarm? Because according to my argument it is immoral ever to use nuclear weapons. But if it is immoral to do something, then it is equally immoral to intend to do it, so it is also immoral to intend to use nuclear weapons. And the only reason we possess nuclear weapons is because we intend to use them if we are attacked. This seems to be the whole idea behind nuclear deterrence: we threaten to use nuclear weapons if we are ever attacked, and threatening to use them implies an intent to use them. Thus, possessing nuclear weapons for deterrent purposes is itself immoral because it involves the immoral intent to use them if attacked. Our only moral option, therefore, is unilaterally to rid ourselves of these weapons and the intent that possessing them implies.

There are several replies that can be made to this objection. First, it is not clear that if it is wrong to do something, then it is equally wrong to intend to do it. Intentions, unlike actions, are not always carried out, so they do not necessarily have the same effects on the world. But second, and more important, it is wrong to claim that threatening to use nuclear weapons implies an intent to use them. Nuclear deterrence is indeed based on a threat, but not all threats are based on intention. When I tell a student that I intend to flunk him if he comes late to class again, and I mean it, then my threat is a declaration of intention. But not all threats are like this. Some threats are based on uncertainty and not on intention. When we say a hurricane is threatening a city, we are not saying that the storm "intends" to destroy the city. A hurricane is a threat because it involves a large element of uncertainty: it may strike us and it may not. That is the kind of threat on which nuclear deterrence can be based: the threat of uncertainty and not the threat of intention. The mere possession of nuclear weapons can deter other nations from attacking, not because there is an intent to use them but because others can never be certain whether or not they will be used. So even if it were wrong to intend to use nuclear weapons, it does not follow that it is necessarily wrong to possess them and have them serve as a threat in virtue of the uncertainty they pose. In fact, the possession of nuclear weapons is morally justified if such possession does in fact deter others from ever using them. In this case, possession prevents the greatest evil that could possibly fall on us: the actual use of nuclear weapons.

I am not arguing, of course, that we are justified in maintaining any and all nuclear armaments. Some nuclear weapons increase the chance of use, others promise more destruction than deterrence requires. Acquiring such weapons is not morally justifiable and we have an obligation to rid ourselves of any that we might have acquired. Neither am I arguing that we should form the fixed intention of refraining from using nuclear weapons, nor am I suggesting that we should then lie or bluff about what our real intentions are so that our enemies will not attack us. I am merely saying that a morally proper deterrence policy requires the absence of any fixed intention to use nuclear weapons.

But note that the absence of a fixed intention to use nuclear weapons does not require the presence of a fixed intention to refrain from using them. Rather, the absence of a fixed intention is simply that: uncertainty about what one will do when the moment of decision comes. Such uncertainty is quite compatible with the sincere formulation of plans to use nuclear weapons and with the sincere promulgation of such plans. Moreover, my own hunch is that such uncertainty is an apt description of our present situation. That is, although we are told that our leaders and the hundreds of people who must execute their orders all plan to use nuclear weapons if we are attacked (and although many of these people may sincerely hope that the plan will be carried out), the fact is that we are uncertain what all of those hundreds of people will actually do when the moment of decision comes. Given the magnitude of the threat that nuclear weapons pose, such uncertainty is all that is required to make deterrence work. There is, thus, no necessary connection between a workable policy of nuclear deterrence and the fixed intent to use nuclear weapons in immoral ways.

# ETHICS AND NUCLEAR DETERRENCE

*Douglas Lackey*

For the first time since the introduction of intercontinental missiles in the early 1960s, the major powers have achieved stable deterrence.

Though the present strategic balance is an improvement over past uncertainties, this gives us no cause to believe that it is the best possible arrangement. For an indefinite period, to preserve this balance, the United States and the Soviet Union must spend large sums on armaments, endure the risk of nuclear accidents, face the possibility that any minor disagreement may escalate into a nuclear war, and maintain an attitude sufficiently bellicose to assure the other side that destruction will swiftly and surely follow upon attack. My purpose in this paper is to examine the extent to which we can rest content with the present strategic *détente*. There are two sorts of criticism possible: first, the utilitarian one that this policy will not produce the best consequences for the world over all the practical alternatives; second, the sterner criticism that our policy is intrinsically abhorrent and ought to be abandoned simply because of what it is. I shall take up each criticism in turn.

## A UTILITARIAN CRITIQUE

Utilitarian critiques are always future-oriented; given the world as it is *now,* with the weapons that actually exist on both sides, which policy will produce the best future results? This prevents retroactive criticism of past military decisions; and though they provide an interesting compendium of missed opportunities and mental lapses, the errors of the 1960s will not concern us here. The costs of the *present* policy (by present policy I mean the policy to maintain force levels at least as high as they now are, subject to the limitations of the SALT I agreement) have already been indicated. *First,* there is the enormous cost of maintaining and operating the present American weapons systems. (Notice that we cannot include present interest on loans taken to develop these systems; that is a critique of *past* action). *Second,* there is the enormous cost of the maintaining and operating of the corresponding arsenal in the Soviet Union. It is not unfair, I believe, to include costs of Soviet arms as part of the utilitarian cost of American policy, even though Americans do not decide whether Russia shall arm. "Cost" in a utilitarian calculation is cost to the human race, and each agent is responsible for such costs as can reasonably be predicted to follow from his policies. It is reasonable to predict, judging from what we know of the Soviet Union and its leadership, that if we maintain our present armament, the Russians will maintain theirs; and also reasonable to predict that if we acted differently as regards the level of arms, the Russians would also. Hence their expenditures should be charged against our policy. By parity of reasoning, the Russian policy must include among its costs the money that Americans, in all their rhetorical fury, can reasonably be predicted to spend in response to Russian armaments. But this would be relevant to a critique of Russian policy, and I am here concerned only with our own. *Third,* since the weapons of destruction exist and are very complex, there is a chance that systems will malfunction and some or all of the world be destroyed by accident. The malfunction may be due to mechanical failure, as is described in the book *Fail Safe,* or to human failure, as is depicted in the movie *Dr. Strangelove.* Though the chances of such accidents are considerably less than they were, say, in October of 1960, when an American nuclear attack was almost ordered against Russia in response to radar signals that had bounced off the moon, the possibility of either sort of failure is still quite real. For reasons quite analogous to those given above as regards the financial burden of armaments, the possibility of malfunction in Russian systems must be charged against our policy, just as much as the possibility of malfunction in American systems. Even though the Russian systems are not supervised by us, they exist in response to ours and their possible malfunctions are concomitants of our policies. Russian expenses and Russian risks are hidden costs of our policies usually ignored even by liberal critics.

The financial burden of armaments is certain; accidental nuclear war is just a possibility. In estimating the value of current defense policy one must subtract some factor for the possibility of accidental war. This factor will be, estimated by the usual methods, the product of the chance of war and the disutility of this result. Though the chance of accidental war is slight, it is not negligible when Russian malfunctions are also considered; and since the disutility of nuclear war is great, the total subtraction from the value of the present policy on this ground alone should be substantial. *Fourth,* since the weapons of destruction exist, there is always the possibility that they will be *deliberately* used, if the leaders of one nation deem some provocation sufficient. The subtraction for this factor, as with the third, is achieved by multiplying the chance that some conflict will escalate to nuclear war by the disutility of that war, which is considerable.

The "gains" that can be attributed to the present policy are said to be threefold. First, the certainty of an American counterattack deters the Russians from launching a nuclear attack on the United States in order to gain some end. To the extent that such attacks are deterred, the world gains and not just the United States. Second, the ability of the United States to launch a devastating counterattack vitiates all Russian attempts to use threats of attack as a regular instrument of policy. If the United States could not attack, the Soviet Union could blackmail the United States at every point, threatening destruction if concessions be not made. Third, if the United States retains its capacity to counterattack, then it has the option, in *extreme* situations, of threatening to attack even though attack is suicidal. Though the Soviet leaders know that any attack is unlikely, they cannot be *certain* that the American leaders will *not* go to war over the issue concerned; and accordingly such threats by the United States will not be totally without effect. President Kennedy used such threats, successfully, to secure the removal of Russian missiles from Cuba. In short, the maintenance of our present military capacity reduces the risk of attack and blackmail, and occasionally can be used to secure goals of policy.

Each of these three "gains" must be carefully analyzed. First, it is claimed that American armaments "reduce the threat of Russian attack." The superficial appeal of this claim disappears when we raise the question: Reduce the chances of attack *relative to what?* Certainly it reduces the chances of attack relative to some anti-Communist fantasy in which the leaders of the Soviet Union daily plot the conquest of the United States. But such fantasies are incredible and it is madness to praise a present policy because it is better than some imaginary evil. The fact is that with the present policy there is a certain chance of war, which can be calculated by combining the possibility of accidental war with the possibility of deliberate attack; and this is an evil of the policy which can only be justified on the grounds that all other policies on balance do even worse.

The same criticism applies to the second "plus" of our deterrence policy: it prevents nuclear blackmail. Our policy can "prevent" nuclear blackmail only if there *is* nuclear blackmail to be prevented. But there is little evidence that either side is prone to blackmail of this sort. On the Russian side, the military tradition is either to act or not to act; threatening to act is not a standard feature of Russian policy. The Soviets did not *threaten* to invade Hungary and Czechoslovakia; they simply invaded them. They did not threaten to attack us if we intercepted their ships steaming toward Cuba in 1962; they merely stopped them. As for the United States, the use of nuclear threats was eschewed in the Acheson era, when there was often something worth blackmailing; and in the Dulles era, though the nuclear sabers were often rattled as a general display, they remained preternaturally still during the Hungarian invasion, the most provocative Soviet act of the 1950s. During this period the United States could have attacked Russia at any time with relative impunity, yet it did not even threaten to attack. In short, the major powers are not given to nuclear blackmail. If this blackmail problem ever does arise, it will arise in the context of nuclear *terrorists*—revolutionary kamikazes with nuclear devices—against whom the threat of counterattack is useless. The true situation is that with the present policy there is not a "reduction" in the chance of nuclear blackmail but rather a set chance of blackmail given present conditions, and no argument has yet been provided that this chance is less than the chance that one would have in all other alternative policies.

The third "plus" of present policy is that if we possess strength we can negotiate from strength—gaining ends we could not attain otherwise. (The latest variant on this theme is the reiterated argument . . . that we must first increase armaments in order to facilitate negotiations to decrease them.) This third plus may be a plus from the perspective of those who make American policy, but it can hardly be considered a plus for humanity in general. "To negotiate from strength" is a euphemism for the making of threats; the making of threats increases the chance of nuclear war. The great disutility of this result outweighs any gains that might result from "negotiating from strength," even if (as is unlikely) the negotiations are aimed at a moral result. In summary, then, even if the present policy results in more good than evil,[1] it is not demonstrated that it results in more good on balance than all alternative policies.

Of the alternative policies, the one that most clearly challenges the present policy of seeking bilateral arms reductions while maintaining the arms race is the policy of gradual unilateral disarmament. The most plausible unilateral disarmament policy at present would be this: first, to cease all nuclear testing; to declare a moratorium on armaments research; to deactivate the implementation of MIRV; to withdraw our strategic air bases from Spain, Thailand, Formosa, etc.; and to phase out all Minuteman missiles and sites. All of this would be merely Stage I, since it would leave the strategic balance completely unimpaired, so long as the Soviet Union built no ABM and the United States retained its fleet of missile submarines. Each one of these steps should be accompanied by requests that similar steps be taken by the Soviet Union, but compliance by the Soviet Union should not be considered a precondition for any of the American initiatives.

Stage II of the disarmament procedure should be as follows: the United States should announce that it will not counterattack if attacked by the Soviet Union and shall progressively deactivate its nuclear submarines,

---

1. Strictly speaking, "an increase in expected value."

down to a point in which the ability of the United States to reply to a Russian attack would be considerably reduced. At the same time, the United States should undertake extensive steps to increase Soviet-American trade, in such areas as exploit the natural specializations of the respective countries.

The consequences of this alternative policy would be, at a minimum, a reduction of the chance of accidental and escalated nuclear war, relative to the present policy, and the diversion of American capital and intellect into enterprises more likely to increase the economic health of the nation. In addition, it is highly likely that a reduction in the American level of armaments would lead to a reduction in Russian armaments, since one principal rationale for the Russian maintenance of these arms is the threat of American attack.

This leaves the question of "nuclear blackmail." If the United States enters into extensive economic arrangements with Russia, provided that these arrangements are not exploitative but based on a national specialization, the Soviet Union would have no cause to blackmail the United States, since an injury to a trading partner is an injury to oneself. Furthermore, the Soviet Union can ill afford to alienate the United States, even if the United States lacks nuclear arms, since the United States holds the balance of power, both military and economic, between the Soviet Union and China, who are at present enemies by geography, by history, and by ideology. In short, though the possibility of nuclear blackmail exists if the United States abandons its armaments, there is little likelihood that there would be such blackmail; and, in my opinion, the small chance of this bad result is far outweighed by the decreased chance of accidental or deliberate nuclear war.

The policy that I recommend bears some resemblance to suggested policies of national pacifism in the 1930s. Since these policies were discredited by events, it is important to see that the problems of the 1970s [and 1980s] are significantly different from those of the 1930s. The principle tension of the 1930s was between Germany and other states, and Germany possessed the most advanced military technology. The principal tension of the 1970s and 1980s will be between the advanced countries and the underdeveloped countries, within which the population bomb will explode. In short, tension in the 1930s was between strong and strong; in the 1980s it will be between strong and weak. The underdeveloped countries do not stand to the world on the same military basis that Germany stood to the rest of Europe. Furthermore, in the 1930s, Germany and Italy were infected with an ideology that contained self-fulfilling prophecies of the inevitability of war. There is no force in the contemporary scene that corresponds to fascism. Neither the ideology of democracy nor the ideology of capitalism preach the inevitability of war, and in the ideology of communism, though there will be inevitable war between *nations,* especially war by socialist states against capitalist states, [the latter] will be defeated not by external invasion but internal contradictions. There is no nation at present which simultaneously has the power, the desire, or the need to go to war.

Historical predictions are a risky business, and the policy of unilateral disarmament may appear unduly risky, even when its probable positive effects are considered. But if disarmament increases the risk of conquest, continued armament increases the risk of war; and of these two, the latter is the more serious, especially if the welfare of the entire world is considered and not the special national interests of the United States. . . .

## A DEONTOLOGICAL CRITIQUE

Suppose that for some reason or lack of reason the Soviet Union launches a nuclear first strike against the United States. Even under these conditions it would be clearly immoral for the United States to retaliate in kind against the Soviet Union, since retaliation by the United States would result in the death of millions of innocent people, for no higher purpose than useless revenge. The present policy of deterrence requires preparations for such retaliation and threats and assurances by us that it will be forthcoming if the United States is attacked. Indeed, if our deterrent is to remain credible, the response of the United States to attack should be semiautomatic. Defenders of armaments justify all the preparations on the grounds that they will prevent an attack *on us;* if retaliation is ever needed, they say, the system has already failed. Now, a Russian attack against the United States would be at least as immoral as our retaliation against the Russians. So one aspect of the moral problem of deterrence is this: Is one justified in *threatening* to do something which is immoral, if the reasoned intention behind one's threat is to prevent something immoral from occurring?

Let us consider some analogous situations.

(1) It would be immoral to kill a man in order to prevent default on a debt, even if one had no intention of killing the man at all, so long as he pays the debt. Indeed, it is immoral to threaten to kill a man in order to pay a debt, even if one has no intention of killing him under any circumstances, including nonpayment of the debt. In this case at least, threatening evil is not justified by good results or an increased chance of good results. Perhaps this lack of justification derives from the inherent wrongfulness of such threats of violence or from the bad results that would follow if everyone regularly made threats of this sort—whatever the cause, the good results that *actually* follow from the threat do not justify it; even, I would say, in a state of nature containing no judicial system. (2) It might be objected that this example is unfair because the stakes in question are not high enough. Would it be equally immoral to threaten to kill Jones if the intention of the threat is to prevent Jones from doing murder himself, and if the threat will *be* carried out only when Jones actually does murder? This, perhaps, is the way deterrence theorists view the present strategic *détente.* It must be admitted that in this situation the threat to kill is not *obviously* immoral. Indeed, anyone who recommends capital punishment for convicted murderers is allowing that such threats, if tempered by due process of law, are *not* immoral.

The difficulty with this example is that it does not truly reflect the structure of our present nuclear policy. Our policy is not to threaten a potential *murderer* with death in order to prevent him from murdering, and to execute *him* when he actually does murder, but rather to threaten *someone else* with death in order to prevent a potential murderer from attacking and to execute *someone else* when the murderer actually strikes. An American counterattack would be directed against the Russian people, and it is not the Russian people who would be ordering an attack on the American people. Similarly, if leaders in the United States ordered an attack on Russia, the Russian counterattack would fall on the American people and not on the leaders who ordered the attack.[2] In the present *détente*, the leaders of each side hold the population of the other hostage, and threaten to execute the hostages if the opposing *leaders* do not meet certain conditions. The proper moral examples, then, with which to analyze the *détente* should be examples of hostage-taking. (3) Suppose that the Hatfields and the McCoys live in an area sufficiently rural that disputes cannot be settled by appeal to a higher authority. For various reasons, the two families take a dislike to each other. Each family, let us assume, possesses hand grenades that could destroy the other family completely; and against these hand grenades there is no adequate defense. Each family, in what it considers to be a defensive move, kidnaps a child from the family of the other and holds it hostage. Each side wires its hostage to a device which will explode and kill the hostage if there is any loud noise nearby—such as the noise of a grenade attack or, what is not likely but still *possible,* the accidental explosion of the captors' own grenades or the sounding of a nearby clap of thunder. This example, I believe, fairly represents the present policies of deterrence.

A defender of Hatfield foreign policy might justify himself as follows: "We have no intention of killing the McCoy child, unless, of course, we are attacked. If we are attacked, we must kill him automatically (or else lose the credibility of this deterrent); but we feel that it is very unlikely that, under these conditions, any attack will occur. True, there is some small chance that the child will die by accident, but this is only a *small* chance, and so we have good reason to believe that this will not happen. At the same time, the presence of the hostage reduces the chance that the McCoys will attack, relative to the chances of attack if we had taken no hostage. If the child dies, we cannot be blamed, since we have good reason to believe that he would not, and if he lives, we are to be commended for adopting a policy which has in fact prevented an attack."

The moral reply here is obvious: the Hatfields have no *right* to seize the McCoy child, whatever dubious advantages they gain by seizing him. True they only *threaten* to kill him, but threatening to kill him increases the chance of his being killed, and they have no right to increase these

---

2. I am assuming that the Russian and American peoples cannot be held responsible for the decisions of their leaders. For the Russians, this is surely the case; for the Americans, who live in a relatively more democratic nation, the issue is more debatable. Still, whatever fraction of responsibility the American people would bear for an attack on Russia, it would hardly be sufficient to justify punishing millions of Americans with injury and death.

chances. The moral repulsiveness of the Hatfield policy derives from its abuse of the innocent for dubious ends. Deterring the McCoys in this manner is like deterring one's neighbors from running into you on the road by seizing their children and tying them to the front bumper of your car.[3] If everyone did this, accidents might decrease and, on balance, more lives [might be] saved than lost. Perhaps it could be predicted that the chances of a single child dying on a car bumper are slight; perhaps, by a miracle, no child would die.[4] Whatever the chances and whatever the gains, no one could claim the right to use a single child in this way. Yet it seems that the present American policy uses the entire Russian population in just this manner. In the preceding section I argued that our deterrence policy does not produce the best results when all alternative policies are considered. These examples show that even if the policy *did* produce the best results, it still ought not to be adopted.

(4) The key step in the preceding criticism is that the Hatfields have no right to increase the chances of the McCoy child dying, and analogously the United States has no right to increase the chances of the Russian population's dying. The threat is illicit if the threat is real. This leads to the interesting possibility that the threat is licit if it is fraudulent. Suppose that the United States *says* that it will counterattack if the Soviet Union attacks and gives every indication that it will counterattack (missile silos are constructed, submarines cruise the oceans, etc.); but, in fact, unknown to anyone except the highest officials in the government, all the American warheads are disarmed and simply cannot go off. In this case the United States does not threaten, but merely *seems* to threaten to counterattack. If the chance of Russian attack is decreased, such a plan would have good results without the intrinsic repulsiveness of the present policy.

But this plan has practical and moral flaws. The practical flaw is that the bogus threat will not serve as a deterrent unless the Soviet Union *does* discover that, according to the usual analysis, the chances of war will be greatly increased. So, it is not obvious that this plan gives good results, since one must balance the decreased chance of war (if the Soviet Union respects the deterrent) against the increased chance of war (if the Soviet Union discovers that the deterrent is bogus). Furthermore, if this plan is successfully put into effect and the Soviet Union does not have a similar plan of its own, the bogus-warhead plan will result in high and wasteful Soviet expenditures and in an increased chance of accidental or deliberate attack from the Soviet side.

The chances of nuclear war have diminished considerably since the early 1960s;[5] our policies now are safer than they were then. But these

3. This example is in Paul Ramsey, *Modern War and the Christian Conscience.*
4. This miracle, in reference to nuclear weapons, we have seen since 1945.
5. In the early 1960s, the American public overestimated the chance that nuclear war would occur. In the early 1970s, I believe that the public underestimates the chance that nuclear war will occur, and public interest in this issue is nil. But it is a good thing that this mistake is common, since lack of expectation that nuclear attacks will occur lessens the chance that nuclear accidents will be interpreted as hostile acts. In this strange world of nuclear deterrence, ignorance may bring bliss.

improvements should not blind us to the inherent abhorrence of the present policies and the dangers that they pose. Mutual deterrence is neither rational, nor prudent, nor moral, compared to other policies that are not beyond the power of rational men.

# THE ETHICS OF NUCLEAR DETERRENCE: A CONTRACTARIAN ACCOUNT

*Christopher W. Morris*

It is a widely accepted moral principle that it is wrong to kill the innocent. Yet this is precisely what we threaten to do in the event of a nuclear attack. In fact, it is an essential part of nuclear deterrence. Is nuclear deterrence then immoral? Many people, both of the left and the right, believe this to be so.

However, the principle prohibiting the killing of the innocent as stated above is implausible since it does not make allowances for accidental and unintended killings. Thus, many moral philosophers distinguish between direct and indirect killings and argue that indirect killings are not always wrong. One very influential way of making this distinction involves the traditional doctrine of double effect, according to which only acts of direct killing are morally prohibited, while acts of indirect killing may be morally permissible. The doctrine is usually stated as follows: in distinguishing between the good and the bad effects of an act of killing, the act is indirect and morally permissible if

1. the act in itself is not impermissible,
2. the bad effect is not the means to the good effect,
3. the good but not the bad effect is intended, and
4. the good effect is not outweighed by the bad effect.

Killing some civilians while bombing an enemy military installation might thus be permissible if the bad effect (killing the civilians) was neither intended nor the means to the good effect (destroying the installation) and if, say, the number of lives saved by the bombing is greater than the number of civilian casualties. The doctrine would justify such killings where the deaths were the unintended side effects of permissible acts.

An appeal to the doctrine of double effect may not, however, help the defender of nuclear deterrence, for the innocent civilians who are slaughtered by nuclear retaliation surely would not be killed indirectly. Consider what is called "countervalue" retaliation, the nuclear targeting of enemy centers of population. Such retaliation clearly would involve acts of direct killing since conditions 2 and 3 of the doctrine of double effect would not be satisfied. The bad effect (killing massive numbers of innocent civilians) would be both intended and a means to the good effect ("punishing" enemy aggression, deterring future aggression, or whatever).

In view of this, some moral philosophers counsel that we use only "counterforce" strategies, that is, strategies that aim our missiles solely at military targets and not at innocent civilians. However, given the huge numbers of Soviet casualties to be expected from counterforce retaliatory strikes, condition 4 of the doctrine of double effect surely is not satisfied. In terms of numbers of lives, the good effect is outweighed by the bad.

Threatening to kill, however, is not the same as actually killing. Perhaps we are justified in *threatening* nuclear retaliation, so long as we do not intend to carry out our threat. That is, perhaps the morally appropriate deterrent strategy is bluffing. Naturally, we should not expect such an insincere threat to be credible once our moral reluctance became known to our adversary. The effectiveness of such a bluff depends on our adversary's belief that we would (or might) launch a retaliatory second strike in the event of nuclear attack. I do not believe that a policy based on such a bluff is acceptable. First, it would depend on deception—or at least dissimulation—for its effectiveness, and this may be impossible to achieve in an open society. Second, a deceptive policy is inconsistent with the values of an open society like ours. Third, it seems incredible that the most effective means of national defense should depend on such deception. Thus it is my belief that this approach will not salvage our deterrence practices.

Faced with such a conclusion, some moral philosophers would recommend unilateral nuclear disarmament. Though I cannot argue here against this alternative, I should note that I find it unacceptable for a number of reasons. The claims of some proponents of disarmament to the effect that the dangers of Soviet domination or Soviet nuclear blackmail are small seem to me to lack credibility.[1] And many cases for unilateral nuclear disarmament depend on such claims. Further, disarmament proposals usually assume a simultaneous build-up of conventional military forces (to deter conventional attack). But citizens of the Western alliance are notoriously unwilling to shoulder the costs of such a rearmament program. Proponents of unilateral disarmament often forget that nuclear weapons are inexpensive in comparison to conventional weapons and forces.

1. See Douglas P. Lackey, "Missiles and Morals: A Utilitarian Look at Nuclear Deterrence," *Philosophy and Public Affairs*, vol. 11 (1980), pp. 189–231; Russell Hardin, "Unilateral Versus Mutual Disarmament," Gregory S. Kavka, "Doubts About Unilateral Nuclear Disarmament," and Douglas P. Lackey, "Disarmament Revisited: A Reply to Kavka and Hardin," *Philosophy and Public Affairs*, vol. 12 (1983), pp. 236–54, 255–60, 261–65.

Given the unacceptability of unilateral nuclear disarmament, how can we justify nuclear deterrence? Nuclear deterrence involves threatening to kill directly massive numbers of innocents in the event of an enemy nuclear attack, an act not justified by the traditional doctrine of double effect. Is nuclear deterrence then morally impermissible? I shall argue that this is not the case.

Let me begin by stating clearly the moral principle that is involved in this issue. Nuclear deterrence involves threatening to kill directly massive numbers of innocents. Directly killing the innocent is thought to be morally wrong, at least in normal circumstances. The relevant moral principle would thus seem to be the following, which I will call principle P: It is wrong directly to kill innocent persons.

The terms involved in this principle should be understood as follows. An act of direct killing is one that is not an act of indirect killing as defined by the doctrine of double effect. A person is any creature that is owed some moral consideration. An innocent person is a person who is not threatening another. (Sometimes this is called the "causal" sense of innocence, in contrast to the "moral" or "juridical" sense, according to which innocence is equivalent to absence of guilt.) Thus, principle P prohibits the killing of nonthreatening persons except in those cases of indirect or unintentional killing justified by the doctrine of double effect.

According to the natural law tradition, killing the innocent directly is absolutely wrong, that is, it is impermissible whatever the consequences.[2] But I reject the interpretation of P as absolute. Interpreting P as absolute commits us to refrain from using (or threatening to use) nuclear weapons. Given what I have said above, interpreting the principle in this manner would commit us to bluffing or, more likely, to unilateral nuclear disarmament and that, I am assuming, is unacceptable in the present circumstances. Further, given that some deterrent strategies reduce considerably the likelihood of nuclear conflict[3] and that absolutist interpretations of P commit us to rejecting such strategies, then surely that is at least a partial reason for rejecting such interpretations.[4]

Does my rejection of the absolute interpretation of P commit me to interpreting P as *defeasible*? A moral principle is defeasible when it may be overridden by other moral considerations. Utilitarianism, for example, supposes that all of our duties are derived from the principle of maximizing the total quantity of the good, where the good is identified with happiness, well-being, or utility. According to such a view, all of our

2. See G.E.M. Anscombe, "Modern Moral Philosophy" and "War and Murder" in G.E.M. Anscombe, *Collected Philosophical Papers*, vol. 3 (Minneapolis: University of Minnesota Press, 1981), pp. 26–42, 51–61; Alan Donagan, *The Theory of Morality* (Chicago: University of Chicago Press, 1977); and Jeffrie G. Murphy, "The Killing of the Innocent," *The Monist*, vol. 57 (1973), pp. 527–50.

3. See Lackey, "Missiles and Morals." See also Gregory S. Kavka, "Deterrence, Utility, and Rational Choice," *Theory and Decision*, vol. 12 (1980), pp. 41–60.

4. If it is thought that the doctrine of double effect does not rule out counterforce retaliation, then the absolutist interpretation of P may commit us to counterforce deterrent strategies, and that would be most destabilizing in the current situation. (Such a move would in the present circumstances likely engender an arms race in space, something that does not appear to frighten the current United States administration.)

duties are defeasible, since whatever maximizes happiness in one situation may very well not do so in another.

Utilitarian interpretations of P are, of course, only one way of rendering the principle defeasible; other moral theories may do this as well. But understanding the inappropriateness of utilitarian accounts will set the stage for the interpretation of P that I wish to defend.

Utilitarianism would have us consider in our moral deliberations the welfare of all individuals that could be affected by our actions. Further, not only are we to do this, we are also to count their well-being equally with ours. Utilitarianism has often been criticized as too flexible a moral theory; depending on the circumstances, it can be said to justify too much that we think is wrong. It is not always clear that such criticisms are correct, but they seem beside the point here. Rather, what is striking about utilitarianism as it is applied to matters of conflict and war is not how flexible but how demanding a theory it is. After all, it requires us to count our enemy's welfare equally with our own.

Utilitarianism, as has often been noted, is a moral theory that takes a certain ideal that is at best suited for close friends or family and applies it to all persons. Countless critics have remarked on the inappropriateness of this transference. However, another point needs to be emphasized, and that is that utilitarianism is very irrational when applied to situations of major conflict, such as nuclear war. While most wars are not zero sum— that is, both sides have some interests in common—it is doubtful that any argument could be given for the rationality of accepting the principle of utility in all such situations, at least if we understand rationality as not requiring total self-sacrifice. After all, the interests in conflict may be too important to be compromised or abandoned so easily. It is one thing to commit oneself to the principle of utility in situations when others are themselves willing to accept the same principle, but it is entirely another matter to commit oneself to the principle of utility in a nonutilitarian world. I conclude, therefore, that the utilitarian interpretation of principle P as defeasible is not acceptable.

Normally, in moral theory it is thought that "absolute" and "defeasible" are contradictory terms. That is, it is assumed that if a principle is not absolute, then it must be defeasible, and vice versa. However, I want to argue that there are circumstances in which P is neither defeasible nor absolute.

The position I wish to defend is this: In certain circumstances respecting P would be irrational. In such circumstances, P (and other principles of justice)[5] is no longer rationally binding.[6] Thus, in such circum-

5. My concern in this essay is with justice. I am assuming that what is true of justice need not be true of the other virtues. For instance, the virtue of benevolence may be binding in situations where justice is not.

6. The notion of rationality I am using here is basically that widely used in the social sciences, especially in economics and game theory, i.e., a person is rational insofar as he maximizes the satisfaction of his preferences. I would want, however, to amend this conception in the manner suggested by David P. Gauthier in "Reason and Maximization," *Canadian Journal of Philosophy*, vol. 4 (1975), pp. 411–33, so as to handle certain types of problems of strategic interaction (namely, prisoners' dilemmas, for those readers familiar with these issues).

stances directly killing the innocent would not be unjust because nothing would be unjust.[7] These circumstances, which I shall call Hobbesian states of nature, are, I believe, exceedingly rare in the modern world, the behavior of nation-states to the contrary. However, an enemy nuclear attack would bring about such circumstances, or so I shall argue. Therefore, massive nuclear retaliation would not, in those circumstances, be unjust because during an enemy nuclear attack nothing would be unjust. P, on this account, would not be absolute, for it would not be wrong to do what P prohibits. But neither would P be defeasible: since considerations of justice would no longer be binding, there would be no considerations of justice that could override it. Let me now turn to defending these claims.

Faced with the apparent choice between interpreting P as absolute (as recommended by many natural law and natural rights theories) and the demand to accord equal weight to the welfare of the enemy (as recommended by utilitarianism), some moral philosophers counsel retreat into moral nihilism: in war, anything goes; nothing is prohibited. In the social sciences and in politics, such a position often goes under the name of "realism." But such talk is dubious, as well as dangerous. For one, it contradicts seemingly entrenched patterns of ordinary discourse.[8] In war, as well as at other times, most people attempt to justify their actions by reference to moral standards. It is extremely difficult to talk about war without using moral language; even slogans such as "war is hell" do not usually allow us to dispense with moral categories.

Equally important, however, is the danger of destabilization that comes from nihilism. Obviously, such a position reinforces mutual suspicion. At present the United States and the Soviet Union greatly distrust each other. Each appears to believe that the other is acquiring or already possesses offensive nuclear weapons. Should either party come to believe, or be reinforced in its belief, that the other thinks nothing is forbidden, then that party would find it difficult to trust the other to refrain from seeking a first-strike advantage. Assurance that the other side is capable and willing to impose constraints on its behavior is crucial to stabilization. Since abstaining from first-strike advantage is stabilizing, it is clear that a retreat to nihilism may have a significant destabilizing effect. In this context, the suspicion that the other side seeks to use allegedly defensive weapons for offensive, first-strike ends can only increase.

Nonetheless, the retreat to nihilism has an important grain of truth to it, and this is the truth expressed in Thomas Hobbes' account of the relations between nations. According to Hobbes, nations find themselves in a "state of nature" in which there are no binding moral obligations. Relations between nations thus are relations of power, unconstrained by moral rules. In a similar fashion, relations between individuals in a state of nature are also mere relations of power, unconstrained by moral considerations. The difference for Hobbes is that individuals have the possi-

---

7. The "nothing" will be qualified later, with regard to uninvolved third parties.
8. Essentially this is the argument of Michael Walzer, *Just and Unjust Wars* (New York: Basic Books, 1977).

bility of establishing an enforcer or sovereign and thus of escaping from their plight, while no such escape is possible in the world of nations.[9]

But Hobbes' account may be defective in two ways. First, it may be possible to accept his analysis of the problem facing rational individuals in a state of nature without accepting his solution of absolute and unconstrained sovereignty, that is, without accepting his view that only the establishment of an all-powerful and indivisible ruler can end the state of nature.[10] Second, it is not clear that Hobbes' account of international relations must be accepted.[11] I shall not pronounce on the accuracy of Hobbes' account in terms of the nations with which he was familiar in the seventeenth century, but nations today are interdependent in ways that transform their situation. Let me explain these two points.

According to contractarian ethics, relations of justice obtain only between parties that find themselves in certain situations. Following John Rawls, we may call these "circumstances of justice."[12] In this view, relations of justice exist only between parties that are interdependent in certain ways. Individuals in the circumstances of justice are roughly equal in physical and mental powers, and thus are unable to dominate one another and are vulnerable to attack; resources are moderately scarce (relative to needs and wants); needs and wants, although in conflict to some degree, are such as to allow for mutually beneficial interaction. The most important condition here for our purposes is that of mutual advantage: individuals find themselves in the circumstances of justice only if there exists the possibility of mutually beneficial interaction. But in the absence of possible mutual advantage, there is no place for justice since individuals have no reason to constrain their self-interested activity.

Cooperative interaction, as I shall define it, is mutually beneficial interaction made possible by constraints on self-interested behavior. Between interdependent nations today there appears to be at least some room for such interaction. Thus, contrary to Hobbes' account of international relations, modern nations meet one of the most important conditions for cooperative interaction. Assuming the remaining circumstances of justice obtain between nations, norms of cooperation such as Hobbes' first few laws of nature would be rationally binding on them.[13]

Such norms, however, would be binding on nations only insofar as others are willing to abide by them.[14] The problem in international rela-

9. Thomas Hobbes, *The Leviathan* (Harmondsworth: Penguin Books, 1968; 1651); see especially chapter 13.

10. See, for example, David Gauthier, *The Logic of Leviathan* (Oxford: Clarendon Press, 1969), especially chapter 4, section 4.

11. See H.L.A. Hart, *The Concept of Law* (Oxford: Clarendon Press, 1972), pp. 208–31.

12. See David Hume, "Enquiry Concerning the Principles of Morals," section 3, in *Enquiries*, 3rd ed., rev. by P. H. Nidditch (Oxford: Clarendon Press, 1975), and John Rawls, *A Theory of Justice* (Cambridge: Harvard University Press, 1971), pp. 126ff.

13. These laws require that one pursue peace, be willing to give up an equal amount of natural liberty on the condition that others do so as well, and keep one's agreements. Hobbes believed that the laws of nature are summarized in the counsel "Do not that to another, which thou wouldest not have done to thy selfe." Hobbes, *Leviathan*, chapters 14–15.

14. "Be willing when others are too. . . ." Hobbes, *Leviathan*, chapter 14.

tions, of course, is to obtain assurances that others are willing to abide by these norms of cooperation. Between nations, there is no absolute sovereign capable of impartial enforcement of agreements and some system of enforcement is necessary if cooperation is to be rational.

Hobbes assumed that the requisite international mechanism would have to be a supranational sovereign. Since no such international sovereign exists, he concluded that norms of cooperation could not be enforced between nations. But this is a mistake. In many relations between individuals where police protection is unavailable, norms of cooperation are often adequately enforced by the parties themselves. Indeed, the threat to retaliate can often provide adequate enforcement without recourse to other measures. In the same way, we may suppose that threats to retaliate when leveled among nations can also provide the requisite enforcement mechanism that makes cooperation possible. If such threats are morally permissible, then we need not search for an international sovereign to ensure international cooperation.

What strategies promise to stabilize the current situation and provide an enforcement mechanism that can make cooperative interaction between nations possible? Let us suppose that

> [i]n the long run, insofar as nuclear weapons are concerned, what each superpower needs for the deterrence of nuclear and conventional attacks on itself and its main allies is the capacity for assured destruction . . . and a limited capacity for actual warfare. A complete counter-force capability would be disastrous for crisis stability if it consisted of vulnerable forces; and even a complete invulnerable counter-force capability might incite the opponent to strike first in order to use his vulnerable weapons.[15]

Thus, we might suppose that the United States should renounce a first strike on the condition that the Soviet Union does so as well.[16] Adoption of the recommendations quoted above—maintaining the capacity for assured destruction—would convince each party that the other renounces striking first and would provide the threat that makes cooperative interaction possible.

But a threat to retaliate with massive strikes is an acceptable means of deterrence only if it does not violate a basic norm of justice like principle P. Such threats will not violate basic norms of justice when norms of justice no longer bind, i.e., when cooperation between the two parties no longer is possible. But in the event of an enemy nuclear attack, cooperative relations have in fact ended. In such circumstances the parties are back in a Hobbesian state of nature and norms of justice no longer bind.[17]

15. Albert Carnesale, Paul Doty, Stanley Hoffman, Samuel P. Huntington, Joseph S. Nye, Jr., and Scott Sagan, *Living with Nuclear Weapons* (New York: Bantam Books, 1983), p. 250.

16. See McGeorge Bundy, George Kennan, Robert McNamara, and Gerard Smith, "Nuclear Weapons and the Atlantic Alliance," *Foreign Affairs*, vol. 60 (1982), pp. 753–68. Of course, renouncing a first strike would require a change in NATO defense policy and an unpopular rise in European conventional defense spending.

17. In the event of an enemy nuclear attack, not only have cooperative relations in fact ended, but cooperative relations are no longer possible on terms acceptable to rational agents. This latter point is controversial and is not a feature of Hobbes' contractarian theory.

In such a state of nature, the prohibition on the direct killing of the innocent, like all other principles of justice, becomes a mere counsel of nonmoral prudence. Threatening an adversary with countervalue retaliation in the event of a nuclear attack is therefore permissible because in the circumstances in which such a threat would be carried out it would not be impermissible to do so. I am assuming here, of course, that a *threat* to do X in circumstances C is morally permissible if *doing* X in those circumstances is not morally impermissible.[18]

In the account above I have assumed that the prohibition against killing the innocent directly is part of an acceptable contractarian morality. Rational agents, in a contractarian choice situation, would find such a prohibition mutually advantageous. Further, I am supposing that this prohibition is a basic principle, one that binds as long as contractarian morality is in force. A morality is "in force," I shall say, when rational agents are in the "circumstances of justice" and are not forced back into a state of nature; in those situations, such a morality is binding on rational agents.

Principle P, then, binds rational agents up until the point at which they are forced back to a state of nature. It is never permissible, I shall

Cooperative relations presuppose a baseline for determining terms of cooperation, and I am supposing that such a baseline precludes worsening the position of the other side prior to negotiating a cooperative agreement. This account is developed in David Gauthier, "Morals by Agreement" (manuscript, University of Pittsburgh, no date); see also Robert Nozick, *Anarchy, State and Utopia* (New York: Basic Books, 1974) for a noncontractarian account of such a condition on cooperation. Should another party first worsen one's position before endeavoring to cooperate, then cooperation is no longer possible on terms acceptable to rational agents. In other words, cooperation is rational only from a baseline of noncoercion.

Let me expand these remarks somewhat. Contractarian moralists suppose that principles of justice are rationally acceptable only if it is advantageous to live in a world where individuals constrain their self-interested behavior. Thus, to be acceptable to all members of a society, such principles must be mutually beneficial. Advantage here is to be determined in reference to some nonmoral state; otherwise, no claim could be made about the nonmoral rationality of moral practices that was not begging the question. Hobbes supposes that the baseline from which contractarian moralities are determined is one in which individuals interact noncooperatively. Thus, if one party, holding a pistol to another's head, secures the latter's "consent" to enslavement, genuine moral obligations are created; the deal is mutually advantageous. Now we need not follow Hobbes here; we need not suppose that such a baseline is the proper starting point for the conventionalist's construction of morality. Would it in fact be rational to comply with an "agreement" that had been secured by coercion? Clearly not, at least once the means of coercion had been withdrawn. Thus we shall say that the proper baseline for adoption of principles of justice is one of noninteraction. Such a standpoint precludes one party worsening the position of another immediately prior to the agreement. I assume, then, that the baseline of contractarian cooperation precludes coercion.

18. I am assuming merely that if an act is not impermissible, then neither is threatening that act. I also think that sincerely threatening an act is not impermissible if and only if the act itself is not impermissible. But this is a stronger and more controversial principle, and my argument in this paper does not require it. On this issue, see Gregory S. Kavka, "Some Paradoxes of Deterrence," *Journal of Philosophy*, vol. 75 (1978), pp. 285–302; David P. Gauthier, "Deterrence, Maximization, and Rationality" (manuscript, University of Pittsburgh, 1983); and Gregory S. Kavka, "Deterrent Intentions and Retaliatory Actions" (manuscript, University of California, Irvine, 1983). Note also the analogy with punishment: one may legitimately threaten another with some specified punishment should this person commit some action, if so punishing would not be impermissible in the event that individual commits the specified action.

assume, to return unilaterally to a state of nature since this would violate Hobbes' first law of nature, which is to seek peace and follow it. But should another nation unilaterally return to a state of nature, e.g., by launching a nuclear attack, then P (and all other principles of justice) become mere counsels of nonmoral prudence. Thus, massive retaliation is not, under such circumstances, morally impermissible, and by extension a threat to retaliate massively is also morally permissible.

Such an account of P would not justify the killing of the innocent in any situation of conflict. The account that I have developed shows how P is suspended in certain situations, namely when an adversary unilaterally returns to a Hobbesian state of nature. In the event, say, of an enemy nuclear attack, the United States (or the Soviet Union) would no longer be bound by P. This does not mean, however, that P is suspended in all conflicts. For surely not all wars involve the complete return to a Hobbesian state of nature. In most wars, there is an important residue of mutual interest, enough to generate binding rules of conduct—those prohibiting certain weapons, protecting noncombatants, governing the treatment of prisoners, and so on. Thus, this argument is not a justification of terror or obliteration bombing, to cite just two examples. For instance, it is doubtful that the Allies during the latter years of World War II were in a situation in which P was suspended.[19] Certainly the American bombings of Tokyo and Hiroshima and Nagasaki could not be justified by the account I offer here; nothing has been said about suspending P in the pursuit of the unconditional surrender of an enemy state. Mere expediency in the conduct of war would not suffice to justify suspending P.

Nevertheless, an important objection deserves to be considered. In the event of an enemy attack, I have argued that massive countervalue retaliation is not prohibited because P (and other principles of justice) no longer would be in force. Thus killing the innocent would not be wrong (or right). Now someone might grant that we would be in a state of nature with regard to the Soviet leaders and other officials involved in the decision to attack, but demur at the idea that innocent Soviet citizens would be in a similar position. After all, the inhabitants of uninvolved third countries would not be placed in a state of nature by Soviet aggression against us, so we would not be relieved of the prohibition against attacking them. Why should Soviet children, for example, be different?

Such an objection to my argument is difficult to meet. I do not wish to argue that all persons are plunged back into a state of nature by enemy aggression and that we would not be acting wrongly were we to use the occasion to drop bombs on other peoples. Yet I do want to hold that we would not be acting wrongly to retaliate against innocent Soviet citizens in the event of a Soviet attack.

May we deter, for instance, an enemy nuclear attack by threatening some third party about which enemy leaders happen to care? Would the

19. Although it is possible that the British were in precisely such a situation in the early years of World War II and that they were only then justified in suspending P and initiating the bombing of German cities. This does not appear to have been the case with the atomic bombings of Hiroshima and Nagasaki. See Walzer, *Just and Unjust Wars*, pp. 255ff.

inhabitants of this otherwise uninvolved nation also be in a state of nature with respect to us in the event of an enemy nuclear attack?

According to my reasoning, members of society A are not prohibited from deterring attack by society B by threatening to kill innocent members of that society. Is A, however, not prohibited from deterring B by threatening to kill members of C, where C is an uninvolved third country? Should I agree, then am I not supposing that members of B are in some way collectively responsible for the aggressive acts of their leaders? It is hard to conceive of a plausible account of collective responsibility that could hold Soviet children responsible for the aggressive acts of Kremlin officials. Yet I must be able to distinguish between innocent Soviets and innocent third parties since I wish to hold that the latter are not placed in a state of nature by the aggressive actions of Soviet leaders. A reply to this objection requires further analysis of the nature of contractarian moral relations between individuals and groups.

Two individuals who find themselves in the contractarian circumstances of justice and who directly interact with one another are bound to one another by obligations of justice. This much is granted by all contractarian moral theories. What if the individuals are in the circumstances of justice yet do not directly interact with one another? Suppose two individuals, Ann and Boris, stand to benefit mutually from cooperative interaction yet do not interact directly because they live very far apart, Ann in the United States, Boris in the Soviet Union. Yet the two are in the circumstances of justice. While Ann and Boris do not stand to benefit mutually from direct cooperative interaction (until they directly interact), they do stand to benefit from indirect cooperative interaction as members of different societies.

Cooperative relations can be direct or indirect. Obligations of justice can thus bind individuals directly, as natural individuals, or indirectly, as members of a group. Ann and Boris each have obligations of the first sort to the individuals with which they directly interact, perhaps most members of their respective societies. They have only obligations of the second sort to one another. These latter obligations they have by virtue of their membership in societies that stand to benefit from cooperative interaction. Obligations of international justice thus bind individuals only as citizens of a society; obligations of individual justice bind natural individuals.

Suppose that cooperative relations between two countries break down due to a nuclear attack of one upon the other. Then Ann and Boris would find themselves in a Hobbesian state of nature with respect to one another. While it is possible that they could be able to return to civil society with greater ease than their aggressive leaders, nonetheless relations of justice no longer obtain between them.

Note, however, that if Boris were visiting Ann in the United States when his leaders launched an attack, then each would be bound by justice to one another as natural individuals, even though neither would be bound to one another as members of different societies. Ann, or any other American, would be bound by justice not to kill Boris, assuming that he is innocent in the relevant sense.

What distinguishes Soviet citizens from third parties is that we remain bound by justice to the latter even when our obligations to the former are dissolved. In the absence of aggressive behavior on their part, relations of justice continue between the United States and third party nations, thus rendering nuclear strikes against them morally impermissible.

I shall briefly note an implication of this reply to the objection just considered. If we remain bound by justice to uninvolved third parties, then the doctrine of double effect (which I accept) obligates us to minimize the adverse side effects of nuclear retaliation on third parties. Were a massive nuclear retaliation against the Soviet Union to destroy human life on the planet, then the fourth condition of the doctrine of double effect would prohibit it. Note, though, that our obligations, according to my account, would be to the third parties and not to the Soviet citizens. My argument thus places some moral restrictions on the nature of a permissible retaliatory strike against an enemy nuclear attack. Such retaliation could not directly kill innocent third parties.

I have sketched a contractarian account of the moral prohibition on the killing of the innocent. If my account should prove to be sound, then I shall have provided reason to believe that threatening massive slaughter of the innocent is not a morally prohibited response to an enemy nuclear threat. Insofar as such an account is necessary in order to justify nuclear deterrence, which is under attack from both the right and the left, then the argument may prove a useful contribution to current debates.

## ACKNOWLEDGMENTS

This essay is essentially a simplified version of the position developed in "A Contractarian Defense of Nuclear Deterrence," forthcoming in a special issue of *Ethics*, vol. 95. I am grateful to Gregory Kavka, Alan Vick, and Manuel Velasquez for comments and criticism, as well as to the participants at the various lectures and conferences where earlier versions of the essay were presented. I am also grateful to David Gauthier and Gregory Kavka for the use they have allowed me to make of their unpublished writings.

# CHAPTER EIGHT
# THE ETHICS OF SUICIDE

Well over a thousand people commit suicide every day. This means that each year a population equivalent to that of the city of Columbus, Ohio, kills itself. And the figures for those who attempt to kill themselves are even higher, estimated at about five million each year. In the United States alone there are three times more suicides than murders.[1]

The particular reasons why an individual will attempt to commit suicide vary. In 1980, Dr. Edwin S. Shneidman, a psychologist, published the following interview with a young woman who tried to kill herself when she was already in the hospital recovering from her first suicide attempt. In the interview his patient describes what happened to her in the hospital:

> Well, after that I was out of danger and they pretty much let me wander around the hospital as I pleased. The next day there was some question about my husband letting me return home. . . . it was sort of like, well, you go and find a place to stay, and there was no place for me to stay. . . . All of a sudden there I was out in the middle of nowhere without any money, and

---

1. For additional statistics and social science research on suicide, see Jacques Choron, *Suicide* (New York: Scribner's, 1972); L. D. Hankoff and Bernice Einsidler, eds., *Suicide: Theory and Clinical Practice* (Littleton, Mass.: PSG Publishing, 1979); Gene Lester and David Lester, *Suicide: The Gamble with Death* (Englewood Cliffs, N.J.: Prentice-Hall, 1971); Louis Wekstein, *Handbook of Suicidology: Principles, Problems, and Practice* (New York: Brunner/Mazel, 1979).

my husband wasn't going to let me come back to the house and I was desperate. And then I went into a terrible state. . . . He kept saying, "I'm not going to let you know, I'm going to keep you on tenterhooks. You should learn what it's like to wait and to have patience." So that at this point I was supposed to be making these arrangements myself. I could barely even speak, you know. . . . I could barely remember my name. . . . And I thought, My God, in heaven, I can hardly even . . . and I was not functioning at all and these people are going to throw me into the street. . . . I was so desperate, I felt, My God, I can't face this thing . . . being thrown out on the street. And everything was like a terrible sort of whirlpool of confusion. And I thought to myself, there's only one thing I can do, I just have to lose consciousness. That's the only way to get away from it. The only way . . . , I thought, was to jump off something good and high. . . . I just figured I had to get outside, but the windows were all locked. So I . . . . slipped out. No one saw me. And I got to the other building by walking across the catwalk thing, sure that someone would see me, you know, out of all those windows. . . . And I just walked around until I found this open staircase. As soon as I saw it, I just made a beeline right up to it. And then I got to the fifth floor and everything just got very dark all of a sudden, and all I could see was this balcony. Everything around it just blacked out. It was just like a circle. That was all I could see, just the balcony . . . and I went over it. . . . (Sobbing) I was so desperate. Just desperation. And the horribleness and the quietness of it. The quiet. Everything became so quiet. There was no sound. And I sort of went into slow motion as I climbed over that balcony. I let go and it was like I was floating. I blacked out. I don't remember any part of the fall. . . . And then, when I woke up . . . I was in an intensive care unit and I was looking at the patterns on the ceiling.[2]

Dr. Shneidman's research also uncovered several suicide notes written by people immediately before they killed themselves. One of these was by Elton Hammond, an Englishman who never quite managed to acquire the recognition he wanted:

To the charge of self-murder I plead not guilty. For there is no guilt in what I have done. Self-murder is a contradiction in terms. If the King who retires from his throne is guilty of high treason; if the man who takes money out of his own coffers and spends it is a thief; if he who burns his own hayrick is guilty of arson; or he who scourges himself of assault and battery, then he who throws up his own life may be guilty of murder,—if not, not. If anything is a man's own, it is surely his life. . . . How we came by the foolish law which considers suicide as felony I don't know; I find no warrant for it in Philosophy. . . . I am free today and avail myself of my liberty. I cannot be a good man, and prefer death to being a bad one. . . . I take my leave of you.[3]

These two remarkable documents, one a troubled young woman's account of her suicide attempt and the other a seemingly reasonable man's carefully composed farewell note, graphically illustrate the moral dilemmas surrounding the two broad approaches to suicide that have

2. Edwin Shneidman, *Voices of Death*. Copyright © 1980 by Edwin S. Shneidman. Quoted by permission of Bantam Books, Inc. All Rights Reserved.
3. Quoted in ibid., pp. 54–55.

emerged in contemporary discussions.[4] One view sees suicide as an evil or an illness that should be prevented, the other regards it as a rational option based on a so-called "right to die" that every human being should be left free to exercise.

Those who advocate the view that suicide is an evil or an illness often point to the fact that, like the young woman who jumped from the fifth floor balcony of the hospital, many suicides are undergoing periods of severe psychological disturbance. A recent study concluded that 93 percent of completed suicides exhibit evidence of mental illness, including depression (70 percent), alcoholism (15 percent), and other mental disorders (8 percent).[5] Severe depression is evident in the distressed voice of the young woman who was abandoned by her husband when she most desperately needed him and who was convinced that her choices had narrowed to a single option. Many people have argued that such desperately confused individuals do not really want to die, although they mistakenly believe they do. Such suicides may be motivated by a belief that suicide will lead to a better existence or that after suicide the person will experience the satisfactions of having others feel bad about the death. Such acts may also be an unconscious appeal for help. These people do not want to end their lives so much as to change them, so their acts should not be seen as fully rational attempts to pursue their real wishes. Therefore, these suicidal acts should not be condemned but excused, and steps should be taken to save potential suicides from themselves and to help them achieve what they really want in more realistic ways. Suicide prevention is therefore a morally justified way of dealing with the potential suicide.

Advocates of the "right to die" view, however, have questioned several of the assumptions underlying the preventive approach to suicide. First, they have argued with the way in which suicide is usually defined. The irrational acts of psychologically disturbed persons, they maintain, should not even be counted as "suicides." In their opinion, we should limit the term to refer to the deliberate and rational act of the mentally competent person who freely and knowingly chooses to end his own life. Second, advocates of the right to die view have claimed that such rational suicides are morally justified. In this way they often appeal to the sort of considerations proposed in the suicide note in which Elton Hammond suggested that the right to do away with oneself is based on a moral principle of freedom. As Hammond wrote, "I am free" morally to commit suicide and am justified if I "avail myself of my liberty." In this view, it would be wrong to interfere with the person's suicide attempt because it is wrong to interfere with a person's free and rational choices.

4. For an excellent overview of the moral issues surrounding suicide, see Margaret Pabst Battin, *Ethical Issues in Suicide* (Englewood Cliffs, N.J.: Prentice-Hall, 1982). For an anthology of articles on these topics, see Margaret Pabst Battin and David J. Mayer, eds., *Suicide: The Philosophical Issues* (New York: St. Martin's, 1980).

5. B. M. Barraclough, J. Bunch, B. Nelson, and P. Sainsbury, "A Hundred Cases of Suicide: Clinical Aspects," *British Journal of Psychiatry,* vol. 124 (1975), pp. 355–73.

However, many critics have held that even if there are a few cases where the prospective suicide is not mentally ill, the act itself should still be prevented because it is immoral. Plato and other philosophers have argued that this is so because human beings belong to God and it is immoral to destroy someone else's possession; others, like Aquinas, have stated that suicide violates our "natural inclination" toward life; still others feel that suicide is wrong because it is an injury to friends, or society.

There are, then, three main philosophical questions associated with the issue of suicide. First, how should suicide be defined? Second, is it always immoral for a rational, mentally competent person to commit suicide? Third, what should be our response to those who attempt to commit suicide?

The articles that follow examine these various issues. The first, "Suicide and Causing One's Own Death" by Germain Grisez and Joseph Boyle, begins by defining the term "suicide." Grisez and Boyle claim that intention is an essential component of the meaning of "suicide in the strict sense," and they argue on the basis of natural law ethics that this cannot morally be justified. Grisez and Boyle distinguish suicide in the strict sense from the suicidal behavior of a person "who is suffering severe psychological stress," and from the self-destructive act of a person who does not want to die but who believes that it is "morally required" for him to do something that will lead to his own death. Such suicidal behavior and such self-destructive acts are not necessarily suicide in the strict sense, and so they are not necessarily immoral. Self-destructive acts, however, can become immoral if they involve a disregard for basic human goods, especially the good of one's own life.

The second selection, "Duties of Human Beings to Themselves," is written by Alan Donagan, a Kantian. Donagan appeals to Kant's principles to argue that "it is impermissible for any human being to take his own life at will." However, he claims that there are "circumstances in which suicide would be permissible." This would be the case, he suggests, if a person killed himself to avoid "unendurable torture" or "a life unfitting to a rational creature." Suicide might also be permissible to save the lives of others or to escape "dehumanization."

In the third article, "The Morality and Rationality of Suicide," Richard B. Brandt takes a utilitarian approach. Brandt argues that it might "maximize the long-run welfare of everybody affected if people were taught that there is a moral obligation to avoid suicide." But the bulk of his discussion is devoted to whether "suicide is rational for a person from the point of view of his own welfare." He argues that a person contemplating suicide should consider his future preferences and determine whether he can expect more "utility" from a future in which he is dead or from a future in which he continues to live. Brandt warns that a person making such a decision will tend to commit various errors as a result of his "depressed" state and he suggests that it is very difficult to make such a decision objectively. Brandt concludes with a discussion of the obligations others have toward a person contemplating suicide.

# SUICIDE AND CAUSING ONE'S OWN DEATH

*Germain Grisez and Joseph M. Boyle, Jr.*

In the strict sense one kills a person when, having considered bringing about a person's death as something one could do, one commits oneself to doing it by adopting this proposal instead of some alternative and by undertaking to execute it. By definition killing in the strict sense is an action contrary to the good of life. The adoption of a proposal to bring about someone's death is incompatible with respect for this good. Thus every act which is an act of killing in the strict sense is immoral. No additional circumstance or condition can remove this immorality. . . .

We turn now to the consideration of cases in which one brings about one's own death. Even in ordinary language some ethically significant distinctions are made in speaking of this, for one does not call "suicide" all cases in which someone causes his or her own death. Most people who consider suicide immoral do not class martyrs and heroes as suicides, since "suicide" suggests an act of killing oneself. Yet not all who commit suicide do a moral act of killing in the strict sense. . . .

In cases in which suicide is an act of killing in the strict sense the proposal to kill oneself is among the proposals one considers in deliberation, and this proposal is adopted by choice as preferable to alternatives. For example, a person who for some reason is suffering greatly might think: "I wish I no longer had to suffer as I am suffering. If I were dead, my suffering would be at an end. But I am not likely to die soon. I could kill myself. But I fear death and what might follow after it. I could put up with my misery and perhaps find some other way out." One thinking in this way is deliberating. In saying "I could kill myself" suicide is proposed. If this proposal is adopted, one's moral act is killing in the strict sense. As in other instances this act is incompatible with the basic good of human life, and it cannot morally be justified, regardless of what else might be the case.

One can propose to kill oneself without saying to oneself "I could kill myself." One might say something which one would accept as equivalent in meaning: "I could destroy myself," "I could rub myself out," or something of the sort. Again, one might say something which one would admit amounts to "I could kill myself" although not equivalent in meaning to it, such as "I could shoot myself," when what one has in mind is shooting oneself in the head and thereby causing death, not merely shooting oneself to cause a wound.

From such suicidal acts which clearly are cases of killing oneself in the strict sense we distinguish deadly deeds people do upon themselves which are not cases of killing in the strict sense. Some of these suicidal deeds are not moral acts at all; others are acts which execute some choice other than a proposal to kill oneself.

A person who is suffering severe psychological stress, even though not mentally ill, can reach a point at which deliberation and choice become impossible. Perhaps the thought of suicide has come back again and again, and the proposal has been rejected as often as it has returned. But at some point the possibility of a deadly deed against oneself can become obsessive. Without one's own choice every alternative is blocked from consciousness. Only one thought remains: "I will kill myself." A person in this state of mind is not necessarily insane. Moreover, the performance which follows carries out a conscious project. But it is not a moral act of killing in the strict sense, because the project is not a proposal adopted by choice. It is an obsessive thought whose appeal draws the individual into its execution without a personal commitment.

As for the more complex and confused states of mind from which suicidal behavior usually emerges, no one can begin to judge the moral quality of another and hardly can begin to judge oneself. A person who is upright certainly will not lightly play with thoughts of suicide and will not easily adopt any ambiguous proposal which could imply that one's own death be brought about. One who has come to disrespect human life in other instances, however, might easily do so.

The impossibility of judging, it should be noticed, is double-edged. People who have killed themselves ought not to be condemned and despised. But people who are contemplating killing themselves ought not to be reassured that such a deed would carry no grave moral responsibility. The innocence of the latter can be ascertained no more than the guilt of the former.

Some deadly deeds against oneself execute choices which are not suicidal choices. One might believe that some fundamental commitment one previously made demands that one here and now kill oneself; perhaps one has so perfectly integrated this commitment that one proceeds with no further deliberation and choice to do what seems necessary and inevitable. For example, a person who believes in God might believe that God is here and now commanding suicide. Given sufficiently blind faith, such an individual might not think of disobeying. Similarly, those in certain cultures where ritual self-destruction is expected in certain situations perhaps carry out the ritual without considering breaking with received customs. . . .

In cases such as these the morally relevant choice and the locus of responsibility is not in respect to the self-destructive deed, about which there was no choice at all, but in respect to the acceptance of the religion or culture which demands such deeds. And even this acceptance might have been voluntary not by being the content of a proposal adopted by choice but only by being uncritically accepted by a person who could and should have examined more carefully the cultural forms which were handed down.

In addition to properly suicidal acts and to deadly deeds against oneself which are not acts of killing in the strict sense, there are still other cases in which individuals contribute to the causation of their own deaths by acts which are morally significant but which in no way execute proposals which are properly suicidal. Typical martyrs lay down their lives. The death could be avoided if the martyr were willing to do something believed wrong or to leave unfulfilled some duty which is accepted as compelling. But the martyr refuses to avoid death by compromise or evasion of duty. Such persons do only what they believe to be morally required; the consequent loss of their own lives is willingly accepted by martyrs, neither sought nor chosen as a means to anything.

The martyr reasons somewhat as follows: "I would like to please everyone and to stay alive. But they are demanding of me that I do what I believe to be wrong or that I omit doing what I believe to be my sacred mission. They threaten me with death if I do not meet their demands. But if I were to comply with their threat, I would be doing evil in order that the good of saving my life might follow from it. This I may not do. Therefore, I must stand as long as I can in accord with my conscience, even though they are likely to kill me or torture me into submission."

Someone who does not understand the martyr's reasoning is likely to consider the martyr a suicide. But martyrs who reason thus do not propose to bring about their own deaths. The martyr bears witness to a profound commitment, first of all before the persecutors themselves. The latter can and in the martyr's view should accept this testimony and approve the rightness of the commitment. The martyr's refusal to give in does not bring about the persecutor's act of killing; the martyr only fails to win over the persecutor and to forestall the deadly deed.

Not all who cause their own deaths as a demonstration of commitment are typical martyrs. A war protestor might propose: "I wish to make clear the horror of war. I could douse myself with gasoline and set myself afire." Someone entertaining this proposal might admit that it is suicidal. If so, the execution of the proposal, adopted by choice, would be an act of killing in the strict sense. But if the suicidal character of this proposal were not admitted, the clearheadedness of deliberation might be questioned. The very point of the proposal seems to be that the horror of this manner of dying will emphatically communicate the horror of the war being protested. If this is so, the proposal is to kill oneself in the service of peace, and the adoption of this means cannot be consistent with respect for the good of human life. Of course, it is quite possible for an upright person to be terribly confused.

Certain nonsuicidal acts which bring about an individual's own death would be held to be morally wrong by most people. For example, a daredevil might accept very high risks of death carrying out performances which do not involve great skill or other excellent qualities. He might do this in order to create a sensation by pandering to morbid curiosity and hoping to acquire great wealth with little effort.

While not proposing to kill himself, while indeed hoping to survive to enjoy the wealth, the daredevil seems clearly to have an immoral attitude toward the good of human life. If he brings about his death, he is not a suicide, but he bears a grave moral responsibility because of his disregard for the goodness of his own life.

In what ways might acts which are not suicidal but are self-destructive, in results be immoral?

In the first place, such acts remove an individual from human community and in doing so are likely to leave behind some unfulfilled responsibilities. The shock of anyone's death always creates a certain burden and hardship for others, especially when the death comes about violently and seems avoidable. Moreover, the example of disrespect for life affects other people who are tempted to destroy themselves or to kill others. Bringing about one's own death, in other words, serves as a bad example.

In the second place, those who unnecessarily cause their own deaths are taking an irreversible step into darkness. A nonbeliever will not accept concerns about an afterlife. But nonbelief cannot eliminate Hamlet's perhaps: "perhaps to dream." It is presumptuous to suppose that one knows that there can be nothing to fear after death.

In the third place, even if there is no offense against others in bringing about one's death unnecessarily and even if the act is not the execution of a suicidal proposal, still such an act seems to undermine morality in a radical way. In bringing about one's death one removes oneself from the range of the primal demand: to serve human goods, to do what one can, to communicate human meaning to every aspect of life and the world. Perhaps this point is what Wittgenstein—himself tormented by a temptation to commit suicide—meant when he wrote that if suicide is allowed, everything is allowed, and he added, "This throws light on the nature of ethics, for suicide is, so to speak, the elementary sin."

Of course, we hold that suicide which is killing in the strict sense is necessarily immoral simply because it violates the basic good of human life. One who deliberately chooses to end his or her own life constitutes by this commitment a self-murderous self. But considerations which tell against even nonsuicidal acts which bring about a person's own death also argue against the moral justifiability of suicidal acts, which execute a proposal to destroy one's own life.

# DUTIES OF HUMAN BEINGS TO THEMSELVES

*Alan Donagan*

I take the fundamental principle of that part of traditional morality which is independent of any theological presupposition to have been expressed in the scriptural commandment, "Thou shalt love thy neighbor as thyself," understanding one's neighbor to be any fellow human being, and love to be a matter, not of feeling, but of acting in ways in which human beings as such can choose to act. The philosophical sense of this commandment was correctly expressed by Kant in his formula that one act so that one treats humanity always as an end and never as a means only.

Since treating a human being, in virtue of its rationality, as an end in itself, is the same as respecting it as a rational creature, Kant's formula of the fundamental principle may be restated in a form more like that of the scriptural commandment that is its original: *Act always so that you respect every human being, yourself or another, as being a rational creature.* And, since it will be convenient that the fundamental principle of the system to be developed be formulated in terms of the concept of permissibility analysed in the preceding section, the canonical form in which that principle will hereafter be cited is: *It is impermissible not to respect every human being, oneself or any other, as a rational creature.* . . . That each human being has duties to himself follows immediately from the fundamental principle; for if it is impermissible not to respect every human being as a rational creature, it is impermissible not to respect oneself as such. As we shall see, the relations which human beings can have to one another are more complex than those they can have to themselves. But they can injure or hurt themselves; and they can take care of themselves, and cultivate their various capacities. Their duties to themselves are classifiable by reference to these powers.

The worst physical injury anybody can do to himself is to kill himself, that is, to commit suicide. Yet there are reasons for which people do kill themselves; and an important question in common morality is whether it is permissible to do so. A possible view, which the Stoics maintained with respect to sages, is that any human being may quit life as he or she pleases. So stated, it is untenable. It seems evident that if one is to respect oneself as a rational creature, one may not hold one's life cheap, as something to be taken at will. Here the Jewish and Christian repudiation of the Stoic position is plainly correct. Conceding, then, that *it is impermissible for any human being to take his own life at will*, it is necessary to inquire whether there are any circumstances at all in which it is permissible.

From Alan Donagan, *The Theory of Morality* (Chicago: University of Chicago Press, 1977), pp. 65–66, 76–79. Copyright © 1977 the University of Chicago.

An opinion sometimes advanced is that the precepts with respect to killing oneself are exactly parallel to those with respect to killing others: so that killing oneself is impermissible only when it is self-murder. And, presuming murder to killing the objectively or materially innocent, most of the circumstances in which killing another is not murder cannot hold for killing oneself; for nobody need kill himself in order to defend himself, or others, or his society, against an attack from himself—all he need do is call off the attack. However, one circumstance traditionally acknowledged by Jews and Christians to be a justification for killing another, namely, that one be an executioner carrying out a lawful capital sentence, would seem to justify suicide also: at least in a jurisdiction in which, sentence of death having been passed, the culprit is permitted to carry it out.

Yet both Jews and Christians have been reluctant to draw this conclusion. In the case of Jews, the reason has been religious. For, as David Daube has pointed out, rabbinical authority held suicide to be forbidden, not by the prohibition of murder in the Mosaic decalogue, but by a revelation to Noah, "Surely your blood of your lives I will require," which was read as implying that it was for God to determine when a man should die, and not for the man himself. It was on this ground that the martyr Rabbi Hanina ben Teradion refused to shorten his sufferings when he was being tortured to death.

Nor can the traditional Christian denial that it is ever permissible to kill oneself be rationally justified on any other ground. Consider Kant's unqualified declaration:

> Man cannot renounce his personality so long as he is a subject of duty, hence so long as he lives. . . . To destroy the subject of morality in one's own person is to root out the existence of morality itself from the world; and yet morality is an end in itself. Consequently, to dispose of oneself as a mere means to an arbitrary end is to abase humanity in one's person.

Here the *ignoratio elenchi* is patent. For to carry out a lawful judicial sentence upon oneself is not to dispose of oneself as a mere means to an arbitrary end. What Kant wrote is only intelligible as expressing the religious conviction that to take one's own life is to repudiate one's existence as a divine creation.

Setting aside religious considerations of this kind, and confining ourselves to those that are purely moral, there are clear reasons for concluding that there may be circumstances in which suicide would be permissible but in which killing another would not. For suicide cannot be against the will of the person killed, whereas killing another can. To kill another for his own good, but against his will, fails to respect him as a rational creature, because respecting a being as a rational creature is respecting him as autonomous—as having the right, subject to the moral law, to decide for himself what his own good is, and how to pursue it. The purely moral question, then, reduces to this: Are there circumstances in which a human being would not fail to respect himself as a rational creature by killing himself? If there are, it will be permissible in those circumstances for him to kill himself, and for another to help him, although not to kill him against his will.

A preponderance of Jewish discussions of this subject acknowledge the permissibility of killing oneself when an external force one is powerless to resist either (1) imposes on one a choice between denying one's fundamental practical allegiance (in particular, one's religious faith) and suffering death or unendurable torture, or (2) credibly threatens to force one into a life unfitting to a rational creature, such as a life of enforced prostitution, or of any other form of dehumanizing slavery. There appears to be no reason to conclude that, in circumstances of either kind, killing oneself would fail to respect oneself as a rational creature. On the contrary, not to kill oneself would be either heroic or cowardly.

Suicide has also been held to be permissible when it is either (1) to ensure the lives or the fundamental well-being of others, or (2) to escape a condition of natural dehumanization.

Three kinds of case in which suicide appears to be necessary to ensure the lives of others may be mentioned. (i) Those represented by the memorable Stoic example of an overloaded boat, which will sink unless some of its load is jettisoned but the entire load of which is innocent human beings. If nobody can be saved unless somebody goes overboard, and if to go overboard would be suicide, then suicide in such circumstances would certainly not be contrary to the respect due to humanity as such. (ii) Those in which a disease makes a man dangerous to others, whether by infection or by making him insanely violent. Kant describes a case of the latter kind.

> A man who had been bitten by a mad dog already felt hydrophobia, and he explained, in a letter he left, that since, so far as he knew, the disease was incurable, he killed himself lest he harm others as well in his madness, the onset of which he already felt.

While Kant was presumably sceptical of the assertion that only by suicide could the hydrophobic have secured others from harm, situations seem perfectly possible in which there would be no other way; and others could obviously occur in connection with infectious diseases. (iii) Those in which suicide relieves others of a duty which they cannot carry out and survive. The suicide of Captain Oates, in Scott's antarctic expedition, in order not to retard his companions as they struggled back to their depot, is rightly considered an act of charity as well as of courage.

In addition, suicide has been justified simply as sparing others excessive burdens. For example, the care of a relative who has contracted an illness or suffered an injury, which incapacitates him for normal life, may call for very great sacrifices by whoever undertakes it. Suppose the sufferer to know that, although those sacrifices are superogatory, somebody will either make them cheerfully or be coerced by family pressure into making them resentfully. In circumstances of either kind, to describe his suicide as wanting in the respect due to humanity would be questionable.

Kant's example of hydrophobia incidentally illustrates a final ground upon which suicide may be held to be permissible: namely, to obtain release from a life that has become, not merely hard to bear, but utterly dehumanized. Supposing hydrophobia to be incurable and its inevitable course to be one of extreme torment, culminating in madness and death: does respect for himself as rational compel a man to submit to it, and not escape by suicide? Or suppose that a man is trapped in a burning vehicle, without hope of getting out: does respect for himself as rational require him to let himself be burned to death, rather than commit suicide? In my own judgement, suicide is in both cases entirely legitimate. The problem is to draw the line between despairing of human life in adversity and perceiving that, owing to illness or injury, the possibility of a genuinely human life will cease before biological death. When that line is crossed, the case for the permissibility of suicide is strong.

# THE MORALITY AND RATIONALITY OF SUICIDE

*Richard B. Brandt*

## THE MORAL REASONS FOR AND AGAINST SUICIDE

Persons who say suicide is morally wrong must be asked which of two positions they are affirming: Are they saying that *every* act of suicide is wrong, *everything considered;* or are they merely saying that there is always *some* moral obligation—doubtless of serious weight—not to commit suicide, so that very often suicide is wrong, although it is possible that there are *countervailing considerations* which in particular situations make it right or even a moral duty? It is quite evident that the first position is absurd; only the second has a chance of being defensible.

   In order to make clear what is wrong with the first view, we may begin with an example. Suppose an army pilot's single-seater plane goes out of control over a heavily populated area; he has the choice of staying in the plane and bringing it down where it will do little damage but at the cost of certain death for himself, and of bailing out and letting the plane fall where it will, very possibly killing a good many civilians. Suppose he chooses to do the former, and so, by our definition, commits suicide. Does anyone want to say that his action is morally wrong? Even Immanuel Kant, who opposed suicide in all circumstances, apparently would not wish to say that it is; he would, in fact, judge that this act is not one of suicide, for he says, "It is no suicide to risk one's life against one's enemies, and even to sacrifice it, in order to preserve one's duties toward oneself." St. Thomas Aquinas, in his discussion of suicide, may seem to take the position that such an act would be wrong, for he says, "It is altogether unlawful to kill oneself," admitting as an exception only the case of being under special command of God. But I believe St. Thomas would, in fact, have concluded that the act is right because the basic intention of the pilot was to save the lives of civilians, and whether an act is right or wrong is a matter of basic intention.

In general, we have to admit that there are things with some moral obligation to avoid which, on account of other morally relevant considerations, it is sometimes right or even morally obligatory to do. There may be some obligation to tell the truth on every occasion, but surely in many cases the consequences of telling the truth would be so dire that one is obligated to lie. The same goes for promises. There is some moral obligation to do what one has promised (with a few exceptions); but, if one can keep a trivial promise only at serious cost to another person (i.e., keep an appointment only by failing to give aid to someone injured in an accident), it is surely obligatory to break the promise.

The most that the moral critic of suicide could hold, then, is that there is *some* moral obligation not to do what one knows will cause one's death; but he surely cannot deny that circumstances exist in which there are obligations to do things which, in fact, will result in one's death. If so, then in principle it would be possible to argue, for instance, that in order to meet my obligation to my family, it might be right for me to take my own life as the only way to avoid catastrophic hospital expenses in a terminal illness. Possibly the main point that critics of suicide on moral grounds would wish to make is that it is never right to take one's own life *for reasons of one's own personal welfare,* of any kind whatsoever. Some of the arguments used to support the immorality of suicide, however, are so framed that if they were supportable at all, they would prove that suicide is *never* moral.

One well-known type of argument against suicide may be classified as *theological.* St. Augustine and others urged that the Sixth Commandment ("Thou shalt not kill") prohibits suicide, and that we are bound to obey a divine commandment. To this reasoning one might first reply that it is arbitrary exegesis of the Sixth Commandment to assert that it was intended to prohibit suicide. The second reply is that if there is not some consideration which shows on the merits of the case that suicide is morally wrong, God had no business prohibiting it. It is true that some will object to this point, and I must refer them elsewhere for my detailed comments on the divine-will theory of morality.

Another theological argument with wide support was accepted by John Locke, who wrote: ". . . Men being all the workmanship of one omnipotent and infinitely wise Maker; all the servants of one sovereign Master, sent into the world by His order and about His business; they are His property, whose workmanship they are made to last during His, not one another's pleasure. . . . Every one . . . is bound to preserve himself, and not to quit his station wilfully. . . ." And Kant: "We have been placed in this world under certain conditions and for specific purposes. But a suicide opposes the purpose of his Creator; he arrives in the other world as one who has deserted his post; he must be looked upon as a rebel against God. So long as we remember the truth that it is God's intention to preserve life, we are bound to regulate our activities in conformity with it. This duty is upon us until the time comes when God expressly commands us to leave this life. Human beings are sentinels on earth and may not leave their posts until relieved by another beneficent hand." Unfortunately, however, even if we grant that it is the duty of human beings to do what God commands or intends them to do, more argument is required to show that God does *not* permit human beings to quit this life when their own personal welfare would be maximized by so doing. How does one draw the requisite inference about the intentions of God? The difficulties and contradictions in arguments to reach such a conclusion are discussed at length and perspicaciously by David Hume in his essay "On Suicide," and in view of the unlikelihood that readers will need to be persuaded about these, I shall merely refer those interested to that essay.

A second group of arguments may be classed as arguments *from natural law*. St. Thomas says: "It is altogether unlawful to kill oneself, for three reasons. First, because everything naturally loves itself, the result being that everything naturally keeps itself in being, and resists corruptions so far as it can. Wherefore suicide is contrary to the inclination of nature, and to charity whereby every man should love himself. Hence suicide is always a mortal sin, as being contrary to the natural law and to charity." Here St. Thomas ignores two obvious points. First, it is not obvious why a human being is morally bound to do what he or she has some inclination to do. (St. Thomas did not criticize chastity.) Second, while it is true that most human beings do feel a strong urge to live, the human being who commits suicide obviously feels a stronger inclination to do something else. It is as natural for a human being to dislike, and to take steps to avoid, say, great pain, as it is to cling to life.

A somewhat similar argument by Immanuel Kant may seem better. In a famous passage Kant writes that the maxim of a person who commits suicide is "From self-love I make it my principle to shorten my life if its continuance threatens more evil than it promises pleasure. The only further question to ask is whether this principle of self-love can become a universal law of nature. It is then seen at once that a system of nature by whose law the very same feeling whose function is to stimulate the futherance of life should actually destroy life would contradict itself and consequently could not subsist as a system of nature. Hence this maxim cannot possibly hold as a universal law of nature and is therefore entirely opposed to the supreme principle of all duty." What Kant finds contradictory is that the motive of self-love (interest in one's own long-range welfare) should sometimes lead one to struggle to preserve one's life, but at other times to end it. But where is the contradiction? One's circumstances change, and, if the argument of the following section in this chapter is correct, one sometimes maximizes one's own long-range welfare by trying to stay alive, but at other times by bringing about one's demise.

A third group of arguments, a form of which goes back at least to Aristotle, has a more modern and convincing ring. These are arguments to show that, in one way or another, a suicide necessarily does harm to other persons, or to society at large. Aristotle says that the suicide treats the *state* unjustly. Partly following Aristotle, St. Thomas says: "Every man is part of the community, and so, as such, he belongs to the community. Hence by killing himself he injures the community." Blackstone held that a suicide is an offense against the king "who hath an interest in the preservation of all his subjects," perhaps following Judge Brown in 1563, who argued that suicide cost the king a subject—"he being the head has lost one of his mystical members." The premise of such arguments is, as Hume pointed out, obviously mistaken in many instances. It is true that Freud would perhaps have injured society had he, instead of finishing his last book, committed suicide to escape the pain of throat cancer. But surely there have been many suicides whose demise was not a noticeable loss to society; an honest man could only say that in some instances society was better off without them.

It need not be denied that suicide is often injurious to other persons, especially the family of a suicide. Clearly it sometimes is. But, we should notice what this fact establishes. Suppose we admit, as generally would be done, that there is some obligation not to perform any action which will probably or certainly be injurious to other people, the strength of the obligation being dependent on various factors, notably the seriousness of the expected injury. Then there is *some* obligation not to commit suicide, when that act would probably or certainly be injurious to other people. But, as we have already seen, many cases of *some* obligation to do something nevertheless are *not* cases of a duty to do that thing, *everything considered*. So it could sometimes be morally justified to commit suicide, even if the act will harm someone. Must a man with a terminal illness undergo excruciating pain because his death will cause his wife sorrow—when she will be caused sorrow a month later anyway, when he is dead of natural causes? Moreover, to repeat, the fact that an individual has some obligation not to commit suicide when that act will probably injure other persons does not imply that, everything considered, it is wrong for him to do it, namely, that in all circumstances suicide *as such* is something there is some obligation to avoid.

Is there any sound argument, convincing to the modern mind, to establish that there is (or is not) *some moral obligation* to avoid suicide *as such*, an obligation, of course, which might be overridden by other obligations in some or many cases? (Captain Oates may have had a moral obligation not to commit suicide as such, but his obligation not to stand in the way of his comrades getting to safety might have been so strong that, everything considered, he was justified in leaving the polar camp and allowing himself to freeze to death.)

To present all the arguments necessary to answer this question convincingly would take a great deal of space. I shall, therefore, simply state one answer to it which seems plausible to some contemporary philosophers. Suppose it could be shown that it would maximize the long-run welfare of everybody affected if people were taught that there is a moral obligation to avoid suicide—so that people would be motivated to avoid suicide just because they thought it wrong (would have anticipatory guilt feelings at the very idea), and so that other people would be inclined to disapprove of persons who commit suicide unless there were some excuse (such as those mentioned in the first section). One might ask: how could it maximize utility to mold the conceptual and motivational structure of persons in this way? To which the answer might be: feeling in this way might make persons who are impulsively inclined to commit suicide in a bad mood, or a fit of anger or jealousy, take more time to deliberate; hence, some suicides that have bad effects generally might be prevented. In other words, it might be a good thing in its effects for people to feel about suicide in the way they feel about breach of promise or injuring others, just as it might be a good thing for people to feel a moral obligation not to smoke, or to wear seat belts. However, it might be that negative moral feelings about suicide as such would stand in the way of action by those persons whose welfare really is best served by suicide and whose suicide is the best thing for everybody concerned.

## WHEN A DECISION TO COMMIT SUICIDE IS RATIONAL FROM THE PERSON'S POINT OF VIEW

The person who is contemplating suicide is obviously making a choice between future world-courses; the world-course that includes his demise, say, an hour from now, and several possible ones that contain his demise at a later point. One cannot have precise knowledge about many features of the latter group of world-courses, but it is certain that they will all end with death some (possibly short) finite time from now.

Why do I say the choice is between *world*-courses and not just a choice between future life-courses of the prospective suicide, the one shorter than the other? The reason is that one's suicide has some impact on the world (and one's continued life has some impact on the world), and that conditions in the rest of the world will often make a difference in one's evaluation of the possibilities. One *is* interested in things in the world other than just oneself and one's own happiness.

The basic question a person must answer, in order to determine which world-course is best or rational for him to choose, is which he *would* choose under conditions of optimal use of information, when *all* of his desires are taken into account. It is not just a question of what we prefer *now*, with some clarification of all the possibilities being considered. Our preferences change, and the preferences of tomorrow (assuming we can know something about them) are just as legitimately taken into account in deciding what to do now as the preferences of today. Since any reason that can be given today for weighting heavily today's preference can be given tomorrow for weighting heavily tomorrow's preference, the preferences of any time-stretch have a rational claim to an equal vote. Now the importance of that fact is this: we often know quite well that our desires, aversions, and preferences may change after a short while. When a person is in a state of despair—perhaps brought about by a rejection in love or discharge from a long-held position—nothing but the thing he cannot have seems desirable; everything else is turned to ashes. Yet we know quite well that the passage of time is likely to reverse all this; replacements may be found or other types of things that are available to us may begin to look attractive. So, if we were to act on the preferences of today alone, when the emotion of despair seems more than we can stand, we might find death preferable to life; but, if we allow for the preferences of the weeks and years ahead, when many goals will be enjoyable and attractive, we might find life much preferable to death. So, if a choice of what is best is to be determined by what we want not only now but later (and later desires on an equal basis with the present ones)—as it should be—then what is the best or preferable world-course will often be quite different from what it would be if the choice, or what is best for one, were fixed by one's desires and preferences now.

Of course, if one commits suicide there are no future desires or aversions that may be compared with present ones and that should be allowed an equal vote in deciding what is best. In that respect the course of action that results in death is different from any other course of action we may undertake. I do not wish to suggest the rosy possibility that it is often or always reasonable to believe that next week "I shall be more interested in living than I am today, if today I take a dim view of continued existence." On the contrary, when a person is seriously ill, for instance, he may have no reason to think that the preference-order will be reversed—it may be that tomorrow he will prefer death to life more strongly.

The argument is often used that one can never be *certain* what is going to happen, and hence one is never rationally justified in doing anything as drastic as committing suicide. But we always have to live by probabilities and make our estimates as best we can. As soon as it is clear beyond reasonable doubt not only that death is now preferable to life, but also that it will be every day from now until the end, the rational thing is to act promptly.

Let us not pursue the question of whether it is rational for a person with a painful terminal illness to commit suicide; it is. However, the issue seldom arises, and few terminally ill patients do commit suicide. With such patients matters usually get worse slowly so that no particular time seems to call for action. They are often so heavily sedated that it is impossible for the mental processes of decision leading to action to occur; or else they are incapacitated in a hospital and the very physical possibility of ending their lives is not available. Let us leave this grim topic and turn to a practically more important problem: whether it is rational for persons to commit suicide for some reason other than painful terminal physical illness. Most persons who commit suicide do so, apparently, because they face a nonphysical problem that depresses them beyond their ability to bear.

Among the problems that have been regarded as good and sufficient reasons for ending life, we find (in addition to serious illness) the following: some event that has made a person feel ashamed or lose his prestige and status; reduction from affluence to poverty; the loss of a limb or of physical beauty; the loss of sexual capacity; some event that makes it seem impossibile to achieve things by which one sets store; loss of a loved one; disappointment in love; the infirmities of increasing age. It is not to be denied that such things can be serious blows to a person's prospects of happiness.

Whatever the nature of an individual's problem, there are various plain errors to be avoided—errors to which a person is especially prone when he is depressed—in deciding whether, everything considered, he prefers a world-course containing his early demise to one in which his life continues to its natural terminus. Let us forget for a moment the relevance to the decision of preferences that he may have tomorrow, and concentrate on some errors that may infect his preference as of today, and for which correction or allowance must be made.

In the first place, depression, like any other severe emotional experience, tends to primitivize one's intellectual processes. It restricts the range of one's survey of the possibilities. One thing that a rational person would do is compare the world-course containing his suicide with his *best* alternative. But his best alternative is precisely a possibility he may overlook if, in a depressed mood, he thinks only of how badly off he is and cannot imagine any way of improving his situation. If a person is disappointed in love, it is possible to adopt a vigorous plan of action that carries a good chance of acquainting him with someone he likes at least as well; and if old age prevents a person from continuing the tennis game with his favorite partner, it is possible to learn some other game that provides the joys of competition without the physical demands.

Depression has another insidious influence on one's planning; it seriously affects one's judgment about probabilities. A person disappointed in love is very likely to take a dim view of himself, his prospects, and his attractiveness; he thinks that because he has been rejected by one person he will probably be rejected by anyone who looks desirable to him. In a less gloomy frame of mind he would make different estimates. Part of the reason for such gloomy probability estimates is that depression tends to repress one's memory of evidence that supports a nongloomy prediction. Thus, a rejected lover tends to forget any cases in which he has elicited enthusiastic response from ladies in relation to whom he has been the one who has done the rejecting. Thus his pessimistic self-image is based upon a highly selected, and pessimistically selected, set of data. Even when he is reminded of the data, moreover, he is apt to resist an optimistic inference.

Another kind of distortion of the look of future prospects is not a result of depression, but is quite normal. Events distant in the future feel small, just as objects distant in space look small. Their prospect does not have the effect on motivational processes that it would have if it were of an event in the immediate future. Psychologists call this the "goal-gradient" phenomenon; a rat, for instance, will run faster toward a perceived food box than a distant unseen one. In the case of a person who has suffered some misfortune, and whose situation now is an unpleasant one, this reduction of the motivational influence of events distant in time has the effect that present unpleasant states weigh far more heavily than probable future pleasant ones in any choice of world-courses.

If we are trying to determine whether we now prefer, or shall later prefer, the outcome of one world-course to that of another (and this is leaving aside the questions of the weight of the votes of preferences at a later date), we must take into account these and other infirmities of our "sensing" machinery. Since knowing that the machinery is out of order will not tell us what results it would give if it were working, the best recourse might be to refrain from making any decision in a stressful frame of mind. If decisions have to be made, one must recall past reactions, in a normal frame of mind, to outcomes like those under assessment. But many suicides seem to occur in moments of despair. What should be clear from the above is that a moment of despair, if one is seriously contemplating suicide, ought to be a moment of reassessment of one's goals and values, a reassessment which the individual must realize is very difficult to make objectively, because of the very quality of his depressed frame of mind.

A decision to commit suicide may in certain circumstances be a rational one. But a person who wants to act rationally must take into account the various possible "errors" and make appropriate rectification of his initial evaluation.

## THE ROLE OF OTHER PERSONS

What is the moral obligation of other persons toward those who are contemplating suicide? The question of their moral blameworthiness may be ignored and what is rational for them to do from the point of view of personal welfare may be considered as being of secondary concern. Laws make it dangerous to aid or encourage a suicide. The risk of running afoul of the law may partly determine moral obligation, since moral obligation to do something may be reduced by the fact that it is personally dangerous.

The moral obligation of other persons toward one who is contemplating suicide is an instance of a general obligation to render aid to those in serious distress, at least when this can be done at no great cost to one's self. I do not think this general principle is seriously questioned by anyone, whatever his moral theory: so I feel free to assume it as a premise. Obviously the person contemplating suicide is in great distress of some sort; if he were not, he would not be seriously considering terminating his life.

How great a person's obligation is to one in distress depends on a number of factors. Obviously family and friends have special obligations to devote time to helping the prospective suicide—which others do not have. But anyone in this kind of distress has a moral claim on the time of any person who knows the situation (unless there are others more responsible who are already doing what should be done).

What is the obligation? It depends, of course, on the situation, and how much the second person knows about the situation. If the individual has decided to terminate his life if he can, and it is clear that he is right in this decision, then, if he needs help in executing the decision, there is a moral obligation to give him help. On this matter a patient's physician has a special obligation, from which any talk about the Hippocratic oath does not absolve him. It is true that there are some damages one cannot be expected to absorb, and some risks which one cannot be expected to take, on account of the obligation to render aid.

On the other hand, if it is clear that the individual should not commit suicide, from the point of view of his own welfare, or if there is a presumption that he should not (when the only evidence is that a person is discovered unconscious, with the gas turned on), it would seem to be the individual's obligation to intervene, prevent the successful execution of the decision, and see to the availability of competent psychiatric advice and temporary hospitalization, if necessary. Whether one has a right to take such steps when a clearly sane person, after careful reflection over a period of time, comes to the conclusion that an end to his life is what is best for him and what he wants, is very doubtful, even when one thinks his conclusion a mistaken one; it would seem that a man's own considered decision about whether he wants to live must command respect, although one must concede that this could be debated.

The more interesting role in which a person may be cast, however, is that of adviser. It is often important to one who is contemplating suicide to go over his thinking with another, and to feel that a conclusion, one way or the other, has the support of a respected mind. One thing one can obviously do, in rendering the service of advice, is to discuss with the person the various types of issues discussed above, made more specific by the concrete circumstances of his case, and help him find whether, in view, say, of the damage his suicide would do to others, he has a moral obligation to refrain, and whether it is rational or best for him, from the point of view of his own welfare, to take this step or adopt some other plan instead.

To get a person to see what is the rational thing to do is no small job. Even to get a person, in a frame of mind when he is seriously contemplating (or perhaps has already unsuccessfully attempted) suicide, to recognize a plain truth of fact may be a major operation. If a man insists, "I am a complete failure," when it is obvious that by any reasonable standard he is far from that, it may be tremendously difficult to get him to see the fact. But there is another job beyond that of getting a person to see what is the rational thing to do; that is to help him *act* rationally, or *be* rational, when he has conceded what would be the rational thing.

How either of these tasks may be accomplished effectively may be discussed more competently by an experienced psychiatrist than by a philosopher. Loneliness and the absence of human affection are states which exacerbate any other problems; disappointment, reduction to poverty, and so forth, seem less impossible to bear in the presence of the affection of another. Hence simply to be a friend, or to find someone a friend, may be the largest contribution one can make either to helping a person be rational or see clearly what is rational for him to do; this service may make one who was contemplating suicide feel that there is a future for him which it is possible to face.

# CHAPTER NINE
# ETHICAL ISSUES IN ABORTION

Linda Bird Francke, the mother of three children, had an abortion in New York City several years ago. This is how she described her experience:

> We were sitting in a bar on Lexington Avenue when I told my husband I was pregnant. It is not a memory I like to dwell on. Instead of the champagne and hope which had heralded the impending births of the first, second and third child, the news of this one was greeted with shocked silence and Scotch. "Jesus," my husband kept saying to himself, stirring the ice cubes around and around, "Oh, Jesus."
>
> Oh, how we tried to rationalize it that night as the starting time for the movie came and went. My husband talked about his plans for a career change in the next year, to stem the staleness that fourteen years with the same investment banking firm had brought him. A new baby would preclude that option.
>
> The timing wasn't right for me either. Having juggled pregnancies and child care with what freelance jobs I could fit in between feedings, I had just taken on a full-time job. A new baby would put me right back in the nursery just when our youngest child was finally school age. It was time for *us* we tried to rationalize. There just wasn't room in our lives now for another baby. We both agreed. And agreed. And agreed.
>
> How very considerate they are at the Women's Services, known formally as the Center for Reproductive and Sexual Health. Yes, indeed, I could have an abortion that very Saturday morning and be out in time to drive to the country that afternoon. . . .

I checked in at nine A.M. . . . The Saturday morning women's group was more dispirited than the men in the waiting room. There were around fifteen of us, a mixture of races, ages and backgrounds. . . . But unlike any other group of women I've been in, we didn't talk. Our common denominator, the one which usually floods across language and economic barriers into familiarity, today was one of shame. We were losing life that day, not giving it. . . . One of the women in my room was shivering and an aide brought her a blanket.

"What's the matter?" the aide asked her. "I'm scared," the woman said. "How much will it hurt?" The aide smiled. "Oh, nothing worse than a couple of bad cramps," she said. "This afternoon you'll be dancing a jig."

I began to panic. Suddenly the rhetoric, the abortion marches I'd walked in, the telegrams sent to Albany to counteract the Friends of the Fetus, the Zero Population Growth buttons I'd worn, peeled away, and I was alone with my microscopic baby. There were just the two of us there, and soon, because it was more convenient for me and my husband, there would be one again.

How could it be that I, who am so neurotic about life that I step over bugs rather than on them, who spend hours planting flowers and vegetables in the spring even though we rent out the house and never see them, who make sure the children are vaccinated and innoculated and filled with vitamin C, could so arbitrarily decide that this life shouldn't be?

"It's not a life," my husband had argued, more to convince himself than me. "It's a bunch of cells smaller than my fingernail."

But any woman who has had children knows that certain feeling in her taut, swollen breasts, and the slight but constant ache in her uterus that signals the arrival of a life. Though I would march myself into blisters for a woman's right to exercise the option of motherhood, I discovered there in the waiting room that I was not the modern woman I thought I was.

When my name was called, my body felt so heavy the nurse had to help me into the examining room. I waited for my husband to burst through the door and yell "stop," but of course he didn't. I concentrated on three black spots in the acoustic ceiling until they grew in size to the shape of saucers, while the doctor swabbed my insides with antiseptic.

"You're going to feel a burning sensation now," he said, injecting Novocaine into the neck of the womb. The pain was swift and severe, and I twisted to get away from him. He was hurting my baby, I reasoned, and the black saucers quivered in the air. "Stop," I cried. "Please stop." He shook his head, busy with his equipment. "It's too late to stop now," he said. "It'll just take a few more seconds."

What good sports we women are. And how obedient. Physically the pain passed even before the hum of the machine signaled that the vacuuming of my uterus was completed, my baby sucked up like ashes after a cocktail party. Ten minutes start to finish. And I was back on the arm of the nurse. . . .

It had certainly been a successful operation. I didn't bleed at all for two days just as they had predicted, and then I bled only moderately for another four days. Within a week my breasts had subsided and the tenderness vanished, and my body felt mine again instead of the eggshell it becomes when it's protecting someone else.

My husband and I are back to planning our summer vacation and his career switch.

And it certainly does make more sense not to be having a baby right now—we say that to each other all the time. But I have this ghost now. A very little ghost that only appears when I'm seeing something beautiful, like the full moon on the ocean last weekend. And the baby waves at me. And I wave at the baby. "Of course, we have room," I cry to the ghost. "Of course, we do."[1]

The agonizing ambivalence that Linda Bird Francke experienced before and after her abortion is symptomatic of the moral issues that surround abortion in our society. Many people believe that abortion is morally permissible because, like Francke's husband, they hold that the fetus is nothing more than "a bunch of cells smaller than my fingernail." But many others are convinced that abortion is a form of murder since they believe the fetus to be another person. These two contrasting views are both evident in Francke's conflicting feelings. On the one hand, she believed she was justified in having an abortion merely for the sake of her own and her husband's careers (thus implying that she did not feel abortion was killing another person); she supported "abortion marches" and "a woman's right" to choose; and she had lobbied against anti-abortion groups such as the "Friends of the Fetus." On the other hand, she says that she and her husband were just trying "to rationalize" what they were doing, that she felt shame because she was "losing life," and she repeatedly refers to her fetus as "my baby," describing pregnancy as "protecting someone else" (thus implying that the fetus is another person).

Many women are torn between the same conflicting moral views that Linda Bird Francke so poignantly expresses. A large number of women choose to end their pregnancies through abortion, yet feel ambivalent about the morality of what they are doing. In the United States, there is one abortion for every three live births; that means over a million abortions are performed each year. One third of the women who have abortions are married; the rest are single.[2]

Women choose to have abortions for a number of reasons.[3] Among married women like Linda Bird Francke, a common reason is that having a child conflicts with other career or financial decisions or with the happiness of the family. Among unmarried women, a common reason is the social stigma of illegitimacy and the financial burden of supporting a child. A number of women choose to have abortions because they learn their pregnancies may produce a child with undesirable characteristics: it may have physical deformities, it may be of the wrong sex, it may be a carrier of defective genes, or it may be mentally defective. In some cases, a woman has an abortion because continued pregnancy may endanger her physical or mental health. On occasion, continued pregnancy may

1. Jane Doe [pseudonym of Linda Bird Francke], "There Just Wasn't Room in Our Lives Now for Another Baby," *The New York Times,* May 14, 1976; reprinted in Linda Bird Francke, *The Ambivalence of Abortion* (New York: Random House, 1978), pp. 3–7. Copyright © 1976 by The New York Times Company. Reprinted by permission.

2. See Francke, *The Ambivalence of Abortion,* pp. 32–33.

3. See R.F.R. Gardner, *Abortion: The Personal Dilemma* (New York: Pyramid Books, 1974).

even endanger her life. And sometimes abortion is chosen because pregnancy is the result of rape or incest.

In its development, the fetus passes through several stages, a number of which have been held to be morally significant in making decisions concerning abortion.[4] Development begins at conception when a male sex cell (a spermatozoon) meets a female sex cell (an ovum) in the Fallopian tube and forms a single cell (a zygote), which contains the full set of twenty-three chromosomes that is called the "genetic code" of the individual who will develop from the zygote.[5] Traditional moralists hold that the fetus is a human being from this moment of conception and that to abort it is therefore the same as killing a human being. For these ethicians, the moment of conception is the most morally significant point in fetal development.

After conception, the zygote begins to divide as it travels down through the Fallopian tube until it reaches the uterus, where it implants itself about two weeks later. After implantation, the developing organism is called an "embryo" until the end of the eighth week, after which it is referred to as a "fetus." About a month after conception, the rudimentary heart, head, eyes, ears, and nose have appeared. Two months after conception, the heart begins to beat, the head increases in size, and brain waves can be detected. At the end of three months, the fetus is about three inches long and has distinct arms, legs, fingers, and toes. This point in fetal development is called the end of the first "trimester." In 1973, the United States Supreme Court, in a split decision, ruled in *Roe* v. *Wade* that up to this point the mother's "right of privacy" entitles her to have an abortion "without regulation by the State."

The second trimester is the period from the fourth to the sixth month. The United States Supreme Court, in the same ruling, also held that during this second trimester, "the State, in promoting its interest in the health of the mother, may, if it chooses, regulate the abortion procedure in ways that are reasonably related to maternal health."

The fetus continues to develop through the fifth month, when "quickening" occurs, i.e., the mother first begins to feel the fetus moving on its own within her. Prior to the modern era, many moralists held that the fetus acquired human life at the moment of quickening, and they consequently held that prior to this stage it was not a human being. In their view, abortion prior to this stage was wrong, but still not equivalent to homicide. By the end of the fifth month, the fetus is about eight inches long and hair is growing on its head. One month later, the end of the second "trimester" is reached.

The seventh month marks the beginning of the third and last tri-

---

4. For a historical survey of different views on the permissibility of abortion at different points of pregnancy, see John T. Noonan, Jr., "An Almost Absolute Value in History," in John T. Noonan, Jr., ed., *The Morality of Abortion: Legal and Historical Perspectives* (Cambridge, Mass.: Harvard University Press, 1970); see also Germain Grisez, *Abortion: The Myths, the Realities, and the Arguments* (New York: Corpus Books, 1970).

5. See Charles E. McLennan and Eugene C. Sandberg, *Synopsis of Obstetrics*, 9th ed. (Saint Louis: C. B. Mosby, 1974), pp. 41–45, from which the medical details in this and the following paragraphs are drawn.

mester. During this month, the fetus becomes "viable" or capable of surviving outside the womb. For many ethicians, it is immoral to abort the fetus at this point. The United States Supreme Court (in *Roe* v. *Wade)* held that "for the stage subsequent to viability, the State, in promoting its interest in the potentiality of human life, may, if it chooses, regulate, and even proscribe, abortion except where it is necessary, in appropriate medical judgment, for the preservation of the life or health of the mother."

The fetus continues to develop until it reaches full term forty weeks after conception. At this point, labor begins and the baby is born. Some philosophers hold that it is only at birth that the human organism acquires moral rights. In addressing this issue, they have distinguished between a "human being" and a "person." For them, the term "human being" is a biological one, indicating that an organism is a member of the species *Homo sapiens.* The term "person," however, is a moral one, indicating that an organism has full moral rights. The fetus, they say, is merely a "human being" and does not become a "person" until birth or sometime after birth. Different philosophers give different criteria for deciding whether or not a certain organism is a "person." According to some of these, humans do not become "persons" (and thus do not have a right to live) until after infancy. However, critics of these views on "personhood" hold that the philosophers espousing them have arbitrarily made up the criteria they use to decide what is to count as a person.

It is clear, then, that abortion raises several troubling ethical questions.[6] Is the fetus a "person" with the moral rights of adult human beings? Is the abortion of a fetus ever morally permissible? Or is abortion morally permissible only in some circumstances? And if abortion is sometimes morally permissible, for what reasons? At what point in the development of the fetus might it no longer be permissible? Does the viability of the fetus make any difference to the morality of abortion? Would "quickening" make a difference? Does anything prior to birth make a difference?

The answers given to these questions generally tend to be based on the positions ethicians have taken on two issues: (1) At what point, if ever, does the fetus become a human being with the same moral right to life that adult human beings possess? (2) When, if ever, do the rights of the mother and other members of society override the moral rights of the fetus? The articles in this chapter are organized around these two basic issues. Because of their complexity, we have provided detailed analyses of their arguments.

The first three readings deal primarily with the first major ethical

6. There are a number of anthologies that bring together different points of view on the morality of abortion: Joel Feinberg, ed., *The Problem of Abortion* (Belmont, Calif.: Wadsworth, 1973); Marshall Cohen, Thomas Nagel, and Thomas Scanlon, eds., *The Rights and Wrongs of Abortion* (Princeton, N.J.: Princeton University Press, 1974); Robert Perkins, ed., *Abortion* (Cambridge, Mass.: Schenkman, 1974); Malcolm Potts, et al., *Abortion* (Cambridge, England: Cambridge University Press, 1977). There are also a number of books that give more extended treatments of some issues: Daniel Callahan, *Abortion: Law, Choice and Morality* (New York: Macmillan, 1975) and L. W. Sumner, *Abortion and Moral Theory* (Princeton, N.J.: Princeton University Press, 1981).

issue raised by abortion: Is the fetus a human being with the same moral right to life that adult human beings possess? The opening article is written by Michael Tooley, a utilitarian. Tooley claims that to have a right to X, a being must be capable of desiring X. And a being is capable of desiring X only if that being understands the concept of X. Consequently, Tooley concludes that a being can have a right to X only if it has the concept of X (i.e., it understands what X is). Do fetuses and newborn babies then have a right to life, that is, a right "to continue to exist as a subject of experiences and other mental states"? They do not, Tooley argues, because they are not capable of understanding the concept of "a subject of experiences and other mental states." Since fetuses and babies do not have a right to life, he concludes that abortion and infanticide shortly after birth "must be morally acceptable."

The next article, "On the Moral and Legal Status of Abortion" by Mary Anne Warren, takes a different approach. She asks: "What characteristics entitle an entity to be considered a person" with full moral rights? She answers this question by claiming that an entity is a person only if it exhibits five traits: consciousness, reasoning, self-motivated activity, the capacity to communicate, and the presence of self-concepts and self-awareness. Since fetuses clearly do not have these traits, she concludes that they are not persons and do not have "full moral rights." Opponents of abortion therefore cannot say that killing a fetus is killing a person with "full moral rights."

In the third article, "Abortion: The Moral Status of the Unborn," Richard Werner discusses the views of both Tooley and Warren. He begins by arguing that from conception to adulthood there is no break in the development of human beings that would make unborn human beings ontologically (i.e., in their real make-up) different kinds of creatures from adult human beings. He argues for this claim by considering various breaks in human development that people have said make adults different from fetuses: the attainment of human form, quickening, evidence of an EEG, viability, birth, and the development of a cluster of traits like those suggested by Warren. But none of these, in Werner's view, is acceptable. Moreover, he argues that conception does signal an ontological change in human development because before conception two organisms exist (the ovum and the sperm), and after conception one organism exists (the zygote) that then continues in an unbroken development to human adulthood. Thus, Werner concludes that fetuses are the same kinds of creatures as adult human beings. From this, it would follow that fetuses are entitled to the same rights as adult human beings. Werner then asks whether Mary Anne Warren and Michael Tooley are correct when they claim that because the fetus does not have certain capacities it does not have the rights that adult human beings have. He concludes that if their views were correct then logically we would have to be willing to treat infants, retarded adults, the mentally ill, and future generations in ways that we are not willing to treat them. Since we are not willing to do this, the views of these people must be false.

The next three articles discuss the second major moral issue in the abortion controversy: When, if ever, do the moral rights of the mother override the moral rights (if any) of the fetus? The article by Judith Jarvis Thomson, "A Defense of Abortion," is a criticism of what she calls the "extreme" view (the view traditionally held by natural law ethicians), which holds that the fetus is a person and that "directly killing" a person is always wrong. She argues that even if the fetus is a person with the full rights of an adult human being, it does not follow that abortion is always wrong; sometimes the rights of the mother override the rights of the fetus. To show this, Thomson asks us to imagine a woman who wakes up in a hospital to find that her circulatory system has been plugged into the circulatory system of a famous violinist. She is told that the violinist will die unless the two of them remain connected for nine months. Thomson then points out that even though the violinist is a person with a "right to life," it would be "outrageous" to say that the woman may not disconnect herself from the violinist. Similarly, Thomson suggests, it is not necessarily wrong for a pregnant woman to disconnect herself from her fetus, even if the fetus is a person with a "right to life" and even if the fetus will not survive. Moreover, Thomson points out, if the hospitalized woman's life is in danger, it would not be murder for her to disconnect the violinist, even though this would "directly kill" the violinist. (Thomson focuses on direct killings because the natural law view she is criticizing holds that direct killings are wrong, while indirect killings may not be wrong.) Similarly, if a pregnant woman's life is in danger, it would not be murder for her to abort the fetus even though this would directly kill the fetus. And third, Thomson states, the violinist has no right to the hospitalized woman's body. Similarly, she suggests, the fetus has no "right" to the pregnant woman's body since a woman "owns" her own body. Thus, Thomson concludes, since disconnecting oneself from a violinist is exactly like an abortion, and since it is not wrong for a woman to unplug herself from the violinist, abortion is also not necessarily wrong, even if it directly kills another person.

John Finnis' article, "The Rights and Wrongs of Abortion," criticizes Thomson's views by adopting a natural law perspective. Finnis begins by briefly sketching his belief that "to be fully reasonable, one must remain open to every basic form of human good" and must not "choose directly against a basic form of good." Finnis then explains that the phrase "must not choose directly against a basic form of good" means that "the bad effects of one's deed must not be intended either as end or as means." (He notes that the phrase also means that the good effect should be proportionate to the bad effect.) But what does it mean to say that "the bad effect is not intended either as end or as means"? Finnis claims that four main factors can be brought to bear on this question. If we look at them, Finnis argues, it will be clear that Thomson's example is not at all like an abortion, i.e., like a craniotomy. (Finnis discusses only one type of abortion, a "craniotomy," in which the brain of the fetus is destroyed and the fetus is then expelled from the mother's body. Finnis deals with this type of abortion because it is a clear case of directly killing a fetus and Thomson is primarily interested in this type of case.

Factor (1), Finnis says, is this: Would the chosen action have been selected if the bad effect had not been present? If the chosen action would have been selected even without the bad effect, then the bad effect is not intended as an end or a means. But Finnis admits that this first factor does not "serve to distinguish a craniotomy from unplugging that violinist."

Factor (2) is this: Is the person who is making the choice the one whose life is threatened by the victim she kills (when killing someone is the "bad effect")? If a woman herself kills someone who is threatening her life, then this is a case of self-defense. In a craniotomy abortion, Finnis points out, another person (a doctor or a "bystander") must kill the fetus of the pregnant woman when her life is in danger. But in Thomson's hypothetical case, "the unplugging of the violinist is done by the very person defending herself." So the act of unplugging the violinist is justified as self-defense, while a craniotomy abortion is not.

Factor (3) is this: Does the chosen action amount to a direct assault on the body of another person? In Thomson's example, the woman does not directly assault the violinist's body (for example, the violinist is not "killed outright, say by drowning or decapitation") when she unplugs him from herself. But in a craniotomy abortion, the body of the fetus is assaulted. So the case of the violinist involves no direct killing, while abortion does.

Factor (4) is this: Does the chosen action harm someone who had a duty not to be where he is, or is it directed against an innocent party who has done no wrong? In Thomson's example, the violinist had a moral duty not to plug himself into the woman. So when the woman unplugs herself from him she is harming someone who had a duty not to be there. In an abortion, the unborn child did not violate any duty in coming to be present in the woman, so the abortion harms an innocent party. Thus, in the case of the violinist the victim is not innocent, while in the abortion the victim is. Finnis concludes that Thomson's violinist case differs from the direct killing involved in abortion in several important ways. Thus her argument is unsound.

The final article, "Abortion and the Golden Rule," is by R. M. Hare, a British philosopher who adopts a Kantian approach to moral issues. Using a version of Kant's Categorial Imperative (which he points out is similar to the golden rule), Hare argues that "we should do to others what we are glad was done to us." Since we are glad we were allowed to be born, we should allow those who will be like us (i.e., who will be glad) to be born. There is therefore a general presumption against abortion. But what about cases where the mother must choose between aborting this child and having another one later, or having this child now and not having the other one later? How does one choose between the two parties (i.e., the two possible children) in such cases of conflict? In this situation Hare argues that I should do to those involved what I would most want done to me if I were all of them by turns (that is, I must ask myself what I would want done if I were actually both of the parties: I must in my imagination put myself in both of their places and ask myself which party has the better case). Hare claims that if I do this I would choose in favor of the child that has the greatest probability of being born and of being happy. He concludes that when there are conflicts among the interests of mothers, of fetuses, and of potential future populations, they should be resolved in the same manner (i.e., by asking: What would I most want done to me if I were all of them by turns?). Consequently, although there is a general presumption against abortion, nevertheless it is sometimes permissible.

# ABORTION AND INFANTICIDE

*Michael Tooley*

This essay deals with the question of the morality of abortion and infanticide. The fundamental ethical objection traditionally advanced against these practices rests on the contention that human fetuses and infants have a right to life. It is this claim which will be the focus of attention here. The basic issue to be discussed, then, is what properties a thing must possess in order to have a serious right to life. My approach will be to set out and defend a basic moral principle specifying a condition an organism must satisfy if it is to have a serious right to life. It will be seen that this condition is not satisfied by human fetuses and infants, and thus that they do not have a right to life. So unless there are other substantial objections to abortion and infanticide, one is forced to conclude that these practices are morally acceptable ones. . . .

Settling the issue of the morality of abortion and infanticide will involve answering the following questions: What properties must something have to be a person, i.e., to have a serious right to life? At what point in the development of a member of the species Homo sapiens does the organism possess the properties that make it a person? The first question raises a moral issue. To answer it is to decide what basic[1] moral

1. A moral principle accepted by a person is *basic for him* if and only if his acceptance of it is not dependent upon any of his (nonmoral) factual beliefs. That is, no change in his factual beliefs would cause him to abandon the principle in question.

From Michael Tooley, "Abortion and Infanticide," *Philosophy & Public Affairs,* vol. 2, no. 1 (Fall 1972), pp. 37, 43–50, 63. Copyright © 1972 by Princeton University Press. Excerpts reprinted by permission of Princeton University Press.

principles involving the ascription of a right to life one ought to accept. The second question raises a purely factual issue, since the properties in question are properties of a purely descriptive sort.

Some writers seem quite pessimistic about the possibility of resolving the question of the morality of abortion. Indeed, some have gone so far as to suggest that the question of whether the fetus is a person is in principle unanswerable: "we seem to be stuck with the indeterminateness of the fetus' humanity."[2] An understanding of some of the sources of this pessimism will, I think, help us to tackle the problem. Let us begin by considering the similarity a number of people have noted between the issue of abortion and the issue of Negro slavery. The question here is why it should be more difficult to decide whether abortion and infanticide are acceptable than it was to decide whether slavery was acceptable. The answer seems to be that in the case of slavery there are moral principles of a quite uncontroversial sort that settle the issue. Thus most people would agree to some such principle as the following: No organism that has experiences, that is capable of thought and of using language, and that has harmed no one, should be made a slave. In the case of abortion, on the other hand, conditions that are generally agreed to be sufficient grounds for ascribing a right to life to something do not suffice to settle the issue. It is easy to specify other, purportedly sufficient conditions that will settle the issue, but no one has been successful in putting forward considerations that will convince others to accept those additional moral principles.

I do not share the general pessimism about the possibility of resolving the issue of abortion and infanticide because I believe it is possible to point to a very plausible moral principle dealing with the question of *necessary* conditions for something's having a right to life, where the conditions in question will provide an answer to the question of the permissibility of abortion and infanticide.

There is a second cause of pessimism that should be noted before proceeding. It is tied up with the fact that the development of an organism is one of gradual and continuous change. Given this continuity, how is one to draw a line at one point and declare it permissible to destroy a member of Homo sapiens up to, but not beyond, that point? Won't there be an arbitrariness about any point that is chosen? I will return to this worry shortly. It does not present a serious difficulty once the basic moral principles relevant to the ascription of a right to life to an individual are established.

Let us turn now to the first and most fundamental question: What properties must something have in order to be a person, i.e., to have a serious right to life? The claim I wish to defend is this: An organism possesses a serious right to life only if it possesses the concept of a self as a continuing subject of experiences and other mental states, and believes that it is itself such a continuing entity.

My basic argument in support of this claim, which I will call the

2. Wertheimer, "Understanding the Abortion Argument," p. 88.

self-consciousness requirement, will be clearest, I think, if I first offer a simplified version of the argument, and then consider a modification that seems desirable. The simplified version of my argument is this. To ascribe a right to an individual is to assert something about the prima facie obligations of other individuals to act, or to refrain from acting, in certain ways. However, the obligations in question are conditional ones, being dependent upon the existence of certain desires of the individual to whom the right is ascribed. Thus if an individual asks one to destroy something to which he has a right, one does not violate his right to that thing if one proceeds to destroy it. This suggests the following analysis: "A has a right to X" is roughly synonymous with "If A desires X, then others are under a prima facie obligation to refrain from actions that would deprive him of it."[3]

Although this analysis is initially plausible, there are reasons for thinking it not entirely correct. I will consider these later. Even here, however, some expansion is necessary, since there are features of the concept of a right that are important in the present context, and that ought to be dealt with more explicitly. In particular, it seems to be a conceptual truth that things that lack consciousness, such as ordinary machines, cannot have rights. Does this conceptual truth follow from the above analysis of the concept of a right? The answer depends on how the term "desire" is interpreted. If one adopts a completely behavioristic interpretation of "desire," so that a machine that searches for an electrical outlet in order to get its batteries recharged is described as having a desire to be recharged, then it will not follow from this analysis that objects that lack consciousness cannot have rights. On the other hand, if "desire" is interpreted in such a way that desires are states necessarily standing in some sort of relationship to states of consciousness, it will follow from the analysis that a machine that is not capable of being conscious, and consequently of having desires, cannot have any rights. I think those who defend analyses of the concept of a right along the lines of this one do have in mind an interpretation of the term "desire" that involves reference to something more than behavioral dispositions. However, rather than relying on this, it seems preferable to make such an interpretation explicit. The following analysis is a natural way of doing that: "A has a right to X" is roughly synonymous with "A is the sort of thing that is a subject of experiences and other mental states, A is capable of desiring X, and if A does desire X, then others are under a prima facie obligation to refrain from actions that would deprive him of it."

The next step in the argument is basically a matter of applying this analysis to the concept of a right to life. Unfortunately the expression "right to life" is not entirely a happy one, since it suggests that the right in question concerns the continued existence of a biological organism. That this is incorrect can be brought out by considering possible ways of violating an individual's right to life. Suppose, for example, that by some technology of the future the brain of an adult human were to be completely

3. Again, compare the analysis defended by Brandt in *Ethical Theory*, pp. 434-441.

reprogrammed, so that the organism wound up with memories (or rather, apparent memories), beliefs, attitudes, and personality traits completely different from those associated with it before it was subjected to reprogramming. In such a case one would surely say that an individual had been destroyed, that an adult human's right to life had been violated, even though no biological organism had been killed. This example shows that the expression "right to life" is misleading, since what one is really concerned about is not just the continued existence of a biological organism, but the right of a subject of experiences and other mental states to continue to exist.

Given this more precise description of the right with which we are here concerned, we are now in a position to apply the analysis of the concept of a right stated above. When we do so we find that the statement "A has a right to continue to exist as a subject of experiences and other mental states" is roughly synonymous with the statement "A is a subject of experiences and other mental states, A is capable of desiring to continue to exist as a subject of experiences and other mental states, and if A does desire to continue to exist as such an entity, then others are under a prima facie obligation not to prevent him from doing so."

The final stage in the argument is simply a matter of asking what must be the case if something is to be capable of having a desire to continue existing as a subject of experiences and other mental states. The basic point here is that the desires a thing can have are limited by the concepts it possesses. For the fundamental way of describing a given desire is as a desire that a certain proposition be true.[4] Then, since one cannot desire that a certain proposition be true unless one understands it, and since one cannot understand it without possessing the concepts involved in it, it follows that the desires one can have are limited by the concepts one possesses. Applying this to the present case results in the conclusion that an entity cannot be the sort of thing that can desire that a subject of experiences and other mental states exist unless it possesses the concept of such a subject. Moreover, an entity cannot desire that it itself *continue* existing as a subject of experiences and other mental states unless it believes that it is now such a subject. This completes the justification of the claim that it is a necessary condition of something's having a serious right to life that it possess the concept of a self as a continuing subject of experiences, and that it believe that it is itself such an entity.

Let us now consider a modification in the above argument that seems desirable. This modification concerns the crucial conceptual claim advanced about the relationship between ascription of rights and ascrip-

---

4. In everyday life one often speaks of desiring things, such as an apple or a newspaper. Such talk is elliptical, the context together with one's ordinary beliefs serving to make it clear that one wants to eat the apple and read the newspaper. To say that what one desires is that a certain proposition be true should not be construed as involving any particular ontological commitment. The point is merely that it is sentences such as "John wants it to be the case that he is eating an apple in the next few minutes" that provide a completely explicit description of a person's desires. If one fails to use such sentences one can be badly misled about what concepts are presupposed by a particular desire.

tion of the corresponding desires. Certain situations suggest that there may be exceptions to the claim that if a person doesn't desire something, one cannot violate his right to it. There are three types of situations that call this claim into question: (i) situations in which an individual's desires reflect a state of emotional disturbance; (ii) situations in which a previously conscious individual is temporarily unconscious; (iii) situations in which an individual's desires have been distorted by conditioning or by indoctrination.

As an example of the first, consider a case in which an adult human falls into a state of depression which his psychiatrist recognizes as temporary. While in the state he tells people he wishes he were dead. His psychiatrist, accepting the view that there can be no violation of an individual's right to life unless the individual has a desire to live, decides to let his patient have his way and kills him. Or consider a related case in which one person gives another a drug that produces a state of temporary depression; the recipient expresses a wish that he were dead. The person who administered the drug then kills him. Doesn't one want to say in both these cases that the agent did something seriously wrong in killing the other person? And isn't the reason the action was seriously wrong in each case the fact that it violated the individual's right to life? If so, the right to life cannot be linked with a desire to live in the way claimed above.

The second set of situations are ones in which an individual is unconscious for some reason—that is, he is sleeping, or drugged, or in a temporary coma. Does an individual in such a state have any desires? People do sometimes say that an unconscious individual wants something, but it might be argued that if such talk is not to be simply false it must be interpreted as actually referring to the desires the individual *would* have if he were now conscious. Consequently, if the analysis of the concept of a right proposed above were correct, it would follow that one does not violate an individual's right if one takes his car, or kills him, while he is asleep.

Finally, consider situations in which an individual's desires have been distorted, either by inculcation of irrational beliefs or by direct conditioning. Thus an individual may permit someone to kill him because he has been convinced that if he allows himself to be sacrificed to the gods he will be gloriously rewarded in a life to come. Or an individual may be enslaved after first having been conditioned to desire a life of slavery. Doesn't one want to say that in the former case an individual's right to life has been violated, and in the latter his right to freedom?

Situations such as these strongly suggest that even if an individual doesn't want something, it is still possible to violate his right to it. Some modification of the earlier account of the concept of a right thus seems in order. The analysis given covers, I believe, the paradigmatic cases of violation of an individual's rights, but there are other, secondary cases where one also wants to say that someone's right has been violated which are not included.

Precisely how the revised analysis should be formulated is unclear. Here it will be sufficient merely to say that, in view of the above, an individual's right to X can be violated not only when he desires X, but also when he *would* now desire X were it not for one of the following: (i) he is in an emotionally unbalanced state; (ii) he is temporarily unconscious; (iii) he has been conditioned to desire the absence of X.

The critical point now is that, even given this extension of the conditions under which an individual's right to something can be violated, it is still true that one's right to something can be violated only when one has the conceptual capability of desiring the thing in question. For example, an individual who would now desire not to be a slave if he weren't emotionally unbalanced, or if he weren't temporarily unconscious, or if he hadn't previously been conditioned to want to be a slave, must possess the concepts involved in the desire not to be a slave. Since it is really only the conceptual capability presupposed by the desire to continue existing as a subject of experiences and other mental states, and not the desire itself, that enters into the above argument, the modification required in the account of the conditions under which an individual's rights can be violated does not undercut my defense of the self-consciousness requirement.[5]

To sum up, my argument has been that having a right to life presupposes that one is capable of desiring to continue existing as a subject of experiences and other mental states. This in turn presupposes both that one has the concept of such a continuing entity and that one believes that one is oneself such an entity. So an entity that lacks such a consciousness of itself as a continuing subject of mental states does not have a right to life.

It would be natural to ask at this point whether satisfaction of this requirement is not only necessary but also sufficient to ensure that a thing has a right to life. I am inclined to an affirmative answer. However, the issue is not urgent in the present context, since as long as the requirement is in fact a necessary one we have the basis of an adequate defense of abortion and infanticide. If an organism must satisfy some other condition before it has a serious right to life, the result will merely be that the interval during which infanticide is morally permissible may be somewhat longer. Although the point at which an organism first achieves self-consciousness and hence the capacity of desiring to continue existing as a subject of experiences and other mental states may be a theoretically incorrect cutoff point, it is at least a morally safe one: any error it involves is on the side of caution. . . .

This completes my discussion of the basic moral principles involved in the issue of abortion and infanticide. But I want to comment upon an

5. There are, however, situations other than those discussed here which might seem to count against the claim that a person cannot have a right unless he is conceptually capable of having the corresponding desire. Can't a young child, for example, have a right to an estate, even though he may not be conceptually capable of wanting the estate? It is clear that such situations have to be carefully considered if one is to arrive at a satisfactory account of the concept of a right. My inclination is to say that the correct description is not that the child now has a right to the estate, but that he will come to have such a right when he is mature, and that in the meantime no one else has a right to the estate. My reason for saying that the child does not now have a right to the estate is that he cannot now do things with the estate, such as selling it or giving it away, that he will be able to do later on.

important factual question, namely, at what point an organism comes to possess the concept of a self as a continuing subject of experiences and other mental states, together with the belief that it is itself such a continuing entity. This is obviously a matter for detailed psychological investigation, but everyday observation makes it perfectly clear, I believe, that a newborn baby does not possess the concept of a continuing self, any more than a newborn kitten possesses such a concept. If so, infanticide during a time interval shortly after birth must be morally acceptable.

# ON THE MORAL AND LEGAL STATUS OF ABORTION

*Mary Anne Warren*

The question which we must answer in order to produce a satisfactory solution to the problem of the moral status of abortion is this: How are we to define the moral community, the set of beings with full and equal moral rights, such that we can decide whether a human fetus is a member of this community or not? What sort of entity, exactly, has the inalienable rights to life, liberty, and the pursuit of happiness? . . .

Can it be established that genetic humanity is sufficient for moral humanity? I think that there are very good reasons for not defining the moral community in this way. I would like to suggest an alternative way of defining the moral community, which I will argue for only to the extent of explaining why it is, or should be, self-evident. The suggestion is simply that the moral community consists of all and only *people*, rather than all and only human beings;[1] and probably the best way of demonstrating its self-evidence is by considering the concept of personhood, to see what sorts of entity are and are not persons, and what the decision that a being is or is not a person implies about its moral rights.

What characteristics entitle an entity to be considered a person? This is obviously not the place to attempt a complete analysis of the concept of personhood, but we do not need such a fully adequate analysis just to determine whether and why a fetus is or isn't a person. All we need is a rough and approximate list of the most basic criteria of personhood, and

1. From here on, we will use 'human' to mean genetically human, since the moral sense seems closely connected to, and perhaps derived from, the assumption that genetic humanity is sufficient for membership in the moral community.

From Mary Anne Warren, "On the Moral and Legal Status of Abortion," reprinted by permission from vol. 57, no. 1 (January 1973), pp. 54–56, of *The Monist*, La Salle, Illinois 61301.

some idea of which, or how many, of these an entity must satisfy in order to properly be considered a person.

In searching for such criteria, it is useful to look beyond the set of people with whom we are acquainted, and ask how we would decide whether a totally alien being was a person or not. (For we have no right to assume that genetic humanity is necessary for personhood.) Imagine a space traveler who lands on an unknown planet and encounters a race of beings utterly unlike any he has ever seen or heard of. If he wants to be sure of behaving morally toward these beings, he has to somehow decide whether they are people, and hence have full moral rights, or whether they are the sort of thing which he need not feel guilty about treating as, for example, a source of food.

How should he go about making this decision? If he has some anthropological background, he might look for such things as religion, art, and the manufacturing of tools, weapons, or shelters, since these factors have been used to distinguish our human from our prehuman ancestors, in what seems to be closer to the moral than the genetic sense of 'human'. And no doubt he would be right to consider the presence of such factors as good evidence that the alien beings were people, and morally human. It would, however, be overly anthropocentric of him to take the absence of these things as adequate evidence that they were not, since we can imagine people who have progressed beyond, or evolved without ever developing, these cultural characteristics.

I suggest that the traits which are most central to the concept of personhood, or humanity in the moral sense, are, very roughly, the following:

(1) consciousness (of objects and events external and/or internal to the being), and in particular the capacity to feel pain;

(2) reasoning (the *developed* capacity to solve new and relatively complex problems);

(3) self-motivated activity (activity which is relatively independent of either genetic or direct external control);

(4) the capacity to communicate, by whatever means, messages of an indefinite variety of types, that is, not just with an indefinite number of possible contents, but on indefinitely many possible topics;

(5) the presence of self-concepts, and self-awareness, either individual or racial, or both.

Admittedly, there are apt to be a great many problems involved in formulating precise definitions of these criteria, let alone in developing universally valid behavioral criteria for deciding when they apply. But I will assume that both we and our explorer know approximately what (1)–(5) mean, and that he is also able to determine whether or not they apply. How, then, should he use his findings to decide whether or not the alien beings are people? We needn't suppose that an entity must have *all* of these attributes to be properly considered a person; (1) and (2) alone may well be sufficient for personhood, and quite probably (1)–(3) are sufficient. Neither do we need to insist that any one of these criteria is *necessary* for personhood, although once again (1) and (2) look like fairly good candidates for necessary conditions, as does (3), if 'activity' is construed so as to include the activity of reasoning.

All we need to claim, to demonstrate that a fetus is not a person, is that any being which satisfies *none* of (1)–(5) is certainly not a person. I consider this claim to be so obvious that I think anyone who denied it, and claimed that a being which satisfied none of (1)–(5) was a person all the same, would thereby demonstrate that he had no notion at all of what a person is—perhaps because he had confused the concept of a person with that of genetic humanity. If the opponents of abortion were to deny the appropriateness of these five criteria, I do not know what further arguments would convince them. We would probably have to admit that our conceptual schemes were indeed irreconcilably different, and that our dispute could not be settled objectively.

I do not expect this to happen, however, since I think that the concept of a person is one which is very nearly universal (to people), and that it is common to both proabortionists and antiabortionists, even though neither group has fully realized the relevance of this concept to the resolution of their dispute. Furthermore, I think that on reflection even the antiabortionists ought to agree not only that (1)–(5) are central to the concept of personhood, but also that it is a part of this concept that all and only people have full moral rights. The concept of a person is in part a moral concept; once we have admitted that *x* is a person we have recognized, even if we have not agreed to respect, *x*'s right to be treated as a member of the moral community. It is true that the claim that *x* is a *human being* is more commonly voiced as part of an appeal to treat *x* decently than is the claim that *x* is a person, but this is either because 'human being' is here used in the sense which implies personhood, or because the genetic and moral senses of 'human' have been confused.

Now if (1)–(5) are indeed the primary criteria of personhood, then it is clear that genetic humanity is neither necessary nor sufficient for establishing that an entity is a person. Some human beings are not people, and there may well be people who are not human beings. A man or woman whose consciousness has been permanently obliterated but who remains alive is a human being which is no longer a person; defective human beings, with no appreciable mental capacity, are not and presumably never will be people; and a fetus is a human being which is not yet a person, and which therefore cannot coherently be said to have full moral rights.

# ABORTION: THE MORAL STATUS OF THE UNBORN

*Richard Werner*

I

Before I begin to show that one is a human being from conception onward, I want to make the following observations. When I claim that the
unborn are human beings, I am not merely stipulating what I will take the
sign "human being" to mean, nor am I giving the results of a random
sample poll conducted among ordinary language users. What I claim to
show is that if you and I are paradigms of human beings, then there is
every reason to believe and no good reason to deny that the unborn are
also human. I intend to show that one cannot refuse to grant that the
unborn are human without either (a) contradicting our present concept of
a human being or (b) radically changing our present concept of a human
being. I will show this by arguing that there are no relevant dissimilarities
between us as human beings and the unborn as human beings. All proposed cut-off points in the development of the unborn will be shown to
lead to unacceptable consequences and, as such, will be deemed arbitrary.
Here is my argument:

1. An adult human being is the end result of the continuous growth of the
   organism from conception.
2. From conception to adulthood, there is no break in this development which
   is relevant to the ontological status of the organism.
3. If $k$ is related to $k'$ such that $k$ is the end result of the continuous growth of
   the organism $k'$ and there is no break in this growth which is relevant to the
   ontological status of the organism, then $k'$ shares the same ontological status
   as does $k$.
4. Therefore, one is a human being from the point of conception onward.

OBJECTION A. Certainly the most troublesome premise in this argument is
2. It assumes that if one is a human being at time $t + 1$, one must also
have been human at time $t$ (given that $t$ is not prior in time to conception).
Why accept this premise at all?

REPLY TO A. Unless one has good reasons for believing that some significant change has occurred to a human being between $t$ and $t + 1$, there is
no reason to believe that such an entity would have changed its onto-

From Richard Werner, "Abortion: The Ontological and Moral Status of the Unborn," in *Today's
Moral Problems*, 2nd ed., Richard Wasserstrom, ed. (New York: Macmillan, 1979); originally
published, in a different version, as "Abortion: The Ontological Status of the Unborn," *Social
Theory and Practice*, vol. 3, no. 2 (Fall 1974), pp. 201–22. Excerpts reprinted by permission.
Copyright © 1975 by *Social Theory and Practice*.

logical status. So, to support *Objection A* one needs to show that premise 2 is false. One must show that $k$ had some significant characteristic(s) that made $k$ a human being at time $t + 1$ but that $k$ lacked at time $t$. In other words, one must be prepared to (i) give some nonarbitrary, non-ad hoc criterion for being human; and (ii) show that this criterion is not met by $k$ at some time $t$ but is met at time $t + 1$.

Let us consider some of the more popular attempts to provide such a necessary condition for being human. We will consider in turn each of the following conditions: (a) attainment of human form, (b) quickening or the achievement of spontaneous movement, (c) the achievement of consciousness as evidenced by an EEG, (d) viability, (e) birth.

Clearly, neither (a) nor (b) will do as necessary conditions since people who become severely disfigured and totally paralyzed are still considered human. Indeed, a disfigured or a paralyzed newborn is considered human even though failing to have attained these supposedly necessary conditions.

Condition (c), the ability to evidence an EEG, seems a more likely candidate than the first two. However, one's EEG may cease and then be revived some short time later after which one continues living one's normal life. Such entities are deemed human both during the lapse of the EEG and after its reappearance.

A more realistic attempt at a condition for being human is the following:

> (c′)  $k$ is a human being · only if · (c)  *or*  ($k$ has been a human
> being before)
> &  ($k$ will have an EEG
> in the future)

Besides the fact that the addition of the clause "one has been a human being before" seems totally ad hoc (the only function it serves is to rule out embryos and fetuses as humans), (c′) also has some rather undesirable consequences. For instance, if a doctor were working to revive the EEG of a patient and someone came into the room and shot the patient in the head, we would not say that the patient, qua human being, was killed by the gun shot wound. Since the patient neither had an EEG, nor would have one in the future, the patient would, by this criterion, have ceased to be a human being prior to the time of the gun shot. Also, even if someone never evidenced a human EEG but had all of the attributes we normally count as human—they looked and acted human, had a personality, could talk, think, remember, move about and so on—we would undoubtedly consider them human. Examples such as these show that there is neither a necessary nor a conceptual connection between EEGs and being human even though, in fact, the two may appear together most frequently.

Condition (d), viability or the ability to survive as an independent organism, is perhaps the most popular pro-abortionist position at the present time. The difficulty with this criterion is that it rules out as human the man on the heart-lung machine, the woman on the pacemaker, or the old person or baby who is totally dependent on others for their continued existence. In modern times it is more and more common for one to rely on some outside device or entity for one's continued existence. And, since the beginning of human life, some members of society have always been dependent on others for the continuance of their life. Yet condition (d) would be unable to account for the humanity of either of these groups.

Even if one were able to spell out the notion of viability in such a way as to capture the above groups but to exclude embryos and fetuses, perhaps by tacking on the notion of not being directly dependent on another human body for continued existence, it would still fall prey to the following sort of counterexample. In some cases of Siamese twins one member of the pair could be parted from his sibling and go on to live a normal life. However, the second twin is directly dependent on the first twin's body for his existence such that a separation would cause this second twin's death. Now this dependent twin is certainly not viable in any sense in which an embryo or fetus is not. Yet he is surely a human being. Hence, even the modified version of (d) lacks credibility as a criterion for being human.

Condition (e), birth, is totally arbitrary. There is no relevant biological, moral or conceptual difference between the newborn and the delivered fetus. The fact that during the last two months of pregnancy we could deliver the fetus at any time shows that birth is a totally ad hoc criterion for being human, since when birth occurs is totally arbitrary and even controllable by outside means.

Further, if it were possible to raise test-tube babies from the point of conception on, just what if anything would count as birth? Suppose in such cases it was necessary to keep the entity in an incubator six months longer than in the case of normal pregnancy, when then is birth? Suppose it was necessary to change the type of incubator every two weeks during this 15-month period, and then to return the child to a controlled environment every night for the first two years of life, when then is birth? Again the arbitrary nature of when birth occurs makes any attempt at drawing a line seem ludicrous.

Unless one is capable of providing a nonarbitrary, non-ad hoc necessary condition for being human that rules out embryos and fetuses as human, *Objection A* does not hold.

OBJECTION B. One might hold that the concept of a human being has vague boundaries. During pregnancy the fetus gradually moves from a nonhuman state into a human one; there is a hazy period in pregnancy during which a fetus gradually becomes a human being.[1] One might defend this position by pointing out that the concept of a human being is so complex that the addition of no one property makes one human. So,

1. M. A. Warren, "On the Moral and Legal Status of Abortion," *The Monist*, 57, No. 1 (January 1973), 43–61 and reprinted in *Today's Moral Problems*, 2nd ed., Richard Wasserstrom, ed. (New York: Macmillan Publishing Co., Inc., 1979), 35–51, with an added postscript. Following page references will be to the latter publication.

the transformation into a human being is a gradual one, taking place over a period of time and requiring the addition of a cluster of properties.

REPLY TO B. If we attempt something like the following, which makes the best possible cluster concept for the pro-abortionist given the properties we stated earlier, we still run into difficulties.

$k$ is a human being · only if · (a) or (b) or (c) or (d) or (e)

One can imagine a severely disfigured, totally paralyzed, nonviable Siamese twin who was conceived and developed in a test tube and whose EEG has ceased during an operation but which will be revived in the next minute and who will then go on to live his life. We would still consider such a twin to be a human being even though he satisfies none of the above criteria.

Another possibility would be to attempt to construct a cluster concept out of the properties suggested by M. A. Warren.[2] Basically, these are the following: (f) consciousness, (g) reasoning ability, (h) self-motivated activity, (i) capacity to communicate, (j) presence of self-concepts. This then, would give us the following sort of analysis.

$k$ is a human being · only if · (f) or (g) or (h) or (i) or (j)

First, it should be noted, according to this criterion a perfectly normal six-month-old child would fail to be human. However, such a child is counted as human by everyone save, perhaps, adherents of infanticide. If this is incapable of convincing the reader, one can easily imagine a society where suspended animation had been developed to a very high degree of sophistication. In this society people could be instantly frozen and then, years later, slowly revived over a two-year period. Further, while in this state of suspended animation, the frozen entity would have none of the properties (f) through (j). Nevertheless, after going through the two-year revitalization period, one's normal bodily functions and abilities would be restored. It is clear that during the state of suspended animation, one would still be a human being. For instance, if someone entered the frozen room housing the bodies and in full possession of his wits, willfully began to destroy the bodies, we would certainly hold him responsible for murder. These frozen persons show that even Warren's list of properties cannot provide the foundation for a cluster concept for being human.

Like the proponents of *Objection A*, those of *Objection B* must be able to give some nonarbitrary, non-ad hoc criteria for being human and then show that a fetus or embryo fails to satisfy them at time $t$, but does satisfy them at time $t + 1$. In neither case can I see any way of carrying that out.

Furthermore, one can agree that the concept of human being, like most interesting notions, is indeed a cluster concept, but deny that fetuses and embryos fall within the hazy boundaries of the concept. For instance, if monkeys throughout the world began giving birth to creatures that looked and behaved much more like humans than monkeys, then we may

2. Warren, 45.

well be perplexed as to whether these entities were human. Cases like these illustrate the unclear boundaries of the concept of a human being rather than cases like embryos and fetuses.

OBJECTION C. One can construct an argument of exactly the same form as the one I constructed in sec. I, but which would yield the absurd conclusion that if a zygote is a human being, then gametes are human beings and always have been. Such a conclusion illustrates the perversity of using a "slippery slope" type of argument to deal with the complex concept of a human being. Just as an acorn is not an oak, an embryo is not a human.[3]

REPLY TO C. The difficulty with the argument proposed in *Objection C* is that it must assume that conception is an irrelevant change in genetic human development. But unlike the fetus immediately prior to birth and the baby immediately afterward, there is a significant and important difference between the ovum or sperm immediately before fertilization and the zygote immediately afterward. Given the proper environment the embryo, qua itself, is a growing, developing organism. All things being equal, the zygote will grow into a person. On the other hand, the ovum or sperm qua itself is neither growing nor developing no matter in what sort of environment one should find it or put it into. A gamete will not, by itself, grow into anything other than what it already is—a gamete. In this sense it is inert and, thereby, nonhuman. A necessary condition of the ovum becoming human is that it begin to grow and develop into a person, that it be fertilized by a sperm cell. Otherwise, it remains inert, never developing or growing into anything whatever and, as such, is no more a human being than is one of my red blood cells. Admittedly an acorn is not an oak, nor is an ovum or sperm cell a human, but an acorn germinated in the soil is indeed an oak and so is the impregnated ovum a human.[4]

In addition, the zygote is the beginning of the spatiotemporal identity of the creature we call a human being. Clearly, any two separate biological units are at least numerically distinct and, accordingly, could not be the same human. We simply are not the sorts of creatures that can be divided over space and time into distinct biological units, such as ovum and sperm are, with all disjoints remaining one and the same human being. Prior to conception there simply is nothing that could count as a *single* growing and developing human being. The zygote is the first link in the spatiotemporal chain of identity we know as a human being.[5]

Basically what my original argument comes to is the following:

3. This point is J. J. Thomson's objection to the type of argument I have presented. "A Defense of Abortion," *Philosophy and Public Affairs* 1, No. 1 (Fall 1977), 47–66.

4. See J. Finnis, "The Rights and Wrongs of Abortion," *Philosophy and Public Affairs* 2, No. 2 (Winter 1973), 144–156, who uses a similar line of argument and the same analogy as the one I have presented.

5. See R. Wertheimer, "Understanding the Abortion Argument," *Philosophy and Public Affairs* 1, No. 1 (Fall 1971), 67–95, who uses a similar line of argument to the one I have presented.

*k* is a human being · *iff* · *k* belongs to a spatiotemporal chain of identity *m* such that *m* is an instance of at least a portion of the archetypal human spatiotemporal chain of identity *l*.

*l* is the archetypal human spatiotemporal chain of identity · *iff* · *l* is that spatiotemporal chain of identity some portion of which is commonly recognized as being paradigmatic of belonging to the human species *and* the rest of the chain *l* is such that there is no break in the chain *l* which is relevant to the human ontological status of the organism.

The following diagram illustrates what I mean.

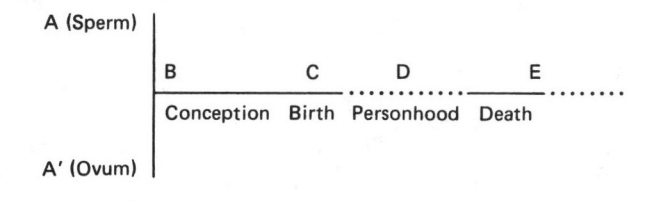

Now, clearly, C through E is that portion of the archetypal spatio-temporal chain of identity that is commonly recognized as being para-digmatic of belonging to the human species. Further, A and A' through B fail to be portions of the archetypal human spatiotemporal chain of identity because (a) prior to conception the characteristic humanness of the chain, evidenced by the growing developing nature of the human organism from B through E, is lacking, (b) the chain of identity breaks down at B since, prior to that moment, there is no single organism that *k* might be. My rejection of other proposed cutoff points is taken as evi-dence that the archetypal chain of identity extends as far back as B, that there is no break in the chain from B onward that is relevant to the human ontological status of the organism. So, the archetypal human chain of identity would be constituted by B through E. All that is needed for my criterion to hold is that *k* evidence some chain of identity *m* such that *m* exemplifies at least a portion of this archetypal human chain of identity *l*.[6] . . .

6. Now that we have answered C we can return to an objection similar to B. One might claim that my arguments are like those which use mathematical induction to show that one cannot draw a clear line between being bald and not and, hence, no one could ever become bald. Unlike the baldness argument, however, we have drawn a clear and sharp line and have given arguments to show why this is the relevant cut-off point. Unlike the baldness argument, our argument is neither slippery nor sophistic.

## II

In the previous section I tried to establish only that one is human from the point of conception onward. In this section I will be concerned with one particular type of argument that has been advanced to establish the morality of abortion. Proponents of this position claim or hold positions that entail that the morally relevant stage in human development begins when one realizes the status of personhood. This type of argument has taken several forms and I will explain each briefly in turn.

First, M. A. Warren holds that the concept of a person is in part a *moral* concept; to be recognized as a person is, *eo ipso*, to be recognized as an entity who is a fully fledged member of the moral community, having all of the rights such membership entails. Having at least one of the characteristics (f) through (j) (mentioned earlier) is a necessary condition of being a person. On the other hand, the concept of a human being in the biological sense is not a moral concept. Hence, simply being human entitles one to no moral rights or considerations. However, other persons may have an interest in having children who are unwanted by their natural parents or an interest in not having their moral sensibilities shocked by infanticide. Infanticide is wrong for reasons analogous to those which make it wrong to wantonly destroy natural resources or great works of art. So long as there are people who want an infant preserved, and who are willing and able to provide the means to care for it, it is wrong to destroy it. Other persons' interest in the unborn does not, however, render abortion wrong. The rights of the mother to freedom, happiness, and self-determination plus the unborn's dependence on the mother override other's interests.[7]

Second, M. Tooley holds that one has a right to life if there is some time at which one is or will be capable of wishing that one had such a right and at which time one *would* so wish if one had all of the relevant information and had not been subjected to influences that distorted one's preferences. Only the unborn and future generations who will have an actual existence as persons have rights and can be wronged.[8]

Third, J. Narveson holds that the reason it is wrong to kill innocent human being V is because V values or desires V's continued existence. Accordingly, at least in the case of persons in Tooley's sense, having values or desires is a necessary condition for a person to have a right not to be killed. Clearly, fetuses lack values and desires of the appropriate sort since they are conceptually incapable of either valuing or desiring to lead a full life. Narveson argues that in the case of the unborn, it is the values or desires of its mother or appropriate parent(s) that are the relevant factor in deciding whether the act of abortion should be performed. Although Narveson does not apply this reasoning to infants, it seems clear where his arguments would lead. Small infants are as conceptually incapable as a fetus of valuing their existence or desiring to lead a full life. As such, the

7. Warren, 44–51.
8. M. Tooley, "Abortion and Infanticide," *Philosophy and Public Affairs*, 2, No. 1 (Fall 1972), 37–65. Also, "Michael Tooley Replies," *Philosophy and Public Affairs*, 2, No. 4 (Summer 1973), 419–432.

values and desires of the child's parents or those interested in adopting or providing support for the child are the relevant factor in deciding whether the act of infanticide should be performed. As with Warren, the child or the unborn *itself* is due neither moral rights nor moral consideration since it lacks the characteristics necessary for such consideration.

There is one type of counterexample that I believe demonstrates the unacceptable consequences of adopting any of the three positions sketched previously. Let us imagine a society that accepts that full moral rights and amenability to moral consideration applies only to persons in the senses prescribed by Warren or Tooley or to humans with values or desires as prescribed by Narveson. Let us suppose further that in such a society no one desires or has an interest in stepping in as parents, trustees, or guardians for infants and the unborn. Such a society could legitimately declare a national open hunting season on infant orphans and other unwanted nonpersons such as the grossly retarded or insane. They could develop a new gourmet delight "roast unwanted infant." They could begin to establish farms such that one buys live abortuses, raises them for food, experimentation, or sport. They could take such young children raised from live abortuses, perform brain operations on them so as to ensure that they will never develop characteristics (f) through (j) or desires or values of the appropriate sort and then use them as pets, servants, slaves, lab animals, and so on. Indeed, it seems that we could not rule out the wanton killing of or medical experimentation upon infants, severely retarded humans, the extremely mentally ill, certain possible future generations and all other nonperson humans.

One might attempt to discount all of this by appealing to Warren's notion of the rights of actually existing persons not to have their values defamed by such goings on, or by bringing in J. Feinberg's notion of guardians or trustees who represent the interests of such beings.[9] But, by hypothesis, in our example these considerations are irrelevant. Further, even if we drop the requirement in our example that states that there are no guardians or morally shocked people available, we can, I believe, take an ideal observer's view, ignore any violations of the rights of actually existing persons, and *still* we would find such activities as I have just described morally repugnant and wrong. What this shows is that it is these human creatures who are being *directly* wronged rather than the mere indirect harm to some trustee or other person. They, the nonperson humans, ought not to be so treated *because of who they are* and regardless of how others' senses are shocked and so on. Neither of the three positions sketched earlier can account for this fact.

---

9. J. Feinberg, "Is There a Right To Be Born?" *Understanding Moral Philosophy*, ed. James Rachels (Enrico and Belmont California: Dickenson Publishing Co., Inc.: 1976), 346–357. The counterexample used here would also apply to Feinberg's analysis. At least the last part of the counterexample would also be telling against L. S. Carrier, "Abortion and the Right to Life," *Social Theory and Practice*, 3, No. 4 (Fall 1975), 381–401, who holds that ". . . an individual who possesses both consciousness *and the potentiality for a heightened consciousness* does have a distinctive right to life." (My emphasis) Carrier, 397. And, "where there is no right to life, then—all else being equal—there is no moral case to be made against abortion as such. . . ." Carrier, 381.

Narveson's point that abortion is allowed and widely practiced in North America and elsewhere, yet people still raise children with love, dedication, and enthusiasm, at best provides cold comfort for the nonperson humans in our example. My concern is with what a moral theory actually entails and not with the inconsistency of actual practices. If one adopts the position that a necessary condition of *x* having a right to A is *x*'s valuing or desiring such a right or *x*'s having one or more of characteristics (f) through (j), then one's position entails that none of the aforementioned beings in our imaginary society has rights in and of himself. One has adopted a moral theory that, at least in instances where no actual person's values or desires are frustrated, cannot disallow as immoral the practices I have sketched.

Similarly unhelpful is Narveson's point that to deny that *x* has a right to life is not the same as saying we may do anything we like to *x*. One could kill or alter all of the creatures in question in a painless and kind manner, one could then treat them with kindness and care, again not causing them pain (perhaps even destroying their capacity for pain in the original alterations), and still, I would think, we would find such killings or alterations morally repugnant. The real question is: Do the human creatures of which I just wrote have *the right* not to be so treated? If one admits that *for their own sake* they ought morally not to be so treated, and ought morally not to be so treated even when no actual person's values or desires are frustrated, then I do not see how one can deny that they, qua themselves, have the right not to be so treated. And this is, after all, the question at issue. I believe that my example shows rather conclusively that we cannot capture our considered moral judgments concerning the treatment of nonperson humans by granting rights only to persons or only to humans with the appropriate values and desires. Accordingly, the three positions sketched all derive from defective moral theories.

# A DEFENSE OF ABORTION[1]

*Judith Jarvis Thomson*

Most opposition to abortion relies on the premise that the fetus is a human being, a person, from the moment of conception. The premise is argued for, but, as I think, not well. Take, for example, the most common argument. We are asked to notice that the development of a human being

1. I am very much indebted to James Thomson for discussion, criticism, and many helpful suggestions.

From Judith Jarvis Thomson, "A Defense of Abortion," *Philosophy & Public Affairs*, vol. 1, no. 1 (Fall 1971), pp. 47–56. Copyright © 1971 by Princeton University Press. Excerpt reprinted by permission of Princeton University Press.

from conception through birth into childhood is continuous; then it is said that to draw a line, to choose a point in this development and say "before this point the thing is not a person, after this point it is a person" is to make an arbitrary choice, a choice for which in the nature of things no good reason can be given. It is concluded that the fetus is, or anyway that we had better say it is, a person from the moment of conception. But this conclusion does not follow. Similar things might be said about the development of an acorn into an oak tree, and it does not follow that acorns are oak trees, or that we had better say they are. Arguments of this form are sometimes called "slippery slope arguments"—the phrase is perhaps self-explanatory—and it is dismaying that opponents of abortion rely on them so heavily and uncritically.

I am inclined to agree, however, that the prospects for "drawing a line" in the development of the fetus look dim. I am inclined to think also that we shall probably have to agree that the fetus has already become a human person well before birth. Indeed, it comes as a surprise when one first learns how early in its life it begins to acquire human characteristics. By the tenth week, for example, it already has a face, arms and legs, fingers and toes; it has internal organs, and brain activity is detectable.[2] On the other hand, I think that the premise is false, that the fetus is not a person from the moment of conception. A newly fertilized ovum, a newly implanted clump of cells, is no more a person than an acorn is an oak tree. But I shall not discuss any of this. For it seems to me to be of great interest to ask what happens if, for the sake of argument, we allow the premise. How, precisely, are we supposed to get from there to the conclusion that abortion is morally impermissible? Opponents of abortion commonly spend most of their time establishing that the fetus is a person, and hardly any time explaining the step from there to the impermissibility of abortion. Perhaps they think the step too simple and obvious to require much comment. Or perhaps instead they are simply being economical in argument. Many of those who defend abortion rely on the premise that the fetus is not a person, but only a bit of tissue that will become a person at birth; and why pay out more arguments than you have to? Whatever the explanation, I suggest that the step they take is neither easy nor obvious, that it calls for closer examination than it is commonly given, and that when we do give it this closer examination we shall feel inclined to reject it.

I propose, then, that we grant that the fetus is a person from the moment of conception. How does the argument go from here? Something like this, I take it. Every person has a right to life. So the fetus has a right to life. No doubt the mother has a right to decide what shall happen in and to her body; everyone would grant that. But surely a person's right to life is stronger and more stringent than the mother's right to decide what happens in and to her body, and so outweighs it. So the fetus may not be killed; an abortion may not be performed.

2. Daniel Callahan, *Abortion: Law, Choice and Morality* (New York, 1970), p. 373. This book gives a fascinating survey of the available information on abortion. The Jewish tradition is surveyed in David M. Feldman, *Birth Control in Jewish Law* (New York, 1968), Part 5, the Catholic tradition in John T. Noonan, Jr., "An Almost Absolute Value in History," in *The Morality of Abortion*, ed. John T. Noonan, Jr. (Cambridge, Mass., 1970).

It sounds plausible. But now let me ask you to imagine this. You wake up in the morning and find yourself back to back in bed with an unconscious violinist. A famous unconscious violinist. He has been found to have a fatal kidney ailment, and the Society of Music Lovers has canvassed all the available medical records and found that you alone have the right blood type to help. They have therefore kidnapped you, and last night the violinist's circulatory system was plugged into yours, so that your kidneys can be used to extract poisons from his blood as well as your own. The director of the hospital now tells you, "Look, we're sorry the Society of Music Lovers did this to you—we would never have permitted it if we had known. But still, they did it, and the violinist now is plugged into you. To unplug you would be to kill him. But never mind, it's only for nine months. By then he will have recovered from his ailment, and can safely be unplugged from you." Is it morally incumbent on you to accede to this situation? No doubt it would be very nice of you if you did, a great kindness. But do you *have* to accede to it? What if it were not nine months, but nine years? Or longer still? What if the director of the hospital says, "Tough luck, I agree, but you've now got to stay in bed, with the violinist plugged into you, for the rest of your life. Because remember this. All persons have a right to life, and violinists are persons. Granted you have a right to decide what happens in and to your body, but a person's right to life outweighs your right to decide what happens in and to your body. So you cannot ever be unplugged from him." I imagine you would regard this as outrageous, which suggests that something really is wrong with that plausible-sounding argument I mentioned a moment ago.

In this case, of course, you were kidnapped; you didn't volunteer for the operation that plugged the violinist into your kidneys. Can those who oppose abortion on the ground I mentioned make an exception for a pregnancy due to rape? Certainly. They can say that persons have a right to life only if they didn't come into existence because of rape; or they can say that all persons have a right to life, but that some have less of a right to life than others, in particular, that those who came into existence because of rape have less. But these statements have a rather unpleasant sound. Surely the question of whether you have a right to life at all, or how much of it you have, shouldn't turn on the question of whether or not you are the product of a rape. And in fact the people who oppose abortion on the ground I mentioned do not make this distinction, and hence do not make an exception in case of rape.

Nor do they make an exception for a case in which the mother has to spend the nine months of her pregnancy in bed. They would agree that would be a great pity, and hard on the mother; but all the same, all persons have a right to life, the fetus is a person, and so on. I suspect, in fact, that they would not make an exception for a case in which, miraculously enough, the pregnancy went on for nine years, or even the rest of the mother's life.

Some won't even make an exception for a case in which continuation of the pregnancy is likely to shorten the mother's life; they regard abortion as impermissible even to save the mother's life. Such cases are nowadays very rare, and many opponents of abortion do not accept this extreme view. All the same, it is a good place to begin: a number of points of interest come out in respect to it.

1. Let us call the view that abortion is impermissible even to save the mother's life "the extreme view." I want to suggest first that it does not issue from the argument I mentioned earlier without the addition of some fairly powerful premises. Suppose a woman has become pregnant, and now learns that she has a cardiac condition such that she will die if she carries the baby to term. What may be done for her? The fetus, being a person, has a right to life, but as the mother is a person too, so has she a right to life. Presumably they have an equal right to life. How is it supposed to come out that an abortion may not be performed? If mother and child have an equal right to life, shouldn't we perhaps flip a coin? Or should we add to the mother's right to life her right to decide what happens in and to her body, which everybody seems to be ready to grant—the sum of her rights now outweighing the fetus' right to life?

The most familiar argument here is the following. We are told that performing the abortion would be directly killing[3] the child, whereas doing nothing would not be killing the mother, but only letting her die. Moreover, in killing the child, one would be killing an innocent person, for the child has committed no crime, and is not aiming at his mother's death. And then there are a variety of ways in which this might be continued. (1) But as directly killing an innocent person is always and absolutely impermissible, an abortion may not be performed. Or, (2) as directly killing an innocent person is murder, and murder is always and absolutely impermissible, an abortion may not be performed.[4] Or, (3) as one's duty to refrain from directly killing an innocent person is more stringent than one's duty to keep a person from dying, an abortion may not be performed. Or, (4) if one's only options are directly killing an innocent person or letting a person die, one must prefer letting the person die, and thus an abortion may not be performed.[5]

Some people seem to have thought that these are not further premises which must be added if the conclusion is to be reached, but that

---

3. The term "direct" in the arguments I refer to is a technical one. Roughly, what is meant by "direct killing" is either killing as an end in itself, or killing as a means to some end, for example, the end of saving someone else's life. See note 6, below, for an example of its use.

4. Cf. *Encyclical Letter of Pope Pius XI on Christian Marriage*, St. Paul Editions (Boston, n.d.), p. 32: "however much we may pity the mother whose health and even life is gravely imperiled in the performance of the duty allotted to her by nature, nevertheless what could ever be a sufficient reason for excusing in any way the direct murder of the innocent? This is precisely what we are dealing with here." Noonan (*The Morality of Abortion*, p. 43) reads this as follows: "What cause can ever avail to excuse in any way the direct killing of the innocent? For it is a question of that."

5. The thesis in (4) is in an interesting way weaker than those in (1), (2), and (3): they rule out abortion even in cases in which both mother *and* child will die if the abortion is not performed. By contrast, one who held the view expressed in (4) could consistently say that one needn't prefer letting two persons die to killing one.

they follow from the very fact that an innocent person has a right to life.[6] But this seems to me to be a mistake, and perhaps the simplest way to show this is to bring out that while we must certainly grant that innocent persons have a right to life, the theses in (1) through (4) are all false. Take (2), for example. If directly killing an innocent person is murder, and thus is impermissible, then the mother's directly killing the innocent person inside her is murder, and thus is impermissible. But it cannot seriously be thought to be murder if the mother performs an abortion on herself to save her life. It cannot seriously be said that she *must* refrain, that she *must* sit passively by and wait for her death. Let us look again at the case of you and the violinist. There you are, in bed with the violinist, and the director of the hospital says to you, "It's all most distressing, and I deeply sympathize, but you see this is putting an additional strain on your kidneys, and you'll be dead within the month. But you *have* to stay where you are all the same. Because unplugging you would be directly killing an innocent violinist, and that's murder, and that's impermissible." If anything in the world is true, it is that you do not commit murder, you do not do what is impermissible, if you reach around to your back and unplug yourself from that violinist to save your life.

The main focus of attention in writings on abortion has been on what a third party may or may not do in answer to a request from a woman for an abortion. This is in a way understandable. Things being as they are, there isn't much a woman can safely do to abort herself. So the question asked is what a third party may do, and what the mother may do, if it is mentioned at all, is deduced, almost as an afterthought, from what it is concluded that third parties may do. But it seems to me that to treat the matter in this way is to refuse to grant to the mother that very status of person which is so firmly insisted on for the fetus. For we cannot simply read off what a person may do from what a third party may do. Suppose you find yourself trapped in a tiny house with a growing child. I mean a very tiny house, and a rapidly growing child—you are already up against the wall of the house and in a few minutes you'll be crushed to death. The child on the other hand won't be crushed to death; if nothing is done to stop him from growing he'll be hurt, but in the end he'll simply burst open the house and walk out a free man. Now I could well understand it if a bystander were to say, "There's nothing we can do for you. We cannot choose between your life and his, we cannot be the ones to decide who is to live, we cannot intervene." But it cannot be concluded that you too can do nothing, that you cannot attack it to save your life. However innocent the child may be, you do not have to wait passively

---

6. Cf. the following passage from Pius XII, *Address to the Italian Catholic Society of Midwives:* "The baby in the maternal breast has the right to life immediately from God.— Hence there is no man, no human authority, no science, no medical, eugenic, social, economic or moral 'indication' which can establish or grant a valid juridical ground for a direct deliberate disposition of an innocent human life, that is a disposition which looks to its destruction either as an end or as a means to another end perhaps in itself not illicit.—The baby, still not born, is a man in the same degree and for the same reason as the mother" (quoted in Noonan, *The Morality of Abortion,* p. 45).

while it crushes you to death. Perhaps a pregnant woman is vaguely felt to have the status of house, to which we don't allow the right of self-defense. But if the woman houses the child, it should be remembered that she is a person who houses it.

I should perhaps stop to say explicitly that I am not claiming that people have a right to do anything whatever to save their lives. I think, rather, that there are drastic limits to the right of self-defense. If someone threatens you with death unless you torture someone else to death, I think you have not the right, even to save your life, to do so. But the case under consideration here is very different. In our case there are only two people involved, one whose life is threatened, and one who threatens it. Both are innocent: the one who is threatened is not threatened because of any fault, the one who threatens does not threaten because of any fault. For this reason we may feel that we bystanders cannot intervene. But the person threatened can.

In sum, a woman surely can defend her life against the threat to it posed by the unborn child, even if doing so involves its death. And this shows not merely that the theses in (1) through (4) are false; it shows also that the extreme view of abortion is false, and so we need not canvass any other possible ways of arriving at it from the argument I mentioned at the outset.

2. The extreme view could of course be weakened to say that while abortion is permissible to save the mother's life, it may not be performed by a third party, but only by the mother herself. But this cannot be right either. For what we have to keep in mind is that the mother and the unborn child are not like two tenants in a small house which has, by an unfortunate mistake, been rented to both: the mother *owns* the house. The fact that she does adds to the offensiveness of deducing that the mother can do nothing from the supposition that third parties can do nothing. But it does more than this: it casts a bright light on the supposition that third parties can do nothing. Certainly it lets us see that a third party who says "I cannot choose between you" is fooling himself if he thinks this is impartiality. If Jones has found and fastened on a certain coat, which he needs to keep him from freezing, but which Smith also needs to keep him from freezing, then it is not impartiality that says "I cannot choose between you" when Smith owns the coat. Women have said again and again "This body is *my* body!" and they have reason to feel angry, reason to feel that it has been like shouting into the wind. Smith, after all, is hardly likely to bless us if we say to him, "Of course it's your coat, anybody would grant that it is. But no one may choose between you and Jones who is to have it."

We should really ask what it is that says "no one may choose" in the face of the fact that the body that houses the child is the mother's body. It may be simply a failure to appreciate this fact. But it may be something more interesting, namely the sense that one has a right to refuse to lay hands on people, even where it would be just and fair to do so, even where justice seems to require that somebody do so. Thus justice might call for somebody to get Smith's coat back from Jones, and yet you have a right to refuse to be the one to lay hands on Jones, a right to refuse to do physical violence to him. This, I think, must be granted. But then what should be said is not "no one may choose," but only "*I* cannot choose," and indeed not even this, but "*I* will not *act*," leaving it open that somebody else can or should, and in particular that anyone in a position of authority, with the job of securing people's rights, both can and should. So this is no difficulty. I have not been arguing that any given third party must accede to the mother's request that he perform an abortion to save her life, but only that he may.

I suppose that in some views of human life the mother's body is only on loan to her, the loan not being one which gives her any prior claim to it. One who held this veiw might well think it impartiality to say "I cannot choose." But I shall simply ignore this possibility. My own view is that if a human being has any just, prior claim to anything at all, he has a just, prior claim to his own body. And perhaps this needn't be argued for here anyway, since, as I mentioned, the arguments against abortion we are looking at do grant that the woman has a right to decide what happens in and to her body.

But although they do grant it, I have tried to show that they do not take seriously what is done in granting it. I suggest the same thing will reappear even more clearly when we turn away from cases in which the mother's life is at stake, and attend, as I propose we now do, to the vastly more common cases in which a woman wants an abortion for some less weighty reason than preserving her own life.

3. Where the mother's life is not at stake, the argument I mentioned at the outset seems to have a much stronger pull. "Everyone has a right to life, so the unborn person has a right to life." And isn't the child's right to life weightier than anything other than the mother's own right to life, which she might put forward as ground for an abortion?

This argument treats the right to life as if it were unproblematic. It is not, and this seems to me to be precisely the source of the mistake.

For we should now, at long last, ask what it comes to, to have a right to life. In some views having a right to life includes having a right to be given at least the bare minimum one needs for continued life. But suppose that what in fact *is* the bare minimum a man needs for continued life is something he has no right at all to be given? If I am sick unto death, and the only thing that will save my life is the touch of Henry Fonda's cool hand on my fevered brow, then all the same, I have no right to be given the touch of Henry Fonda's cool hand on my fevered brow. It would be frightfully nice of him to fly in from the West Coast to provide it. It would be less nice, though no doubt well meant, if my friends flew out to the West Coast and carried Henry Fonda back with them. But I have no right at all against anybody that he should do this for me. Or again, to return to the story I told earlier, the fact that for continued life that violinist needs the continued use of your kidneys does not establish that he has a right to be given the continued use of your kidneys. He certainly has no right against you that *you* should give him continued use of your kidneys. For nobody has any right to use your kidneys unless you give him such a right; and nobody has the right against you that you shall give him this right—if you do allow him to go on using your kidneys, this is a kindness on your part, and not something he can claim from you as his due. Nor has he any right against anybody else that *they* should give him continued use of your kidneys. Certainly he had no right against the Society of Music Lovers that they should plug him into you in the first place. And if you now start to unplug yourself, having learned that you will otherwise have to spend nine years in bed with him, there is nobody in the world who must try to prevent you, in order to see to it that he is given something he has a right to be given.

Some people are rather stricter about the right to life. In their view, it does not include the right to be given anything, but amounts to, and only to, the right not to be killed by anybody. But here a related difficulty arises. If everybody is to refrain from killing that violinist, then everybody must refrain from doing a great many different sorts of things. Everybody must refrain from slitting his throat, everybody must refrain from shooting him—and everybody must refrain from unplugging you from him. But does he have a right against everybody that they shall refrain from unplugging you from him? To refrain from doing this is to allow him to continue to use your kidneys. It could be argued that he has a right against us that *we* should allow him to continue to use your kidneys. That is, while he had no right against us that we should give him the use of your kidneys, it might be argued that he anyway has a right against us that we shall not now intervene and deprive him of the use of your kidneys. I shall come back to third-party interventions later. But certainly the violinist has no right against you that *you* shall allow him to continue to use your kidneys. As I said, if you do allow him to use them, it is a kindness on your part, and not something you owe him.

The difficulty I point to here is not peculiar to the right to life. It reappears in connection with all the other natural rights; and it is something which an adequate account of rights must deal with. For present purposes it is enough just to draw attention to it. But I would stress that I am not arguing that people do not have a right to life—quite to the contrary, it seems to me that the primary control we must place on the acceptability of an account of rights is that it should turn out in that account to be a truth that all persons have a right to life. I am arguing only that having a right to life does not guarantee having either a right to be given the use of or a right to be allowed continued use of another person's body—even if one needs it for life itself. So the right to life will not serve the opponents of abortion in the very simple and clear way in which they seem to have thought it would.

# THE RIGHTS AND WRONGS OF ABORTION: A REPLY TO JUDITH THOMSON

*John Finnis*

Like Thomson's moral language . . . in her "A Defense of Abortion"[1] . . . (setting off the "permissible" against the "impermissible"), the traditional rule about killing doubtless gets its peremptory sharpness primarily (historically speaking) from the injunction, respected as divine and revealed: "Do not kill the innocent and just."[2] But the handful of peremptory negative moral principles correspond to the handful of really basic aspects of human flourishing, which in turn correspond to the handful of really basic and controlling human needs and human inclinations. To be fully reasonable, one must remain *open* to every basic aspect of human flourishing, to every basic form of human good. For is not each irreducibly basic, and none merely means to end? Are not the basic goods incommensurable? Of course it is reasonable to concentrate on realizing those forms of good, in or for those particular communities and persons (first of all oneself), which one's situation, talents and opportunities most fit one for. But concentration, specialization, particularization is one thing; it is quite another thing, rationally and thus morally speaking, to make a choice which cannot but be characterized as a choice *against* life (to kill), *against* communicable knowledge of truth (to lie, where truth is at stake in communication), *against* procreation, *against* friendship and the justice that is bound up with friendship. Hence the strict negative precepts.[3] . . .

But how does one choose "directly against" a basic form of good? When is it the case, for example, that one's choice, one's intentional act, "cannot but be" characterized as "inescapably" anti-life? Is abortion always (or ever) such a case? . . .

. . . Thomson has not recorded in her brief footnote (p. 50 n. 3) the technical meaning given to the term "direct" by moralists using the "doctrine" [of the double effect] to analyze the relation between choices and basic values, namely that the "doctrine" requires more than that a certain bad effect or aspect (say, someone's being killed) of one's deed be not

1. *Philosophy & Public Affairs* 1, no. 1 (Fall 1971): 47–66. Otherwise unidentified page references in the text are to this article.

2. Exodus 23:7; cf. Exodus 20:13, Deuteronomy 5:17, Genesis 9:6, Jeremiah 7:6 and 22:3.

3. These remarks are filled out somewhat in my "Natural Law and Unnatural Acts," *Heythrop Journal* II (1970): 365. See also Germain Grisez, *Abortion: the Myths, the Realities and the Arguments* (New York 1970), chap. 6. My argument owes much to this and other works by Grisez.

From John Finnis, "The Rights and Wrongs of Abortion: A Reply to Judith Thomson," *Philosophy & Public Affairs*, vol. 2, no. 2 (Winter 1973), pp. 117–45. Excerpts are taken from pp. 125–26, 129, 134–35, 137–43. Copyright © 1973 by Princeton University Press. Excerpts reprinted by permission of Princeton University Press.

intended either as end or as means. If one is to establish that one's death-dealing deed need not be characterized as directly or intentionally against the good of human life, the "doctrine" requires further that the good effect or aspect, which *is* intended, should be proportionate (say, saving someone's life), i.e. sufficiently good and important relative to the bad effect or aspect: otherwise (we may add, in our own words) one's choice, although not directly and intentionally to kill, will reasonably be counted as a choice inadequately open to the value of life.[4] And this consideration alone might well suffice to rule out abortions performed in order simply to remove the unwanted foetus from the body of women who conceived as a result of forcible rape, even if one were to explicate the phrase "intended directly as end or as means" in such a way that the abortion did not amount to a directly intended killing (e.g. because the mother desired only the removal, not the death of the foetus, and would have been willing to have the foetus reared in an artificial womb had one been available).[5]

Well, how *should* one explicate these central requirements of the "doctrine" of double effect? When *should* one say that the expected bad effect or aspect of an action is not intended either as end or as means and hence does not determine the moral character of the act as a choice not to respect one of the basic human values? . . .

A variety of factors are appealed to explicitly or relied on implicitly in making a judgment that the bad effect is to count as intended-as-a-means; Bennett would call the set of factors a "jumble";[6] but they are even more various than he has noted. It will be convenient to set them out while at the same time observing their bearing on the two cases centrally in dispute, the craniotomy to save a mother's life and that notable scenario in which "you reach around to your back and unplug yourself from that violinist to save your life."

(1) Would the chosen action have been chosen if the victim had not been present? If it would, this is ground for saying that the bad aspects of the action, viz, its death-dealing effects on the victim (child or violinist), are not being intended or chosen either as end or means, but are genuinely incidental side effects that do not necessarily determine the character of one's action as (not) respectful of human life. This was the principal reason the ecclesiastical moralists had for regarding as permissible the operation to remove the cancerous womb of the pregnant woman.[7] And

4. *Ibid.*, p. 7. This is the fourth of the four usual conditions for the application of the "Doctrine of Double Effect"; see e.g. Grisez, *Abortion: The Myths, the Realities and the Arguments*, p. 329. G.E.M. Anscombe, "War and Murder," in *Nuclear Weapons and Christian Conscience*, ed. W. Stein (London, 1961), p. 57, formulates the "principle of double effect," in relation to the situation where "someone innocent will die unless I do a wicked thing," thus: "you are no murderer if a man's death was neither your aim nor your chosen means, *and if you had to act in the way that led to it or else do something absolutely forbidden*" (emphasis added).

5. Grisez argues thus, *op. cit.*, p. 343; also in "Toward a Consistent Natural-Law Ethics of Killing," *American Journal of Jurisprudence* 15 (1970): 95.

6. Jonathan Bennett, " 'Whatever the Consequences,' " *Analysis* 26 (1966): p. 92 n. 1.

7. See the debate between A. Gemelli and P. Vermeersch, summarized in *Ephemerides Theologicae Lovaniensis* II (1934): 525-561; see also Noonan, *The Morality of Abortion*, p. 49; Zalba, *Theologiae Moralis Compendium* I, p. 885.

the "bitter" reaction which Foot cites and endorses—"If you are permitted to bring about the death of the child, what does it matter how it is done?"—seems, here, to miss the point. For what is in question, here, is not a mere matter of technique, of different ways of doing something. Rather it is a matter of the very reason one has for acting in the way one does, and such reasons can be constitutive of the act as an intentional performance. One has no reason even to want to be rid of the foetus within the womb, let alone to want to kill it; and so one's act, though certain, causally, to kill, is not, intentionally, a choice against life.

But of course, *this* factor does not serve to distinguish a craniotomy from unplugging that violinist; in both situations, the oppressive presence of the victim is what makes one minded to do the act in question.

(2) Is the person making the choice the one whose life is threatened by the presence of the victim? Thomson rightly sees that this is a relevant question, and Thomas Aquinas makes it the pivot of his discussion of self-defensive killing (the discussion from which the "doctrine" of double effect, as a theoretically elaborated way of analyzing intention, can be said to have arisen). He says:

> Although it is not permissible to intend to kill someone else in order to defend oneself (since it is not right to do the act "killing a human being," except [in some cases of unjust aggression] by public authority and for the general welfare), still it is not morally necessary to omit to do what is strictly appropriate to securing one's own life simply in order to avoid killing another, for to make provision for one's own life is more strictly one's moral concern than to make provision for the life of another person.[8]

As Thomson has suggested, a bystander, confronted with a situation in which one innocent person's presence is endangering the life of another innocent person, is in a different position; to choose to intervene, in order to kill one person to save the other, involves a choice to make himself a master of life and death, a judge of who lives and who dies; and (we may say) this context of his choice prevents him from saying, reasonably, what the man defending himself can say: "I am not choosing to kill; I am just doing what—as a single act and not simply by virtue of remote consequences or of someone else's subsequent act—is strictly needful to protect my own life, by forcefully removing what is threatening it." Now the traditional condemnation of abortion concerns the bystander's situation: a bystander cannot but be choosing to kill if (a) he rips open the mother, in a way foreseeably fatal to her, in order to save the child from the threatening enveloping presence of the mother (say, because the placenta has come adrift and the viable child is trapped and doomed unless it can be rescued, or because the mother's blood is poisoning the child, in a situation in which the bystander would prefer to save the child, either because he wants to save it from eternal damnation, or because the child is of royal blood and the mother low born, or because the mother is in any case sick, or old, or useless, or "has had her turn," while the child has a whole

8. *Summa Theologiae* II-II, q.64, art. 7.

rich life before it); or if (b) he cuts up or drowns the child in order to save the mother from the child's threatening presence. "Things being as they are, there isn't much a woman can safely do to abort herself," as Thomson says (p. 52)—at least, not without the help of bystanders, who by helping (directly) would be making the same choice as if they did it themselves. But the unplugging of the violinist is done by the very person defending herself. Thomson admits (p. 52) that this gives quite a different flavor to the situation, but she thinks that the difference is not decisive, since bystanders have a decisive reason to intervene in favor of the *mother* threatened by her child's presence. And she finds this reason in the fact that the mother *owns* her body, just as the person plugged in to the violinist owns his own kidneys and is entitled to their unencumbered use (p. 53). Well, this too has always been accounted a factor in these problems, as we can see by turning to the following question.

(3) Does the chosen action involve not merely a denial of aid and succor to someone but an actual intervention that amounts to an assault on the body of that person? . . . Sometimes, as here, it is the causal structure of one's activity that involves one willy-nilly in a choice for or against a basic value. The connection between one's activity and the destruction of life may be so close and direct that intentions and considerations which would give a different dominant character to mere nonpreservation of life are incapable of affecting the dominant character of a straightforward taking of life. This surely is the reason why Thomson goes about and about to represent a choice to have an abortion as a choice *not* to provide assistance or facilities, *not* to be a Good or at any rate a Splendid Samaritan; and why, too, she carefully describes the violinist affair so as to minimize the degree of intervention against the violinist's body, and to maximize the analogy with simply refusing an invitation to volunteer one's kidneys for his welfare (like Henry Fonda's declining to cross America to save Judith Thomson's life). "If anything in the world is true, it is that you do not commit murder, you do not do what is impermissible, if you reach around to your back and unplug yourself from that violinist to save your life" (p. 52). Quite so. It might nevertheless be useful to test one's moral reactions a little further: suppose, not simply that "unplugging" required a *bystander's* intervention, but also that (for medical reasons, poison in the bloodstream, shock, etc.) unplugging could not safely be performed unless and until the violinist had first been dead for six hours and had moreover been killed outright, say by drowning or decapitation (though not necessarily while conscious). Could one then be *so* confident, as a bystander, that it was right to kill the violinist in order to save the philosopher? But I put forward this revised version principally to illustrate *another* reason for thinking that, within the traditional casuistry, the violinist-unplugging in Thomson's version is *not* the "direct killing" which she claims it is, and which she *must* claim it is if she is to make out her case for rejecting the traditional principle about direct killing.

Let us now look back to the traditional rule about abortion. If the mother needs medical treatment to save her life, she gets it, subject to one proviso, even if the treatment is certain to kill the unborn child—for after all, her body is *her* body, as "women have said again and again" (and they have been heard by the traditional casuists!). And the proviso? That the medical treatment not be *via* a straightforward assault on or intervention against the child's body. For after all *the child's body is the child's body, not the woman's.* The traditional casuists have admitted the claims made on behalf of one "body" up to the very limit where those claims become *mere (understandable) bias, mere (understandable) self-interested* refusal to listen to the *very same* claim ("This body is *my* body") when it is made by or on behalf of another person.[9] Of course, a traditional casuist would display an utter want of feeling if he didn't most profoundly sympathize with women in the desperate circumstances under discussion. But it is vexing to find a philosophical Judith Thomson, in a cool hour, unable to see when an argument cuts both ways, and unaware that the casuists have seen the point before her and have, unlike her, allowed the argument to cut both ways impartially. The child, like his mother, has a "just prior claim to his own body," and abortion involves laying hands on, manipulating, that body. And here we have perhaps the decisive reason why abortion cannot be assimilated to the range of Samaritan problems and why Thomson's location of it within that range is a mere (ingenious) novelty.

(4) But is the action action against someone who had a duty not to be doing what he is doing, or not to be present where he is present? There seems no doubt that the "innocence" of the victim whose life is taken makes a difference to the characterizing of an action as open to and respectful of the good of human life, and as an intentional killing. Just how and why it makes a difference is difficult to unravel; I shall not attempt an unraveling here. We all, for whatever reason, recognize the difference and Thomson has expressly allowed its relevance (p. 52).

But her way of speaking of "rights" has a final unfortunate effect at this point. We can grant, and have granted, that the unborn child has no Hohfeldian *claim-right* to be allowed to stay within the mother's body under all circumstances; the mother is not under a strict duty to allow it to stay under all circumstances. In *that* sense, the child "has no right to be there." But Thomson discusses also the case of the burglar in the house; and he, too, has "no right to be there," even when she opens the window! But beware of the equivocation! The burglar not merely has no claim-right to be allowed to enter or stay; he also has a strict duty *not* to enter or stay, i.e. he has no Hohfeldian *liberty*—and it is *this* that is uppermost in our minds when we think that he "has no right to be there": it is actually unjust for him to be there. Similarly with Jones who takes Smith's coat, leaving Smith freezing (p. 53). And similarly with the violinist. He and his agents had a strict duty not to make the hook-up to Judith Thomson or her gentle reader. Of course, the violinist himself may have been unconscious and so not himself at fault; but the whole affair is a gross injustice to the person whose kidneys are made free with, and the injustice to that

9. Not, of course, that they have used Thomson's curious talk of "owning" one's own body with its distracting and legalistic connotations and its dualistic reduction of subjects of justice to objects.

person is not measured simply by the degree of moral fault of one of the parties to the injustice. Our whole view of the violinist's situation is colored by this burglarious and persisting wrongfulness of his presence plugged into his victim.

But can any of this reasonably be said or thought of the unborn child? True, the child had no *claim-right* to be allowed to come into being within the mother. But it was not in breach of any *duty* in coming into being nor in remaining present within the mother; Thomson gives no arguments at all in favor of the view that the child is in breach of duty in being present (though her counter examples show that she is often tacitly assuming this). (Indeed, if we are going to use the wretched analogy of owning houses, I fail to see why the unborn child should not with justice say of the body around it: "That is my house. No one *granted* me property rights in it, but equally no one *granted* my mother any property rights in it." The fact is that both persons *share* in the use of this body, both by the same sort of title, viz., that this is the way they happened to come into being. But it would be better to drop this ill-fitting talk of "ownership" and "property rights" altogether.) So though the unborn child "had no right to be there" (in the sense that it never had a claim-right to be allowed to *begin* to be there), in another straightforward and more important sense it *did* "have a right to be there" (in the sense that it was not in breach of duty in being or continuing to be there). All this is, I think, clear and clearly different from the violinist's case. Perhaps forcible rape is a special case; but even then it seems fanciful to say that the child is or could be in any way at fault, as the violinist is at fault or would be but for the adventitious circumstance that he was unconscious at the time.

Still, I don't want to be dogmatic about the justice or injustice, innocence or fault, involved in a rape conception. (I have already remarked that the impermissibility of abortion in any such case, where the mother's life is not in danger, does not depend necessarily on showing that the act is a choice directly to kill.) It is enough that I have shown how in three admittedly important respects the violinist case differs from the therapeutic abortion performed to save the life of the mother. As presented by Thomson, the violinist's case involves (i) no bystander, (ii) no intervention against or assault upon the body of the violinist, and (iii) an indisputable injustice to the agent in question. Each of these three factors is absent from the abortion cases in dispute. Each has been treated as relevant by the traditional casuists whose condemnations Thomson was seeking to contest when she plugged us into the violinist.

# ABORTION AND THE GOLDEN RULE

*R. M. Hare*

Approaching our moral question in the most general way, let us ask whether there is *anything* about the fetus *or* about the person it may turn into that should make us say that we ought not to kill it. If, instead of asking this question, somebody wants to go on asking, indirectly, whether the fetus is a person, and whether, *therefore,* killing it is wrong, he is at liberty to do so; but I must point out that the reasons he will have to give for saying that it is a person, and that, therefore, killing it is wrong (or that it is not a person and, therefore, killing it is not wrong) will be the very same moral reasons as I shall be giving for the answer to my more direct question. Whichever way one takes it, one cannot avoid giving a reasoned answer to this moral question; so why not take it the simplest way? To say that the fetus is (or is not) a person gives *by itself* no moral reason for or against killing it; it merely incapsulates any reasons we may have for including the fetus within a certain category of creatures that it is, or is not, wrong to kill (i.e. persons or nonpersons). The word "person" is doing no work here (other than that of bemusing us). . . .

The single, or at least the main, thing about the fetus that raises the moral question is that, if not terminated, the pregnancy is highly likely to result in the birth and growth to maturity of a person just like the rest of us. The word "person" here reenters the argument, but in a context and with a meaning that does not give rise to the old troubles; for it is clear at least that we ordinary adults are persons. If we knew beyond a peradventure that a fetus was going to miscarry anyway, then little would remain of the moral problem beyond the probably minimal sufferings caused to the mother and just possibly the fetus by terminating the pregnancy now. If, on the other hand, we knew (to use Professor Tooley's science-fiction example)[1] that an embryo kitten would, if not aborted but given a wonder drug, turn into a being with a human mind like ours, then that too would raise a moral problem. Perhaps Tooley thinks not; but we shall see. It is, to use his useful expression, the "potentiality" that the fetus has of becoming a person in the full ordinary sense that creates the problem. It is because Tooley thinks that, once the "potentiality principle" (see below) is admitted, the conservatives or extreme antiabortionists will win the case hands down, that he seeks reasons for rejecting it; but, again, we shall see.

We can explain why the potentiality of the fetus for becoming a person raises a moral problem if we appeal to a type of argument which, in one guise or another, has been the formal basis of almost all theories of moral

1. "Abortion and Infanticide," *Philosophy & Public Affairs* 2, no. 1 (Fall 1972): 60; *RWA*, p. 75. It will be clear what a great debt I owe to this article.

From R. M. Hare, "Abortion and the Golden Rule," *Philosophy & Public Affairs*, vol. 4, no. 3 (Spring 1975), pp. 206–9, 211–14, 218. Copyright © 1975 by R. M. Hare. Reprinted by permission of the author and of Princeton University Press.

reasoning that have contributed much that is worth while to our understanding of it. I am alluding to the Christian (and indeed pre-Christian) "Golden Rule," the Kantian Categorical Imperative, the ideal observer theory, the rational contractor theory, various kinds of utilitarianism, and my own universal prescriptivism.[2] I would claim that the last of these gives the greatest promise of putting what is common to all these theories in a perspicuous way, and so revealing their justification in logic; but it is not the purpose of this paper to give this justification. Instead, since the problem of abortion is discussed as often as not from a Christian standpoint, and since I hope thereby to find a provisional starting point for the argument on which many would agree, I shall use that form of the argument which rests on the Golden Rule that we should do to others as we wish them to do to us.[3] It is a logical extension of this form of argument to say that we should do to others what *we are glad was* done to us. Two (surely readily admissible) changes are involved here. The first is a mere difference in the two tenses which cannot be morally relevant. Instead of saying that we should do to others as we wish them (in the future) to do to us, we say that we should do to others as we wish that they had done to us (in the past). The second is a change from the hypothetical to the actual; instead of saying that we should do to others as we wish that they had done to us, we say that we should do to others as we are glad that they did do to us. I cannot see that this could make any difference to the spirit of the injunction, and logical grounds could in any case be given, based on the universal prescriptivist thesis, for extending the Golden Rule in this way.

The application of this injunction to the problem of abortion is obvious. If we are glad that nobody terminated the pregnancy that resulted in *our* birth, then we are enjoined not, *ceteris paribus*, to terminate any pregnancy which will result in the birth of a person having a life like ours. Close attention obviously needs to be paid to the *"ceteris paribus"* clause, and also to the expression "like ours." The "universalizability" of moral judgments, which is one of the logical bases of the Golden Rule, requires us to make the same moral judgment about qualitatively identical cases, and about cases which are *relevantly* similar. Since no cases in this area are going to be qualitatively *identical*, we shall have to rely on relevant similarity. Without raising a very large topic in moral philosophy, we can perhaps avoid the difficulty by pointing out that the relevant respects here are going to be those things about our life which make us glad that we were born. These can be stated in a general enough way to cover all those persons who are, or who are going to be or would be, glad that they were born. Those who are not glad they were born will still have a reason for not aborting those who would be glad; for even the former wish that,

2. See my "Rules of War and Moral Reasoning," *Philosophy & Public Affairs* 1, no. 2 (Winter 1972), fn. 3; reprinted in *War and Moral Responsibility*, ed. Marshall Cohen, Thomas Nagel, and Thomas Scanlon (Princeton, N.J., 1974). See also my review of John Rawls, *A Theory of Justice*, in *Philosophical Quarterly* 23 (1973): 154f.; and my "Ethical Theory and Utilitarianism" in *Contemporary British Philosophy*, series 4, ed. H.D. Lewis (London, forthcoming).

3. St. Matthew 7:12. There have been many misunderstandings of the Golden Rule, some of which I discuss in my "Euthanasia: A Christian View," *Proceedings of the Center for Philosophic Exchange*, vol. 6 (SUNY at Brockport, 1975).

if they had been going to be glad that they were born, nobody should have aborted them. So, although I have, for the sake of simplicity, put the injunction in a way that makes it apply only to the abortion of people who will have a life just like that of the aborter, it is generalizable to cover the abortion of any fetus which will, if not aborted, turn into someone who will be glad to be alive.

I now come back to Professor Tooley's wonder kitten. He says that if it became possible by administering a wonder drug to an embryo kitten to cause it to turn into a being with a human mind like ours, we should still not feel under any obligation either to administer the drug to kittens or to refrain from aborting kittens to whom the drug had been administered by others. He uses this as an argument against the "potentiality principle," which says that if there are any properties which are possessed by adult human beings and which endow any organisms possessing them with a serious right to life, then "at least one of those properties will be such that any organism *potentially* possessing that property has a serious right to life even now, simply by virtue of that potentiality, where an organism possesses a property potentially if it will come to have that property in the normal course of its development."[4] Putting this more briefly and in terms of "wrong" instead of "rights," the potentiality principle says that if it would be wrong to kill an adult human being because he has a certain property, it is wrong to kill an organism (e.g. a fetus) which will come to have that property if it develops normally.

Why does Tooley think that, if the potentiality principle is once granted, the extreme conservative position on abortion becomes impregnable? Obviously because he has neglected to consider some other potential beings. Take, to start with, the next child that this mother will have if this pregnancy is terminated but will not have if this pregnancy is allowed to continue. Why will she not have it? For a number of alternative reasons. The most knockdown reason would be that the mother would die or be rendered sterile if this pregnancy were allowed to continue. Another would be that the parents had simply decided, perhaps for morally adequate reasons, that their family would be large enough if and when this present fetus was born. I shall be discussing later the morality of family limitation; for the moment I shall assume for the sake of argument that it is morally all right for parents to decide, after they have had, say, fifteen children, not to have any more, and to achieve this modest limitation of their family by remaining completely chaste.

In all these cases there is, in effect, a choice between having this child now and having another child later. Most people who oppose abortion make a great deal of the wrongness of stopping the birth of this child but say nothing about the morality of stopping the birth of the later child. My own intuition (on which I am by no means going to rely) is that they are wrong to make so big a distinction. The basis of the distinction is supposed to be that the fetus already exists as a single living entity all in one place, whereas the possible future child is at the moment represented

4. Tooley, "Abortion and Infanticide," pp. 55–56; *RWA*, pp. 70–71 (my italics).

only by an unfertilized ovum and a sperm which may or may not yet exist in the father's testes. But will this basis support so weighty a distinction?

First, why is it supposed to make a difference that the genetic material which causes the production of the future child and adult is in two different places? If I have a duty to open a certain door, and two keys are required to unlock it, it does not seem to me to make any difference to my duty that one key is already in the lock and the other in my trousers. This, so far, is an intuition, and I place no reliance on it; I introduce the parallel only to remove some prejudices. The real argument is this: when I am glad that I was born (the basis, it will be remembered, of the argument that the Golden Rule therefore places upon me an obligation not to stop others being born), I do not confine this gladness to gladness that they did not abort me. I am glad, also, that my parents copulated in the first place, without contraception. So from my gladness, in conjunction with the extended Golden Rule, I derive not only a duty not to abort, but also a duty not to abstain from procreation. In the choice-situation that I have imagined, in which it is either this child or the next one but not both, I cannot perform both these duties. So, in the words of a wayside pulpit report to me by Mr. Anthony Kenny, "if you have conflicting duties, one of them isn't your duty." But which?

I do not think that any general answer can be given to this question. If the present fetus is going to be miserably handicapped if it grows into an adult, perhaps because the mother had rubella, but there is every reason to suppose that the next child will be completely normal and as happy as most people, there would be reason to abort this fetus and proceed to bring to birth the next child, in that the next child will be much gladder to be alive than will this one. The Golden Rule does not directly guide us in cases where we cannot help failing to do to *some* others what we wish were done to us, because if we did it to some, we should thereby prevent ourselves from doing it to others. But it can guide us indirectly, if further extended by a simple maneuver, to cover what I have elsewhere called "multilateral" situations. We are to do to the others affected, taken together, what we wish were done to us if we had to be all of them by turns in random order.[5] In this case, by terminating this pregnancy, I get, on this scenario, no life at all in one of my incarnations and a happy life in the other; but by not terminating it, I get a miserable life in one and no life at all in the other. So I should choose to terminate. In order to reach this conclusion it is not necessary to assume, as we did, that the present fetus will turn into a person who will be positively miserable; only that that person's expectation of happiness is so much less than the expectation of the later possible person that the other factors (to be mentioned in a moment) are outweighed.

In most cases, the probability that there will be another child to replace this one is far lower than the probability that this fetus will turn into a living child. The latter probability is said in normal cases to be

5. See C. I. Lewis, *An Analysis of Knowledge and Valuation* (La Salle, 1946), p. 547; D. Haslett, *Moral Rightness* (The Hague, 1974), chap. 3. Cf. my *Freedom and Reason* (Oxford, 1963), p. 123.

about 80 percent; the probability of the next child being born may be much lower (the parents may separate; one of them may die or become sterile; or they may just change their minds about having children). If I do not terminate in such a normal case, I get, on the same scenario, an 80 percent chance of a normal happy life in one incarnation and no chance at all of any life in the other; but if I do terminate, I get a much lower chance of a normal happy life in the second incarnation and no chance at all in the first. So in this case I should not terminate. By applying this kind of scenario to different cases, we get a way of dramatizing the application of the Golden Rule to them. The cases will all be different, but the relevance of the differences to the moral decision becomes clearer. It is these differences in probabilities of having a life, and of having a happy one, that justify, first of all the presumptive policy, which most people would follow, that abortions in general ought to be avoided, and secondly the exceptions to this policy that many people would now allow—though of course they will differ in their estimation of the probabilities.

I conclude, therefore, that the establishment of the potentiality principle by no means renders impregnable the extreme conservative position, as Tooley thinks it does. It merely creates a rebuttable or defeasible presumption against abortion, which is fairly easily rebutted if there are good indications. The interests of the mother may well, in many cases, provide such good indications, although, because hers is not the only interest, we have also to consider the others. Liberals can, however, get from the present form of argument all that they could reasonably demand, since in the kinds of cases in which they would approve of termination, the interests of the mother will usually be predominant enough to tip the balance between those of the others affected, including potential persons. . . .

It might be objected, as we have seen, that the view I have advocated would require unlimited procreation, on the ground that not to produce any single child whom one might have produced lays one open to the charge that one is not doing to that child as one is glad has been done to oneself (viz. causing him to be born). But there are, even on the present view, reasons for limiting the population. Let us suppose that fully-grown adults were producible ad lib., not by gestation in human mothers or in the wombs of cats or in test tubes, but instantaneously by waving a wand. We should still have to formulate a population policy for the world as a whole, and for particular societies and families. There would be a point at which the additional member of each of these units imposed burdens on the other members great enough in sum to outweigh the advantage gained by the additional member. In utilitarian terms, the classical or total utility principle sets a limit to population which, although higher than the average utility principle, is nevertheless a limit. In terms of the Golden Rule, which is the basis of my present argument, even if the "others" to whom we are to do what we wish, or what we are glad, to have done to us are to include potential people, good done to them may be outweighed by harm done to other actual or potential people. If we had to submit to all their lives or nonlives in turn, we should have a basis for choosing a population policy which would not differ from that yielded by the classical utility principle. How restrictive this policy would be would depend on assumptions about the threshold effects of certain increases in population size and density. I think myself that even if potential people are allowed to be the objects of duties, the policy will be fairly restrictive; but this is obviously not the place to argue for this view.

# CHAPTER TEN
# THE ETHICS OF EUTHANASIA

The following letter was written to one of the authors by a nurse who is an administrator in a hospital cancer treatment program:

> What is it like to hold someone you love in your arms while he takes his last breath? How do you feel when you hear a little child whom you love deeply, screaming in pain? These are some of the things I need to share with you and that I said I wanted to write you about.
>
> I met Danny when he was seven years old. It was instant love but the circumstances were anything but happy. Danny had been admitted to the hospital where I was the pediatric supervisor and he had just been diagnosed with acute lymphocytic leukemia. His parents were having a very difficult time with the diagnosis and were still in a state of shock. Danny needed to be told his diagnosis, but no one wanted to be the one to tell him. Somehow I was elected.
>
> We talked about the different kinds of cells that make up your blood: white and red. We played a game. On one side were the white soldiers, and on the other side were the red soldiers. Most of the time there was peace, but now war had broken out and the white soldiers were winning, crowding out the good red soldiers. He seemed to understand. At least enough for now. As time went on, he would understand a whole lot more: lab tests, chemotherapy, blood transfusions, platelets, loss of hair, pain, and eventual death. No need to rush. One day at a time.
>
> In the beginning, his doctor admitted Danny to the hospital for chemotherapy, lumbar punctures, bone marrows, etc. Since he was in and out of

the hospital frequently, we became very close friends. As time went on, Danny understood and accepted more about his disease and he became a source of strength for his family. But sometimes he would panic and become frightened. Then he would need reassurance and extra T.L.C.

Danny was almost eleven before he started having real serious problems. Prior to that, he led a fairly normal life. He had made up his mind that he was going to play all sports: baseball, football, basketball, no matter what. He was a determined young boy.

At one point, Danny had come home from the hospital and took his Dad aside. He said that he needed to talk to him and his brother because he was going to die and it was not very far away. He also would need their help to talk to his mother and sister because he was worried about them. He explained to his family that they were his "Godparents," and he had only been loaned to them. Now he had to go to God, his Father. His dad said later that Danny had talked a lot about heaven and what he thought it would be like.

Not long after this I was called to their home one night, about midnight. Danny's condition was poor and he was in a considerable amount of pain. From my long experience with cancer patients I knew that Danny wouldn't live much longer. At first he didn't want to go to the hospital. But his pain was so intense that I knew it couldn't be controlled at home. After some discussion, his family decided that it would be best for Danny to be admitted to the hospital where his pain could be controlled and he could be made more comfortable. I sat down on the bed beside him and talked to him for a long time. The next morning Danny was admitted to the hospital.

His condition remained precarious for several days. During this time he was so brave and strong. He was an inspiration for all of us on the hospital floor.

But though he was so brave and strong, his last day was filled with terror. The pain was excruciating and we had been unable to get it under control. His family was beside themselves to see him suffer so. I couldn't keep the tears from my eyes as I watched my little friend writhing in pain. How could we let him suffer? I went to the desk and called the doctor for an order to increase the morphine we were giving him. We all stood around his bed and watched and waited for this miracle drug to take effect. Finally some relief came. But it lasted only a little while. So I called the doctor again and got another order, a larger dose. I remembered my instructor in nurses training impressing upon us that morphine is a respiratory depressant and that in sufficiently high dosages it will induce respiratory failure. Now we waited and Danny did too. The painful minutes ticked away slowly. The room somehow seemed smaller. Perspiration was rolling down Danny's father's face. His mother was silently crying as she gently caressed his forehead. At last Danny relaxed and he dozed for awhile. But when he awoke we could all see the agony on his face, although he tried to hide it. I felt the tears flowing freely down my own cheeks. No, this should not be! This innocent little child should not suffer like this. I left the room and returned with the resident doctor.

She took one look at Danny and realized how much pain he was in. She left the room and a nurse soon returned with another shot. Danny continued to cry. Gradually we were giving him morphine almost every fifteen minutes, and still he was crying in agony. He had had a tremendous amount of morphine! At the back of our minds was the realization that this amount, in a child his age and size, would probably kill him. This did not matter now. The important thing was to keep Danny from suffering. I picked him up and held him close. "Just let go, Danny," I whispered. "Just let go. Relax and let the medicine help you. Just relax. Let go." Suddenly he stopped crying and started to go limp in my arms. "Am I a loser, Dad?" "No, son, you're a winner." With that, he looked up at all of us and gave us a beautiful radiant smile, then closed his eyes, never to feel pain again.

Was this euthanasia or was this love? Was it morally wrong or was it right? Did we have the right to make the decisions we made for Danny? In my heart I feel I know the answer. Am I wrong?

The word "euthanasia" derives from the Greek for "happy death." In modern usage, the term has come to refer to any action that knowingly results in the death of a person who is suffering from a painful and incurable disease and that is carried out for reasons presumed to be merciful. Is euthanasia morally right or is it always wrong? This is the question the hospital administrator asked and that the articles in this chapter address.[1]

There are a number of distinctions ethicians make when discussing the morality of particular euthanasia cases: Was the death voluntary or involuntary? Was the death brought about through active or passive euthanasia? Was the patient killed or was the patient allowed to die of natural causes? What were the intentions of the persons whose action or inaction led to the patient's death? If the patient was allowed to die, was it because the medical staff withheld extraordinary treatment or did they withhold ordinary treatment?[2]

The distinction between voluntary and involuntary euthanasia turns on whether or not the patient consented. Euthanasia is voluntary when the patient gives his informed consent to the action that will result in his death. Some ethicians hold that euthanasia is moral so long as the patient has consented. The consent may be given at the time of death or the patient may have expressed his wishes earlier, either in writing or verbally. Euthanasia is involuntary when the patient failed to give such consent. Perhaps he was unconscious or perhaps, as in the case of newborns, he was incompetent. Involuntary euthanasia poses many difficulties, even

1. There are a number of fine anthologies on the moral issues involved in euthanasia: Tom L. Beauchamp and Seymour Perlin, eds., *Ethical Issues in Death and Dying* (Englewood Cliffs, N.J.: Prentice-Hall, 1978); Marvin Kohl, ed., *Beneficient Euthanasia* (Buffalo, N.Y.: Prometheus Books, 1975); Robert Weir, ed., *Ethical Issues in Death and Dying* (New York: Columbia University Press, 1977); John A. Behnke and Sissela Bok, eds., *The Dilemmas of Euthanasia* (Garden City, N.Y.: Anchor Books, 1975); John Ladd, ed., *Ethical Issues Relating to Life and Death* (New York: Oxford University Press, 1979).

2. For full discussions of these and other distinctions related to euthanasia, see Paul Ramsey, *Ethics at the Edges of Life* (New Haven, Conn.: Yale University Press, 1978); Tom L. Beauchamp and James F. Childress, *Principles of Biomedical Ethics* (New York: Oxford University Press, 1979), esp. chs. 4 and 7; A. B. Downing, *Euthanasia and the Right to Die* (New York: Humanities Press, 1970); Jonathan Glover, *Causing Death and Saving Lives* (Harmondsworth, England: Penguin Books, 1977); Marvin Kohl, *The Morality of Killing* (New York: Humanities Press, 1974); Germain Grisez and Joseph M. Boyle, Jr., *Life and Death with Liberty and Justice: A Contribution to the Euthanasia Debate* (Notre Dame: University of Notre Dame Press, 1979); Daniel C. McGuire, *Death by Choice* (Garden City, N.Y.: Doubleday, 1974); Peter Singer, *Practical Ethics* (New York: Cambridge University Press, 1979), ch. 7; Robert Veatch, *Death, Dying and the Biological Revolution* (New Haven, Conn.: Yale University Press, 1976).

for those who hold that voluntary euthanasia is always moral. For example, in Danny's case could we say that he was old enough to understand the nature of the medications he was receiving and was he old enough to give his consent? If he was not old enough, was there someone who could have given consent for him? Who, then, had the right to decide whether or not to administer euthanasia to Danny? Danny himself? His parents? His doctor? His friend?

The distinction between active and passive euthanasia is based on the difference between killing someone and allowing someone to die. In passive euthanasia, death is caused by the patient's disease, which is allowed to run its natural course without any treatment that might lead to a prolongation of the patient's life. In active euthanasia, the immediate cause of death is not the patient's disease; instead, something is done to or given to the patient that causes his death. For example, the patient might be administered a lethal dose of medication. The active/passive distinction is important because some ethicians (including J. Gay-Williams, author of one of the articles in this chapter) hold that although active euthanasia is always immoral, passive euthanasia may be permissible. In fact, some authors hold that passive euthanasia is not really a form of euthanasia at all.

Was Danny's death the result of active or passive euthanasia? It would seem to be the former, but the situation is complicated by the fact that some ethicians would hold that in active euthanasia the person who brings about the death must intend to kill the patient. Were the nurses who administered the morphine intending to kill Danny? Or were they merely trying to ease his pain? Was his death a tragically necessary but unintended side effect of their attempts to control his pain?

Some ethicians argue that the active/passive distinction has no moral significance, that it does not matter how death is caused. Instead, they argue that we are morally responsible for a death whether it comes about through our withholding of life-saving treatment or through our administration of a death-inducing measure. In his essay, James Rachels argues in this manner. Tom L. Beauchamp, however, challenges Rachels' view. If the active/passive distinction is rejected, then what would be important in Danny's case would be the morality or immorality of terminating his life, regardless of how it was done.

Some ethicians hold that the morality of passive euthanasia depends on the kind of treatment that is refused or withheld, making a distinction between ordinary and extraordinary treatment. The former consists of routine care, such as feeding, while the latter involves medical treatment or life support systems that are not routine care for a sick person insofar as they probably would not benefit the patient or would involve excessive pain, expense, or other human costs. Whereas it is moral to refuse or withhold extraordinary treatment of a disease, these ethicians claim, it is immoral to refuse or withhold ordinary treatment. In Danny's case, for example, it was judged that any additional attempt to combat the cancer would probably have no beneficial effects and that it would certainly be quite painful and costly. Such treatment would thus be extraordinary, and so it was not administered. On the other hand, Danny continued to be given nourishment, some of it intravenously, which helped to prolong his life. Such nourishment was judged to be ordinary treatment and it was felt to be wrong to withhold or refuse it.

The first reading in this chapter focuses on one of the important distinctions we have been discussing. In his article, "Active and Passive Euthanasia," James Rachels cites a number of reasons for his view that the active/passive distinction is not morally significant. First, he argues that when doctors rely on this distinction they will only allow passive euthanasia and thereby make their patients suffer longer than they would if active euthanasia were administered. Second, he claims that by relying on the active/passive distinction, people are sometimes led to make life and death decisions on irrelevant grounds. Third, Rachels says that if we compare killing a child by drowning it and allowing a child to drown by watching and doing nothing, it will be clear that the morality of the act does not depend on the difference between killing and letting die.

Tom L. Beauchamp discusses Rachels' arguments in "A Reply to Rachels on Active and Passive Euthanasia." In this essay, Beauchamp points out that Rachels' example (of drowning a child versus allowing it to drown) shows only that the active/passive distinction is sometimes not important; it does not, however, show that this is always so. Using a different example (the Karen Quinlan case) Beauchamp claims that the active/passive distinction is important when a patient might continue to live even if we "passively" cease using extraordinary means, and when "actively" terminating a patient's life would "preempt the possibility of life." Beauchamp then appeals to rule utilitarianism to argue that rules permitting active euthanasia are wrong because they might reduce respect for human life.

J. Gay-Williams adopts a natural law approach in "The Wrongfulness of Euthanasia" to support his view that such practices are morally forbidden. Gay-Williams defines euthanasia as "intentionally taking the life of a presumably hopeless person." He notes that this definition is meant to include only cases of deliberately and intentionally killing a patient, thus excluding cases of passive euthanasia. He then argues that euthanasia as he defines it (i.e., active euthanasia) is morally wrong because (1) it violates the natural inclination to life, (2) it can be used against us and can harm our own self-interest, and (3) it can lead to a decline in the quality of medical care and to dangerous social policies.

In "Rights, Justice, and Euthanasia," Bertram and Elsie Bandman adopt Rawls' social contract view of morality to argue that voluntary euthanasia is morally permissible except in cases where prolonging the patient's life would involve less injustice than allowing the patient to die. They argue that everyone has an equal right to be free, and this right includes the freedom to decide whether to live or die. Thus, in a just society people must be allowed freely to choose whether to live or die. However, if allowing a person to exercise the right to die (or live) would violate justice, then society need not respect this right. A person's decision to die (or live) would violate justice if it would lead to the deaths of two or more other people and thereby violate their right to be free to live. According to the Bandmans, "if there is a conflict between two or more people's equal rights to live, two or more equal rights outweigh one person's equal right." The Bandmans formulate three principles (a Kantian principle, a utilitarian principle, and a "compromise" principle) that are usually appealed to when discussing cases involving conflicts between people's rights to live or die. They claim that their way of resolving such conflicts can still be maintained and defended in the face of these principles and these cases of conflict.

# ACTIVE AND PASSIVE EUTHANASIA

*James Rachels*

The distinction between active and passive euthanasia is thought to be crucial for medical ethics. The idea is that it is permissible, at least in some cases, to withhold treatment and allow a patient to die, but it is never permissible to take any direct action designed to kill the patient. This doctrine seems to be accepted by most doctors, and it is endorsed in a statement adopted by the House of Delegates of the American Medical Association on December 4, 1973:

> The intentional termination of the life of one human being by another—mercy killing—is contrary to that for which the medical profession stands and is contrary to the policy of the American Medical Association.
> The cessation of the employment of extraordinary means to prolong the life of the body when there is irrefutable evidence that biological death is imminent is the decision of the patient and/or his immediate family. The advice and judgment of the physician should be freely available to the patient and/or his immediate family.

However, a strong case can be made against this doctrine. In what follows I will set out some of the relevant arguments, and urge doctors to reconsider their views on this matter.

To begin with a familiar type of situation, a patient who is dying of incurable cancer of the throat is in terrible pain, which can no longer be satisfactorily alleviated. He is certain to die within a few days, even if present treatment is continued, but he does not want to go on living for

From James Rachels, "Active and Passive Euthanasia," *New England Journal of Medicine*, vol. 292 (January 9, 1975), pp. 78–80. Reprinted by permission of the *New England Journal of Medicine*.

those days since the pain is unbearable. So he asks the doctor for an end to it, and his family joins in the request.

Suppose the doctor agrees to withhold treatment, as the conventional doctrine says he may. The justification for his doing so is that the patient is in terrible agony, and since he is going to die anyway, it would be wrong to prolong his suffering needlessly. But now notice this. If one simply withholds treatment, it may take the patient longer to die, and so he may suffer more than he would if more direct action were taken and a lethal injection given. This fact provides strong reason for thinking that, once the initial decision not to prolong his agony has been made, active euthanasia is actually preferable to passive euthanasia, rather than the reverse. To say otherwise is to endorse the option that leads to more suffering rather than less, and is contrary to the humanitarian impulse that prompts the decision not to prolong his life in the first place.

Part of my point is that the process of being "allowed to die" can be relatively slow and painful, whereas being given a lethal injection is relatively quick and painless. Let me give a different sort of example. In the United States about one in 600 babies is born with Down's syndrome. Most of these babies are otherwise healthy—that is, with only the usual pediatric care, they will proceed to an otherwise normal infancy. Some, however, are born with congenital defects such as intestinal obstructions that require operations if they are to live. Sometimes, the parents and the doctor will decide not to operate, and let the infant die. Anthony Shaw describes that happens then:

> ... When surgery is denied [the doctor] must try to keep the infant from suffering while natural forces sap the baby's life away. As a surgeon whose natural inclination is to use the scalpel to fight off death, standing by and watching a salvageable baby die is the most emotionally exhausting experience I know. It is easy at a conference, in a theoretical discussion, to decide that such infants should be allowed to die. It is altogether different to stand by in the nursery and watch as dehydration and infection wither a tiny being over hours and days. This is a terrible ordeal for me and the hospital staff—much more so than for the parents who never set foot in the nursery.[1]

I can understand why some people are opposed to all euthanasia, and insist that such infants must be allowed to live. I think I can also understand why other people favor destroying these babies quickly and painlessly. But why should anyone favor letting "dehydration and infection wither a tiny being over hours and days?" The doctrine that says that a baby may be allowed to dehydrate and wither, but may not be given an injection that would end its life without suffering, seems so patently cruel as to require no further refutation. The strong language is not intended to offend, but only to put that point in the clearest possible way.

My second argument is that the conventional doctrine leads to decisions concerning life and death made on irrelevant grounds.

1. Anthony Shaw, "Doctor, Do We Have a Choice?" *New York Times Magazine* (January 30, 1972), p. 54.

Consider again the case of the infants with Down's syndrome who need operations for congenital defects unrelated to the syndrome to live. Sometimes, there is no operation, and the baby dies, but when there is no such defect, the baby lives on. Now, an operation such as that to remove an intestinal obstruction is not prohibitively difficult. The reason why such operations are not performed in these cases is, clearly, that the child has Down's syndrome and the parents and doctor judge that because of that fact it is better for the child to die.

But notice that this situation is absurd, no matter what view one takes of the lives and potentials of such babies. If the life of such an infant is worth preserving, what does it matter if it needs a simple operation? Or, if one thinks it better that such a baby should not live on, what difference does it make that it happens to have an unobstructed intestinal tract? In either case, the matter of life and death is being decided on irrelevant grounds. It is the Down's syndrome, and not the intestine, that is the issue. The matter should be decided, if at all, on that basis, and not be allowed to depend on the essentially irrelevant question of whether the intestinal tract is blocked.

What makes this situation possible, of course, is the idea that when there is an intestinal blockage, one can "let the baby die," but when there is no such defect there is nothing that can be done, for one must not "kill" it. The fact that this idea leads to such results as deciding life or death on irrelevant grounds is another good reason why the doctrine should be rejected.

One reason why so many people think that there is an important moral difference between active and passive euthanasia is that they think killing someone is morally worse than letting someone die. But is it? Is killing, in itself, worse than letting die? To investigate this issue, two cases may be considered that are exactly alike except that one involves killing whereas the other involves letting someone die. Then, it can be asked whether this difference makes any difference to the moral assessments. It is important that the cases be exactly alike, except for this one difference, since otherwise one cannot be confident that it is this difference and not some other that accounts for any variation in the assessments of the two cases. So, let us consider this pair of cases:

In the first, Smith stands to gain a large inheritance if anything should happen to his six-year-old cousin. One evening while the child is taking his bath, Smith sneaks into the bathroom and drowns the child, and then arranges things so that it will look like an accident.

In the second, Jones also stands to gain if anything should happen to his six-year-old cousin. Like Smith, Jones sneaks in planning to drown the child in his bath. However, just as he enters the bathroom Jones sees the child slip and hit his head, and fall face down in the water. Jones is delighted; he stands by, ready to push the child's head back under if it is necessary, but it is not necessary. With only a little thrashing about, the child drowns all by himself, "accidentally," as Jones watches and does nothing.

Now Smith killed the child, whereas Jones "merely" let the child die.

That is the only difference between them. Did either man behave better, from a moral point of view? If the difference between killing and letting die were in itself a morally important matter, one should say that Jones's behavior was less reprehensible than Smith's. But does one really want to say that? I think not. In the first place, both men acted from the same motive, personal gain, and both had exactly the same end in view when they acted. It may be inferred from Smith's conduct that he is a bad man, although that judgment may be withdrawn or modified if certain further facts are learned about him—for example, that he is mentally deranged. But would not the very same thing be inferred about Jones from his conduct? And would not the same further considerations also be relevant to any modification of this judgment? Moreover, suppose Jones pleaded, in his own defense, "After all, I didn't do anything except just stand there and watch the child drown. I didn't kill him; I only let him die." Again, if letting die were in itself less bad than killing, this defense should have at least some weight. But it does not. Such a "defense" can only be regarded as a grotesque perversion of moral reasoning. Morally speaking, it is no defense at all.

Now, it may be pointed out, quite properly, that the cases of euthanasia with which doctors are concerned are not like this at all. They do not involve personal gain or the destruction of normal healthy children. Doctors are concerned only with cases in which the patient's life is of no further use to him, or in which the patient's life has become or will soon become a terrible burden. However, the point is the same in these cases: the bare difference between killing and letting die does not, in itself, make a moral difference. If a doctor lets a patient die, for humane reasons, he is in the same moral position as if he had given the patient a lethal injection for humane reasons. If his decision was wrong—if, for example, the patient's illness was in fact curable—the decision would be equally regrettable no matter which method was used to carry it out. And if the doctor's decision was the right one, the method used is not in itself important.

The AMA policy statement isolates the crucial issue very well; the crucial issue is "the intentional termination of the life of one human being by another." But after identifying this issue, and forbidding "mercy killing," the statement goes on to deny that the cessation of treatment is the intentional termination of a life. This is where the mistake comes in, for what is the cessation of treatment, in these circumstances, if it is not "the intentional termination of the life of one human being by another?" Of course it is exactly that, and if it were not, there would be no point to it.

Many people will find this judgment hard to accept. One reason, I think, is that it is very easy to conflate the question of whether killing is, in itself, worse than letting die, with the very different question of whether most actual cases of killing are more reprehensible than most actual cases of letting die. Most actual cases of killing are clearly terrible (think, for example, of all the murders reported in the newspapers), and one hears of such cases every day. On the other hand, one hardly ever hears of a case of letting die, except for the actions of doctors who are motivated by humanitarian reasons. So one learns to think of killing in a much worse light than of letting die. But this does not mean that there is something about killing that makes it in itself worse than letting die, for it is not the bare difference between killing and letting die that makes the difference in these cases. Rather, the other factors—the murderer's motive of personal gain, for example, contrasted with the doctor's humanitarian motivation—account for different reactions to the different cases.

I have argued that killing is not in itself any worse than letting die; if my contention is right, it follows that active euthanasia is not any worse than passive euthanasia. What arguments can be given on the other side? The most common, I believe, is the following:

> The important difference between active and passive euthanasia is that, in passive euthanasia, the doctor does not do anything to bring about the patient's death. The doctor does nothing, and the patient dies of whatever ills already afflict him. In active euthanasia, however, the doctor does something to bring about the patient's death; he kills him. The doctor who gives the patient with cancer a lethal injection has himself caused his patient's death; whereas if he merely ceases treatment, the cancer is the cause of the death.

A number of points need to be made here. The first is that it is not exactly correct to say that in passive euthanasia the doctor does nothing, for he does do one thing that is very important: he lets the patient die. "Letting someone die" is certainly different, in some respects, from other types of action—mainly in that it is a kind of action that one may perform by way of not performing certain other actions. For example, one may let a patient die by way of not giving medication, just as one may insult someone by way of not shaking his hand. But for any purpose of moral assessment, it is a type of action nonetheless. The decision to let a patient die is subject to moral appraisal in the same way that a decision to kill him would be subject to moral appraisal: it may be assessed as wise or unwise, compassionate or sadistic, right or wrong. If a doctor deliberately let a patient die who was suffering from a routinely curable illness, the doctor would certainly be to blame for what he had done, just as he would be to blame if he had needlessly killed the patient. Charges against him would then be appropriate. If so, it would be no defense at all for him to insist that he didn't "do anything." He would have done something very serious indeed, for he let his patient die.

Fixing the cause of death may be very important from a legal point of view, for it may determine whether criminal charges are brought against the doctor. But I do not think that this notion can be used to show a moral difference between active and passive euthanasia. The reason why it is considered bad to be the cause of someone's death is that death is regarded as a great evil—and so it is. However, if it has been decided that euthanasia—even passive euthanasia—is desirable in a given case, it has also been decided that in this instance death is no greater an evil than the patient's continued existence. And if this is true, the usual reason for not wanting to be the cause of someone's death simply does not apply.

Finally, doctors may think that all of this is only of academic interest—the sort of thing that philosophers may worry about but that has no practical bearing on their own work. After all, doctors must be concerned about the legal consequences of what they do, and active euthanasia is clearly forbidden by the law. But even so, doctors should also be concerned with the fact that the law is forcing upon them a moral doctrine that may well be indefensible, and has a considerable effect on their practices. Of course, most doctors are not now in the position of being coerced in this matter, for they do not regard themselves as merely going along with what the law requires. Rather, in statements such as the AMA policy statement that I have quoted, they are endorsing this doctrine as a central point of medical ethics. In that statement, active euthanasia is condemned not merely as illegal but as "contrary to that for which the medical profession stands," whereas passive euthanasia is approved. However, the preceding considerations suggest that there is really no moral difference between the two, considered in themselves (there may be important moral differences in some cases in their *consequences*, but, as I pointed out, these differences may make active euthanasia, and not passive euthanasia, the morally preferable option). So, whereas doctors may have to discriminate between active and passive euthanasia to satisfy the law, they should not do any more than that. In particular, they should not give the distinction any added authority and weight by writing it into official statements of medical ethics.

# A REPLY TO RACHELS ON ACTIVE AND PASSIVE EUTHANASIA

*Tom L. Beauchamp*

James Rachels has recently argued that the distinction between active and passive euthanasia is neither appropriately used by the American Medical Association nor generally useful for the resolution of moral problems of euthanasia.[1] Indeed he believes this distinction—which he equates

1. "Active and Passive Euthanasia," *New England Journal of Medicine* 292, pp. 78–80 (January 9, 1975).

From Tom L. Beauchamp, "A Reply to Rachels on Active and Passive Euthanasia," in *Ethical Issues in Death and Dying,* Tom L. Beauchamp and Seymour Perlin, eds. (Englewood Cliffs, N.J.: Prentice-Hall, 1978), pp. 246–58. Copyright © 1978 by Tom L. Beauchamp. Excerpts reprinted by permission of the author.

with the killing/letting die distinction—does not in itself have any moral importance. The chief object of his attack is the following statement adopted by the House of Delegates of the American Medical Association in 1973:

> The intentional termination of the life of one human being by another— mercy killing—is contrary to that for which the medical profession stands and is contrary to the policy of the American Medical Association.
>
> The cessation of the employment of extraordinary means to prolong the life of the body when there is irrefutable evidence that biological death is imminent is the decision of the patient and/or his immediate family. The advice and judgment of the physician should be freely available to the patient and/or his immediate family.

Rachels constructs a powerful and interesting set of arguments against this statement. In this paper I both (1) challenge his contentions on the grounds that he does not appreciate the moral reasons which give weight to the active/passive distinction and (2) provide a constructive account of the moral relevance of the active/passive distinction.

## I

I would concede that the active/passive distinction is *sometimes* morally irrelevant. Of this Rachels convinces me. But it does not follow that it is *always* morally irrelevant. What we need, then, is a case where the distinction is a morally relevant one and an explanation why it is so. Rachels himself uses the method of examining two cases which are exactly alike except that "one involves killing, whereas the other involves letting die. . . ." We may profitably begin by comparing the kinds of cases governed by the AMA's doctrine with the kinds of cases adduced by Rachels in order to assess the adequacy and fairness of his cases.

The second paragraph of the AMA statement is confined to a narrowly restricted range of passive euthanasia cases, viz., those (a) where the patients are on extraordinary means, (b) where irrefutable evidence of imminent death is available, and (c) where patient or family consent is available. Rachels' two cases involve conditions notably different from these:

> In the first, Smith stands to gain a large inheritance if anything should happen to his six-year-old cousin. One evening while the child is taking his bath, Smith sneaks into the bathroom and drowns the child, and then arranges things so that it will look like an accident.
>
> In the second, Jones also stands to gain if anything should happen to his six-year-old cousin. Like Smith, Jones sneaks in planning to drown the child in his bath. However, just as he enters the bathroom Jones sees the child slip and hit his head, and fall face down in the water. Jones is delighted; he stands by, ready to push the child's head back under if it is necessary, but it is not necessary. With only a little thrashing about, the child drowns all by himself, "accidentally," as Jones watches and does nothing.

> Now Smith killed the child, whereas Jones "merely" let the child die. That is the only difference between them.

Rachels says there is no moral difference between the cases in terms of our moral assessments of Smith and Jones' behavior. This seems fair enough, but what can Rachels' cases be said to prove, as they are so markedly disanalogous to the sorts of cases envisioned by the AMA proposal? Rachels concedes important disanalogies, but thinks them irrelevant:

> The point is the same in these cases: the bare difference between killing and letting die does not, in itself, make a moral difference. If a doctor lets a patient die, for humane reasons, he is in the same moral position as if he had given the patient a lethal injection for humane reasons.

Three observations are immediately in order. First, Rachels seems to infer that from such cases we can conclude that the distinction between killing and letting die is *always* morally irrelevant. This conclusion is fallaciously derived. What the argument in fact shows, being an analogical argument, is only that in all *relevantly similar* cases the distinction does not in itself make a moral difference. Since Rachels concedes that other cases are disanalogous, he seems thereby to concede that his argument is as weak as the analogy itself. (We shall see in the next section how weak the analogy is.) Second, Rachels' cases involve two *unjustified* actions, one of killing and the other of letting die. The AMA statement distinguishes one set of cases of unjustified killing and another of *justified* cases of allowing to die. Nowhere is it claimed by the AMA that what *makes* the difference in these cases is the active/passive distinction itself. It is only implied that one set of cases, the justified set, *involves* (passive) letting die while the unjustified set *involves* (active) killing. While it is said that justified euthanasia cases are passive ones and unjustified ones active, it is not said either that what *makes* some acts justified is the fact of their being passive or that what *makes* others unjustified is the fact of their being active. This fact will prove to be of vital importance.

The third and most important point is that in both of Rachels' cases the respective moral agents—Smith and Jones—are morally responsible for the death of the child and are morally blameworthy—even though Jones is not *causally* responsible. In the first case death is caused by the agent, while in the second it is not; yet the second agent is no less morally responsible. While the law might find only the first homicidal, morality condemns the motives in each case as equally wrong, and it holds that the duty to save life in such cases is as compelling as the duty not to take life. I suggest that it is largely because of this equal degree of moral responsibility that there is no morally relevant difference in Rachels' cases. In the cases envisioned by the AMA, however, an agent is held to be responsible for taking life by actively killing but is not held to be morally required to preserve life, and so not responsible for death, when removing the patient from extraordinary means (under conditions a–c above). I shall elaborate this latter point as a defense of the AMA position momentarily. My only conclusion thus far is the negative one that Rachels' arguments rest on weak foundations. His cases are not relevantly similar to euthanasia cases and do not support his apparent conclusion that the active/passive distinction is *always* morally irrelevant.

## II

I wish now to provide a positive account of the moral relevance of the active/passive distinction. I shall adduce two arguments in justification of a limited use of the distinction. The first elaborates the theme of responsibility, and the second a rather more speculative reason for invoking the distinction. I begin with an actual case, the celebrated Quinlan case.[2] Karen Quinlan was in a coma, and was on a mechanical respirator which artificially sustained her vital processes and which her parents wished to cease. At least some physicians believed there was irrefutable evidence that biological death was imminent and the coma irreversible. This case, under this description, closely conforms to the passive cases envisioned by the AMA. During an interview the father, Mr. Quinlan, asserted that he did not wish to kill his daughter, but only to remove her from the machines in order to see whether she would live or would die a natural death.[3] Suppose he had said—to envision now a second and hypothetical, but parallel case—that he wished only to see her die painlessly and therefore wished that the doctor could induce death by an overdose of morphine. Most of us would think the second act, which involves active killing, morally unjustified in these circumstances, while many of us would think the first act morally justified. (This is not the place to consider whether in fact it is justified, and if so under what conditions.) What accounts for the apparent morally relevant difference?

I have considered these two cases in order to follow Rachels' method of entertaining parallel cases where the only difference is that the one case involves killing and the other letting die. However, there is a further difference, and an important one which crops up in the euthanasia context. The difference rests in our judgments of medical fallibility and moral responsibility. Mr. Quinlan seems to think that, after all, the doctors might be wrong. There is a remote possibility that she might live without the aid of a machine. But whether or not the medical prediction of death turns out to be accurate, if she dies then no one is morally responsible for directly bringing about or causing her death, as they would be if they caused her death by killing her. Rachels finds explanations which appeal to causal conditions unsatisfactory; but this is perhaps only because he fails to see the nature of the causal link. To bring about her death is by that act to preempt the possibility of life. To "allow her to die" by removing artificial equipment is to allow for the possibility of wrong diagnosis or incorrect prediction and hence to absolve oneself of moral responsibility for the taking of life under false assumptions. There may, of course, be

2. As recorded in the Opinion of Judge Robert Muir, Jr., Docket No. C-201-75 of the Superior Court of New Jersey, Chancery Division, Morris County (November 10, 1975).
3. See Judge Muir's Opinion, p. 18—a slightly different statement but on the subject.

utterly no empirical possibility of recovery in some cases since recovery would violate a law of nature. However, judgments of empirical impossibility in medicine are notoriously problematic—my reason for emphasizing medical fallibility. And in all the hard cases I think we do not *know* that recovery is empirically impossible, even if *good evidence* is available.

The above reason for invoking the active/passive distinction can now be generalized: Active termination of life removes all possibility of life for the patient, while passively ceasing extraordinary means may not. This is not trivial since patients have survived in several celebrated cases where, in knowledgeable physicians' judgments, there was "irrefutable" evidence that death was imminent.[4]

One may, of course, be entirely responsible and culpable for another's death *either* by killing him *or* by letting him die. In such cases, of which Rachels' are examples, there is no morally significant difference between killing and letting die precisely because whatever one does, omits, or refrains from doing does not absolve one of responsibility. Either active or passive involvement renders one responsible for the death of another, and both involvements are equally wrong for the same principled moral reason: it is (prima facie) morally wrong to bring about the death of an innocent person capable of living whenever the causal intervention or negligence is intentional. (I use causal terms here because causal involvement need not be active, as when by one's negligence one is nonetheless causally responsible.) But not all cases of killing and letting die fall under this same moral principle. One is sometimes culpable for killing, because morally responsible as agent for death, as when one pulls the plug on a respirator sustaining a recovering patient (a murder). But one is sometimes not culpable for letting die because not morally responsible as agent, as when one pulls the plug on a respirator sustaining an irreversibly comatose and unrecoverable patient (a routine procedure, where one is *merely* causally responsible).[5] Different degrees and means of involvement assess different degrees of responsibility, and our assessments of culpability can become intricately complex. The only point which now concerns us, however, is that because different moral principles may govern very similar circumstances, we are sometimes morally culpable for killing but not for letting die.

A second argument may now be adduced in defense of the active/passive distinction. I shall develop this argument by combining (1) so-called wedge or slippery slope arguments with (2) recent arguments in defense of rule utilitarianism. I shall explain each in turn and show how in combination they may be used to defend the active/passive distinction.

(1) *Wedge arguments* proceed as follows: if killing were allowed, even

---

4. This problem of the strength of evidence also emerged in the Quinlan trial, as physicians disagreed whether the evidence was "irrefutable." Such disagreement, when added to the problems of medical fallibility and causal responsibility just outlined, provides one important argument against the *legalization* of active euthanasia, as perhaps the AMA would agreed.

5. Among the moral reasons why one is held to be responsible in the first sort of case and not responsible in the second sort are, I believe, the two grounds for the active/passive distinction under discussion in this section.

under the guise of a merciful extinction of life, a dangerous wedge would be introduced which places all "undesirable" or "unworthy" human life in a precarious condition. Proponents of wedge arguments believe the initial wedge places us on a slippery slope for at least one of two reasons: (i) It is said that our justifying principles leave us with no principled way to avoid the slide into saying that all sorts of killings would be justified under similar conditions. Here it is thought that once killing is allowed, a firm line between justified and unjustified killings cannot be securely drawn. It is thought best not to redraw the line in the first place, for redrawing it will inevitably lead to a downhill slide. It is then often pointed out that as a matter of historical record this is precisely what has occurred in the darker regions of human history, including the Nazi era, where euthanasia began with the best of intentions for horribly ill, non-Jewish Germans and gradually spread to anyone deemed an enemy of the people. (ii) Second, it is said that our basic principles against killing will be gradually eroded once some form of killing is legitimated. For example, it is said that permitting voluntary euthanasia will lead to permitting involuntary euthanasia, which will in turn lead to permitting euthanasia for those who are a nuisance to society (idiots, recidivist criminals, defective newborns, and the insane, e.g.). Gradually other principles which instill respect for human life will be eroded or abandoned in the process.

I am not inclined to accept the first reason.[6] If our justifying principles are themselves justified, then any action they warrant would be justified. Accordingly, I shall only be concerned with the second approach.

(2) *Rule utilitarianism* is the position that a society ought to adopt a rule if its acceptance would have better consequences for the common good (greater social utility) than any comparable rule could have in that society. Any action is right if it conforms to a valid rule and wrong if it violates the rule. Sometimes it is said that alternative *rules* should be measured against one another, while it has also been suggested that whole moral *codes* (complete sets of rules) rather than individual rules should be compared. While I prefer the latter formulation (Brandt's), this internal dispute need not detain us here. The important point is that a particular rule or a particular code of rules is morally justified if and only if there is no other competing rule or moral code whose acceptance would have a higher utility value for society, and where a rule's acceptability is contingent upon the consequences which would result if the rule were made current.

Wedge arguments, when conjoined with rule utilitarian arguments, may be applied to euthanasia issues in the following way. We presently subscribe to a no-active-euthanasia rule (which the AMA suggests we retain). Imagine now that in our society we make current a restricted-active-euthanasia rule (as Rachels seems to urge). Which of these two moral rules would, if enacted, have the consequence of maximizing social utility? Clearly a restricted-active-euthanasia rule would have *some* utility value, as

---

6. An intelligent argument of this form, but one I find unacceptable for reasons given below, is Arthur Dyck, "Beneficent Euthanasia and Benemortasia: Alternative Views of Mercy," in M. Kohl, ed., *Beneficent Euthanasia* (Buffalo: Prometheus Books, 1975), pp. 120f.

Rachels notes, since some intense and uncontrollable suffering would be eliminated. However, it may not have the highest utility value in the structure of our present code or in any imaginable code which could be made current, and therefore may not be a component in the ideal code for our society. If wedge arguments raise any serious questions at all, as I think they do, they rest in this area of whether a code would be weakened or strengthened by the addition of active euthanasia principles. For the disutility of introducting legitimate killing into one's moral code (in the form of active euthanasia rules) may, in the long run, outweigh the utility of doing so, as a result of the eroding effect such a relaxation would have on rules in the code which demand respect for human life. If, for example, rules permitting active killing were introduced, it is not implausible to suppose that destroying defective newborns (a form of involuntary euthanasia) would become an accepted and common practice, that as population increases occur the aged will be even more neglectable and neglected than they now are, that capital punishment for a wide variety of crimes would be increasingly tempting, that some doctors would have appreciably reduced fears of actively injecting fatal doses whenever it seemed to them propitious to do so, and that laws of war against killing would erode in efficacy even beyond their already abysmal level. A hundred such possible consequences might easily be imagined. But these are sufficient to make the larger point that such rules permitting killing could lead to a general reduction of respect for human life. Rules against killing in a moral code are not *isolated* moral principles; they are pieces of a web of rules against killing which forms a moral code. The more threads one removes, the weaker the fabric becomes. And if, as I believe, moral principles against active killing have the deep and continuously civilizing effect of promoting respect for life, and if principles which allow passively letting die (as envisioned in the AMA statement) do not themselves cut against this effect, then this seems an important reason for the maintenance of the active/passive distinction. (By the logic of the above argument passively letting die would also have to be prohibited if a rule permitting it had the serious adverse consequence of eroding acceptance of rules protective of respect for life. While this prospect seems to me highly improbable, I can hardly claim to have refuted those conservatives who would claim that even rules which sanction letting die place us on a precarious slippery slope.)

A troublesome problem, however, confronts my use of utilitarian and wedge arguments. Most all of us would agree that both killing and letting die are justified under some conditions. Killings in self-defense and in "just" wars are widely accepted as justified because the conditions excuse the killing. If society can withstand these exceptions to moral rules prohibiting killing, then why is it not plausible to suppose society can accept another excusing exception in the form of justified active euthanasia? This is an important and worthy objection, but not a decisive one. The defenseless and the dying are significantly different classes of persons from aggressors who attach individuals and/or nations. In the case of aggressors, one does not confront the question whether their lives are no longer *worth living*. Rather, we reach the judgment that the aggressors' morally blameworthy actions justify counteractions. But in the case of the dying and the otherwise ill, there is no morally blameworthy action to justify our own. Here we are required to accept the judgment that their lives are no longer *worth living* in order to believe that the termination of their lives is justified. It is the latter sort of judgment which is feared by those who take the wedge argument seriously. We do not now permit and never have permitted the taking of morally blameless lives. I think this is the key to understanding why recent cases of intentionally allowing the death of defective newborns (as in the famous case at Johns Hopkins Hospital) have generated such protracted controversy. Even if such newborns could not have led meaningful lives (a matter of some controversy), it is the wedged foot in the door which creates the most intense worries. For if we once take a decision to allow a restricted infanticide justification or any justification at all on grounds that a life is not meaningful or not worth living, we have qualified our moral rules against killing. That this qualification is a matter of the utmost seriousness needs no argument. I mention it here only to show why the wedge argument has moral force even though we *already* allow some very different conditions to justify intentional killing.

I reach only a guarded conclusion. While I am unsure about the predictions made in wedge arguments, I find it equally impossible to ignore them. They point to a fearful and not unlikely danger inherent in the legalization of active euthanasia. It is hard to say where the burden of proof rests. The evidence is everywhere imperfect, yet sufficient to generate controversy. Those who would endorse limited euthanasia rules, however, have given scant attention to the problems of legalizing active euthanasia which are pointed to by wedge arguments. Yet the matter is sufficiently momentous that I think we ought to be most cautious in embracing even highly restricted active euthanasia rules, which involve a rather fundamental change in our moral code, until some further assurance on this score is received. And this provides a second reason for insisting upon the moral relevance of the active/passive distinction.

## III

It may still be insisted that my case has not touched Rachels' leading claim, for I have not shown, as Rachels puts it, that it is "the bare difference between killing and letting die that makes the difference in these cases." True, I have not shown this, and in my judgment it cannot be shown. But this concession does not require capitulation to Rachels' argument. I adduced a case which is at the center of our moral intuition that killing is morally different (in at least some cases) from letting die; and I then attempted to account for at least part of the grounds for this belief. The grounds turn out to be other than the *bare* difference, but nevertheless *make* the distinction morally relevant.

It is also worth noticing that there is nothing in the AMA statement which says that the bare difference between killing and letting die itself and alone makes the difference in our differing moral assessments of rightness and wrongness. Rachels forces this interpretation on the statement. Some philosophers may have thought bare difference makes the difference, but there is scant evidence that the AMA or any thoughtful ethicist *must* believe it in order to defend the relevance and importance of the active/passive distinction. When this conclusion is coupled with my earlier argument that from Rachels' paradigm cases it follows only that the active/passive distinction is sometimes, but not always, morally irrelevant, it would seem that his case against the AMA is decisively impaired.

# THE WRONGFULNESS OF EUTHANASIA

*J. Gay-Williams*

My impression is that euthanasia—the idea, if not the practice—is slowly gaining acceptance within our society. Cynics might attribute this to an increasing tendency to devalue human life, but I do not believe this is the major factor. The acceptance is much more likely to be the result of unthinking sympathy and benevolence. Well-publicized, tragic stories like that of Karen Quinlan elicit from us deep feelings of compassion. We think to ourselves, "She and her family would be better off if she were dead." It is an easy step from this very human response to the view that if someone (and others) would be better off dead, then it must be all right to kill that person. Although I respect the compassion that leads to this conclusion, I believe the conclusion is wrong. I want to show that euthanasia is wrong. It is inherently wrong, but it is also wrong judged from the standpoints of self-interest and of practical effects.

Before presenting my arguments to support this claim, it would be well to define "euthanasia." An essential aspect of euthanasia is that it involves taking a human life, either one's own or that of another. Also, the person whose life is taken must be someone who is believed to be suffering from some disease or injury from which recovery cannot reasonably be expected. Finally, the action must be deliberate and intentional. Thus, euthanasia is intentionally taking the life of a presumably hopeless

From J. Gay-Williams, "The Wrongfulness of Euthanasia," in Ronald Munson, ed., *Intervention and Reflection, Basic Issues in Medical Ethics*, 2nd ed. (Belmont, Calif.: Wadsworth Publishing Company, 1983), pp. 156–59. Copyright © 1983 by Wadsworth, Inc. Reprinted by permission of Wadsworth Publishing Company, Belmont, California 94002.

person. Whether the life is one's own or that of another, the taking of it is still euthanasia.

It is important to be clear about the deliberate and intentional aspect of the killing. If a hopeless person is given an injection of the wrong drug by mistake and this causes his death, this is wrongful killing but not euthanasia. The killing cannot be the result of accident. Furthermore, if the person is given an injection of a drug that is believed to be necessary to treat his disease or better his condition and the person dies as a result, then this is neither wrongful killing nor euthanasia. The intention was to make the patient well, not kill him. Similarly, when a patient's condition is such that it is not reasonable to hope that any medical procedures or treatments will save his life, a failure to implement the procedures or treatments is not euthanasia. If the person dies, this will be as a result of his injuries or disease and not because of his failure to receive treatment.

The failure to continue treatment after it has been realized that the patient has little chance of benefitting from it has been characterized by some as "passive euthanasia." This phrase is misleading and mistaken. In such cases, the person involved is not killed (the first essential aspect of euthanasia), nor is the death of the person intended by the withholding of additional treatment (the third essential aspect of euthanasia). The aim may be to spare the person additional and unjustifiable pain, to save him from the indignities of hopeless manipulations, and to avoid increasing the financial and emotional burden on his family. When I buy a pencil it is so that I can use it to write, not to contribute to an increase in the gross national product. This may be the unintended consequence of my action, but it is not the aim of my action. So it is with failing to continue the treatment of a dying person. I intend his death no more than I intend to reduce the GNP by not using medical supplies. His is an unintended dying, and so-called "passive euthansia" is not euthanasia at all.

## 1. THE ARGUMENT FROM NATURE

Every human being has a natural inclination to continue living. Our reflexes and responses fit us to fight attackers, flee wild animals, and dodge out of the way of trucks. In our daily lives we exercise the caution and care necessary to protect ourselves. Our bodies are similarly structured for survival right down to the molecular level. When we are cut, our capillaries seal shut, our blood clots, and fibrogen is produced to start the process of healing the wound. When we are invaded by bacteria, antibodies are produced to fight against the alien organisms, and their remains are swept out of the body by special cells designed for clean-up work.

Euthanasia does violence to this natural goal of survival. It is literally acting against nature because all the processes of nature are bent towards the end of bodily survival. Euthanasia defeats these subtle mechanisms in a way that, in a particular case, disease and injury might not.

It is possible, but not necessary, to make an appeal to revealed religion in this connection. Man as trustee of his body acts against God, its rightful possessor, when he takes his own life. He also violates the commandment to hold life sacred and never to take it without just and compelling cause. But since this appeal will persuade only those who are prepared to accept that religion has access to revealed truths, I shall not employ this line of argument.

It is enough, I believe, to recognize that the organization of the human body and our patterns of behavioral responses make the continuation of life a natural goal. By reason alone, then, we can recognize that euthanasia sets us against our own nature. Furthermore, in doing so, euthanasia does violence to our dignity. Our dignity comes from seeking our ends. When one of our goals is survival, and actions are taken that eliminate that goal, then our natural dignity suffers. Unlike animals, we are conscious through reason of our nature and our ends. Euthanasia involves acting as if this dual nature—inclination towards survival and awareness of this as an end—did not exist. Thus, euthanasia denies our basic human character and requires that we regard ourselves or others as something less than fully human.

## 2. THE ARGUMENT FROM SELF-INTEREST

The above arguments are, I believe, sufficient to show that euthanasia is inherently wrong. But there are reasons for considering it wrong when judged by standards other than reason. Because death is final and irreversible, euthanasia contains within it the possibility that we will work against our own interest if we practice it or allow it to be practiced on us.

Contemporary medicine has high standards of excellence and a proven record of accomplishment, but it does not possess perfect and complete knowledge. A mistaken diagnosis is possible, and so is a mistaken prognosis. Consequently, we may believe that we are dying of a disease when, as a matter of fact, we may not be. We may think that we have no hope of recovery when, as a matter of fact, our chances are quite good. In such circumstances, if euthanasia were permitted, we would die needlessly. Death is final and the chance of error too great to approve the practice of euthanasia.

Also, there is always the possibility that an experimental procedure or a hitherto untried technique will pull us through. We should at least keep this option open, but euthanasia closes it off. Furthermore, spontaneous remission does occur in many cases. For no apparent reason, a patient simply recovers when those all around him, including his physicians, expected him to die. Euthanasia would just guarantee their expectations and leave no room for the "miraculous" recoveries that frequently occur.

Finally, knowing that we can take our life at any time (or ask another to take it) might well incline us to give up too easily. The will to live is strong in all of us, but it can be weakened by pain and suffering and feelings of hopelessness. If during a bad time we allow ourselves to be killed, we never have a chance to reconsider. Recovery from a serious illness requires that we fight for it, and anything that weakens our determination by suggesting that there is an easy way out is ultimately against our own interest. Also, we may be inclined towards euthanasia because of our concern for others. If we see our sickness and suffering as an emotional and financial burden on our family, we may feel that to leave our life is to make their lives easier. The very presence of the possibility of euthanasia may keep us from surviving when we might.

## 3. THE ARGUMENT FROM PRACTICAL EFFECTS

Doctors and nurses are, for the most part, totally committed to saving lives. A life lost is, for them, almost a personal failure, an insult to their skills and knowledge. Euthanasia as a practice might well alter this. It could have a corrupting influence so that in any case that is severe doctors and nurses might not try hard enough to save the patient. They might decide that the patient would simply be "better off dead" and take the steps necessary to make that come about. This attitude could then carry over to their dealings with patients less seriously ill. The result would be an overall decline in the quality of medical care.

Finally, euthanasia as a policy is a slippery slope. A person apparently hopelessly ill may be allowed to take his own life. Then he may be permitted to deputize others to do it for him should he no longer be able to act. The judgment of others then becomes the ruling factor. Already at this point euthanasia is not personal and voluntary, for others are acting "on behalf of" the patient as they see fit. This may well incline them to act on behalf of other patients who have not authorized them to exercise their judgment. It is only a short step, then, from voluntary euthanasia (self-inflicted or authorized), to directed euthanasia administered to a patient who has given no authorization, to involuntary euthanasia conducted as part of a social policy. Recently many psychiatrists and sociologists have argued that we define as "mental illness" those forms of behavior that we disapprove of. This gives us license then to lock up those who display the behavior. The category of the "hopelessly ill" provides the possibility of even worse abuse. Embedded in a social policy, it would give society or its representatives the authority to eliminate all those who might be considered too "ill" to function normally any longer. The dangers of euthanasia are too great to all to run the risk of approving it in any form. The first slippery step may well lead to a serious and harmful fall.

I hope that I have succeeded in showing why the benevolence that inclines us to give approval of euthanasia is misplaced. Euthanasia is inherently wrong because it violates the nature and dignity of human beings. But even those who are not convinced by this must be persuaded that the potential personal and social dangers inherent in euthanasia are sufficient to forbid our approving it either as a personal practice or as a public policy.

Suffering is surely a terrible thing, and we have a clear duty to comfort those in need and to ease their suffering when we can. But suffering is also a natural part of life with values for the individual and for others that we should not overlook. We may legitimately seek for others and for ourselves an easeful death, as Arthur Dyck has pointed out. Euthanasia, however, is not just an easeful death. It is a wrongful death. Euthanasia is not just dying. It is killing.

# RIGHTS, JUSTICE, AND EUTHANASIA

*Bertram and Elsie Bandman*

[I]f there are any moral rights at all, there is at least one prior right founded on justice—the equal right of all persons to be free to decide to live or die. Such a prior moral right, we shall argue, is moreover one whose claims are nearly incontestable and can only be overridden under extraordinary circumstances (a) favoring the continuation of a person's life and (b) involving the least injustice. The type of exception to be noted is justified only on the grounds that it provides the least injustice to everyone's otherwise inviolably equal right to be free.

The equal right to be free to decide to live or die, we hold, is based largely on John Rawls' point that "to respect persons is to recognize that they possess an inviolability founded on justice that even the welfare of society as a whole cannot override." We demur, ever so slightly, however, to Rawls' implication that "the welfare of society as a whole" makes no morally just claim. There is also justice in being on the side of "the welfare of society as a whole." A conflict between moral rights and claims involving difficult choices calls for a just procedure to effect the least possible injustice, which does not, however, override the claims of justice. That is, justice, as "the first virtue of social institutions," cannot be overturned in principle; only in some of the circumstances of its application is a just claim ever overridden, but always and only by some other just claim. But justice and just claims are never morally overridden by injustice or by unjust claims, only by those that effect the least injustice. According to Rawls, with whom we agree on this point, "the interests requiring the violation of justice have no value. Having no merit in the first place, they cannot override its claims."

From Bertram and Elsie Bandman, "Rights, Justice, and Euthanasia," in Marvin Kohl, ed., *Beneficent Euthanasia* (Buffalo, N.Y.: Prometheus Books, 1975), pp. 81–89, 91–94. Reprinted by permission of the publisher.

## THE RIGHT TO BE FREE TO DECIDE TO LIVE OR DIE

But first this explication of what it means to have the prior right to be free to decide to live or die.

A corollary of the right to be free is the right to live. One cannot be free if one is not alive. Almost no one wants to die. There is such a thing as living well, but not dying well. Almost no one to whom beneficent euthanasia applies wants to die. Justice is connected to what a person wants. The first moral right, if there is one, is the equal right to be free. And this freedom involves the freedom to live as unimpaired, as uninjured, and as long as possible.

To die is to lose whatever freedom one has. The moral right to be free, if there is any moral right at all, implies the equal right to be free to live. One cannot exercise freedom in death. Death is not "only an event not lived through," as Wittgenstein said; it is an event devoutly feared by most people. People do not march to the gallows in euphoria. Death is the end of life. There is just no way to add spice to death by calling it "beneficent" or "kind" or by referring to it as "death with dignity." Death is not the end, like a destination or terminal or time as when one goes to sleep; one does not wake up from death. Nor is death like a long voyage from which one returns. The person who goes on the "trip" of death never returns; he never again carries on life functions, never experiences boredom, frustration, joy or sorrow, hunger or thirst, or sexual desire; nor does he see the squirrels in the park in the winter or the bikinis in the summer. He experiences not at all.

What, then, is so beneficent about death? Alleviation of suffering? That has to be weighed against the possibility of the discovery of a new drug or of remission the next day. At best, death is to the person who dies a necessary evil, among the worst of evils, from which there is neither return, revival, nor relief. Death is the termination of the process of life; it is necessary and inevitable, not a freedom and so not a right. Nothing connected with a person's death is a right. No one has freedom in death or rights in death. The dead have no rights. If everyone has an equal right to be free, this entails the equal right to be free to live as well and as long as possible. The only way to exercise such a right is to be put in a corresponding position to *claim* it.

A just society is here distinguishable from one that is unjust. An unjust society makes no provision for the physically weak and infirm to have their moral rights respected and recognized and put into effect. A just society is one that respects a person's inviolable right to be free even if he is in no position to make the needed physical movements to assume and safeguard his rights. Others protect but do not usurp or assume the right to live of the debilitated person. . . .

. . . A just society utilizes its resources to respect the wishes of its people, young and old, and does more to prevent and also to attempt to cure fatal diseases than does an unjust society. A just society places its priorities on values that make possible the long and good life equally for everyone.

Even those who welcome death seldom do so in the belief that death is another phase of a better life rather than the end of life.

Notwithstanding such a desire, the requirement to respect a person's autonomy implies that a person is capable of being rational, that he is adequately informed and freely gives consent, and that he alone has not only the equal moral right to be free to live but also that he has, ultimately and finally, the equal right to be free to decide to live or die.

As bad as death is to most persons who want to live, the right of a person to decide includes the last decision for which one may be free, to decide to die, "to end it all" in Hamlet's phrase. Only the patient has the moral right to decide the question of his death; and to assure that his right to live or die shall be respected, restrictive conditions accompany those who would, with his consent, terminate his life. . . .

But even for a person, the right to die is not as high a priority right as the right to live, because a consequence of the exercise of the right to die is the final elimination of a person's freedom. A person who chooses to die cannot take back his decision after it has been acted on. So safeguards are needed to assure that the desire to die is the firm conviction of the patient.

There may even be extenuating circumstances in which the prolonged suffering of a person may have beneficial consequences that enhance other persons' possibilities of living. The right to live outweighs the right to die. So, in a pinch where the lives of others depend on overruling a person's right to die, his right to die justly gives way to their prior right to live.

But the converse is not ordinarily just. Sacrificing a person's life to save others is not necessarily just. It may be done, it may be necessary, but necessity is not morality. It is only moral if it is the least unjust thing to do. Would sacrificing one life to save others be the least unjust thing to do in some circumstances? If so, it would be the moral thing to do. But the following priorities must be recognized within the right to decide to live or die: (1) a person's right to decide to live or die overrides anyone else's right to decide for that person; (2) a person's right to live overrides another person's right to die; (3) in a situation involving two or more person's rights to live or die, taking 1 and 2 into consideration, the least injustice overrides anyone's right to live or die—that is, the equal rights of several persons to live outweighs one person's right to live.

Least injustice can be explained as follows. Every person has the equal right to be free to decide to live or die. Justice as the *equal* right to be free and to be treated fairly and impartially means that a person's right to be free is made less equal if unjust exception is taken to 1 and 2. And, in 3, everyone's equal right to live (assuming that all rights are at least partly derived from needs) means that in a "catastrophe case" the equal rights of several persons to live overrides one person's equal right to live. The sacrifice of one's life in certain emergency situations to save the lives of many may constitute the least injustice. A fireman may sense that the least evil and also the least injustice is in his risking his life, or an elderly person in a life raft may sense that the least injustice is in giving up his life. On the other hand, the person in a life raft who is best qualified to guide it to safety ought, on the grounds of the survival of the majority, to be the last to sacrifice himself.

The point is that the least injustice in life-and-death cases consists in an equal consideration of every person's need to live. The reason for 3 is that in a "catastrophe case" one person's equal right to be free to live or die may be overridden by another person's right to live if it results in the least injustice. Killing a person is morally wrong unless it can be shown that killing that person effects the least injustice in a given situation. At any rate, as a matter of moral priority, only after settling the question of whether or under what conditions to permit beneficent euthanasia does the question of having to administer beneficent euthanasia arise. But under no circumstances is killing a person with "mercy" or "kindness," inducing a "good death," or effecting "death with dignity" without recognition of the recipient's rights morally desirable. Are these expressions even logically free of a category mistake?

We will examine the right to be free to decide to live or die in relation to four hypothetical examples that illustrate conflicting claims. After presenting these examples, we will cite principles appealed to and consider whether, in the face of hard examples and other principles, the moral right cited at the outset can still be maintained and defended.

## SOME EXAMPLES

*Hypothetical Case 1:*   ($A_1$) Mr. Black, a gifted pathologist, can cure a disease that will save others' lives but is himself cancer-ridden and wants to die. Black is still functioning but would rather die. According to $A_1$ Black has a right to die.

($B_1$) There is an overriding reason to deny Black the right to die. If Black were not gifted, $B_1$'s response would be that Black has the right to die. But $B_1$ appeals to Black's capacity to help others. That is, Black, although painfully suffering from an incurable disease, is the only one who knows how to cure his disease, which will extinguish life in his community.

Does Black in this instance have the incontestable right to decide to live or die? If commonsense moral intuitions are consulted, one might, in this instance, invoke $B_1$'s argument, thus restricting Black's right to decide. What happened to Black's inviolable right?

*Hypothetical Case 2:*   ($A_2$) Mr. Blue, cancer ridden, wants to live, but his family is seriously inconvenienced by the cost of Blue's care. The family finances are depleted. Yet, according to $A_2$ Blue has the right to live.

($B_2$) Blue's right to live is overridden by his family's needs and claims. Blue is a drain on the family finances, which effectively prevents his four sons from going to college. Moreover, the physician believes that Blue will be a drag on society and that he would be better off dead than living in a public home at the taxpayer's expense. According to $B_2$ Blue will only become a burden to society and so his right to live is overridden by the greater needs of society.

$A_2$ says that Blue was not only deprived of his right to live but that his right to decide whether to live or die also was *violated*. On the contrary, $B_2$ says, it was Blue's family that suffered the most. Blue no longer had the right to decide, and even if he did, it was overruled by the needs, claims, and interests of his family and of society.

One's sense of justice this time seems to favor $A_2$'s side, perceiving that Blue's right to decide to live or die was violated. Moreover, favoring $A_2$ accords with Blue's equal right to be free to decide whether to live or die. So, although there may be a problem, which we will consider, in resolving the case 1 conflict, there seems to be no problem of consistency or explanation in case 2; for the decision favoring $A_2$ is consistent with Blue's prior right to decide to live or die.

*Hypothetical Case 3:* ($A_3$) Let us next imagine the following: Mrs. Green, a woman of wealth and an accomplished pianist, has twins, each of whom needs an immediate kidney transplant to live. She is the only available donor. She has heart trouble and an operation would risk her life. There is a 50 percent chance of her dying in surgery, but if she dies in surgery, then both kidneys may be transplanted and both children can be saved. According to $A_3$ her children have a right to live, but not at the risk of her life. Her right to live overrides their right.

($B_3$) Mrs. Green's twins have a right to live, either of whom can do so only if she gives up a kidney for either child, possibly by drawing lots. Better to risk one life, Mrs. Green's, and save at least one of the twins. If Mrs. Green dies during surgery, then both children will live. In either case, her risk means that two people will live in good health. If she refuses, she lives, but both sons will die. To $B_3$ it is two lives to one in any case. Therefore, the right of at least one son to live overrides the right of the mother to refuse to take a 50 percent risk.

Case 2 offered us little difficulty; case 3 is indeed difficult to judge. Here Mrs. Green, in exercising her right to live or die, chooses to live, which overrides the right to die. But Mrs. Green's right to live—more precisely, her right to refuse to risk her life for the sake of saving the life of at least one other person in a pinch case—is overridden by her twins' rights to live because it is the least unjust thing to do in the situation. This appeal will also subsequently be defended.

*Hypothetical Case 4:* ($A_4$) Brown, aged sixteen, the brilliant only child of professional parents, suffers from advanced leukemia, following years of painful drug administration, radiation, transfusions, and hospitalizations. He has seen other children die of the same illness and can no longer bear the painful process of the disease and wishes to die. $A_4$ holds that Brown has the right to die. The doctor's prognosis coincides with the boy's. He sees no point in prolonging a painful and hopeless process.

($B_4$) Brown's parents are heartbroken. They are able to supply every possible means of medical assistance and care to prolong his life and keep hoping for a remission or the discovery of a lifesaving drug, despite the obvious terminal phase of their son's illness. They want him to live. According to $B_4$ Brown's right to decide to die is overridden by his parents' wishes.

$A_4$ overrides $B_4$ because Brown's right to be free to decide to live or die outweighs the preferences of his parents and even Brown's right to prefer death to life, which although a lower priority than the right to life is in accord with Brown's prior right to decide. Case 4 is different from Case 1 in that Brown, unlike Black, does not have the lives of others depending on his continuing to live. So Brown has the equal moral right to decide to die. In Black's case that right is not equal since others' lives depend on Black. In case 2 Blue's right to live overrides his family's concerns with serious financial difficulty; nor does the inconvenience to society count. And unlike the Green case, Blue's right involves no pinch or "either/or," as Black's case does. According to the principles of justice so far developed, in cases 1 and 3, B's argument overrides A's; and in cases 2 and 4 A's argument overrides B's.

We consider next the principles each disputant appeals to in justifying his conclusion, as well as the grounds for our conclusions.

## PRINCIPLES

A appeals to a modified deontological or Kantian view that bases all action on exceptionless principles. B appeals to utilitarian consequentialist principles, which are concerned with maximizing flourishing and minimizing the total amount of pain and has been called the "aggregative principle." A appeals to a principle K: Every person without exception has the equal moral right to be free. Therefore, treat every person with respect and justice as an end, never as a means to be sacrificed without his consent for the convenience, welfare, or the lives of others. B, however, appeals to a principle U: Always maximize happiness and flourishing for everyone without regard for the rights of any given person and minimize the total amount of suffering in the world. Regarding euthanasia, maximize kindness and minimize cruelty.

In case 1 our moral intuitions, it seems, favor $B_1$. But does this mean that Black has no right to decide whether to live or die? He has, but his right is overridden by appeal to U, which coincides with the priority of life over death. In case 2 A's appeal to K coincides with everyone's equal right to be free to decide to live or die, and with Blue's right to live, which has priority over financial inconvenience to Blue's family. In case 3, Mrs. Green's right to live without risking her life is overridden by appealing to U, which maximizes the saving of life. In case 4, Brown's right to decide is not overridden by the rights of others, in this case the preferences of his family. Black (case 1) and Brown (case 4) want euthanasia. Black's right is overridden by the equal right of others to live. This is not so with Brown, who has the right to have his life ended. Case 4 clearly rules in favor of beneficent euthanasia, whereas case 1 rules against it. So, even one's right to end life is not sacrosanct. Blue and Green (cases 2 and 3) both want to live. Blue's right involves no other person's equal right to live and so his right overrides his family's financial concerns. Case 2 accordingly clearly rules in favor of Blue and reveals in this type of case the strength of K over U.

But on what basis do we decide to favor B in case 3? Gertrude Ezorsky tells us in a similar connection that in dire cases of this sort—"catastrophic cases" or "pinch cases"—one appeals to a compromise principle "to referee the outcome." We accordingly appeal in a pinch case to the following principle, KU: Consider happiness, flourishing, pleasure, and pain, but do the least injustice possible. Hence, Mrs. Green's right to live and not to risk her life is overridden, but by appeal to the compromise principle KU.

Appeal to KU gives the equal rights of Mrs. Green's twins a moral edge over Mrs. Green's right not to risk her life. In case 1, in conjunction with the principles of justice stated initially, appeal to U suffices to decide between Black's desire to die and the needs of those whose lives depend on his staying alive. If there is doubt about whether to appeal to U or to K, appeal to KU, being closest to our initial principles, settles the issue in favor of those who need help to live that only Black can give.

In case 2, in conjunction with our initial principles, appeal to K is also sufficient. Again, if a doubt arises, further appeal to KU settles the question in favor of Blue's right to live. Finally, in cases 3 and 4, appeal to U and K, respectively, settles the matter. But, if a doubt arises, appeal to KU in Green's case favors the saving of more lives and in Brown's case favors his right to live or die over the preferences of others. Consequently, wherever a doubt arises, one may appeal finally to KU to decide any of the four cases. But what is the basis for appeal to KU? . . .

## THE RIGHT TO DIE IS LIMITED AND HEDGED ROUND WITH RESTRICTIONS

. . . Conditions for justified euthanasia are the fully informed and freely given consent of the recipient.

These conditions can be overridden only if prolonging a person's life (or risking it) against his will results in saving the lives of others (as in cases 1 and 3). Otherwise a person's will cannot be overridden (as in cases 2 and 4).

Everyone has an *equal* moral right to decide to live or die, and one person's right to decide is *not equal* to that of others if their lives depend on overriding his right. That was one reason for appealing to KU in a pinch case such as 1 or 3. Extraneous family financial factors (case 2) or family preferences (case 4) do not carry moral weight against every person's equal right to decide. Where there is a conflict, the right to live overrides the right to die (as in case 1); and if there is a conflict between two or more people's equal rights to live, two or more equal rights outweigh one person's equal right (as in case 3). Only with such exceptions to restrict euthanasia does one provide the least injustice in pinch cases, thereby safeguarding the beneficence of euthanasia.

Even a rational and just society occasionally calls on a person to perform the supererogatory and heroic acts of living with unbearable pain or of risking one's life (as in cases 1 and 3) for the good of others. There are otherwise no rational grounds for weakening restrictions against justified euthanasia. A society that compels people to make premature life or death decisions may foreclose alternatives for improving and lengthening life and is, to that extent, cruel and unjust for not assuring every person's equal right to be free; for if a person is free, he will ordinarily choose to live.

The saying "where there is life there is hope" suggests that even a patient who is considered to be terminally ill may have a reversal or remission of his disease, assuming a just society in which every person receives medical benefits equal to those of the most advantaged members of society.

# CHAPTER ELEVEN
# SEXUAL ETHICS

People's views on the morality of sexual activities vary enormously. Forms of sex that are condemned as "perversions" by some people are highly desirable to others. Consider the following statement written by a teenage boy:

> I am sixteen and my mom is forty-eight. It all started one night when I came home from a date. I went right upstairs to bed, and I was lying there [nude] . . . and my mom walked in and turned the light on. We both just stood still for a while. She said she had come up to put my sheet on my bed. She sat on the bed and I got up and put my underwear on, and sat next to her. . . . Then she asked me if I wanted to make love. . . . My fantasy now is that I will sleep in my mom's bedroom.[1]

Or consider this statement, also written by a young male:

> I have as far back as I can remember always been greatly fascinated by ladies' dainty and elegant footwear when worn by women who have nice shapely legs and well-formed feet so the shoe or boot hugs and fits the contours of their feet and legs, often to such perfection that it gives the viewer the concept of it being a part of her own personal charms, or one might say fitting almost like a second skin. And so whenever and wherever I

---

1. Nancy Friday, ed., *Men in Love: Men's Sexual Fantasies; The Triumph of Love over Rage,* p. 165. Copyright © 1980 by Nancy Friday. Reprinted by permission of Delacorte Press, New York.

feast my eyes on such ladies wearing shiny black high-heeled patent leather shoes or boots, I become sexually stimulated. . . . When I become infatuated with the lady's sexy shoes or boots, I make a real study of admiring the high curved arch of her instep which the high slim heel serves to emphasize and I get the urge to kneel down and fervently lick and kiss the shiny, sexy shoe leather in humble homage and become the lady's personal boot slave.[2]

Or consider this newspaper report on a college teacher's course:

[T]he glib former professor of the psychology of sex [Dr. Singer] . . . was suspended with pay . . . after he said in a published interview that he had been "romantically involved" with some of his students, attended student parties where there was nudity and sex, and openly discussed giving home-work credit for sexual experimentation. . . . Singer insisted that he gave students credit for optional sexual experimentation only when he believed the experience would be safe for them. But he conceded that there may be "some legitimate controversy" over what is safe. Those who elected to use the option included a woman who was living with a man and wanted to have a bisexual student join them in bed, and several heterosexual women who decided to try lesbian experiences, Singer said. "I happen to think that a straight woman having a lesbian experience is just fine," he said, "that there is virtually no risk involved."[3]

Are the sexual activities mentioned in the accounts above morally wrong?[4] Are parental incest, shoe fetishism, and homosexuality moral perversions or, as Dr. Singer suggests, are they "just fine" so long as there is no risk of danger to the parties involved?

Traditional moralists have condemned all sexual activities outside of marriage.[5] Some have argued that the natural purpose or end of sex is the continuation of the human race through procreation,[6] and that sexual activity intentionally carried on apart from this end is unnatural and therefore immoral. In this view, incest, fetishism, and homosexuality are all unnatural and immoral. In fact, to the traditionalist all sexual activity

2. Ibid., pp. 187–88.

3. *San Jose Mercury,* January 25, 1983.

4. For additional research on sexual behavior, see: Virginia E. Johnson and William H. Masters, *Human Sexual Response* (Boston: Little, Brown, 1966); Gilbert D. Bartell, *Group Sex: A Scientist's Eyewitness Report on Swinging in the Suburbs* (New York: Wyden, 1970); Eleanor S. Morrison and Vera Borosage, eds., *Human Sexuality: Contemporary Perspectives,* 2nd ed. (Palo Alto, Calif.: Mayfield, 1977); James McCary, *Human Sexuality,* 3rd ed. (New York: Van Nostrand, 1978); John H. Gagnon and William Simon, eds., *Sexual Conduct* (Chicago: Aldine, 1973); Harold Greenwald, *The Elegant Prostitute: A Social and Psychoanalytic Study* (New York: Walker, 1970); Hendrick M. Ruitenbeck, ed., *Homosexuality: A Changing Picture* (Atlantic Highlands, N.J.: Humanities Press, 1974).

5. For some traditional approaches to the morality of sex, see Peter A. Bertocci, *Sex, Love and the Person* (New York: Sheed and Ward, 1967) and John F. Dedek, *Contemporary Sexual Morality* (New York: Sheed and Ward, 1971). For a historical overview of ancient and contemporary views on sexuality, see D. P. Verene, ed., *Sexual Love and Western Morality* (New York: Harper and Row, 1972).

6. See, for example, Sacred Congregation for the Doctrine of the Faith, *Declaration on Certain Questions Concerning Sexual Ethics* (Washington, D.C.: U. S. Catholic Publications Office, Dec. 29, 1975).

outside of marriage is immoral because sex is linked to the institution of marriage, which is necessary to continue the human race through the procreation and raising of children. However, critics of this view claim that to say something is unnatural does not imply that it is immoral.[7] To them, the term "unnatural" merely means "unusual" and does not automatically carry moral connotations.

Other traditional moralists have argued that the welfare of society depends on the stability of family life and that allowing sexual activities outside of marriage is wrong because it weakens the institution of the family.[8] In this view, incest and homosexuality would be immoral not because they are unnatural but because they do not contribute to the well-being of society. On the other hand, something like fetishism would not be immoral, so long as it did not affect the family.

Less traditional thinkers have claimed that sexual activities are moral so long as they take place between partners who love each other and are exclusively committed to each other.[9] In other words, sexual activities should be exclusive in the sense that they should be limited to the one person with whom one has a relationship of love and commitment. Thus, fetishism would be immoral because it is not a relationship with another person, but homosexuality would be moral so long as it was practiced by two people who loved each other and were exclusively committed to each other. Incest, on the other hand, would be immoral because it would occur between people who were not exclusively committed to each other.

In contrast, liberal ethicians have argued that sexual activity is immoral only when it involves coercion, deception, or harm of some kind to others.[10] In this view, any sexual activity between consenting rational adults is not immoral, but other forms of sex could be. For example, incest would be immoral because it is a relationship between an adult and a minor who, without knowing it, may be unable to consent with full freedom because he is too young and too vulnerable to parental pressure or manipulation. Adultery, or sex between two people who are married to others, would also be wrong because the two people are deceiving their spouses, breaking the marriage promises they made to them. But homosexuality or fetishism would be morally permissible so long as the parties involved were rational adults who freely and knowingly consented to what they were doing and so long as they were not deceiving or harming others.

Some critics of the liberal view have argued that adult consent does

7. See Burton Leiser, *Liberty, Justice and Morals*, 2nd ed. (New York: Macmillan, 1979), esp. ch. 2.

8. For an analysis of these and other arguments on the morality of sexual behavior, see Ronald Atkinson, *Sexual Morality* (London: Hutchinson, 1965).

9. See, for example, the views in Richard F. Hettlinger, *Living with Sex: The Student's Dilemma* (New York: Seabury, 1966), esp. ch. 10. For an analysis of the philosophical arguments concerning premarital sex, see Carl Wellman, *Morals and Ethics* (Glenview, Ill.: Scott, Foresman, 1975), ch. 5.

10. See, for example, Russell Vannoy, *Sex Without Love: A Philosophical Exploration* (Buffalo, N.Y.: Prometheus, 1980). For a dated but classic discussion of this point of view, see Bertrand Russell, *Marriage and Morals* (New York: Liveright, 1929).

not necessarily render every form of sex morally acceptable. To them, some forms of sex are seen as evidence of personality disorders or are conducive to such disorders. Traditional Freudian psychologists, for example, have claimed that homosexuality is a harmful personality disorder that should be cured.[11] Others believe that fetishism is also harmful because it fixates an individual on impersonal objects and makes him less willing to enter into interpersonal relationships, which are psychologically preferable. Such personally destructive forms of sex are immoral, these critics argue, because we have a moral duty not to harm ourselves.

The readings that follow examine the issues we have been discussing,[12] attempting to answer a number of questions. Is there such a thing as a sexual perversion? Is sex outside of marriage immoral? Must sex involve love and exclusivity? What makes an action unnatural and does such a label make that action wrong?

The first four selections deal with the definition of sexual perversion and whether or not it is immoral. In his famous essay, "Sexual Perversion," Thomas Nagel describes adult sexual capacity as in part made up of persons and their partners seeing and desiring one another in a way that is mutual and reciprocal. He then argues that perversion is the result of some interference with this capacity. Where does this leave homosexuality? In Nagel's view, it is not perverse.

In "Sex and Perversion," Robert Solomon disagrees with Nagel's way of defining sexual perversion, contending that sexuality is a language used to communicate with others. From this perspective, sexual perversion can be seen as a "breach of comprehensibility." Using this analogy with language to discuss varieties of sexual experience, Solomon claims that sexuality is not inherently a matter for moral evaluation or concern by others. Rather, sex is of relevance only to the persons involved.

Alan Goldman's essay, "Plain Sex," points out that much of the difficulty in analyzing the morality of sexual activity is due to confusion about what it is that is being evaluated. He reminds us that in and of themselves, neither sexual desire nor sexual activity are matters of morality. Perversion, Goldman claims, is always defined in relation to normal sex, and what is normal is statistically determined in terms of those desires that diverge from so-called "plain sex."

In his article, "Perversion and the Unnatural as Moral Categories," Donald Levy summarizes and criticizes the views of Nagel, Solomon, and Goldman. Then, as an alternative, he offers his own natural law account of sexual perversion. Traditionally, perversion is treated as unnatural, but before we can know what is unnatural we must determine what human

11. Sigmund Freud, *Collected Papers of Sigmund Freud*, vol. 8, *Sexuality and the Psychology of Love* (New York: Collier Books, n.d.).

12. For further reading on these and other issues concerning sexual morality, see: Robert Baker and Frederick Elliston, eds., *Philosophy and Sex* (Buffalo, N.Y.: Prometheus, 1975); J.F.M. Hunter, *Thinking About Sex and Love* (New York: St. Martin's, 1980); Alan Soble, ed., *Philosophy of Sex* (Totowa, N.J.: Littlefield, Adams and Co., 1980); C. H. Whiteley and W. N. Whiteley, *Sex and Morals* (New York: Basic Books, 1967); John Wilson, *Logic and Sexual Morality* (Harmondsworth, England: Penguin Books, 1965).

nature is. Pursuing this line of reasoning, Levy argues that we all have a common nature that can be understood. In his view, there are certain "basic goods" in life, and these are desired by everyone. Therefore, an unnatural act is one that denies a person a basic good, without needing to do so, for the sake of some other end. According to Levy, this sort of action is always wrong, and is a necessary component of perversion. Pleasure—which is not a basic good—is the motive for acting in the case of perversion, and so the action is wrong.

The next two articles, by John Finnis and Burton Leiser, discuss the meaning of "unnatural" as applied to sexual activities. In "Natural Law and Unnatural Acts," Finnis adopts a natural law position, arguing that all wrongful acts (not just wrongful sexual acts) are defined as such by reason of being unnatural. Finnis claims that human "intelligence naturally and spontaneously grasps" that certain things are "values that give sense and worth" to our lives. We must remain open to all of these values, and so it is wrong "to choose directly against" one of them. Among these naturally known values is the common pursuit in marriage of the procreation and education of children, or the "bringing of the child into a community of love." In Finnis' opinion, sexual acts that deliberately "exclude the possibility of procreation" involve "a choice directly and immediately against [this] basic value." They are thus unnatural in the sense that they involve a choice against those values that intelligence "naturally and spontaneously grasps."

In "Homosexuality and the 'Unnaturalness Argument,'" Burton Leiser is also concerned with the unnatural. However, he directs his attention toward refuting the claim that homosexuality can be defined as such. To do this, he examines the various meanings of the words "natural" and "unnatural" and argues that none of them equate natural with good or unnatural with bad. Since this is so, he claims that showing homosexuality to be unnatural does not automatically show it to be wrong.

In the last essay in this chapter, "A Philosophical Analysis of Sexual Ethics," Raymond Belliotti offers the Kantian-based view that "sex is immoral if and only if it involves deception, promise-breaking and/or the treatment of the other merely as a means to one's own ends." Given this premise, acts such as rape and bestiality always turn out to be immoral, but necrophilia, incest, promiscuity, and adultery are immoral only when they involve deception or do not include the rational consent of the persons involved. Belliotti points out that his evaluation differs from a religious one that would be based on adherence to God's law. He closes by noting that even though some sexual behaviors are not immoral, they may still be tasteless or psychologically harmful.

# SEXUAL PERVERSION

*Thomas Nagel*

There is something to be learned about sex from the fact that we possess a concept of sexual perversion. I wish to examine the idea, defending it against the charge of unintelligibility and trying to say exactly what about human sexuality qualifies it to admit of perversions. Let me begin with some general conditions that the concept must meet if it is to be viable at all. These can be accepted without assuming any particular analysis.

First, if there are any sexual perversions, they will have to be sexual desires or practices that are in some sense unnatural, though the explanation of this natural/unnatural distinction is of course the main problem. Second, certain practices will be perversions if anything is, such as shoe fetishism, bestiality, and sadism; other practices, such as unadorned sexual intercourse, will not be; about still others there is controversy. Third, if there are perversions, they will be unnatural sexual *inclinations* rather than just unnatural practices adopted not from inclination but for other reasons. . . . I shall offer a psychological account of sexual perversion that depends on a theory of sexual desire and human sexual interactions. . . . Sexual desire involves a kind of perception, but not merely a single perception of its object, for in the paradigm case of mutual desire there is a complex system of superimposed mutual perceptions—not only perceptions of the sexual object, but perceptions of oneself. Moreover, sexual awareness of another involves considerable self-awareness to begin with— more than is involved in ordinary sensory perception. The experience is felt as an assault on oneself by the view (or touch, or whatever) of the sexual object.

Let us consider a case in which the elements can be separated. For clarity we will restrict ourselves initially to the somewhat artificial case of desire at a distance. Suppose a man and a woman, whom we may call Romeo and Juliet, are at opposite ends of a cocktail lounge, with many mirrors on the walls which permit unobserved observation, and even mutual unobserved observation. Each of them is sipping a martini and studying other people in the mirrors. At some point Romeo notices Juliet. He is moved, somehow, by the softness of her hair and the diffidence with which she sips her martini, and this arouses him sexually. Let us say that *X senses Y* whenever *X* regards *Y* with sexual desire. (*Y* need not be a person, and *X*'s apprehension of *Y* can be visual, tactile, olfactory, etc., or purely imaginary; in the present example we shall concentrate on vision.) So Romeo senses Juliet, rather than merely noticing her. At this stage he

From Thomas Nagel, "Sexual Peversion," *The Journal of Philosophy,* vol. 66, no. 1 (1969), pp. 5, 10–13, 14–17. Reprinted by permission.

is aroused by an unaroused object, so he is more in the sexual grip of his body than she of hers.

Let us suppose, however, that Juliet now senses Romeo in another mirror on the opposite wall, though neither of them yet knows that he is seen by the other (the mirror angles provide three-quarter views). Romeo then begins to notice in Juliet the subtle signs of sexual arousal, heavy-lidded stare, dilating pupils, faint flush, etc. This of course intensifies her bodily presence, and he not only notices but senses this as well. His arousal is nevertheless still solitary. But now, cleverly calculating the line of her stare without actually looking her in the eyes, he realizes that it is directed at him through the mirror on the opposite wall. That is, he notices, and moreover senses, Juliet sensing him. This is definitely a new development, for it gives him a sense of embodiment not only through his own reactions but through the eyes and reactions of another. Moreover, it is separable from the initial sensing of Juliet; for sexual arousal might begin with a person's sensing that he is sensed and being assailed by the perception of the other person's desire rather than merely by the perception of the person.

But there is a further step. Let us suppose that Juliet, who is a little slower than Romeo, now senses that he senses her. This puts Romeo in a position to notice, and be aroused by, her arousal at being sensed by him. He senses that she senses that he senses her. This is still another level of arousal, for he becomes conscious of his sexuality through his awareness of its effect on her and of her awareness that this effect is due to him. Once she takes the same step and senses that he senses her sensing him, it becomes difficult to state, let alone imagine, further iterations, though they may be logically distinct. If both are alone, they will presumably turn to look at each other directly, and the proceedings will continue on another plane. Physical contact and intercourse are natural extensions of this complicated visual exchange, and mutual touch can involve all the complexities of awareness present in the visual case, but with a far greater range of subtlety and acuteness.

Ordinarily, of course, things happen in a less orderly fashion—sometimes in a great rush—but I believe that some version of this overlapping system of distinct sexual perceptions and interactions is the basic framework of any full-fledged sexual relation and that relations involving only part of the complex are significantly incomplete. The account is only schematic, as it must be to achieve generality. Every real sexual act will be psychologically far more specific and detailed, in ways that depend not only on the physical techniques employed and on anatomical details, but also on countless features of the participants' conceptions of themselves and of each other, which become embodied in the act. (It is [a] familiar enough fact, for example, that people often take their social roles and the social roles of their partners to bed with them.) . . . But the most characteristic feature of a specifically sexual immersion in the body is its ability to fit into the complex of mutual perceptions that we have described. Hunger leads to spontaneous interactions with food; sexual desire leads to spontaneous interactions with other persons, whose bodies are asserting their sovereignty in the same way, producing involuntary reactions and spontaneous impulses in *them*. These reactions are perceived, and the perception of them is perceived, and that perception is in turn perceived; at each step the domination of the person by his body is reinforced, and the sexual partner becomes more possessible by physical contact, penetration, and envelopment.

Desire is therefore not merely the perception of a pre-existing embodiment of the other, but ideally a contribution to his further embodiment which in turn enhances the original subject's sense of himself. This explains why it is important that the partner be aroused, and not merely aroused, but aroused by the awareness of one's desire. It also explains the sense in which desire has unity and possession as its object: physical possession must eventuate in creation of the sexual object in the image of one's desire, and not merely in the object's recognition of that desire, or in his or her own private arousal. . . . Even if this is a correct model of the adult sexual capacity, it is not plausible to describe as perverted every deviation from it. For example, if the partners in heterosexual intercourse indulge in private heterosexual fantasies, thus avoiding recognition of the real partner, that would, on this model, constitute a defective sexual relation. It is not, however, generally regarded as a perversion. Such examples suggest that a simple dichotomy between perverted and unperverted sex is too crude to organize the phenomena adequately.

Still, various familiar deviations constitute truncated or incomplete versions of the complete configuration, and may be regarded as perversions of the central impulse. If sexual desire is prevented from taking its full interpersonal form, it is likely to find a different one. The concept of perversion implies that a normal sexual development has been turned aside by distorting influences. I have little to say about this causal condition. But if perversions are in some sense unnatural, they must result from interference with the development of a capacity that is there potentially.

It is difficult to apply this condition, because environmental factors play a role in determining the precise form of anyone's sexual impulse. Early experiences in particular seem to determine the choice of a sexual object. To describe some causal influences as distorting and others as merely formative is to imply that certain general aspects of human sexuality realize a definite potential whereas many of the details in which people differ realize an indeterminate potential, so that they cannot be called more or less natural. What is included in the definite potential is therefore very important, although the distinction between definite and indeterminate potential is obscure. Obviously a creature incapable of developing the levels of interpersonal sexual awareness I have described could not be deviant in virtue of the failure to do so. (Though even a chicken might be called perverted in an extended sense if it had been conditioned to develop a fetishistic attachment to a telephone.) But if humans will tend to develop some version of reciprocal interpersonal sexual awareness unless prevented, then cases of blockage can be called unnatural or perverted.

Some familiar deviations can be described in this way. Narcissistic practices and intercourse with animals, infants, and inanimate objects seem to be stuck at some primitive version of the first stage of sexual feeling. If the object is not alive, the experience is reduced entirely to an awareness of one's own sexual embodiment. Small children and animals permit awareness of the embodiment of the other, but present obstacles to reciprocity, to the recognition by the sexual object of the subject's desire as the source of his (the object's) sexual self-awareness. Voyeurism and exhibitionism are also incomplete relations. The exhibitionist wishes to display his desire without needing to be desired in return; he may even fear the sexual attentions of others. A voyeur, on the other hand, need not require any recognition by his object at all: certainly not a recognition of the voyeur's arousal.

On the other hand, if we apply our model to the various forms that may be taken by two-party heterosexual intercourse, none of them seem clearly to qualify as perversion. Hardly anyone can be found these days to inveigh against oral-genital contact, and the merits of buggery are urged by such respectable figures as D. H. Lawrence and Norman Mailer. In general, it would appear that any bodily contact between a man and a woman that gives them sexual pleasure is a possible vehicle for the system of multi-level interpersonal awareness that I have claimed is the basic psychological content of sexual interaction. Thus a liberal platitude about sex is upheld.

The really difficult cases are sadism, masochism, and homosexuality. The first two are widely regarded as perversions and the last is controversial. In all three cases the issue depends partly on causal factors; do these dispositions result only when normal development has been prevented? Even the form in which this question has been posed is circular, because of the word 'normal'. We appear to need an independent criterion for a distorting influence, and we do not have one.

It may be possible to class sadism and masochism as perversions because they fall short of interpersonal reciprocity. Sadism concentrates on the evocation of passive self-awareness in others, but the sadist's engagement is itself active and requires a retention of deliberate control which may impede awareness of himself as a bodily subject of passion in the required sense. De Sade claimed that the object of sexual desire was to evoke involuntary responses from one's partner, especially audible ones. The infliction of pain is no doubt the most efficient way to accomplish this, but it requires a certain abrogation of one's own exposed spontaneity. A masochist on the other hand imposes the same disability on his partner as the sadist imposes on himself. The masochist cannot find a satisfactory embodiment as the object of another's sexual desire, but only as the object of his control. He is passive not in relation to his partner's passion but in relation to his nonpassive agency. In addition, the subjection to one's body characteristic of pain and physical restraint is of a very different kind from that of sexual excitement: pain causes people to contract rather than dissolve. These descriptions may not be generally accurate. But to the extent that they are, sadism and masochism would be disorders of the second stage of awareness—the awareness of oneself as an object of desire.

Homosexuality cannot similarly be classed as a perversion on phenomenological grounds. Nothing rules out the full range of interpersonal perceptions between persons of the same sex. . . . Let me close with some remarks about the relation of perversion to good, bad, and morality. The concept of perversion can hardly fail to be evaluative in some sense, for it appears to involve the notion of an ideal or at least adequate sexuality which the perversions in some way fail to achieve. . . .

Whether it is a moral evaluation, however, is another question entirely—one whose answer would require more understanding of both morality and perversion than can be deployed here.

# SEX AND PERVERSION

*Robert Solomon*

## SEX AS LANGUAGE

. . . Whatever else sexuality might be and for whatever purposes it might be used or abused, it is first of all language. When spoken it tends to result in pregnancy, in scandal, in jealousy and divorce (the "perlocutionary" effects of language, in Austin's terminology). It is a language that, like verbal language, but sometimes more effectively, can be used to manipulate people, to offend and to ingratiate oneself with them. It can be enjoyable, not just on account of its phonetics, which are neither enjoyable nor meaningful in themselves, but because of *what* is said. One enjoys not just the tender caress but the message it carries; and one welcomes a painful thrust or bite not because of masochism but because of the meaning, in context, that it conveys. Most sexologists, one might add, commit the McLuhanesque fallacy of confusing the medium with the message. . . .

## SEXUAL PERVERSION REINTERPRETED

If sexuality is a form of language that can be used to express almost anything, it follows that the use of sexuality admits of any number of creative as well as forced variations. As a language it also admits of breaches in comprehension, and it is here that we can locate what little is left of our conception of "sexual perversion." It should now be clear that

From Robert Solomon, "Sex and Perversion," in Robert Baker and Frederick Elliston, eds., *Philosophy and Sex* (Buffalo, N.Y.: Prometheus Books, 1975), pp. 279–86. Copyright © 1975 by Prometheus Books.

this is not a moral term but more a logical category, a breach of comprehensibility. Accordingly, it would be advisable to drop the notion of perversion altogether and content ourselves with "sexual incompatibility" or "sexual misunderstanding." It is not always easy to distinguish abuses of the language from abuses expressed by the language, or to separate nonsense from sophistry, sexual fanaticism from sexual "politics." It is not always clear what is to count as a literal expression, a metaphorical usage, an imaginative expression, a pun, a solecism, or a bad joke. And so what might be taken as incomprehensibility and perversion by a sexual conservative would be taken as poetry or pun by someone else. Perversion, then, is a communication breakdown; it may have general guidelines but ultimately rests in the context of the bodily mutual understanding of the people involved. Quite the contrary of a moral or quasi-moral category, "sexual incompatibility" is strictly relativized, within the language, to the particular people involved.

If sexuality is essentially a language, it follows that masturbation, while not a perversion, is a deviation and not, as Freud thought, the primary case. Masturbation is essentially speaking to oneself. But not only children, lunatics, and hermits speak to themselves; so do poets and philosophers. And so masturbation might, in different contexts, count as wholly different extensions of language. . . .

It is clear that between two people almost any activity *can* be fully sexual when it is an attempt to communicate mutual feelings through bodily gestures, touches, and movements. But this requires serious qualification. Expressions of domination and dependence are among the most primitive vocabulary items in our body language. But these may go beyond mere expressions and gestures to become a kind of "acting out"; and there is a difference, if only of degree, between gestures and full-blooded actions. When expressions of domination and dependence turn into actions, they become sadism and masochism, respectively. If these feelings are not complementary, they can only be interpreted as a communication breakdown, as sexual incompatibility. When sadistic actions are not expected, they are to sexuality as real bullets in a supposedly prop gun are to the stage. Again, the possible extension of sexual language depends mutually upon the participants. The subtlety and explicitness of a language depends upon the perceptivity of the conversationalists. For the articulate and the quick, sadism and masochism may consist of an apparently minor change in sexual positions, a slight but degrading change of posture that is ample expression of mutually negative or hostile feelings or of complementary dominance and submission. For the more dense or uninitiated, such expression may require outright infliction of pain or discomfort, a painful pinch or punch. In many cases we might want to say that, as Billy Budd was inarticulate, and violent as a result, sadism and masochism may be matters of inarticulateness and lack of interpersonal perception as well as products of the hostile feelings to be expressed. . . .

To other so-called perversions the same considerations apply, and the degree of the breakdown in communication is not always clear. Sexual activities themselves are not perverted; people are perverted. Fetishism in general might be a product of stupidity, poor vocabulary, or fear of communicating, but it might be extreme ingenuity in the face of an impoverished sexual field. A voyeur might be someone with nothing to say, but the voyeur might count as a good listener in those cases in which he makes himself known. Sexual *in*versions, as Freud calls them, are not deviations of *sex* (according to the theory developed here, homosexuality is not such an inversion), but relations with children or animals would be like carrying on an adult conversation with a child who does not have the vocabulary to understand or a dog who nods dumb agreement to every proposal. Multiple sexual encounters are surely not in themselves perversions; quite the contrary, languages are not designated for exclusive two-party use. But it is clear that such multiple relationships, like trying to hold several conversations at once or working on several books at the same time, can be distracting, confusing, and ultimately disastrous.

# PLAIN SEX

*Alan H. Goldman*

## 1. SEX AS THE DESIRE FOR PHYSICAL CONTACT

. . . I shall suggest here that sex continues to be misrepresented in recent writings, at least in philosophical writings, and I shall criticize the predominant form of analysis which I term "means-end analysis." Such conceptions attribute a necessary external goal or purpose to sexual activity, whether it be reproduction, the expression of love, simple communication, or interpersonal awareness. They analyze sexual activity as a means to one of these ends, implying that sexual desire is a desire to reproduce, to love or be loved, or to communicate with others. All definitions of this type suggest false views of the relation of sex to perversion and morality by implying that sex which does not fit one of these models or fulfill one of these functions is in some way deviant or incomplete.

The alternative, simpler analysis with which I will begin is that sexual desire is desire for contact with another person's body and for the pleasure which such contact produces; sexual activity is activity which tends to fulfill such desire of the agent. Whereas Aristotle and Butler were correct in holding that pleasure is normally a byproduct rather than

From Alan H. Goldman, "Plain Sex," *Philosophy & Public Affairs*, vol. 6, no. 3 (Spring 1977), pp. 267–71, 280–81, 284–86. Copyright © 1977 by Princeton University Press. Excerpts reprinted by permission of Princeton University Press.

a goal of purposeful action, in the case of sex this is not so clear. The desire for another's body is, principally among other things, the desire for the pleasure that physical contact brings. On the other hand, it is not a desire for a particular sensation detachable from its causal context, a sensation which can be derived in other ways. This definition in terms of the general goal of sexual desire appears preferable to an attempt to more explicitly list or define specific sexual activities, for many activities such as kissing, embracing, massaging, or holding hands may or may not be sexual, depending upon the context and more specifically upon the purposes, needs, or desires into which such activities fit. The generality of the definition also represents a refusal (common in recent psychological texts) to overemphasize orgasm as the goal of sexual desire or genital sex as the only norm of sexual activity (this will be hedged slightly in the discussion of perversion below).

Central to the definition is the fact that the goal of sexual desire and activity is the physical contact itself, rather than something else which this contact might express. By contrast, what I term "means-end analyses" posit ends which I take to be extraneous to plain sex, and they view sex as a means to these ends. Their fault lies not in defining sex in terms of its general goal, but in seeing plain sex as merely a means to other separable ends. I term these "means-end analyses" for convenience, although "means-separable-end analyses," while too cumbersome, might be more fully explanatory. The desire for physical contact with another person is a minimal criterion for (normal) sexual desire, but is both necessary and sufficient to qualify normal desire as sexual. Of course, we may want to express other feelings through sexual acts in various contexts, but without the desire for the physical contact in and for itself, or when it is sought for other reasons, activities in which contact is involved are not predominantly sexual. Furthermore, the desire for physical contact in itself, without the wish to express affection or other feelings through it, is sufficient to render sexual the activity of the agent which fulfills it. Various activities with this goal alone, such as kissing and caressing in certain contexts, qualify as sexual even without the presence of genital symptoms of sexual excitement. The latter are not therefore necessary criteria for sexual activity. . . .

## SEX AND MORALITY

. . . To the question of what morality might be implied by my analysis, the answer is that there are no moral implications whatever. Any analysis of sex which imputes a moral character to sex acts in themselves is wrong for that reason. There is no morality intrinsic to sex, although general moral rules apply to the treatment of others in sex acts as they apply to all human relations. We can speak of a sexual ethic as we can speak of a business ethic, without implying that business in itself is either moral or immoral or that special rules are required to judge business practices which are not derived from rules that apply elsewhere as well. Sex is not in itself a moral category, although like business it invariably places us into relations with others in which moral rules apply. It gives us opportunity to do what is otherwise recognized as wrong, to harm others, deceive them or manipulate them against their wills. Just as the fact that an act is sexual in itself never renders it wrong or adds to its wrongness if it is wrong on other grounds (sexual acts toward minors are wrong on other grounds, as will be argued below), so no wrong act is to be excused because done from a sexual motive. If a "crime of passion" is to be excused, it would have to be on grounds of temporary insanity rather than sexual context (whether insanity does constitute a legitimate excuse for certain actions is too big a topic to argue here). Sexual motives are among others which may become deranged, and the fact that they are sexual has no bearing in itself on the moral character, whether negative or exculpatory, of the actions deriving from them. Whatever might be true of war, it is certainly not the case that all's fair in love or sex.

Our first conclusion regarding morality and sex is therefore that no conduct otherwise immoral should be excused because it is sexual conduct, and nothing in sex is immoral unless condemned by rules which apply elsewhere as well. The last clause requires further clarification. Sexual conduct can be governed by particular rules relating only to sex itself. But these precepts must be implied by general moral rules when these are applied to specific sexual relations or types of conduct. The same is true of rules of fair business, ethical medicine, or courtesy in driving a car. In the latter case, particular acts on the road may be reprehensible, such as tailgating or passing on the right, which seem to bear no resemblance as actions to any outside the context of highway safety. Nevertheless their immorality derives from the fact that they place others in danger, a circumstance which, when avoidable, is to be condemned in any context. This structure of general and specifically applicable rules describes a reasonable sexual ethic as well. To take an extreme case, rape is always a sexual act and it is always immoral. A rule against rape can therefore be considered an obvious part of sexual morality which has no bearing on nonsexual conduct. But the immorality of rape derives from its being an extreme violation of a person's body, of the right not to be humiliated, and of the general moral prohibition against using other persons against their wills, not from the fact that it is a sexual act.

## PERVERTED SEX

While my initial analysis lacks moral implications in itself, as it should, it does suggest by contrast a concept of sexual perversion. Since the concept of perversion is itself a sexual concept, it will always be defined relative to some definition of normal sex; and any conception of the norm will imply a contrary notion of perverse forms. The concept suggested by my account again differs sharply from those implied by the means-end analyses examined above. Perversion does not represent a deviation from the reproductive function (or kissing would be perverted), from a loving relationship (or most sexual desire and many heterosexual acts would be perverted), or from efficiency in communicating (or unsuccessful seduction attempts would be perverted). It is a deviation from a norm, but the norm in question is merely statistical. Of course, not all sexual acts that are statistically unusual are perverted—a three-hour continuous sexual act would be unusual but not necessarily abnormal in the requisite sense. The abnormality in question must relate to the *form of the desire* itself in order to constitute sexual perversion; for example, desire, not for contact with another, but for merely looking, for harming or being harmed, for contact with items of clothing. This concept of sexual abnormality is that suggested by my definition of normal sex in terms of its typical desire. However not all unusual desires qualify either, only those with the typical physical sexual effects upon the individual who satisfies them. These effects, such as erection in males, were not built into the original definition of sex in terms of sexual desire, for they do not always occur in activities that are properly characterized as sexual, say, kissing for the pleasure of it. But they do seem to bear a closer relation to the definition of activities as perverted. (For those who consider only genital sex sexual, we could build such symptoms into a narrower definition, then speaking of sex in a broad sense as well as "proper" sex.) . . .

The only proper evaluative norms relating to sex involve degrees of pleasure in the acts and moral norms, but neither of these scales coincides with statistical degrees of abnormality, according to which perversion is to be measured. The three parameters operate independently (this was implied for the first two when it was held above that the pleasure of sex is a good, but not necessarily a moral good). Perverted sex may be more or less enjoyable to particular individuals than normal sex, and more or less moral, depending upon the particular relations involved. Raping a sheep may be more perverted than raping a woman, but certainly not more condemnable morally. It is nevertheless true that the evaluative connotations attaching to the term "perverted" derive partly from the fact that most people consider perverted sex highly immoral. Many such acts are forbidden by long standing taboos, and it is sometimes difficult to distinguish what is forbidden from what is immoral. Others, such as sadistic acts, are genuinely immoral, but again not at all because of their connection with sex or abnormality. The principles which condemn these acts would condemn them equally if they were common and nonsexual. It is not true that we properly could continue to consider acts perverted which were found to be very common practice across societies. Such acts, if harmful, might continue to be condemned properly as immoral, but it was just shown that the immorality of an act does not vary with its degree of perversion. If not harmful, common acts previously considered abnormal might continue to be called perverted for a time by the moralistic minority; but the term when applied to such cases would retain only its emotive negative connotation without consistent logical criteria for application. It would represent merely prejudiced moral judgments.

# PERVERSION AND THE UNNATURAL AS MORAL CATEGORIES

*Donald Levy*

For whatever reasons, the recent revival of philosophical interest in problems relating to love and sexuality began with attempts to analyze the concept of sexual perversion. Is it essentially an incoherent idea, one we moderns ought to seek to do without in thinking about sex? Is a revival of one or other of the traditional theologically based accounts of sexual perversion to be undertaken, perhaps updated, by the addition of the latest psychiatric findings? Or does the concept conceal hitherto unsuspected patterns of meaning which philosophical analysis might uncover for the first time? If sexual perversion is to be taken seriously, problems of definition demand solution at the start: What makes a sexual practice perverted? What differentiates sexual perversions from nonsexual perversions, if there are any such things? What makes a human activity perverted at all?

The range of human sexual activities commonly called sexual perversions is very wide and vague in outline. Its vagueness will be clear from the following list, which I have adapted from Michael Balint: (1) First of all, there are the various kinds of homosexuality; (2) next, the several forms of sadism and masochism; (3) then, exhibitionism, voyeurism, and the use of other parts of the body (i.e., other than the genitals); (4) fetishism, transvestism, and possibly kleptomania; (5) bestiality; and (6) finally, necrophilia and pedophilia. I should add that this list can be misleading by its abstractness—fetishism, for example, may cover a great variety of behaviors. . . .

Recent philosophical attempts to define sexual perversion have not achieved any greater success than have the efforts of the psychoanalysts. Thomas Nagel conceives of sexual perversion in psychological terms, he says, but it is nothing psychoanalytic he has in mind. Sexual perversions, according to Nagel, are incomplete versions of the "multi-level interpersonal awareness" which is "the basic psychological content of sexual interaction." Perversions are incomplete versions of the complete configuration. Nagel's view seems close to the one usually ascribed to Freud, fixation on an infantile level being a kind of incompleteness. Nagel's view seems even closer to the idea contained in Catholic canon law, which defines as immoral any sex act which is "designed to be preparatory to the complete act," but which is "entirely divorced from the complete act." Nagel does not indicate why it is important or noteworthy that some people seem to want only incomplete versions of sex instead of the complete ones—why do we need the classification "perversion" at all? (After all, we have no special

From Donald Levy, "Perversion and the Unnatural as Moral Categories," *Ethics*, vol. 90, no. 2 (January 1980), pp. 191, 193–202. Copyright © 1980 by the University of Chicago Press.

designation for those who select their meals from the à la carte menu instead of ordering the complete dinner.) Another trouble with Nagel's view is that the prostitute, for example, who hardly participates at all in the interpersonal awareness Nagel refers to, would be perverted, yet neither ordinary usage nor any traditional classification of the perversions has such a result. (Nagel seems to be aware of this problem but does not regard it as crucial.) Besides, the sadomasochistic pair do complete the psychological process Nagel refers to, that is, there is interpersonal awareness between them on many levels, yet they would commonly be classified as perverted. It is surprising and puzzling that Nagel claims that sexual perversions ". . . will have to be sexual desires or practices that can be plausibly described as in some sense unnatural, though the explanation of this natural/unnatural distinction is of course the main problem." Yet he does not attempt to explain the distinction or relate the concept of perversion to it. . . .

Robert C. Solomon faults Nagel's definition of perversion for emphasizing the form of the interpersonal awareness in sex rather than its content. According to Solomon, sadism, for example, is not so much a breakdown in communication as ". . . an excessive expression of a particular content, namely the attitude of domination, perhaps mixed with hatred, fear, and other negative attitudes." Solomon offers no account explaining at what point the expression of attitudes of domination becomes excessive enough to warrant being labeled perversion; more important, it is hard to see why being excessive in the expression of domination should count as perversion at all and not merely as rudeness, perhaps. . . .

The opposite extreme is Alan H. Goldman's purely statistical interpretation, according to which those sexual desires are perverted which are statistically abnormal in form. Identifying the form of a desire is problematic, however. Goldman gives the following examples of desires whose abnormality in form makes them perverted desires: ". . . desire, not for contact with another, but for merely looking, for harming or being harmed, for contact with items of clothing." Desiring to engage in sex continuously for three hours is not, it seems, abnormal in form in the requisite sense. Nevertheless, plausible counterexamples seem to be available; the male office worker whose lustful desires are restricted exclusively to his female superiors would seem to be one, since his sexual desires are abnormal (statistically), yet hardly perverted. It might at first appear that this example involves only an abnormality in the content of the desire, not in its form. But if the office-worker case is dismissed as a case of perverison on account of the form-content distinction, there is the danger that the heterosexual transvestite, necrophiliac, or child molester will also lie outside the definition of perversion. This problem with the form-content distinction arises again when Goldman writes that "raping a sheep may be more perverted than raping a woman, but certainly not more condemnable morally." It is hard to see how raping a woman could be perverted at all on Goldman's account, since the form of the act would appear to be normal. (Incidentally, I doubt that it even makes sense to speak of raping a sheep, whose consent or lack of it cannot exist.) . . .

Perhaps in despair at the problems such efforts at definition as these confront, the temptation arises to declare the concepts of perversion and the unnatural to be empty, idle, or meaningless. Such a trend (with regard to the unnatural) can be traced as far back as Mill's essay *On Nature,* Diderot's *D'Alembert's Dream,* Descartes's *Sixth Meditation,* and perhaps the ancient sophists. The most recent expression of this position is Michael Slote's "Inapplicable Concepts and Sexual Perversion." The best response to this temptation would be a theory of perversion and the unnatural that succeeds in overcoming the difficulties to be found in Nagel, Ruddick, Solomon, Fried, Goldman, Gray, and Slote. . . .

First of all, the traditional treatments (in Plato, Aquinas, and Kant, e.g.) discuss perversion under the heading of the unnatural, and this is where I shall begin, too. Modern philosophers tend to ignore the concept of the natural—and so, too, of the unnatural—perhaps out of verification-ist concern about the apparent impossibility of giving nonemotive sense to talk about the unnatural in moral matters, and perhaps also out of considerations of the sort Sartre offers in *Existentialism Is a Humanism.* To talk of human nature, he argues, is possible only on the assumption that man is an artifact, a product of divine handicraft, made for a purpose. Apart from that framework, that view of the universe, no sense can be given to talk of human nature. I intend to take issue with that view; indeed, my argument will have the implication that, whatever may be the case with other things in the universe, man is one thing we can know has a nature—we can know man's nature regardless of whether man is seen as created for a purpose or created at all.

To define the unnatural, of which the perverted is a subcategory, I shall need first to make a distinction between a limited set of basic human goods on the one hand, and the indefinitely large set of nonbasic, nonessential goods on the other. Among the latter, I include such things as enjoying one's dinner, getting to be famous in one's profession, winning at the next drawing of the state lottery, winning at some drawing or other of the state lottery, having children of whom one can be proud. It should be clear from these examples that classifying something as a nonbasic human good is not at all to claim that it is unimportant. By contrast, what I count as the basic human goods can be rather completely listed: life, health, control of one's bodily and psychic functions, the capacity for knowledge and love. These goods seem to be basic in the (Rawlsian) sense that these will be desired no matter whatever else will, insofar as they are necessary for the getting of any other human goods; but two other ways occur to me to identify the basic human goods and distinguish them from the others.

One mark of a basic human good is that it is hard to make literal sense of the claim that a person has too much of it; what is commonly called being loved too much, that is, being spoiled, is really a case of having been loved badly. Hence, too, I exclude wealth from the list. I doubt that much disagreement about what belongs on the list is possible, though different cultures may order them differently in importance. My reasons for claiming that much disagreement is not possible may be connected with the other, major way of picking out the basic human goods, which is this: A basic human good is a feature of human life one can actively seek to reduce to a minimum among humans only at the expense of one's own status as a human being. For example, a creature (perhaps human in appearance) who acts out of a "moral" obligation to reduce health among humans as much as possible in the way we normally feel obliged to avoid causing disease as much as possible (i.e., on principle) would be a creature whom we would not perceive as human. (Imagine a creature who sincerely offered excuses for having failed to spread disease in a particular situation in which he had the opportunity.) It is at that point that simple people begin to speak of creatures as being possessed by evil demons, that is, the point at which a creature manifests negative concern for the basic human goods. (The zombie and Frankenstein's monster are variants of demon possession; in them, absence of awareness or care about the basic human goods is manifested.) People around the world intuitively avoid dealing with human wickedness as if it consisted of an infinite continuum with no lower end; instead, they cut off at a certain point and call whatever lies on the other side alien, nonhuman, demonic, possessed. I offer this general, though not universal, fact as evidence of a deep distinction between basic and nonbasic human goods; it also seems to me to pick out as basic those goods I listed as such. Any creature, however rational or articulate, who does not value the basic human goods is not human. The basic human goods may be defined as those aspects of human existence such that principled lack of concern for them by a creature is a sufficient condition of the creature's nonhumanity.

As a first approximation, I suggest that an unnatural act is one that denies a person (oneself or another) one or more of these basic human goods without necessity, that is, without having to do so in order to prevent losing some other basic human good. A person might intelligibly deny himself or another one or more of these basic human goods for the sake of another basic human good. A priest, for example, might adopt celibacy, admitting that it is against nature to seek to live without human love. An artist might sacrifice his health for his art. (A sacrifice is the giving up of something valued; we cannot sacrifice our garbage to the city dump.) But denying oneself or another a basic human good without some other basic human good being expected or intended to be made possible thereby is always wrong; it is also, as I shall show, a necessary condition of perversion. Sports-car racers enjoy risking their lives, partly at least for the gain in skill achieved thereby. Although the likelihood may be great that they may die in a racing accident, it is not probable that they will die in any particular race. If this were likely, they might well seem unnatural, even perverted. Similar arguments apply in the case of the smoker, the drinker, the drug user.

The perverted is a subclass of the unnatural. When a person denies himself or another one of the basic human goods (or the capacity for it) and no other basic human good is seen as resulting thereby, and when pleasure is the motive of the denial, the act is perverted. When the pleasure is sexual, the perversion is sexual. It should be clear from this definition of perversion that pleasure is assumed not to be a basic human good. First, because one can have too much of it—to see this, consider the case of a person hooked up to a machine stimulating the pleasure center of the brain. Suppose he were unwilling to disconnect himself even long enough to obtain food to sustain life. He would have died for a bit of extra pleasure. Besides, a person can seek to minimize human pleasure quite generally (perhaps as an obstacle to the maximization of knowledge or other basic human goods) without casting his humanity into doubt—a rather extreme Puritan might illustrate this.

This account distinguishes sexual from nonsexual perversions. An example of the latter would be the man who takes pleasure in frightening small children by holding them close up to speeding trains. His pleasure would be perverted, since the effects on his victims can be expected to be traumatic. Killing for pleasure, or maiming for the fun of it, would, of course, also be perverted; but neither would be a sexual perversion. A surgeon who performs operations for the excitement, when not required for the health of the patient, is perverted. In individual cases it may be difficult to determine just what motivated someone to do what he did— rationalizations may be common. But this uncertainty of verification is distinguishable from the blurring of the line *defining* perverted and non-perverted acts. I shall assume that the child molester is a case of sexual perversion, even though it is not the sort of case central to (or even mentioned in) several familiar accounts of the concept; it has the requisite completeness for natural sex in the canon law sense, its form is normal, it can lead to reproduction, so that Aquinas does not consider it in his treatment of the unnatural in sex. Nevertheless, the young girl sexually initiated by an older person can easily be traumatized; that there is no way of undoing the harmful effects with the ease and certainty with which they were induced establishes the correctness of classifying the case as one of sexual perversion. (The mere intensity of the seducer's sexual feeling can be traumatic to a child, even if the seducer is not strange or threatening.)

The sort of damage I refer to is properly called degradation, corruption. That perversion degrades is a necessary truth (perhaps a trivial one) as I have defined perversion. To categorize some activity as perverted is to say something important about what is wrong with it. One advantage of this account of sexual peversion is that accepting it does not commit us to accepting any one of the common views of particular sex acts, although it does, in fact, capture many of our intuitions about what is perverted. How the concept of perversion as defined here would apply, for instance, to homosexuality is not obvious if only because homosexuality is a complex phenomenon: it can be viewed merely as an activity, one among many engaged in by those whose lives at the same time include other sexual activities, for example, heterosexual activities. But homosexuality can also occur as an institution, which it is in many societies other than our own; there, it is often typical of one stage of normal development, leading to, and compatible with, heterosexual functioning in marriage. Last, homosexuality can also be considered as a form of life when it practically excludes heterosexuality. It is this that modern gay liberation intends, and about which little can be learned from other societies. However, consideration of homosexuality as a form of life would take us far from the question of perversion and the unnatural.

Although the definition of the concept does not, by itself, produce criteria strong enough to allow us to be decisive in the important case of homosexuality, the definition might seem to require rape to be included among the sexual perversions, contrary to the traditional accounts. Rape does degrade—this would seem to be a necessary truth—but whether in the way the definition of perversion requires is unclear. (All perversions degrade, but not all degrading acts or experiences are cases of perversion.) What more must be added to the definition of perversion in order to generate criteria applicable to homosexuality deserves a paper of its own, as does the question of why rape has not traditionally been perceived as perversion at all.

# NATURAL LAW AND UNNATURAL ACTS[1]

*John M. Finnis*

Plato has situated the problem of sexual vice at the core of ethical speculation. In his great early dialogue, the *Gorgias,* in which he declares unequivocal 'war and battle' (cf. 447A) against the enlightened contemporary society, Plato has Socrates confront Callicles, the exponent of a prag-

1. This paper was read to the Scotus Society, Campion Hall, Oxford in May 1970. In the first part, on the general theory of natural law, I am obviously and greatly indebted to: *(a)* Germain G. Grisez, 'Methods of Ethical Inquiry', *Proc. American Catholic Philosophical Assoc.,* 41 (1967), p. 160; 'The First Principle of Practical Reason: A Commentary on the *Summa Theologiae,* 1–2, Question 94, Article 2', *Natural Law Forum,* 10 (1965), p. 168. *(b)* J. de Finance, *Essai sur l'agir humain* (Rome, 1962). *(c)* B. J. F. Lonergan, *Insight* (London, 1957). *(d)* G. de Broglie, 'Malice intrinsèque du péché et péchés heureux par leurs conséquences', RSR XXIV (1934), p. 302, p. 578; XXV (1935), p. 5; XXVI (1936), p. 46, p. 297; XXVII (1937), p. 275.

In the second part, on sexual ethics, I am indebted to: *(a)* Germain G. Grisez, *Contraception and the Natural Law* (Milwaukee, 1964); 'A New Formulation of a Natural-Law Argument against Contraception', *The Thomist,* XXX (1966), p. 343. *(b)* J. de Finance, 'Sur la notion de loi naturelle', *Doctor Communis,* XXII (1969), p. 201. *(c)* B. J. F. Lonergan, 'Finality, Love, Marriage', ThSt 4 (1943), p. 477, reprinted as Ch. 2 of his *Collection* (New York, 1967). *(d)* G. de Broglie, 'Pour la morale conjugale traditionelle', *Doctor Communis,* XXI (1968), p. 117.

From John M. Finnis, "Natural Law and Unnatural Acts," *The Heythrop Journal,* vol. 11, no. 4 (October 1970), pp. 365–87. Twelve pages (365–67, 375–76, 380–86) of this twenty-three page article are reprinted here. Finnis' ethical theory is more fully expressed in his books, *Natural Law and Natural Rights* (Oxford: Oxford University Press, 1980) and *Fundamentals of Ethics* (Oxford: Oxford University Press, 1983).

matic and egoistic hedonism. The crisis of their discussion, perhaps of the whole dialogue, is the question whether there are bad pleasures. Callicles maintains that the happy life consists in having many appetites which one can satisfy with enjoyment. Socrates asks whether a man is indeed happy who itches and wants to scratch, and can spend his life scratching. The question is vulgar and absurd, thinks Callicles; but he will not give way: a life of pleasurable scratching is a happy life. 'But suppose the itch were not confined to one's head. Must I go on with my questions? Think what you will answer, Callicles, if you are asked the questions which naturally follow. To bring the matter to a head—take the life of one who wallows in unnatural vices. . . . Isn't that shocking and shameful and miserable?' (494E). The question makes Callicles squirm. Socrates presses him: 'Can it be, my good friend, that good is not identical with enjoyment of *whatever* kind? If it is, the shocking things I hinted at just now must obviously follow, and many other things as well' (495B). 'That's what *you* think, Socrates', retorts Callicles—it is the classical retort to all ethical speculation and teaching. But in fact the back of Callicles's resistance has been broken.

The appeal of Socrates–Plato has not been to any ethical doctrine of natural law. It has been to Callicles's, and the reader's, confused, submerged but real grasp of what is good and what is a falling away, an aversion, a flight from good. Natural law is not a doctrine. It is one's permanent dynamic orientation towards an understanding grasp of the goods that can be realized by free choice, together with a bias (like the bias in one's 'speculation' towards raising questions that will lead one on from data to insight and from insight to judgement) towards actually making choices that are intelligibly (because intelligently) related to the goods which are understood to be attainable, or at stake, in one's situation. Now the jargon-laden sentence just uttered is a piece of speculation, theorizing, doctrine about natural law. But the point of all such theorizing can be little more than to uncover what is already available to everyone, submerged and confused, perhaps, but shaping everyone's practical attitudes and choices of what to do, what to love and what to respect.

So much for the phrase 'natural law' in my title. What about 'unnatural acts'? I have deliberately courted every kind of misunderstanding by putting sexual deviation at the forefront of my paper. People will think of some gross biologicist ethics of conformity to natural functions, respect for natural faculties—and then what about shaving? But in fact I have given prominence to the sexual question only because it is the subject of current debate, and too often is debated without sufficient understanding of its relation to other questions and more general 'principles of ethics'. What I hope to do is to restate the traditional reasons for thinking that:

*(i)* all wrongful acts are wrongful by reason of being unnatural;

*(ii)* some acts, describable without reference to virtue or vice, are always wrongful;

*(iii)* some sexual acts, describable without reference to virtue or vice, are always wrongful.

Part I of this paper concerns the first two propositions, Part II the third. . . .

## PART I

The actual pattern or structure of one's living, and even more so the range of opportunities in some sense open to one, can seem very complex and resistant to analysis. But the analysis is not impossible—anthropologists, for example, are trained to undertake it, not indeed reflexively but in order to understand other people—and what emerges is a limited number of basic and controlling inclinations towards a limited number of basic goods which can, however, be attained or realized in a limitless variety of ways and combinations. In each case, one's desire for a good can be completely spontaneous and concrete—for this food, for that protection, for the approval or satisfaction of that friend, for the answer to this problem—but in each case, too, intelligence naturally and spontaneously grasps that this good is an *instance* of a *value*—life, friendship, knowledge . . . —which can be realized not only by me in this instance but by other men in other instances and in an infinite variety of modes and ways. Human life-styles are malleable and plastic, yet not formless; the range of opportunities of flourishing that are open to one can be stated in principle (the statement being not so much a piece of speculation about 'human nature' as an appeal to the reader to reflect on his own experience and self-understanding and to agree that for him, too, these are the basic forms of flourishing). One might attempt a list (to cut a long story short) as follows:

> living, in health and some security; the acquisition of arts and skills to be cultivated for their own sake; the relishing of beauty; the seeking of knowledge and understanding; the cultivation of friendships, immediate, communal and political; effecive and intelligent freedom; a right relation in this passing life to the lasting principles of reality, 'the gods'; the procreation of children and their education so that they can attain for themselves, and in their own mode, the foregoing values. . . .

Like any values, all these appear in practical discourse principally as principles of the form, 'Such-and-such is a good-to-be-pursued, and what threatens it avoided.' And certainly one can question the list I have offered, and suggest reformulations and additions. But I think it can be seen, both by observation and (more relevantly) by reflexion on one's own living, that these are the values which give sense and worth, in some immediate (and, as we shall see, questionable) measure, to the utterly varied and complex routines and projects in which we are engaged. . . .

[W]here one of these irreducible values falls immediately under our choice directly to realize it or to spurn it, then, in the Christian understanding, we must remain open to that value, that basic component of the human order, as the only reasonable way to remain open to the ground of all values, all order. To choose directly against it in favour of some other basic value is arbitrary, for each of the basic values is equally basic, equally irreducibly and self-evidently attractive. Expected total consequences do not, here, provide a ground for choosing directly against a basic value, for . . . 'expected total consequences' cannot be given a definitive evaluation, while a choice directly against a basic good provides its own definitive evaluation of itself. To foreclose on a basic value in pursuit of some hoped-for and expected better state of affairs that may be brought about by one's action is to assume a knowledge of the future, its meaning and its measure of worth, that we simply do not have. Of course, we must plan for the future, and pursue the construction of a future that will, as far as we can see, be for the best—i.e. be the best realization of the fundamental values. But our plans and constructions must at every point remain open to every one of the basic values where they come directly into play, and if this openness demands a sacrifice of what otherwise would seem to be for the best, then so be it; every man's willingness should be fixed on the basic goods which God has set before us, here and now as each one directly falls to be realized or rejected by us, rather than perhaps and by some chain of indirect causation or by the choices of other men, in a future which we cannot assess.

So:  *no suicide, no killing of the innocent: for human life is a fundamental value;*
     *no blasphemy: for a right relationship to God is a fundamental value;*
     *no injustice: for friendship in society is a fundamental value;*
     *no lying: for truth is a basic value and can be directly at stake in communication;*
and so on.

In short, there are acts—specified not by appeal to virtues and vices, but by reference to their direct and immediate relationship to one of the fundamental forms of human flourishing—which are always, as such, wrongful; always, as acts, a failure of virtue; because always representing an inadequate openness to the unconditionally Good as it presents itself to us in this life in the forms of human goods.

## PART II

[On] sexual intercourse or interplay between the intelligent young:

The idea that morality could enter into it is one I refuse to discuss—I find it so laughable. Sex is natural, wonderful, something to be shared, like a marvellous meal. I don't know when, or even if, I shall get married, so why should I wait indefinitely to enjoy it?[2]

How do some people respond to this rhetorical question (which I have taken, more or less at random, from an interview with an educated

2. See the *Daily Mail*, 23 September, 1969, 'Femail' section.

and respectable young woman in London, commenting on the decade or so since she gave up her virginity)?

The Dutch Catechism says:

> sexual intercourse . . . has by its very nature a definitive character. It implies that it is for good. If they surrender themselves to it, there is an inner change in the young man and the young woman. From then on they experience each other as husband and wife, and each act of union conjures up one to follow. This brings with it on the one hand the sense of being married, and on the other, the conflict of knowing that they are not married. And a step backwards—at any rate if a long period is involved—is only possible at the cost of profound inner tensions. From all these human reasons we can deduce God's will and law—that only married people should live together [p. 387].

Now it may be that this passage (as its context suggests) is concerned only with the psychology of engaged couples. In this case the apparent generality of the final deduction (I am assuming, to preserve the Christian sense of the Catechism, that 'live together' is a euphemism) is unwarranted (quite apart from the fact that the major premise of the deduction appears to be the negative, neo-utilitarian precept, 'Avoid inner tensions and conflicts'). And if the propositions preceding the deduction are concerned with young people generally—those contemplating not marriage but some years of contracepted (or in some other way non-procreative) sexual play, before settling down to a serious and disciplined marriage in which adultery will be excluded or at any rate prudently moderated for the sake of the children and as a sign of the completeness of one's devotion to one's spouse—then I am afraid that this Catechism has nothing to say to (or about) such people. I am afraid it is not true to say that their sexual intercourse 'has by its very nature a definitive character' and 'implies that it is for good'. Our London girl and her partners could have a good laugh at the claim that 'they experience each other as husband and wife'! They *can* experience each other in this way, of course, and some do (often involuntarily), but they need not, and many do not: it is mainly a matter of what you make of it, and the avoidance of the risks which preachers put before you—unwanted children and hang-ups of one sort and another—is just a challenge to intelligence and an invitation to cultivate a dash of the worldly wisdom of moderation. One can even be prayerful about it, since apart from moderation, there seems to be in sexual play no moral implication that could come between God and me (except the *ipse dixit* of the Catechism).

The relevant Committee of the Lambeth Conference in 1958, addressing itself to young unmarried people, said:[3]

> The full giving and receiving of a whole person which sexual intercourse expresses is only possible within the assurance and protection of the faithful, life-long promise of each to the other, 'forsaking all others'.

3. Report of the Committee on the Family in Contemporary Society, *The Lambeth Conference 1958* (London, 1958), **2**, 156.

This is well said. But the more relevant question is: Why should sexual intercourse be engaged in *only* in order to express a full giving and receiving? Why not to express . . . well, what we express in parties, in dancing, in dining out together, in comforting each other (just acquaintances) in times of stress . . . and so on? And if it is said that, *despite* one's intentions and the context, *the physical form of the act* 'has a definitive character' or 'expresses the full giving and receiving of a human person', then we must respond with two questions: (*i*) Really? What is it about the physical form of the act that has or bestows this extraordinary significance? (*ii*) Anyway, so what? After all, on no plausible ethical theory are we bound to respect the natural, given physical form of an act simply because it is its physical form. So why should we respect the 'natural significance' of that form (if the latter conception be granted)? At this point the Dutch and Lambeth seem to run out of breath. But more needs to be said.

We talk easily, these days, about the 'significance', for example the 'unitive significance' *(significatio unitatis),* of sexual intercourse. Now the English, 'unitive significance', rather more than the Latin, suggests that this act of physical union of bodies in some way has the meaning of bringing about a uniting of the partners, as if it had (perhaps in some realm of meanings) an effect. But the latter proposition, as it stands and as far as I understand it, seems to be false, for the reasons I have suggested. There seems no reason at all to accept that intercourse engaged in promiscuously, or as play or in sympathy or otherwise, need have any such effect. On the other hand, the Latin, *significatio unitatis,* rather suggests that intercourse expresses, is a symbol of, a union that already exists; and no doubt this is true: *ex hypothesi,* sexual intercourse is a union of bodies, and *as such* can express a common affection, a common playfulness, a common celebration, more vividly than dining out together . . . or dancing. It is 'something to be shared, like a marvellous meal'. But of course, *this* doesn't bear the load we want to put on the notion of *significatio unitatis.* Moreover, to say that intercourse 'has' this expressive sense or force obscures the fact that often intercourse actually expresses no more than a mutual taste for diversion, or a mutual *libido dominandi.*

What then is the source of the appeal and apparent plausibility of talk about the unitive significance of sexual intercourse? I think it is this: *granted* an ideal of a profound, life-long, exclusive, loving union between man and woman, then intercourse between these spouses is to be regarded as a very apt expression of their union, their common and exclusive project. And then one may wish to add, with the Lambeth Conference Committee again, that this apt expression is somehow made less apt (or perhaps is impossible?) unless 'the partners bring to each other a complete offering of self-hood unspoiled by any liaison'—hence 'premarital intercourse can never be right'.[4]

But before one leaps with relief to this conclusion, let us raise a few questions, not so much about the all-too-questionable assertion that casual sexual play 'spoils one's self-hood', but rather about the premise that

4. Loc. cit.

intercourse is a peculiarly apt expression of the ideal of marriage. *(i)* Once more: What is it about intercourse, the union of bodies and members in *this* way (rather than that. . .), that makes it so apt an expression? *(ii)* Granted that this is the most apt expression of the ideal of marriage, does it follow that it is the only apt use of one's sexual powers? And even if it does follow, what is *morally* offensive about an inapt use of a physical capacity? *(iii)* More radically: What is the sense of the ideal of a profound, life-long, exclusive, loving union between one man and one woman?

This last question emerges, not out of a cheap cynicism, but from reflection on the meaning of friendship. It is self-evidently lovely for a person to go out from himself in friendship. *Bonum sui diffusivum* ["goodness goes out from itself"] is the principle of a whole philosophical and theological civilization.[5] The mutual sharing of the good things of life is itself an unsurpassed good. So' friendship does not rest satisfied with one friend, but seeks to extend itself to one's friend's friends, to widen the circle of love; it even dreams of a love of all men. For the union between one man and another man is deepened and strengthened, not weakened and dissipated, by its extension to other persons, the friends of my friends, sharing an ever-greater good, namely the ever-extending sharing of the goods open to man. Into this meditation on friendship erupts the peremptory demand that *one* friendship be exclusive and share its highest good with no one. Or rather, to reverse the challenge: into contemporary Christian rhapsodies about 'the couple' *we* (married people) must inject the blunt question: Why is it not perhaps vice, rather than virtue, to cultivate the exclusive life of the couple, and to reserve certain good things for *one* other person? No amount of praise of unity or of acts signifying unity will be an adequate response to this question; indeed, it will only increase the urgency of the question.

The only eligible answer to the question, I think, is that given in the terse and masterly summary of the Christian ideal of marriage which prefaces the analysis of that ideal in the encyclical *Humanae Vitae*.[6] It runs: "through their mutual gift of themselves, a gift which is specific and exclusive to them, the spouses seek that sharing of persons by which they perfect one another, IN ORDER THAT they may co-operate with God in the procreation and education of new lives." There's the . . . challenge to 'the couple' to find their mutually fulfilling communion and friendship not in an inexplicably exclusive cultivation of each other, but in a common pursuit, the pursuit of a good that *de facto* cannot be adequately realized otherwise than by single-minded devotion to that good, by the *only* two people who can be *the* mother and *the* father of *that* child. Now to say this is not to draw any further conclusions (which would in fact be unwarranted)—such as that marriage should be entered upon primarily with the motive of having children, or that intercourse within marriage ought to be so motivated. No,

5. Cf. Per Erik Persson, *Sacra Doctrina: Reason and Revelation in Aquinas* (Oxford, 1970), pp. 132–8, on the difference between the neo-Platonist and Thomist worlds of thought, and the corresponding treatments of the tag, *bonum sui diffusivum* ["goodness goes out from itself"].

6. Para. 8.

the point is simply to issue a reminder about that dimension of sexuality which had not yet been mentioned, and to suggest in passing (because the emphasis of much modern catechetics seems to me profoundly awry) that what, in the last analysis, makes sense of the conditions of the marital enterprise, its stability and exclusiveness, is not the worthy and delightful sentiments of love and affection which invite one to marry, but the desire for and demands of a *procreative* community, a family.

However, to show that it is sensible to reserve a *complete and procreative self-giving* to the context of a stable and exclusive union is very far from showing that it is sensible to reserve *sexual intercourse* to that context. For a sexual movement, like any other bodily motion, has as a human action the meaning one gives it in context, and can be engaged in without any pretence that one is either establishing or expressing a stable and exclusive union.

The meaning one gives it—this meaning-giving is an act of choice. Now an intelligent choice to engage in sexual intercourse has to take into account a plain fact—not a 'meaning' so much as a biological fact of physical causality—*viz.* that intercourse may bring about procreation; that a child may be conceived; that intercourse is procreative (cause and effect, nothing more). One can accept this fact and seek to capitalize on it, or one can ignore this fact and proceed regardless, or one can by simple means prevent the effect following from the cause. But in any case, one is willy nilly engaged, in sexual intercourse, with the basic human value of procreation. When I get into my car to drive home at night, I am not on a life-saving mission, but the causal potentialities of my activity bring me willy nilly within the range of the basic human value of life, and in terms of that value my actions can be characterized as sufficiently respectful of life, careless of life or wilfully violative of life, as the case may be. I am not bound to be always cultivating life, to be always cultivating God, or truth or social justice, or to be always procreating. But sometimes I find myself in (or bring myself within) situations which by their brute causal structure require of me an attention or a choice that will be adequately open to a basic value whose realization or violation is, by reason of that structure, at stake or in question in the situation. And then the call of reason reaching up toward the source of all intelligible good is to remain fully open to that basic intelligible good which now immediately confronts me.

From this point, and from no other, unfolds naturally the whole Christian understanding of the morality of sexual activity. Certainly, the Christian grasp of this basic value, procreation, is distinctively intense— "begotten not made"—and what is demanded in procreation is not just its existence but its good existence, not a spawning, but the bringing of the child into a community of love which will provide the substance of his education into a loving ability to realize all the human values. But this peculiarly intense grasp of the basic natural value does not distort or render peculiar or non-natural the development of the norm of *prudentia* [prudence] in response to the call of the value. As always, the question is: What actions, by their causal structure, involve a choice adequately open to the basic values, and what actions involve, by their causal structure, a choice immediately against a basic value?

The Christian weighting of the value of procreation, as the value of procreation and education within a "sharing of persons," means that fornication, in which procreation may follow but not within an assured "sharing of persons," involves an inadequate openness to procreation (so understood). Nor can this conclusion be avoided by pointing to the fact that it is easy to exclude the possibility of procreation from fornication. For the choice to exclude the possibility of procreation while engaging in intercourse is always, and in an obvious and unambiguous way (which it requires no Christian weighting of the value of procreation to see), a choice directly and immediately against a basic value. (To this last remark it is perhaps unnecessary to add that taking steps to prevent procreation when one has brought oneself or is about to bring oneself within the range of the procreative value by engaging in sexual intercourse is obviously very different from the policy of *not* bringing oneself fully within the range of the value at times when procreation might follow, but engaging in intercourse at other times within the framework of the procreative "sharing of persons.") And if a question is raised about solitary sexual acts or sexual intercourse outside the vagina (whether homo- or hetero-sexual), the Christian response, making explicit the confused natural sense of the question which Plato was able to appeal to even in a Callicles, turns on the fact that all sexual activity involves an inchoate version, or perhaps a kind of reminder, of the procreative causal potency of 'full' sexual intercourse; this reminder or inchoate version brings a sensitive man sufficiently within the range of the procreative value for that value to make its ordinary imperious claim (like the other basic values) to a sufficient openness and respect towards it. And it is this sense of the symbolic relation of sexual movements to the value of procreation (understood as the rich familial "sharing of persons")[7] that makes the fornication of even the 'naturally' sterile seem, to the Christian, an inadequate openness to a basic good.

So, since the value of procreation, like other basic values, is a permanent and irreducible part of the structure of our will, of our thirst for the intelligible good, and since, like other basic values, its realization or rejection are permanent possibilities always implicit in certain of our situations, it is possible to see (given the vertical perspective towards the Good that can confront us in the immediate form of our choice) that some sexual acts are (as types of choice) always wrong because an inadequate response, or direct closure, to the basic procreative value that they put in question.[8]

7. It is this symbolic relation of intra-marital sexual acts to the value of procreation so understood that makes sense of marriage of the naturally sterile; their permanent and exclusive union honours the procreative community as a value they would wish to have devoted themselves to in common had they been able to effectively as well as symbolically.

8. Hence the 'sanctity' of the seminative genital movement in the vagina is the *form* of the relevant moral principle, but it is not the *point* of the principle. There is no question of respecting the physical structure 'for its own sake'. Failure to distinguish the explicit form(ulation) from the implicit point of the Christian rule radically vitiates the analyses in John T. Noonan, *Contraception* (New York, Mentor Omega edition, 1967), Ch. 8 ('The

By a trick of certain European languages, we call the more visibly non-procreative of these acts 'unnatural';[9] but whether the opposition or indifference to procreation as a value be visible or merely causal, symbolic or effective, all such acts are morally of a kind. If someone wishes to distinguish within the class, we must ask him to reflect: 'Think what you will answer, Callicles, if you are asked the questions which naturally follow . . . the shocking things I hinted at just now must obviously follow, and many other things as well.'

# HOMOSEXUALITY AND THE "UNNATURALNESS ARGUMENT"

*Burton M. Leiser*

[The alleged "unnaturalness" of homosexuality] raises the question of the meaning of *nature, natural,* and similar terms. Theologians and other moralists have said that [homosexual acts] violate the "natural law," and that they are therefore immoral and ought to be prohibited by the state.

The word *nature* has a built-in ambiguity that can lead to serious misunderstandings. When something is said to be "natural" or in confor-

---

Rationale of the Prohibition'), and G. Egner, *Birth Regulation and Catholic Belief* (London, 1966), Ch. 3. Noonan says: 'What is taken as sacral is the act of intercourse resulting in insemination' (p. 294; also p. 628). It is true that, in the same context (pp. 294, 628), he adds: 'If coitus was taken as sacred, it was because generation was only achievable through this means.' But his misunderstanding of what, in the tradition, is meant by the 'sanctity' of the seminative act of intercourse, is clearly shown by his remark (p. 628) that the foregoing position 'would, however, be consistent with a position which permitted the use of anovulants as agents not affecting the sacral act of coitus itself'. Plainly Noonan thinks that the tradition is based on a concern for the physical, visible structure rather than a concern that the value of procreation should not be violated (as of course it is violated, in a straightforward way, by contraceptive use of anovulants). Egner too thinks that the tradition 'takes the natural norm as a special pattern of anatomical contact rather than as the generative finality of sexual relations' (p. 48). He fails to show that one can play off 'special pattern' against 'generative finality' without engaging in some arbitrary consequentialist calculus of 'total good'; or that 'the "moral centre of gravity" of the Roman Position [lies] in the status accorded to the physiological structure of intercourse' (p. 260).

9. Cf. André Pellicer, *Natura: étude sémantique et historique du mot latin* (Paris, 1966), pp. 357-67.

mity with "natural law" or the "law of nature," this may mean either (1) that it is in conformity with the descriptive laws of nature, or (2) that it is not artificial, that man has not imposed his will or his devices upon events or conditions as they exist or would have existed without such interference.

1. *The descriptive laws of nature.*    The laws of nature, as these are understood by the scientist, differ from the laws of man. The former are purely descriptive, whereas the latter are prescriptive. When a scientist says that water boils at 212° Fahrenheit or that the volume of a gas varies directly with the heat that is applied to it and inversely with the pressure, he means merely that as a matter of recorded and observable fact, pure water under standard conditions always boils at precisely 212° Fahrenheit and that as a matter of observed fact, the volume of a gas rises as it is heated and falls as pressure is applied to it. These "laws" merely *describe* the manner in which physical substances *actually behave.* They differ from municipal and federal laws in that they *do not prescribe behavior.* Unlike manmade laws, natural laws are not passed by any legislator or group of legislators; they are not proclaimed or announced; they impose no obligation upon anyone or anything; their "violation" entails no penalty, and there is no reward for "following" them or "abiding by" them. When a scientist says that the air in a tire "obeys" the laws of nature that "govern" gases, he does *not* mean that the air, having been informed that it *ought* to behave in a certain way, behaves appropriately under the right conditions. He means, rather, that as a matter of fact, the air in a tire *will* behave like all other gases. In saying that Boyle's law "governs" the behavior of gases, he means merely that gases do, as a matter of fact, behave in accordance with Boyle's law, and that Boyle's law enables one to predict accurately what will happen to a given quantity of a gas as its pressure is raised; he does *not* mean to suggest that some heavenly voice has proclaimed that all gases should henceforth behave in accordance with the terms of Boyle's law and that a ghostly policeman patrols the world, ready to mete out punishments to any gases that "violate" the heavenly decree. In fact, according to the scientist, it does not make sense to speak of a natural law being violated. For if there were a true exception to a so-called law of nature, the exception would require a change in the description of those phenomena, and the "law" would have been shown to be no law at all. The laws of nature are revised as scientists discover new phenomena that require new refinements in their descriptions of the way things actually happen. In this respect they differ fundamentally from human laws, which are revised periodically by legislators who are not so interested in *describing* human behavior as they are in *prescribing* what human behavior *should* be.

2. *The artificial as a form of the unnatural.*    On occasion when we say that something is not natural, we mean that it is a product of human artifice. My typewriter is not a natural object, in this sense, for the substances of which it is composed have been removed from their natural state—the state in which they existed before men came along—and have been trans-

formed by a series of chemical and physical and mechanical processes into other substances. They have been rearranged into a whole that is quite different from anything found in nature. In short, my typewriter is an artificial object. In this sense, the clothing that I wear as I lecture before my students is not natural, for it has been transformed considerably from the state in which it was found in nature; and my wearing of clothing as I lecture before my students is also not natural, in this sense, for in my natural state, before the application of anything artificial, before any human interference with things as they are, I am quite naked. Human laws, being artificial conventions designed to exercise a degree of control over the natural inclinations and propensities of men, may in this sense be considered to be unnatural.

Now when theologians and moralists speak of homosexuality, contraception, abortion, and other forms of human behavior as being unnatural, and say that for that reason such behavior must be considered to be wrong, in what sense are they using the word *unnatural?* Are they saying that homosexual behavior and the use of contraceptives are contrary to the scientific laws of nature, are they saying that they are artificial forms of behavior, or are they using the terms *natural* and *unnatural* in some third sense?

They cannot mean that homosexual behavior (to stick to the subject presently under discussion) violates the laws of nature in the first sense, for, as we have pointed out, in *that* sense it is impossible to violate the laws of nature. Those laws, being merely descriptive of what actually does happen, would have to *include* homosexual behavior if such behavior does actually take place. Even if the defenders of the theological view that homosexuality is unnatural were to appeal to a statistical analysis by pointing out that such behavior is not normal from a statistical point of view, and therefore not what the laws of nature require, it would be open to their critics to reply that any descriptive law of nature must account for and incorporate all statistical deviations, and that the laws of nature, in this sense, do not *require* anything. These critics might also note that the best statistics available reveal that about half of all American males engage in homosexual activity at some time in their lives, and that a very large percentage of American males have exclusively homosexual relations for a fairly extensive period of time; from which it would follow that such behavior is natural, for them, at any rate, in this sense of the word *natural.*

If those who say that homosexual behavior is unnatural are using the term *unnatural* in the second sense, it is difficult to see why they should be fussing over it. Certainly nothing is intrinsically wrong with going against nature (if that is how it should be put) in this sense. That which is artificial is often far better than what is natural. Artificial homes seem, at any rate, to be more suited to human habitation and more conducive to longer life and better health than caves and other natural shelters. There are distinct advantages to the use of such unnatural (i.e. artificial) amenities as clothes, furniture, and books. Although we may dream of an idyllic return to nature in our more wistful moments, we would soon discover, as Thoreau did in his attempt to escape from the artificiality of civilization, that needles and thread, knives and matches, ploughs and nails, and countless other products of human artifice are essential to human life. We would discover, as Plato pointed out in the *Republic,* that no man can be truly self-sufficient. Some of the by-products of industry are less than desirable; but neither industry itself, nor the products of industry, are intrinsically evil, even though both are unnatural in this sense of the word.

Interference with nature is not evil in itself. Nature, as some writers have put it, must be tamed. In some respects man must look upon it as an enemy to be conquered. If nature were left to its own devices, without the intervention of human artifice, men would be consumed with disease, they would be plagued by insects, they would be chained to the places where they were born with no means of swift communication or transport, and they would suffer the discomforts and the torments of wind and weather and flood and fire with no practical means of combating any of them. Interfering with nature, doing battle with nature, using human will and reason and skill to thwart what might otherwise follow from the conditions that prevail in the world, is a peculiarly human enterprise, one that can hardly be condemned merely because it does what is not natural.

Homosexual behavior can hardly be considered to be unnatural in this sense. There is nothing "artificial" about such behavior. On the contrary, it is quite natural, in this sense, to those who engage in it. And even if it were not, even if it were quite artificial, this is not in itself a ground for condemning it.

It would seem, then, that those who condemn homosexuality as an unnatural form of behavior must mean something else by the word *unnatural,* something not covered by either of the preceding definitions. A third possibility is this:

*3. Anything uncommon or abnormal is unnatural.*    If this is what is meant by those who condemn homosexuality on the ground that it is unnatural, it is quite obvious that their condemnation cannot be accepted without further argument. For the fact that a given form of behavior is uncommon provides no justification for condemning it. Playing viola in a string quartet is no doubt an uncommon form of human behavior. I do not know what percentage of the human race engages in such behavior, or what percentage of his life any given violist devotes to such behavior, but I suspect that the number of such people must be very small indeed, and that the total number of manhours spent in such activity would justify our calling that form of activity uncommon, abnormal (in the sense that it is statistically not the the kind of thing that people are ordinarily inclined to do), and therefore unnatural, in this sense of the word. Yet there is no reason to suppose that such uncommon, abnormal behavior is, by virtue of its uncommonness, deserving of condemnation or ethically or morally wrong. On the contrary, many forms of behavior are praised precisely because they are so uncommon. Great artists, poets, musicians, and scientists are "abnormal" in this sense; but clearly the world is better off for having them, and it would be absurd to condemn them or their activities for their failure to be common and normal. If homosexual behavior is wrong, then, it must be for some reason other than its "unnaturalness" in this sense of the word.

*4. Any use of an organ or an instrument that is contrary to its principal purpose or function is unnatural.* Every organ and every instrument—perhaps even every creature—has a function to perform, one for which it is particularly designed. Any use of those instruments and organs that is consonant with their purposes is natural and proper, but any use that is inconsistent with their principal functions is unnatural and improper, and to that extent, evil or harmful. Human teeth, for example, are admirably designed for their principal functions—biting and chewing the kinds of food suitable for human consumption. But they are not particularly well suited for prying the caps from beer bottles. If they are used for the latter purpose, which is not natural to them, they are liable to crack or break under the strain. The abuse of one's teeth leads to their destruction and to a consequent deterioration in one's overall health. If they are used only for their proper function, however, they may continue to serve well for many years. Similarly, a given drug may have a proper function. If used in the furtherance of that end, it can preserve life and restore health. But if it is abused, and employed for purposes for which it was never intended, it may cause serious harm and even death. The natural uses of things are good and proper, but their unnatural uses are bad and harmful.

What we must do, then, is to find the proper use, or the true purpose, of each organ in our bodies. Once we have discovered that, we will know what constitutes the natural use of each organ, and what constitutes an unnatural, abusive, and potentially harmful employment of the various parts of our bodies. If we are rational, we will be careful to confine our behavior to our proper functions and to refrain from unnatural behavior. According to those philosophers who follow this line of reasoning, the way to discover the "proper" use of any organ is to determine what it is perculiarly suited to do. The eye is suited for seeing, the ear for hearing, the nerves for transmitting impulses from one part of the body to another, and so on.

What are the sex organs peculiarly suited to do? Obviously, they are peculiarly suited to enable men and women to reproduce their own kind. No other organ in the body is capable of fulfilling that function. It follows, according to those who follow the natural-law line, that the "proper" or "natural" function of the sex organs is reproduction, and that strictly speaking, any use of those organs for other purposes is unnatural, abusive, potentially harmful, and therefore wrong. The sex organs have been given to us in order to enable us to maintain the continued existence of mankind on this earth. All perversions—including masturbation, homosexual behavior, and heterosexual intercourse that deliberately frustrates the design of the sexual organs—are unnatural and bad. As Pope Pius XI once said, "Private individuals have no other power over the members of their bodies than that which pertains to their natural ends."

But the problem is not so easily resolved. Is it true that every organ has one and only one proper function? A hammer may have been designed to pound nails, and it may perform that particular job best. But it is not sinful to employ a hammer to crack nuts if I have no other more suitable tool immediately available. The hammer, being a relatively versatile tool, may be employed in a number of ways. It has no one "proper" or "natural" function. A woman's eyes are well adapted to seeing, it is true. But they seem also to be well adapted to flirting. Is a woman's use of her eyes for the latter purpose sinful merely because she is not using them, at that moment, for their "primary" purpose of seeing? Our sexual organs are uniquely adapted for procreation, but that is obviously not the only function for which they are adapted. Human beings may—and do—use those organs for a great many other purposes, and it is difficult to see why any *one* use should be considered to be the only proper one. The sex organs, for one thing, seem to be particularly well adapted to give their owners and others intense sensations of pleasure. Unless one believes that pleasure itself is bad, there seems to be little reason to believe that the use of the sex organs for the production of pleasure in oneself or in others is evil. In view of the peculiar design of these organs, with their great concentration of nerve endings, it would seem that they were designed (if they *were* designed) with that very goal in mind, and that their use for such purposes would be no more unnatural than their use for the purpose of procreation.

Nor should we overlook the fact that human sex organs may be and are used to express, in the deepest and most intimate way open to man, the love of one person for another. Even the most ardent opponents of "unfruitful" intercourse admit that sex does serve this function. They have accordingly conceded that a man and his wife may have intercourse even though she is pregnant, or past the age of child bearing, or in the infertile period of her menstrual cycle.

Human beings are remarkably complex and adaptable creatures. Neither they nor their organs can properly be compared to hammers or to other tools. The analogy quickly breaks down. The generalization that a given organ or instrument has one and only one proper function does not hold up, even with regard to the simplest manufactured tools, for, as we have seen, a tool may be used for more than one purpose—less effectively than one especially designed for a given task, perhaps, but "properly" and certainly not *sinfully*. A woman may use her eyes not only to see and to flirt, but also to earn money—if she is, for example, an actress or a model. Though neither of the latter functions seems to have been a part of the original "design," if one may speak sensibly of *design* in this context, of the eye, it is difficult to see why such a use of the eyes of a woman should be considered sinful, perverse, or unnatural. Her sex organs have the unique capactiy of producing ova and nurturing human embryos, under the right conditions; but why should any other use of those organs, including their use to bring pleasure to their owner or to someone else, or to manifest love to another person, or even, perhaps, to earn money, be regarded as perverse, sinful, or unnatural? Similarly, a man's sexual organs possess the unique capacity of causing the generation of another human being, but if a man chooses to use them for pleasure, or for the expression of love, or for some other purpose—so long as he does not interfere with the rights of some other person—the fact that his sex organs do have their unique capabilities does not constitute a convincing justification for condemning their other uses as being perverse, sinful, unnatural, or criminal. If a man "perverts" himself by wiggling his ears for the entertainment of his neighbors instead of using them exclusively for their "natural" function of hearing, no one thinks of consigning him to prison. If he abuses his teeth by using them to pull staples from memos—a function for which teeth were clearly not designed—he is not accused of being immoral, degraded, and degenerate. The fact that people *are* condemned for using their sex organs for their own pleasure or profit, or for that of others, may be more revealing about the prejudices and taboos of our society than it is about our perception of the true nature or purpose or "end" (whatever that might be) of our bodies.

To sum up, then, the proposition that any use of an organ that is contrary to its principal purpose or function is unnatural assumes that organs *have* a principal purpose or function, but this may be denied on the ground that the purpose or function of a given organ may vary according to the needs or desires of its owner. It may be denied on the ground that a given organ may have more than one principal purpose or function, and any attempt to call one use or another the only natural one seems to be arbitrary, if not questionbegging. Also, the proposition suggests that what is unnatural is evil or depraved. This goes beyond the pure description of things, and enters into the problem of the evaluation of human behavior, which leads us to the fifth meaning of "natural."

*5. That which is natural is good, and whatever is unnatural is bad.*    When one condemns homosexuality or masturbation or the use of contraceptives on the ground that it is unnatural, one implies that whatever is unnatural is bad, wrongful, or perverse. But as we have seen, in some senses of the word, the unnatural (i.e., the artificial) is often very good, whereas that which is natural (i.e., that which has not been subjected to human artifice or improvement) may be very bad indeed. Of course, interference with nature may be bad. Ecologists have made us more aware than we have ever been of the dangers of unplanned and uninformed interference with nature. But this is not to say that *all* interference with nature is bad. Every time a man cuts down a tree to make room for a home for himself, or catches a fish to feed himself or his family, he is interfering with nature. If men did not interfere with nature, they would have no homes, they could eat no fish, and, in fact, they could not survive. What, then, can be meant by those who say that whatever is natural is good and whatever is unnatural is bad? Clearly, they cannot have intended merely to reduce the word *natural* to a synonym of *good, right,* and *proper,* and *unnatural* to a synonym of *evil, wrong, improper, corrupt,* and *depraved.* If that were all they had intended to do, there would be very little to discuss as to whether a given form of behavior might be proper even though it is not in strict conformity with someone's views of what is natural; for *good* and *natural* being synonyms, it would follow inevitably that whatever is good must be natural, and vice versa, by definition. This is certainly not what the opponents of homosexuality have been saying when they claim that homosexuality, being unnatural, is evil. For if it were, their claim would be quite empty. They would be saying merely that homosexuality, being evil, is evil—a redundancy that could as easily be reduced to the simpler assertion that homosexuality is evil. This assertion, however, is not an argument. Those who oppose homosexuality and other sexual "perversions" on the ground that they are "unnatural" are saying that there is some objectively identifiable quality in such behavior that is unnatural; and that that quality, once it has been identified by some kind of scientific observation, can be seen to be detrimental to those who engage in such behavior, or to those around them; and that *because* of the harm (physical, mental, moral, or spiritual) that results from engaging in any behavior possessing the attribute of unnaturalness, such behavior must be considered to be wrongful, and should be discouraged by society. "Unnaturalness" and "wrongfulness" are not synonyms, then, but different concepts. The problem with which we are wrestling is that we are unable to find a meaning for *unnatural* that enables us to arrive at the conclusion that homosexuality is unnatural or that if homosexuality is unnatural, it is therefore wrongful behavior. We have examined four common meanings of *natural* and *unnatural,* and have seen that none of them performs the task that it must perform if the advocates of this argument are to prevail. Without some more satisfactory explanation of the connection between the wrongfulness of homosexuality and its alleged unnaturalness, the argument must be rejected.

# A PHILOSOPHICAL ANALYSIS OF SEXUAL ETHICS

*Raymond A. Belliotti*

I shall advance and defend what can be labeled a secular analysis of sexual ethics. As a secular analysis it shall make no appeal to religious considerations; it shall, in fact, consider religious factors irrelevant to the analysis. In doing so it should be obvious that the account will seem unsatisfactory to fervent religious believers.

From Raymond A. Belliotti, "A Philosophical Analysis of Sexual Ethics," *Journal of Social Philosophy,* vol. 10, no. 3 (September 1979), pp. 8–11. Reprinted by permission of the *Journal of Social Philosophy.*

I

I begin with what I take to be a fundamental ethical maxim: it is morally wrong for someone to treat another merely as a means to his own ends. Immanuel Kant first formulated the maxim in this way, but I think it can be considered uncontroversially true by most, if not all, moral thinkers. We often speak disparagingly of a person who "uses" or "exploits" another. What do we mean by this? It seems that we are suggesting that the former is morally culpable because he has treated the latter in a way that is morally wrong for one human to treat another. The culpable individual has "objectified" his victim; he has treated the other as an object to be manipulated and used, much as we might utilize a tool. One of the worst things that one person can do to another is to recognize the other as something less than human or as something less than the other really is: to recognize the other, not as an end in himself, but rather as an object to be used merely as a means to the user's ends. If we believe, and I think we do, that each person has an intrinsic worth and value which demands that we treat all others as subjects of experience and as being as fully human as ourselves, then we are following the general pattern of Kant's ethical maxim.

Notice that the maxim does not state that we cannot treat others as a means to our ends. It only states that we cannot *merely* treat the other in this way. We often need others to fulfill our goals, but immorality occurs only if we treat them merely as a means to these goals and not as an equal subject of experience.

So in all our human interactions we have a moral obligation to treat others as more than just means to our ends. This obligation becomes even more important when considering sexual interactions since very important feelings, desires, and drives are involved.

The second stage of the argument concerns the nature of sexual interactions. I contend that the nature of these interactions is contractual and involves the important notion of reciprocity. When two people voluntarily consent to interact sexually they create obligations to each other based on their needs and expectations. Every sexual encounter has as its base the needs, desires, and drives of the individuals involved. That we choose to interact sexually is an acknowledgment that none of us is totally self-sufficient. We interact with others in order to fulfill certain desires which we cannot fulfill by ourselves. This suggests that the basis of the sexual encounter is contractual; i.e., it is a voluntary agreement on the part of both parties to satisfy the expectations of the other.

Some might recoil at the coldness of such an analysis. Is the sexual encounter as business-like a contract as the relationship between two corporations or the agreements one makes with his insurance agent? Of course it is not. Very important feelings of intimacy are involved which make the consenting parties emotionally vulnerable. But all this shows is that the sexual contract may well be the most important agreement that one makes from an emotional standpoint; it does not show that the interaction itself is not contractual. The contractual basis of the sexual interaction involves the notion of a voluntary agreement founded on the expectations of fulfillment of reciprocal needs.

The final stage of the argument consists of two acknowledgements: (1) That voluntary contracts are such that the parties are under a moral obligation, other things being equal, to fulfill that which they agreed upon, and (2) that promise-breaking and deception are, other things equal, immoral actions. The acknowledgement of the second makes the recognition of the first redundant, since the non-fulfillment of one's contractual duties is a species of promise-breaking. Ordinarily we feel that promise-breaking and deception are paradigm cases of immoral actions, since they involve violations of moral duties, and often, explicit or implicit lying. If it is true that sexual interactions entail contractual relationships then any violation of that which one has voluntarily consented to perform is morally wrong, since it involves promise-breaking and the non-fulfillment of the moral duty to honor one's voluntary agreements.

It is clear, then, that both parties must perform that which they voluntarily contracted to do for the other, unless the other agrees to the non-performance of the originally agreed upon action. Although sexual contracts are not as formal or explicit as corporation agreements, the rule of thumb should be the concept of reasonable expectation. If a woman smiles at me and agrees to have a drink I cannot reasonably assume, at least at this point, that she has agreed to spend the weekend with me. On the other hand if she did agree to share a room and bed with me for the weekend I could reasonably assume that she had agreed to have sexual intercourse with me. Although all examples are not clearcut, in general, the notion of reasonable expectation should guide us here. If there is any doubt concerning whether or not someone has agreed to perform a certain sexual act with another, I would suggest that the doubting party simply ask the other and make the contract more explicit. In lieu of this, prudence dictates that we be cautious in assuming what the other has offered, and when in doubt assume nothing until a more explicit overture has been made.

The conclusion of the argument is that sex is immoral if and only if it involves deception, promise-breaking, and/or the treatment of the other merely as a means to one's own ends.

## II

The results of this analysis can now be applied to various sexual activities.

(1) *Rape* is intrinsically immoral because it involves the involuntary participation of one of the parties. Since the basis of the sexual encounter is contractual it should be clear that any coercion or force renders the interaction immoral; contracts are not validly consummated if one of the parties is compelled to agree by force or fraud. An interesting question concerns whether it is possible for a husband to rape his wife. I tend to think that this is possible. Some contend that the marriage contract allows both parties unrestricted sexual access to the other, and that, therefore,

rape cannot occur in a marital situation. Others define rape as a sexual interaction which occurs when one individual forcibly uses another and the parties are not married to each other. But I think of rape as any case of forcibly using another in a sexual encounter without the other's consent. Under this definition it would be possible for a man to rape his wife, and in doing so commit an immoral act.

(2) *Bestiality* is intrinsically immoral because it too involves the involuntary participation of one of the parties. No non-human animal is capable of entering into a valid sexual contract with a human; as such all cases of bestiality can be considered instances of animal rape. A critic might argue that bestiality is only a form of sex with an object since only a non-human animal is involved. Kant, himself, felt that animals could be used merely as a means to the ends of humans. But this is mistaken from a moral point of view. Animals, unlike objects, have interests, desires, and are capable of experiencing pleasure and pain; i.e., they are sentient beings. As sentient beings their interests ought to be taken into account. As it seems clear that the interests of non-human animals are not advanced by being used as sexual objects by humans, it also seems clear that to do so cannot be morally justified. The differences between mere objects, which can be legitimately used merely as means to human ends, and non-human animals, who are sentient beings, are obvious. To use or totally objectify the latter is morally wrong; although probably less wrong than the use or objectification of other human beings.

(3) *Necrophilia* is immoral since it also involves the involuntary participation of one of the parties. The corpse cannot voluntarily enter into a contract with a living human; hence cases of necrophilia can be considered instances of the rape of dead humans. Now it may seem that corpses *are* mere objects; certainly they cannot feel pleasure and pain. But are they mere objects in the sense that rocks, stones, and desks are objects? The corpse was once a sentient being and it may still be the case that even as a corpse it has interests. This may seem absurd at first glance. But we really acknowledge this very fact by honoring death bed promises made to the dying, by taking care when handling and displaying the bodies of the dead, and by being careful not to defame maliciously the reputations of dead people. Don't we feel that there is a difference between being buried with dignity and being hung and mutilated after we die? Wouldn't we prefer the former? And the reason we would involves the fact that no *mere* object is involved, but rather a human corpse.

There are imaginable instances in which necrophilia would not be immoral. Suppose the will of man X contains a clause stipulating that "anyone wishing to use my corpse for sexual purposes between the hours of 7–9 P.M. on Thurdays at the Greenmount Cemetery may do so." As long as X made the stipulation rationally and sincerely my analysis would consider sexual acts performed on the appointed day and time as not immoral; the law, however, might take a dimmer view of this activity.

(4) *Incest* is immoral when it involves a child who cannot be considered capable of entering into a contractual relationship. Children cannot know the ramifications of a sexual interaction with their parent(s);

hence they cannot be thought of as fully responsible agents. Any contract, sexual or otherwise, can only be legitimately consummated with fully responsible parties.

Incest would also be immoral if the parties knowingly conceived a child with the likelihood of genetic defect, since this is an act which would contribute to the needless misery of another.

But there are times when incest is not immoral. Suppose a 50 year old father and his 30 year old daughter voluntarily agree, rationally and sincerely, to a sexual interaction. Both parties are fully responsible agents knowing the ramifications of their actions, and employ proper birth control methods to eliminate the possibility of conceiving a defective child, or engage in a sexual act in which no child could possibly be conceived. This, repugnant though it may seem, would not be an immoral act.

(5) *Promiscuity and adultery* are immoral only if they involve promise-breaking, deceit, or exploitation. Promise-breaking and deceit can occur in a number of ways: one party may deceive another concerning his real feelings for the other; he may break promises to his spouse in order that he might be with the other; he may explicitly lie in order to sustain the two relationships. In romantic triangles of this nature, immorality can occur from the actions of any of the parties in relation to the two other parties.

Some would argue that the nature of the marriage contract itself entails that *any* extramarital encounter on the part of either party is immoral (i.e., it involves promise-breaking) since one provision of the marriage contract is sexual exclusivity. But under my analysis the parties to the marriage contract may legitimately amend the contract at any time, and an extramarital sexual encounter need not be immoral as long as both marital partners agree prior to the encounter that it is permissible. If the marriage relationship is construed as a voluntary reciprocal contract the partners are free to amend its provisions insofar as they can both agree on the alterations involved.

## III

The religious argument against many of the aforementioned sexual activities is often straightforward:

(A)   If an action is a violation of God's law then it is immoral.
(B)   X breaks the law of God.
      X is an immoral action.

Substitute the acts in question for X and we see the essence of the religious argument against these acts. For the believer a supernatural being, possessing certain qualities, has created us and set down a variety of laws. To transgress these laws is to violate morality, since the ultimate lawgiver has set forth the basis for morality in these laws. All the believer need do is point to the relevant biblical scripture or the relevant source of these laws to show that certain acts are immoral. These acts are seen as *intrinsically* immoral, regardless of whether promise-breaking, deception, or exploitation are involved. Surely these latter factors are viewed as immoral, but even if they do not occur the action in question is still immoral because it violates the law of God. Violating the law of God is considered a sufficient condition for an act to be immoral by the religious believer.

Of course to someone who does not believe in any supernatural being or to one who believes in a supernatural being of a radically different nature from the Christian God, this argument is not convincing. Without a religious conviction premise (A) is vacuous.

Yet it is true that many non-believers share the believer's convictions regarding the immorality of certain of the sexual practices we have considered. Why is this so? I think that an important reason is that many religious convictions about practical moral issues have become imbedded into our considered moral judgments. Because of the influence and historical power of Christianity throughout the ages certain beliefs about the immorality of particular actions became an integral part of our moral education and customs. Hence many nonbelievers still think that adultery, promiscuity, etc. are morally pernicious even though they deny the existence of the Christian God. Under my analysis, however, these actions are not immoral (presupposing no promise-breaking, deception, or exploitation) once belief in the Christian God is abrogated. Once sexual interactions are viewed as being contractual and reciprocal we have a basis for judging their morality independent of any reliance upon the laws of a supernatural being.

## IV

The results of my analysis are in certain cases more liberal than conventional moralists (e.g., adultery, promiscuity, necrophilia, and incest are not immoral if certain conditions pertain), and in other cases more conservative (e.g., "teasing" without the intention to fulfill that which the other reasonably can be expected to think was offered is immoral, since it involves the nonfulfillment of that which the other could reasonably be expected to think was agreed upon).

It must be pointed out that to state that a certain act is not immoral does not entail that it is advisable to pursue. I have argued that under certain conditions these acts are not immoral, but I would certainly advise against most, if not all, of these actions. Often these actions still are offensive to our tastes, not in our best long term interests, and may be psychologically harmful. Because our most important feelings and emotions are involved in sexual interactions we must be cautious about engaging in certain acts which may be damaging in the long run. Just as we should be careful in agreeing to *any* voluntary contract involving a reciprocal exchange of goods and services, we should be most careful before agreeing upon what may be our most important kind of contract. The sexual contract is one in which our most valuable intangible commodities are at stake; in fact our self-esteem may well be on the line. And although we may freely enter into certain sexual contracts it is important to know the ramifications and long range effects to our own interests and the interests of others.

The purpose of this essay, then, is not to endorse or encourage certain of the sexual practices mentioned, but rather to show that the basis of our secular aversion to them often cannot be the notion of morality.

# CHAPTER TWELVE
# AID FOR THE NEEDY

What should we do about people who are unable to provide themselves with the basic necessities of life? What should governments do? We have all heard of famines and disasters that ravage populations in distant locations across the globe, but there are more and more needy people in the United States as well. For example, according to a congressional subcommittee there may be as many as 2.5 million Americans who do not have a place to live:

> [When] the first cold spell of winter hit Atlanta with subfreezing weather . . . it dipped to 24 degrees in the night . . . Isaac Williamson, 53, chose to sleep near an incinerator behind the Omni Shopping and Sports Complex. He was wearing a thin yellow coat and a pullover shirt. Police found him dead the next afternoon. It is believed that Williamson died of exposure and that, homeless, he had tried to hide from the cold winds amid the bold new buildings of Atlanta. . . .
>
> Holly Reed died in Denver . . . in the car that had been her home for six months. She was seven months old. A 30-degree evening claimed her life as her unemployed father ate dinner in the restaurant that employed her mother.
>
> "He didn't want to put a burden on parents or brothers or sisters," a police detective said of the father. "He's got some pride. He didn't want to go on welfare."
>
> So, when the last in a series of fast-food jobs expired for him, Michael Anthony Reed, 21, started living in his Toyota with his 21-year-old wife and

infant daughter. Holly Reed . . . died . . . of hypothermia while bundled in blankets in the family car.

In Huston, Anita Weber, a 59-year-old "bag lady" roams the downtown streets at night, often barefoot, carrying the shopping bags filled with scraps of cloth and paper that are meaningful only to her. Out of pity, desk clerks at the Texas State Hotel permit her to sleep in a straight-backed chair in the hotel lobby. . . .

Joe Wilkerson, 25, and his wife, Sheila, 22, are from Chicago. They are typical of the "new homeless.". . . Joe lost his $25,000-a-year job as a forklift operator. . . . So they sold all they had, left the house they rented in Chicago, and headed west to Denver with their two sons. In a month, their money—about $500—was gone. . . .

"The hardest part of my life [said Mrs. Wilkerson] was the night we came here (to the Samaritan Shelter in Denver). . . . We left a friend's house; they were on hard times. My husband, myself and my two sons were walking in the cold and the kids asked, 'Where are we going?' and we said, 'We don't know.' I told them the truth. 'I don't know. We're going with the Lord.' "[1]

Starvation, exposure, illness, death: all characterize the plight of the needy. But what ought to be done for them? And who ought to do it? There are rich and poor, both among nations and among citizens of the same nation. Do the rich owe anything to the poor? Should the wealthy give up some of their affluence to help the needy? Do all humans have rights that entitle them to the satisfaction of their needs? And, if so, who should satisfy those needs?[2]

Philosophers who have addressed these questions have tended to take several positions. One of the major ones, held by libertarians,[3] says that freedom is a basic right and that it is always wrong to force others to do something they would not freely choose, except when such force is needed to prevent one person from harming another. Because freedom is a basic right, libertarians claim that people must be left to do whatever they want with their own property and wealth. In this view, governments may tax citizens in order to finance the police and militia that are needed to prevent people from harming each other, but not for the sake of financing social welfare programs for the needy or providing foreign aid to less wealthy nations. A tax whose only purpose is to provide assistance for the needy is, to the libertarian, a form of forced theft if it is imposed on citizens who are unwilling to provide that assistance. For this reason, the tax is immoral. Thus, a libertarian government has no obligation to provide aid for the needy, and the Isaac Williamsons, Holly Reeds, Anita

1. *Los Angeles Times*, December 26, 1982.
2. There are several fine anthologies of articles that discuss these issues: William Aiken and Hugh La Follette, eds., *World Hunger and Moral Obligation* (Englewood Cliffs, N.J.: Prentice-Hall, 1977); Peter G. Brown and Douglas MacLean, eds., *Human Rights and U.S. Foreign Policy* (Lexington, Mass.: Lexington Books, 1979); Peter G. Brown and Henry Shue, eds., *Food Policy: The Responsibility of the United States in the Life and Death Choices* (New York: Free Press, 1977); George Lucas and Thomas W. Ogletree, eds., *Lifeboat Ethics* (New York: Harper and Row, 1976).
3. This is the view of Robert Nozick, *Anarchy, State and Utopia* (New York: Basic Books, 1974).

Webers, and Sheila Wilkersons of the world should not look to such a government for aid.

Some thinkers also believe that private individuals have no significant obligations in regard to the needy. To them, one's first duty is to provide for oneself and those one loves or those to whom one has special obligations, such as family members. If anything is left over, then it is meritorious but not obligatory to help those who are less fortunate. In other words, the needy do not have any moral claims on the property and wealth of others.

This view has also been advanced by two highly influential American philosophies, the Puritan ethic and social Darwinism.[4] The Puritan ethic, which developed in this country during the colonial period, held that every person had a religious obligation to work hard at his "calling," and that God justly rewarded hard work with wealth and success, while justly punishing laziness with poverty and failure. Today this Puritan ethic has evolved into a secularized work ethic that places a high value on personal effort and assumes that since hard work leads to success, poverty must be a shameful sign of laziness that should be punished.

Social Darwinism, a nineteenth-century philosophy, held that just as competition in the animal world ensures the survival of the fittest, so free competition in human societies ensures that only the best people succeed. And just as survival of the fittest results in the continuing progress and improvement of an animal species, so the free competition that enriches some individuals and reduces others to poverty will result in the gradual improvement of the human race. Because of this, governments should not interfere with competition, however harsh it may be, since this would only impede progress by allowing misfits to survive.

Both the Puritan ethic and social Darwinism come to the same conclusion: poverty is the fault of the poor. Thus, anyone who is poor is either lazy or defective, and in either case he should feel shame and should not ask for handouts. In other words, to rely on aid is to admit that you are lazy or defective. The influence of these philosophies is evident in the views of some of the needy people described earlier. Consider, for example, the attitude of Michael Reed: "He's got some pride. He didn't want to go on welfare." Similarly, Sheila Wilkerson says that "the hardest part of my life" was having to ask for housing at the Samaritan Shelter. But the view that poverty is the fault of the poor is perhaps most evident in the arguments some philosophers make concerning aid to poor foreign nations—that if they are impoverished it is the fault of their governments or their populations. In either case, wealthy nations should not help them out since this would merely make their problems worse.[5]

4. On the Puritan work ethic, see A. Whitner Griswold, "Three Puritans on Prosperity," *The New England Quarterly*, vol. 7 (1934), pp. 475–88, and Daniel T. Rodgers, *The Work Ethic in Industrial America* (Chicago: University of Chicago Press, 1978). On social Darwinism, see Richard Hofstadter, *Social Darwinism in American Thought* (Boston: Beacon Press, 1955) and Donald Fleming, "Social Darwinism," in Arthur Schlesinger, Jr., and Morton White, eds., *Paths of American Thought* (Boston: Houghton Mifflin, 1970), pp. 123–46.

5. This is the view of Garrett Hardin in "Living on a Lifeboat," *Bioscience*, vol. 24 (October 1974) and "The Tragedy of the Commons," *Science*, vol. 162 (December 13, 1968).

The less harsh view on aid to the needy is often called the liberal one. According to this perspective, people have a right to be provided with whatever goods they must have to meet their basic needs.[6] The United Nations 1948 "Universal Declaration of Human Rights," for example, is a liberal document that states that every human being has a right to basic "food, clothing, housing, and medical care." Because each person has a right to these basic necessities, other people and governments have a duty to provide them when a person is unable to do so for himself. Thus, in the liberal view, governments and individuals must give aid to the needy. Individuals have a duty to provide for others, and governments also have an obligation to tax their citizens to finance such aid whenever necessary.

A final influential position is that of the socialist.[7] There are various kinds of socialist philosophies, but a fundamental element of most of them is the idea that societies should be communities in which benefits and burdens are distributed on the model of the family. Just as able individuals willingly contribute to the family, and just as needy individuals are willingly supported by the family, so also should the more fortunate members of a society take up its burdens, allowing the needy to share in its benefits. Many socialists also espouse the position known as egalitarianism: that everyone should be given an equal share in society's benefits. Critics of this position, however, have argued that socialism simply won't work. They point out that human nature is essentially self-interested, and that outside the family people cannot be motivated by such fraternal willingness to share and help. In their opinion, people simply would not be motivated to work if they knew they would receive the same rewards, whether they worked or not.

The articles in this chapter discuss the various issues raised by the positions we have been discussing. All of them are concerned with the question, "What are our obligations to the needy?" In "Famine, Affluence, and Morality," Peter Singer, a utilitarian, addresses the problem of starvation. He begins with an apparently uncontroversial pair of assumptions: (1) suffering and death from lack of food, shelter, and medical care are bad, and (2) if it is in our power to prevent something bad from happening, without thereby sacrificing anything of comparable moral importance, we ought, morally, to do it. These assumptions, however, lead to some provocative conclusions. If we accept them, Singer says we can no longer morally distinguish duty from charity because one's obligation is to do that which will prevent another person from starving. If Singer is right, people would be obligated to introduce significant changes into their attitudes and their lives.

---

For a critical evaluation of Hardin, see Daniel Callahan, "Doing Well by Doing Good: Garrett Hardin's 'Lifeboat Ethic,' " *The Hastings Center Report*, vol. 4 (December 1974).

6. For an example of this view, see Henry Shue, *Basic Rights: Subsistence, Affluence, and U. S. Foreign Policy* (Princeton, N.J.: Princeton University Press, 1980).

7. The socialist viewpoint is presented alongside libertarian, utilitarian, and liberal points of view in John Arthus and William H. Shaw, eds., *Justice and Economic Distribution* (Englewood Cliffs, N.J.: Prentice-Hall, 1978).

In the next article, "Carrying Capacity as an Ethical Concept," Garrett Hardin looks at foreign aid from a utilitarian perspective but reaches conclusions diametrically opposed to those of Singer. Hardin starts by examining the concept of the "commons," an area owned by a community and available for any herdsman to use as grazing ground. So long as the commons is not overpopulated, all works smoothly. But in a situation of overpopulation, the commons will go to ruin because "each herdsman has more to gain individually by increasing the size of his herd than he has to lose by . . . lowering the carrying capacity" of the commons. (By "carrying capacity" Hardin means the number of organisms that can be supported by a given environment.) This concept of an overpopulated commons is important to Hardin's views, for he argues that an overpopulated country is like an overpopulated commons. Such countries would actually be harmed if they were provided with limited foreign aid (which is all other countries can provide), especially if they were provided with food. For with additional food, more people in the disadvantaged country would survive and thus consume even more of the limited resources of their common areas. This irretrievably depletes the natural resources of the already disadvantaged country (like a commons that is overgrazed until it can no longer produce grass), and the disadvantaged country will then never be able to better itself. Thus, it is wrong to provide such aid.

Alan Gewirth is also concerned with famine relief. In his essay, "Starvation and Human Rights," he claims that freedom and well-being are both fundamental rights because a person cannot act voluntarily unless he attributes these rights to himself. (Gewirth's position has similarities to Kant's argument that a person cannot act unless he attributes freedom to himself. Gewirth calls freedom and well-being "generic features" of action. Moreover, Gewirth claims that it would be a contradiction for me to hold that I have these rights but that others do not. (Here again, Gewirth's position is an echo of Kant.) Since freedom and well-being are also necessary generic features of the voluntary acts of other people, if they are fundamental rights for me, they are fundamental rights for others as well. Gewirth expresses this conclusion in what he calls the "Principle of Generic Consistency": "Act in accord with the generic rights of your recipients as well as of yourself." In light of this Kantian analysis, Gewirth argues that the needy have a right not only to freedom but also to the goods that are necessary for their well-being. But how is the right to freedom of the wealthy person to be balanced against the right to well-being of the needy? Can the wealthy person be forced to help the needy or would this violate the wealthy person's freedom? Gewirth replies that the rights of starving people to be fed take precedence over others' rights to make use of their property as they wish because the former are more important. Gewirth ends by applying his principle to nations as well as individuals, arguing that starving nations likewise have a right to what is necessary for well-being and that nations with a surplus have the duty to feed them.

James Sterba also seeks to determine how the right of private property and the right to life should be ranked against one another. And in his essay, "Human Rights: A Social Contract Perspective," he provides a Rawlsian social contract method of answering this question, stating that the more important right is the one that will best satisfy people's basic needs—that is, their needs for "food, shelter, medical care, protection, companionship, and self-development." Sterba then answers objections that might be offered by a libertarian, socialist, and a natural law theorist.

In the final essay, "The Concept of Health and the Right to Health Care," Joseph Boyle discusses the obligation to provide medical care to the needy citizens of one's own nation. He argues from a natural law position, concluding that health is a basic good of all persons. Thus, because the aim of health care is to provide the basic good of health, everyone is entitled to whatever care is necessary to attain or maintain that basic good. In other words, the recognition of and the commitment to the achievement of the basic good of health generates the right to health care.

# FAMINE, AFFLUENCE, AND MORALITY

*Peter Singer*

*Singer's premise*

. . . I begin with the assumption that suffering and death from lack of food, shelter, and medical care are bad. I think most people will agree about this, although one may reach the same view by different routes. I shall not argue for this view. People can hold all sorts of eccentric positions, and perhaps from some of them it would not follow that death by starvation is in itself bad. It is difficult, perhaps impossible, to refute such positions, and so for brevity I will henceforth take this assumption as accepted. Those who disagree need read no further.

My next point is this: if it is in our power to prevent something bad from happening, without thereby sacrificing anything of comparable moral importance, we ought, morally, to do it. By "without sacrificing anything of comparable moral importance" I mean without causing anything else comparably bad to happen, or doing something that is wrong in itself, or failing to promote some moral good, comparable in significance to the bad thing that we can prevent. This principle seems almost as uncontroversial as the last one. It requires us only to prevent what is bad, and not to promote what is good, and it requires this of us only when we can do it without sacrificing anything that is, from the moral point of view, comparably important. I could even, as far as the application of my

From Peter Singer, "Famine, Affluence, and Morality," *Philosophy and Public Affairs,* vol. 1, no. 3 (Spring 1972), pp. 231–35, 238–40, 242–43. Copyright © 1972 by Princeton University Press. Excerpts reprinted by permission of Princeton University Press.

argument to the Bengal emergency is concerned, qualify the point so as to make it: if it is in our power to prevent something very bad from happening, without thereby sacrificing anything morally significant, we ought, morally, to do it. An application of this principle would be as follows: if I am walking past a shallow pond and see a child drowning in it, I ought to wade in and pull the child out. This will mean getting my clothes muddy, but this is insignificant, while the death of the child would presumably be a very bad thing.

The uncontroversial appearance of the principle just stated is deceptive. If it were acted upon, even in its qualified form, our lives, our society, and our world would be fundamentally changed. For the principle takes, firstly, no account of proximity or distance. It makes no moral difference whether the person I can help is a neighbor's child ten yards from me or a Bengali whose name I shall never know, ten thousand miles away. Secondly, the principle makes no distinction between cases in which I am the only person who could possibly do anything and cases in which I am just one among millions in the same position.

I do not think I need to say much in defense of the refusal to take proximity and distance into account. The fact that a person is physically near to us, so that we have personal contact with him, may make it more likely that we *shall* assist him, but this does not show that we *ought* to help him rather than another who happens to be further away. If we accept any principle of impartiality, universalizability, equality, or whatever, we cannot discriminate against someone merely because he is far away from us (or we are far away from him). Admittedly, it is possible that we are in a better position to judge what needs to be done to help a person near to us than one far away, and perhaps also to provide the assistance we judge to be necessary. If this were the case, it would be a reason for helping those near to us first. This may once have been a justification for being more concerned with the poor in one's own town than with famine victims in India. Unfortunately for those who like to keep their moral responsibilities limited, instant communication and swift transportation have changed the situation. From the moral point of view, the development of the world into a "global village" has made an important, though still unrecognized, difference to our moral situation. Expert observers and supervisors, sent out by famine relief organizations or permanently stationed in famine-prone areas, can direct our aid to a refugee in Bengal almost as effectively as we could get it to someone in our own block. There would seem, therefore, to be no possible justification for discriminating on geographical grounds.

There may be a greater need to defend the second implication of my principle—that the fact that there are millions of other people in the same position, in respect to the Bengali refugees, as I am, does not make the situation significantly different from a situation in which I am the only person who can prevent something very bad from occurring. Again, of course, I admit that there is a psychological difference between the cases; one feels less guilty about doing nothing if one can point to others, similarly placed, who have also done nothing. Yet this can make no real difference to our moral obligations. Should I consider that I am less obliged to pull the drowning child out of the pond if on looking around I see other people, no further away than I am, who have also noticed the child but are doing nothing? One has only to ask this question to see the absurdity of the view that numbers lessen obligation. It is a view that is an ideal excuse for inactivity; unfortunately most of the major evils—poverty, overpopulation, pollution—are problems in which everyone is almost equally involved.

The view that numbers do make a difference can be made plausible if stated in this way: if everyone in circumstances like mine gave £5 to the Bengal Relief Fund, there would be enough to provide food, shelter, and medical care for the refugees; there is no reason why I should give more than anyone else in the same circumstances as I am; therefore I have no obligation to give more than £5. Each premise in this argument is true, and the argument looks sound. It may convince us, unless we notice that it is based on a hypothetical premise, although the conclusion is not stated hypothetically. The argument would be sound if the conclusion were: if everyone in circumstances like mine were to give £5, I would have no obligation to give more than £5. If the conclusion were so stated, however, it would be obvious that the argument has no bearing on a situation in which it is not the case that everyone else gives £5. This, of course, is the actual situation. It is more or less certain that not everyone in circumstances like mine will give £5. So there will not be enough to provide the needed food, shelter, and medical care. Therefore by giving more than £5 I will prevent more suffering than I would if I gave just £5.

It might be thought that this argument has an absurd consequence. Since the situation appears to be that very few people are likely to give substantial amounts, it follows that I and everyone else in similar circumstances ought to give as much as possible, that is, at least up to the point at which by giving more one would begin to cause serious suffering for oneself and one's dependents—perhaps even beyond this point to the point of marginal utility, at which by giving more one would cause oneself and one's dependents as much suffering as one would prevent in Bengal. If everyone does this, however, there will be more than can be used for the benefit of the refugees, and some of the sacrifice will have been unnecessary. Thus, if everyone does what he ought to do, the result will not be as good as it would be if everyone did a little less than he ought to do, or if only some do all that they ought to do.

The paradox here arises only if we assume that the actions in question—sending money to relief funds—are performed more or less simultaneously, and are also unexpected. For if it is to be expected that everyone is going to contribute something, then clearly each is not obliged to give as much as he would have been obliged to had others not been giving too. And if everyone is not acting more or less simultaneously, then those giving later will know how much more is needed, and will have no obligation to give more than is necessary to reach this amount. To say this is not to deny the principle that people in the same circumstances have the same obligations, but to point out that the fact that others have given, or may be expected to give, is a relevant circumstance: those giving after it has become known that many others are giving and those giving before are not in the same circumstances. So the seemingly absurd consequence of the principle I have put forward can occur only if people are in error about the actual circumstances—that is, if they think they are giving when others are not, but in fact they are giving when others are. The result of everyone doing what he really ought to do cannot be worse than the result of everyone doing less than he ought to do, although the result of everyone doing what he reasonably believes he ought to do could be.

If my argument so far has been sound, neither our distance from a preventable evil nor the number of other people who, in respect to that evil, are in the same situation as we are, lessens our obligation to mitigate or prevent that evil. I shall therefore take as established the principle I asserted earlier. As I have already said, I need to assert it only in its qualified form: if it is in our power to prevent something very bad from happening, without thereby sacrificing anything else morally significant, we ought, morally, to do it.

The outcome of this argument is that our traditional moral categories are upset. The traditional distinction between duty and charity cannot be drawn, or at least, not in the place we normally draw it. Giving money to the Bengal Relief Fund is regarded as an act of charity in our society. The bodies which collect money are known as "charities." These organizations see themselves in this way—if you send them a check, you will be thanked for your "generosity." Because giving money is regarded as an act of charity, it is not thought that there is anything wrong with not giving. The charitable man may be praised, but the man who is not charitable is not condemned. People do not feel in any way ashamed or guilty about spending money on new clothes or a new car instead of giving it to famine relief. (Indeed, the alternative does not occur to them.) This way of looking at the matter cannot be justified. When we buy new clothes not to keep ourselves warm but to look "well-dressed" we are not providing for any important need. We would not be sacrificing anything significant if we were to continue to wear our old clothes, and give the money to famine relief. By doing so, we would be preventing another person from starving. It follows from what I have said earlier that we ought to give money away, rather than spend it on clothes which we do not need to keep us warm. To do so is not charitable, or generous. Nor is it the kind of act which philosophers and theologians have called "supererogatory"—an act which it would be good to do, but not wrong not to do. On the contrary, we ought to give the money away, and it is wrong not to do so. . . .

It may still be thought that my conclusions are so wildly out of line with what everyone else thinks and has always thought that there must be something wrong with the argument somewhere. In order to show that my conclusions, while certainly contrary to contemporary Western moral standards, would not have seemed so extraordinary at other times and in other places, I would like to quote a passage from a writer not normally thought of as a way-out radical, Thomas Aquinas.

Now, according to the natural order instituted by divine providence,

material goods are provided for the satisfaction of human needs. Therefore the division and appropriation of property, which proceeds from
human law, must not hinder the satisfaction of man's necessity from such
goods. Equally, whatever a man has in superabundance is owed, of natural right, to the poor for their sustenance. So Ambrosius says, and it is
also to be found in the *Decretum Gratiani:* "The bread which you withhold
belongs to the hungry; the clothing you shut away, to the naked; and the
money you bury in the earth is the redemption and freedom of the
penniless."[1]

I now want to consider a number of points, more practical than
philosophical, which are relevant to the application of the moral conclusion we have reached. These points challenge not the idea that we ought
to be doing all we can to prevent starvation, but the idea that giving away
a great deal of money is the best means to this end.

It is sometimes said that overseas aid should be a government responsibility, and that therefore one ought not to give to privately run
charities. Giving privately, it is said, allows the government and the non-
contributing members of society to escape their responsibilities.

This argument seems to assume that the more people there are who
give to privately organized famine relief funds, the less likely it is that the
government will take over full responsibility for such aid. This assumption is unsupported, and does not strike me as at all plausible. The opposite view—that if no one gives voluntarily, a government will assume that
its citizens are uninterested in famine relief and would not wish to be
forced into giving aid—seems more plausible. In any case, unless there
were a definite probability that by refusing to give one would be helping
to bring about massive government assistance, people who do refuse to
make voluntary contributions are refusing to prevent a certain amount of
suffering without being able to point to any tangible beneficial consequence of their refusal. So the onus of showing how their refusal will
bring about government action is on those who refuse to give. . . .

Another, more serious reason for not giving to famine relief funds is
that until there is effective population control, relieving famine merely
postpones starvation. If we save the Bengal refugees now, others, perhaps
the children of these refugees, will face starvation in a few years' time. In
support of this, one may cite the now well-known facts about the population explosion and the relatively limited scope for expanded production.

This point, like the previous one, is an argument against relieving
suffering that is happening now, because of a belief about what might
happen in the future; it is unlike the previous point in that very good
evidence can be adduced in support of this belief about the future. I will
not go into the evidence here. I accept that the earth cannot support
indefinitely a population rising at the present rate. This certainly poses a
problem for anyone who thinks it important to prevent famine. Again,

1. *Summa Theologica,* II-II, Question 66, Article 7, in *Aquinas, Selected Political Writings,*
ed. A. P. d'Entreves, trans. J. G. Dawson (Oxford, 1948), p. 171.

however, one could accept the argument without drawing the conclusion that it absolves one from any obligation to do anything to prevent famine. The conclusion that should be drawn is that the best means of preventing famine, in the long run, is population control. It would then follow from the position reached earlier that one ought to be doing all one can to promote population control (unless one held that all forms of population control were wrong in themselves, or would have significantly bad consequences). Since there are organizations working specifically for population control, one would then support them rather than more orthodox methods of preventing famine.

Discussion, though, is not enough. What is the point of relating philosophy to public (and personal) affairs if we do not take our conclusions seriously? In this instance, taking our conclusion seriously means acting upon it. The philosopher will not find it any easier than anyone else to alter his attitudes and way of life to the extent that, if I am right, is involved in doing everything that we ought to be doing. At the very least, though, one can make a start. The philosopher who does so will have to sacrifice some of the benefits of the consumer society, but he can find compensation in the satisfaction of a way of life in which theory and practice, if not yet in harmony, are at least coming together.

# CARRYING CAPACITY AS AN ETHICAL CONCEPT

*Garrett Hardin*

Lifeboat ethics is merely a special application of the logic of the commons. The classic paradigm is that of a pasture held as common property by a community and governed by the following rules: first, each herdsman may pasture as many cattle as he wishes on the commons; and second, the gain from the growth of cattle accrues to the individual owners of the cattle. In an underpopulated world the system of the commons may do no harm and may even be the most economic way to manage things, since management costs are kept to a minimum. In an overpopulated (or overexploited) world a system of the commons leads to ruin, because each herdsman has more to gain individually by increasing

Abridged from Garrett Hardin, "Carrying Capacity as an Ethical Concept," in George R. Lucas, Jr., and Thomas W. Ogletree, eds., *Lifeboat Ethics: The Moral Dilemmas of World Hunger* (New York: Harper & Row, 1976), pp. 120–31. Copyright © 1976 by Vanderbilt University and The Society for Values in Higher Education. Reprinted by permission of Harper & Row, Publishers, Inc.

the size of his herd than he has to lose as a single member of the community guilty of lowering the carrying capacity of the environment. Consequently he (with others) overloads the commons.

Even if an individual fully perceives the ultimate consequences of his actions he is most unlikely to act in any other way, for he cannot count on the restraint *his* conscience might dictate being matched by a similar restraint on the part of *all* the others. (Anything less than all is not enough.) Since mutual ruin is inevitable, it is quite proper to speak of the *tragedy* of the commons.

Tragedy is the price of freedom in the commons. Only by changing to some other system (socialism or private enterprise, for example) can ruin be averted. In other words, in a crowded world survival requires that some freedom be given up. (We have, however, a choice in the freedom to be sacrificed.) Survival is possible under several different politico-economic systems—but not under the system of the commons. When we understand this point, we reject the ideal of distributive justice stated by Karl Marx a century ago, "From each according to his ability, to each according to his needs." This ideal might be defensible if "needs" were defined by the larger community rather than by the individual (or individual political unit) *and if "needs" were static.* But in the past quarter-century, with the best will in the world, some humanitarians have been asserting that rich populations must supply the needs of poor populations even though the recipient populations increase without restraint. At the United Nations conference on population in Bucharest in 1973 spokesmen for the poor nations repeatedly said in effect: "We poor people have the right to reproduce as much as we want to; you in the rich world have the responsibility of keeping us alive."

Such a Marxian disjunction of rights and responsibilities inevitably tends toward tragic ruin for all. It is almost incredible that this position is supported by thoughtful persons, but it is. How does this come about? In part, I think, because language deceives us. When a disastrous loss of life threatens, people speak of a "crisis," implying that the threat is temporary. More subtle is the implication of quantitative stability built into the pronoun "they" and its relatives. Let me illustrate this point with quantified prototype statements based on two different points of view.

*Crisis analysis:* "*These* poor people (1,000,000) are starving, because of a crisis (flood, drought, or the like). How can we refuse *them* (1,000,000)? Let us feed *them* (1,000,000). Once the crisis is past those who are still hungry are few (say 1,000) and there is no further need for our intervention."

*Crunch analysis:* "*Those* (1,000,000) who are hungry are reproducing. We send food to *them* (1,010,000). *Their* lives (1,020,000) are saved. But since the environment is still essentially the same, the next year *they* (1,030,000) ask for more food. We send it to *them* (1,045,000); and the next year *they* (1,068,000) ask for still more. Since the need has not gone away, it is a mistake to speak of a passing crisis: it is evidently a permanent crunch that this growing 'they' face—a growing disaster, not a passing state of affairs."

"They" increases in size. Rhetoric makes no allowance for a balloon-ing pronoun. Thus we can easily be deceived by language. We cannot deal adequately with ethical questions if we ignore quantitative matters. This attitude has been rejected by James Sellers, who dismisses prophets of doom from Malthus to Meadows as "chiliasts." Chiliasts (or millenialists, to use the Latin-derived equivalent of the Greek term) predict a catastrophic end of things a thousand years from some reference point. The classic example is the prediction of Judgment Day in the year 1000 anno Do-mini. Those who predicted it were wrong, of course; but the fact that this specific prediction was wrong is no valid criticism of the use of numbers in thinking. Millenialism is numerology, not science.

In science, most of the time, it is not so much exact numbers that are important as it is the relative size of numbers and the direction of change in the magnitude of them. Much productive analysis is accomplished with only the crude quantitation of "order of magnitude" thinking. First and second derivatives are often calculated with no finer aim than to find out if they are positive or negative. Survival can hinge on the crude issue of the sign of change, regardless of number. This is a far cry from the spurious precision of numerology. Unfortunately the chasm between the "two cul-tures," as C. P. Snow called them, keeps many in the non-scientific culture from understanding the significance of the quantitative approach. One is tempted to wonder also whether an additional impediment to understand-ing may not be the mortal sin called Pride, which some theologians regard as the mother of all sins.

Returning to Marx, it is obvious that the *each* in "to each according to his needs" is not—despite the grammar—a unitary, stable entity: "each" is a place-holder for a ballooning variable. Before we commit ourselves to saving the life of *each* and every person in need we had better ask this question: "*And then what?*" That is, what about tomorrow, what about posterity? As Hans Jonas has pointed out, traditional ethics has almost entirely ignored the claims of posterity. In an overpopulated world humanity cannot long endure under a regime governed by poster-ity-blind ethics. It is the essence of ecological ethics that it pays attention to posterity. . . .

[F]oreign aid is a tough nut to crack. The literature is large and contradictory, but it all points to the inescapable conclusion that a quarter of a century of earnest effort has not conquered world poverty. To many observers the threat of future disasters is more convincing now than it was a quarter of a century ago—and the disasters are not all in the future either. Where have we gone wrong in foreign aid?

We wanted to do good, of course. The question, "How can we help a poor country?" seems like a simple question, one that should have a simple answer. Our failure to answer it suggests that the question is not as simple as we thought. The variety of contradictory answers offered is dishearten-ing.

How can we find our way through this thicket? I suggest we take a cue from a mathematician. The great algebraist Karl Jacobi (1804–1851) had a simple stratagem that he recommended to students who found themselves butting their heads against a stone wall. *Umkehren, immer umkehren*—"Invert, always invert." Don't just keep asking the same old question over and over: turn it upside down and ask the opposite question. The answer you get then may not be the one you want, but it may throw useful light on the question you started with.

Let's try a Jacobian inversion of the food/population problem. To sharpen the issue, let us take a particular example, say India. The question we want to answer is, "How can we help India?" But since that approach has repeatedly thrust us against a stone wall, let's pose the Jacobian invert, "How can we *harm* India?" After we've answered this perverse question we will return to the original (and proper) one.

As a matter of method, let us grant ourselves the most malevolent of motives: let us ask, "How can we harm India—*really* harm her?" Of course we might plaster the country with thermonuclear bombs, speedily wiping out most of the 600 million people. But, to the truly malevolent mind, that's not much fun: a dead man is beyond harming. Bacterial warfare could be a bit "better," but not much. No: we want something that will really make India suffer, not merely for a day or a week, but on and on and on. How can we achieve this inhumane goal?

Quite simply: by sending India a bounty of food, year after year. The United States exports about 80 million tons of grain a year. Most of it we sell: the foreign exchange it yields we use for such needed imports as petroleum (38 percent of our oil consumption in 1974), iron ore, bauxite, chromium, tin, etc. But in the pursuit of our malevolent goal let us "unselfishly" tighten our belts, make sacrifices, and do without that foreign exchange. Let us *give* all 80 million tons of grain to the Indians each year.

On a purely vegetable diet it takes about 400 pounds of grain to keep one person alive and healthy for a year. The 600 million Indians need 120 million tons per year; since their nutrition is less than adequate presumably they are getting a bit less than that now. So the 80 million tons we give them will almost double India's per capita supply. With a surplus, Indians can afford to vary their diet by growing some less efficient crops; they can also convert some of the grain into meat (pork and chickens for the Hindus, beef and chickens for the Moslems). The entire nation can then be supplied not only with plenty of calories, but also with an adequate supply of high quality protein. The people's eyes will sparkle, their steps will become more elastic; and they will be capable of more work. "Fatalism" will no doubt diminish. (Much so-called fatalism is merely a consequence of malnutrition.) Indians may even become a bit overweight, though they will still be getting only two-thirds as much food as the average inhabitant of a rich country. Surely—we think—surely a well-fed India would be better off?

Not so: *ceteris paribus*, they will ultimately be worse off. Remember, "We can never do merely one thing." A generous gift of food would have not only nutritional consequences: it would also have political and economic consequences. The difficulty of distributing free food to a poor people is well known. Harbor, storage, and transport inadequacies result in great losses of grain to rats and fungi. Political corruption diverts food from those who need it most to those who are more powerful. More abundant supplies depress free market prices and discourage native farmers from growing food in subsequent years. Research into better ways of agriculture is also discouraged. Why look for better ways to grow food when there is food enough already?

There are replies, of sorts, to all the above points. It may be maintained that all these evils are only temporary ones: in time, organizational sense will be brought into the distributional system and the government will crack down on corruption. Realizing the desirability of producing more food, for export if nothing else, a wise government will subsidize agricultural research in spite of an apparent surplus. Experience does not give much support to this optimistic view, but let us grant the conclusions for the sake of getting on to more important matters. Worse is to come.

The Indian unemployment rate is commonly reckoned at 30 percent, but it is acknowledged that this is a minimum figure. *Under*-employment is rife. Check into a hotel in Calcutta with four small bags and four bearers will carry your luggage to the room—with another man to carry the key. Custom, and a knowledge of what the traffic will bear, decree this practice. In addition malnutrition justifies it in part. Adequately fed, half as many men would suffice. So one of the early consequences of achieving a higher level of nutrition in the Indian population would be to increase the number of unemployed.

India needs many things that food will not buy. Food will not diminish the unemployment rate (quite the contrary); nor will it increase the supply of minerals, bicycles, clothes, automobiles, gasoline, schools, books, movies, or television. All these things require energy for their manufacture and maintenance.

Of course, food is a form of energy, but it is convertible to other forms only with great loss; so we are practically justified in considering energy and food as mutually exclusive goods. On this basis the most striking difference between poor and rich countries is not in the food they eat but in the energy they use. On a per capita basis rich countries use about three times as much of the primary foods—grain and the like—as do poor countries. (To a large extent this is because the rich convert much of the grain to more "wasteful" animal meat.) But when it comes to energy, rich countries use ten times as much per capita. (Near the extremes Americans use 60 times as much per person as Indians.) By reasonable standards much of this energy may be wasted (e.g., in the manufacture of "exercycles" for sweating the fat off people who have eaten too much), but a large share of this energy supplies the goods we regard as civilized: effortless transportation, some luxury foods, a variety of sports, clean space-heating, more than adequate clothing, and energy-consuming arts—music, visual arts, electronic auxiliaries, etc. Merely giving food to a people does almost nothing to satisfy the appetite for any of these other goods.

But a well-nourished people is better fitted to try to wrest more energy from its environment. The question then is this: Is the native environment able to furnish more energy? And at what cost?

In India energy is already being gotten from the environment at a fearful cost. In the past two centuries millions of acres of India have been deforested in the struggle for fuel, with the usual environmental degradation. The Vale of Kashmir, once one of the garden spots of the world, has been denuded to such an extent that the hills no longer hold water as they once did, and the springs supplying the famous gardens are drying up. So desperate is the need for charcoal for fuel that the Kashmiri now make it out of tree leaves. This wasteful practice denies the soil of needed organic mulch.

Throughout India, as is well known, cow dung is burned to cook food. The minerals of the dung are not thereby lost, but the ability of dung to improve soil tilth is. Some of the nitrogen in the dung goes off into the air and does not return to Indian soil. Here we see a classic example of the "vicious circle": because Indians are poor they burn dung, depriving the soil of nitrogen and making themselves still poorer the following year. If we give them plenty of food, as they cook this food with cow dung they will lower still more the ability of their land to produce food. . . .

So the answer to our Jacobian question, "How can we harm India?" is clear: send food *only*. Escaping the Jacobian by reinverting the question we now ask, "How can we *help* India?" Immediately we see that we must *never* send food without a matching gift of non-food energy. But before we go careening off on an intoxicating new program we had better look at some more quantities.

On a per capita basis, India uses the energy equivalent of one barrel of oil per year; the U.S. uses sixty. The world average of all countries, rich and poor, is ten. If we want to bring India only up to the present world average, we would have to send India about $9 \times 600$ million bbls. of oil per year (or its equivalent in coal, timber, gas or whatever). That would be more than five billion barrels of oil equivalent. What is the chance that we will make such a gift?

Surely it is nearly zero. For scale, note that our total yearly petroleum use is seven billion barrels (of which we import three billion). Of course we use (and have) a great deal of coal too. But these figures should suffice to give a feeling of scale.

More important is the undoubted psychological fact that a fall in income tends to dry up the springs of philanthropy. Despite wide disagreements about the future of energy it is obvious that from now on, for at least the next twenty years and possibly for centuries, our per capita supply of energy is going to fall, year after year. The food we gave in the past was "surplus." By no accounting do we have an energy surplus. In fact, the perceived deficit is rising year by year.

India has about one-third as much land as the United States. She has about three times as much population. If her people-to-land ratio were the same as ours she would have only about seventy million people (instead of 600 million). With the forested and relatively unspoiled farmlands of four centuries ago, seventy million people was probably well within the carrying capacity of the land. Even in today's India, seventy

million people could probably make it in comfort and dignity—provided
they didn't increase!

To send food only to a country already populated beyond the carrying capacity of its land is to collaborate in the further destruction of the
land and the further impoverishment of its people.

Food plus energy is a recommendable policy; but for a large population under today's conditions this policy is defensible only by the logic of
the old saying, "If wishes were horses, beggars would ride." The fantastic
amount of energy needed for such a program is simply not in view. (We
have mentioned nothing of the equally monumental "infrastructure" of
political, technological, and educational machinery needed to handle unfamiliar forms and quantities of energy in the poor countries. In a short
span of time this infrastructure is as difficult to bring into being as is an
abundant supply of energy.)

In summary, then, here are the major foreign-aid possibilities that
tender minds are willing to entertain:

a. Food plus energy—a conceivable, but practically impossible program.

b. Food alone—a conceivable and possible program, but one which
would destroy the recipient.

. . . If *any* gift of food to overpopulated countries does more harm
than good, it is not necessary to decide which countries get the gift and
which do not. For posterity's sake we should never send food to any
population that is beyond the realistic carrying capacity of its land.


# STARVATION AND HUMAN RIGHTS

*Alan Gewirth*


Do persons threatened with starvation have a strict right to be given
food by those who have it in abundance? The question is, of course, far
from academic. But its analysis and development can throw light not only
on one of the most pressing moral issues of our time but also on the
ability of moral philosophy to deal with such issues. The reason why this
ability is called into question is that the topic of rights and duties bearing
on relief of starvation involves serious conflicts both of interests and of

From Alan Gewirth, "Starvation and Human Rights," in K. E. Goodpaster and K. M. Sayre,
eds, *Ethics and Problems of the 21st Century* (Notre Dame, Ind.: University of Notre Dame
Press, 1979), pp. 139–59. Copyright, 1979, University of Notre Dame Press, Notre Dame,
Indiana 46556. Professor Gewirth's article has been abridged for the purpose of this anthology.

moral criteria. The capacity of a moral philosophy for clarifying and resolving such conflicts provides an important test of its adequacy.

## I

. . . We may distinguish at least two criterial questions about moral rights. First, there is the general question: How, if at all, can it be known that any persons have any such rights? Second, there is the more specific question: Who has moral rights to what, and how, if at all, can this be known? Both questions ask for the ground or reason for having moral rights. Although moral rights, by definition, have moral grounds or criteria, there still remain the questions of whether moral reasons can justify anyone's having rights at all, what are those reasons, and what rights do they justify as belonging to which persons. . . .

I shall now approach the problem of the criterion for having rights through their familiar connection with claims. . . .

All moral and other practical precepts, regardless of their varying specific contents, are concerned directly or indirectly with how persons ought to act. Insofar as actions are the possible objects of any such precepts, they are performed by purposive agents. As is shown by the endeavor which each agent contributes to achieving his purposes, he regards his purposes as good according to whatever criteria (not necessarily moral ones) are involved in his acting to fulfill them. Hence, the agent also a fortiori regards as necessary goods the proximate necessary conditions of his acting to achieve his purposes. These conditions, which pertain alike to all actual or prospective agents, are freedom and well-being, where freedom consists in controlling one's behavior by one's unforced choice while having knowledge of relevant circumstances, and well-being consists in having the other general abilities and conditions required for agency. . . . I shall call freedom and well-being the *generic features* of action, since they characterize all action, or at least all successful action, in the respect in which "action" has been delimited above.

Every rational agent logically must claim or accept, at least implicitly, that he has rights to freedom and well-being. If any agent were to deny that he has these rights, he would contradict himself. For in holding, as he rationally must, that freedom and well-being are necessary conditions of his agency, he holds that they are necessary goods; and because of his conative attachment to his purposes he holds that it is necessary that he have these goods in that he (prudentially) ought to have them. The meaning of this "ought" includes the idea of necessary restrictions on the interference of other persons with his having freedom and well-being. The agent holds that these restrictions are justified and are owed to him, from the standpoint of his own prudential purposes, because of their necessity for his engaging in action. If he were to deny that he has rights to freedom and well-being, then he would hold that it is permissible for other persons to interfere with his having these goods, so that it is all right that he not have them. This, however, would contradict his conviction that it is necessary that he have them because they are necessary goods without which he cannot be an agent. Hence, every agent must hold or claim, on pain of self-contradiction, that he has rights to freedom and well-being. I shall call them *generic rights,* because they are rights to the generic features of action. They are not yet moral rights but only prudential ones, since their ground is the agent's own pursuit of his purposes, whatever they may be. For the rights to be also moral ones, they must be shown to have a further ground in the agent's favorable consideration of the purposes or interests of other persons besides himself. Let us see why the agent must also take this further step.

Every agent must hold that he has the generic rights on the ground or for the sufficient reason that he is a prospective agent who has purposes he wants to fulfill. Suppose some agent A were to hold that he has these rights only for some more restrictive reason R. Since this would entail that in lacking R he would lack the generic rights, A would thereby contradict himself. For since, as was shown above, it is necessarily true of every agent that he holds implicitly that he has rights to freedom and well-being, A would be in the position of saying both that he has the generic rights and that, as lacking R, he does not have these rights. Thus, on pain of self-contradiction, every agent must accept the generalization that all prospective purposive agents have the generic rights, because, as we have seen, he must hold that being a prospective purposive agent is a sufficient condition or reason for having the generic rights. This generalization entails that the agent ought to refrain from interfering with the freedom and well-being of all other persons insofar as they are prospective purposive agents. Since to refrain from such interference is to act in such a way that one's actions are in accord with the generic rights of all other persons, every agent is logically committed, on pain of inconsistency, to accept the following precept: Act in accord with the generic rights of your recipients as well as of yourself. I shall call this the Principle of Generic Consistency (PGC), since it combines the formal consideration of consistency with the material consideration of the generic features and rights of agency. To act in accord with someone's right to freedom is to refrain from coercing him; to act in accord with someone's right to well-being is to refrain from harming him. These rights, as thus upheld, are now moral ones because they are concerned to further the interests or goods of persons other than or in addition to the agent.... The main point, put succinctly, is that what for any agent are necessarily goods of action, namely, freedom and well-being, are equally goods to his recipients, and he logically must admit that they have as much right to these goods as he does, since the ground or reason for which he rationally claims them for himself also pertains to his recipients. . . .

Since all humans are such agents, the generic rights to freedom and well-being are human rights. They are strict rights in that they entail correlative obligations on the part of persons other than the right-holder. But they are also primarily negative rights in that the primary obligation of these other persons is to refrain from interfering with the right-holder's freedom and well-being. There are, however, certain kinds of situations where, if some person A is inactive in the face of serious harm impending to another person B, A interferes with B's basic well-being. In such situations the PGC with its criterion of rights requires action rather than refraining from action because to refrain is to interfere with someone's basic well-being and hence constitutes a violation of his right to well-being. . . .

## II

. . . Such interference may occur in different ways. Persons may quite involuntarily cause obstacles to be put in the way of A's having food, with the result that he lacks food. For example, from ignorance of methods of scientific farming, from lack of required fertilizer, or through other circumstances beyond their control, persons may bring about a crop failure, with the result that A starves. Such persons do not, however, violate A's right to have food, for this violation would be a failure to fulfill their duty to refrain from interfering with A's having food—the duty which is entailed by A's having a right to food. Insofar as "ought" implies "can," since the persons in question are assumed to be unable to refrain from interfering with A's having food, it follows that they do not have the duty to refrain from such interference. (I here use "duty" in the general sense in which it is equivalent to a practical "ought," not in the more restricted sense in which it signifies a task assigned by social rules to some role or status.) Similarly, if other persons do not have enough food to supply their own minimal needs, then they are unable to provide food for A so that they have no duty to do so. Here again A's right to have food is so far not violated.

It is also possible that A may himself be the cause of his lack of food. He may intentionally starve himself for a variety of reasons, including a desire to lose weight or to go on a hunger strike. Or he may be too lazy to take care of himself or to work and hence to supply his basic needs. In such cases A's lack of food does not show that other persons have interfered with his having food; hence, they have not violated his right to have food.

In order to determine, then, whether A's right to have food has been violated and by whom, we must exclude both the involuntary actions and nonactions of other persons and the voluntary actions of A himself. What remains is the voluntary actions of other persons. For these persons to have the duty of supplying A with food, so that their interfering with his having food constitutes a violation of his right, they must both be aware that he lacks food from causes beyond his control and be able to repair this lack. They must have sufficient resources to have a surplus from their own basic food needs so as to be able to transfer some to A. By virtue of this ability, it is within their control to determine by their own unforced choice whether or not A has food. If, under these circumstances, A lacks food and they withhold food from him, then they voluntarily interfere with his having food and hence inflict basic harm on him. Thereby they violate his right to have food.

The better to understand this argument, which is derived from the PGC, let us apply it to a particular case of interpersonal morality. Suppose Ames, a bachelor, has a very large amount of food while Bates, another bachelor who lives nearby, is starving to death. None of the voluntary factors mentioned above applies to Bates. Ames knows of Bates's plight but doesn't want to give away any of his food, despite Bates's appeals for help. Bates dies of starvation.

In depicting this situation I have intentionally provided only the most meagre details about Bates's involuntary starvation, omitting all reference to any other psychological, historical, or institutional contexts. In the situation as thus depicted, the PGC supplies the sufficient ground for Ames's duty to give food to Bates. The principle prescribes, as a matter of strict duty, that agents refrain from inflicting basic harms on their recipients where such infliction violates the recipients' rights to basic well-being. But since Ames, in failing to give food to Bates, inflicts a basic harm on him, Ames violates Bates's right to food. Ames thereby violates a strict duty imposed by the PGC. Since to violate the PGC is to incur self-contradiction, Ames's violation is shown to lack the most basic kind of rational justification.

Certain questions must now be considered about this application of the PGC. The principle sets a requirement for every agent, that he act in accord with the generic rights of his recipients. Since, however, Ames is passive and inert in the face of Bates's starving, it may be objected that Ames is here not an agent and hence not subject to the PGC's requirement. In reply, we must note that for someone to be an agent he need not engage in gross physical movement; it is sufficient that he engages in voluntary and purposive behavior. Ames is here an agent because his inaction in the face of Bates's plight is something he unforcedly chooses for purposes of his own while knowing of Bates's urgent need for food. Bates, moreover, is here Ames's recipient, since Ames's intentional knowing inaction crucially affects Bates's effective possession of the right to basic well-being. If Ames had given food to Bates, Bates would not have died; since he did not give food to Bates, Bates died. . . .

## III

This conclusion has an obvious bearing on one of the central sociopolitical problems of our age: the extreme contrast between the great affluence of some nations and the great poverty of others, where millions of persons in Asia and Africa are threatened or actually engulfed by famine. . . .

The relation of states to one another may be assimilated to the relation between individual persons when one nation, through the actions of its government, is able to affect the basic well-being of sizeable numbers of persons in the other nation. It is true that these actions lack certain elements of the voluntariness or freedom and purposiveness which are the generic features of individual actions: In constitutional regimes the behavior of government officials is controlled and directed not by their individual choices and purposes but rather by legal rules. Nevertheless, insofar as these rules result in turn from the advocacy of individuals and groups within the society, the rules and the ensuing actions or inactions may be assimilated to the voluntary and purposive behavior of individual agents. And just as individuals implicitly claim rights to freedom and well-being on the ground of their being prospective purposive agents, a similar implicit claim may be attributed to states insofar as freedom and well-being are required at least for the actions of their corporate representatives as well as for the population at large. The recipient states, in turn, may also be assimilated to the individual recipients of particular actions, for at least two reasons. The states consist of individual persons who are prospective purposive agents, and their basic well-being may be drastically affected by the action or inaction of other states. The actions of states toward one another are not, then, devoid of the personal cognitive and volitional controls which characterize the actions of individuals so that the causal and moral responsibility found among the latter may also be attributed to the conduct of societies and their relevant political officials. Thus the requirements of personal morality may be extended, with due qualifications, to the morality of the relations between states or nations.

From this it follows that, just as Ames had a strict duty to give food to Bates, so Nation A has a strict duty to give food to Nation B where Nation A has an overabundance of food while Nation B lacks sufficient food to feed its population so that sizeable numbers are threatened with starvation. Nation B has a correlative strict right to be given this food, for it is relatively similar to Nation A in that regard in which the members of the latter implicitly claim for themselves rights to freedom and well-being. The members of Nation B, like those of Nation A, need food for survival and hence for agency, and they necessarily claim a right to food on this ground. To give this food is a moral duty for Nation A quite apart from considerations of self-interest. It may well be the case that underdeveloped nations will promote increasing international tension and unrest unless they are given relief from the pressures of underdevelopment and resulting insecurity, including the danger or actuality of famine. But even if such threatening tendencies can be kept securely in check, the moral duty is no less urgent.

# HUMAN RIGHTS: A SOCIAL CONTRACT PERSPECTIVE

*James P. Sterba*

There are many perspectives from which one might attempt to defend a conception of human rights. In this paper I argue that, from a social contract perspective, every human person possesses a right to life interpreted as a right to noninterference with that person's attempts to acquire the goods and resources necessary for satisfying his or her basic needs, and a right to property interpreted as a right to retain goods and resources acquired either by appropriation from nature or by voluntary agreement. I argue, moreover, that a person's right to life will generally have priority over other persons' rights to property. Finally, I defend this social contract justification of human rights against objections that arise from libertarian, socialist, and natural law perspectives.

The social contract perspective from which I defend this concept of human rights does not presuppose any actual agreement as the basis for a person's right to life or a person's right to property. Rather, with John Rawls, I contend that a suitably constrained hypothetical agreement suffices as the moral basis for such fundamental human rights. The main constraint I would place on such a hypothetical agreement is that the agreement be reached by persons who discount the knowledge of which particular interests happen to be their own. Persons who were so constrained obviously would know what their particular interests are; they would just not be taking that knowledge into account when agreeing to a conception of human rights. Rather, in agreeing to such a conception, they would be reasoning from their knowledge of all the particular interests of everyone affected by their agreement, but not from their knowledge of which particular interests happen to be their own. Persons who were so constrained would (like judges who discount prejudicial information in order to reach fair decisions) be able to give a fair hearing to everyone's particular interests. Assuming further that they were well-informed of the particular interests that would be affected by their agreement and were fully capable of rationally deliberating with respect to that information, then their deliberations would culminate in a unanimous agreement. This is because each of them would be deliberating in a rationally correct manner with respect to the same information and would be constrained so as to give a uniform evaluation of the alternatives; consequently, each of them would favor the same conception of human rights.

But what conception of human rights would result from such a constrained hypothetical agreement? Since in reaching such an agreement persons would not be using their knowledge of which particular interests happen to be their own, they would be quite concerned about the pattern according to which goods and resources happened to be distributed. They would be especially concerned that their particular interests might be either those of persons with the largest share of goods and resources or those of persons with the smallest share of goods and resources. On the one hand, if their interests were those of persons with the largest share of goods and resources then it would presumably be in their interest to favor a virtually unconditional right to property. On the other hand, if their interests were those of persons with the smallest share of goods and resources then it would presumably be in their interest to favor a virtually unconditional right to life. But it would not be reasonable for persons who have discounted their knowledge of which particular interests happen to be their own either to exclusively favor the interests of persons with the largest share of goods and resources by endorsing a virtually unconditional right to property or to favor exclusively the interests of persons with the smallest share of goods and resources by endorsing a virtually unconditional right of life. Rather it would be reasonable for them to compromise by endorsing a right to life interpreted as a right to noninterference with a person's attempts to acquire the goods and resources necessary for satisfying his or her basic needs and a right to property interpreted as a right to retain the goods and resources acquired by appropriation from nature or by free agreement provided that doing so does not violate anyone's right to life.

Now clearly the right to life that would be favored by persons constrained to discount the knowledge of which particular interests happen to be their own would not be as demanding as the right to life that would be most beneficial to those who have the smallest share of goods and resources. For the right to life that would be most beneficial to this group would be a virtually unconditional right to receive the highest possible minimum of goods and resources. By contrast, the right to life that would be favored by persons constrained to discount the knowledge of which particular interests happen to be their own normally would only require that others not interfere with a person's attempts to take advantage of opportunities made available by others for meeting his or her basic needs by engaging in mutually beneficial work. Only when such opportunities are not available or when the person is unable to take advantage of them would this right to life also require that others not interfere with the person's attempts simply to appropriate from the surplus possessions of the more advantaged what is required to meet his or her basic needs. And even when a person's right to life would make this more demanding requirement, there would still be an obligation to return the equivalent of those surplus possessions once the person is able to do so and still satisfy his or her basic needs.

Moreover, just as the right to life that would be favored by persons constrained to discount the knowledge of which particular interests happen to be their own would not be as demanding as the right to life that would be most beneficial to those who have the smallest share of goods and resources, so likewise the right to property favored by persons so constrained would not be as demanding as the right to property that would be most beneficial to those who have the largest share of goods and resources. For the right to property that would be most beneficial to this group would be a right to property that is unrestricted by a right to life under almost any interpretation. By contrast, the right to property favored by persons constrained to discount the knowledge of which particular interests happen to be their own would be a right to property that is restricted by a right to life under the favored interpretation.

Obviously by agreeing to this conception of human rights persons constrained to discount the knowledge of which particular interests happen to be their own would be giving priority to the satisfaction of people's basic needs. Now a person's basic needs are simply those needs which must be satisfied in order not to endanger seriously the person's health and sanity. Thus the needs a person has for food, shelter, medical care, protection, companionship, and self-development are at least in part needs of this sort. Naturally, societies vary in their ability to satisfy a person's basic needs but the needs themselves would not seem to be similarly subject to variation unless there were a corresponding variation in what constitutes health and sanity in different societies. Consequently, even though the criterion of need would not be an acceptable standard for distributing all social goods because, among other things, of the difficulty of determining both what a person's nonbasic needs are and how they should be arranged according to priority, the criterion of need does appear to be an acceptable standard for determining when a right to life should have priority over a right to property.

In order to better assess the merits of this social contract conception of human rights, let us now consider how this conception might be defended against representative objections from libertarian, socialist, and natural law perspectives.

First of all, from a libertarian perspective this social contract conception of human rights would appear to be flawed in its foundation. Libertarians, like Robert Nozick and John Hospers, might grant that persons who were so constrained to discount the knowledge of which particular interests happen to be their own would agree to this conception of human rights, but they would surely deny that such a constrained hypothetical agreement shows that the conception of human rights is morally defensible. For libertarians would maintain that the ultimate moral foundation for a conception of human rights is not a constrained hypothetical agreement but rather an ideal of liberty. Taking liberty to be the absence of interference by other persons, libertarians would contend that an ideal of liberty justifies a conception of human rights that is quite different from the conception that would emerge from a constrained hypothetical agreement. More specifically, libertarians would contend that an ideal of liberty justifies a conception of human rights which features a virtually unconditional right to property.

Suppose, however, for the sake of argument we accept a libertarian's contention that the ultimate moral foundation for a conception of human rights is an ideal of liberty and not a constrained hypothetical agreement. And suppose further that we also accept the libertarian's contention that liberty is to be understood as the absence of interference by other persons. From these assumptions it would follow that when the poor take what is necessary for meeting their basic needs from the surplus possessions of the rich (case 1), the poor would be restricting the liberty of the rich. But it also follows that when the rich interfere with the poor's taking what is necessary for meeting their basic needs from the surplus possessions of the rich (case 2), the rich would be restricting the liberty of the poor. For in both cases we have people performing actions that interfere with the actions of others. Thus given the practical impossibility of avoiding both of these competing restrictions of liberty, the key question is how to assess these restrictions from a moral point of view.

Libertarians, of course, would want to maintain that restricting the liberty of the poor as in case (2) is morally preferable to restricting the liberty of the rich as in case (1); but if we assume that, however else we specify the requirements of morality, they cannot be contrary to reason then it would seem that we cannot justify this preference. For while it would surely be contrary to reason to ask the poor to restrict their liberty as in case 2 and thus sacrifice the fulfillment of their basic needs, it would not at all seem contrary to reason to ask the rich to restrict their liberty as in case 1 and thus sacrifice the fulfillment of some of their nonbasic needs (e.g., their needs for exotic food, expensive wardrobes, and multiple dwellings). Surely restricting the liberty of the rich to satisfy their non-basic needs is morally preferable to restricting the liberty of the poor to satisfy their basic needs.

Needless to say, this moral preference for restricting the liberty of the rich depends upon the willingness of the poor to take advantage of whatever opportunities are available to them for satisfying their basic needs by engaging in mutually beneficial work, so that failure of the poor to take advantage of such opportunities would normally either cancel or at least significantly reduce the obligation of the rich to restrict their own liberty for the benefit of the poor. In addition, the poor would be required to return the equivalent of any surplus possessions they have simply taken from the rich once they are able to do so and still satisfy their basic needs. Accordingly, a moral assessment of the competing liberties as determined by the libertarian's ideal of liberty leads to the same conception of human rights as would emerge from a constrained hypothetical agreement. It follows, then, that even if we accepted the libertarian's contention that an ideal of liberty is the ultimate moral foundation for a conception of human rights we should still endorse a social contract conception of human rights.

Turning now to a socialist perspective, we find a more practical objection to a social contract conception of human rights. For socialists would contend that while a social contract conception of human rights has considerable merit as an ideal, it fails to make clear that the proper implementation of such an ideal would require socialization of the means of production. For example, C. B. Macpherson claims

> It is not difficult to show . . . that a socialist system can meet the requirements of [a social contract conception of human rights]. But it can do so not as a "modification" of the capitalist market system, but by its rejection of exploitative property institutions.

Nevertheless, for persons who accept a social contract conception of human rights, the question of whether or not to socialize the means of production may not be as momentous as Macpherson takes it to be. The reason for this is that in order for a system of private ownership of the means of production to satisfy the high minimum requirements of this conception, it would appear necessary to limit and redistribute private holdings to such a degree that the ownership of all the means of production would, as a result, be widely dispersed throughout the society. For example, in the United States where 5% of the population owns 83% of corporate stock and 63% of businesses and professions, the ownership of income-bearing investments would have to be significantly limited and redistributed in order to meet the requirements of this conception of human rights. As Marx pointed out, the widespread exploitation of laborers associated with early capitalism only began when large numbers "had been robbed of all their own means of production and of all the guarantees of existence afforded by the old feudal system" by persons and economic groups who already had considerable wealth and power. But the concentration of wealth and power necessary to carry out such exploitation is not likely to be found in a society which in accordance with a social contract conception of human rights provides for the basic needs of all its members as well as for the basic needs of distant peoples and future generations. Consequently, a shift from such restricted private ownership of the means of production to socialization of those means may in fact have little practical consequence.

Of course, socialists might respond that merely providing a minimum sufficient to satisfy the basic needs of each and every person does not go far enough in eliminating alienation and injustice from a society since these defects can manifest themselves in failure to satisfy nonbasic needs as well as basic needs. And it is just in this regard, so socialists might claim, that a socialist state would significantly differ from the welfare state usually endorsed by defenders of a social contract conception of human rights. For presumably in a welfare state after basic needs have been met, appropriation from nature and free agreement would determine the distribution of property, and hence, determine whose nonbasic needs would be satisfied whereas in a socialist state there would be a willingness to provide both for the basic and the nonbasic needs of each and every person.

But even granting that theoretically there may be this difference, practically speaking, in either a welfare state or a socialist state the scope for the satisfaction of nonbasic needs would be so drastically limited by the necessity of meeting not only the basic needs of the members of one's own society but also the basic needs of distant peoples and future generations as well that there would not appear to be any net benefit to be gained from enforcing some particular distribution of the relatively few social goods that could legitimately be used to satisfy nonbasic needs. Consequently, socialists would have little reason to object to a welfare state in which in accordance with a social contract conception of human rights people fulfill their obligation to provide a minimum for their fellow citizens as well as for distant peoples and future generations.

Finally, from a natural law perspective this social contract conception of human rights faces both a theoretical objection to its ultimate moral foundation and a practical objection to the completeness of its requirements.

The theoretical objection challenges the social contract theorist to show why the ultimate moral foundation for a conception of human rights should be a constrained hypothetical agreement rather than an adequate account of human nature. For at least some natural law theorists would surely maintain that grounding a conception of human rights on a constrained hypothetical agreement introduces an unwarranted element of conventionality into a conception of human rights. For such theorists, only by grounding a conception of human rights on an adequate account of human nature can we preserve the essential nonconventionality of a conception of human rights.

This theoretical objection to a social contract conception of human rights however, fails to take into account the fact that the constrained hypothetical agreement is itself made with a full appreciation of the morally relevant facts of human nature. Indeed, the only knowledge about human nature that is not taken into account in fashioning a social contract conception of human rights is the knowledge of which particular interests happen to belong to the persons making the constrained hypothetical agreement, and that knowledge, assuming that the social contract theorist is correct, is morally suspect and should be discounted. Thus, insofar as the knowledge of human nature can legitimately determine a conception of human rights, a social contract theorist can maintain that his conception of human rights would be determined by that knowledge. Accordingly, there is no reason to think that by employing a constrained hypothetical agreement, a social contract theorist cannot provide an essentially nonconventional moral foundation for a conception of human rights.

The second and more practical objection which natural law theorists would raise to this social contract conception of human rights concerns the completeness of the conception's practical requirements. For natural law theorists might grant that this social contract conception of human rights is correct as far as it goes. St. Thomas, for example, allowed that when there is no other remedy

> . . . it is lawful for a man to satisfy his own need by means of another's property, by taking it either openly or secretly. . . .

And obviously a claim of this sort is, practically speaking, quite close to the requirements of this social contract conception of human rights. But even granting that this social contract conception of human rights is correct as far as it goes, natural law theorists would still maintain that the conception is incomplete as a moral ideal, since, for example, it neither provides an account of self-regarding virtues nor an account of the requirements of supererogation.

Here, I think, it must be conceded that this objection is sound as an objection to the social contract theory so far elaborated. On the other hand, there does not seem to be any reason why this social contract theory could not be further elaborated to provide a relatively complete moral ideal. Particularly, once we recognize that a constrained hypothetical agreement can take into account all the morally relevant facts about human nature, there seems to be no reason to think that such an agreement could not be reached concerning a relatively complete moral ideal. Thus, while it is true that social contract theorists have generally directed their energies at determining basic human rights, there appears to be no reason why a social contract perspective might not also be used to determine a relatively complete moral ideal.

Summing up, I have argued that from a social contract perspective each human person possesses a right to life that places fairly strong demands on others to provide the means for meeting the person's basic needs and a right to property that is restricted by this right to life. I have also considered representative objections to this social contract conception of human rights arising from libertarian, socialist, and natural law perspectives. Of course, the fact that all of these objections proved ultimately unsuccessful does not suffice to show that some other objection might not yet succeed. However, given the representative character of the objections that have failed, there would seem to be a strong presumptive case in favor of this social contract conception of human rights.

# THE CONCEPT OF HEALTH AND THE RIGHT TO HEALTH CARE

*Joseph M. Boyle, Jr.*

The understanding that someone has a certain right plays an important role in ethics. The claim that someone has a right also plays an important role in political discourse. If one has an unqualified right, that

From Joseph M. Boyle, Jr., "The Concept of Health and the Right to Health Care," *Social Thought*, vol. 3, no. 3 (Summer 1977), pp. 10–15.

right must be honored; other moral and social considerations are cut short. Deliberation must stop. The right must be honored. However, claims to rights are often in conflict and in recent years the claims to rights have become extravagant. These facts suggest that claims to rights need justification. Such claims are not self-evident nor is the application of these claims in particular situations.

There are a number of ways to justify rights. I will briefly sketch only one of these—a kind of natural law justification.

Human beings recognize that certain basic goods or values are worthy of their allegiance and that the pursuit of these goods constitutes human flourishing. Life and health, friendship and peace, truth and beauty are some of these. We also recognize that these goods are the object not only of individual pursuit but are the goals of our common activity. The obligation placed on us by these goods is not only individual but also common. The community of men—like individuals—ought to pursue and respect these values. The community *respects* these values in much the same way as individuals do. A community should not act against these values as they are realized in the lives of its members and other people and communities, nor should it allow individuals within the community to do so. Thus, we have the foundation of such negative rights as the right to life, the right to religious expression, and so on.

When it comes to the *pursuing* of these values by the community, however, things become more complex. Not all communities need pursue all that is good, and the pursuit of different values in a complex community is undertaken by dividing labor, separating tasks, and thus creating roles. Thus, not everyone in a community pursues the values of the community in the same way. Moreover, this pursuit of values which are common to the entire community by diversification of roles generates positive duties on the part of those who fulfill the various roles and entitlements on the part of others in the community. These roles are founded upon the common commitment of the community to the values which define the roles. This fact implies that the person who carries out a role does so on behalf of the community and for the good of its members insofar as they share in the commitment to the good in question. Thus, the person fulfilling a role has certain duties and members of the community have certain claims upon the benefits achieved through his specialized activities.

This brief and abstract sketch is sufficient to show why there is a right to a degree of health care. The aim of health care is health, which is a perfection of bodily life. As such, it is a component of human life—a basic good for man. Moreover, we live in a complex community which *is* committed to this value. The medical professions carry out this commitment in a specialized way and should do so for the common good. Thus, there is an obligation that the medical professions provide the results of their specialized activities to the members of the community. Similarly, the members of the community are entitled to a fair measure of these results: they have a right to health care, and especially to that care which—because they do not as individuals have the expertise of the medical professions—they cannot provide for themselves.

On this account, the right to health care is not a tendentious slogan or a mysterious ethical absolute; rather, it arises from the same source as individual obligations—the human good. Our entitlement to health care arises from the common commitment we have to the good of health. It follows that if a responsible moral agent's personal commitment to this good is lacking, his participation in the community of health seekers is, as it were, accordingly diminished, and his claim on the community's resources is to that extent weakened. The need for health care is thus not sufficient by itself to generate the right to health care. For those who are moral agents, a personal commitment to the good of health is also required.

Therefore, a practical policy for implementing the right to health care—National Health Insurance, for example—could justly include penalties or exclusions for those individuals whose illnesses arise primarily because of their own neglect of their health.

These considerations do not immediately indicate how much health care one is entitled to by right. They do, however, provide a basis for answering this question. One might suppose that the right to health care requires that the best care which is technologically feasible should be provided for all. This supposition is unreasonable. Societies such as our own pursue—and morally should pursue—many goals other than health. Defense, education, cultural enrichment, and aid to poorer societies are only some of these. The right to health care requires that the community's pursuit of health through the specialization of the medical professions be of benefit to each of the members of the community on a fair basis. It does not imply that health is the only important goal for the community or even that it is the most important goal. The ordering of a society's priorities is a matter of social choice which cannot be settled only by an appeal to rights. The community must consider the whole set of obligations by which it is directed and the whole set of values which it can pursue. Like a person it must constitute itself by choice; a people must decide what kind of people it will be. Thus, even if health care should have a higher priority than it now has, this issue cannot be settled by the right to health care. Obviously, it would require such a reordering of priorities if the delivery of the maximal level of health care were considered a right.

It is perhaps more reasonable, therefore, to suppose that a minimally decent level of health care is what the right to health care guarantees. Such a level of health care is certainly required by the right to health care in a society such as ours. But perhaps something more is required as well. If the resources committed to health care allow for more than a minimally decent level for all, then this too should be available to all as a matter of right. In other words, members of a community have a right to *ordinary* health care—that is, to a fair share of what is available to the community at a given time.

With one exception, the basis for a fair distribution of health care resources is medical need—or, more precisely, that level of need compatible with the fulfillment of the similar needs of other persons in the community. There are other possible bases for a fair distribution, but in the case of health care, need is the most reasonable. Other bases—such as merit or wealth—are only accidentally related to the community's goal of helping its members to promote their health. Merit, for example, can be a fair basis for distributing opportunities for higher education. Sophisticated training, however, is not based on an elemental need of the persons who may be given the opportunity. Deprivation of the benefits of such opportunities does not involve the pain, debility, and even the loss of life which may follow from the deprivation of health care.

To sum up: there is a right to health care. This right does not by itself require that the community commit more of its resources to the health sector. Moreover, it does not demand that everything that some people regard as medical care be provided. Only that care which is directed to health is a matter of entitlement. To demand more is to demand what might not be part of the common good of the community and what might even be opposed to this good, or what might render impossible a common agreement about what constitutes this good. Nor does this right absolve individuals from responsibility for their own health; on the contrary, it presupposes this responsibility. What the right to health care *does* require is that the members of a community committed to health be provided on an equal basis with the medical care they need. This conclusion, although limited, has important practical implications, since what the right to health care demands clearly does not obtain in the United States today. Justice thus requires that some community response—possibly but not necessarily National Health Insurance—be made.

# CHAPTER THIRTEEN
# RACISM AND SEXISM

Sexism can be defined as the unequal treatment of persons on the basis of sex. Similarly, racism involves unequal treatment on the basis of race. What is such discrimination like? Consider the following statement of a woman hired to work in an office job:

> I am twenty-three years old, I have a B.A. in Spanish literature. . . . During my interview for this job my interviewer kept looking at my legs and talking about how interesting he thought the job would be for me because I would be around men doing interesting work. . . . "We usually don't hire married girls," he said. "We like to have young, pretty and available girls around the office." "You know," he added, "it cheers things up a lot." I was hired and took the job because I was desperate. I was told I was awfully pretty and would most certainly be an asset to the office. . . . When I was hired I was told that two people constitute a team that would work on a specific project. . . . [T]he "team" turned out to be a male, making around [twice what the] female [was] making. Most "girls" have the same degrees as the men, or higher ones, but are still in the lower positions. The reason for this, I was told, was that most foreigners (whom the office deals with) don't "respect" women and would feel slighted if they had to deal with "one." (Wasn't that the reason given for not hiring blacks in offices and shops?—blacks would turn away customers!). . . . In my office all the men go out to eat together and all the women go out to eat together. . . .

[T]he three blacks in the mailroom eat inside. They are not permitted to go out to eat.[1]

Most people would say that the kind of treatment described above is morally wrong. But there is disagreement about exactly why this is so.[2] Some hold that such behavior fails to show the kind of respect all human beings should have for one another. But why should all human beings be given "equal" respect? Others say that unequal treatment is wrong because of a basic principle of justice, which states that individuals should be treated as equals unless there is some relevant difference between them. In this view, it is unjust to treat people unequally on the basis of race or sex because these are not relevant differences. But why aren't race and sex relevant? The female office worker was told that "most foreigners (whom the office deals with) don't 'respect' women and would feel slighted if they had to deal with 'one.' " Would the preferences of foreign customers make a woman's sex a relevant reason for treating her differently from men? Would anything justify such remarks as, "We like to have young, pretty and available girls around the office"?

It has also been suggested that it is unjust to treat people differently on the basis of characteristics over which they have no control, such as the color of their eyes or hair, their race, or their sex. But schools often take a person's I.Q. into account when determining admission into an academic program, and we do not control our I.Q. Similarly, police departments usually set certain height requirements for applicants. And a director casting the parts for a play will always keep sex and race in mind when determining whether a person can handle a particular role. Moreover, some people have claimed that there are natural differences between men and women, and because of this it is morally permissible to treat men and women differently.

Exactly why, then, is it usually morally wrong to treat people differently on the basis of their race or sex? That is, what makes racial or sexual discrimination morally wrong? This is one of the issues the articles in this chapter address.

During the last two decades, special programs have been set up for

1. Anonymous, "We Usually Don't Hire Married Girls," quoted in Richard C. Edwards, Michael Reich, and Thomas E. Weisskopf, eds., *The Capitalist System*, 2nd. ed. (Englewood Cliffs, N.J.: Prentice-Hall, 1978), pp. 13–15.

2. For discussions of racism, see Richard A. Wasserstrom, "Racism, Sexism, and Preferential Treatment: An Approach to the Topics," *UCLA Law Review*, vol. 24 (1977), pp. 581–622; Bernard Boxill, "Self-Respect and Protest," *Philosophy & Public Affairs*, vol. 6 (1976), p. 58; Irving Thalberg, "Visceral Racism," *The Monist*, vol. 56 (1972), p. 43; Irving Thalberg, "Justifications of Institutional Racism," *The Philosophical Forum*, vol. 3 (1972), p. 243. For several other philosophical articles on racism see *Philosophia*, vol. 8, nos. 1–2 (1978). For discussions of sexism, see, besides Wasserstrom's article, Jane English, ed., *Sex Equality* (Englewood Cliffs, N.J.: Prentice-Hall, 1977); Steven Goldberg, *The Inevitability of Patriarchy* (New York: Morrow, 1973); Shirley Weitz, *Sex Roles* (New York: Oxford University Press, 1977); Carol C. Gould and Marx W. Wartofsky, eds., *Women and Philosophy* (New York: Putnam's, 1976); Mary Vetterling-Braggin, Frederick A. Elliston, and Jane English, eds., *Feminism and Philosophy* (Totowa, N.J.: Littlefield, Adams & Co., 1977). For several other philosophical articles on sexism, see *The Monist*, vol. 57, no. 1 (1973) and *The Philosophical Forum*, vol. 5, nos. 1–2 (1973–74).

sexual and racial groups that have been systematically discriminated against in the past. Whether they are called "affirmative action" or "preferential treatment," these programs are designed to rectify wrongs by giving women and minorities special consideration in hiring and admissions. Here is an example of such a program:

> The Kaiser Aluminum plant in Gramercy, Louisiana, opened in 1958. From the beginning, the Kaiser Gramercy plant had relatively few black workers. By 1965, although 39 percent of the local work force was black, Kaiser had hired only 4.7 percent blacks. In 1970, a federal review of the Gramercy plant found that none of the higher-paying skilled craft worker positions were filled by blacks. A 1973 federal review found that although Kaiser had allowed several whites with no prior craft experience to transfer into the skilled craft positions, blacks were not transferred unless they possessed at least five years of prior craft experience. A third federal review in 1975 found that 2.2 percent of Kaiser Gramercy's 290 craft workers were black. Moreover, although the local labor market in 1975 was still 39 percent black, the Kaiser Gramercy plant's overall work force was only 13.3 percent black. Only the lowest paying category of jobs—unskilled laborers—included a large proportion (35.5 percent) of blacks.
>
> In 1974 Kaiser set up a training program that was intended to eliminate the manifest racial imbalance in its crafts positions. One half of the slots in the crafts training program would be reserved for blacks until the percentage of black skilled craft workers in the plant approximated the percentage of blacks in the local labor force. Openings in the program would be filled by alternating between the most senior qualified white employee (i.e., the white employee who had worked the longest at the plant) and the most senior qualified black employee. The U.S. Supreme court later ruled that this program did not violate U.S. law.
>
> During the first year of the program, thirteen workers were selected for the crafts training program: seven blacks and six whites. Brian Weber, a young white worker who had applied to the program, was not among those selected. Brian, a talkative, likeable Southerner and father of three, had been working in a blue-collar "semi-skilled" position. He wanted very much to enter one of the higher paying skilled craft positions. Upon investigation, Weber found that he had several months more seniority than two of the black workers who had been admitted into the training program. Forty-three other white workers who were also rejected had even more seniority than he did. Junior black employees were thus receiving training in preference to white employees with more seniority. Weber later found that none of the black workers who had been admitted to the program had themselves been the subject of any prior employment discrimination by Kaiser.[3]

The kind of affirmative action program just described has been the source of a great deal of ethical controversy.[4] The debate centers on one

3. Adapted from Manuel Velasquez, *Business Ethics: Concepts and Cases* (Englewood Cliffs, N.J.: Prentice-Hall, 1982), pp. 288–89.

4. There is a large literature on the morality of affirmative action programs: Marshall Cohen, Thomas Nagel, and Thomas Scanlon, eds., *Equality and Preferential Treatment* (Princeton, N.J.: Princeton University Press, 1977); Barry Gross, ed., *Reverse Discrimination* (Buffalo, N.Y.: Prometheus Books, 1977); William T. Blackstone and Robert D. Heslep, eds., *Social Justice and Preferential Treatment* (Athens, Ga.: University of Georgia Press, 1977); Robert K.

crucial question: Does society have a moral obligation to use these programs to rectify the wrongs produced by past discrimination? Some people have held that affirmative action is required by a principle of compensatory justice, which holds that compensation or reparation must be made to parties who have been wrongfully injured. In the case of the Kaiser program, for example, the company was compensating blacks for past injustices. However, critics have claimed that such programs do not compensate those specific individuals who were discriminated against in the past. Moreover, they unjustly penalize individuals like Brian Weber, who had nothing to do with previous discriminatory practices.

Some ethicians have defended affirmative action programs on utilitarian grounds. They argue that the racial and sexual inequalities caused by past discrimination now produce a great many social problems. By gradually eliminating such inequalities, affirmative action on the whole will produce more good consequences than any other alternative. But critics of these arguments hold that an affirmative action program is an unjust means being used to achieve an admittedly good end. In their eyes, affirmative action programs are a form of "reverse discrimination." That is, such programs discriminate against white males on the basis of morally irrelevant characteristics: race and sex. For this reason, they are immoral.

The readings that follow are concerned with the two main issues we have been discussing. The first two articles focus on determining exactly why racism and sexism are wrong. In other words, what exactly is wrong with the kind of treatment the woman office worker in our first example received? The last two articles discuss the morality of the kind of affirmative action program that was instituted in the Kaiser plant. They attempt to discover whether such programs are morally justified or whether they are violations of justice.

In the article, "Servility and Self-Respect," Thomas E. Hill, Jr., argues that the "Uncle Tom," the "Self-Deprecator," and the "Deferential Wife" allow themselves to be subjected to unequal treatment, thus demonstrating a lack of self-respect. Following Kant, Hill argues that this is a moral defect, that is to say, a lack of respect for one's own moral rights. In effect, Hill claims that by choosing to be servile these individuals do not have that respect for moral law that Kant said all human beings must have. The servile person who allows himself to be subjected to unequal treatment does not acknowledge his rights because he does not respect the moral law—and thereby he does wrong.

Some people claim that if there are natural differences between men and women that make women better suited for some jobs and men for others, then discrimination on the basis of sex is not wrong. Joyce Trebilcot criticizes three versions of these arguments in the article, "Sex Roles: The Argument from Nature." First, she says, some people believe that since sex differences are natural, role differences are inevitable. But if

---

Fullinwider, *The Reverse Discrimination Controversy* (Totowa, N.J.: Rowman and Littlefield, 1980); Alan Goldman, *Justice and Reverse Discrimination* (Princeton, N.J.: Princeton University Press, 1979).

role differences are inevitable, why force men and women to accept certain roles? If freedom is valued, then forcing men and women to conform to sex-related roles is wrong. Second, some people have argued that members of each sex are happier in certain roles than in others because they are naturally better suited to them. Hence, to promote well-being, society should encourage people to make the appropriate role choices. Trebilcot criticizes such arguments because they presume that the unhappiness resulting from the wrong role choice will be worse than the unhappiness resulting from the lack of freedom to make a role choice. Third, some have argued that society would be better off if only those who were naturally suited to certain tasks were allowed to assume them. It would be more efficient, easier, and cheaper to train such naturally adept individuals. Trebilcot replies that such restrictions would violate liberty, equality of opportunity, and justice, and that efficiency should not take precedence over these values.

The next group of articles discusses the morality of affirmative action. In "Preferential Policies in Hiring and Admissions: A Jurisprudential Approach," James Nickel explores the problems involved in three ways of justifying preferential treatment programs. First, he examines the principle of compensatory justice, which requires that when individuals have been wrongfully harmed they should be compensated by those who harmed them. Preferential programs are supposed to provide such compensation for minorities and women who were the victims of past discrimination. However, Nickel claims that this argument is unclear about whether compensatory benefits should be given only to those minority individuals who have been harmed or to all members of minority groups. Compensatory justice seems to require that only the former should be compensated. Second, Nickel considers the view that preferential programs can be justified on the basis of distributive justice—in other words, that preferential programs allot benefits more justly than is presently the case among women and minorities. However, Nickel points out that the present distribution of benefits might be due to differences in culture and background and not to discrimination. Third, Nickel turns to the claim that preferential programs can be justified on the basis of utilitarianism, that inequality has bad social effects and that the purpose of preferential programs is to get rid of any inequalities. The problem here, however, is that preferential programs involve social costs, and these costs may outweigh their benefits. In closing, Nickel turns to a discussion of several objections that are often brought against preferential programs, arguing that they are all mistaken. Thus, in Nickel's view, although there are problems with the three kinds of arguments people give to justify preferential treatment, there are, at the same time, no good objections to such treatment.

In the final article, "Justifying Reverse Discrimination in Employment," George Sher approaches preferential treatment from a utilitarian perspective, asking whether past discrimination justifies choosing a less qualified candidate for a position on the basis of race or sex. Sher considers several arguments supporting preferential treatment and rejects each of them. First, some have stated that since members of certain groups have been denied employment in the past, members of those same groups should now be given more employment as compensation. Sher rejects this because it is not groups that were wronged but individuals. Second, some have argued that since certain groups have been denied employment, it is likely that these groups are deprived in other ways as well because of this lack of employment. Preferential programs are thus intended to make up for such deprivation. The problem here, according to Sher, is that it is unclear why this kind of compensation is appropriate rather than some other kind. Indeed, other forms of redress may in fact be fairer than preferential hiring. Third, some have claimed that discrimination has impoverished some groups and that this in turn has affected their mental and physical development. If people are developmentally handicapped, they will be less likely to be employed, thus keeping them deprived and impoverished. Sher responds that not all problems produced by such deprivation could be remedied by preferential programs. Fourth, some have argued that the privations produced by past discrimination are by themselves sufficient grounds for granting preferential treatment to certain groups. However, Sher believes that only privations that undermine the ability to compete are relevant. In the case of women, although there may be psychological disadvantages, these affect the inclination rather than the ability to do certain work. And as for minorities, Sher claims that it is unlikely that their abilities have been reduced by past discrimination. Thus, preferential treatment is not a good solution in this case either.

# SERVILITY AND SELF-RESPECT

*Thomas E. Hill, Jr.*

Three examples may give a preliminary idea of what I mean by *servility*. Consider, first, an extremely deferential black, whom I shall call the *Uncle Tom*. He always steps aside for white men; he does not complain when less qualified whites take over his job; he gratefully accepts whatever benefits his all-white government and employers allot him, and he would not think of protesting its insufficiency. He displays the symbols of deference to whites, and of contempt towards blacks; he faces the former with bowed stance and a ready 'sir' and 'ma'am'; he reserves his strongest

From Thomas E. Hill, Jr., "Servility and Self-Respect," reprinted by permission from vol. 57, no. 1 (January 1973), pp. 88–89, 93–94, 97–101, of *The Monist*, La Salle, Illinois 61301.

obscenities for the latter. Imagine, too, that he is not playing a game. He is not the shrewdly prudent calculator, who knows how to make the best of a bad lot and mocks his masters behind their backs. He accepts without question the idea that, as a black, he is owed less than whites. He may believe that blacks are mentally inferior and of less social utility, but that is not the crucial point. The attitude which he displays is that what he values, aspires for, and can demand is of less importance than what whites value, aspire for, and can demand. He is far from the picture book's carefree, happy servant, but he does not feel that he has a right to expect anything better.

Another pattern of servility is illustrated by a person I shall call the *Self-Deprecator*. Like the Uncle Tom, he is reluctant to make demands. He says nothing when others take unfair advantage of him. When asked for his preferences or opinions, he tends to shrink away as if what he said should make no difference. His problem, however, is not a sense of racial inferiority but rather an acute awareness of his own inadequacies and failures as an individual. These defects are not imaginary: he has in fact done poorly by his own standards and others'. But, unlike many of us in the same situation, he acts as if his failings warrant quite unrelated mal-treatment even by strangers. His sense of shame and self-contempt make him content to be the instrument of others. He feels that nothing is owed him until he has earned it and that he has earned very little. He is not simply playing a masochist's game of winning sympathy by disparaging himself. On the contrary, he assesses his individual merits with painful accuracy.

A rather different case is that of the *Deferential Wife*. This is a woman who is utterly devoted to serving her husband. She buys the clothes *he* prefers, invites the guests *he* wants to entertain, and makes love whenever *he* is in the mood. She willingly moves to a new city in order for him to have a more attractive job, counting her own friendships and geographi-cal preferences insignificant by comparison. She loves her husband, but her conduct is not simply an expression of love. She is happy, but she does not subordinate herself as a means to happiness. She does not simply defer to her husband in certain spheres as a trade-off for his deference in other spheres. On the contrary, she tends not to form her own interests, values, and ideals; and, when she does, she counts them as less important than her husband's. She readily responds to appeals from Women's Lib-eration that she agrees that women are mentally and physically equal, if not superior, to men. She just believes that the proper role for a woman is to serve her family. As a matter of fact, much of her happiness derives from her belief that she fulfills this role very well. No one is trampling on her rights, she says; for she is quite glad, and proud, to serve her husband as she does.

Each one of these cases reflects the attitude which I call servility. It betrays the absence of a certain kind of self-respect. What I take this attitude to be, more specifically, will become clearer later on. . . . Why, then, is servility a moral defect? There is, I think, another sort of answer which is worth exploring. The first part of this answer must be an attempt to isolate the objectionable features of the servile person; later we can ask why these features are objectionable. As a step in this direction, let us examine again our three paradigm cases. The moral defect in each case, I suggest, is a failure to understand and acknowledge one's own moral rights. I assume, without argument here, that each person has moral rights. Some of these rights may be basic human rights; that is, rights for which a person needs only to be human to qualify. Other rights will be derivative and contingent upon his special commitments, institutional affiliations, etc. Most rights will be prima facie ones; some may be absolute. Most can be waived under appropriate conditions; perhaps some cannot. Many rights can be forfeited; but some, presumably, cannot. The servile person does not, strictly speaking, violate his own rights. At least in our paradigm cases he fails to acknowledge fully his own moral status because he does not fully understand what his rights are, how they can be waived, and when they can be forfeited.

The defect of the Uncle Tom, for example, is that he displays an attitude that denies his moral equality with whites. He does not realize, or apprehend in an effective way, that he has as much right to a decent wage and a share of political power as any comparable white. His gratitude is misplaced; he accepts benefits which are his by right as if they were gifts. The Self-Deprecator is servile in a more complex way. He acts as if he has forfeited many important rights which in fact he has not. He does not understand, or fully realize in his own case, that certain rights to fair and decent treatment do not have to be earned. He sees his merits clearly enough, but he fails to see that what he can expect from others is not merely a function of his merits. The Deferential Wife *says* that she understand her rights vis-à-vis her husband, but what she fails to appreciate is that her consent to serve him is a valid waiver of her rights only under certain conditions. If her consent is coerced, say, by the lack of viable options for women in her society, then her consent is worth little. If socially fostered ignorance of her own talents and alternatives is responsible for her consent, then her consent should not count as a fully legitimate waiver of her right to equal consideration within the marriage. All the more, her consent to defer constantly to her husband is not a legitimate setting aside of her rights if it results from her mistaken belief that she has a moral duty to do so. (Recall: "The *proper* role for a woman is to serve her family.") If she believes that she has a *duty* to defer to her husband, then whatever she may say, she cannot fully understand that she has a *right* not to defer to him. When she says that she freely gives up such a right, she is confused. Her confusion is rather like that of a person who has been persuaded by an unscrupulous lawyer that it is legally incumbent on him to refuse a jury trial but who nevertheless tells the judge that he understands that he has a right to a jury trial and freely waives it. He does not really understand what it is to have and freely give up the right if he thinks that it would be an offense for him to exercise it.

. . . The objectional feature of the servile person, as I have described him, is his tendency to disavow his own moral rights either because he misunderstands them or because he cares little for them. The question remains: why should anyone regard this as a moral defect? After all, the rights which he denies are his own. He may be unfortunate, foolish, or even distasteful; but why *morally* deficient? One sort of answer, quite different from those reviewed earlier, is suggested by some of Kant's remarks. Kant held that servility is contrary to a perfect nonjuridical duty to oneself. To say that the duty is perfect is roughly to say that it is stringent, never overridden by other considerations (e.g. beneficence). To say that the duty is nonjuridical is to say that a person cannot legitimately be coerced to comply. Although Kant did not develop an explicit argument for this view, an argument can easily be constructed from materials which reflect the spirit, if not the letter, of his moral theory. The argument which I have in mind is prompted by Kant's contention that respect for persons, strictly speaking, is respect for moral law. If taken as a claim about all sorts of respect, this seems quite implausible. If it means that we respect persons only for their moral character, their capacity for moral conduct, or their status as "authors" of the moral law, then it seems unduly moralistic. My strategy is to construe the remark as saying that at least one sort of respect for persons is respect for the rights which the moral law accords them. If one respects the moral law, then one must respect one's own moral rights; and this amounts to having a kind of self-respect incompatible with servility.

The premises for the Kantian argument, which are all admittedly vague, can be sketched as follows:

*First,* let us assume, as Kant did, that all human beings have equal basic human rights. Specific rights vary with different conditions, but all must be justified from a point of view under which all are equal. Not all rights need to be earned, and some cannot be forfeited. Many rights can be waived but only under certain conditions of knowledge and freedom. These conditions are complex and difficult to state; but they include something like the condition that a person's consent releases others from an obligation only if it is autonomously given, and consent resulting from underestimation of one's moral status is not autonomously given. Rights can be objects of knowledge, but also of ignorance, misunderstanding, deception, and the like.

*Second,* let us assume that my account of servility is correct; or, if one prefers, we can take it as a definition. That is, in brief, a servile person is one who tends to deny or disavow his own moral rights because he does not understand them or has little concern for the status they give him.

*Third,* we need one formal premise concerning moral duty, namely, that each person ought, as far as possible, to respect the moral law. In less Kantian language, the point is that everyone should approximate, to the extent that he can, the ideal of a person who fully adopts the moral point of view. Roughly, this means not only that each person ought to do what is morally required and refrain from what is morally wrong but also that each person should treat all the provisions of morality as valuable—worth preserving and prizing as well as obeying. One must, so to speak, take up the spirit of morality as well as meet the letter of its requirements. To keep one's promises, avoid hurting others, and the like, is not sufficient; one should also take an attitude of respect towards the principles, ideals, and goals of morality. A respectful attitude towards a system of rights and duties consists of more than a disposition to conform to its definite rules of behavior; it also involves holding the system in esteem, being unwilling to ridicule it, and being reluctant to give up one's place in it. The essentially Kantian idea here is that morality, as a system of equal fundamental rights and duties, is worthy of respect and hence a completely moral person would respect it in word and manner as well as in deed. And what a completely moral person would do, in Kant's view, is our duty to do so far as we can.

The assumptions here are, of course, strong ones, and I make no attempt to justify them. They are, I suspect, widely held though rarely articulated. In any case, my present purpose is not to evaluate them but to see how, if granted, they constitute a case against servility. The objection to the servile person, given our premises, is that he does not satisfy the basic requirement to respect morality. A person who fully respected a system of moral rights would be disposed to learn his proper place in it, to affirm it proudly, and not to tolerate abuses of it lightly. This is just the sort of disposition that the servile person lacks. If he does not understand the system, he is in no position to respect it adequately. This lack of respect may be no fault of his own, but it is still a way in which he falls short of a moral ideal. If, on the other hand, the servile person knowingly disavows his moral rights by pretending to approve of violations of them, barring special explanations, he shows an indifference to whether the provisions of morality are honored and publicly acknowledged. This avoidable display of indifference, by our Kantian premises, is contrary to the duty to respect morality. The disrespect in this second case is somewhat like the disrespect a religious believer might show toward his religion if, to avoid embarrassment, he laughed congenially while nonbelievers were mocking the beliefs which he secretly held. In any case, the servile person, as such, does not express disrespect for the system of moral rights in the obvious way by violating the rights of others. His lack of respect is more subtly manifested by his acting before others as if he did not know or care about his position of equality under that system.

The central idea may be illustrated by an analogy. Imagine a club, say, an old German dueling fraternity. By the rules of the club, each member has certain rights and responsibilities. These are the same for each member regardless of what titles he may hold outside the club. Each has, for example, a right to be heard at meetings, a right not to be shouted down by the others. Some rights cannot be forfeited: for example, each may vote regardless of whether he has paid his dues and satisfied other rules. Some rights cannot be waived: for example, the right to be defended when attacked by several members of the rival fraternity. The members show respect for each other by respecting the status which the rules confer on each member. Now one new member is careful always to allow the others to speak at meetings; but when they shout him down, he does nothing. He just shrugs as if to say, 'Who am I to complain?' When he fails to stand up in defense of a fellow member, he feels ashamed and refuses to vote. He does not deserve to vote, he says. As the only commoner among illustrious barons, he feels that it is his place to serve them and defer to their decisions. When attackers from the rival fraternity come at him with swords drawn, he tells his companions to run and save themselves. When they defend him, he expresses immense grati-tude—as if they had done him a gratuitous favor. Now one might argue that our new member fails to show respect for the fraternity and its rules. He does not actually violate any of the rules by refusing to vote, asking others not to defend him, and deferring to the barons, but he symboli-cally disavows the equal status which the rules confer on him. If he ought to have respect for the fraternity, he ought to change his attitude. Our servile person, then, is like the new member of the dueling fraternity in having insufficient respect for a system of rules and ideals. The differ-ence is that everyone ought to respect morality whereas there is no com-parable moral requirement to respect the fraternity.

The conclusion here is, of course, a limited one. Self-sacrifice is not always a sign of servility. It is not a duty always to press one's rights. Whether a given act is evidence of servility will depend not only on the attitude of the agent but also on the specific nature of his moral rights, a matter not considered here. Moreover, the extent to which a person is responsible, or blameworthy, for his defect remains an open question. Nevertheless, the conclusion should not be minimized. In order to avoid servility, a person who gives up his rights must do so with a full apprecia-tion for what they are. A woman, for example, may devote herself to her husband if she is uncoerced, knows what she is doing, and does not pretend that she has no decent alternative. A self-contemptuous person may decide not to press various unforfeited rights but only if he does not take the attitude that he is too rotten to deserve them. A black may demand less than is due to him provided he is prepared to acknowledge that no one has a right to expect this of him. Sacrifices of this sort, I suspect, are extremely rare. Most people, if they fully acknowledged their rights, would not autonomously refuse to press them.

# SEX ROLES: THE ARGUMENT FROM NATURE

*Joyce Trebilcot*

I am concerned here with the normative question of whether, in an ideal society, certain roles should be assigned to females and others to males. In discussions of this issue, a great deal of attention is given to the claim that there are natural psychological differences between the sexes.

From Joyce Trebilcot, "Sex Roles: The Argument from Nature," *Ethics*, vol. 85, no. 3 (April 1975), pp. 249–55. Copyright © 1975 by the University of Chicago Press.

Those who hold that at least some roles should be sex roles generally base their view primarily on an appeal to such natural differences, while many of those advocating a society without sex roles argue either that the sexes do not differ in innate psychological traits or that there is no evidence that they do. In this paper I argue that whether there are natural psychological differences between females and males has little bearing on the issue of whether society should reserve certain roles for females and others for males.

Let me begin by saying something about the claim that there are natural psychological differences between the sexes. The issue we are dealing with arises, of course, because there are biological differences among human beings which are bases for designating some as females and others as males. Now it is held by some that, in addition to biological differences between the sexes, there are also natural differences in temperament, interests, abilities, and the like. In this paper I am concerned only with arguments which appeal to these psychological differences as bases of sex roles. Thus I exclude, for example, arguments that the role of jockey should be female because women are smaller than men or that boxers should be male because men are more muscular than women. Nor do I discuss arguments which appeal directly to the reproductive functions peculiar to each sex. If the physiological processes of gestation or of depositing sperm in a vagina are, apart from any psychological correlates they may have, bases for sex roles, these roles are outside the scope of the present discussion.

It should be noted, however, that virtually all those who hold that there are natural psychological differences between the sexes assume that these differences are determined primarily by differences in biology. According to one hypothesis, natural psychological differences between the sexes are due at least in part to differences between female and male nervous systems. As the male fetus develops in the womb, the testes secrete a hormone which is held to influence the growth of the central nervous system. The female fetus does not produce this hormone, nor is there an analogous female hormone which is significant at this stage. Hence it is suggested that female and male brains differ in structure, that this difference is due to the prenatal influence of testicular hormone, and that the difference in brains is the basis of some later differences in behavior.

A second view about the origin of allegedly natural psychological differences between the sexes, a view not incompatible with the first, is psychoanalytical. It conceives of feminine or masculine behavior as, in part, the individual's response to bodily structure. On this view, one's more or less unconscious experience of one's own body (and in some versions, of the bodies of others) is a major factor in producing sex-specific personality traits. The classic theories of this kind are, of course, Freud's; penis envy and the castration complex are supposed to arise largely from perceptions of differences between female and male bodies. Other writers make much of the analogies between genitals and genders: the uterus is passive and receptive, and so are females; penises are active and penetrating, and so are males. But here we are concerned not with the etiology of allegedly natural differences between the sexes but rather with the question of whether such differences, if they exist, are grounds for holding that there should be sex roles.

That a certain psychological disposition is natural only to one sex is generally taken to mean in part that members of that sex are more likely to have the disposition, or to have it to a greater degree, than persons of the other sex. The situation is thought to be similar to that of height. In a given population, females are on the average shorter than males, but some females are taller than some males, as suggested by figure 1. The

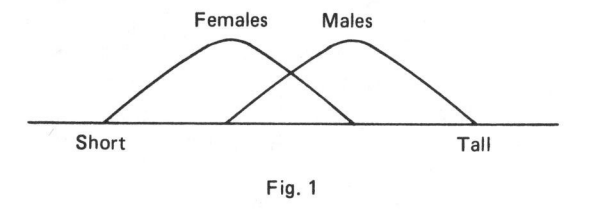

Fig. 1

shortest members of the population are all females, and the tallest are all males, but there is an area of overlap. For psychological traits, it is usually assumed that there is some degree of overlap and that the degree of overlap is different for different characteristics. Because of the difficulty of identifying natural psychological characteristics, we have of course little or no data as to the actual distribution of such traits.

I shall not undertake here to define the concept of role, but examples include voter, librarian, wife, president. A broad concept of role might also comprise, for example, being a joker, a person who walks gracefully, a compassionate person. The genders, femininity and masculinity, may also be conceived as roles. On this view, each of the gender roles includes a number of more specific sex roles, some of which may be essential to it. For example, the concept of femininity may be construed in such a way that it is necessary to raise a child in order to be fully feminine, while other feminine roles—teacher, nurse, charity worker—are not essential to gender. In the arguments discussed below, the focus is on sex roles rather than genders, but, on the assumption that the genders are roles, much of what is said applies, *mutatis mutandis,* to them.

A sex role is a role performed only or primarily by persons of a particular sex. Now if this is all we mean by "sex role," the problem of whether there should be sex roles must be dealt with as two separate issues: "Are sex roles a good thing?" and "Should society enforce sex roles?" One might argue, for example, that sex roles have value but that, even so, the demands of individual autonomy and freedom are such that societal institutions and practices should not enforce correlations between roles and sex. But the debate over sex roles is of course mainly a discussion about the second question, whether society should enforce these correlations. The judgment that there should be sex roles is generally taken to mean not just that sex-exclusive roles are a good thing, but that society should promote such exclusivity.

In view of this, I use the term "sex role" in such a way that to ask whether there should be sex roles is to ask whether society should direct women into certain roles and away from others, and similarly for men. A role is a sex role then (or perhaps an "institutionalized sex role") only if it is performed exclusively or primarily by persons of a particular sex *and* societal factors tend to encourage this correlation. These factors may be of various kinds. Parents guide children into what are taken to be sex-appropriate roles. Schools direct students into occupations according to sex. Marriage customs prescribe different roles for females and males. Employers and unions may refuse to consider applications from persons of the "wrong" sex. The media carry tales of the happiness of those who conform and the suffering of the others. The law sometimes penalizes deviators. Individuals may ridicule and condemn role crossing and smile on conformity. Societal sanctions such as these are essential to the notion of sex role employed here.

I turn now to a discussion of the three major ways the claim that there are natural psychological differences between the sexes is held to be relevant to the issue of whether there should be sex roles.

*1. Inevitability.*   It is sometimes held that if there are innate psychological differences between females and males, sex roles are inevitable. The point of this argument is not, of course, to urge that there should be sex roles, but rather to show that the normative question is out of place, that there will be sex roles, whatever we decide. The argument assumes first that the alleged natural differences between the sexes are inevitable; but if such differences are inevitable, differences in behavior are inevitable, and if differences in behavior are inevitable, society will inevitably be structured so as to enforce role differences according to sex. Thus, sex roles are inevitable.

For the purpose of this discussion, let us accept the claim that natural psychological differences are inevitable. We assume that there are such differences and ignore the possibility of their being altered, for example, by evolutionary change or direct biological intervention. Let us also accept the second claim, that behavioral differences are inevitable. Behavioral differences could perhaps be eliminated even given the assumption of natural differences in disposition (for example, those with no natural inclination to a certain kind of behavior might nevertheless learn it), but let us waive this point. We assume then that behavioral differences, and hence also role differences, between the sexes are inevitable. Does it follow that there must be sex roles, that is, that the institutions and practices of society must enforce correlations between roles and sex?

Surely not. Indeed, such sanctions would be pointless. Why bother to direct women into some roles and men into others if the pattern occurs regardless of the nature of society? Mill makes the point elegantly in *The Subjection of Women:* "The anxiety of mankind to interfere in behalf of nature, for fear lest nature should not succeed in effecting its purpose, is an altogether unnecessary solicitude."

It may be objected that if correlations between sex and roles are inevitable societal sanctions enforcing these correlations will develop because people will expect the sexes to perform different roles and these expectations will lead to behavior which encourages their fulfillment. This can happen, of course, but it is surely not inevitable. One need not act so as to bring about what one expects.

Indeed, there could be a society in which it is held that there are inevitable correlations between roles and sex but institutionalization of these correlations is deliberately avoided. What is inevitable is presumably not, for example, that every woman will perform a certain role and no man will perform it, but rather that most women will perform the role and most men will not. For any individual, then, a particular role may not be inevitable. Now suppose it is a value in the society in question that people should be free to choose roles according to their individual needs and interests. But then there should not be sanctions enforcing correlations between roles and sex, for such sanctions tend to force some individuals into roles for which they have no natural inclination and which they might otherwise choose against.

I conclude then that, even granting the assumptions that natural psychological differences, and therefore role differences, between the sexes are inevitable, it does not follow that there must be sanctions enforcing correlations between roles and sex. Indeed, if individual freedom is valued, those who vary from the statistical norm should not be required to conform to it.

*2. Well-being.*  The argument from well-being begins with the claim that, because of natural psychological differences between the sexes, members of each sex are happier in certain roles than in others, and the roles which tend to promote happiness are different for each sex. It is also held that if all roles are equally available to everyone regardless of sex, some individuals will choose against their own well-being. Hence, the argument concludes, for the sake of maximizing well-being there should be sex roles: society should encourage individuals to make "correct" role choices.

Suppose that women, on the average, are more compassionate than men. Suppose also that there are two sets of roles, "female" and "male," and that because of the natural compassion of women, women are happier in female than in male roles. Now if females and males overlap with respect to compassion, some men have as much natural compassion as some women, so they too will be happier in female than in male roles. Thus, the first premise of the argument from well-being should read: Suppose that, because of natural psychological differences between the sexes, *most* women are happier in female roles and *most* men in male roles. The argument continues: If all roles are equally available to everyone, some of the women who would be happier in female roles will choose against their own well-being, and similarly for men.

Now if the conclusion that there should be sex roles is to be based on these premises, another assumption must be added—that the loss of potential well-being resulting from societally produced adoption of unsuitable roles by individuals in the overlapping areas of the distribution is *less* than the loss that would result from "mistaken" free choices if there were no sex roles. With sex roles, some individuals who would be happier in roles assigned to the other sex perform roles assigned to their own sex, and so there is a loss of potential happiness. Without sex roles, some individuals, we assume, choose against their own well-being. But surely we are not now in a position to compare the two systems with respect to the number of mismatches produced. Hence, the additional premise required for the argument, that overall well-being is greater with sex roles than without them, is entirely unsupported.

Even if we grant, then, that because of innate psychological differences between the sexes members of each sex achieve greater well-being in some roles than ,in others, the argument from well-being does not support the conclusion that there should be sex roles. In our present state of knowledge, there is no reason to suppose that a sex role system which makes no discriminations within a sex would produce fewer mismatches between individuals and roles than a system in which all roles are open equally to both sexes.

*3. Efficiency.* If there are natural differences between the sexes in the capacity to perform socially valuable tasks, then, it is sometimes argued, efficiency is served if these tasks are assigned to the sex with the greatest innate ability for them. Suppose, for example, that females are naturally better than males at learning foreign languages. This means that, if everything else is equal and females and males are given the same training in a foreign language, females, on the average, will achieve a higher level of skill than males. Now suppose that society needs interpreters and translators and that in order to have such a job one must complete a special training program whose only purpose is to provide persons for these roles. Clearly, efficiency is served if only individuals with a good deal of natural ability are selected for training, for the time and effort required to bring them to a given level of proficiency is less than that required for the less talented. But suppose that the innate ability in question is normally distributed within each sex and that the sexes overlap (see fig. 2). If we assume that a sufficient number of candidates can be re-

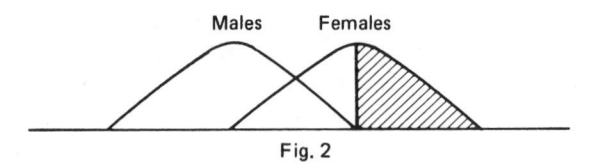

Fig. 2

cruited by considering only persons in the shaded area, they are the only ones who should be eligible. There are no men in this group. Hence, although screening is necessary in order to exclude nontalented women, it would be inefficient even to consider men, for it is known that no man is as talented as the talented women. In the interest of efficiency, then, the occupational roles of interpreter and translator should be sex roles; men should be denied access to these roles but women who are interested in them, especially talented women, should be encouraged to pursue them.

This argument is sound. That is, if we grant the factual assumptions and suppose also that efficiency for the society we are concerned with has some value, the argument from efficiency provides one reason for holding that some roles should be sex roles. This conclusion of course is only prima facie. In order to determine whether there should be sex roles, one would have to weigh efficiency, together with other reasons for such roles, against reasons for holding that there should not be sex roles. The reasons against sex roles are very strong. They are couched in terms of individual rights—in terms of liberty, justice, equality of opportunity. Efficiency by itself does not outweigh these moral values. Nevertheless, the appeal to nature, if true, combined with an appeal to the value of efficiency, does provide one reason for the view that there should be sex roles.

The arguments I have discussed here are not the only ones which appeal to natural psychological differences between the sexes in defense of sex roles, but these three arguments—from inevitability, well-being, and efficiency—are, I believe, the most common and the most plausible ones. The argument from efficiency alone, among them, provides a reason—albeit a rather weak reason—for thinking that there should be sex roles. I suggest, therefore, that the issue of natural psychological differences between women and men does not deserve the central place it is given, both traditionally and currently, in the literature on this topic.

It is frequently pointed out that the argument from nature functions as a cover, as a myth to make patriarchy palatable to both women and men. Insofar as this is so, it is surely worthwhile exploring and exposing the myth. But of course most of those who use the argument from nature take it seriously and literally, and this is the spirit in which I have dealt with it. Considering the argument in this way, I conclude that whether there should be sex roles does not depend primarily on whether there are innate psychological differences between the sexes. The question is, after all, not what women and men naturally are, but what kind of society is morally justifiable. In order to answer this question, we must appeal to the notions of justice, equality, and liberty. It is these moral concepts, not the empirical issue of sex differences, which should have pride of place in the philosophical discussion of sex roles.

# PREFERENTIAL POLICIES IN HIRING AND ADMISSIONS: A JURISPRUDENTIAL APPROACH

*James W. Nickel*

. . . Preferential hiring and admissions policies give an advantage in competitions for jobs or places in educational institutions to members of particular groups. The most common use of preferential policies in the United States has been to provide special educational and employment opportunities for veterans, but the recent controversy over preferential policies has to do with their use in recent years to provide special opportunities to blacks and members of other disadvantaged groups.

It is important to recognize that preferential policies need not be used in combination with racial or other classifications based on inherent characteristics. One might apply them, for example, to all persons who are on welfare or who have an income below a certain level. Hence, after discussing some justifications for using preferential policies, I will divide my discussion of objections to preferential policies into two parts. The first part will discuss objections to preferential policies that have nothing to do with the use of racial or ethnic classifications to define the preferred group, and the second part will discuss objections that focus on the use of racial (and ethnic) classifications. My approach, put broadly, is that of a defender of preferential policies, but I hope that my analysis of the issues involved will be helpful even to those who disagree.

## I. JUSTIFICATIONS AND CONCEPTIONS

As a means of clarifying these matters, I will discuss the different sorts of justifications that might be offered for programs that use preferential policies, and the difficulties with each.

### A. Compensatory Justice

To argue that programs which use preferential policies to provide greater opportunities to members of disadvantaged minorities are justifiable on grounds of compensatory justice is to argue that either the *actual* recipients or the persons that one thinks *ought* to be the recipients deserve compensation for wrongs they have suffered. Compensatory justice requires that counterbalancing benefits be provided to those individuals who have been wrongfully injured which will serve to bring them up to the level of wealth and welfare that they would now have if they had not been disadvantaged. Compensatory programs differ from redistributive programs mainly in regard to their concern with the past. Redistribution is concerned with eliminating present inequities, while compensatory justice is concerned not only with this but with providing compensation for unfair burdens borne in the past.

There are a number of difficulties involved in using considerations of compensatory justice to justify programs that use preferential policies to assist the disadvantaged. These include: (1) questions about whether compensatory benefits are owed only to those particular individuals who have been harmed substantially by discrimination and hardship or to all members of those groups that have been frequent targets of discrimination; (2) questions about whether a person who was once harmed by discrimination but who has overcome his losses through his own efforts still deserves compensation now; (3) questions about whether governments, companies, institutions and individuals have obligations to compensate losses they did not cause; and (4) questions about how far back into the past the view of compensatory justice should extend. Although I cannot undertake here the extended discussion that would be needed for an adequate exploration of these questions, the first one must be given some attention since it is crucial to how justifications in terms of compensatory justice are conceived.

It is sometimes maintained that in addition to compensatory principles that apply to individuals there are compensatory principles that create obligations between groups when one group injures another group or is unjustly enriched at the other group's expense. Paul W. Taylor, for example, argues that there is a principle of compensatory justice which requires that "[w]hen an injustice has been committed to a group of persons, some form of compensation or reparation must be made to that group." In Taylor's view, a group's right to compensation does not derive from the right to compensation of individuals in that group and cannot be satisfied by only compensating those within the group who as individuals deserve compensation. Furthermore, a member of a wronged group who has not personally been wronged may have a right to compensation as a member of the group. Taylor's approach offers a basis for giving preference to all members of wronged groups without regard to their personal histories. Group rights to compensation are not rights against particular wrongdoers but are against society as a whole: "The obligation to offer such benefits to the group as a whole is an obligation that falls on society in general, not on any particular person. For it is society in general that through its established social practice brought upon itself the obligation." Finally, Taylor thinks that "affirmative action" programs are an appropriate way for a government to discharge society's obligation to wronged groups.

Although compensatory principles that apply directly to groups are frequently advocated, I personally do not find them appealing. Although there may well be moral principles that apply directly to groups, I find the principle that Taylor advocates implausible because it would unnecessarily duplicate many of the rights and obligations created by compensatory principles that apply to individuals, and would provide compensatory benefits to persons who personally have sustained no injury and therefore need not be made whole. It may be desirable to offer special opportunities to, say, all young blacks, whether or not they have personally been significantly harmed by discrimination, but the justification would have to be based on considerations of redistribution, utility, or administrative convenience, not on the claim that all blacks, whatever their situation, have a *right* to such benefits on the grounds of compensatory justice. . . .

### B. Distributive Justice

Programs using preferential policies are also conceived as a means of promoting the redistribution of income and other important benefits. This approach would claim that the justification for such programs lies in the reduction of distributive inequities that they bring about. Since good educations lead to good jobs, and good jobs provide income, security, and status, altering the ways in which educations and jobs are distributed so as to give a bigger share to the previously deprived is one way of bringing about redistribution. A concern with distributive justice is a concern with whether people have fair shares of benefits and burdens. Distributive justice does not require that all people have the same income or equally good jobs, the requirement is rather that benefits and burdens be distributed in accordance with relevant considerations such as the rights, deserts, merits, contributions and needs of the recipients. Thus, if both Jones and Smith have had adequate opportunities for self-development, and if Jones is qualified for a desirable and prestigious job as a director of an art museum, while Smith is only qualified for janitorial positions, then there will be no injustice in hiring Jones as the director and Smith as the janitor. . . .

Those who take this approach are likely to point to large statistical differences between the incomes of blacks and whites or men and women as evidence of unjustifiable inequalities. It is beyond doubt that there has been and still is discrimination in employment against blacks and women, and that blacks and women have had fewer opportunities to develop qualifications. The difficulty, however, in arguing from such statistics is in distinguishing the extent to which the differences derive from discrimination rather than from other factors which may vary in strength between sexes and among groups. When there are groups which have different histories and cultures and emphasize different personal goals, it is unlikely that their members will uniformly utilize the same opportunities, go into the same areas of employment, and have the same attitudes towards vocational achievement. The ideal of having all groups represented at all levels of income and achievement in proportion to their numbers in the country's population may therefore be unrealistic, and perhaps even unappealing. This ideal, which might be called the ideal of proportional equality, has been criticized by many of those who are opposed to preferential policies for women or blacks, but the case for the use of preferential policies does not stand or fall with its acceptance or rejection.

## C. Utility

Redistribution of important benefits may also be advocated because it is believed that the public welfare, on the whole and over the long term, can be promoted by reducing poverty and inequality. On this approach a program using preferential policies to increase educational and employment opportunities would be seen as one means of promoting the public welfare by eliminating poverty and its attendant evils and by eliminating the sort of economic inequality that leads to resentment and strife. Extreme poverty is objectionable to one who is concerned with utility because of what it involves, namely unmet needs and suffering, and because of what it leads to, namely crime, family strife, lack of self-respect and social discontent. Economic inequality of the sort that we currently have, with wide extremes of income and wealth and with some groups largely concentrated at the bottom of the economic ladder is objectionable under this view because it perpetuates stereotypes, deprives people in low-income groups of role models, fosters lack of self-respect, and makes understanding and cooperation between groups more difficult. As long as there are, for example, few black doctors, lawyers, or executives, it will be easy for people, blacks included, to believe that blacks generally lack the abilities to fill these positions, and the maintenance of such beliefs can only perpetuate inequality with its untoward consequences.

Considerations about unmet needs and suffering may only require the elimination of extreme poverty, but considerations about the bad effects of economic inequality—especially the sort that sees some groups concentrated at the lower levels—suggest stronger measures to facilitate upward mobility for those at lower levels. Hence, moving towards proportional representation might be desirable on grounds of utility even if it is not required by distributive justice.

I have discussed some of the utilitarian benefits which are thought to follow from the use of preferential policies to increase the educational and employment opportunities available to disadvantaged minorities, but on any utilitarian approach these benefits must be balanced against the accompanying costs. Taking money or other benefits away from those who have much in order to promote the public good by giving these benefits to the disadvantaged is not without its costs. The rich person now has some of his money taken to finance job programs, or the young person who finds it difficult or impossible to get into professional school because of programs designed to increase the number of economically disadvantaged persons applying or accepted will not normally be made happier or better off as a result. There may also be attendant social costs, for the rich person may have invested the appropriated money in a way that would have benefited more people, or the young professional school applicant may have been more qualified. These costs cannot be ignored; utilitarian advocates of preferential policies must claim that they are outweighed by greater benefits. This is probably true in many cases, but judgments about this depend on particular facts and must be made in particular cases.

## II. GENERAL OBJECTIONS TO PREFERENTIAL POLICIES

### A. Problems of Incompetency

Insofar as the use of preferential policies led to the admission or hiring of unqualified persons, significant reductions in the efficiency and productivity of companies and institutions would be likely to follow. Those who are opposed to preferential policies often raise the specter of illiterate students, highway patrolmen who do not know how to drive, teachers who cannot handle children and surgeons who remove tonsils by cutting throats. Although these dangers are easily exaggerated, the importance of competent personnel to institutional efficiency must be recognized, and it can be readily conceded that preferential policies should be restricted to those who are adequately qualified, or who, with the training provided, can become adequately qualified for the position sought. This will mean that if a person is unable to perform the task adequately, then preferential policies will not apply to him with respect to the position.

### B. Problems of Unfair Burdens

A second objection is that preferential policies unfairly place the burden of helping those who are preferred on those who are thereby excluded.

If we assume that preference is only given to adequately qualified candidates, and hence that both preferential and non-preferential policies are compatible with the requirements of efficiency, what is it that makes it worse when those excluded are persons who are better qualified than some of those hired? An answer to this question will obviously refer to the better qualifications of the persons excluded by the preferential policy, but why is it worse to exclude better qualified persons than to deprive less qualified candidates of preferences indicated by considerations of compensation, distributive justice, or utility? One possibility is to say that better qualifications confer upon their holders a prima facie right to be chosen in preference to anyone who is less qualified. This claim is plausible because, other things being equal, the best way of distributing jobs is to give them to the best qualified candidate. Although this is normally the best way, it does not seem to be the only permissible way. If in a case where small differences in competence had little impact on institutional efficiency, a company chose to save money and effort by hiring the first adequately qualified person who applied or to select among the adequately qualified candidates by lot, no one would have good grounds for complaint. It is unclear whether these cases show that there is no right to be hired in preference to less qualified candidates, or simply that this right is one that can be overridden by considerations of efficiency in some cases, but these cases do at least show that the policy of selecting in accordance with the best qualifications is not sacrosanct.

## III. OBJECTIONS TO PREFERENTIAL POLICIES THAT USE RACIAL, ETHNIC, OR SEXUAL CLASSIFICATIONS

### A. Race as an Irrelevant Characteristic

When a black person is preferentially awarded a job, and a nonblack person is thereby denied it, both the award and the denial seem to be on the basis of an irrelevant characteristic, namely the race of the candidates. Awarding and denying benefits on the basis of such an irrelevant characteristic seems to be no different in principle—even though the motives may be more defensible—from traditional sorts of discrimination against blacks and in favor of whites. Preferential hiring or admissions policies for blacks are therefore likely to be charged with being discriminatory, even though they are done in the name of rectifying discrimination and other evils. If one condemns the original discrimination against blacks because it was based on an irrelevant characteristic, and hence was unreasonable, one is likely to be charged with inconsistency if one now advocates policies that award and deny benefits on the basis of the same characteristic.

The defect in this charge is that it mistakenly assumes that race is the justification for preferential treatment. This is only apparently so. If preference is given to blacks because of past discrimination and present poverty, the basis for this preference is not that these people are black but rather that they are likely to have been victimized by discrimination, to have fewer benefits and more burdens than is fair, to be members of an underrepresented group, or to be the sorts of persons that can help public institutions meet the needs of those who are now poorly served. Being black does not itself have any relevancy to these goals, but the facts which are associated with being black often do in the present context.

### B. Administrative Convenience as Inadequate Justification

When this defect is pointed out, the person arguing that racially based preferential policies are discriminatory may formulate a new version of his objection. This version recognizes that the *justifying basis* for preferential policies is discrimination, injustice, unmet needs, and so forth, but it notes that being black is often a necessary condition for receiving preference and therefore forms the *administrative basis* for preferential programs. Those who defend the use of race as part of the administrative basis allow that race in itself is irrelevant, but they assert that the use of racial classifications in administering preferential policies is justified by the high correlation between being black and having the characteristics that form the justifying basis. Having noted this, the critic of preferential policies using racial classifications is likely to point out that a similar claim was and is made by racists. Racists claim that they do not treat blacks worse than whites simply because they are black, but rather because blacks are lazy or untrustworthy or have some other characteristic that makes them undeserving of good treatment. Like the advocates of preferential policies for blacks, racists deny that they base differential treatment on an irrelevant characteristic such as race. They claim that the justifying basis for their differential treatment of blacks is something relevant such as being lazy or untrustworthy, not something irrelevant such as race. Race only forms, the racist might say, the administrative basis for his policy of treating blacks worse than whites. The critic of preference on the basis of racial classifications will argue, therefore, that an approach to the justifications of preferential policies which distinguishes between the justifying basis—for example, having been harmed by discrimination—and the administrative basis—for example, being a low-income black—makes the same mistake as the racist since the form of reasoning is exactly the same. Thus, the objection continues, if the advocate of preferential policies can use this distinction between the justifying and the administrative bases to show that he is not practicing invidious discrimination, then so can the racist. But since this defense will not work for the racist, neither will it work for the defender of preferential policies.

But there is a way of distinguishing these cases, and it can be seen by comparing the premises that are used to connect being black with having a relevant characteristic. When these premises are compared, it becomes apparent that for the racist to defend his position, he has to make claims which can be proven to be erroneous about the correlation between being black and having some relevant defect such as being lazy or untrustworthy, while the defender of racially administered preferential policies can make a plausible case without using erroneous premises. Hence, one important way of distinguishing justifiable from unjustifiable uses of racial classifications is in terms of the soundness of the alleged correlation between race and a relevant characteristic. . . . Efficiency in administering large-scale programs requires that detailed investigations of individual cases be kept to a minimum, and this means that many allocative decisions will have to be made on the basis of gross but easily discernible characteristics. By giving preferences to all applicants who are members of certain disadvantaged groups, administrative costs can be kept to a minimum. The alternative is to investigate on an individual basis. . . . An approach of this sort might be workable and desirable in some circumstances, but it would be expensive both for the applicant and for the institution processing the applications. For this reason, there are considerable advantages in using gross indicators, including racial, ethnic and sexual ones, as indicators of the presence of the characteristics that provide the justifying basis.

### C. Problems of Stigmatization and Loss of Self-Respect

It may be the case, however, that the use of racial classifications in preferential programs favoring blacks may confirm a sense of inferiority among black recipients, since the presupposition of such programs is that blacks deserve or are in need of assistance. . . . Although special admissions procedures for blacks may, if misunderstood, be taken to imply black inferiority and thereby to stigmatize blacks, it seems to be an exaggeration to say, as Justice Douglas does, that programs designed to remedy injustices and overcome handicaps nevertheless stigmatize blacks no less than policies that required blacks to attend segregated schools. Indeed, if the stigmatizing effect of preferential programs were as great as that of segregated schools, one would expect to find blacks avoiding such programs, black organizations opposing them, and black leaders denouncing them. In practice, however, one finds nothing of the sort and indeed finds the opposite.

# JUSTIFYING REVERSE DISCRIMINATION IN EMPLOYMENT

*George Sher*

    A currently favored way of compensating for past discrimination is to afford preferential treatment to the members of those groups which have been discriminated against in the past. I propose to examine the rationale behind this practice when it is applied in the area of employment. I want to ask whether, and if so under what conditions, past acts of discrimination against members of a particular group justify the current hiring of a member of that group who is less than the best qualified applicant for a given job. Since I am mainly concerned about exploring the relations between past discrimination and present claims to employment, I shall make the assumption that each applicant is at least minimally competent to perform the job he seeks; this will eliminate the need to consider the claims of those who are to receive the services in question. Whether it is ever justifiable to discriminate in favor of an incompetent applicant, or a less than best qualified applicant for a job such as teaching, in which almost any increase in employee competence brings a real increase in services rendered, will be left to be decided elsewhere. Such questions, which turn on balancing the claim of the less than best qualified applicant against the competing claims of those who are to receive his services, are not as basic as the question of whether the less than best qualified applicant ever *has* a claim to employment.

I

It is sometimes argued, when members of a particular group have been barred from employment of a certain kind, that since this group has in

From George Sher, "Justifying Reverse Discrimination in Employment," *Philosophy & Public Affairs*, vol. 4, no. 2 (Winter 1975), pp. 159–70. Copyright © 1975 by Princeton University Press. Reprinted by permission of Princeton University Press.

the past received *less* than its fair share of the employment in question, it now deserves to receive *more* by way of compensation. This argument, if sound, has the virtue of showing clearly why preferential treatment should be extended even to those current group members who have not themselves been denied employment: if the point of reverse discrimination is to compensate a wronged *group*, it will presumably hardly matter if those who are preferentially hired were not among the original victims of discrimination. However, the argument's basic presupposition, that groups as opposed to their individual members are the sorts of entities that can be wronged and deserve redress, is itself problematic. Thus the defense of reverse discrimination would only be convincing if it were backed by a further argument showing that groups can indeed be wronged and have deserts of the relevant sort. No one, as far as I know, has yet produced a powerful argument to this effect, and I am not hopeful about the possibilities. Therefore I shall not try to develop a defense of reverse discrimination along these lines.

Another possible way of connecting past acts of discrimination in hiring with the claims of current group members is to argue that even if these current group members have not (yet) been denied *employment*, their membership in the group makes it very likely that they have been discriminatorily deprived of *other* sorts of goods. It is a commonplace, after all, that people who are forced to do menial and low-paying jobs must often endure corresponding privations in housing, diet, and other areas. These privations are apt to be distributed among young and old alike, and so to afflict even those group members who are still too young to have had their qualifications for employment bypassed. It is, moreover, generally acknowledged by both common sense and law that a person who has been deprived of a certain amount of one sort of good may sometimes reasonably be compensated by an equivalent amount of a good of another sort. (It is this principle, surely, that underlies the legal practice of awarding sums of money to compensate for pain incurred in accidents, damaged reputations, etc.) Given these facts and this principle, it appears that the preferential hiring of current members of discriminated-against groups may be justified as compensation for the *other* sorts of discrimination these individuals are apt to have suffered.

But, although this argument seems more promising than one presupposing group deserts, it surely cannot be accepted as it stands. For one thing, insofar as the point is simply to compensate individuals for the various sorts of privations they have suffered, there is no special reason to use reverse discrimination rather than some other mechanism to effect compensation. There are, moreover, certain other mechanisms of redress which seem prima facie preferable. It seems, for instance, that it would be most appropriate to compensate for past privations simply by making preferentially available to the discriminated-against individuals equivalent amounts of the very same sorts of goods of which they have been deprived; simple cash settlements would allow a far greater precision in the adjustment of compensation to privation than reverse discriminatory hiring ever could. Insofar as it does not provide any reason to adopt reverse discrimination rather than these prima facie preferable mechanisms of redress, the suggested defense of reverse discrimination is at least incomplete.

Moreover, and even more important, if reverse discrimination is viewed simply as a form of compensation for past privations, there are serious questions about its fairness. Certainly the privations to be compensated for are not the sole responsibility of those individuals whose superior qualifications will have to be bypassed in the reverse discriminatory process. These individuals, if responsible for those privations at all, will at least be no more responsible than others with relevantly similar histories. Yet reverse discrimination will compensate for the privations in question at the expense of these individuals alone. It will have no effect at all upon those other, equally responsible persons whose qualifications are inferior to begin with, who are already entrenched in their jobs, or whose vocations are noncompetitive in nature. Surely it is unfair to distribute the burden of compensation so unequally.

These considerations show, I think, that reverse discriminatory hiring of members of groups that have been denied jobs in the past cannot be justified simply by the fact that each group member has been discriminated against in other areas. If this fact is to enter into the justification of reverse discrimination at all, it must be in some more complicated way.

## II

Consider again the sorts of privations that are apt to be distributed among the members of those groups restricted in large part to menial and low-paying jobs. These individuals, we said, are apt to live in substandard homes, to subsist on improper and imbalanced diets, and to receive inadequate educations. Now, it is certainly true that adequate housing, food, and education are goods in and of themselves; a life without them is certainly less pleasant and less full than one with them. But, and crucially, they are also goods in a different sense entirely. It is an obvious and well-documented fact that (at least) the sorts of nourishment and education a person receives as a child will causally affect the sorts of skills and capacities he will have as an adult—including, of course, the very skills which are needed if he is to compete on equal terms for jobs and other goods. Since this is so, a child who is deprived of adequate food and education may lose not only the immediate enjoyments which a comfortable and stimulating environment bring but also the subsequent ability to compete equally for other things of intrinsic value. But to lose this ability to compete is, in essence, to lose one's access to the goods that are being competed for; and this, surely, is itself a privation to be compensated for if possible. It is, I think, the key to an adequate justification of reverse discrimination to see that practice, not as the redressing of *past* privations, but rather as a way of neutralizing the *present* competitive disadvantage *caused* by those past privations and thus as a way of restoring equal access to those goods which society distributes competitively. When reverse discrimination is justified in this way, many of the difficulties besetting the simpler justification of it disappear.

For whenever someone has been irrevocably deprived of a certain good and there are several alternative ways of providing him with an equivalent amount of another good, it will ceteris paribus be preferable to choose whichever substitute comes closest to actually replacing the lost good. It is this principle that makes preferential access to decent housing, food, and education especially desirable as a way of compensating for the experiential impoverishment of a deprived childhood. If, however, we are concerned to compensate not for the experiential poverty, but for the effects of childhood deprivations, then this principle tells just as heavily for reverse discrimination as the proper form of compensation. If the lost good is just the *ability* to compete on equal terms for first-level goods like desirable jobs, then surely the most appropriate (and so preferable) way of substituting for what has been lost is just to remove the *necessity* of competing on equal terms for these goods—which, of course, is precisely what reverse discrimination does.

When reverse discrimination is viewed as compensation for lost ability to compete on equal terms, a reasonable case can also be made for its fairness. Our doubts about its fairness arose because it seemed to place the entire burden of redress upon those individuals whose superior qualifications are bypassed in the reverse discriminatory process. This seemed wrong because these individuals are, of course, not apt to be any more responsible for past discrimination than others with relevantly similar histories. But, as we are now in a position to see, this objection misses the point. The crucial fact about these individuals is not that they are more *responsible* for past discrimination than others with relevantly similar histories (in fact, the dirty work may well have been done before any of their generation attained the age of responsibility), but rather that unless reverse discrimination is practiced, they will *benefit* more than the others from its effects on their competitors. They will benefit more because unless they are restrained, they, but not the others, will use their competitive edge to claim jobs which their competitors would otherwise have gotten. Thus, it is only because they stand to *gain* the most from the relevant effects of the *original* discrimination, that the bypassed individuals stand to *lose* the most from *reverse* discrimination. This is surely a valid reply to the charge that reverse discrimination does not distribute the burden of compensation equally.

III

So far, the argument has been that reverse discrimination is justified insofar as it neutralizes competitive disadvantages caused by past privations. This may be correct, but it is also oversimplified. In actuality, there are many ways in which a person's environment may affect his ability to compete; and there may well be logical differences among these ways which affect the degree to which reverse discrimination is called for. Consider, for example, the following cases:

(1) An inadequate education prevents someone from acquiring the degree of a certain skill that he would have been able to acquire with a better education.

(2) An inadequate diet, lack of early intellectual stimulation, etc., lower an individual's ability, and thus prevent him from acquiring the degree of competence in a skill that he would otherwise have been able to acquire.

(3) The likelihood that he will not be able to use a certain skill because he belongs to a group which has been discriminated against in the past leads a person to decide, rationally, not even to try developing that skill.

(4) Some aspect of his childhood environment renders an individual incapable of putting forth the sustained effort needed to improve his skills.

These are four different ways in which past privations might adversely affect a person's skills. Ignoring for analytical purposes the fact that privation often works in more than one of these ways at a time, shall we say that reverse discrimination is equally called for in each case?

It might seem that we should say it is, since in each case a difference in the individual's environment would have been accompanied by an increase in his mastery of a certain skill (and, hence, by an improvement in his competitive position with respect to jobs requiring that skill). But this blanket counterfactual formulation conceals several important distinctions. For one thing, it suggests (and our justification of reverse discrimination seems to require) the possibility of giving *just enough* preferential treatment to the disadvantaged individual in each case to restore to him the competitive position that he would have had, had he not suffered his initial disadvantage. But in fact, this does not seem to be equally possible in all cases. We can roughly calculate the difference that a certain improvement in education or intellectual stimulation would have made in the development of a person's skills if his efforts had been held constant (cases 1 and 2); for achievement is known to be a relatively straightforward compositional function of ability, environmental factors, and effort. We cannot, however, calculate in the same way the difference that improved prospects or environment would have made in degree of *effort* expended; for although effort is affected by environmental factors, it is not a known compositional function of them (or of anything else). Because of this, there would be no way for us to decide how much preferential treatment is just enough to make up for the efforts that a particular disadvantaged individual would have made under happier circumstances.

There is also another problem with (3) and (4). Even if there were a way to afford a disadvantaged person just enough preferential treatment to make up for the efforts he was prevented from making by his environment, it is not clear that he *ought* to be afforded that much preferential treatment. To allow this, after all, would be to concede that the effort he *would* have made under other conditions is worth just as much as the effort that his rival actually *did* make; and this, I think, is implausible. Surely a person who *actually has* labored long and hard to achieve a given degree of a certain skill is more deserving of a job requiring that skill than another who is equal in all other relevant respects, but who merely *would* have worked and achieved the same amount under different conditions. Because actual effort creates desert in a way that merely possible effort does not, reverse discrimination to restore precisely the competitive position that a person would have had if he had not been prevented from working harder would not be desirable even if it were possible.

There is perhaps also a further distinction to be made here. A person who is rationally persuaded by an absence of opportunities not to develop a certain skill (case 3) will typically not undergo any sort of character transformation in the process of making this decision. He will be the same person after his decision as before it, and, most often, the same person without his skill as with it. In cases such as (4), this is less clear. A person who is rendered incapable of effort by his environment does in a sense undergo a character transformation; to become truly incapable of sustained effort is to become a different (and less meritorious) person from the person one would otherwise have been. Because of this (and somewhat paradoxically, since his character change is itself apt to stem from factors beyond his control), such an individual may have less of a claim to reverse discrimination than one whose lack of effort does not flow from even an environmentally induced character fault, but rather from a justified rational decision.

## IV

When reverse discrimination is discussed in a nontheoretical context, it is usually assumed that the people most deserving of such treatment are blacks, members of other ethnic minorities, and women. In this last section, I shall bring the results of the foregoing discussion to bear on this assumption. Doubts will be raised both about the analogy between the claims of blacks and women to reverse discrimination and about the propriety, in absolute terms, of singling out either group as the proper recipient of such treatment.

For many people, the analogy between the claims of blacks and the claims of women to reverse discrimination rests simply upon the undoubted fact that both groups have been discriminatorily denied jobs in the past. But on the account just proposed, past discrimination justifies reverse discrimination only insofar as it has adversely affected the competitive position of present group members. When this standard is invoked, the analogy between the claims of blacks and those of women seems immediately to break down. The exclusion of blacks from good jobs in the past has been only one element in an interlocking pattern of exclusions and often has resulted in a poverty issuing in (and in turn reinforced by) such other privations as inadequate nourishment, housing, and health care, lack of time to provide adequate guidance and intellectual stimulation for the young, dependence on (often inadequate) public education, etc. It is this whole complex of privations that undermines the ability of the young to compete; and it is largely because of its central causal role in this complex that the past unavailability of good jobs for blacks justifies reverse discrimination in their favor now. In the case of women, past discrimination in employment simply has not played the same role. Because children commonly come equipped with both male *and* female parents, the inability of the female parent to get a good job need not, and usually does not, result in a poverty detracting from the quality of the nourishment, education, housing, health, or intellectual stimulation of the female child (and, of course, when such poverty does result, it affects male and female children indifferently). For this reason, the past inaccessibility of good jobs for women does not seem to create for them the same sort of claim on reverse discrimination that its counterpart does for blacks.

Many defenders of reverse discrimination in favor of women would reply at this point that although past discrimination in employment has of course not played the *same* causal role in the case of women which it has in the case of blacks, it has nevertheless played *a* causal role in both cases. In the case of women, the argument runs, that role has been mainly psychological: past discrimination in hiring has led to a scarcity of female "role-models" of suitably high achievement. This lack, together with a culture which in many other ways subtly inculcates the idea that women should not or cannot do the jobs that men do, has in turn made women psychologically less able to do these jobs. This argument is hard to assess fully, since it obviously rests on a complex and problematic psychological claim. The following objections, however, are surely relevant. First, even if it is granted without question that cultural bias and absence of suitable role-models do have some direct and pervasive effect upon women, it is not clear that this effect must take the form of a reduction of women's *abilities* to do the jobs men do. A more likely outcome would seem to be a reduction of women's *inclinations* to do these jobs—a result whose proper compensation is not preferential treatment of those women who have sought the jobs in question, but rather the encouragement of others to seek those jobs as well. Of course, this disinclination to do these jobs may in turn lead some women not to develop the relevant skills; to the extent that this occurs, the competitive position of these women will indeed be affected, albeit indirectly, by the scarcity of female role-models. Even here, however, the resulting disadvantage will not be comparable to those commonly produced by the poverty syndrome. It will flow solely from lack of effort, and so will be of the sort (cases 3 and 4) that neither calls for nor admits of full equalization by reverse discrimination. Moreover, and conclusively, since there is surely the same dearth of role-models, etc., for blacks as for women, whatever psychological disadvantages accrue to women because of this will beset blacks as well. Since blacks, but not women, must also suffer the privations associated with poverty, it follows that they are the group more deserving of reverse discrimination.

Strictly speaking, however, the account offered here does not allow us to speak this way of *either* group. If the point of reverse discrimination is to compensate for competitive disadvantages caused by past discrimination, it will be justified in favor of only those group members whose abilities have actually been reduced; and it would be most implausible to suppose that *every* black (or *every* woman) has been affected in this way. Blacks from middle-class or affluent backgrounds will surely have escaped many, if not all, of the competitive handicaps besetting those raised under less fortunate circumstances; and if they have, our account provides no reason to practice reverse discrimination in their favor. Again, whites from impoverished backgrounds may suffer many, if not all, of the competitive handicaps besetting their black counterparts; and if they do, the account provides no reason *not* to practice reverse discrimination in their favor. Generally, the proposed account allows us to view racial (and sexual) boundaries only as roughly suggesting which individuals are likely to have been disadvantaged by past discrimination. Anyone who construes these boundaries as playing a different and more decisive role must show us that a different defense of reverse discrimination is plausible.

# CHAPTER FOURTEEN
# CAPITAL PUNISHMENT

John Evans III grew up in Beaumont, Texas. He was on parole from an Indiana prison in 1977 when he went on a ten-state crime spree that allegedly included scores of robberies, kidnappings, killings, and other violent crimes. In one incident, Evans entered the pawnshop of Edward Nassar in Mobile, Alabama, and murdered Nassar while the man's two daughters looked on in horror. Evans was finally captured in Little Rock, Arkansas, and returned to Alabama, where he stood trial for the killing. During the proceedings, Evans demanded that if he was found guilty he should be given the death sentence. When the jury convicted him, his demand was granted.

John Evans was executed on April 22, 1983, after receiving his last meal—steak and shrimp—and the last rites of the Roman Catholic Church. The next day, newspapers across the country carried the following story:

> Prison officials could not explain yesterday why it took 10 minutes and three jolts of electricity to execute convicted murderer John Louis Evans III in what his lawyer called "a barbaric ritual."
>
> "John Evans was burned alive by the state of Alabama," attorney Russell F. Canan said of Friday night's execution. "John Evans was tortured in the name of vengeance and the disguise of justice."
>
> After the U.S. Supreme Court dissolved a last-minute stay of execution granted by a federal judge, Evans' head was shaved, and he was dressed in a

white cotton uniform and taken the 25 steps from his Death Row cell to "Big Yellow Mama," Alabama's electric chair at Holman Prison.

The 33-year-old condemned man appeared calm as he was strapped in the brightly painted electric chair and the death warrant was read. A skull cap of electrodes was fitted on his head, his chin was strapped tight to the chair back and his face covered by a black mask that draped over his chest.

The first 30-second surge of 1,900 volts of electricity came at 5:30 p.m. P.S.T. Evans tensed and the electrode on his left leg snapped off. The second jolt came at 5:33 p.m. Evans did not move but a puff of smoke and a small tongue of flame burst from the leather strap on his left temple. Doctors said he was still not dead.

Canan, a witness to the execution, then sought clemency from Gov. George Wallace, saying the protracted execution was "cruel and unusual." The governor's office quickly reported back that Wallace would not intervene.

The third surge of electricity was administered at 5:40 p.m. and Evans was declared dead four minutes later. Prison spokesman Ron Tate said he could not explain why the first jolt did not kill Evans.

"He was dead for all practical purposes after the second. He never knew what hit him after the first one," Tate said. "Why it took more than one, I don't know."

Tate said the electric chair had been tested every day last week with gauges to make sure it had a high enough current level.

This was supposed to be a very clean manner of administering death," he said. "The chair checked out fine. I don't know that it can be explained."

Inez Nassar, the mother of pawnbroker Edward Nassar, the man Evans killed during a 1977 robbery attempt, said, "He got what he deserved." However, she added, "I feel sorry for his mother; she has my sympathy."

"I was proud of him," said Evans' mother, Betty Evans Dickson, after her son was put to death. "He left this life as a true Christian. The smile at the end was in anticipation of stepping into the arms of his Savior."

She said the family's only regret "was the agony we felt caused by the method used to carry out the execution. We abhor the needless cruelty of electrocution."[1]

Inflicting the death penalty is obviously an ugly business, especially when it is accomplished in the manner just described. How then can such punishment be justified? Traditionally, ethicians have done so on the basis of four theories.

According to the first theory, the presence and threat of punishment are intended to deter others who might contemplate the commission of similar crimes. This is usually called the deterrence theory.[2] For example, the horrifying execution of John Evans was intended to strike fear into the hearts of other people who might consider committing the kind of crime for which Evans was executed. After seeing what happened to Evans, the theory implies, other criminals will be deterred from doing the

1. *San Francisco Sunday Examiner and Chronicle*, April 24, 1983, p. A2.

2. For a defense of the deterrent effects of the death penalty, see Ernest van den Haag, "On Deterrence and the Death Penalty," *Ethics*, vol. 78 (1968), pp. 280–87; this is criticized in Hugo Bedau, "The Death Penalty as a Deterrent: Argument and Evidence," *Ethics*, vol. 80 (1970), pp. 205–16; van den Haag replies in "Deterrence and the Death Penalty: A Rejoinder," *Ethics*, vol. 81 (1970), pp. 74–75.

same. However, critics of deterrence claim that capital punishment does not in fact produce this result. They point out that states and nations that allow the death penalty do not uniformly have lower crime rates than those that employ it. Moreover, a person who is engaged in committing a crime is usually in such a confused or psychologically impaired state of mind that he does not stop to consider the legal consequences of his act. For example, when Evans went on his crime spree he certainly was not cooly weighing the costs and benefits of his behavior.

A second theory holds that punishment is intended to prevent the person who receives it from committing future crimes. (The deterrence theory, by contrast, holds that punishment is supposed to deter óthers from committing future crimes.) Imprisonment, for example, incapacitates the criminal during the period of confinement, while the death penalty ensures that he is permanently unable to commit crimes. This is generally called the preventative theory of punishment. But opponents of the death penalty have argued that execution is too severe a way of incapacitating a criminal when permanent imprisonment can accomplish the same purpose. They may argue, for example, that John Evans should have been given a life sentence instead of being sentenced to death in such a "cruel" and "barbaric ritual."

A third theory of punishment, which concentrates on reform or rehabilitation, is a variant of the preventative theory insofar as it also holds that punishment is intended to prevent the person who is punished from committing future crimes.[3] The rehabilitative theory, however, adds that punishment should change the criminal so he will obey society's laws in the future. Obviously, the death penalty could not be justified on the basis of this theory. Moreover, critics have argued that punishments that attempt to reform the criminal are manipulative because they do not allow him to choose his own values (and take the consequences of doing so) but instead force him to accept the values society imposes on him. Such critics might point out that John Evans explicitly asked for the death penalty at his trial. Consequently, they might argue that it would have been wrong to put Evans in prison and attempt to manipulate or change his psychology so as to force him to conform to society's values instead of respecting his explicit wishes.

The fourth theory of punishment is the retributive one.[4] According to this view, the criminal, by wrongfully and deliberately injuring others, becomes deserving of punishment. Justice then requires that he accept a form of retribution as severe as the injury he inflicted on someone else. This is the opinion expressed by the mother of Edward Nassar, the man John Evans murdered, when she says: "He got what he deserved." It is also the opinion Evans' lawyer, Russell F. Canan, was criticizing when he exclaimed, "John Evans was tortured in the name of vengeance and the

3. Discussions of the morality of rehabilitation may be found in Jeffrie G. Murphy, ed., *Punishment and Rehabilitation* (Belmont, Calif.: Wadsworth, 1973).

4. For a defense of the retributive theory óf capital punishment, see Walter Berns, *For Capital Punishment* (New York: Basic Books, 1979).

disguise of justice." Opponents of the retributive theory hold that it is merely a socially accepted way of extracting revenge. And it is immoral, these critics add, for society to impose the death penalty simply to extract revenge.

There are, then, a number of questions raised by the issue of capital punishment.[5] Even if a person takes a human life, is it acceptable for the state to take the murderer's life in return? Or is human life so sacred that killing is never justified, even in response to an act of murder? Furthermore, since humans are subject to error, should capital punishment be exercised when there is the slightest possibility of executing an innocent person? The essays that follow deal with these and other related questions.

In "Does Capital Punishment Deter?" Steven Goldberg, a utilitarian, tries to show that such punishment can be justified on the basis of a deterrence theory. He approaches the issue not by asking what effect the punishment had on the murderer, but by asking what effect it had on those who do not commit murder: how exactly did punishment deter the rest of us from committing murder? His view is that punishment does not deter at the moment of the crime. Instead, long before the crime would have been committed, capital punishment has created in us a strong internalized prohibition against murder. In other words, we are deterred from murdering when society inculcates in us the value of refraining from murder, and society does this by inflicting the most severe of its punishments on murderers. If this is how capital punishment deters, Goldberg reasons, then it works even if statistical studies show that criminals are not always deterred—and even if criminals are not deterred more in nations with capital punishment than in nations without capital punishment. Moreover, Goldberg argues, it is better (from a utilitarian point of view) to gamble on the deterrent effect of capital punishment than risk innocent lives by eliminating such a punishment.

David A. Conway also discusses the deterrence theory in his essay, "Capital Punishment and Deterrence: Some Considerations in Dialogue Form." Here he considers several arguments for and against capital punishment, using the device of a conversation between two individuals with opposing views. The first argument Conway discusses is what he calls the "preference" argument, which holds that if given the choice between life imprisonment and the death penalty most people would prefer the former. For this reason, the death penalty must be a more severe punishment and a stronger deterrent than life imprisonment. Conway replies, however, that since both execution and life imprisonment are extremely severe, the deterrent value of the two is very likely indistinguishable. The second argument is the "rational person–deterrent argument," according to which the death penalty will at least deter rational persons. To this,

5. Further discussions of the death penalty may be found in Hugo A. Bedau, ed., *The Death Penalty in America*, rev. ed. (Garden City, N.Y.: Doubleday, 1967) and James McCafferty, ed., *Capital Punishment* (New York: Lieber-Atherton, 1972). For a discussion of the factual issues associated with capital punishment, see Hugo Adam Bedau and C. M. Pierce, eds., *Capital Punishment in the United States* (New York: AMS Press, 1976).

Conway replies that it is not clear why rational persons seldom murder. The third and most important argument Conway considers is the "best-bet argument." (Which is similar to the one Goldberg presents in the closing paragraphs of his essay.) According to the best-bet argument, it is better to use capital punishment and be mistaken about its deterrent effect than to get rid of capital punishment and be mistaken about its failure to deter. For if we use capital punishment and it turns out that such punishment does not deter, we have merely lost the lives of the criminals we needlessly executed. But if we get rid of capital punishment and it turns out that such punishment would in fact have deterred some criminals, then we have lost the lives of the innocent people who were their victims. In other words, it is better to gamble on losing the lives of criminals than on losing the lives of innocent people. Conway replies that this argument assumes that people (criminals) can be treated as means rather than as ends in themselves, which violates Kant's moral principles. Although one might feel that the life of an innocent person is worth more than the life of a guilty one, such a feeling is mistaken. All human lives have the same intrinsic value. Moreover, Conway points out, if we use capital punishment, then we are not gambling that lives will be lost, since we will know for sure that we are losing lives, i.e., the lives of the criminals we execute.

Jeffrie Murphy approaches the issue of punishment from a retributive point of view in "Marxism and Retribution." His first proposition is that all utilitarian theories of punishment are mistaken because they treat criminals as means and not as ends in themselves. If people are to be treated as ends and not merely as means, he argues, then they must be subjected only to punishments they have somehow consented to accept. Murphy then offers an account of punishment that is based on a social contract theory that draws on both Kant and Rawls. According to this theory, a person who accepts the legitmate authority of the state freely consents to the principle that the state may impose punishment on those who break the law. Because of this consent, when the state punishes some person it is merely treating that person in the way he has freely and rationally consented to be treated. This retributive theory of punishment, Murphy claims, treats people as ends and not as means. However, following Marx, he then argues that this social contract view is defective in three ways. First, it is egoistic insofar as it assumes that individuals rationally calculate what they must consent to in order to get as many benefits for themselves as they can. Second, it is unjust because it punishes people for acting out of motives fostered by capitalism: greed and selfishness. Third, people do not consent freely to the state since for all practical purposes they are not free to choose whether to stay in it or leave it.

Richard Brandt, a utilitarian, gives his own analysis of punishment in "A Utilitarian Theory of Criminal Punishment." He begins by outlining the traditional utilitarian argument that punishment "maximizes expectable utility" because (1) punishment deters other lawbreakers, (2) punishment changes the person so that he will not commit future crimes, and (3) punishment removes lawbreakers from society. In addition, utilitarianism holds that the severity of punishment should balance the probable benefit it produces. Brandt then dismisses several objections to this utilitarian account. First, he points out, the utilitarian principle would not be false even if premises (1) and (2) were false. Second, utilitarianism can distinguish between exculpating excuses (i.e., excuses that remove a person's guilt altogether) and mitigating excuses (i.e., excuses that lessen a person's guilt) just as well as any other moral theory can.

# DOES CAPITAL PUNISHMENT DETER?

*Steven Goldberg*

Those who deny the ability of capital punishment to deter invoke a number of lines of reasoning—none of which is particularly convincing. They point out, quite correctly, that the murderer often does not believe that he will be caught (so that it does not matter to the murderer whether the punishment for murder is a small fine or death). The problem with this attempt to deny the deterrent effect of capital punishment is that no one who supports capital punishment and who has thought the problem through would predicate his support on the ability of capital punishment to deter the murderer; by definition the murderer has not been deterred by anything. The question that is of determinative importance, and the question that the opponents of capital punishment rarely attempt to even consider on a theoretical level, is what is it that deters those who are deterred; that is, not the murderer, but the rest of us? . . .

A determinative factor affecting the degree to which murder will be committed in any given society may be the strength with which the value prohibiting murder is inculcated in the society's individual members, and this strength may be a function of the penalty with which the society backs up the value. It may be that individuals give values an internal weight concomitant with the weight they perceive the value as being given by their society, and this perception may judge the weight given to the value by the society in terms of—among other things—the weight of the punishment with which the society backs up the value. This seems a reasonable explanation of why the forces deterring murder defeat, in most individuals, those encouraging murder.

If our description of the way in which individuals develop the resistance to emotional and environmental factors encouraging murder is cor-

From Steven Goldberg, "Does Capital Punishment Deter?" *Ethics*, vol. 85, no. 1 (October 1974), pp. 68, 69, 70–74. Copyright © 1974 by the University of Chicago Press.

rect, society inculcates in the individual the value prohibiting murder (or any other value) on the basis of its "saying" (through its severe punishment) that the value is a very important one and *not* primarily through the threat of punishment. One might argue that threat is always the initiator in the development of the individual's perception of the strength of a value, and this might well be correct, but it is important to note that this is very different from the assertion that threat deters at the time of the act. We who do not murder refrain from murdering because of the strength of the internalized value that one does not murder and not because the present threat of punishment is so great that present fear of punishment precludes our committing the murderous act. . . .

It should be clear that capital punishment deters—if it does deter—not because the individual who is considering murder weighs the potential murder against the punishment and decides that, while life imprisonment is a cheap price to pay, execution is too dear. He is deterred by capital punishment—if he is deterred by capital punishment—because he has perceived, from childhood on, that murder is the most serious of social offenses. He has accepted this assessment of the seriousness of murder and internalized it in part because his society has emphasized the importance of this value by punishing it with a penalty stronger than that it imposes for any other crime. It is possible, of course, that this reasoning is all correct, but that one weighs internalized values only in relative terms so that the internal energies working against the emotions that would utilize murder (and the environmental factors that encourage murder) would be equally strong if life imprisonment were the most severe penalty invoked by the society. Or it is possible that absolute severity is crucial, but that it is so only up to a maximal threshold (ten years' imprisonment, for example) past which the individual's internal resistance no longer increases its strength. However, one is not justified in *assuming* that either of these possibilities in reality obtains.

So we can begin at least to approach the question of what it is that does deter most people from committing murder, a question that the opponents of capital punishment rarely even attempt to address. We can agree that many of those individuals who do commit murder are following irrational imperatives before which social sanctions are impotent, yet suggest that it is reasonable to assume that the behavior of most individuals conforms to social values, that the likelihood of the failure of most of these individuals to conform to social values (the likelihood of, for example, an individual failing to conform his behavior to the value prohibiting murder) is related to the importance of the value, and that the individual comes to appreciate the degree of importance placed upon the value by society through—among other things—the severity of the punishment for ignoring the value.

Thus even if one views the majority of murderers as individuals for whom irrational forces render social values irrelevant and/or individuals who purposely choose negative sanctions (i.e., individuals who seek the punishment rather than the rewards of the crime), this view leaves unanswered the question of what deters those who do not murder. One could, on the other hand, see all or some murderers as individuals in whom the battle between those emotions which, as Freud tells us, would "murder even for trifles" (and the environmental factors which tend to encourage murder) and the necessities of social life (to which the individual conforms as he internalizes the culture that his society inculcates in him) is won by the former. This view would see the majority of society's members as not murdering because, for this group, society's values have been instilled with sufficient strength to defeat the emotions for which murder is merely another way of dealing with environmental pressure. This view would then—without invoking individual irrational forces or a desire for punishment—have to explain why, for the group of murderers, social values failed to deter. It would then have to ask whether more severe punishment would have served to imbue the social values with enough strength to defeat the forces and emotions which, in the murderer, had won the battle and generated murderous behavior.

I do not know whether capital punishment deters, but I do know that it makes sense that it would and that the arguments attempting to demonstrate that it does not are unpersuasive. Given the nature of a modern society with its heterogeneity infusing every aspect of social life and its encouragement of diversity and freedom of speech, it does not seem likely that, save perhaps the society in the throes of religious or revolutionary rebirth, any society will ever again be able to count on the strength of a single shared culture and familial authority to maintain even the minimal amount of social control necessary for a society to survive. If we cannot rely on shared values and familial authority as the sole sources of social control it behooves us to understand the mechanisms which serve to permit society to survive. Such understanding is rendered impossible if we categorically assume the correctness of an explanation which may well be incorrect. This is what we do when we assert the inability of capital punishment to deter.

I suspect that we would all *like* to believe that capital punishment does not deter. This relieves us of the weight of a moral decision. The strength of human reaction reflects perceived proximity, and most of us feel the responsibility inherent in supporting the execution of real murderers more intensely than the responsibility for a hypothetical group of victims who—if capital punishment does deter—will be murdered if our opposition to capital punishment prevails but who will not be murdered if our opposition fails and capital punishment is maintained. Our seeming sympathy may well be an act of moral cowardice, an acceptance of a position that caters to fears of potential guilt rather than to responsibility to real, if unnameable, people. For if the proponent of capital punishment is incorrect in his assumption that capital punishment deters and is successful in his efforts to convince his society to invoke capital punishment, he is responsible "merely" for the deaths of *guilty* individuals who, if deterrence is the rationale for execution, should not be executed. If the opponent of capital punishment, on the other hand, is incorrect in his assumption that capital punishment does not deter and is successful in his efforts to convince his society to refrain from invoking capital punishment, *he* is responsible for the deaths of *innocent* people. Moreover, the number of innocent people who would not have been murdered if the deterrent of capital punishment had been invoked will be far greater than the number of innocent people who could conceivably be executed as a result of the mistaken conviction of innocent individuals for crimes they did not commit in a society that invokes capital punishment, and considerably greater, in all probability, than the total number of individuals who will be executed (guilty plus executed by mistaken conviction) in a society that invokes capital punishment. An awareness of this reduces considerably the persuasiveness of the position that argues that since we do not know whether capital punishment deters we should not invoke it.

# CAPITAL PUNISHMENT AND DETERRENCE: SOME CONSIDERATIONS IN DIALOGUE FORM

*David A. Conway*

*[A] lively dialogue between a retentionist, a proponent (P) of capital punishment, and an abolitionist, an opponent (O) of capital punishment.*

P:  I am happy to learn that our state legislature is trying to restore C.P.[1] Many of the legislators think they can pass a bill prescribing C.P. that the Supreme Court would not find unconstitutional.

O:  Yes, that is true in many legislatures. But it is hardly something I am happy about. Not only do I think C.P. is wrong, but I see a great danger in the present situation. The prime question in the minds of too many legislators seems to be, How do we draft laws that the court would not object to? The more basic question, Is C.P. ethically justifiable? may be lost sight of altogether.

P:  Perhaps, but if necessary, I think C.P. can be justified easily enough.

O:  Are you some sort of retributivist?

P:  Not at all. I hold that deterrence is the aim of punishment and that it is the central issue in the minds of legislators. They, as I am, are worried about the sheer lack of personal safety in our society.

1. I shall use "C.P." for "capital punishment" throughout this paper.

From David A. Conway, "Capital Punishment and Deterrence: Some Considerations in Dialogue Form," *Philosophy & Public Affairs*, vol. 3, no. 4 (Summer, 1974), pp. 431–37, 439–43. Copyright © 1974 by Princeton University Press. Excerpts reprinted by permission of Princeton University Press.

O: I didn't know that you had any strong feelings on this subject.
P: I didn't until recently. Then I read an interview in a newspaper. Ernest van den Haag, in response to questions from Philip Nobile, gives some arguments for C.P. that I find very convincing.[2] And I would bet that legislators do too.

## I. THE PREFERENCE ARGUMENT

O: How can you think that C.P. is an effective deterrent? What about all of the statistical studies that have failed to show that this is true?[3]
P: I admit that such studies are inconclusive. But I am not relying on them to show the deterrent value of C.P. A simpler fact will do the job. Consider this exchange in the van den Haag interview:

> *Nobile:* Is it true that capital punishment is a better deterrent than irrevocable life imprisonment?
>
> *van den Haag:* Yes, and that I can prove. I noticed a story in the paper the other day about a French heroin smuggler who pleaded guilty in a New York court because, as his lawyer admitted, he preferred irrevocable life imprisonment here to the guillotine in France.
>
> In fact, all prisoners prefer life. For even if the sentence is irrevocable, as long as there's life, psychologically, there's hope.

O: That argument is pretty popular among policemen and some editorial writers. In fact, Hugo Bedau in *The Death Penalty in America* includes a passage from Police Chief Allen which gives this argument. Bedau also mentions it in one of his essays in that volume, but he does not argue against it, although he does argue against some pro-C.P. views of Sidney Hook and Jacques Barzun.
P: What does that mean? That serious philosophers do not bother to argue against policemen and editorial writers? or that this particular argument is too stupid to bother with?
O: I'm not sure what it means. But I do think this argument is worth taking seriously. For it is intuitively plausible, and it rests on an empirical premise which seems to me to be almost indisputably true. That is, almost all of us would, at least consciously, given the present choice between being subjected to life imprisonment and to C.P., choose the former. Still, the argument is not convincing.
P: Why not?
O: There are a couple of reasons. First, you are saying that if, given that I must choose between some punishment x and another punishment

2. *St. Louis Globe-Democrat*, 6–7 January 1973. The arguments that van den Haag puts forth in this interview are currently quite popular among "intellectual conservatives" (e.g. writers for the *National Review* and conservative newspapers). The importance of his views is much greater than would be indicated just by the fact that one person happened to express them in a newspaper interview.

3. See, for instance, Hugo Bedau, *The Death Penalty in America* (Garden City: Doubleday, 1967), especially chapters 6 and 7.

*y*, I would strongly prefer *y*, then it follows that knowing that *x* will be inflicted on me if I perform some action will more effectively deter me from performing that action than will knowing that *y* will be inflicted. But consider that, given the choice, I would strongly prefer one thousand years in hell to eternity there. Nonetheless, if one thousand years in hell were the penalty for some action, it would be quite sufficient to deter me from performing that action. The additional years would do nothing to discourage me further.

Similarly, the prospect of the death penalty, while worse, may not have any greater deterrent effect than does that of life imprison-ment. In fact, I would imagine that either prospect would normally deter the rational man, while the man irrational enough not to be deterred by life imprisonment wouldn't be deterred by anything. So, the deterrent value of the two may be indistinguishable in practice even though one penalty may be definitely preferable to the other, if one is forced to choose between them.

P:  I see. Still there could be potential killers who are deterred by one and not by the other.

O:  Of course there *could be*. But have you forgotten what this discussion is about? You were supposed to have a proof that there are such people.

P:  OK. What is your other argument?

O:  Well, before, I argued that C.P. may not be an additional deterrent even if we assume that the criminal expects to be caught. But surely most do not expect to be caught or they hold no expectations at all, i.e. they are acting in "blind passion." In these cases, the punishment is irrelevant. If, however, we assume at least minimal rationality on the part of the criminal, he knows that there is some chance that he will be caught. Let us say that he believes that there is a one in ten chance that he will be, and also that the actuality of punishment *x* is sufficient to deter him from performing some actions from which punishment *y* would not deter him. It does not follow from this that a one in ten chance of *x* would deter him from performing any actions that a one in ten chance of *y* would not. To put it abstractly, we can assign to the death penalty 100 "disutility units" and to life imprisonment 50 "disutility units" to represent a significant difference between their undesirability. If the chance of either punishment actually being inflicted, however, is only one in ten, the difference becomes much less significant (i.e. $1/10 \cdot 100$ vs. $1/10 \cdot 50$, or 10 vs. 5 disutility units). We do not, of course, actually think in such precise terms of probability and utility units, but we do often approximate such reasoning. For instance, if it is impor-tant that I get to my destination quickly, I may be willing to (actu-ally) be fined for speeding while I am not willing to (actually) smash up my car and possibly myself. The difference between the two "penalties," if actually inflicted, is very great, great enough that one deters and the other does not. If, however, I know that there is only a slight chance of either occurring, the deterrent effect of the threats may be virtually indistinguishable, and I may speed on my way.

There are, then, at least two reasons for not equating "what we fear the most" with "what will most effectively deter us." Both of these are overlooked by those of you who give the "preference argument."


## II. THE RATIONAL PERSON–DETERRENT ARGUMENT

O:   What else did you find in the van den Haag interview?
P:   Well, there is this.

> *Nobile:* Most capital crimes are crimes of passion in which family members or friends kill each other. You can't stop this sort of thing with the threat of execution.
>
> *van den Haag:* It's perfectly true that the irrational person won't be deterred by any penalty. But to the extent that murder is an act of passion, the death penalty has already deterred all rational persons.

O:   And you agree with that?
P:   I suppose not. It does seem to be a pretty clear case of *post hoc, ergo propter hoc* reasoning. Still, there is a smaller point to be made here. Van den Haag says that C.P. has deterred rational persons. We do not know that it has. But, we also don't know that it hasn't. You opponents of C.P. are always saying something like, "Virtually all capital crimes are committed by persons in an irrational frame of mind. Therefore, C.P. (or any other punishment) cannot be regarded as a deterrent." So, you say, rational persons just do not (often) murder; I say, maybe they do not because of the threat of C.P. And so you cannot simply cite the fact that they do not as an argument against C.P.
O:   I have to grant you that point. What you say has been often enough said before, and, yet, without attempting to answer the point, my fellow opponents of C.P. too often just go on saying "rational people seldom murder." We must seriously try to show that rational people seldom murder even in the absence of C.P., rather than just continuing to recite "rational people seldom murder."


## III. THE BEST-BET ARGUMENT

O:   Do you have any more arguments to trot out?
P:   There is another in the van den Haag interview, and I have been saving the best for last.
O:   Let's hear it.
P:   All right.

*Nobile:* You're pretty cavalier about executions, aren't you?

*van den Haag:* If we have capital punishment, our risk is that it is unnecessary and no additional deterrence is achieved. But if we do not have it, our risk is that it might have deterred future murderers and spared future victims. Then it's a matter of which risk you prefer and I prefer to protect the victims.

*Nobile:* But you're gambling with the lives of condemned men who might otherwise live.

*van den Haag:* You're right. But we're both gambling. I'm gambling by executing and you're gambling by not executing.

We can see the force of this more clearly if we specify all of the possible outcomes. ("C.P. works" means "C.P. is a uniquely effective deterrent.")

|  | C.P. Works | C.P. Does Not Work |
|---|---|---|
| We bet C.P. works | (a) We win: Some murderers die, but innocents, who would otherwise die, are spared. | (b) We lose: Some murderers die for no purpose. The lives of others are unaffected. |
| We bet C.P. does not work | (c) We lose: Murderers live, but some innocents needlessly die. | (d) We win: Murderers live and the lives of others are unaffected. |

To make it more clear, suppose that we assign utility values in this way:

| | |
|---|---|
| Each murderer saved (not executed) | $+5$ |
| Each murderer executed | $-5$ |
| Each innocent person saved (not murdered) | $+10$ |
| Each innocent person murdered | $-10$ |

And assume also that, if C.P. works, each execution saves five innocents (a conservative estimate, surely). Potential gains and losses can be represented as:

$$
\begin{array}{ll}
\text{(a)} & \begin{array}{r} -5 \\ +50 \\ \hline +45 \end{array} \qquad \text{(b)} \quad -5 \\
\\
\text{(c)} & \begin{array}{r} +5 \\ -50 \\ \hline -45 \end{array} \qquad \text{(d)} \quad +5
\end{array}
$$

Now we can clearly see that not only do we have less to lose by betting on C.P., but we also have more to gain. It would be quite irrational not to bet on it.

O:    Pascal lives.

P:    What's that?

O:    Nothing. But look, you have to admit that there is an unsavory air about the argument. Nobile is right; the very notion of gambling with human lives seems morally repugnant.

P:    Maybe. But the fact is, as van den Haag says, we are also gambling if we do not execute, so you would do so as much as I.

O:    If so, then what your argument does is make very apparent the sort of point retributivists have always made. In Kantian terms, this sort of gambling with human lives is a particularly crude form of treating human beings as means rather than ends.

P:    You are willing to take a retributivist position in order to avoid the force of the argument?

O:    No. I will leave vengeance to the Lord, if he wants it. Anyway, I am not convinced there are not other reasons for rejecting your argument. I cannot get over the feeling that, in some sense, you are gambling with lives in a way I am not.

P:    Maybe that is a feeling that requires therapy to get over. Let me say it once more: If either of us loses our wager, human lives are needlessly lost. Granted, if you win yours, no life is lost at all, while if I win mine, the criminal loses his; but since he loses it and others gain theirs, that cannot be what is disturbing you. There is nothing disturbing about the prospect of saving many innocents.

O:    Wait now. I think that I am beginning to see what is going on here. . . . Van den Haag says, "It's a matter of which risk you prefer and I prefer to protect the victims." This immediately makes us think of the situation in a misleading way, for it seems to imply that while I would risk the lives of potential victims, he would risk the lives of convicted criminals. Or, minimally, it implies that there are risks of a like kind on both sides. But he isn't *risking* the lives of criminals; he is taking their lives and risking that some further good will come of this.

Put the same thing a slightly different way. It has been said in our discussion that on either bet, the result could be the needless loss of life. This makes the bets look more parallel than they are. If we bet your way, lives *have been lost,* and the risk is that this is needless. If we bet my way, it is *possible* that *lives may be lost,* needlessly. The difference between *lives lost,* perhaps needlessly, and *perhaps lives lost,* strikes me as a very significant one.

Now it should be clear that there is a sense in which you are gambling and I am not. It is exactly the sense in which I would be gambling if I used my last ten dollars to buy a lottery ticket but would not be if I used the money for groceries. Opting for a certain good, rather than risking it on a chance of a greater future good, is exactly what we mean when we say we refuse to gamble. Not gambling is taking the sure thing.

On the plausible moral principle, gambling with human lives is wrong, I can, then, reject the "Best-bet Argument."

P:   But if you understand "gambling" as not taking the sure thing, that moral principle is much too strong. Unless you have infallible knowledge that C.P. deters, on that principle it could never be justified, even under conditions in which you would want to adopt it. For even if it were ninety *percent* certain that it deters, you would still be gambling. And there are other circumstances in which we must gamble with lives in this way. Suppose you were almost, but not quite, certain a madman was about to set off all the bombs in the Western hemisphere. On that principle, you would not be justified in shooting him, even if it were the only possible way to stop him.

O:   Yes, I suppose that I must grant you that. But perhaps my suppositions that gambling is taking the risk and that gambling with human lives is wrong, taken together, at least partially account for my intuitive revulsion with van den Haag's argument.

P:   That may be. But so far, your intuitions have come to nothing in producing a genuine objection to the argument. I might add that I cannot even agree with your intuition that not gambling is taking the sure thing. Don't we sometimes disapprove of the person who refuses to take out life insurance or automobile liability insurance on the grounds that he is unwisely gambling that he will not die prematurely or be responsible for a highway accident? And he is taking the sure thing, keeping the premium money in his pocket. So, in common sense terms, failure to take a wise bet is sometimes "gambling."

O:   You are right again. And I thank you.

P:   For what?

O:   For saying just what I needed to hear in order to get straight on this whole business. As I indicated before, once we properly set out the betting situation, it does not appear that you proponents *have* such a good bet. But, in addition, I have (along with Nobile) been plagued by the feeling that there is something *in principle* wrong with the argument, that you would gamble with human lives while I would not. Now I understand that these two objections are actually only one objection.

P:   How so?

O:   Your insurance examples make the point. They show that what we intuitively think of as "gambling" is simply taking the more risky course of action, i.e. making a bad bet. So, my intuitive worry resulted simply from my conviction that your bet on C.P. is "gambling," i.e. that it is the riskier course of action; or, and this comes to the same thing, it is a *bad* bet.

P:   So you admit that there is nothing in principle wrong with my argument. That it all depends on whether the bet on C.P. is a good bet.

O:   I think I must. But that does not change my views about C.P. Once the bet is clarified, it should be clear that you are asking us to risk too much, to actually take a human life on far too small a chance of saving others. It is just a rotten bet.

P:  But it is not. As I have said, the life of each murderer is clearly worth much less than the life of an innocent, and, besides, each criminal life lost may save many innocents.

O:  This business about how much lives are "worth" seems pretty suspicious to me. According to some, human life qua human life is sacred and so all lives have the same value. According to others, the continued life of an innocent child is of much less importance than that of a criminal, since it is the criminal, qua criminal, who needs a chance to cleanse his soul. Or we could consider the potential social usefulness of the individual. If we do this, it is by no means obvious that the average murderer has less potential than the average person (consider Chessman or Leopold).

P:  How can you talk like that? Have you ever seen the battered, maimed body of an innocent child, raped and brutally murdered? Compare the value of that life against that of the beast who performed the deed, and then can you doubt that the child is worth 10,000 times the criminal?

O:  That seems to me to be based on a desire for revenge against "the beast," rather than on any evaluation of the "value of different lives." I admit to sharing such feelings, in some moods, at least, but it is not at all clear how they are relevant. Anyway, let's drop this. I am willing to rely on my feelings and grant, for argument purposes, that the life of a murderer is worth somewhat less than that of an innocent.

The basic problem with your wager is simply that we have no reason to think C.P. does work, and in the absence of such reason, the probability that it does is virtually zero. In general, you proponents seem confused about evidence. First, you say C.P. deters. Then you are confronted with evidence such as: State A and State B have virtually identical capital crime rates but State A hasn't had C.P. for one hundred years. You reply, for instance, that this could be because State A has more Quakers, who are peace-loving folk and so help to keep the crime rate down. And, you say, with C.P. and all those Quakers, State A, perhaps, could have had an even lower crime rate. Since we do not know about all such variables, the evidence is "inconclusive." Here, "inconclusive" can only mean that while the evidence does not indicate that C.P. deters, it also does not demonstrate that it does not.

The next thing we see is you proponents saying that we just do not know whether C.P. deters or not, since the evidence is "inconclusive." But for this to follow, "inconclusive" must mean something like "tends to point both ways." The only studies available, on your own account, fail to supply any evidence at all that it *does* deter. From this, we cannot get "inconclusive" in the latter sense; we can't say that "we just don't know" whether it deters; we can only conclude, "we have no reason to think it does." Its status as a deterrent is no different from, e.g. prolonged tickling of murderers' feet. It could deter, but why think it does?

P:  That's an absurd comparison that only a professional philosopher could think of. Common sense tells us that C.P. is a likely deterrent and foot-tickling is not.

O: I don't see how we can rely very heavily on the common sense of a law-abiding man to tell us how murderers think and why they act. Common sense also tells us that pornography should inflame the passions and therefore increase sex crimes, but Denmark's recent experience indicates quite the opposite.

P: So you demand that we have definite, unequivocal evidence and very high probability that C.P. deters before it could be said to be justifiable.

O: No, I never said that. That is what most of my fellow opponents of C.P. seem to demand. In fact, even though this would probably horrify most opponents, I think the "Best-bet Argument" shows that that demand is too strong. Given the possible gains and losses, if there is even a strong possibility that it works, I do not think it would be irrational to give it another try. But we should do so in full cognizance of the betting situation. We would be taking lives on the chance that there will be more than compensating saving of lives. And, I also think that it is damned difficult to show that there is even a strong possibility that C.P. deters.

P: Not really. Consider the fact that, given a choice between life imprisonment and C.P., prisoners always prefer . . .

O: Good night.

# MARXISM AND RETRIBUTION

*Jeffrie G. Murphy*

Philosophers have written at great length about the moral problems involved in punishing the innocent—particularly as these problems raise obstacles to an acceptance of the moral theory of Utilitarianism. Punishment of an innocent man in order to bring about good social consequences is, at the very least, not always clearly wrong on utilitarian principles. This being so, utilitarian principles are then to be condemned by any morality that may be called Kantian in character. For punishing an innocent man, in Kantian language, involves using that man as a mere means or instrument to some social good and is thus not to treat him as an end in himself, in accord with his dignity or worth as a person.

From Jeffrie G. Murphy, "Marxism and Retribution," *Philosophy & Public Affairs*, vol. 2, no. 3 (Spring 1973), pp. 218–41. Copyright © 1973 by Princeton University Press. Excerpts reprinted by permission of Princeton University Press.

The Kantian position on the issue of punishing the innocent, and the many ways in which the utilitarian might try to accommodate that position, constitute extremely well-worn ground in contemporary moral and legal philosophy. I do not propose to wear the ground further by adding additional comments on the issue here. What I do want to point out, however, is something which seems to me quite obvious but which philosophical commentators on punishment have almost universally failed to see—namely, that problems of the very same kind and seriousness arise for the utilitarian theory with respect to the punishment of the guilty. For a utilitarian theory of punishment (Bentham's is a paradigm) must involve justifying punishment in terms of its social results—e.g., deterrence, incapacitation, and rehabilitation. And thus even a guilty man is, on this theory, being punished because of the instrumental value the action of punishment will have in the future. He is being used as a means to some future good—e.g., the deterrence of others. Thus those of a Kantian persuasion, who see the importance of worrying about the treatment of persons as mere means, must, it would seem, object just as strenuously to the punishment of the guilty on utilitarian grounds as to the punishment of the innocent. Indeed the former worry, in some respects, seems more serious. For a utilitarian can perhaps refine his theory in such a way that it does not commit him to the punishment of the innocent. However, if he is to approve of punishment at all, he must approve of punishing the guilty in at least some cases. This makes the worry about punishing the guilty formidable indeed, and it is odd that this has gone generally unnoticed. It has generally been assumed that if the utilitarian theory can just avoid entailing the permissibility of punishing the innocent, then all objections of a Kantian character to the theory will have been met. This seems to me simply not to be the case.

What the utilitarian theory really cannot capture, I would suggest, is the notion of persons having rights. And it is just this notion that is central to any Kantian outlook on morality. Any Kantian can certainly agree that punishing persons (guilty or innocent) may have either good or bad or indifferent consequences and that insofar as the consequences (whether in a particular case or for an institution) are good, this is something in favor of punishment. But the Kantian will maintain that this consequential outlook, important as it may be, leaves out of consideration entirely that which is most morally crucial—namely, the question of rights. Even if punishment of a person would have good consequences, what gives us (ie., society) the moral right to inflict it? If we have such a right, what is its origin or derivation? . . .

Now one fairly typical way in which others acquire rights over us is by our own consent. If a neighbor locks up my liquor cabinet to protect me against my tendencies to drink too heavily, I might well regard this as a presumptuous interference with my own freedom, no matter how good the result intended or accomplished. He had no right to do it and indeed violated my rights in doing it. If, on the other hand, I had asked him to do this or had given my free consent to his suggestion that he do it, the same sort of objection on my part would be quite out of order. I had given him the right to do it, and he had the right to do it. In doing it, he violated no rights of mine—even if, at the time of his doing it, I did not desire or want the action to be performed. Here then we seem to have a case where my autonomy may be regarded as intact even though a desire of mine is thwarted. For there is a sense in which the thwarting of the desire can be imputed to me (my choice or decision) and not to the arbitrary intervention of another.

How does this apply to our problem? The answer, I think, is obvious. What is needed, in order to reconcile my undesired suffering of punishment at the hands of the state with my autonomy (and thus with the state's right to punish me), is a political theory which makes the state's decision to punish me in some sense my own decision. If I have willed my own punishment (consented to it, agreed to it) then—even if at the time I happen not to desire it—it can be said that my autonomy and dignity remain intact. Theories of the General Will and Social Contract theories are two such theories which attempt this reconciliation of autonomy with legitimate state authority (including the right or authority of the state to punish). Since Kant's theory happens to incorporate elements of both, it will be useful to take it for our sample.

## MORAL RIGHTS AND THE RETRIBUTIVE THEORY OF PUNISHMENT

Kant thinks that laws may require of a person some action that he does not desire to perform. This is not a violent invasion of his freedom, however, if it can be shown that in some antecedent position of choice (what John Rawls calls "the original position"), he would have been rational to adopt a Rule of Law (and thus run the risk of having some of his desires thwarted) rather than some other alternative arrangement like the classical State of Nature. This is, indeed, the only sense that Kant is able to make of classical Social Contract theories. Such theories are to be viewed, not as historical fantasies, but as ideal models of rational decison. For what these theories actually claim is that the only coercive institutions that are morally justified are those which a group of rational beings could agree to adopt in a position of having to pick social institutions to govern their relations. . . .

How does this bear specifically on punishment? Kant, as everyone knows, defends a strong form of a retributive theory of punishment. He holds that guilt merits, and is a sufficient condition for, the infliction of punishment. And this claim has been universally condemned—particularly by utilitarians—as primitive, unenlightened and barbaric.

But why is it so condemned? Typically, the charge is that infliction of punishment on such grounds is nothing but pointless vengeance. But what is meant by the claim that the infliction is "pointless"? If "pointless" is tacitly being analyzed as "disutilitarian," then the whole question is simply being begged. You cannot refute a retributive theory merely by noting that it is a retributive theory and not a utilitarian theory. This is to confuse redescription with refutation and involves an argument whose circularity is not even complicated enough to be interesting.

Why, then, might someone claim that guilt merits punishment? Such a claim might be made for either of two very different reasons. (1) Someone (e.g., a Moral Sense theorist) might maintain that the claim is a primitive and unanalyzable proposition that is morally ultimate—that we can just intuit the "fittingness" of guilt and punishment. (2) It might be maintained that the retributivist claim is demanded by a general theory of political obligation which is more plausible than any alternative theory. Such a theory will typically provide a technical analysis of such concepts as crime and punishment and will thus not regard the retributivist claim as an indisputable primitive. It will be argued for as a kind of theorem within the system. . . .

Kant's theory is of the second sort. He does not opt for retributivism as a bit of intuitive moral knowledge. Rather he offers a theory of punishment that is based on his general view that political obligation is to be analyzed, quasi-contractually, in terms of reciprocity. If the law is to remain just, it is important to guarantee that those who disobey it will not gain an unfair advantage over those who do obey voluntarily. It is important that no man profit from his own criminal wrongdoing, and a certain kind of "profit" (i.e., not bearing the burden of self-restraint) is intrinsic to criminal wrongdoing. Criminal punishment, then, has as its object the restoration of a proper balance between benefit and obedience. The criminal himself has no complaint, because he has rationally consented to or willed his own punishment. That is, those very rules which he has broken work, when they are obeyed by others, to his own advantage as a citizen. He would have chosen such rules for himself and others in the original position of choice. And, since he derives and voluntarily accepts benefits from their operation, he owes his own obedience as a debt to his fellow-citizens for their sacrifices in maintaining them. If he chooses not to sacrifice by exercising self-restraint and obedience, this is tantamount to his choosing to sacrifice in another way—namely, by paying the prescribed penalty. . . .

This analysis of punishment regards it as a debt owed to the law-abiding members of one's community; and, once paid, it allows reentry into the community of good citizens on equal status.

Now some of the foregoing no doubt sounds implausible or even obscurantist. Since criminals typically desire not to be punished, what can it really mean to say that they have, as rational men, really willed their own punishment? Or that, as Hegel says, they have a right to it? Perhaps a comparison of the traditional retributivist views with those of a contemporary Kantian—John Rawls—will help to make the points clearer. Rawls (like Kant) does not regard the idea of the social contract as an historical fact. It is rather a model of rational decision. Respecting a man's autonomy, at least on one view, is not respecting what he now happens, however uncritically, to desire; rather it is to respect what he desires (or would desire) as a rational man. (On Rawls's view, for example, rational men are said to be unmoved by feelings of envy; and thus it is not regarded as unjust to a person or a violation of his rights, if he is placed in a situation where he will envy another's advantage or position. A rational man would object, and thus would never consent to, a practice where another might derive a benefit from a position at his expense. He would not, however, envy the position *simpliciter,* would not regard the position as itself a benefit.) Now on Kant's (and also, I think, on Rawls's) view, a man is genuinely free or autonomous only in so far as he is rational. Thus it is man's rational will that is to be respected.

Now this idea of treating people, not as they in fact say that they want to be treated, but rather in terms of how you think they would, if rational, will to be treated, has obviously dangerous (indeed Fascistic) implications. Surely we want to avoid cramming indignities down the throats of people with the offhand observation that, no matter how much they scream, they are really rationally willing every bit of it. It would be particularly ironic for such arbitrary repression to come under the mask of respecting autonomy. And yet, most of us would agree, the general principle (though subject to abuse) also has important applications—for example, preventing the suicide of a person who, in a state of psychotic depression, wants to kill himself. What we need, then, to make the general view work, is a check on its arbitrary application; and a start toward providing such a check would be in the formulation of a public, objective theory of rationality and rational willing. It is just this, according to both Kant and Rawls, which the social contract theory can provide. On this theory, a man may be said to rationally will X if, and only if, X is called for by a rule that the man would necessarily have adopted in the original position of choice—i.e., in a position of coming together with others to pick rules for the regulation of their mutual affairs. This avoids arbitrariness because, according to Kant and Rawls at any rate, the question of whether such a rule would be picked in such a position is objectively determinable given certain (in their view) noncontroversial assumptions about human nature and rational calculation. Thus I can be said to will my own punishment if, in an antecedent position of choice, I and my fellows would have chosen institutions of punishment as the most rational means of dealing with those who might break the other generally beneficial social rules that had been adopted. . . .

The question of primary interest to Marx, of course, is whether this formal respect also involves a material respect, i.e., does the theory have application in concrete fact in the actual social world in which we live? Marx is confident that it does not, and it is to this sort of consideration that I shall now pass.

## ALIENATION AND PUNISHMENT

In outline, then, I want to argue the following: that when Marx challenges the material adequacy of the retributive theory of punishment, he is suggesting (a) that it presupposes a certain view of man and society that is false and (b) that key concepts involved in the support of the theory (e.g., the concept of "rationality" in Social Contract theory) are given analyses which, though they purport to be necessary truths, are in fact mere reflections of certain historical circumstances. . . .

. . . At what points will this challenge the credentials of the contractarian retributive theory as outlined above? I should like to organize my answer to this question around three basic topics:

*1. Rational choice.*   The model of rational choice found in Social Contract theory is egoistic—rational institutions are those that would be agreed to by calculating egoists ("devils" in Kant's more colorful terminology). The obvious question that would be raised by any Marxist is: Why give egoism this special status such that it is built, a priori, into the analysis of the concept of rationality? Is this not simply to regard as necessary that which may be only contingently found in the society around us? Starting from such an analysis, a certain result is inevitable—namely, a transcendental sanction for the status quo. Start with a bourgeois model of rationality and you will, of course, wind up defending a bourgeois theory of consent, a bourgeois theory of justice, and a bourgeois theory of punishment.

*2. Justice, benefits, and community.*   The retributive theory claims to be grounded on justice; but is it just to punish people who act out of those very motives that society encourages and reinforces? If Bonger is correct, much criminality is motivated by greed, selfishness, and indifference to one's fellows; but does not the whole society encourage motives of greed and selfishness ("making it," "getting ahead"), and does not the competitive nature of the society alienate men from each other and thereby encourage indifference—even, perhaps, what psychiatrists call psychopathy? The moral problem here is similar to one that arises with respect to some war crimes. When you have trained a man to believe that the enemy is not a genuine human person (but only a gook, or a chink), it does not seem quite fair to punish the man if, in a war situation, he kills indiscriminately. For the psychological trait you have conditioned him to have, like greed, is not one that invites fine moral and legal distinctions. There is something perverse in applying principles that presuppose a sense of community in a society which is structured to destroy genuine community.

*3. Voluntary acceptance.*   Central to the Social Contract idea is the claim that we owe allegiance to the law because the benefits we have derived have been voluntarily accepted. This is one place where our autonomy is supposed to come in. That is, having benefited from the Rule of Law when it was possible to leave, I have in a sense consented to it and to its consequences—even my own punishment if I violate the rules. To see how silly the factual presuppositions of this account are, we can do no better than quote a famous passage from David Hume's essay "Of the Original Contract":

> Can we seriously say that a poor peasant or artisan has a free choice to leave his country—when he knows no foreign language or manners, and lives

from day to day by the small wages which he acquires? We may as well assert that a man, by remaining in a vessel, freely consents to the dominion of the master, though he was carried on board while asleep, and must leap into the ocean and perish the moment he leaves her.

A banal empirical observation, one may say. But it is through ignoring such banalities that philosophers generate theories which allow them to spread iniquity in the ignorant belief that they are spreading righteousness.

It does, then, seem as if there may be some truth in Marx's claim that the retributive theory, though formally correct, is materially inadequate. At root, the retributive theory fails to acknowledge that criminality is, to a large extent, a phenomenon of economic class. To acknowledge this is to challenge the empirical presupposition of the retributive theory— the presupposition that all men, including criminals, are voluntary participants in a reciprocal system of benefits and that the justice of this arrangement can be derived from some eternal and ahistorical concept of rationality.

# A UTILITARIAN THEORY OF CRIMINAL PUNISHMENT

*Richard B. Brandt*

The broad questions to be kept in the forefront of discussion are the following: (1) What justifies anyone in inflicting pain or loss on an individual on account of his past acts? (2) Is there a valid general principle about the punishments proper for various acts? (Possibly there should be no close connection between offense and penalty; perhaps punishment should be suited to the individual needs of the criminal, and not to his crime.) (3) What kinds of defense should excuse from punishment? . . .

## THE UTILITARIAN THEORY

. . . The essence of the rule-utilitarian theory, we recall, is that our actions, whether legislative or otherwise, should be guided by a set of prescriptions, the conscientious following of which by all would have maximum net expectable utility. As a result, the utilitarian is not, just as such, committed to any particular view about how anti-social behavior should be

From Richard B. Brandt, *Ethical Theory* (Englewood Cliffs, N.J.: Prentice-Hall, 1959), pp. 480–81, 489, 490–96, 498–99. Copyright © by Richard B. Brandt.

treated by society—or even to the view that society should do anything at all about immoral conduct. It is only the utilitarian principle *combined* with statements about the kind of laws and practices which will maximize expectable utility that has such consequences. Therefore, utilitarians are free to differ from one another about the character of an ideal system of criminal justice; some utilitarians think that the system prevalent in Great Britain and the United States essentially corresponds to the ideal, but others think that the only system that can be justified is markedly different from the actual systems in these Western countries. We shall concentrate our discussion, however, on the more traditional line of utilitarian thought which holds that roughly the actual system of criminal law, say in the United States, is morally justifiable, and we shall follow roughly the classic exposition of the reasoning given by Jeremy Bentham—but modifying this freely when we feel amendment is called for. At the end of the chapter we shall look briefly at a different view.

Traditional utilitarian thinking about criminal justice has found the rationale of the practice, in the United States, for example, in three main facts. (Those who disagree think the first two of these "facts" happen not to be the case.) (1) People who are tempted to misbehave, to trample on the rights of others, to sacrifice public welfare for personal gain, can usually be deterred from misconduct by fear of punishment, such as death, imprisonment, or fine. (2) Imprisonment or fine will teach malefactors a lesson; their characters may be improved, and at any rate a personal experience of punishment will make them less likely to misbehave again. (3) Imprisonment will certainly have the result of physically preventing past malefactors from misbehaving, during the period of their incarceration.

In view of these suppositions, traditional utilitarian thinking has concluded that having laws forbidding certain kinds of behavior on pain of punishment, and having machinery for the fair enforcement of these laws, is justified by the fact that it maximizes expectable utility. Misconduct is not to be punished just for its own sake; malefactors must be punished for their past acts, according to law, as a way of maximizing expectable utility.

The utilitarian principle, of course, has implications for decisions about the severity of punishment to be administered. Punishment is itself an evil, and hence should be avoided where this is consistent with the public good. Punishment should have precisely such a degree of severity (not more or less) that the probable disutility of greater severity just balances the probable gain in utility (less crime because of the more serious threat). The cost, in other words, should be counted along with the value of what is bought; and we should buy protection up to the point where the cost is greater than the protection is worth. How severe will such punishment be? Jeremy Bentham had many sensible things to say about this. Punishment, he said, must be severe enough so that it is to no one's advantage to commit an offense even if he receives the punishment; a fine of $10 for bank robbery would give no security at all. Further, since many criminals will be undetected, we must make the penalty heavy enough in comparison with the prospective gain from crime, that a prospective criminal will consider the risk hardly worth it, even considering that it is not certain he will be punished at all. Again, the more serious offenses should carry the heavier penalties, not only because the greater disutility justifies the use of heavier penalties in order to prevent them, but also because criminals should be motivated to commit a less serious rather than a more serious offense. Bentham thought the prescribed penalties should allow for some variation at the discretion of the judge, so that the actual suffering caused should roughly be the same in all cases; thus, a heavier fine will be imposed on a rich man than on a poor man.

Bentham also argued that the goal of maximum utility requires that certain facts should *excuse* from culpability, for the reason that punishment in such cases "must be inefficacious." He listed as such (1) the fact that the relevant law was passed only after the act of the accused, (2) that the law had not been made public, (3) that the criminal was an infant, insane, or was intoxicated, (4) that the crime was done under physical compulsion, (5) that the agent was ignorant of the probable consequences of his act or was acting on the basis of an innocent misapprehension of the facts, such that the act the agent thought he was performing was a lawful one, and (6) that the motivation to commit the offense was so strong that no threat of law could prevent the crime. Bentham also thought that punishment should be remitted if the crime was a collective one and that the number of the guilty so large that great suffering would be caused by its imposition, or if the offender held an important post and his services were important for the public, or if the public or foreign powers would be offended by the punishment; but we shall ignore this part of his view.

Bentham's account of the logic of legal "defenses" needs amendment. What he should have argued is that *not* punishing in certain types of cases (cases where such defenses as those just indicated can be offered) reduces the amount of suffering imposed by law and the insecurity of everybody, and that failure to impose punishment in these types of cases will cause only a negligible increase in the incidence of crime.

How satisfactory is this theory of criminal justice? Does it have any implications that are far from being acceptable when compared with concrete justified convictions about what practices are morally right?

Many criminologists would argue that Bentham was mistaken in his facts: The deterrence value of the threat of punishment, they say, is much less than he imagined, and criminals are seldom reformed by spending time in prison. If these contentions are correct, then the ideal rules for society's treatment of malefactors are very different from what Bentham thought, and from what actual practice is today in the United States. To say all this, however, is not to show that the utilitarian *principle* is incorrect, for in view of these facts presumably the attitudes of a "qualified" person would not be favorable to criminal justice as practiced today. Utilitarian theory might still be correct, but its implications would be different from what Bentham thought—and they might coincide with justified ethical judgments. . . .

The whole utilitarian approach, however, has been criticized on the grounds that it ought not in consistency to approve of *any* excuses from criminal liability. Or at least, it should do so only after careful empirical inquiries. It is not obvious, it is argued, that we increase net expectable utility by permitting such defenses. At the least, the utilitarian is committed to defend the concept of "strict liability." Why? Because we could get a more strongly deterrent effect if everyone knew that *all behavior* of a certain sort would be punished, irrespective of mistaken supposals of fact, compulsion, and so on. The critics admit that knowledge that all behavior of a certain sort will be punished will hardly deter from crime the insane, persons acting under compulsion, persons acting under erroneous beliefs about facts, and others, but, as Professor Hart points out, it does not follow from this that general knowledge that certain acts will always be punished will not be salutary.

The utilitarian, however, has a solid defense against charges of this sort. We must bear in mind (as the critics do not) that the utilitarian principle, *taken by itself, implies nothing whatever* about whether a system of law should excuse persons on the basis of certain defenses. What the utilitarian does say is that, when we *combine* the principle of utilitarianism with *true* propositions about a certain thing or situation, then we shall come out with true statements about obligations. The utilitarian is certainly not committed to saying that one will derive true propositions about obligations if one starts with *false* propositions about fact or about what will maximize welfare, or with *no* such propositions at all. Therefore the criticism sometimes made (for example, by Hart), that utilitarian theory does not render it "obviously" or "necessarily" the case that the recognized excuses from criminal liability should be accepted as excusing from punishment, is beside the point. Moreover, in fact the utilitarian can properly claim that we do have excellent reason for believing that the general public would be no better motivated to avoid criminal offenses than it now is, if the insane and others were also punished along with intentional wrongdoers. Indeed, he may reasonably claim that the example of punishment of these individuals could only have a hardening effect—like public executions. Furthermore, the utilitarian can point out that abolition of the standard exculpating excuses would lead to serious insecurity. Imagine the pleasure of driving an automobile if one knew one could be executed for running down a child whom it was absolutely impossible to avoid striking! One certainly does not maximize expectable utility by eliminating the traditional excuses. In general, then, the utilitarian theory is not threatened by its implications about exculpating excuses.

It might also be objected against utilitarianism that it cannot recognize the validity of *mitigating* excuses. Would not consequences be better if the distinction between premeditated and impulsive acts were abolished? The utilitarian can reply that people who commit impulsive crimes, in the heat of anger, do not give thought to legal penalties; they would not be deterred by a stricter law. Moreover, such a person is unlikely to repeat his crime, so that a mild sentence saves an essentially good man for society.

# CHAPTER FIFTEEN
# ETHICS AND THE
# ENVIRONMENT

Modern technology has created a material prosperity that is unequaled in our history. It has also created environmental threats of almost inconceivable magnitude. The build-up of carbon dioxide produced by burning coal and oil now threatens to result in a global warming trend that could cause world-wide climatic changes, including devastating droughts coupled with large-scale coastal flooding.[1] Widespread industrialization has put serious strains on our energy and mineral resources; it is now believed that the production of oil, aluminum, manganese, mercury, tungsten, and zinc will peak and begin to diminish before the end of this century.[2]

Each year, American automobiles and industrial smokestacks spew some 200 million tons of pollutants into the air we breathe, causing widespread emphysema, lung cancer, bronchitis, and other lethal human and animal diseases. Emissions of sulfur and nitrogen oxides are particularly troubling because these combine with water vapor in the atmosphere to form acid rain that kills fish and other water organisms, destroys trees and other plants, and corrodes building materials.[3]

The ozone layer of the upper atmosphere, which protects the earth

1. See John Gribbin, *Future Weather and the Greenhouse Effect* (New York: Delacorte, 1982).
2. W. Jackson Davis, *The Seventh Year* (New York: W.W. Norton, 1979), pp. 131–32.
3. Council on Environmental Quality and the Department of State, *The Global 2000 Report to the President,* vol. 1 (Washington, D.C.: U.S. Government Printing Office, 1980), p. 36.

from harmful ultraviolet light, is being destroyed by chlorofluorocarbon emissions from aerosol cans and refrigeration equipment, by nitrous oxide emissions from the breakdown of nitrogen fertilizers, and possibly by the effects of high-altitude aircraft flights. An increase in the ultraviolet rays reaching the earth can induce skin cancers in humans and animals, as well as damage the oceans' plankton, which produces much of the world's oxygen, and destroy many other plant and animal species.[4]

Intensive farming and logging methods have razed large woodland areas. By the year 2000, 40 percent of the forests still remaining in less developed countries will have been destroyed. Each year, the world's desert areas expand by an area equal to the size of the state of Maine.

Nuclear power plants produce about 612,000 gallons of liquid and 2,300 tons of solid high-level radioactive wastes every year; in the same period, a medium-sized nuclear reactor yields 265 pounds of plutonium, a highly toxic cause of cancer that will threaten future populations for a quarter of a million to a million years.[5] (A dust particle of plutonium can cause death within a few weeks; twenty pounds, if properly distributed, could give lung cancer to everyone on earth.)

The Environmental Protection Agency estimates that modern industries generate about 80 billion pounds of solid hazardous wastes each year (about 350 pounds for every U.S. citizen) and only 10 percent are properly disposed of. Much of the remaining 78 billion pounds will eventually find its way into the nation's rivers, lakes, and ground water, where it will poison the drinking supplies of future generations. Many areas are already heavily polluted with industrial wastes from pulp and paper mills, tanneries, slaughterhouses, oil refineries, chemical plants, and pesticides.[6] These can have devastating effects, as the following 1978 news story indicates:

NIAGARA FALLS, N.Y.—They thought they bought the American Dream on 97th and 99th streets, but instead they invested their lives in a neighborhood where the mailman wears a gas mask. The basements of their small wooden houses reek with chemicals that smell like dead animals, and the radishes in their gardens have turned coal black. The ash trees in their backyards have withered and died, and some of their dogs are festered with sores. Most unspeakable are the children: one with an extra row of teeth, another with a club foot, a third whose mind is slowed by retardation. And their mothers are pregnant again with what could be the first chemically mutated generation.

These families bought houses that were built over Love Canal, an old waste disposal facility of Hooker Chemical Co. More than 80 different chemical compounds—11 of them probably capable of causing cancer—were placed in the old canal and covered with clay. Heavy rains during recent years brought the long-buried chemicals bubbling up through the ground and into the backyards and basements of the houses. Last week, New York

4. "The Effects of Ozone Depletion," *Science*, October 4, 1974.

5. Scott Fenn, *The Nuclear Power Debate* (Washington, D.C.: Investor Responsibility Research Center, 1980).

6. See Samuel S. Epstein, Lester O. Brown, and Carl Pope, *Hazardous Waste in America* (San Francisco: Sierra Club Books, 1982).

state officials warned of "an extremely serious threat and danger" to the people living there and recommended the immediate evacuation of all pregnant women and children under the age of 2.

"I'm taking my wife and babies away and we're never coming back here again. This thing—we can't fight it," said Robert Huryn, who tossed his infant son's crib in the back of his van and fled his brown-shingled house on 97th Street last week.

Huryn's wife, Janet, 25, talked softly about breast-feeding her three-month-old son. Her voice squeaked with nervous exhaustion. "I might be poisoning him and don't even know," she said. "I could be killing him. I don't know what's going on."

The bombshell fell late last month when the families were mailed official Environmental Protection Agency reports that identified the chemical which had invaded their homes and their bodies. The letters listed 11 chemicals, two of which definitely cause cancer. Even more wrenching was the state health department's report issued last Wednesday. It recommended immediate evacuation. The report was based on a survey of the 100 or so families whose homes border Love Canal. There was a significant number of miscarriages among pregnant mothers on 99th Street, especially during last summer, the report said, and five children had been born with congenital defects. The report was preliminary and officials fear it may be just the tip of the iceberg.

Karen Schroeder's 9-year-old daughter was born slightly retarded with a cleft palate, two rows of bottom teeth and an enlarged liver. Her son has blisters on his eyes and another daughter's brown hair is falling out in clumps. Lois Heisner's 3-year-old daughter was born with a defective ureter and will probably have to undergo an operation this fall. Mrs. Heisner has also had a miscarriage. Other mothers wearily tick off family ailments—skin rashes, breathing problems, hearing difficulties, heart murmurs, and a variety of cancers.[7]

Humans are not the only victims of modern technology. Environmental pressures are currently destroying animals in massive numbers. The Environmental Protection Agency estimates that between half a million and two million species—15 to 20 percent of all those on earth— could be killed off by the year 2000, partly because of loss of wild habitat and partly because of pollution. Extinction of animal species on this scale is without precedent in human history.[8] Moreover, modern industry and the production of new chemical substances have led to the widespread use of animals to test new products. These tests often involve extreme discomfort and lead to prolonged and excruciatingly painful deaths for their animal victims.

One standard method of measuring toxicity is the Draize test (named after J. H. Draize), in which concentrated solutions of cosmetics or other substances are dripped into the eyes of rabbits. The animals are then examined for swelling, redness, and eye injuries. Other procedures are just as distasteful. Consider, for example, the following report, which describes the testing of a nasal decongestant called Amidephrine Mesylate:

7. *San Francisco Sunday Examiner & Chronicle*, August 13, 1978, p. A16.
8. See *The Global 2000 Report to the President*, p. 37.

J. Weikel, Jr., and K. Harper, of the Mead Johnson Research Center at Evansville, Indiana, and the Huntingdon Research Center, Huntingdon, England, studied the acute toxicity of Amidephrine Mesylate in ninety-six rabbits, sixteen rhesus monkeys, eight squirrel monkeys, five cats, 376 rats, and an unstated number of dogs and mice. The substance was administered to the animals by mouth, by injection, into the nostrils, and tested for irritancy on the eyes and penises of rabbits. Rats and mice, regardless of the mode of administration, lost the power of muscular coordination, their eyes watered and their eyeballs protruded. Lethal doses caused, in addition, salivation, convulsions, and hemorrhage about the nose and mouth. Rabbits showed similar symptoms. Cats had a profuse watery discharge from the nose, diarrhea and vomiting. Dogs lost muscular coordination, salivated, and had diarrhea.[9]

In addition, modern industrialized societies have applied intensive forms of farming technology to the production of meat and poultry products. These mass-production methods inflict high levels of pain, discomfort, and stress on their animal victims. Cattle are castrated, branded, and slaughtered without anesthetics; calves are starved to produce veal; chickens are confined to one-foot-square wire cages.

Thus our modern industrial advances have created major environmental and technological risks that threaten the lives and well-being not only of ourselves but of future generations and other animal species as well. These threats raise large and unsettling ethical questions. For it is obvious that we cannot simply do away with the industry and technology that create these threats. Not only does our present welfare rest on this technology, but our future welfare may also depend on it. Indeed, if we are to raise the standard of living of underdeveloped nations, we must deploy the very industrial technology that threatens that standard. By the same token, the painful animal tests that are now in such wide use are often necessary in order to prevent equally painful human diseases. And eliminating a particular form of technology—such as the use of chlorofluorocarbons for refrigeration—will impose staggering economic penalties on the millions of people who are dependent on that technology. What moral obligations do we have, then, to modify our industries and technologies so as to protect ourselves, our environment, future generations, and other animal species? These are the questions that are addressed in this chapter.

Discussions of such matters have raised a number of puzzling moral issues. One major issue concerns the question of how far our moral obligations extend. Obviously, we have moral obligations to those human beings with whom we presently share our world, and these obligations imply that we should not damage the environment in ways that will injure those human beings. But do we owe any moral obligations to anyone else? Do we have any obligations, for example, to human generations who are not yet born—and who may never be born? And what about present and future generations of nonhumans? Do our obligations extend beyond the

9. Quoted in Peter Singer, *Animal Liberation* (New York: Random House, 1975), p. 49.

scope of the human community to embrace living nonhumans such as plants and animals? Do our obligations extend even to nonliving entities— a wild river, a mountain, a forest? If we do have some moral duties toward nonhumans, are these duties owed only to individuals (such as an individual animal) or do we also have a duty to protect entire groups (such as an endangered species)? These are difficult questions, and philosophers have taken a variety of positions on them.[10]

Some philosophers have assumed that our moral duty not to pollute the environment is based primarily on our moral duty not to harm other presently living human beings. The most important question for these philosophers is how we are to balance the duty not to damage the environment against other moral duties, such as not inflicting economic harm and respecting people's freedom. To what extent, for example, can we adopt environmental regulations that impose severe economic injuries on one group in order to improve the environment for another group? And how should the government's duty to respect the freedom of business people be balanced against its duty to protect the health of citizens?

Other philosophers have focused their discussions on the rights of future generations. Much of the resource depletion and environmental degradation that we bring about will have a negligible effect on us, but will cause major problems for our descendants. They are the ones who will bear most of the burden of carbon dioxide build-up, nuclear and industrial wastes, pesticide contamination of water supplies, ozone depletion, destruction of energy and mineral resources, and so on. What obligations do we owe to these future generations? Some philosophers have argued that future generations simply do not have any moral rights since they do not now exist and may never exist. Others have contended that we can say someone has a certain right only if we know he has a certain interest or need which that right protects. Because we do not know what interests or needs future generations will develop, we cannot say that they have any rights.

Other philosophers, however, have argued that our descendants have the same rights we have, since it is virtually certain that at least some human beings will exist in the future. Furthermore, we know that many of their needs and interests will be the same as ours. Thus, we have an obligation to preserve an unpolluted environment for them. Still other

10. There are several anthologies that discuss these issues: Donald Scherer and Thomas Attig, eds., *Ethics and the Environment* (Englewood Cliffs, N.J.: Prentice-Hall, 1983); William Blackstone, ed., *Philosophy and the Environmental Crisis* (Athens, Ga.: University of Georgia Press, 1974); Ernest Partridge, ed., *Responsibilities to Future Generations* (Buffalo, N.Y.: Prometheus Books, 1981); Brian Barry and R. I. Sikora, eds., *Obligations to Future Generations* (Philadelphia: Temple University Press, 1978); Peter Brown and Douglas Mac-Lean, eds., *Energy Policy and Future Generations* (Totowa, N.J.: Rowman and Littlefield, 1981); Kenneth Goodpaster and K. M. Sayre, eds., *Ethics and Problems of the 21st Century* (Notre Dame, Ind.: University of Notre Dame Press, 1979). In addition, the reader might consult the issues of a journal devoted entirely to environmental issues: *Environmental Ethics.* Two books that have become classics in this area are John Passmore, *Man's Responsibility for Nature* (London: Scribner's, 1974) and Aldo Leopold, *A Sand County Almanac* (Oxford: Oxford University Press, 1949).

philosophers have responded that our moral theories are designed to deal only with moral conflicts between contemporaneous persons, hence they cannot adequately treat moral issues involving the future. Utilitarianism, for example, implies that we should maximize happiness, and this seems to suggest that we should multiply the number of future persons who could experience happiness. But multiplying future persons would put even more severe strains on the environment. Social contract theory, on the other hand, seems to imply that people have obligations only toward those with whom they have entered a mutual contract. But clearly future generations cannot enter a contract with us. Moreover, although we can sacrifice for the sake of future generations, it is clear that future generations cannot do anything for us; why, then, should we do anything for them?

A further problem concerns our obligations to nonhumans.[11] Recent philosophers have distinguished two important aspects of this issue: What obligations do we have toward individual nonhuman entities, and what obligations do we have toward particular classes of nonhuman entities, such as a plant or animal species? Some philosophers have argued that our obligations toward individual animals are no different from our obligations toward individual human beings: just as we are obliged not to inflict pain on humans, we also have an obligation not to inflict pain on animals. We do not have similar obligations to plants and nonliving entities, however, because they cannot experience pain. Other philosophers have countered that we should respect all life, including plant life, and that our obligations should extend not only to animals but to plants as well. Still others have resisted these attempts to extend our obligations to nonhumans. They have argued that plants clearly do not have rights and, moreover, that individual animals do not have the same rights that human beings have. In this view, there are important differences between animals and human beings, differences which imply that human interests have more weight than the interests of animals. Accordingly, it is immoral to inflict pain on animals for trivial reasons, but it is not wrong to inflict pain on them or kill them in order to meet important human needs.

Opinion is similarly divided about our obligations to nonliving entities and to classes of wildlife such as endangered species. Some philosophers have held that any obligations we owe nonlivng entities depend wholly on our obligations to human beings: we must not injure these parts of the environment when doing so will impose indirect injuries on humans. Other philosophers have urged an "environmental ethic" that views all such entities as "sacred," not to be injured or destroyed. Although such views are not yet widespread, they are certainly becoming more popular.

---

11. For further reading on the moral issues raised by our treatment of animals, see Richard Knowles Morris and Michael W. Fox, eds., *On the Fifth Day: Animal Rights and Human Ethics* (Washington, D.C.: Acropolis Press, 1978); Tom Ragan and Peter Singer, eds., *Animal Rights and Human Obligations* (Englewood Cliffs, N.J.: Prentice-Hall, 1976); Peter Singer, *Animal Liberation* (New York: Random House, 1975); R. G. Frey, *Interests and Rights: The Case Against Animals* (Oxford: Clarendon Press, 1980); Mary Midgley, *Beast and Man* (Ithaca, N.Y.: Cornell University Press, 1979).

The discussions in the articles that follow cross back and forth over these various issues. The first article, by William T. Blackstone, argues that we must not pollute the environment because of our duties to present generations of human beings. The second, by Ronald Green, states that we must not pollute the environment for future generations because of our duties to those generations. The third, by Joel Feinberg, discusses not only our environmental duties to future human generations but those we owe to plants, animals, and animal species as well. The fourth, by Peter Singer, is devoted wholly to a discussion of our duties to animals, as is the last article, by Martin Benjamin.

In "Ethics and Ecology," William T. Blackstone adopts a Kantian approach, claiming that human rights are based on our "capacities for rationality and freedom," which are essential aspects of being human. Because of this, we have a right to what we need to fulfill these capacities. He then argues that since a clean environment is necessary to fulfill our capacities for rationality and freedom, it follows that we have a right to a clean environment. Moreover, economic rights and property rights should be limited when they come into conflict with this right to a clean environment.

In "Intergenerational Distributive Justice and Environmental Responsibility," Ronald M. Green proposes three axioms concerning our environmental obligations to future generations. The first is that we are bound to real future persons by ties of justice, not by utilitarian considerations. According to Green, utilitarianism cannot deal with our obligations to the future because it holds that the world's future populations should increase indefinitely, and this position is clearly foolish. Instead, Green claims, we must see morality as an instrument for adjudicating conflicts in a just and impartial manner. Rawls' social contract method of moral reasoning provides such an instrument. Using Rawls' method, we can see that we have certain ties of justice to future generations; in particular, we have an obligation to limit population growth for the sake of those real (and not merely possible) persons who will be born in the future. Green's second axiom is that we should not make the lives of future persons worse than our own. This axiom is also based on Rawls. Green illustrates the axiom by arguing that since widespread production of plutonium by present generations will benefit the present but make things worse for the future, we should reject a plutonium economy. The third axiom is that sacrifices for future generations must be distributed in a just manner among those living today. Rawls' social contract reasoning, as Green interprets it, implies that the poor should not be excessively burdened by the sacrifices our generation makes for the future.

In "The Rights of Animals and Unborn Generations," Joel Feinberg states that to have a right is "to have a claim to something and against someone." Although animals are incapable of having duties, or of being able to claim their rights, Feinberg argues that they nevertheless have interests. This is sufficient to make individual animals the kind of creatures that can also have rights. Since (1) individual animals can have rights and since (2) we hold that we ought to treat animals humanely for their own sake, it follows that we do in fact attribute rights to individual animals and that there is nothing wrong with doing so. However, since neither plants nor species have interests, they do not have rights. Feinberg also claims that if we assume future generations will come into existence, then they too have environmental rights. However, in his view, future generations do not necessarily have a right to be born.

The selection "Not for Humans Only: The Place of Nonhumans in Environmental Issues" is written by Peter Singer, a utilitarian. Singer distinguishes between the duties we owe to individual animals and those we owe to an entire species. Turning first to individual animals, Singer notes that the predominant Western view is that only the welfare of humans has intrinsic moral significance. According to this view, the only duty we owe individual nonhuman animals is to avoid treating them in ways that might directly or indirectly harm humans. Singer argues that this traditional view is as arbitary as racism: it assumes that the suffering of individuals of other species has no moral significance, just as racism assumes that the suffering of individuals of other races has no moral significance. Instead, Singer believes, the interests of any individual animal that can experience pleasure or pain should be given a consideration equal to that which we give to the interests of our fellow human beings. Singer draws the utilitarian conclusion that just as we have a duty to reduce the suffering we cause individual human beings, we have an equal duty to reduce the suffering we cause individual nonhuman animals. However, he claims that an animal species (as distinct from individual animals) does not have any interests. Consequently, we do not seem to have any direct duties to preserve entire species of animals, except when doing so will (indirectly) benefit human beings or other individual animals.

In "Ethics and Animal Consciousness," Martin Benjamin examines three philosophical views on our obligations to animals: indirect obligation theories, no obligation theories, and direct obligation theories. He argues that none of these is "entirely satisfactory," although each provides a correct "fundamental insight." Accordingly, Benjamin puts these fundamental insights together into a fourth theory, which holds that since persons have "reflective consciousness," they have a "higher status" and "greater worth" than animals, which have only "simple consciousness." Consequently, inflicting suffering on animals is justified when necessary to meet "important needs" of persons, but not when inflicted merely to satisfy "trivial tastes or desires."

# ETHICS AND ECOLOGY

*William T. Blackstone*

## THE RIGHT TO A LIVABLE ENVIRONMENT
## AS A HUMAN RIGHT

Let us first ask whether the right to a livable environment can properly be considered to be a human right. For the purposes of this paper, however, I want to avoid raising the more general question of whether there are any human rights at all. Some philosophers do deny that any human rights exist. In two recent papers I have argued that human rights do exist (even though such rights may properly be overridden on occasion by other morally relevant reasons) and that they are universal and inalienable (although the actual exercise of such rights on a given occasion is alienable).[1] My argument for the existence of universal human rights rests, in the final analysis, on a theory of what it means to be human, which specifies the capacities for rationality and freedom as essential, and on the fact that there are no relevant grounds for excluding any human from the opportunity to develop and fulfill his capacities (rationality and freedom) as a human. This is not to deny that there are criteria which justify according human rights in quite different ways or with quite different modes of treatment for different persons, depending upon the nature and degree of such capacities and the existing historical and environmental circumstances.

If the right to a livable environment were seen as a basic and inalienable human right, this could be a valuable tool (both inside and outside of legalistic frameworks) for solving some of our environmental problems, both on a national and on an international basis. Are there any philosophical and conceptual difficulties in treating this right as an inalienable human right? Traditionally we have not looked upon the right to a decent environment as a human right or as an inalienable right. Rather, inalienable human or natural rights have been conceived in somewhat different terms; equality, liberty, happiness, life, and property. However, might it not be possible to view the right to a livable environment as being entailed by, or as constitutive of, these basic human or natural rights recognized in our political tradition? If human rights, in other words, are those rights which each human possesses in virtue of the fact that he is human and in virtue of the fact that those rights are essential in permitting him to live a

---

1. See my "Equality and Human Rights," *Monist* 52, no. 4 (1968): 616–639 and my "Human Rights and Human Dignity," in Laszlo and Gotesky, eds., *Human Dignity*.

human life (that is, in permitting him to fulfill his capacities as a rational and free being), then might not the right to a decent environment be properly categorized as such a human right? Might it not be conceived as a right which has emerged as a result of changing environmental conditions and the impact of those conditions on the very possibility of human life and on the possibility of the realization of other rights such as liberty and equality?[2] Let us explore how this might be the case.

Given man's great and increasing ability to manipulate the environment, and the devastating effect this is having, it is plain that new social institutions and new regulative agencies and procedures must be initiated on both national and international levels to make sure that the manipulation is in the public interest. It will be necessary, in other words, to restrict or stop some practices and the freedom to engage in those practices. Some look upon such additional state planning, whether national or international, as unnecessary further intrusion on man's freedom. Freedom is, of course, one of our basic values, and few would deny that excessive state control of human action is to be avoided. But such restrictions on individual freedom now appear to be necessary in the interests of overall human welfare and the rights and freedoms of *all* men. Even John Locke with his stress on freedom as an inalienable right recognized that this right must be construed so that it is consistent with the equal right to freedom of others. The whole point of the state is to restrict unlicensed freedom and to provide the conditions for equality of rights for all. Thus it seems to be perfectly consistent with Locke's view and, in general, with the views of the founding fathers of this country to restrict certain rights or freedoms when it can be shown that such restriction is necessary to insure the equal rights of others. If this is so, it has very important implications for the rights to freedom and to property. These rights, perhaps properly seen as inalienable (though this is a controversial philosophical question), are not properly seen as unlimited or unrestricted. When values which we hold dear conflict (for example, individual or group freedom and the freedom of all, individual or group rights and the rights of all, and individual or group welfare and the welfare of the general public) something has to give; some priority must be established. In the case of the abuse and waste of the environmental resources, less individual freedom and fewer individual rights for the sake of greater public welfare and equality of rights seem justified. What in the past had been properly regarded as freedoms and rights (given what seemed to be unlimited natural resources and no serious pollution problems) can no longer be so construed, at least not without additional restrictions. We must recognize both the need for such restrictions and the fact that none of our rights can be realized without a

2. Almost forty years ago, Aldo Leopold stated that "there is as yet no ethic dealing with man's relationship to land and to the non-human animals and plants which grow upon it. Land, like Odysseus' slave girls, is still property. The land relation is still strictly economic entailing privileges but not obligations." (See Leopold's "The Conservation Ethic," *Journal of Forestry*, 31, no. 6 (October 1933): 634–643. Although some important changes have occurred since he wrote this, no systematic ethic or legal structure has been developed to socialize or institutionalize the obligation to use land properly.

livable environment. Both public welfare and equality of rights now require that natural resources not be used simply according to the whim and caprice of individuals or simply for personal profit. This is not to say that all property rights must be denied and that the state must own all productive property, as the Marxist argues. It is to insist that those rights be qualified or restricted in the light of new ecological data and in the interest of the freedom, rights, and welfare of all.

The answer then to the question, Is the right to a livable environment a human right? is yes. Each person has this right qua being human and because a livable environment is essential for one to fulfill his human capacities. And given the danger to our environment today and hence the danger to the very possibility of human existence, access to a livable environment must be conceived as a right which imposes upon everyone a correlative moral obligation to respect.[3] . . .

# INTERGENERATIONAL DISTRIBUTIVE JUSTICE AND ENVIRONMENTAL RESPONSIBILITY

*Ronald M. Green*

From the beginning of the nuclear age, through the Pugwash Conferences of the late 1950s, down to the environmental movement of our own decade, scientists have played a leading role in alerting us to the dangers posed by our present habits and technologies. Each problem in what Platt has termed the "storm of crisis problems" facing mankind today—population growth, resource depletion, environmental degradation, and the control of nuclear energy—has typically first been identified and publicized by members of the scientific community.[1]

Since a distinguishing feature of all these problems is that they

---

3. The right to a livable environment might itself entail other rights, for example, the right to population control. Population control is obviously essential for quality human existence. This issue is complex and deserves a separate essay, but I believe that the moral framework explicated above provides the grounds for treating population control both as beneficial and as moral.

1. John Platt, "What We Must Do," *Science,* 166 (1969), 1115–1121.

threaten massive evil for generations yet unborn, scientists have also performed the important task of reminding us of our moral responsibility to future generations. More than many of us, scientists have been alert to the fact that our moral obligations extend beyond our contemporaries to the generations that will follow us. But although scientists have tended to assume the existence of a responsibility to the future, they have not commonly discussed the more abstract question of the nature of that responsibility, its basis, extent, or limits.

As an ethicist, I want to take the modest step here of remedying this lack of discussion by proposing three very basic guides to our thinking about obligations to the future. I call these "axioms" of intergenerational responsibility. They are so "commonsensical" that I suspect that most scientists concerned with the future already share them. Nevertheless, each does involve some serious conceptual difficulties, and it may be useful to look at these moral axioms with some of the same care that scientists bring to questions of fact.

## BONDS WITH THE FUTURE

The first axiom is: *We are bound by ties of justice to real future persons.*

Even though the belief that we have obligations to future generations is widely held, the very idea of obligations to persons in the future is quite odd. In a discussion of this issue, Stearns pointed this out when he asked: "Why should there be obligations to future generations? We have made no commitments to them. We have entered no social compacts with them. . . . Under any moral theory, why should there be obligations to nonexistent persons?"[2]

One response to these puzzling questions may be offered by utilitarian moral theory, which reduces all obligation to the single requirement that we act to produce "the greatest happiness for the greatest number of persons."[3] Since, from a utilitarian point of view, it is immaterial where or for whom happiness is produced, this requirement clearly extends to the future and helps explain our obligation to future persons.

Though this may be so, utilitarianism also entails some puzzling difficulties of its own. For example, if we are obligated to maximize happiness, might we not be obligated to multiply the number of persons who could experience happiness? Indeed, so long as the aggregate or overall gains to happiness produced this way proved greater than the corresponding loss to per capita well-being resulting from crowding, a utilitarian approach might even counsel indefinite growth in population. A utilitarian utopia might thus be characterized by burgeoning populations living at or near the subsistence level.

This possible utilitarian conclusion seems to illustrate the old saw

2. J. B. Stearns, "Ecology and the Indefinite Unborn," *Monist*, 56 (1972), 612–625.
3. J. S. Mill, *Utilitarianism* (London: Longman, 1864); H. Sidgwick, *The Methods of Ethics*, 7th ed. (New York: Dover Publications, 1907).

that there is no position so foolish that some philosopher has not defended it. But utilitarianism is not just foolish. It represents a serious effort to answer the question of why we should be obligated to persons who are not yet even alive.

Nevertheless, we do not have to accept utilitarianism or its possible conclusions to understand our obligations to the future. In fact, the utilitarian error is a very basic one. Morality does not really involve any kind of lofty commitment to maximizing human happiness, nor even, as some have believed, to minimizing suffering.[4] Rather, morality has a far more mundane purpose: It is primarily an instrument for adjudicating possible conflicts between persons and for facilitating a noncoercive settlement of social disputes. It is an effort to replace the play of force and power in human affairs with principles to guide our conduct derived from reasoned, common agreement.[5]

### Moral Reasoning

This understanding of morality is reflected in the recent return by some philosophers to a social contract method of moral reasoning. According to Rawls, for example, moral principles may be thought of as those basic rules agreed to by free, equal, self-interested and rational persons under conditions of strict impartiality.[6] Specifically, Rawls proposes that we view our moral principles as deriving from a hypothetical (not real) contract situation in which each of us seeks best to protect our possible interests. To prevent an unfair distortion of the outcome and to produce a result acceptable to all, however, he asks that we also think of ourselves as deprived of knowledge of our own particular strengths and weaknesses, advantages or disadvantages. The outcome of this hypothetical reasoning process would be a set of principles to which all could agree.

Rawls' view has many complexities, but the basic idea is as familiar as the everyday counsel to "put yourself in the other fellow's shoes." What Rawls is telling us is that if we are rationally to settle our social disputes and to construct a harmonious social order, we must adopt a moral point of view that involves choosing rationally but impartially before the array of competing interests and claims.

These considerations suggest just why we are obligated to future generations. It is not, as utilitarians mistakenly believe, because we have a duty to promote human happiness. Rather, it is because our wishes and behavior can conflict with those of future persons. We live, after all, in a finite world with limited space, resources, and opportunites, and not even the most optimistic prospects of technological change in the future are likely to remove all limits. By reducing these resources or opportunities, our conduct in the present can injure those who follow us, and they, in

4. J. Narveson, "Utilitarianism and New Generations," *Mind,* 76 (1967), 62–72.
5. D. Baier, *The Moral Point of View* (Ithaca, N.Y.: Cornell University Press, 1958); G. J. Warnock, *The Object of Morality* (London: Methuen, 1971).
6. J. Rawls, *A Theory of Justice* (Cambridge, Mass.: Harvard University Press, 1971).

turn, in anger, resentment, or ignorance can inflict injury on their descendants.

For these reasons, moral obligations between generations are as important as any obligations we possess. In fact, they clearly form a part of the total requirements of distributive justice that bear upon us; as we must equitably distribute scarce goods and opportunities in the present, so must we do so over time. If we fail to do so, if we neglect our just responsibilities to the future, we risk reducing ongoing human relations to the Hobbesian "war of all with all" that morality aims to prevent.

### Who Is the Future?

As elemental as this understanding is, it has some important implications. For one thing, it suggests that we need not morally concern ourselves with the welfare of merely "possible" future persons—with those human beings whose very coming into existence depends on our reproductive decisions. Persons who will never come into being cannot conceivably occasion social conflict, so merely "possible" persons need not enter into our moral thinking at all. Concretely, this means that there is no such thing as a "right to come into being" or a "right to be born."[7] It also means that in our collective population decisions we are primarily called upon to minimize injury to *real* future persons. Zero population growth, with its goal of improved life circumstances for smaller future numbers, is a valid conclusion from these basic premises.

Actually, the population issue is a bit more complex than this. Even with merely "possible" persons out of the picture, population policy can involve a conflict between generations. To some degree, it is in the interests of certain segments of present generations to have unrestrained procreative liberty, whereas it is generally in the interests of future generations to have earlier population growth limited. Apart from the emotional satisfactions produced by children, for example, there are often concrete reasons why parents in agrarian societies opt for numerous offspring. At the same time, larger family size can disadvantage the children themselves, a fact that has led some demographers to speak of the "parental exploitation of children" in the underdeveloped setting.[8]

This raises the question of how disputes of this sort are to be settled. The answer, I think, is furnished by the kind of contract method Rawls proposes. Specifically, each of us must ask: "If I were a member of a hypothetical contract situation seeking my possible advantage, but if I were denied knowledge of which generation I live in, what population policy would I propose?" Elsewhere I have tried to consider this question at length,[9] but a general answer seems clear: In view of the many future generations aided by stationary population levels, and the relatively slight

---

7. J. Feinberg, "The Rights of Animals and Unborn Generations," in *Philosophy and Environmental Crisis*, ed. W. T. Blackstone (Athens, Ga.: University of Georgia Press, 1974).
8. T. P. Schultz, "An Economic Perspective on Population Growth," in National Academy of Sciences, *Rapid Population Growth* (Baltimore, Md.: Johns Hopkins Press, 1971).
9. R. Green, *Population Growth and Justice* (Missoula, Mont.: Scholars Press, 1976).

sacrifices imposed on the present, a no-growth policy is a good choice under conditions of radical impartiality. Zero population growth is right. Indeed, negative growth rates to enhance the circumstances of future generations are also justifiable, and it goes without saying that rampant population growth under conditions of poverty is absolutely unacceptable. Quite apart from the question of whether such growth threatens physical survival, the miserable survival it produces is a severe injustice to those born into progressively more impoverished generations.

More important than this almost undisputed conclusion, however, is the method of arriving at it. What I am trying to suggest under the heading of this first axiom is a way of thinking about our obligations to the future and, at the same time, a rational way of determining the extent of those obligations. This method, moreover, is as applicable to other problems of intergenerational justice, including environmental responsibility and re- source planning, as it is to population policy. In each of these cases, I suggest, we are called upon to ask a simple question: "Which policy would I find most advantageous if I were deprived of the knowledge of the genera- tion to which I belonged?" Obviously, this question alone will not solve our problems. Complex factual matters must also be faced on each issue, and the expertise of many disciplines must be drawn upon. But it may be of some help at the outset to see that the right question is being asked.

## FUTURE SHOULD BE BETTER

The second axiom is: *The lives of future persons ought ideally to be "better" than our own and certainly no worse.*

Ordinarily, when we act out of respect for other persons, we can at least entertain the possibility that when their turn comes, they will act out of respect for us as well. But virtually no possibility of such reciprocity exists between generations. Except, perhaps, by respecting our memory, future generations cannot really compensate us for the sacrifices we make on their behalf. This consideration has led some philosophers to suggest that human history displays a kind of chronological unfairness; the earli- est generations are called upon to make sacrifices whose benefits they can never enjoy.[10] A similar oddity has been noted by economists and others who have discussed the matter of capital savings for the future. A policy of savings, they observe, benefits every generation but the first, which experiences only sacrifice.[11]

It is tempting to conclude that policies which disadvantage one indi- vidual or group for the sake of others must be unjust. This need not be true. Where circumstances allow no alternative, policies of this sort can be just, and this seems to be the case where obligations to the future are

10. I. Kant, "Idea for a Universal History with a Cosmopolitan Purpose," in *Kant's Political Writings,* ed. H. Reiss (Cambridge, Eng.: Cambridge University Press, 1970).
11. D. C. Mueller, "Intergenerational Justice and the Social Discount Rate," *Theory and Decision,* 5 (1974), 263–273; Rawls, *A Theory of Justice.*

concerned. Not only is restraint on behalf of the future required, but deliberate sacrifices on our part aimed at making life better for all our descendants also are justified.

To see this, we need only regard the choices impartially. We can refuse to sacrifice or save, and we can insist on a strict equality of expectations across generations. This probably is to our advantage if we happen to be in any initial generation when savings are proposed. But it is clearly to our disadvantage if we belong to any subsequent generation. Each of these receives something from its predecessors and benefits generally from the process of savings as the circumstances of life continue to improve. Deprived of knowledge of the generation to which we belong, therefore, it seems reasonable to opt for some kind of savings policy. Morally this expresses itself as the duty to strive, even at some expense to ourselves, for the betterment of the conditions of life of those who follow us.

My use of the terms *savings* and *betterment* interchangeably may suggest that I construe this duty to improve the welfare of our descendants primarily in economic terms—as some kind of unending growth in material productivity. Certainly, money income and consumer goods of one sort or another are candidates for consideration among the values we ought to increase for our descendants. But they cannot be the sole goods because we know that increase in these goods has characteristically been accompanied by the degradation of other important and choice-worthy values, including human emotional health, cultural richness, and environmental quality.

The fact that many evils associated with an expanding economy are external to any one generation has led some economists to view commodity production and consumption as an undisputed good, something that persons with divergent ends can all support. But any perspective which takes future generations into account must question this emphasis. Even responsible economists today agree that adequate income measurements must encompass the cross-generational costs of environmental deterioration and resource depletion.[12]

### The Quality of Life

These considerations raise the complex question of "quality of life." If we agree that we ought to improve the real quality of life of our descendants, which criteria should we select for doing so? What constitutes a good or "better" life? So many moralists have tried to answer this question, that it would be presumptuous of me to try to resolve it here. But a few modest suggestions may be in order. For one thing, the fact that it is far easier to identify what constitutes a deterioration in the quality of life than what constitutes an improvement makes it minimally

---

12. E. Dolan, *Tanstaafl: The Economic Strategy for Environmental Crisis* (New York: Holt, Rinehart & Winston, 1971); E. F. Schumacher, *Small Is Beautiful* (New York: Harper & Row, 1973); J. Spengler, "The Aesthetics of Population," *Population Bulletin*, 13 (1957), 61–75; J. Spengler, "The Economist and the Population Question," *American Economic Review*, 56 (1966), 1–24.

incumbent upon us not to worsen the lot of our successors. This means that we must be careful not to squander or dissipate the legacy of natural and cultural values we have inherited from the past. In particular, we must respect the integrity of our physical environment, since all future progress presumes environmental stability.

In considering the direction actual progress in the future should take, we might keep in mind the fact that, here as elsewhere, moral choice requires a process of impartial but informed reasoning. This means that we must not allow our choices for the future to be guided by narrow preferences and special interest groups. Neither those who would make us into insatiable consumers nor those who would have us all become philosophers deserve our exclusive attention. A realistic assessment of the plurality of human ends must guide our thinking about the world we hand down to the future.

The fact that moral choice requires impartiality, however, does not mean that it presumes ignorance. On the contrary, full general information is essential to sound moral reasoning. Even the hypothetical contractors of Rawls' theory are assumed to know all the "general laws and theories" that bear on their choices.[13] This means that scientists have a particularly important role in helping us make our choices for the future. True, in choosing goods and weighing values, or even in judging scientific matters outside their areas of competence, scientists have no more expertise than educated laymen.[14] But within their broad areas of specialization scientists have the vital task of alerting us to the dangers and opportunities in our actions and of identifying for us the natural conditions of human flourishing. In this respect, science is an irreplaceable "instrument of service" to the total moral community.[15]

It may well be that scientific inquiry will inform us that an overall improvement in our condition requires *less* of some of the goods or activities we presently cherish, or even, perhaps, a measure of deliberately programmed austerity and hardship in our lives.[16] Keeping this in mind, we should not forget that it is still our obligation to help improve the lives of those who follow us. Whatever the intent, appeals for an end to economic growth may have recently had the effect of casting the very idea of progress into disrepute.[17] Although this conclusion is understandable, it can encourage a defection from our obligation to the future. Our responsibility is not to abandon a striving for progress so much as to identify and develop those areas where significant human progress remains possible.

13. Rawls, *A Theory of Justice.*
14. B. Glass, *Science and Ethical Values* (Chapel Hill, N.C.: University of North Carolina Press, 1965).
15. K. Thimann, "Science as an Instrument of Service," *Science,* 164 (1969), 1013.
16. R. DuBos, *Man Adapting* (New Haven, Conn.: Yale University Press, 1965); V. R. Potter, *Bioethics* (Englewood Cliffs, N.J.: Prentice-Hall, 1971).
17. K. E. Boulding, "The Economics of the Coming Spaceship Earth," in *Environmental Quality in a Growing Economy,* ed. H. Jarrett (Baltimore, Md.: Johns Hopkins Press, 1966); D. H. Meadows, D. L. Meadows, J. Randers, and W. W. Behrens III, *The Limits of Growth* (New York: Universe Books, 1972); E. J. Mishan, *The Costs of Economic Growth* (New York: Praeger, 1967).

Whatever positive directions we select for the future, it remains true that we are minimally required not to worsen the future quality of life. Any historical process displaying a retrogression in human prospects would violate the deepest possibilities of the human enterprise. Unfortunately, an unprecedented capacity to inflict deliberate, mammoth, and irreversible injury on our descendants is a distinguishing feature of our era. Our exercise of this capacity is illustrated by our near exhaustion of petroleum resources and by the serious insults we inflict on delicate environmental systems. Among the most vivid illustrations of irresponsibility to the future, however, are the recent proposals for development of a plutonium recycle economy. Since these proposals furnish virtually a textbook case of how *not* to treat our descendants, I want briefly to dwell on them.

### Possibility of a Plutonium Economy

The arguments in favor of a plutonium economy are fairly straightforward. Not only would such an economy enable us to use what is presently a troublesome waste-product of nuclear reactors, but with the development of the Liquid Metal Fast Breeder Reactor (LMFBR) we would be in a position to exploit abundantly available uranium 238 and thus vastly expand our energy resources. This would lower energy costs for decades to come and might also save lives by reducing the number of persons needed for uranium mining.[18]

The difficulties with this proposal are equally clear. Plutonium is one of the most toxic substances known. Lung burdens no larger than a millionth of a gram (the weight of a grain of pollen) produce cancer in animals with certainty. The problem is exacerbated by the fact that, with a half-life of 24,000 years, plutonium's radioactivity is undiminished within the span of human imagining.[19]

The fact that plutonium is virtually unknown in nature also means that we are uniquely responsible for every grain of this substance introduced into the environment. We have been creating plutonium, of course, from the beginning of the nuclear age, because it is a by-product of fission reactions. But the problem would assume new dimensions if we were to develop a plutonium recycle economy. Not only would this greatly increase the amount of plutonium produced—some projections foresee a cumulative flow of 100,000 tons of plutonium through the fuel cycle within roughly the next half-century—but because this plutonium would be in pure form it would be especially subject to theft and accidental dispersion.[20] The special safety problems of breeder reactors only further compound the risks.

By even the most conservative standards of intergenerational justice,

18. Environmental Protection Agency, *Proceedings of Public Hearings: Plutonium and Other Transuranium Elements* (Washington, D.C.: Environmental Protection Agency, 1974).

19. J. G. Speth, A. R. Tamplin, and T. B. Cochrane, "Plutonium Recycle: The Fateful Step," *Bulletin of the Atomic Scientists*, 30 (1974), 15–22.

20. B. T. Feld, "The Menace of a Fission Power Economy," *Bulletin of the Atomic Scientists*, 30 (1974), 32–34; L. Scheinman, "Safeguarding Nuclear Materials," *Bulletin of the Atomic Scientists*, 30 (1974), 34–36.

these proposals seem grossly irresponsible. How can we justify introducing into the environment a substance that can seriously jeopardize the health and lives of countless future generations? The argument advanced at a recent government hearing—that because we will not be dependent on plutonium for more than a few hundred years it "will not be an important problem indefinitely"—entirely misses the point.[21] Though we may rely on plutonium for only a relatively brief period, the plutonium produced during that period may be with us indefinitely, and it may jeopardize the lives of many times the number of generations that profit from its use. Assuming there are alternatives to plutonium recycle, it is not the kind of policy that people deprived of knowledge of the generation to which they belong would favor. For a small probability of gain in the earlier generations, they would assume eons of risk to life and health.

It may be objected here that it is not possible to make such long-term calculations of risk. As some have observed, our future is "very open" with all sorts of scientific change possible.[22] We may someday be in a position to develop protective medical technologies against the somatic and genetic dangers plutonium represents.[23]

The reply to this, of course, is that we may. But if we look at the matter impartially, it hardly seems acceptable to embark on programs that presently pose great foreseeable dangers merely in the hope that these dangers will vanish in the future. In matters of intergenerational responsibility, just as in more familiar moral choices, caution is in order where great evils are involved. This suggests that in considering policies that affect the future, we must evaluate our actions in terms of the best *available* estimate of their consequences.[24] By this standard, the proposals for a plutonium economy seem presently unacceptable.

It may finally be objected, however, that this kind of discussion proceeds in a vacuum. There is no such thing as an absolute evil. All the evils of any policy must be weighed against the evils of alternative policies. But any such weighing seems to favor a plutonium economy. All of our present energy alternatives, after all, involve serious risks. Do not the lives of hundreds of persons killed, maimed, or disabled in each generation by coal mining mean anything? And what about the many ordinary citizens whose health is jeopardized and whose lives are cut short by the air pollution caused by fossil fuels?

These are weighty arguments. Certainly it is true that policies involving generations, no less than individual moral choices, require a relative evaluation of goods and evils. Moral choices are always balancing judgments. It is also true that if we regard the matter impartially, it is very difficult to weigh a sure risk to the life and health of a series of present

21. Environmental Protection Agency, *Proceedings of Public Hearings.*
22. M. Golding, "Obligations to Future Generations," *Monist*, 56 (1972), 85–99; K. Nielsen, "The Enforcement of Morality and Future Generations," *Philosophia*, 3 (1973), 443–448.
23. G. Garvey, *Energy, Ecology, Economy* (New York: W. W. Norton, 1972).
24. D. Callahan, "What Obligations Do We Have to Future Generations?" *American Ecclesiastical Review*, 144 (1971), 265–280.

generations against the grave possible risks plutonium holds for future generations. If that were the choice before us, it would be a difficult one indeed. But is that the choice? Must we continue expending lives in order to protect distant future generations?

One answer to this, I suspect, is that the choice before us is not quite as dramatic as the defenders of a plutonium economy (or similar deleterious policies) would have us believe. Many of the present evils to which they allude can be eliminated or substantially reduced if we are prepared to spend money to do so. Thus, the dangers of coal mining and air pollution can both be substantially reduced for a price. Then, too, there is a prospect of developing relatively nonpolluting solar energy (or, less certainly, fusion energy) to replace much of our dependence on fossil fuel. The choice before us, in other words, is not the sacrifice of present life for future life. Rather, it is the choice of accepting material sacrifices in the present—in the form of higher energy and conservation costs—in order to protect the lives and health of our descendants.

By now it is clear that I believe we should choose against plutonium (and, perhaps by extension, any fission energy policy as well). Regarding the matter as though we did not know which generation were our own, it seems unreasonable to risk our lives and health in countless future generations (and the lives and health of those we love) simply to preserve high material living standards in the present.

Of course, sacrifices in material living standards are important. For some persons, a decline in such living standards can adversely affect life and health. This consideration raises a new question: When sacrifices on behalf of future generations are morally demanded, how shall these sacrifices be distributed? Who shall bear the burden? This digression into the issue of energy policy, therefore, serves as a fitting prelude to consideration of the third axiom of intergenerational justice.

## DISTRIBUTING SACRIFICES FOR THE FUTURE

The third axiom is: *Sacrifices on behalf of the future must be distributed equitably in the present, with special regard for those presently least advantaged.*

From the beginning of my remarks, I have tried to suggest that our obligations to the future are obligations of justice. They form part of the total moral question of how we are to distribute the limited material resources and opportunities our environment affords. There is nothing new in this understanding. It was emphasized almost two centuries ago by Thomas Robert Malthus, one of the pioneers in intergenerational thinking, when he argued against unrestrained procreation. The procreatively irresponsible, Malthus said, can be thought of as unjustly pushing their numerous offspring forward to the limited places at some future banquet table of life.[25] Recently, in a classic article, Hardin made the same point by

25. T. R. Malthus, *Essay on the Principle of Population*, 2nd ed. (London: J. Johnson, 1802).

comparing groups or nations with high fertility to abusers of the commons.[26] Even more than Malthus, Hardin's discussion indicates the element of injustice in abuse over time of a shared environment.

However, if we grant that it is unjust to force our excess progeny on others or that it is unjust to consume more than our generation's share of resources, what does this imply for our total moral responsibility and particularly for the question of how we ought to distribute needed sacrifices in the present? Very specifically, can we demand just treatment for the future while neglecting justice in the present? Can we require some persons to sacrifice on behalf of all our descendants while we refuse to treat those same persons by the strictest standards of justice? Can justice itself be compartmentalized in this way?

I believe the answer to these questions must be no. Just regard for the future is inseparable from just policies in the present. We cannot pick and choose our areas of moral exertion, encouraging or demanding regard for some persons but not for others. Unfortunately, this awareness has sometimes escaped participants in the population and resource debate. From Malthus to Hardin, many proponents of environmental responsibility have been quick to champion just policies protective of the future. But they have sometimes been equally slow to recognize the just claims of less advantaged groups or individuals in the present. In the case of Malthus, this partiality was a deliberate expression of his aristocratic and antidemocratic bias, and it deservedly earned him the enmity of radical defenders of the poor.[27]

Malthus' followers have not always shared his social preferences. Some have been convinced that restraints on consumption and population are very much to everybody's eventual advantage. Although this may be true, it obscures the fact that just demands on behalf of the future are first of all precisely that—demands. As such, they necessarily bring up the whole question of distributive justice.

### What Distributive Justice Entails

This is all rather abstract, but it has some important concrete implications. Within our own nation it suggests that we must be especially careful to see that when we institute policies to protect the future, we do not disproportionately injure our less advantaged citizens in the present. I do not want to maintain that individuals or families earning less than, say, the median income are being unjustly treated. Justice need not require equality of income.[28] But certainly departures from equality require justification, and even when they are justified lesser shares of income can frequently generate resentment. To ask our less affluent fellow citizens to bear a special share of the burden of protecting the future, therefore, risks compounding injustice or exacerbating resentment.

26. G. Hardin, "The Tragedy of the Commons," *Science*, 162 (1968), 1243–1248.

27. R. Meek, *Marx and Engels on Malthus* (London: Lawrence & Wishart, 1953).

28. Rawls, *A Theory of Justice;* N. Rescher, *Distributive Justice* (Indianapolis, Ind.: Bobbs-Merrill, 1967).

We might also keep in mind the fact that the less affluent and the poor often have fewer reasons to identify with the future generations we seek to protect. Neither inner-city residents nor blue-collar workers, for example, typically enjoy optimum natural environments. One government report recently termed our urban poor as among our environmentally "most endangered" citizens.[29] Therefore, we should not be surprised if appeals for environmental responsibility go unheeded by members of these groups, or if they reject these appeals as an "elitist" preoccupation.

More serious than this is the fact that the less affluent can rarely afford the special sacrifices needed for the future, although these sacrifices very often tend to fall directly on them. Both in this country and abroad, for example, high fertility is usually associated with low income groups partly because members of these groups have the greatest need for the various kinds of basic security that large families can provide.[30] However necessary, and however much it may eventually benefit all families, therefore, population limitation can often severely disadvantage low income parents by requiring them to limit the size of their families before alternative social security programs are available and before adequate local health care can guarantee survival of all their children.

The same is true of the related environmental and resource issues. Recently, for example, measures aimed at protecting our environment have tended to strike lower-middle class or poor workers the hardest. Not only can these workers barely afford to pay the extra costs or taxes for these measures, but they often depend for a livelihood on marginal firms whose viability is jeopardized by demands for pollution control or recycling equipment.

The energy issue offers a similar picture. As recent hearings on United States energy policy make clear, it is the poor and middle class that most sorely feel the bite of added energy costs.[31] Members of these groups tend to pay a large percentage of their income for fuel and gasoline, and they are tied to aging homes or automobiles, whose energy consumption is disproportionately high.

## Implications

All those engaged in efforts to marshall support for programs protective of future generations should keep these facts in mind. It is not only that we potentially commit an injustice against the less privileged members of our community by causing them to bear a larger share of our intergenerational distributive responsibility. It is also that, in doing so, we

29. Environmental Protection Agency, *Report to the Administration of the Environmental Protection Agency by the Task Force on Environmental Problems of the Inner City* (Washington, D.C.: Environmental Protection Agency, 1971).

30. L. S. El-Hamamsy, "Belief Systems and Family Planning in Peasant Societies," in *Are Our Descendants Doomed?* ed. H. Brown and E. Hutchings, Jr. (New York: Viking Press, 1972); J. B. Gordon and J. E. Wyon, *The Khanna Study* (Cambridge, Mass.: Harvard University Press, 1971).

31. Federal Energy Administration, *Project Independence* (Washington, D.C.: Government Printing Office, 1974).

endanger our very efforts to protect future generations. When those who are less well-off are treated in a way they regard as unjust, they may respond with resentment and resistance, which can paralyze efforts on behalf of future generations. Indeed, the recent erosion of public support for environmental programs during this recessionary period, and particularly the resistance of lower-middle class workers fearful of losing their jobs, may serve as warning that these dangers are very real.

The third axiom of intergenerational justice has implications for a number of policy issues, ranging from the very specific matter of establishing fair rate schedules for promoting energy conservation to the broader matter of how we can best formulate strategies for eliciting environmental concern. It also has application to the international arena, where it may counsel a change in the tone, if not the content, of demands for population restraint on the part of the poorer nations. These demands rightly proceed from a sense of the injustice of such unrestrained procreation (injustice to *all* our descendants).

But some of the most strident of these demands have been voiced by citizens of other nations or by indigenous elites whose own conduct, not only in matters of population or resource consumption but in a host of other social relations as well, has been morally questionable. Strict justice in the matter of population does not, as some have mistakenly believed and objected, require toleration of serious reproductive irresponsibility.[32] Those who fail to limit the number of their offspring are themselves guilty of violating strict standards of justice. The recognition that our objection to this behavior is based on considerations of justice, however, may caution us to be aware of our own inadequacies when we call on the procreatively irresponsible to respect our common future.


## CONCLUSIONS

This is not the place to explore all the implications and applications of these axioms. My aim, instead, has been to present a way of thinking about intergenerational responsibility. Working out all the details of these axioms and the method that underlies them is an important but separate task. In moral reasoning, as in science, the method of thinking about problems may be more important than specific conclusions, "the act of judging more critical than the judgment."[33]

Although these three axioms may be taken singly, there is some value in regarding them all together. Like organic life, justice is a seamless web.[34] If these axioms offer any lesson, it is that, although we are responsible to the future, our efforts to improve the future quality of life must not become an excuse for neglecting our responsibilities to our neighbors in the present.

32. G. Hardin, "Living on a Lifeboat," *BioScience*, 24 (1974), 561–568.
33. J. Bronowski, *Science and Human Values* (New York: Julian Messner, 1956).
34. R. Neuhaus, *In Defense of People* (New York: Macmillan, 1971).

The last point may have special importance for scientists. Perhaps because they work so closely with the delicate natural systems on which all of our lives depend, or perhaps just because they naturally have "the future in their bones," as C. P. Snow puts it,[35] scientists, and particularly biologists, have been at the forefront of efforts at environmental preservation. In the very urgent task of protecting the environment, however, scientists must be careful not to align themselves with those privileged individuals, groups, or nations whose calls for sacrifice are directed primarily at the poor.

Scientists must also be careful that their efforts to shock us into responsibility do not help generate the "me-first" attitude of survival more appropriate to a battlefield or lifeboat than an ongoing human community. If scientists allow their foresight to be used as an ideology by the privileged, if they fail to keep in mind the strict relationship between justice to the future and justice to the less fortunate in the present, both science and future generations will be the losers.

# THE RIGHTS OF ANIMALS AND UNBORN GENERATIONS

*Joel Feinberg*

Every philosophical paper must begin with an unproved assumption. Mine is the assumption that there will still be a world five hundred years from now, and that it will contain human beings who are very much like us. We have it within our power now, clearly, to affect the lives of these creatures for better or worse by contributing to the conservation or corruption of the environment in which they must live. I shall assume furthermore that it is psychologically possible for us to care about our remote descendants, that many of us in fact do care, and indeed that we ought to care. My main concern then will be to show that it makes sense to speak of the rights of unborn generations against us, and that given the moral judgment that we ought to conserve our environmental inheritance for them, and its grounds, we might well say that future generations *do* have

35. C. P. Snow, *The Two Cultures and the Scientific Revolution* (London: Cambridge University Press, 1959).

rights correlative to our present duties toward them. Protecting our environment now is also a matter of elementary prudence, and insofar as we do it for the next generation already here in the persons of our children, it is a matter of love. But from the perspective of our remote descendants it is basically a matter of justice, of respect for their rights. My main concern here will be to examine the concept of a right to better understand how that can be.

## THE PROBLEM

To have a right is to have a claim[1] *to* something and *against* someone, the recognition of which is called for by legal rules or, in the case of moral rights, by the principles of an enlightened conscience. In the familiar cases of rights, the claimant is a competent adult human being, and the claimee is an officeholder in an institution or else a private individual, in either case, another competent adult human being. Normal adult human beings, then, are obviously the sorts of beings of whom rights can meaningfully be predicated. Everyone would agree to that, even extreme misanthropes who deny that anyone in fact has rights. On the other hand, it is absurd to say that rocks can have rights, not because rocks are morally inferior things unworthy of rights (that statement makes no sense either), but because rocks belong to a category of entities of whom rights cannot be meaningfully predicated. That is not to say that there are no circumstances in which we ought to treat rocks carefully, but only that the rocks themselves cannot validly claim good treatment from us. In between the clear cases of rocks and normal human beings, however, is a spectrum of less obvious cases, including some bewildering borderline ones. Is it meaningful or conceptually possible to ascribe rights to our dead ancestors? to individual animals? to whole species of animals? to plants? to idiots and madmen? to fetuses? to generations yet unborn? Until we know how to settle these puzzling cases, we cannot claim fully to grasp the concept of a right, or to know the shape of its logical boundaries.

One way to approach these riddles is to turn one's attention first to the most familiar and unproblematic instances of rights, note their most salient characteristics, and then compare the borderline cases with them, measuring as closely as possible the points of similarity and difference. In the end, the way we classify the borderline cases may depend on whether we are more impressed with the similarities or the differences between them and the cases in which we have the most confidence.

It will be useful to consider the problem of individual animals first because their case is the one that has already been debated with the most thoroughness by philosophers so that the dialectic of claim and rejoinder has now unfolded to the point where disputants can get to the end game quickly and isolate the crucial point at issue. When we understand pre-

---

1. I shall leave the concept of a claim unanalyzed here, but for a detailed discussion, see my "The Nature and Value of Rights," *Journal of Value Inquiry* 4 (Winter 1971): 263–277.

cisely what *is* at issue in the debate over animal rights, I think we will have
the key to the solution of all the other riddles about rights.

## INDIVIDUAL ANIMALS

Almost all modern writers agree that we ought to be kind to animals, but
that is quite another thing from holding that animals can claim kind treatment from us as their due. Statutes making cruelty to animals a crime are
now very common, and these, of course, impose legal duties on people not
to mistreat animals; but that still leaves open the question whether the
animals, as beneficiaries of those duties, possess rights correlative to them.
We may very well have duties *regarding* animals that are not at the same
time duties *to* animals, just as we may have duties regarding rocks, or
buildings, or lawns, that are not duties *to* the rocks, buildings, or lawns.
Some legal writers have taken the still more extreme position that animals
themselves are not even the directly intended beneficiaries of statutes prohibiting cruelty to animals. During the nineteenth century, for example, it
was commonly said that such statutes were designed to protect human
beings by preventing the growth of cruel habits that could later threaten
human beings with harm too. Prof. Louis B. Schwartz finds the rationale of
the cruelty-to-animals prohibition in its protection of animal lovers from
affronts to their sensibilities. "It is not the mistreated dog who is the ultimate object of concern," he writes. "Our concern is for the feelings of other
human beings, a large proportion of whom, although accustomed to the
slaughter of animals for food, readily identify themselves with a tortured
dog or horse and respond with great sensitivity to its sufferings."[2] This
seems to me to be factitious. How much more natural it is to say with John
Chipman Gray that the true purpose of cruelty-to-animals statutes is "to
preserve the dumb brutes from suffering."[3] The very people whose sensibilities are invoked in the alternative explanation, a group that no doubt
now includes most of us, are precisely those who would insist that the
protection belongs primarily to the animals themselves, not merely to their
own tender feelings. Indeed, it would be difficult even to account for the
existence of such feelings in the absence of a belief that the animals deserve
the protection in their own right and for their own sakes.

   Even if we allow, as I think we must, that animals are the intended
direct beneficiaries of legislation forbidding cruelty to animals, it does not
follow directly that animals have legal rights, and Gray himself, for one,[4]
refused to draw this further inference. Animals cannot have rights, he
thought, for the same reason they cannot have duties, namely, that they
are not genuine "moral agents." Now, it is relatively easy to see why

   2. Louis B. Schwartz, "Morals, Offenses and the Model Penal Code," *Columbia Law
Review* 63 (1963): 673.
   3. John Chipman Gray, *The Nature and Sources of the Law*, 2d ed. (Boston: Beacon
Press, 1963), p. 43.
   4. And W. D. Ross for another. See *The Right and the Good* (Oxford: Clarendon Press,
1930), app. 1, pp. 48–56.

animals cannot have duties, and this matter is largely beyond controversey. Animals cannot be "reasoned with" or instructed in their responsibilities; they are inflexible and unadaptable to future contingencies; they are subject to fits of instinctive passion which they are incapable of repressing or controlling, postponing or sublimating. Hence, they cannot enter into contractual agreements, or make promises; they cannot be trusted; and they cannot (except within very narrow limits and for purposes of conditioning) be blamed for what would be called "moral failures" in a human being. They are therefore incapable of being moral subjects, of acting rightly or wrongly in the moral sense, of having, discharging, or breeching duties and obligations.

But what is there about the intellectual incompetence of animals (which admittedly disqualifies them for duties) that makes them logically unsuitable for rights? The most common reply to this question is that animals are incapable of *claiming* rights on their own. They cannot make motion, on their own, to courts to have their claims recognized or enforced; they cannot initiate, on their own, any kind of legal proceedings; nor are they capable of even understanding when their rights are being violated, of distinguishing harm from wrongful injury, and responding with indignation and an outraged sense of justice instead of mere anger or fear.

No one can deny any of these allegations, but to the claim that they are the grounds for disqualification of rights of animals, philosophers on the other side of this controversy have made convincing rejoinders. It is simply not true, says W. D. Lamont,[5] that the ability to understand what a right is and the ability to set legal machinery in motion by one's own initiative are necessary for the possession of rights. If that were the case, then neither human idiots nor wee babies would have any legal rights at all. Yet it is manifest that both of these classes of intellectual incompetents have legal rights recognized and easily enforced by the courts. Children and idiots start legal proceedings, not on their own direct initiative, but rather through the action of proxies or attorneys who are empowered to speak in their names. If there is no conceptual absurdity in this situation, why should there be in the case where a proxy makes a claim on behalf of an animal? People commonly enough make wills leaving money to trustees for the care of animals. Is it not natural to speak of the animal's right to his inheritance in cases of this kind? If a trustee embezzles money from the animal's account,[6] and a proxy speaking in the dumb brute's behalf presses the animal's claim, can he not be described as asserting the animal's *rights*? More exactly, the animal itself claims its rights through the vicarious actions of a human proxy speaking in its name and in its behalf. There appears to be no reason why we should require the animal to understand what is going on (so the argument concludes) as a condition for regarding it as a possessor of rights.

5. W. D. Lamont, *Principles of Moral Judgment* (Oxford: Clarendon Press, 1946), pp. 83–85.

6. Cf. H. J. McCloskey, "Rights," *Philosophical Quarterly* 15 (1965): 121, 124.

Some writers protest at this point that the legal relation between a principal and an agent cannot hold between animals and human beings. Between humans, the relation of agency can take two very different forms, depending upon the degree of discretion granted to the agent, and there is a continuum of combinations between the extremes. On the one hand, there is the agent who is the mere "mouthpiece" of his principal. He is a "tool" in much the same sense as is a typewriter or telephone; he simply transmits the instructions of his principal. Human beings could hardly be the agents or representatives of animals in this sense, since the dumb brutes could no more use human "tools" than mechanical ones. On the other hand, an agent may be some sort of expert hired to exercise his professional judgment on behalf of, and in the name of, the principal. He may be given, within some limited area of expertise, complete independence to act as he deems best, binding his principal to all the beneficial or detrimental consequences. This is the role played by trustees, laywers, and ghost-writers. This type of representation requires that the agent have great skill, but makes little or no demand upon the principal, who may leave everything to the judgment of his agent. Hence, there appears, at first, to be no reason why an animal cannot be a totally passive principal in this second kind of agency relationship.

There are still some important dissimilarities, however. In the typical instance of representation by an agent, even of the second, highly discretionary kind, the agent is hired by a principal who enters into an agreement or contract with him; the principal tells his agent that within certain carefully specified boundaries "You may speak for me," subject always to the principal's approval, his right to give new directions, or to cancel the whole arrangement. No dog or cat could possibly do any of those things. Moreover, if it is the assigned task of the agent to defend the principal's rights, the principal may often decide to release his claimee, or to waive his own rights, and instruct his agent accordingly. Again, no mute cow or horse can do that. But although the possibility of hiring, agreeing, contracting, approving, directing, canceling, releasing, waiving, and instructing is present in the typical (all-human) case of agency representation, there appears to be no reason of a logical or conceptual kind why that *must* be so, and indeed there are some special examples involving human principals where it is not in fact so. I have in mind legal rules, for example, that require that a defendant be represented at his trial by an attorney, and impose a state-appointed attorney upon reluctant defendants, or upon those tried *in absentia*, whether they like it or not. Moreover, small children and mentally deficient and deranged adults are commonly represented by trustees and attorneys, even though they are incapable of granting their own consent to the representation, or of entering into contracts, of giving directions, or waiving their rights. It may be that it is unwise to permit agents to represent principals without the latters' knowledge or consent. If so, then no one should ever be permitted to speak for an animal, at least in a legally binding way. But that is quite another thing than saying that such representation is logically incoherent or conceptually incongruous—the contention that is at issue.

H. J. McCloskey,[7] I believe, accepts the argument up to this point, but he presents a new and different reason for denying that animals can have legal rights. The ability to make claims, whether directly or through a representative, he implies, is essential to the possession of rights. Animals obviously cannot press their claims on their own, and so if they have rights, these rights must be assertable by agents. Animals, however, cannot be represented, McCloskey contends, and not for any of the reasons already discussed, but rather because representation, in the requisite sense, is always of interests, and animals (he says) are incapable of having interests.

Now, there is a very important insight expressed in the requirement that a being have interests if he is to be a logically proper subject of rights. This can be appreciated if we consider just why it is that mere things cannot have rights. Consider a very precious "mere thing"—a beautiful natural wilderness, or a complex and ornamental artifact, like the Taj Mahal. Such things ought to be cared for, because they would sink into decay if neglected, depriving some human beings, or perhaps even all human beings, of something of great value. Certain persons may even have as their own special job the care and protection of these valuable objects. But we are not tempted in these cases to speak of "thing-rights" correlative to custodial duties, because, try as we might, we cannot think of mere things as possessing interests of their own. Some people may have a duty to preserve, maintain, or improve the Taj Mahal, but they can hardly have a duty to help or hurt it, benefit or aid it, succor or relieve it. Custodians may protect it for the sake of a nation's pride and art lovers' fancy; but they don't keep it in good repair for "its own sake," or for "its own true welfare," or "well-being." A mere thing, however valuable to others, has no good of its own. The explanation of that fact, I suspect, consists in the fact that mere things have no conative life: no conscious wishes, desires, and hopes: or urges and impulses; or unconscious drives, aims, and goals; or latent tendencies, direction of growth, and natural fulfillments. Interests must be compounded somehow out of conations; hence mere things have no interests. *A fortiori,* they have no interests to be protected by legal or moral rules. Without interests a creature can have no "good" of its own, the achievement of which can be its due. Mere things are not loci of value in their own right, but rather their value consists entirely in their being objects of other beings' interests.

So far McCloskey is on solid ground, but one can quarrel with his denial that any animals but humans have interests. I should think that the trustee of funds willed to a dog or cat is more than a mere custodian of the animal he protects. Rather his job is to look out for the interests of the animal and make sure no one denies it its due. The animal itself is the beneficiary of his dutiful services. Many of the higher animals at least have appetites, conative urges, and rudimentary purposes, the integrated satisfaction of which constitutes their welfare or good. We can, of course, with consistency treat animals as mere pests and deny that they have any

7. Ibid.

rights; for most animals, especially those of the lower orders, we have no choice but to do so. But it seems to me, nevertheless, that in general, animals *are* among the sorts of beings of whom rights can meaningfully be predicated and denied.

Now, if a person agrees with the conclusion of the argument thus far, that animals are the sorts of beings that *can* have rights, and further, if he accepts the moral judgment that we ought to be kind to animals, only one further premise is needed to yield the conclusion that some animals do in fact have rights. We must now ask ourselves for whose sake ought we to treat (some) animals with consideration and humaneness? If we conceive our duty to be one of obedience to authority, or to one's own conscience merely, or one of consideration for tender human sensibilities only, then we might still deny that animals have rights, even though we admit that they are the kinds of beings that *can* have rights. But if we hold not only that we ought to treat animals humanely but also that we should do so for the animals' own sake, that such treatment is something we owe animals as their due, something that can be claimed for them, something the withholding of which would be an injustice and a wrong, and not merely a harm, then it follows that we do ascribe rights to animals. I suspect that the moral judgments most of us make about animals do pass these phenomenological tests, so that most of us do believe that animals have rights, but are reluctant to say so because of the conceptual confusions about the notion of a right that I have attempted to dispel above.

Now we can extract from our discussion of animal rights a crucial principle for tentative use in the resolution of the other riddles about the applicability of the concept of a right, namely, that the sorts of beings who *can* have rights are precisely those who have (or can have) interests. I have come to this tentative conclusion for two reasons: (1) because a right holder must be capable of being represented and it is impossible to represent a being that has no interests, and (2) because a right holder must be capable of being a beneficiary in his own person, and a being without interests is a being that is incapable of being harmed or benefitted, having no good or "sake" of its own. Thus, a being without interests has no "behalf" to act in, and no "sake" to act for. My strategy now will be to apply the "interest principle," as we can call it, to the other puzzles about rights, while being prepared to modify it where necessary (but as little as possible), in the hope of separating in a consistent and intuitively satisfactory fashion the beings who can have rights from those which cannot.

## VEGETABLES

It is clear that we ought not to mistreat certain plants, and indeed there are rules and regulations imposing duties on persons not to misbehave in respect to certain members of the vegetable kingdom. It is forbidden, for example, to pick wildflowers in the mountainous tundra areas of national parks, or to endanger trees by starting fires in dry forest areas. Members of Congress introduce bills designed, as they say, to "protect" rare redwood trees from commercial pillage. Given this background, it is surprising that no one[8] speaks of plants as having rights. Plants, after all, are not "mere things"; they are vital objects with inherited biological propensities determining their natural growth. Moreover, we do say that certain conditions are "good" or "bad" for plants, thereby suggesting that plants, unlike rocks, are capable of having a "good." (This is a case, however, where "what we say" should not be taken seriously: we also say that certain kinds of paint are good or bad for the internal walls of a house, and this does not commit us to a conception of walls as beings possessed of a good or welfare of their own.) Finally, we are capable of feeling a kind of affection for particular plants, though we rarely personalize them, as we do in the case of animals, by giving them proper names.

Still, all are agreed that plants are not the kinds of beings that can have rights. Plants are never plausibly understood to be the direct intended beneficiaries of rules designed to "protect" them. We wish to keep redwood groves in existence for the sake of human beings who can enjoy their serene beauty, and for the sake of generations of human beings yet unborn. Trees are not the sorts of beings who have their "own sakes," despite the fact that they have biological propensities. Having no conscious wants or goals of their own, trees cannot know satisfaction or frustration, pleasure or pain. Hence, there is no possibility of kind or cruel treatment of trees. In these morally crucial respects, trees differ from the higher species of animals.

· · ·

## WHOLE SPECIES

The topic of whole species, whether of plants or animals, can be treated in much the same way as that of individual plants. A whole collection, as such, cannot have beliefs, expectations, wants, or desires, and can flourish or languish only in the human interest-related sense in which individual plants thrive and decay. Individual elephants can have interests, but the species elephant cannot. Even where individual elephants are not granted rights, human beings may have an interest—economic, scientific, or sentimental—in keeping the species from dying out, and *that* interest may be protected in various ways by law. But that is quite another matter from recognizing a right to survival belonging to the species itself. Still, the preservation of a whole species may quite properly seem to be a morally more important matter than the preservation of an individual animal. Individual animals can have rights but it is implausible to ascribe them a right to life on the human model. Nor do we normally have duties to keep individual animals alive or even to abstain from killing them provided we do it humanely and nonwantonly in the promotion of legitimate human interests. On the other hand, we do have duties to protect threatened

8. Outside of Samuel Butler's *Erewhon*.

species, not duties to the species themselves as such, but rather duties to future human beings, duties derived from our housekeeping role as temporary inhabitants of this planet.

• • •

## FUTURE GENERATIONS

We have it in our power now to make the world a much less pleasant place for our descendants than the world we inherited from our ancestors. We can continue to proliferate in ever greater numbers, using up fertile soil at an even greater rate, dumping our wastes into rivers, lakes, and oceans, cutting down our forests and polluting the atmosphere with noxious gases. All thoughtful people agree that we ought not to do these things. Most would say that we have a duty not to do these things, meaning not merely that conservation is morally required (as opposed to merely desirable) but also that it is something due our descendants, something to be done for their sakes. Surely we owe it to future generations to pass on a world that is not a used up garbage heap. Our remote descendants are not yet present to claim a livable world as their right, but there are plenty of proxies to speak now in their behalf. These spokesmen, far from being mere custodians, are genuine representatives of future interests.

Why then deny that the human beings of the future have rights which can be claimed against us now in their behalf? Some are inclined to deny them present rights out of fear of falling into obscure metaphysics, by granting rights to remote and unidentifiable beings who are not yet even in existence. Our unborn great-great-grandchildren are in some sense "potential" persons, but they are far more remotely potential, it may seem, than fetuses. This, however, is not the real difficulty. Unborn generations are more remotely potential than fetuses in one sense, but not in another. A much greater period of time with a far greater number of causally necessary and important events must pass before their potentiality can be actualized, it is true; but our collective posterity is just as certain to come into existence "in the normal course of events" as is any given fetus now in its mother's womb. In that sense the existence of the distant human future is no more remotely potential than that of a particular child already on its way.

The real difficulty is not that we doubt whether our descendants will ever be actual, but rather that we don't know who they will be. It is not their temporal remoteness that troubles us so much as their indeterminacy—their present facelessness and namelessness. Five centuries from now men and women will be living where we live now. Any given one of them will have an interest in living space, fertile soil, fresh air, and the like, but that arbitrarily selected one has no other qualities we can presently envision very clearly. We don't even know who his parents, grandparents or great-grandparents are, or even whether he is related to us. Still, whoever these human beings may turn out to be, and whatever they might reasonably be expected to be like, they will have interests that we can affect, for better or worse, right now. That much we can and do know about them. The identity of the owners of these interests is now necessarily obscure, but the fact of their interest-ownership is crystal clear, and that is all that is necessary to certify the coherence of present talk about their rights. We can tell, sometimes, that shadowy forms in the spatial distance belong to human beings, though we know not who or how many they are; and this imposes a duty on us not to throw bombs, for example, in their direction. In like manner, the vagueness of the human future does not weaken its claim on us in light of the nearly certain knowledge that it will, after all, be human.

Doubts about the existence of a right to be born transfer neatly to the question of a similar right to come into existence ascribed to future generations. The rights that future generations certainly have against us are contingent rights: the interests they are sure to have when they come into being (assuming of course that they will come into being) cry out for protection from invasions that can take place now. Yet there are no actual interests, presently existent, that future generations, presently nonexistent, have now. Hence, there is no actual interest that they have in simply coming into being, and I am at a loss to think of any other reason for claiming that they have a right to come into existence (though there may well be such a reason). Suppose then that all human beings at a given time voluntarily form a compact never again to produce children, thus leading within a few decades to the end of our species. This of course is a wildly improbable hypothetical example but a rather crucial one for the position I have been tentatively considering. And we can imagine, say, that the whole world is converted to a strange ascetic religion which absolutely requires sexual abstinence for everyone. Would this arrangement violate the rights of anyone? No one can complain on behalf of presently nonexistent future generations that their future interests which give them a contingent right of protection have been violated since they will never come into existence to be wronged. My inclination then is to conclude that the suicide of our species would be deplorable, lamentable, and a deeply moving tragedy, but that it would violate no one's rights. Indeed if, contrary to fact, all human beings could ever agree to such a thing, that very agreement would be a symptom of our species' biological unsuitability for survival anyway.

## CONCLUSION

For several centuries now human beings have run roughshod over the lands of our planet, just as if the animals who do live there and the generations of humans who will live there had no claims on them whatever. Philosophers have not helped matters by arguing that animals and future generations are not the kinds of beings who can have rights now, that they don't presently qualify for membership, even "auxiliary membership," in our moral community. I have tried in this essay to dispel the conceptual confusions that make such conclusions possible. To acknowledge their rights is the very least we can do for members of endangered species (including our own). But that is something.


# NOT FOR HUMANS ONLY: THE PLACE OF NONHUMANS IN ENVIRONMENTAL ISSUES

*P. Singer*


When we humans change the environment in which we live, we often harm ourselves. If we discharge cadmium into a bay and eat shellfish from that bay, we become ill and may die. When our industries and automobiles pour noxious fumes into the atmosphere, we find a displeasing smell in the air, the long-term results of which may be every bit as deadly as cadmium poisoning. The harm that humans do the environment, however, does not rebound solely, or even chiefly, on humans. It is nonhumans who bear the most direct burden of human interference with nature.

By "nonhumans" I mean to refer to all living things other than human beings, though for reasons to be given later, it is with nonhuman animals, rather than plants, that I am chiefly concerned. It is also important, in the context of environmental issues, to note that living things may be regarded either collectively or as individuals. In debates about the environment the most important way of regarding living things collectively has been to regard them as species. Thus, when environmentalists worry about the future of the blue whale, they usually are thinking of the blue whale as a species, rather than of individual blue whales. But this is not, of course, the only way in which one can think of blue whales, or other animals, and one of the topics I shall discuss is whether we should be concerned about what we are doing to the environment primarily insofar as it threatens entire species of nonhumans, or primarily insofar as it affects individual nonhuman animals.

The general question, then, is how the effects of our actions on the environment of nonhuman beings should figure in our deliberations about what we ought to do. There is an unlimited variety of contexts in which this issue could arise. To take just one: Suppose that it is considered necessary to build a new power station, and there are two sites, A and B, under consideration. In most respects the sites are equally suitable, but building the power station on site A would be more expensive because the greater depth of shifting soil at that site will require deeper foundations; on the other hand to build on site B will destroy a favored breeding ground for thousands of wildfowl. Should the presence of the wildfowl enter into the decision as to where to build? And if so, in what manner should it enter, and how heavily should it weigh?

In a case like this the effects of our actions on nonhuman animals could be taken into account in two quite different ways: directly, giving the lives and welfare of nonhuman animals an intrinsic significance which must count in any moral calculation; or indirectly, so that the effects of our actions on nonhumans are morally significant only if they have consequences for humans.

It is the latter view which has been predominant in the Western tradition. Aristotle was among the founders of this tradition. He regarded nature as a hierarchy, in which the function of the less rational and hence less perfect beings was to serve the more rational and more perfect. So, he wrote:

> Plants exist for the sake of animals, and brute beasts for the sake of man—domestic animals for his use and food, wild ones (or at any rate most of them) for food and other accessories of life, such as clothing and various tools.
>
> Since nature makes nothing purposeless or in vain, it is undeniably true that she has made all animals for the sake of man.[1]

If one major strain of Western thought came from Greece, the other dominant influence was that of Christianity. The early Christian writers were no more ready than Aristotle to give moral weight to the lives of non-human animals. When St. Paul, in interpreting the old Mosaic law against putting a muzzle on the ox that treads out the corn, asked: "Doth God care for oxen?" it is clear that he was asking a rhetorical question, to which the answer was "No"; the law must have somehow been meant "altogether for our sakes."[2] Augustine agreed, using as evidence for the view that there are no common rights between humans and lesser living things, the incidents in the Gospels when Jesus sent devils into a herd of swine, causing them to hurl themselves into the sea, and with a curse withered a fig tree on which he had found no fruit.[3]

It was Thomas Aquinas, blending Aristotle and the Christian writings, who put most clearly the view that any consideration of the lives or welfare of animals must be because of the indirect consequences of such consideration for humans. Echoing Aristotle, he maintained that plants

---

1. *Politics*, 1256b.
2. 1 *Corinthians* 9: 9–10.
3. St. Augustine, *The Catholic and Manichean Ways of Life*, tr. D. A. Gallagher and I. J. Gallagher (Boston: Catholic University Press, 1966), p. 102.

exist for the sake of animals, and animals for the sake of man. Sins can only be against God, one's human neighbors, or against oneself. Even charity does not extend to "irrational creatures," for, among other things, they are not included in "the fellowship of everlasting happiness." We can love animals only "if we regard them as the good things that we desire for others," that is, "to God's honor and man's use." Yet if this was the correct view, as Aquinas thought, there was one problem that needed explaining: Why does the Old Testament have a few scattered injunctions against cruelty to animals, such as "The just man regardeth the life of his beast, but the bowels of the wicked are cruel?" Aquinas did not overlook such passages, but he did deny that their intention was to spare animals pain. Instead, he wrote, "it is evident that if a man practices a pitiable affection for animals, he is all the more disposed to take pity on his fellow-men." So, for Aquinas, the only sound reason for avoiding cruelty to animals was that it could lead to cruelty to humans.[4]

The influence of Aquinas has been strong in the Roman Catholic church. Not even that oft-quoted exception to the standard Christian view of nature, Francis of Assisi, really broke away from the orthodox theology of his co-religionists. Despite his legendary kindness to animals, Francis could still write: "every creature proclaims: 'God made me for your sake, O man!'"[5] As late as the nineteenth century, Pope Pius IX gave evidence of the continuing hold of the views of Paul, Augustine, and Aquinas by refusing to allow a society for the prevention of cruelty to animals to be established in Rome because to do so would imply that humans have duties toward animals.[6]

It is not, however, only among Roman Catholics that a view like that of Aquinas has found adherents. Calvin, for instance, had no doubt that all of nature was created specifically for its usefulness to man;[7] and in the late eighteenth century, Immanuel Kant, in lecturing on ethics, considered the question of our duties to animals, and told his students: "So far as animals are concerned, we have no direct duties. Animals are not self-conscious and are there merely as a means to an end. That end is man." And Kant then repeated the line that cruelty to animals is to be avoided because it leads to cruelty to humans.[8]

The view that the effects of our actions on other animals has no direct moral significance is not as likely to be openly advocated today as it was in the past; yet it is likely to be accepted implicitly and acted upon. When planners perform cost-benefit studies on new projects, the costs and benefits are costs and benefits for human beings only. This does not

4. See the *Summa Theologica*, I, II, Q72, art. 4; II, I, Q102, art. 6; II, II, Q25, art. 3; II, II, Q64, art. 1; II, II, Q159, art. 2; and the *Summa Contra Gentiles* III, II, 112.

5. *St. Francis of Assisi, His Life and Writings as Recorded by His Contemporaries*, tr. L. Sherley-Price (London, 1959); see also John Passmore, *Man's Responsibility for Nature* (New York: Charles Scribner's Sons, 1974), p. 112.

6. E. S. Turner, *All Heaven in a Rage* (London: Michael Joseph, 1964), p. 163.

7. See the *Institutes of Religion*, tr. F. C. Battles (London, 1961), Bk. 1, chs. 14, 22; vol. 1, p. 182 and elsewhere. I owe this reference to Passmore, *Responsibility for Nature*, p. 13.

8. *Lectures on Ethics*, tr. L. Infield (New York: Harper & Row, 1963), pp. 239–40.

mean that the impact of the power station or highway on wildlife is ignored altogether, but it is included only indirectly. That a new reservoir would drown a valley teeming with wildlife is taken into account only under some such heading as the value of the facilities for recreation that the valley affords. In calculating this value, the cost-benefit study will be neutral between forms of recreation like hunting and shooting and those like bird watching and bush walking—in fact hunting and shooting are likely to contribute more to the benefit side of the calculations because larger sums of money are spent on them, and they therefore benefit manufacturers and retailers of firearms as well as the hunters and shooters themselves. The suffering experienced by the animals whose habitat is flooded is not reckoned into the costs of the operation; nor is the recreational value obtained by the hunters and shooters offset by the cost to the animals that their recreation involves.

Despite its venerable origins, the view that the effects of our actions on nonhuman animals have no intrinsic moral significance can be shown to be arbitrary and morally indefensible. If a being suffers, the fact that it is not a member of our own species cannot be a moral reason for failing to take its suffering into account. This becomes obvious if we consider the analogous attempt by white slaveowners to deny consideration to the interests of blacks. These white racists limited their moral concern to their own race, so the suffering of a black did not have the same moral significance as the suffering of a white. We now recognize that in doing so they were making an arbitrary distinction, and that the existence of suffering, rather than the race of the sufferer, is what is really morally significant. The point remains true if "species" is substituted for "race." The logic of racism and the logic of the position we have been discussing, which I have elsewhere referred to as "speciesism," are indistinguishable; and if we reject the former then consistency demands that we reject the latter too.[9]

It should be clearly understood that the rejection of speciesism does not imply that the different species are in fact equal in respect of such characteristics as intelligence, physical strength, ability to communicate, capacity to suffer, ability to damage the environment, or anything else. After all, the moral principle of human equality cannot be taken as implying that all humans are equal in these respects either—if it did, we would have to give up the idea of human equality. That one being is more intelligent than another does not entitle him to enslave, exploit, or disregard the interests of the less intelligent being. The moral basis of equality among humans is not equality in fact, but the principle of equal consideration of interests, and it is this principle that, in consistency, must be extended to any nonhumans who have interests.

There may be some doubt about whether any nonhuman beings have interests. This doubt may arise because of uncertainty about what it is to have an interest, or because of uncertainty about the nature of some nonhuman beings. So far as the concept of "interest" is the cause of

---

9. For a fuller statement of this argument, see my *Animal Liberation* (New York: A New York Review Book, 1975), especially ch. 1.

doubt, I take the view that only a being with subjective experiences, such as the experience of pleasure or the experience of pain, can have interests in the full sense of the term; and that being with such experiences does have at least one interest, namely, the interest in experiencing pleasure and avoiding pain. Thus consciousness, or the capacity for subjective experience, is both a necessary and a sufficient condition for having an interest. While there may be a loose sense of the term in which we can say that it is in the interests of a tree to be watered, this attenuated sense of the term is not the sense covered by the principle of equal consideration of interests. All we mean when we say that it is in the interests of a tree to be watered is that the tree needs water if it is to continue to live and grow normally; if we regard this as evidence that the tree has interests, we might almost as well say that it is in the interests of a car to be lubricated regularly because the car needs lubrication if it is to run properly. In neither case can we really mean (unless we impute consciousness to trees or cars) that the tree or car has any preference about the matter.

The remaining doubt about whether nonhuman beings have interests is, then, a doubt about whether nonhuman beings have subjective experiences like the experience of pain. I have argued elsewhere that the commonsense view that birds and mammals feel pain is well founded;[10] but more serious doubts arise as we move down the evolutionary scale. Vertebrate animals have nervous systems broadly similar to our own and behave in ways that resemble our own pain behavior when subjected to stimuli that we would find painful; so the inference that vertebrates are capable of feeling pain is a reasonable one, though not as strong as it is if limited to mammals and birds. When we go beyond vertebrates to insects, crustaceans, mollusks and so on, the existence of subjective states becomes more dubious, and with very simple organisms it is difficult to believe that they could be conscious. As for plants, though there have been sensational claims that plants are not only conscious, but even psychic, there is no hard evidence that supports even the more modest claim.[11]

The boundary of beings who may be taken as having interests is therefore not an abrupt boundary, but a broad range in which the assumption that the being has interests shifts from being so strong as to be virtually certain to being so weak as to be highly improbable. The principle of equal consideration of interests must be applied with this in mind, so that where there is a clash between a virtually certain interest and a highly doubtful one, it is the virtually certain interest that ought to prevail.

In this manner our moral concern ought to extend to all beings who have interests. Unlike race or species, this boundary does not arbitrarily exclude any being; indeed it can truly be said that it excludes nothing at all, not even "the most contemptible clod of earth" from equal consideration of interests—for full consideration of no interests still results in no

10. Ibid.
11. See, for instance, the comments by Arthur Galston in *Natural History* 83, no. 3 (March 1974): 18, on the "evidence" cited in such books as *The Secret Life of Plants*.

weight being given to whatever was considered, just as multiplying zero by a million still results in zero.[12]

Giving equal consideration to the interests of two different beings does not mean treating them alike or holding their lives to be of equal value. We may recognize that the interests of one being are greater than those of another, and equal consideration will then lead us to sacrifice the being with lesser interests, if one or the other must be sacrificed. For instance, if for some reason a choice has to be made between saving the life of a normal human being and that of a dog, we might well decide to save the human because he, with his greater awareness of what is going to happen, will suffer more before he dies; we may also take into account the likelihood that it is the family and friends of the human who will suffer more; and finally, it would be the human who had the greater potential for future happiness. This decision would be in accordance with the principle of equal consideration of interests, for the interests of the dog get the same consideration as those of the human, and the loss to the dog is not discounted because the dog is not a member of our species. The outcome is as it is because the balance of interests favors the human. In a different situation—say, if the human were grossly mentally defective and without family or anyone else who would grieve for it—the balance of interests might favor the nonhuman.[13]

The more positive side of the principle of equal consideration is this: where interests are equal, they must be given equal weight. So where human and nonhuman animals share an interest—as in the case of the interest in avoiding physical pain—we must give as much weight to violations of the interest of the nonhumans as we do to similar violations of the human's interest. This does not mean, of course, that it is as bad to hit a horse with a stick as it is to hit a human being, for the same blow would cause less pain to the animal with the tougher skin. The principle holds between similar amounts of felt pain, and what this is will vary from case to case.

It may be objected that we cannot tell exactly how much pain another animal is suffering, and that therefore the principle is impossible to apply. While I do not deny the difficulty and even, so far as precise measurement is concerned, the impossibility of comparing the subjective experiences of members of different species, I do not think that the problem is different in kind from the problem of comparing the subjective experience of two members of our own species. Yet this is something we do all the time, for instance when we judge that a wealthy person will suffer less by being taxed at a higher rate than a poor person will gain

12. The idea that we would logically have to consider "the most contemptible clod of earth" as having rights was suggested by Thomas Taylor, the Cambridge Neo-Platonist, in a pamphlet he published anonymously, entitled *A Vindication of the Rights of Brutes* (London, 1792) which appears to be a satirical refutation of the attribution of rights to women by Mary Wollstonecraft in her *Vindication of the Rights of Woman* (London, 1792). Logically, Taylor was no doubt correct, but he neglected to specify just what interests such contemptible clods of earth have.

13. Singer, *Animal Liberation*, pp. 20–23.

from the welfare benefits paid for by the tax; or when we decide to take our two children to the beach instead of to a fair, because although the older one would prefer the fair, the younger one has a stronger preference the other way. These comparisons may be very rough, but since there is nothing better, we must use them; it would be irrational to refuse to do so simply because they are rough. Moreover, rough as they are, there are many situations in which we can be reasonably sure which way the balance of interests lies. While a difference of species may make comparisons rougher still, the basic problem is the same, and the comparisons are still often good enough to use, in the absence of anything more precise.

The principle of equal consideration of interests and the indefensibility of limiting this principle to members of our own species means that we cannot deny, as Aquinas and Kant denied, that we have direct duties to members of other species. It may be asked whether this means that members of other species have rights against us. This is an issue on which there has been a certain amount of dispute,[14] but it is, I believe, more a dispute about words than about substantive issues. In one sense of "right," we may say that it follows immediately from that fact that animals come within the scope of the principle of equal consideration. This is, admittedly, an odd kind of right—it is really a necessary foundation for having rights, rather than a right in itself. But some other rights could be derived from it without difficulty: the right not to have gratuitous pain inflicted would be one such right. There is, however, another sense of "right," according to which rights exist only among those who are part of a community, all members of whom have rights and in turn are capable of respecting the rights of others. On this view, rights are essentially contractual, and hence cannot exist unless both parties are capable of honoring the contract.[15] It would follow that most, if not all, nonhuman animals have no rights. It should be noted, though, that this is a narrower notion of rights than that commonly used in America today; for it follows from this notion of rights that not only nonhuman animals, but also human infants and young children, as well as mentally defective humans, have no rights. Those who put forward this view of rights do not believe that we may do what we like with young or mentally defective humans or nonhuman animals; rather they would say that moral rights are only one kind of constraint on our conduct, and not necessarily the most important. They might, for instance, take account of utilitarian considerations which would apply to all beings capable of pleasure or pain. Thus actions which proponents of the former, broader view of rights may condemn as violations of the rights of animals could also be condemned by those who hold the narrower view, though they would not classify such actions as infringing rights. Seen in this light the question of whether animals have rights becomes less important than it

14. See the selection of articles on this question in part IV of *Animal Rights and Human Obligations*, ed. Tom Regan and Peter Singer (Englewood Cliffs, N.J.: Prentice-Hall, 1976).

15. A clear statement of this view is to be found in H. L. A. Hart, "Are There Any Natural Rights?" *The Philosophical Review* 64 (1955).

might otherwise appear, for what matters is how we think animals ought to be treated, and not how we employ the concept of a right. Those who deny animals rights will not be likely to refuse to consider their interests, as long as they are reminded that the denial of rights to nonhuman animals does no more than place animals in the same moral category as human infants. Hence I doubt if the claim that animals have rights is worth the effort required in its defense; it is a claim which invites replies which, whatever their philosophical merits, serve as a distraction from the central practical question.

We can now draw at least one conclusion as to how the existence of nonhuman living things should enter into our deliberations about actions affecting the environment: Where our actions are likely to make animals suffer, that suffering must count in our deliberations, and it should count equally with a like amount of suffering by human beings, insofar as rough comparisons can be made.

The difficulty of making the required comparison will mean that the application of this conclusion is controversial in many cases, but there will be some situations in which it is clear enough. Take, for instance, the wholesale poisoning of animals that is euphemistically known as "pest control." The authorities who conduct these campaigns give no consideration to the sufferings they inflict on the "pests," and invariably use the method of slaughter they believe to be cheapest and most effective. The result is that hundreds of millions of rabbits have died agonizing deaths from the artificially introduced disease, myxomatosis, or from poisons like "ten-eighty"; coyotes and other wild dogs have died painfully from cyanide poisoning; and all manner of wild animals have endured days of thirst, hunger, and fear with a mangled limb caught in a leg-hold trap.[16] Granting, for the sake of argument, the necessity for pest control—though this has rightly been questioned—the fact remains that no serious attempts have been made to introduce alternative means of control and thereby reduce the incalculable amount of suffering caused by present methods. It would not, presumably, be beyond modern science to produce a substance which, when eaten by rabbits or coyotes, produced sterility instead of a drawn-out death. Such methods might be more expensive, but can anyone doubt that if a similar amount of human suffering were at stake, the expense would be borne?

Another clear instance in which the principle of equal consideration of interests would indicate methods different from those presently used is in the timber industry. There are two basic methods of obtaining timber from forests. One is to cut only selected mature or dead trees, leaving the forest substantially intact. The other, known as clear-cutting, involves chopping down everything that grows in a given area, and then reseeding. Obviously when a large area is clear-cut, wild animals find their whole living area destroyed in a few days, whereas selected felling makes a relatively minor disturbance. But clear-cutting is cheaper, and timber

16. See J. Olsen, *Slaughter the Animals, Poison the Earth* (New York: Simon and Schuster, 1971), especially pp. 153–64.

companies therefore use this method and will continue to do so unless forced to do otherwise.[17]

This initial conclusion about how the effects of our actions on nonhuman animals should be taken into account is the only one which follows directly from the argument that I have given against the view that only actions affecting our own species have intrinsic moral significance. There are, however, other suggestions which I shall make more tentatively which are at least consistent with the preceding argument, although much more discussion would be needed to establish them.

The first of these suggestions is that while the suffering of human and nonhuman animals should, as I have said, count equally, the killing of nonhuman animals is in itself not as significant as the killing of normal human beings. Some of the reasons for this have already been discussed—the probable greater grief of the family and friends of the human, and the human's greater potential. To this can be added the fact that other animals will not be made to fear for their own lives, as humans would, by the knowledge that others of their species have been killed. There is also the fact that normal humans are beings with foresight and plans for the future, and to cut these plans off in midstream seems a greater wrong than that which is done in killing a being without the capacity for reflection on the future.

All these reasons will seem to some not to touch the heart of the matter, which is the killing itself and not the circumstances surrounding it; and it is for this reason that I have put forward this view as a suggestion rather than a firm conclusion. For it might be held that the taking of life is intrinsically wrong—and equally wrong whatever the characteristics of the life that was taken. This, perhaps, was the view that Schweitzer held and which has become famous under his memorable if less than crystal-clear phrase, "reverence for life." If this view could be supported, then of course we would have to hold that the killing of nonhuman animals, however painless, is as serious as the killing of humans. Yet I find Schweitzer's position difficult to justify. What is it that is so valuable in the life of, say, a fly, which presumably does not itself have any awareness of the value of its own life, and the death of which will not be a source of regret to any member of its own species or of any other species?

It might be said—and this is a possible interpretation of Schweitzer's remark that there is the same "will-to-live" in all other forms of life as in myself—that while I may see my own life as all-important to me, so is the life of any living thing all-important to it, and hence I cannot justifiably claim greater importance for my own life. If I do, the claim will be true only from my own point of view. But this argument is weak in two respects. First, the idea of a being's life being important *for that being* depends, I think, on the assumption that the being is conscious, and perhaps even on the stronger assumption that the being is aware that it is alive and

17. See R. and V. Routley, *The Fight for the Forests* (Canberra: Australian National University Press, 1974), for a thoroughly documented indictment of clear-cutting in Australia; and for a recent report of the controversy about clear-cutting in America, see *Time*, May 17, 1976.

that its life is something that it could lose. This would exclude many forms of life from the scope of the argument, particularly if on reflection we decide that it is the stronger assumption that the argument requires. Second, the argument appears to rest on the implicit claim that if two things are each all-important for two independent beings, it is impossible to make a comparison which would show that in some objective or at least intersubjective sense that thing is more important for one than for the other. There is, however, no theoretical difficulty in a comparison of this kind, great as the practical difficulties may be. In theory, all I have to do is imagine myself living simultaneously the lives of both myself and the other being, experiencing whatever the two beings experience. I then ask myself which life I would choose to cease living if I could continue to live only one of the two lives. Since I would be making this decision from a position that is impartial between the two lives, we may conclude that the life I would choose to continue living is objectively or at least intersubjectively of greater value than the life I would choose to give up.[18] If one of the living beings in this thought experiment had *no* conscious experiences, then when imagining myself living the life of this being I would be imagining myself as having no experiences at all. It is hardly necessary to add that it would be no great sacrifice to cease living such a life. This suggests that, just as nonconscious beings have no interests, so nonconscious life lacks intrinsic value.

For Schweitzer, life itself is sacred, not even consciousness being necessary. So the truly ethical man, he says, will not tear a leaf from a tree or break off a flower unnecessarily.[19] Not surprisingly, given the breadth of its coverage, it is impossible for the ethic of reverence for life to be absolute in its prohibitions. We must take plant life, at least, if we are to eat and live. Schweitzer therefore accepts the taking of one form of life to preserve another form of life. Indeed, Schweitzer's whole life as a doctor in Africa makes no sense except on the assumption that the lives of the human beings he was saving are more valuable than the lives of the germs and parasites he was destroying in their bodies, not to mention the plants and probably animals that those humans would kill and eat after Schweitzer had cured them.[20] So I suggest that the idea that all life has equal value, or

18. This way of putting the question derives from C. I. Lewis, *An Analysis of Knowledge and Valuation* (La Salle, Ill.: Open Court, 1946), p. 547, via the work of R. M. Hare, especially *Freedom and Reason* (Oxford: Oxford University Press, 1963) and "Ethical Theory and Utilitarianism," in *Contemporary British Philosophy,* 4th series, ed. H. D. Lewis (London: Allen and Unwin, 1976).

19. *Civilization and Ethics,* tr. John Naish, reprinted in *Animal Rights and Human Obligations,* p. 134. (Nor, say Schweitzer in the same sentence, will the truly ethical man shatter an ice crystal that sparkles in the sun—but he offers no explanation of how this prohibition is derived from the ethic of reverence for life. The example may suggest that for Schweitzer killing is wrong because it is unnecessary destruction, a kind of vandalism. For discussion of this view when applied to whole species of animals, as it more commonly is, see p. 488.)

20. There is, I suppose, an alternative rationale for Schweitzer's medical activities: that while all life is of equal value, we owe loyalty to our own species and have a duty to save their lives over the lives of members of other species when there is a conflict. But I can find nothing in Schweitzer's writings to suggest that he would take so blatantly a speciesist line, and much to suggest that he would not.

is equally sacred, lacks a plausible theoretical basis and was not, in practice, adhered to even by the man whose name is most often linked with it.

I shall conclude this discussion of the comparative seriousness of killing human and nonhuman animals by admitting that I have been unable to say anything about *how much* less seriously we should regard the killing of a nonhuman. I do not feel that the death of an animal like a pig or dog is a completely trivial matter, even if it should be painless for the animal concerned and unnoticed by any other members of the species; on the other hand I am quite unable to quantify the issue so as to say that a certain number of porcine and canine deaths adds up to one human death, and in the absence of any such method of comparison, my feeling that the deaths of these animals must count for something lacks both proper justification and practical significance. Perhaps, though, this will not leave practical decision making about the environment in as bad a way as it might seem to. For when an environmental decision threatens the lives of animals and birds, it almost always does so in a way that causes suffering to them or to their mates, parents, offspring, or pack-members. Often, the type of death inflicted will itself be a slow and painful one, caused, for instance, by the steady build-up of a noxious chemical. Even when death itself is quick and painless, in many species of birds and mammals it leaves behind survivors whose lives may be disrupted. Birds often mate for life, in some species separating after the young have been reared but meeting again, apparently recognizing each other as individuals, when the breeding season comes round again. There are many species in which a bird who has lost its mate will not mate again. The behavior of mammals who have lost their young also suggests sorrow and distress, and infant mammals left without a mother will usually starve miserably. In other social species the death of one member of a group can cause considerable disturbance, especially if the dead animal is a group leader. Now, since, as we have already seen, the suffering of nonhuman animals must count equally with the like suffering of human beings, the upshot of these facts is that quite independently of the intrinsic value we place on the lives of nonhuman animals any morally defensible decision affecting the environment should take care to minimize the loss of animal life, particularly among birds and mammals.

To this point we have been discussing the place of individual nonhuman animals in environmental issues, and we have seen that an impartial consideration of their interests provides sufficient reason to show that present human attitudes and practices involving environmental issues are morally unjustifiable. Although this conclusion is, I think, obvious enough to anyone who thinks about the issue along the lines just discussed, there is one aspect of it that is in sharp contrast to an underlying assumption of much environmental debate, an assumption accepted even by many who consider themselves for animals and against the arrogant "human chauvinism" that sees all of nature as a resource to be harvested or a pit for the disposal of wastes. This assumption is that concern for nonhuman animals is appropriate when a whole species is endangered, but not when the threat is only to individual animals. It is in accordance with this assumption that the National Wildlife Federation has sought and obtained a court injunction preventing the U.S. Department of Transportation from building an interstate highway interchange in an area frequented by the extremely rare Mississippi sandhill crane, while the same organization openly supports what it calls "the hunter-sportsman who, during legal hunting seasons, crops surplus wildlife."[21] Similarly the National Audubon Society has fought to preserve rare birds and other animals but opposed moves to stop the annual slaughter of 40,000 seals on the Pribilof Islands of Alaska on the grounds that this "harvest" could be sustained indefinitely, and the protests were thus "without foundation from a conservation and biological viewpoint."[22] Other "environmentalist" organizations which either actively support or refuse to oppose hunting include the Sierra Club, the Wilderness Society, and the World Wildlife Fund.[23]

Since we have already seen that animals' interests in avoiding suffering are to be given equal weight to our own, and since it is sufficiently obvious that hunting makes animals suffer—for one thing, no hunter kills instantly every time—I shall not discuss the ethics of hunting, though I cannot resist inviting the reader to think about the assumptions behind the use of such images as the "cropping" of surplus wildlife" or the "harvesting" of seals. The remaining ethical issue that needs to be discussed is whether it is still worse to hunt or otherwise to kill animals of endangered species than it is to kill those of species that are plentiful. In other words, suppose that groups like the National Wildlife Federation were to see the error of their prohunting views, and swing round to opposition to hunting. Would they nevertheless be justified in putting greater efforts into stopping the shooting of the Mississippi sandhill crane than into stopping duck-shooting? If so, why?

Some reasons for an affirmative answer are not hard to find. For instance, if we allow species to become extinct, we shall deprive ourselves and our descendents of the pleasures of observing all of the variety of species that we can observe today. Anyone who has ever regretted not being able to see a great auk must have some sympathy with this view. Then again, we never know what ecological role a given species plays, or may play under some unpredictable change of circumstances. Books on ecology are full of stories about how farmers/the health department/ the army/the Forestry Commission decided to get rid of a particular rodent/bird/fish/insect because it was a bit of a nuisance, only to find that that particular animal was the chief restraint on the rate of increase of some much nastier and less easily eradicated pest. Even if a species has already been reduced to the point where its total extinction could not

21. For the attempt to obtain a court injunction, see *The Wall Street Journal*, January 9, 1976, and for the statement in support of hunting, Lewis Regenstein, *The Politics of Extinction* (New York: Macmillan, 1975), p. 32.

22. Victor Scheffer, *A Voice for Wildlife* (New York: Charles Scribner's Sons, 1974), p. 64, quoting "Protest, Priorities and the Alaska Fur Seal," *Audubon* 72 (1970): 114–15.

23. Regenstein, *Politics of Extinction*, p. 33. There are, of course, some who argue for the preservation of species precisely because otherwise there will be no animals left to hunt; for a brief discussion see Passmore, *Responsibility for Nature*, p. 103.

have much "environmental impact" in the sense of triggering off other changes, it is always possible that in the future conditions will change, the species will prove better adapted to the new conditions than its rivals, and will flourish, playing an important part in the new ecological balance in its area to the advantage of humans living there. Yet another reason for seeking to preserve species is that, as is often said, the removal of a species depletes the "gene pool" and thus reduces the possibility of "improving" existing domestic or otherwise useful animals by cross-breeding with related wild animals. We do not know what qualities we may want domestic animals to have in the future. It may be that existing breeds lack resistance to a build-up of toxic chemicals or to a new disease that may break out in some remote place and sweep across our planet; but by interbreeding domestic animals with rare wild varieties, we might be able to confer greater resistance on the former, or greater usefulness to humans on the latter.

These reasons for preserving animals of endangered species have something in common: They are all concerned with benefits or dangers for humans. To regard these as the only reasons for preserving species is to take a position similar to that of Aquinas and Kant, who, as we saw earlier, thought cruelty to animals wrong only because it might indirectly harm human beings. We dismissed that argument on the grounds that if human suffering is intrinsically bad, then it is arbitrary to maintain that animal suffering is of no intrinsic significance. Can we similarly dismiss the view that species should be preserved only because of the benefits of preservation to humans? It might seem that we should, but it is not easy to justify doing so. While individual animals have interests, and no morally defensible line can be drawn between human interests and the interests of nonhuman animals, species as such are not conscious entities and so do not have interests above and beyond the interests of the individual animals that are members of the species. These individual interests are certainly potent reasons against killing rare animals, but they are no more potent in the case of rare animals than in the case of common animals. The rarity of the blue whale does not cause it to suffer any more (nor any less) when harpooned than the more common sperm whale. On what basis, then, other than the indirect benefits to humans, can we justifiably give preference to the preserving of animals of endangered species rather than animals of species that are not in any danger?

One obvious answer, on the basis of the foregoing, is that we ought to give preference to preserving animals of endangered species if so doing will have indirect benefits for nonhuman animals. This may sometimes be the case, for if the extinction of a species can lead to far-reaching ecological damage, this is likely to be bad for nonhuman animals as well as for humans. Yet this answer to our question, while extending the grounds for preserving species beyond the narrow limits of human benefits, still provides no basis for attributing intrinsic value to preservation. To find such a basis we need an answer to the following modified version of the question asked above: On what basis, other than the indirect benefits to humans or other animals, can we justifiably give preference to the preserving of animals of endangered species rather than animals of species that are not in danger?

To this question I can find no satisfactory answer. The most promising suggestion, perhaps, is that the destruction of a whole species is the destruction of something akin to a great work of art; that the tiger, or any other of the "immensely complex and inimitable items produced in nature" has its own, noninstrumental value, just as a great painting or cathedral has value apart from the pleasure and inspiration it brings to human beings.[24] On this view, to exterminate a species is to commit an act of vandalism, like setting about Michelangelo's *Pietà* with a hammer; while allowing an endangered species to die out without taking steps to save it is like allowing Angkor Wat to fall into ruins and be obliterated by the jungle.

My difficulty with this argument is a difficulty with the allegedly less controversial case on which the analogy is built. If the analogy is to succeed in persuading us that there may be intrinsic value quite independently of any benefits for sentient beings in the existence of a species, we must believe that there is this kind of intrinsic value in the existence of works of art; but how can it be shown that the *Pietà* has value independently of the appreciation of those who have seen or will see it? If, as philosophers are fond of asking, I were the last sentient being on earth, would it matter if, in a moment of boredom, I entertained myself by making a bonfire of all the paintings in the Louvre? My own view is that it would not matter—provided, of course, I really could exclude the possibility that, as I stood around the dying embers, a flying saucer would not land and disgorge a load of tourists from Alpha Centauri who had come all the way solely in order to see the Mona Lisa. But there are those who take the opposite view, and I would agree that *if* works of art have intrinsic value, then it is plausible to suppose that species have too.

I conclude, then, that unless or until better grounds are advanced, the only reasons for being more concerned about the interests of animals from endangered species than about other animals are those which relate the preservation of species to benefits for humans and other animals. The significance of these reasons will vary from case to case, depending on such factors as just how different the endangered species really is from other nonendangered species. For instance, if it takes an expert ornithologist to tell a Mississippi sandhill crane from other, more common cranes (and I have no knowledge of whether this is so), then the argument for preservation based on the pleasures of observing a variety of species cannot carry much weight in this case, for this pleasure would be available only to a few people. Similarly, the value of retaining species that perhaps

24. Val Routley, "Critical Notice of *Man's Responsibility for Nature*," *Australasian Journal of Philosophy* 53, no. 2 (1975): 175. Routley uses this argument more as an ad hominem against Passmore (who accepts that works of art can have intrinsic value) than as the basis for her own view. For further discussion of this view, see Passmore, *Responsibility for Nature*, p. 103; and Stanley Benn, "Personal Freedom and Environmental Ethics: The Moral Inequality of Species," paper presented to the World Congress on Philosophy of Law and Social Philosophy, St. Louis, Mo., August 1975, especially p. 21.

will one day be usefully crossbred with domestic species will not apply to species that have no connection with any domestic animal; and the importance we place on this reason for preserving species will also depend on the importance we place on domestic animals. If, as I have argued elsewhere, it is generally both inefficient and inhumane to raise animals for food, we are not going to be greatly moved by the thought of "improving" our livestock.[25] Finally, although the argument that the greater the variety of species, the better the chances of a smooth adjustment to environmental changes, is usually a powerful one, it has little application to endangered species that differ only marginally and in ecologically insignificant ways—like minor differences in the markings of birds—from related, nonendangered species.

This conclusion may seem unfavorable to the efforts of environmental groups to preserve endangered species. I would not wish it to be taken in that way. Often the indirect reasons for preservation will make an overwhelming case for preservation; and in any case we must remember that what we have been discussing is not whether to defend animals against those who would kill them and deprive them of their habitat but whether to give preference to defending animals of endangered species. Defending endangered species is, after all, defending individual animals too. If we are more likely to stop the cruel form of commercial hunting known as whaling by pointing out that blue whales may become extinct than by pointing out that blue whales are sentient creatures with lives of their own to lead, then by all means let us point out that blue whales may become extinct. If, however, the commercial whalers should limit their slaughter to what they call the "maximum sustainable yield" and so cease to be a threat to blue whales as a species, let us not forget that they remain a threat to thousands of individual blue whales. My aim throughout this essay has been to increase the importance we give to individual animals when discussing environmental issues, and not to decrease the importance we presently place on defending animals which are members of endangered species.

25. Singer, *Animal Liberation,* esp. chs. 3 and 4.

# ETHICS AND ANIMAL CONSCIOUSNESS

*Martin Benjamin*

## INTRODUCTION

Are there any ethical restrictions on the ways in which human beings may use and treat nonhuman animals? If so, what are they and how are they to be justified? In what follows, I will first review three standard responses to these questions and briefly indicate why none of them is entirely satisfactory. Next I will identify what I take to be the kernel of truth in each of the three responses and then I will attempt to blend them into a fourth, more adequate, position. In so doing, I hope to suggest the importance, from an ethical point of view, of further inquiry into the nature and extent of consciousness in nonhuman animals.

## THREE STANDARD POSITIONS

Historically, Western philosophers have responded to questions about the nature and extent of ethical restrictions on the human use and treatment of nonhuman animals in three ways. First, those who hold what I label "Indirect Obligation" theories maintain that ethical restrictions on the use and treatment of animals can be justified *only if* they can be derived from direct obligations to human beings. The second type of response, which I label "No Obligation" theories, holds that there are no restrictions whatever on what humans may do to other animals. And the third type of response, which I label "Direct Obligation" theories, maintains that ethical restrictions on the use and treatment of animals can sometimes be justified solely for the sake of animals themselves. I will now elaborate each of these positions.

### 1. Indirect Obligation

Among the most noted philosophers in the Western tradition, St. Thomas Aquinas (1225–1274) and Immanuel Kant (1724–1804) have acknowledged restrictions on human conduct with regard to the use and treatment of nonhuman animals, but these restrictions are, in their view, ultimately grounded upon obligations to other human beings. Blending views that can be traced both to the Bible and Aristotle, Aquinas held a hierarchial or means-end view of the relationship between plants, animals, and humans, respectively:

> There is no sin in using a thing for the purpose for which it is. Now the order of things is such that the imperfect are for the perfect . . . things, like plants which merely have life, are all alike for animals, and all animals are for man. Wherefore it is not unlawful if men use plants for the good of animals, and animals for the good of man, as the Philosopher states (*Politics*, i, 3).
> Now the most necessary use would seem to consist in the fact that animals use plants, and men use animals, for food, and this cannot be done unless these be deprived of life, wherefore it is lawful both to take life from plants for the use of animals, and from animals for the use of men. In fact this is in keeping with the commandment of God himself (*Genesis* i, 29, 30 and *Genesis* ix, 3).[1]

Nevertheless, it does not follow, for Aquinas, that one can do anything to an animal. For example, one is still prohibited from killing another person's ox: "He that kills another's ox, sins, not through killing the ox, but through injuring another man in his property. Wherefore this is not a species of the sin of murder but of the sin of theft or robbery." And there may even be similarly *indirect* grounds for not harming animals who are no one's property. Thus, Aquinas explains,

> if any passages of Holy Writ seem to forbid us to be cruel to dumb animals, for instance to kill a bird with its young: this is either to remove man's thoughts from being cruel to other men, and lest through being cruel to animals one become cruel to human beings: or because injury to an animal leads to the temporal hurt of man, either of the doer of the deed, or of another.[2]

Kant, too, held that insofar as humans are obligated to restrain themselves in their dealings with animals, it is due to their obligations to other humans. Thus,

> so far as animals are concerned, we have no direct duties. Animals are not self-conscious and are there merely as a means to an end. That end is man. . . . Our duties towards animals are merely indirect duties towards humanity. Animal nature has analogies to human nature, and by doing our duties to animals in respect of manifestations of human nature, we indirectly do our duty to humanity. . . . If . . . any acts of animals are analogous to human acts and spring from the same principles, we have duties towards the

---

1. St. Thomas Aquinas, *Summa Theologica*, literally translated by the English Dominican Fathers (Benziger Brothers, 1918), Part II, Question 64, Article 1. Reprinted in Tom Regan and Peter Singer, eds., *Animal Rights and Human Obligations* (Prentice-Hall, 1976), p. 119.

2. St. Thomas Aquinas, *Summa Contra Gentiles*, literally translated by the English Dominican Fathers (Benziger Brothers, 1928), Third Book, Part II, Chap. CXII. Reprinted in Regan and Singer, p. 59.

animals because thus we cultivate the same duties towards human beings. If a man shoots his dog because the animal is no longer capable of service, he does not fail in his duty to the dog, for the dog cannot judge, but his act is inhuman and damages in itself that humanity which it is his duty to show towards mankind. If he is not to stifle his human feelings, he must practice kindness towards animals, for he who is cruel to animals becomes hard also in his dealings with men.[3]

Thus Aquinas and Kant both hold what I have labeled "Indirect Obligation" theories with regard to ethical restrictions on the use and treatment of animals. Although they agree that we have obligations *with regard* to animals, these obligations are *not*, at bottom, *owed to* the animals themselves but rather they are owed to other human beings.

There are, nonetheless, significant problems with Aquinas's and Kant's positions, at least in their present forms. First, insofar as Aquinas assumes that it is necessary for humans to use animals for food and thus to deprive them of life, his position must be reconsidered in the light of modern knowledge about nutrition. It has been maintained, for example, that a perfectly nutritious diet may require little or no deprivation of animal life and, even if it does, that the average American consumes twice as much animal protein as his or her body can possibly use.[4] Insofar as we continue to consume large quantities of animal foodstuff requiring pain and the deprivation of life, then, we do so, not so much to serve vital nutritional demands, but rather to indulge our acquired tastes. Secondly, insofar as Aquinas's view is based upon a hierarchial world-view and assumes that those lower in the order or less perfect are to serve the good of those higher or more perfect, it is open to a serious theoretical objection. It is, unfortunately, not difficult to imagine a group of beings— perhaps from another part of the universe—who are more rational and more powerful than we. Assuming that such beings are more perfect than we are, it seems to follow, if we adopt the principles underlying Aquinas's view, that we ought to acquiesce in their using us for whichever of their purposes they fancy we would serve. But do we want to agree with the rightness of this? And if we take Aquinas's view, would we have any grounds on which to disagree?

As for Kant's view, the main difficulties have to do first with his emphasis on self-consciousness as a condition for being the object of a direct obligation, and second with his assumption that all and only human beings are self-conscious. I will postpone consideration of the first difficulty until later. For the moment, let me simply develop the second. Even supposing that being self-conscious is a necessary condition for being the object of a direct obligation, it does not follow either that *all* human beings are the objects of direct obligations or that *no* animal can be the object of such an obligation. First, advances in medical knowledge, techniques, and technology have, among other things, preserved and pro-

3. Immanuel Kant, "Duties to Animals and Spirits," in *Lectures on Ethics*, translated by Louis Infield (Harper and Row, 1963). Reprinted in Regan and Singer, p. 122.
4. Francis Moore Lappé, "Fantasies of Famine," *Harper's*, 250 (February 1975), p. 53.

longed the lives of a number of human beings who are severely retarded or otherwise mentally impaired due to illness or accident and the irreversibly comatose (e.g., Karen Ann Quinlan). In our day, then, if not in Kant's, one cannot assume that all human beings are self-conscious. Second, some contemporary researchers have suggested that at least some non-human animals have a capacity for becoming self-conscious that has, until recently, been undetected or ignored by humans. Thus, even if we follow Kant and accept self-consciousness as a condition for being the object of direct obligations, it does not follow that *all* and *only* humans satisfy this condition. Some humans, it may turn out, will not be the objects of direct obligations and some animals will.

### 2. No Obligation

If animals are not conscious—that is, if they are not sentient and have no capacity for pleasure, pain, or any other mental states—they may not even be the objects of indirect obligations. Insofar as Aquinas says that it is possible to be "cruel to dumb animals" and Kant says that "he who is cruel to animals becomes hard in his dealings with men," each presupposes that animals, unlike plants and machines, are sentient and are thereby capable of sensation and consciousness. Thus it is surprising to find René Descartes (1596–1650), a renowned philosopher, mathematician, and scientist, comparing animals to machines. Nonetheless, this is just what he did in his influential *Discourse on Method* when he compared machines made by the hand of man with human and nonhuman animal bodies made by the hand of God: "From this aspect the body is regarded as a machine which, having been made by the hands of God, is incomparably better arranged, and possesses in itself movements which are much more admirable than any of those which can be invented by man."[5] Living *human* bodies were, for Descartes, distinguished from living *animal* bodies by the presence of an immortal soul which was a necessary condition for mental experiences. Without a soul, a living biological body was a natural automaton, "much more splendid," but in kind no different from those produced by humans.

For Descartes, the criterion for distinguishing those living bodies which were ensouled from those which were not was the capacity to use language. The former, he believed, included all and only human beings. Among humans, he maintained,

> there are none so depraved and stupid, without even exempting idiots, that they cannot arrange different words together, forming of them a statement by which they make known their thoughts; while on the other hand, there is no other animal, however perfect and fortunately circumstanced it may be, which can do the same.[6]

5. René Descartes, *Discourse on Method*, in *Philosophical Works of Descartes*, translated by E. S. Haldane and G. R. T. Ross (Cambridge University Press), Vol. 1. Reprinted in Regan and Singer, p. 61.
6. Ibid.

Insofar as nonhuman animals do appear to do some things better than we do, Descartes added, "it is nature which acts in them according to the disposition of their organs, just as a clock, which is only composed of wheels and weights is able to tell the hours and measure the time more correctly than we can do with all our wisdom."[7] As for the ethical implications of his view, Descartes, in a letter to Henry More, noted that his "opinion is not so much cruel to animals as indulgent to men . . . since it absolves them from the suspicion of crime when they eat or kill animals."[8]

Insofar as Descartes's position presupposes that all and only human beings have the capacity to use language, it is open to the same sort of criticisms and objections that we raised against Kant. That is, advances in medicine are providing more nonlinguistic humans and advances in science are suggesting that at least some nonhuman animals have more linguistic facility or capacity than we previously supposed. Moreover, even if Descartes were correct in believing that the capacity to use language is uniquely human, why should this, rather than the capacity to feel pain and experience distress, be the principal criterion for determining the nature and extent of ethical restrictions on the use and treatment of animals? It is this objection which sets the stage for positions which hold that humans have direct obligations to at least some animals.

### 3. Direct Obligation

Jeremy Bentham (1748–1832), the father of modern utilitarianism, held that pain and pleasure were what governed behavior and that any ethical system which was founded on anything but maximizing the net balance of pleasure over pain, dealt in "sounds instead of sense, in caprice instead of reason, in darkness instead of light." Every action, for Bentham was to be assessed in terms of its likelihood of maximizing the net balance of happiness. But, he noted, if the capacity to experience pleasure and pain was what qualified one to be taken into account in estimating the effects of various courses of action, then nonhuman as well as human animals would have to be taken into account insofar as they, too, had the capacity to experience pleasure and pain. Thus, for Bentham, it is sentience, or the capacity for pleasure and pain, that determines whether a being qualifies for moral consideration.

> What else is it that should trace the insuperable line? Is it the faculty of reason, or perhaps the faculty of discourse? But a full-grown horse or dog is beyond comparison a more rational, as well as a more conversable animal than an infant of a day or a week or even a month old. But suppose they were otherwise, what would it avail? The question is not, Can they *reason* nor Can they *talk?* but, *Can they suffer?*[9]

7. Ibid, p. 62.
8. René Descartes, Letter to Henry More, in *Descartes: Philosophical Letters*, translated and edited by Anthony Kenny (Oxford University Press, 1970). Reprinted in Regan and Singer, p. 66.
9. Jeremy Bentham, *The Principles of Morals and Legislation* (1789), Chapter XVII, Section 1. Reprinted in Regan and Singer, p. 129.

The question now is, what grounds do we have to believe that animals *can* suffer, can feel pain, or can experience distress? If a being lacks the capacity to convey his suffering, pain, or distress linguistically how do we know that it actually has such experiences and isn't a rather splendid automaton going through the motions?

In response to such skepticism, one holding a utilitarian direct obligation theory must show why he or she believes that nonhuman animals are conscious. There are a number of ways one might go about this. First, one could stress behavioral similarities between human and nonhuman animals in their respective responses to certain standard pain- and pleasure-producing stimuli. Comparing the behavior of nonhuman animals with human infants would be especially forceful here. Second, we could stress relevant neurophysiological similarities between humans and nonhumans. After making these comparisons we may then be inclined to agree with Richard Sergeant when he claims that:

> Every particle of factual evidence supports the contention that the higher mammalian vertebrates experience pain sensations at least as acute as our own. To say that they feel less because they are lower animals is an absurdity; it can easily be shown that many of their senses are far more acute than ours—visual acuity in certain birds, hearing in most wild animals, and touch in others; these animals depend more than we do on the sharpest possible awareness of a hostile environment.[10]

So, if Sergeant is correct in this, at least some animals are conscious and hence, on utilitarian grounds, qualify as the objects of direct obligation.

There are, nonetheless, significant limitations to this view. First, although utilitarianism takes nonhuman animals directly into account in determining ethical obligations, there is no guarantee that animals will, in fact, fare better on this view than they will on an Indirect Obligation view like that of Aquinas or Kant. Contemporary animal welfare advocates who find utilitarianism hospitable to their position have not fully appreciated utilitarianism's indifference to any outcome apart from the maximization of happiness. Thus, for example, on utilitarian grounds, a policy which causes a great amount of pain to animals which also causes an even greater amount of offsetting pleasure to humans, would appear to be ethically justified. Second, one who adopts utilitarianism because it takes direct account of animal suffering, must recognize all of its implications. One of the standard objections to utilitarianism is that it seems, on the face of it, more suited to animals than it is to human beings. Thus Bentham's version was initially caricatured as philosophy for swine because it seemed to imply that it was better to be a satisfied pig than a dissatisfied human; or better to be a fool satisfied than Socrates dissatisfied.

10. Richard Sergeant, *The Spectrum of Pain* (London, Hart-Davis, 1969), p. 72. Cited by Peter Singer in Tom Regan, ed., *Matters of Life and Death* (Random House, 1980), p. 225.

## A FOURTH POSITION

Although none of the positions we have examined is entirely satisfactory, each, I believe, has something to recommend it. *Indirect Obligation* theories are correct to stress the difference between what I will call "simple consciousness" and "reflective-consciousness," but they have not adequately characterized the difference nor have they fully appreciated its ethical significance. *No Obligation* theories, at least that of Descartes, are correct in emphasizing the relationship between the use of language and the development of reflective-consciousness. And, finally, *Direct Obligation* theories are correct in noting that the possession of simple consciousness (or sentience) in human or nonhuman animals is, by itself, sufficient to give them independent standing in the ethical deliberations of beings who are reflectively-conscious. I will now, very briefly, outline each of these fundamental insights and suggest how they may be integrated into a fourth, more adequate position.

The fundamental insight of *Indirect Obligation* theories is their recognition of a difference between simple and reflective consciousness. Beings having only simple consciousness can experience pain, have desires, and make choices. But they are not capable of reflecting upon their experiences, desires, and choices and altering their behavior as a result of such self-conscious evaluation and deliberation. Beings who can do this I will, following John Locke (1632–1704), label "persons." A person, in Locke's view, is "A thinking intelligent being that has reason and reflection and can consider itself as itself, the same thinking thing, in different times and places."[11] Although they were mistaken in believing that the class of persons fully coincided with the class of human beings, *Indirect Obligation* theorists were correct to emphasize the special status of persons. For only persons are capable of tracing the consequences and implications of various courses of action and then deliberating and deciding to embark on one rather than another on grounds other than self-interest. To do this is part of what it means to have a morality, and it is the capacity for taking the moral point of view (that is, voluntarily restricting one's appetite or desires for the sake of others) that gives the persons their special worth.

The fundamental insight of Descartes's *No Obligation* theory was to recognize the connection between the development and exercise of personhood and the development and exercise of language. As Stuart Hampshire has recently pointed out, although people often associate the use of language primarily with communication, "language's more distinctive and far-reaching power is to bring possibilities before the mind. Culture has its principal source in the use of the word 'if,' in counterfactual speculation."[12] Only language, then, gives us the power to entertain complex unrealized possibilities. "The other principal gift of language to culture," Hampshire

11. John Locke, *Essay Concerning Human Understanding*, ed. by John Yolton (J. M. Dent & Sons, 1961), Vol. One, Book II, Ch. XXVII, p. 281.
12. Stuart Hampshire, *"Human Nature," New York Review of Books*, XXVI (December 6, 1979), Special Supplement, p. d.

continues, "is the power to date, and hence to make arrangements for tomorrow and to regret yesterday."[13] Thus a being cannot become a person and, in Locke's words, "consider itself as itself, the same thinking thing, in different times and places," without the use of language.

Finally, the fundamental insight of *Direct Obligation* theories was to note that one needn't be a person to be the object of a moral obligation. Simple consciousness or sentience is sufficient to entitle a being to be considered *for its own sake* in the ethical deliberations of persons. If, for example, the capacity to feel pain is sufficient ground for a *prima facie* obligation not to cause gratuitous pain to persons, why is it not also a sufficient ground for a similar obligation not to cause pain to beings having simple consciousness? With regard to the evil of avoidable and unjustifiable pain, the question is, as Bentham emphasized, not "Can they reason nor Can they talk? but, Can they suffer?"

Putting all of this together, we may say that persons, who are characterized as possessing reflective consciousness, may have a higher status than beings having only simple consciousness. Their special worth is a function of the extent to which they use language "to bring possibilities before the mind" and then restrain their more trivial desires for the sake of not harming others whom they recognize, from the moral point of view, as their equals in certain respects. Among the beings whose interests must be taken into account *for their own sake* in the moral deliberations of persons are beings possessing only simple consciousness. To the extent that persons reluctantly cause pain, suffering, and even death to beings possessing simple consciousness in order to meet *important needs*, what they do may be justified by appeal to their higher status or greater worth. But, to the extent that persons inflict avoidable pain and suffering on such beings merely to satisfy certain *trivial tastes or desires*, they pervert their greater capacities. In so doing, they ironically undermine their claim to higher status or worth and thereby weaken any justification they may have had for sacrificing beings having only simple consciousness for important ends.

Whether something is to be classified as an "important need" or a "trivial taste or desire" will frequently be a matter of debate and uncertainty. Yet we should not allow disputes over difficult cases to blind us to the existence of relatively easy cases. There is, for example, little doubt that well-designed, nonduplicative research on animals aimed at preventing or treating disease serves an important need. And it seems just as certain that causing pain to animals in order to test the toxicity of "new and improved" floor polishes or cosmetics serves trivial tastes or desires. And even cases that are not so immediately clear may be resolved by a bit of thoughtful investigation. Thus I suspect that most people who care to learn something about human nutrition and the treatment of animals on modern "factory farms" will be strongly inclined to conclude that factory

13. *Ibid.*

farming causes pain and suffering to animals for the sake of trivial tastes and desires.[14]

## FURTHER INQUIRY

The foregoing is at best a sketch or outline of a position on the ethical significance of animal awareness. A number of refinements need to be made and a number of questions need to be answered before we can confidently use it to make particular judgments and decisions about the use and treatment of nonhuman animals. First, we must do more in the way of spelling out the crucial distinction between simple consciousness and reflective consciousness. In addition, we must determine the extent to which *various degrees* of both types of consciousness are distributed or realized within members of various classes of human and nonhuman animals. It is important to note here that since there is nothing in the distinction between simple and reflective consciousness that requires it to follow species lines, the investigations in question will involve infants and severely retarded and severely brain-damaged human beings, as well as nonhuman animals.

Among the important questions we must ask is whether, and if so, to what extent, beings who lack reflective consciousness can experience things other than pain and pleasure. For example, can chimps, dogs, pigs, or chickens experience sadness, boredom, loneliness, frustration, apprehensiveness, disappointment, anxiety, and other states that are not as closely identified with determinate behavioral responses as is pain? If so, how would we know? Questions of this kind will, I hope, be soon addressed by philosophers of mind, ethologists, psychologists, neurophysiologists, and others. My principal aim has been to show why, from an ethical point of view, they are important questions.

14. See, for example, Peter Singer, *Animal Liberation* (New York: New York Review, 1975); and Jim Mason and Peter Singer, *Animal Factories* (New York: Crown Publishers, 1980).

# THE NEW YORK ARCHIPELAGO

DRAWN BY OLD MAN MUD FLAP DURING HIS TRAVELS

ISBNs:
978-0-9859010-2-8 (paperback)
978-0-9859010-0-4 (Kindle)
978-0-9859010-1-1 (ePub)

*Cover design by Ed Schneider*

*Print layout by eBooks by Barb for booknook.biz*

**BIRTHRIGHT PUBLISHING**
WASHINGTON DC

For Ed and Sam

The characters presented here, whether real or imagined, may not actually come to exist in the 22nd century. And if it turns out any of them do, then more power to them. This is a work of fiction. (Please keep that in mind, Larry King.)

# THE NEW YORK ARCHIPELAGO 2120

## CHAPTER 1.

MARGARET HUGHES POURED herself a second cup of koffey, eased into her office chair and began to peruse the day's appointments. Can't get the real stuff any more, she lamented. Columbian? Kenyan? Kona? Sometimes she wished she didn't have such a great memory. Practically photographic. A shot of Starbucks espresso? Mmmm. She could almost smell the beans grinding.

Margaret first started acquiring memories near the turn of the last century and although more than a hundred years had passed since she spat out her pacifier, she readily recalled her early childhood. And she was as sharp as ever, a quality much to be desired in a neurosurgeon regardless of her age.

Her brain was a beauty. It showed no lesions, no plaque, no signs of senility whatsoever. Of course, she had only been using it for the past five years. The same was true of her body, which appeared to be that of an athletic teenager, although she'd much prefer to look her body's actual age of twenty-four. It was embarrassing when strangers mistook her for an intern despite her capable manner and a nametag that helpfully read "Dr. M. Hughes."

She did, of course, struggle with the adolescent urges that sometimes overrode her common sense. It was part of the transition. As a bio-engineer and neurologist, Margaret was more aware of the problem than most of her patients. Her prefrontal cortex, the part of the brain that controls impulses and makes moral judgments, wouldn't be fully functional until she was, say twenty-six. Maybe even older.

It was no big deal. Honestly. What was she, blonde? It's not like she was going to get knocked up. Her father had actually warned her… Like he was so mature. Gawd.

Margaret drained her cup, wriggled into her white coat and strung a stethoscope over her shoulder. She felt this added years and drew the respect she damned well deserved – especially from Stepper Goodwin. The family lawyer was flying his wife in from the Palisades for a pre-operative viewing. Stepper was such a skeeze. On the way to the rooftop via the family's private elevator, Margaret vowed to ignore his jibes no matter how cringe-worthy.

The helipad was empty and she felt the heat of the reflective coating through her clogs. The Goodwins weren't

due for another few minutes so she sheltered in the shade of the flight chief's shack, tapped a cigarette from her platinum case and lit it with a matching lighter. They had been gifts from a grateful patient. He had been a quadriplegic before she renewed him. A super nice guy.

Margaret took a drag and blew a perfect chain of smoke rings. As she watched them float toward the water tower and gradually break apart, a small helicopter came into view and began to hover over the helipad. It was a Dragonfly, speedy, fairly quiet and more maneuverable than a full-size helo. A sweet little bird. She wished she had taken time to get a pilot's license.

Stepper Goodwin waved from the cockpit as the aircraft settled onto the huge red cross marking the center of the helipad. A pair of security guards rushed past Margaret to check Stepper's credentials, unaware perhaps that he was the family lawyer and had been since long before Hurricane Adolf churned Manhattan and environs into Big Apple sauce. Stepper could afford a flight of Dragonflies on his retainer alone.

Margaret waved off the guards, who reluctantly gave way as she reached the aircraft. Stepper was helping his seventh wife, Zoë, from the chopper. Zoë was afraid of flying; she was afraid of just about everything as far as Margaret could tell. She reminded her of Bambi, the orphaned fawn in the Disney movie: Saucer-eyed and baby-faced, exactly Stepper's type.

"Stepper, Zoë," Margaret reached for his, then Zoë's hand.

"Baby Doc," Stepper boomed. "You all ready for us?"

"Right on schedule," Margaret assured him as they walked toward the elevator. "How about you, Zoë? Any last minute concerns?"

Zoë flashed a nervous smile.

"She's fine," Stepper intervened.

"Is that right?" Margaret turned to face Zoë. "We'll have a chat before pre-op and if you need him, we have a great psychiatric consultant on staff."

Margaret ushered them into the elevator. A cloud of Zoë's floral perfume filled the car, which gently lowered them to the viewing rooms on the fifth floor. Margaret sneezed.

Zoë was only thirty-four and that was far too young for the procedure in Margaret's opinion. But many of her patients were robbing the cradle now that transfers were safer and the results more predictable. At the same time, it was brain surgery, not a frigging tonsillectomy.

Zoë clung to Stepper's arm, her eyes shiny with potential tears.

"Is it like she's dead?" Zoë blurted.

"She?" Margaret asked.

"It. How many times do we have to go over this?" Stepper demanded.

Margaret frowned at Stepper. "She's new at this, Step."

He grunted his acquiescence.

Margaret turned to Zoë. "Your vessel isn't dead. It's comatose. The higher brain functions are inactive."

"Nobody's home," Stepper added, pointing to his temple. "It won't even know we're there."

Zoë looked at Margaret, who provided her with a reassuring nod.

The elevator slowed and opened onto a spacious, lavishly carpeted corridor suffused with a golden light that made even Stepper's reddened skin seem to glow from within. Zoë was stunning despite the slightest softening of her jaw line and her sun-damaged skin. Sun block didn't prevent the damage, it only lessened it. People don't listen. Why did she bother?

"Follow me," said Margaret, turning down the corridor to the left. "We're in the next room."

"I'm scared," Zoë said, still hanging back.

"Don't be ridiculous," Stepper growled.

"You don't have to be so mean," Zoë protested.

"Zoë, I swear to God."

"Here we are." Margaret pressed her palm against the scanner, which read her DNA and unlocked the door of the viewing room. Stepper pushed his hesitant wife after Margaret, who turned up the lights so the couple could get a better look at Zoë's vessel, the naked female floating in a glass-topped holding tank.

"It's gorgeous, isn't it?" Margaret smiled at Zoë's vessel.

"You've done yourself proud, Baby Doc," said Stepper, unable to suppress a boner.

Zoë, her fear defeated by her curiosity, peered into the tank. "Oh, my God," she gasped, "Oh, my God. She looks exactly like me. Except younger."

"That's the idea," Margaret agreed.

"It's like looking into a mirror," Zoë said.

"Close. Not exactly," Margaret said.

Zoë placed her hand against the glass and stared at the closed eyes. "Are you sure they're the right color?"

"Absolutely," Margaret answered.

Zoë continued to inspect her vessel, which was suspended in a lime green gel and looked vaguely alien.

"How long before the color wears off?" she asked.

"It isn't a dye," Margaret said.

"Will I have a belly button?"

"Did you want one?" Margaret was losing patience. "Look if you're finished with the inspection," she began when Zoë gasped.

"What is it?" Margaret asked the horrified young woman.

"They're so small." Fat tears rolled down her apple cheeks.

"They?"

"My bosoms." Zoë looked at Stepper for confirmation.

"She-eet, she's right."

Margaret took a look. "I assure you they are to exact specifications."

Stepper shook his head. "No, ma'am. We ordered D-cups. Those look like fucking tea cups."

"Do I have to show you the papers?"

Stepper ignored her question. "Can you fix them?" he asked.

Margaret swallowed hard, bit back a smug retort, then took a deep breath. "Yes. But it'll have to be cosmetic and it'll cost more."

"Well, she sure as hell can't go around looking like that. Make 'em bigger. Lots bigger. Got that?"

"I shall look to the pyramids for inspiration."

"That's the ticket, Doc." He slapped Margaret on the shoulder, then turned to leave.

"Before you go, Zoë will have to decide what to do with the remains?"

"Th-the remains?" Zoë blurted.

"Yeah. Did you want to donate them to charity? Most patients do. We can cremate them, but…"

Zoë's lip quivered; she looked at Stepper for an answer.

"It's tax deductible," Margaret added. "But you know that already."

"She'll make a donation," Stepper said.

Margaret handed him a small folder. "Make sure to fill out the forms and have them registered with the city well before her surgery."

"Will do," Stepper said.

"In the meantime, I'll set up an appointment with Dr. English. Miles and I were at Columbia together. He's the best in the business."

Margaret moved toward the door. "I've got another appointment," she lied. "If you want, you can stay a little longer."

"No need," said Stepper, who put an arm around Zoë and walked into the hallway. "Give a shout-out to your old man for me."

"Will do," said Margaret making a beeline for her office. Her secretary had provided another pot of koffey along with a clean mug and a plate of ginger snaps. She plopped down in her chair and helped herself to both. Mmmm. She licked her lips and wiggled her toes. Just like her mother, Ann, used to make... if her mother had been the cookie-making type, which she hadn't.

Ann had been a trophy wife, blonde and petite like Zoë. Margaret hoped she had been more assertive than Zoë, though it was never easy to stand up to her dad who could be as persuasive as he was charming. Morgan Hughes had never forgiven Ann for leaving them on their own while Margaret was still eating her own boogers.

Margaret picked up a framed, faded snapshot of Morgan and Ann that had been taken on their honeymoon in Hawaii. They were wearing leis and toasting each other with fruity cocktails mixed in coconut shells. Ann had a gorgeous tan.

Margaret's own skin was a creamy white. Despite her Irish ancestry, she was freckle-free. Her dead sister, Lily, had had a sprinkling on her nose. Otherwise, they might have

passed for twins with their flaming hair and heart-shaped little faces.

# CHAPTER 2.

HE AND ANN had loved each other once, Morgan was certain of it. At the same time, he had to admit that he had never loved anyone quite so much as he loved himself before Lily arrived. He had been smitten by his adorable, good-natured daughter from the moment he first laid eyes on her, squalling, wrinkled and red. Before Lily, Morgan's focus had been on his business – buying up and demolishing Manhattan's outmoded buildings, then erecting the most ostentatious structures conceivable in their stead.

Morgan had wanted to hire a filmmaker to record the birth, but his wife Ann vehemently refused to grunt and writhe for the cameras. So Lily came into his world unchronicled and au naturel on July 5, 1996, a birthday she

shared with a lamb named Dolly. The creature was neither a lamb of God nor a lamb of sheep. Dolly was a lamb of man – the first mammal ever cloned from an adult of its species.

Lily's birth was greeted with oohing and cooing, champagne and caviar. Morgan passed out cigars. Ann complained that her breasts were too big. The house was fragrant with floral arrangements and the baby's rosy room was crowded with presents.

In contrast, Dolly's delivery was both toasted and flambéed. Cameras rolled and the ink poured. While Dolly suckled, TV reporters broadcast from her pen in Edinburgh. Talk show guests shouted their differing opinions. Tabloids dubbed the poor little lamb, "Frankensheep."

"Next thing you know they'll be cloning people," became a mantra of the masses.

" 'What if' wasn't the question," declared the talking heads, "it was 'how soon.' "

The pope and the president of United States of America along with lesser world leaders jointly denounced the cloning of human beings as unethical, unnecessary and grotesque beyond all comprehension. They envisioned bizarre, but not altogether unlikely scenarios beyond eugenic apocalypse:

Clones would be grown as slaves; they would be born brain dead and their organs harvested; the gene pool would be exhausted, corrupted, maybe even dried up; familial relations would become hopelessly tangled.

Leaders of various religious communities – except the

Episcopalians – more or less agreed with the Right Reverend Orville Hast Sr. "Cloning a human being… well, you
might as well walk right up to the Lord and slap Him
upside the head."

But argued the bio-geneticists, we will cure diseases,
retard the aging process, extend life far beyond four score
and ten. Given the enormous strides in cognitive neuro-
science, why we could build a body for Ted Williams'
frozen noggin!

Though Morgan now wondered if he hadn't been subcon-
sciously influenced by the synonymous birth dates of girl
and lamb, the coincidence resonated little to the besotted
new parents. Lily was a happy baby who suckled tenderly,
slept soundly and chortled readily. She had inherited her
mother's warmth and her father's charm, but looked
nothing like either of them. Instead she took after Morgan's
great-aunt Glory, who with his mother had come to
America by way of Ellis Island. At every family gathering,
the relatives would marvel at the child's eerie resemblance
to Glory: green, almond-shaped eyes, fair skin and hair the
red of dying embers.

"Why, you are the spitting image of your great auntie,"
they exclaimed.

Morgan doubted Lily knew what spitting image
meant, but the picture it painted in her head drove her from
the room. Then again, maybe she was simply bored.

Anyhow she would skip off to her room and pretend to be a princess with a pet unicorn and a prince whom, if he displeased her, she would zap into a frog.

Ann had been tucking Lily and her stuffed animals in one night when she noticed the little girl sounded congested. She had smoothed back Lily's hair and felt her forehead for fever. (Probably a case of the sniffles, the nanny suggested.) If she was no better tomorrow, they would pay a visit to the pediatrician. The next morning, Lily was wheezy and gulping for air. The doctor ordered tests.

Memories of Lily were best left buried in the back of his mind, though Morgan sometimes unearthed them without quite grasping why. She had been such a brave kid. Like the time, she assured them she wasn't afraid of the big donut machine. He and Ann held hands as she disappeared inside for a CT scan of her chest and abdomen.

The procedure was over in minutes and the results were soon in the hands of a prominent radiologist. His findings couldn't have been much worse. Morgan had read the verdict in the doctor's face. "We found a tumor," he said, "a lymphoma winding around Lily's windpipe like a python."

The diagnosis sent Ann, a lapsed Catholic, to the nearest church, where she daubed herself with holy water, lighted rows of votives and prayed to Rita, saint of lost causes. After a few weeks, Ann's knees were bruised from

kneeling, yet Lily grew weaker with every dose of chemo. As for watching her child suffer bravely… Well, Ann would rather die herself.

Morgan dealt with the tumor like the invader it was. He mounted a fierce campaign. He sought the finest doctors and the latest treatments, but none was able to heal his adorable, good-natured daughter. He refused to give up even after the oncologist uttered those dreadful words: "We have done all we can. It's a matter of weeks, months if we're lucky."

That night, he had looked in on Lily, sleeping sweetly, her arm around her favorite stuffed animal, a fuzzy pink lamb that baahed when squeezed. Morgan, fighting back tears, had tiptoed from the room. He was sitting in the dark, stirring the ice cubes in his scotch when the light bulb came on and he began his search for a different kind of doctor.

The next day he began to make discreet inquiries that lead to Dr. Ylan Wu. The South Korean bio-engineer claimed not only to have cloned thirteen human embryos, but also to have implanted one in Cecilia del Pomodoro, the wife of an Italian pasta-sauce scion. Although Wu's work had since been questioned, rumor had it that the doctor had been set up by a jealous colleague. Morgan thought it was more likely to be an agent of another Asian country, eager to corner the burgeoning bio-tech market.

That evening, Morgan told Ann he was going to Hong Kong on business. He made no mention of his plans to meet with Dr. Wu or of Wu's expertise. Had she known

about either, Ann would have been no less angry at her husband for abandoning Lily on her death bed.

"The doctor said she has weeks," Morgan protested.

Ann hit him over the head with a six-hundred-year-old Ming vase, went into their bedroom and refused to come out before he left for JFK.

# CHAPTER 3.

DR. YLAN WU had not only been her father's business partner, but Margaret's godfather. She always thought that was pretty funny. Wu didn't see the irony or preferred not to. He took the appointment seriously and had greatly influenced her life, particularly her brilliant medical career. After graduating from med school, she joined him in testing the Lang-Verret methodology on early human volunteers – a crucial step in the chain of events that lead Wu-Hughes Laboratories to originate the life-extension process.

In 2060, alas, Wu left for a scientific expedition in the Himalayas and never returned. Neither his body nor the bodies of his fellow travelers were ever recovered. Margaret still missed Wu, especially when she craved *Doenjang jigae*.

They had shared many a bowl of the hearty Korean stew after working until all hours. He reminisced about the good old days, about how he had been treated like a superstar until a lab assistant accused him of falsifying his results.

The South Korean government took him to court. He lost his credibility, his funding, his professorship at Seoul University. He did not, however, intend to lose his freedom and with the help of those who still believed in him, he fled South Korea for Hong Kong. "Tall branches are apt to be broken," he cautioned Margaret.

He often told her the tale of his first meeting with her father, which he recalled right down to the beverages consumed. Wu, who feared he was under surveillance, awaited Morgan's arrival at Hong Kong International in the darkest corner of a crowded airport bar. He was sipping a South Korean lager and munching wasabi peas when Morgan entered the bar and immediately spotted the scientist.

Morgan ordered a single malt scotch, threw it back and ordered another for himself and a second beer for Wu. As soon as the waiter left, he leaned toward Wu conspiratorially and got right to the point. "So is it true? Can you clone a human being?"

"Why do you ask?" Wu inquired suspiciously.

"Lily, my little girl, is dying."

"I commiserate, Mr. Hughes."

"I don't want your commiserations, Doc. I want you to save her. So can you or can't you?"

"Can I heal your Lily? No, I cannot. Can I replace your daughter? Also, no. Can I duplicate her? Under the right circumstances, it might be possible."

"And the right circumstances…"

"Would be costly, Mr. Hughes."

"How much would you need?"

"Enough for a laboratory, equipment, a place to live. Not in America. There is more flexibility in Singapore."

"I can make that happen," Morgan said.

Wu picked up his glass and drained half of it. "Before we go any further, Mr. Hughes, there is something you should know."

"I'm listening."

"A clone will not be an exact copy. It would share your daughter's DNA, but other variables will affect the outcome. Your wife is older, for example. Conditions inside the womb will differ. If she were to become ill or deliver prematurely, the baby would be as vulnerable to death and disabilities as any other infant."

"I'll risk it," Morgan said.

"I'm not finished."

"Go on."

"The baby's personality won't be identical. A child's brain develops based on what she learns as well as when and how she learns it. I remind you that you and your wife are not the same people you were when your daughter was born. The world you live in is not the same world. All this will have a large impact on your second child."

Morgan shrugged, downed the last of his scotch and threw a wad of cash on the table. "Let's get started."

As soon as his plane landed in New York, Morgan went to Children's Hospital to check on Lily. She was practically a ghost, so pale and thin in her Powerpuff Girls pajamas. He sat by her bed watching her chest rise and fall as she slept and tried not to weep.

Awakened by her father's crying, Lily reached up and patted his cheek. "It's okay, Daddy. Don't cry. Mommy says I'm going to heaven."

"You're not going anywhere. I'll never let you go, sweetheart. I promise."

When she fell asleep again, Morgan scraped a bit of skin from her arm and placed it in a tiny, sterile tube provided by Wu.

A few days later, Lily died and was buried in a white dress in a white casket covered with lilies of the valley. Ann took one of the flowers and pressed it to her lips as she and Morgan walked from the gravesite hand in hand. That night, they held each other for the first time in years. She wept in his arms and he stroked her hair.

"I miss her," Ann whispered.

Morgan kissed the top of her head. "I miss her, too."

"I don't think I can live without her. I really don't."

"You don't have to live without her, my love. It's all taken care of."

Eleven months later, Margaret Morgan Hughes came into the world squinting against the light and squalling bloody murder. She looked like Lily, though as Dr. Wu had cautioned, in temperament and personality she was anything but an exact copy. Morgan attempted to recreate the circumstances of Lily's life – same nanny, same toys, same preschool, even the same pacifier. So they told her.

Only Margaret never got the message: She preferred the chauffeur to the nanny, no school to preschool and her thumb to a pacifier. Lily's prized dolls became sacrificial offerings, sometimes headless, to the monster who dwelled under the bed. Ann rescued them all, wrapped them in tissue paper and hid them away. Margaret had spied on her. She realized she was a disappointment to her mother, but she didn't know why until Morgan finally decided she was old enough to hear about "the miracle of her birth."

Lily had been Ann's dream child, all ruffles and ribbons, a girly girl's girl who loved to play dress up and believed in fairy tales. Instinctively Margaret tried to be more Lily-like. She clomped about in her mother's Ferragamos and pretended to embrace glitter, pink and happily ever after. She sensed her mother knew she was trying to be worthy of her love. Only Ann had run out and simply didn't have any love left to give.

On Margaret's sixth birthday, her dad came home to find dinner in the oven and a packet of signed divorce papers on the kitchen counter. Margaret was devastated

when he told her Ann had gone and was never coming home again.

"It's all my fault, Daddy," she said.

Morgan insisted it had nothing to do with her and that one day she would understand why Mommy left them. He was right, only it didn't make being abandoned feel any better. One hundred-fourteen years later, Margaret was still pissed.

# CHAPTER 4.

CHASE WAS ASLEEP before he hit the bed, which was a mattress on the floor, so you know he was dead tired. His sweaty gear – tights, vest, chaps and pads – were still wet when the implant in his head starting buzzing. He slapped at his ear. The thing sounded a lot like a mosquito and the bitch of it was, you couldn't turn it off unless it was yours.

Chase couldn't afford a pinkie phone of his own. This was a one-way device between the inline skater and Fleet, the small company that employed him as a medical courier. Commonly known as grinders, Fleet's employees specialized in the speedy transport of human organs from Hughes Renewal Center to the public hospital.

"Damn it. What now?" Chase groaned as he groggily put his thumb to his ear and his little finger to his lips.

"Lyman here."

"It's Fra–" a crackle of static "–issio–"

"Fran, you're breaking up."

"–urgen–"

"Piece of shit…" He'd been issued the cheapest model.

"Who's a piece of…" static again.

"I'm talking about the phone not you." Chase moved to the window and stuck his head out over the fire escape.

"Fran? Can you hear me now?"

"Yeah. That's better."

"You woke me up."

"I got a run for you."

"Too tired. Must sleep."

"Sorry, sweet cheeks, but that ain't happening."

"Pick on somebody else… by the way, you've got lipstick on your teeth."

"You can't see me."

"Don't have to."

Chase knew Fran would check her reflection in the window of her office, see he was right and rub the crimson smear off her incisors.

"That's better," he said.

"Yeah, yeah. We got a kid needs a liver by morning. So get a move on."

"What about Ali?"

"He's on a run."

"Heysoos?"

"On a run."

"Vash?"

"AWOL."

Chase sighed. "Okay… I'm on it."

"I knew I could count on you."

Chase grumbled some more, then lit a candle and rummaged in the closet till he found some spare tights and a dry wife-beater. He put the soggy vest and chaps on top of these and with his Aero-Dynes over his shoulder, clambered down the fire escape to the alley. He waited till he reached the street before strapping on his blades, not that the pothole-pocked streets were much more navigable than the brick-paved passageway.

Though this mission was high-priority – most were – the visibility called for caution, not speed. The streetlights were broken and the sliver of a moon had disappeared behind a thicket of clouds. Except for an occasional candle in an upstairs window, the tenements were dark and the narrow streets deserted.

This was home turf. *I can shred this sucker with a bucket over my head,* he told himself as he tucked his dirty blond ponytail under his helmet, then pulled down the visor and switched on the headlamp. All around him the eyes of rats glimmered in its beam. Looked to be armies of them.

All the more reason to get the fuck out of here, he decided, forcing his weary legs into motion. The fatigue

would wear off, he knew, when he fell into the rhythm of his stride, arms and legs moving in perfect tandem. With the street to himself at this hour, he picked up his pace and focused on avoiding potholes, broken pavement and loose gravel.

Maybe it was instinct or maybe a slight movement caught his eye. Chase couldn't be sure, but for whatever reason, he looked up and saw a stray billy goat, a 170-pounder grazing in the gutter dead ahead. Fuck. He was closing too fast. He yelled. The goat looked up and non-chalantly went right back to enjoying the litter.

Chase veered sharply to the left, but the turn was too tight. His right skate skidded from under him and he pitched forward, flailing his arms in an unsuccessful attempt to regain his balance. Instead he fell forward into the gutter, all but a whisker's-length from the goat. The animal continued to nosh.

Chase got up slowly, all the while cursing himself for hot-dogging on the job and the goat for escaping its pen.

"Hey, I nearly busted my ass," Chase shouted.

"Meh-heh-heh-heh," the goat bleated.

"This is no joke. I could have been killed. You could have been killed."

"Heh-heh." The goat went back to the gutter.

"Fuck you, too."

Chase reached for the tag on the animal's collar. He wanted a word with the owner. The goat lowered its head and grunted a warning. The son of a bitch was going to ram

him. This one, a black-and white Nubian, most likely strayed from Old Man Mud Flap's pasture. He'd have a serious talk with the goatherd tomorrow.

"Don't think this is over, pal," Chase said, turning his blades toward a bustling stretch of brothels, bars and casinos known as Lowtide. Folks went there on a Saturday night so they'd have something to pray about on Sunday morning. Some folks anyway. He didn't believe in much, aside from himself and his friends.

The neighborhood's distinctive odor of bug spray, boozer's breath and smoldering charcoal told him he was only blocks away from the district's working streetlights and even pavement. The merchants paid for the upkeep themselves. Sin sold and Lowtide was always rocking sin.

That's where I ought to be, thought Chase, as he slid by Potholes, a grinders' bar known for harsh music and lukewarm beer. Later, he promised himself, as he soldiered through the crowds waiting to get into the pub. Revelers bought fried fish and pickled eel from women carrying baskets on their heads. His stomach rumbled as he was reminded how hungry he was.

Club bouncers stood in the doorways with their arms folded over their bulky chests while pickpockets lifted the wallets and watches of the unwary. Jugglers, beggars and Jack smugglers likewise attempted to part people from their money, though they did offer something, however worthless, in exchange.

Jack was some sick drug. No way he'd ever try the

stuff, Chase vowed as he approached a knot of tourists who had stopped to stare at Lowtide's prostitutes. Male and female, they preened under the streetlights for block after block. Always a terrific show. Do not get distracted, he warned himself.

He prided himself on keeping his eyes on the road, but he wasn't entirely immune to the charms of hot, half-naked women. He did try to focus. Only the ladies disliked being ignored and called out seductive invitations as he passed. The flesh was weak and the will was out-voted when Chase glimpsed a luscious chica in a baby doll skirt blow him a kiss.

He not only turned his head and returned the gesture, but continued to ogle her in his helmet's rearview mirror. As she bent over to pick up… uh, something… Her ass was bare. A full moon. "There is a God," he moaned.

He was still gaping when one of the pros shouted a warning. "In front of you! Look out!"

He whipped around and spotted a swank up-towner helping his lady friend into a cab. Chase was moments from colliding with the guy, who locked eyes with him and stood his ground.

"Watch it, punk!" he yelled.

Chase swerved to miss him, but hit a puddle and splashed the up-towner with urban stew. "Sorry, man," Chase apologized as he blew past.

Chase chastised himself for ogling chicks on the job, which was a slap on the wrist compared with the other

dude's spit-flying rant: "Come back here and I'll kick your skinny ass. I'm reporting you. You won't get away with this."

Chase caught some of the screed, but was soon too far away to hear the rest. It sounded pretty much like "You motherfucker… don't own the fucking road… dick wad?"

What could he do? He flipped him off, as required by the grinder's code.

"Do you know who I am? Do you?" The man continued to yell.

"I don't think he does," the woman said.

Chase's lungs felt as if they were bursting as he scaled Old Washington Street, the steep, gingko-lined avenue that led to the Hughes Renewal Center. The exclusive medical compound was built on the former site of the Revolutionary War-era Ft. Washington. At 265.05 feet above sea level, the site was the highest point on Northattan Island. Like the Palisades across the Hudson, the bluff provided a safe haven during the Inundations.

The center's main facility, several stories of which were underground, was imposing, but not so grand as Hughes' earlier, downtown projects. Constructed of schist quarried from the bluff itself, the ten floors rising above ground seemed to be rooted into the earth. The architecture wasn't soaring, it was sturdy. The place had been built to withstand hurricanes and had survived Adolf.

To Chase, it looked kind of like a giant wart, but he

was mighty pleased to see the brownish-red building come into view. It meant the rest of the trip would be downhill. He was even more relieved to see that the fundamentalist Right-to-Death protestors had gone home for the night. He hated fighting his way through the confrontational crowds of zealots. Fucking fundies. He didn't have a cat in this fight, but he'd been cursed at, spit on and whacked in the head with one of their handmade placards: "Heaven Can't Wait," "Death Is Life," and "Dump the Dupes."

For the record, Chase was pretty sure he'd never ever met a dupe. He had no way of telling even if he had. It wasn't like they were tattooed or anything. Furthermore, he had given little thought to whether or not dupes did or didn't have a soul. They were rich people. He didn't give a shit whether they went to hell or not. What pissed him off was that security precautions had been beefed up as a result of the protests.

The complex had been well-fortified before the fundies grew restive. An electric fence, which was camouflaged by a wall of thorny evergreen shrubbery, ran around the perimeter. Rumor had it that behind this hedge was a moat teeming with alligators. Now Hughes had added brighter lights, more barriers, stocked the armory with bigger guns and carved out tunnels for use by off-Center personnel.

Chase hated the tunnels. They were narrow, dark and dank inside, like intestines. And if penetrated by an unauthorized individual, they could be sealed and pumped

full of gas in an instant. It was only natural there would be an asshole at the other end.

Officer Drat was always on sentry duty when Chase had a run. Drat was a rigid rule follower, a nonentity when he wasn't in his little booth sporting his badge and his uniform. He was a stickler for stupidity and seemingly the more dire a grinder's mission, the more bureaucratic the bastard became.

Chase tried to look like he had all the time in the world, but Drat wasn't buying it. After scanning the grinder for weapons, he patted him down and did a retinal scan. After all that, Drat demanded to see his ID.

"Come on, man," Chase said, "You know I got a life-and-death mission."

"Do I look like I give a fuck?"

Chase had to admit that he didn't and handed over his ID.

"Where'd you say you were going?" Drat asked.

"You know damn well where I'm going," Chase answered, as only one establishment sat beyond the barrier.

"I got no patience for smart asses," Drat said, placing his hand on the holster of his service revolver.

Chase didn't think the guard would shoot him, but he didn't want to test that theory. "Capaldini and Gross," he said with as much courtesy as he could muster.

# CHAPTER 5.

LEON GROSS AND Irv Capaldini supervised the Department of Reclamation located in the crypt-like space beneath the Hughes Renewal Center. Giant refrigerators and empty black body bags lined the walls and battered Styrofoam coolers were neatly stacked in the entryway.

Jars of eyeballs, trays of teeth and a thermos of chicory sat on Capaldini's antique mahogany desk. His partner's smart rat, Mr. Pebbles, stuck his head from a drawer and seeing all was well, scurried across the wooden surface. Capaldini slipped it a crust from his pigeon salad sandwich.

If there were any good guys in the renewal industry, then Capaldini and Gross were good guys. And they made a

splendid team: Capaldini was a people person and Gross was a dead people person. Your typical, lovable odd couple.

When Chase arrived, he found the affable Capaldini, a squat cigar between his fingers, on the holo-phone pitching a repeat customer. The man's ghostly image emanated from the HP, its screen coated with greasy fingerprints and dust from the bone saw.

Capaldini nodded at Chase, gestured that he'd be right with him.

"Yeah, sure you will," mumbled Chase over Capaldini's inquiries into the health of the customer's family.

"Born with twelve toes. You don't say," Capaldini bellowed.

Dr. Gross, eyes looming behind thick glasses, labored over a middle-aged woman's corpse. From Chase's vantage point, she appeared to be perfectly made-up. Weird, but he'd seen it before. Rich bitches didn't go anywhere without their faces on – not even inside a black bag.

Chase once made a crack about their vanity to Gross, who chided the grinder for his "stab at humor." Capaldini confided that Gross was under the impression the ladies were dolling up for him. As a bachelor, he had never learned that women wore make-up to please themselves. Chase nodded knowingly.

As was his habit, Gross wore a heavy black rubber apron over a tatty, acid-spotted mink coat. The fur had belonged to his late mother and in this way, he kept her memory alive.

"I could have arranged her renewal," he once told Chase, "Only Ma never wanted one. 'Eighty years was enough already,' she'd tell us kids. 'If I had a chance to do it all over again, which I do, I wouldn't either. Wait till you're sixty-five, bucko. You'll see.'"

Gross took out a scalpel and cut into the body. Chase watched the steam rise from the still warm cadaver as the doctor, now engrossed, began to harvest vital organs from her midriff. Gross was happy in his work. When he was cutting corpses, it was like he was the one who had died and gone to heaven.

Not the perfect metaphor, Chase knew, because the body donors weren't exactly dead and according to the fundies, they hadn't gone to heaven. He or she had merely moved from one body to the next – a practice that drove the shrill, seemingly eternal debate on the ethics of neural transfer and body replication. A bunch of hooey about playing God.

Chase cleared his throat, then cleared it again, louder this time. Gross continued to poke about inside the cadaver. Chase was about to give Capaldini a piece of his mind when Gross shouted, "Eureka," and proudly held up his grisly find.

"Got a damn, fine pancreas here," he crowed. "Irv, take a look-see."

"That's a beaut all right, Leon," Capaldini said, taking a quick gander.

"Need a pancreas, Burt?" Capaldini asked the blurry image on the HP.

"Nah, man. You know we're overstocked. Not much call for 'em."

"Well, we got a beaut. A quality piece. I'll make you a good price."

"Pass. If you come across a decent spleen though-"

"You will be the first to know."

Chase cleared his throat.

"My best to the wife."

Capaldini finally clicked off and turned his attention to Chase. "Sorry. Old customer. So howzitgoin', chief?"

"If you really want to know," Chase snapped. "I'm pissed off and I'm staying pissed off. I'm late and you're making me later. You may not give a crap-"

"Sure I do. Of course, I do."

"Bullshit, you do."

Capaldini turned to his partner. "Leon, stop playing with that pancreas and get the boy his liver. We don't want to keep our young friend waiting."

Gross reluctantly returned the pancreas to the body, took a baggie from the fridge and checked the contents. "Slightly damaged," he apologized to Chase for the sclerotic organ.

"That's nothing new. Right, pal?" Capaldini took the baggie and placed it in a Styrofoam backpack he filled with ice.

"Are you sure there's enough ice?" Chase asked. "Last time I had to buy another bag at the 24-7. I can't afford-"

"Not to worry, son," Gross assured him. "I used to pack giblets in a chicken-plucking factory. It's how I paid my way through medical school."

"That would be reassuring, Mr. G, if this liver had originally belonged to a chicken," said Chase, hoisting the cooler on his back while Capaldini readjusted the harness. Gross opened the door. Chase put on his helmet and headed for the tunnel.

"Godspeed," chorused the partners.

# CHAPTER 6.

CHASE EMERGED FROM the tunnel and hung a right onto the back end of Old Washington Street, which quickly became a precipitous, one-lane slalom ride that ran directly into the old elevated freeway below. Grinders called it the Graveyard Express. Whatever. He had to skate the sucker to reach the hospital in time.

He stopped for a minute, studied the course, then pushed off. All he had to do was stay upright, he told himself as he headed downhill, his skates clattering as he negotiated the steeps and curves of the road. His thighs were already on fire before he dropped lower into his tuck to gain speed. He needed all the momentum he could

muster when he challenged the uphill ramp onto the elevated freeway.

The Old El couldn't support cars or trucks, which were rare enough on city streets. Those who traveled the roadway employed lighter modes of transportation: horses, mules, scooters, bikes, golf carts, goat carts, shopping carts, riding mowers and of course, blades.

Two of the road's six lanes had collapsed and the stanchions upon which it had been built were pitted with rust and the pilings sunk into the river below were under attack by concrete-eating, marine termites. Sumac, black-berry bushes and poison ivy obscured the safety railings and would have covered the remaining lanes if it weren't for wild goats and hungry deer.

Seabirds squawked below. Chase imagined them hovering over the men and women fishing from the stanchions. The gulls could do their own fishing, yes, but they were content to bitch and wrangle over fish guts, bits of bait or crumbs from the fishermen's breakfasts.

Chase thanked the powers that be, for sparing him the seagulls. They crapped more than pigeons and the last thing he needed was a roadway slippery with bird shit. Not that he'd have a choice in any case. Whatever its shortcomings, the El was the fastest route to Mercy Municipal Hospital – better known by doctors and patients as Lawd Hav' Mercy.

The sun was inching above the horizon, the temper-ature was rising and Chase could feel melted ice water trickling down his back. Fuck. The liver would be boiled

before he reached the exit ramp if he didn't fire his retro burners. Chase hesitated. The fuel was costly and the company docked your pay if you couldn't prove a burn was justified.

Deciding to chance it, the grinder pushed his heel against a disc inside his left skate and immediately shot forward. He fought to control his skates, their wheels clattering violently as he rocketed over the rough roadway. The exit ramp came up so fast, he had to swerve hard to the right to hit it. Centrifugal force was all that kept him from flying off the ramp and into the streets below.

As Mercy came into view, Chase glimpsed a gang of off-duty grinders sitting on the stairs outside the hospital's emergency entrance. Some of them were probably betting on whether or not he was going to land pretty or scrape off his face. Not his friend Heysoos, who cheered him on from atop the wide balustrade, as Chase sped past and screeched to a stop at the ER doors.

Heysoos ran down the stairs to congratulate his buddy amid the cheers of their fist-pumping peers. Chase, spattered with grease, mud and dead bugs, chest-butted Heysoos and began making his bows to the others. His antics were cut short when Big Beulah, Mercy's Valkyrie of an admitting nurse, grabbed Chase by the shoulder.

"Ouch, what the hell," Chase yelled.

"Ain't got no time for your foolishness," Beulah said, pointing him toward the entrance.

"Messenger's here. Clear the way," she boomed at the gawkers gathered in the doorway. She nodded at Chase. "OR 314. Haul your ass, little brother."

"Yes, ma'am." Chase saluted her and set off down a dim, narrow corridor, dodging orderlies pushing gurneys and disoriented patients trailing IVs as he raced toward the operating room. He knew he was late, but damn. By the time he arrived, the five-year-old patient was anesthetized and the surgeons were in the process of removing the child's diseased liver. Gasping for breath, Chase, shrugged out of the straps of the Styrofoam container on his back.

"Where the hell have you been?" demanded one surgeon as he opened the box, peered in, and scowled at the poor condition of the liver.

"Good Christ, is this the best you can do?"

"I don't make 'em, Doc. I just schlep 'em," Chase fired back and stalked off down the corridor.

"Prick could have at least said, 'Thank you,'" Chase complained as he made his way back to admitting. The big nurse took in his downcast look.

"Don't let 'em get you down, brother. They're too angry to be grateful," said Beulah, nearly knocking him over with a hearty slap on the back.

Chase managed a grudging smile.

"Lawd have mercy on youse," she called after him.

"And youse," mumbled Chase.

# CHAPTER 7.

GABRIEL MUNRO, HEAD of Hughes security operation, placed his team on high alert and planted spies all along the route of the Day of the Dead Parade. Sure, it was billed as a peaceful event, but this year the Right Reverend Dr. Orville Hast III was the grand marshal and when it came to Hast and his cockamamie cult - the Evangelicals for Natural Death (END) - Gabe didn't take chances.

Sure they looked peaceful now. Only like he'd told the boss, they are some nutty, motherfucking shit bags and Hast gets his cashews off riling them the fuck up. But if Hast was planning to do anything other than throw candy to the kiddies, Gabe was more than ready to stop him. Hell, he had been a top operative with the National Peace Patrol.

And he didn't go anywhere – not even to bed – without his piece, now comfortably tucked into his belt.

The security chief focused his binoculars on the Reverend as the parade turned the corner and headed up the boulevard toward the center. The short, barrel-chested cleric was sausaged into a dark cloak and his round face, painted white, was shadowed by his hood. He shook a bloody scythe from his perch atop a horse-drawn wagon while disciples attired as skeletons ran alongside tossing licorice and death's head marzipan to screaming onlookers.

Hast was meant to represent the Grim Reaper – an annual honor bestowed by the Holy Council of Churches, Temples and Mosques upon the cleric whose congregation increased the most the previous year. The fucker looked more like one of Santa's elves in mourning, solemnly waving to the crowd as the four horses trudged up the hill.

Children darted from the curb into the animals' path, scattering marigolds, daisies and yellow mums. Now and again, one of the animals would lift its tail in answer to nature's call. Piles of steaming road apples marked their passing. Pilgrims, in Jesus sandals, walked behind, purposefully trampling the flowers and the horse manure into a gooey mash.

"Do you believe that?" Gabe asked one of the men of his squad.

"Sir?"

"They go out of their way to step in the stuff."

"The shit, sir?"

Gabe nodded. "They're called holy shits. The shoes and the assholes wearing them, too. Like it's some big honor."

Gabe wrinkled his nose though he was too far away to smell the pungent potpourri and turned his sights on the bone-rattlin' men, who marched past followed by the cacophonious Jews with Kazoos. The Mimes for Jesus passed in silence, pretending to walk on water and then to turn water into wine.

Pretty girls and animal mascots threw more candy and flowers from floats sponsored by communion supply companies, the Union of Ministers, Deacons and Choir Masters as well as some of the larger congregations. Buddhists, Wicca, Vegi-Baptists, Eskafarians, Ladder-Day Mortons, and Catholites – all God's children joined the joyous throngs.

So far the only crime Gabe observed – aside from the idolatry of an asshole – was trespassing. Hast's flock milled in the road and picnicked on the grassy hem of the Hughes Center. They had been waiting at the crest of the hill since sunrise with their blankets and baskets, singing hymns and entertaining the kids with games of "Matthew, Mark, Luke or John?"

Still when Hast came into view and the crowd hurried to greet him, Gabe ordered his Para-military team to take up arms and to be obvious about their intent to use them. The effect was not what he had expected. Instead of intimidating Hast, the show of force seemed to delight him.

Gabe swore. He had played into the Reverend's hand. He had taken him seriously.

Morgan Hughes looked down on the spectacle from his penthouse office. The crowd had surrounded Hast's wagon and the Reverend was gesticulating wildly. Morgan trusted Gabe to keep them under control.

Margaret, still wearing green surgical scrubs and booties, slipped into the room and joined her father at the window.

"END again?" she asked.

"His holiness is leading the parade today. Happy Day of the Dead by the way."

"Did you get me anything?"

Morgan rolled his eyes.

"Looks peaceful enough," said Margaret, putting an arm around her father's shoulder.

"You never know with that lunatic."

She nodded her assent.

"Want a drink? I'm having one." Hughes took two cut crystal tumblers and a decanter of scotch from the walnut liquor cabinet. He poured each of them a double.

"Here," he said, handing her the glass before he sank into the cushy leather sofa alongside his daughter.

"You smell like Lysol."

"My signature fragrance," Margaret said, propping her legs on the glistening, glass coffee table.

Morgan reached over and patted her knee. "So how about you, honey? Did you have a good day?"

She took a gulp of her scotch.

"Not exactly. I had a consult with your pal, Stepper. Major ass plug."

"I wish you wouldn't talk like that, Maggie."

"Dad, I'm a big girl. I think I can talk anyway I want."

Morgan grinned, waited for her to continue.

"So Stepper goes ballistic over Zoë's vessel."

Morgan frowned. "Was there a problem?"

"It was fine, gorgeous."

"But–"

"Her girls were too small. Size doesn't seem to matter when it comes to her brain, but her tits…"

"What's so wrong with that?"

"You better be kidding."

"I'm just saying…"

"They were exactly as specified."

Margaret got up and returned to look out the window. The Reverend seemed to be pointing his scythe toward her, an action cheered and applauded by the crowd.

"I think he's putting a curse on us – 'a pox on your house and upon your children,'" she joked before turning her attention back to the Reverend. He now had a bullhorn, had hopped down from his perch and was prancing about the wagon as if he were a 20th century rock star.

Margaret and Morgan couldn't hear his exhortations, but they could hear the cheers, ululations and shouts of

"amen" from the increasingly energized crowd. The more he preached, the more he waved his arms, the more excitable the congregants became. One minute they were shaking their fists; the next they were throwing bottles over the hedge.

Gabe's men dispersed the crowd with a fusillade of tear gas cartridges. The more belligerent stragglers were chased down, thrown into paddy wagons and driven to the city jail. The Reverend knelt and clasped his hands in prayer, occasionally looking up either at heaven or the Hughes.

# CHAPTER 8.

WHEN THE MAN who would become Mud Flap regained consciousness, he was sitting in a Mister Softee van atop a pyramid of road-going wreckage: Cars, trucks, buses, motorcycles, RVs and wiener wagons piled high. He didn't know why he was there or who he was, but he realized he had better get the hell out of the teetering ice cream van. With cat-like caution he eased himself from the vehicle and crept to the edge of the heap.

He looked around in all directions, but recognized no landmarks, be they geographic or architectural. He saw nothing but corpses – animal and human – caught in the branches of splintered trees or stranded on rooftops. Signs and sounds of life eluded him. The stench of death was all

around him. Nothing moved except the rising water. So lonely.

The rain began again, so he hunkered under a black, vinyl convertible top, where he fell asleep. Days went by. He hoped to die here, but the sun returned and it got so hot under the vinyl that he was forced to crawl out. Weak from dehydration, he lapped warm water from puddles in the rubble. He saw mirages in broken windshields and dreamed of pitchers filled with iced tea.

He was heartened when from the bottom of his roost, someone yelled, "Anybody up there?" He looked over the edge and beheld a little girl and her exhausted mother staring up from a rowboat. He waved. "Are you all right?" called the mother, beckoning him to come down and join them.

He nodded. Then he realized he hadn't a thing to wear. His shirt was filthy and his pants were soiled. These he removed and threw aside. He did keep the belt in hopes of completing the outfit with a garbage bag.

"What's taking so long?" called the mother after he failed to return in a few minutes.

"Need time to clean up," he hollered as he hurriedly searched through the rubble for something to wear. The convertible top was too large and no garbage bags had turned up. He stopped digging when he uncovered a pair of mud flaps.

"These will do nicely," he exclaimed and began to

fashion a loincloth by belting one flap over his privates and the other over his butt cheeks.

When the woman and her daughter saw him, they laughed for the first time since Adolf. Because the man had forgotten his name, they decided to call him Mud Flap or sometimes simply Flaps.

Mud Flap and the two women had been among the thousands who survived the twenty-three-foot tidal wave that swamped the city. Most eventually starved, committed suicide or were murdered for food, clean water, drugs, batteries or guns. Disease took the rest. When his rescuers died of malaria the following month, Mud Flap prayed to join them to no avail.

Seven decades later, he was a little bent and wore his gray hair in a tidy braid that ended at his waist. He was also a little deaf, but was too proud to acknowledge this infirmity. Now known as Old Man Mud Flap, he kept a produce stand on Water Street. Every morning he and his goat, Houdini, brought a cart laden with yogurt and cheese, fresh berries, herbs and edible weeds. These were displayed in baskets he had woven from wild grape vine and wisteria which flourished during the long summers.

The vendor was extolling the curative powers of dandelion wine and sassafras tea – "Available by special order only." – and the first customers were filling their baskets when Chase, sleepy and disheveled, arrived to speak with Mud Flap on behalf of himself and all the other grinders who had problems with his goat.

"Git yer 'shrooms 'n weeds and teas for yer knees," Mud Flap sang.

Chase didn't wait for the spiel to end. He walked up behind him and tapped him on the shoulder. "Hey, Mud Flap. I got a beef–"

"Sorry, no cows around these parts. Only goats."

Chase leaned nearer Mud Flap's ear. "It's about your goat."

"I thought you were interested in beef."

Mud Flap turned and frowned at a customer who was fondling the pokeweed leaves. "Those bruise easily, Madame."

When he returned to Chase, the grinder hurriedly described his run-in with Houdini the night before.

"I could have been killed," Chase said. "All of a sudden, I'm on a collision course with your goat. I'm carving so hard I nearly take a header."

Houdini butted Mud Flap's thigh, batted his bedroom-eyes and bleated. Mud Flap listened intently.

"He says 'No problem, no harm, no foul,'" Mud Flap translated.

"I'm forgiven. Oh, wow. That makes everything all better."

Mud Flap shook his hand. "Here, have some mustard greens, on the house. They're good for the penis."

"My penis is fine."

"These will keep it from falling off. The Indians swore

by it. Course, they're all dead. At least I believe that to be the case."

"Oh, for Christ's sake." Chase took the greens, shoved them under his shirt and skated away.

He has grown into a fine young man considering, thought Mud Flap as he recalled the evening he found the triplets abandoned in a doorway.

On the occasions he had more food than he could sell, he carted the extra goat cheese, milk or greens to the Cabrini Orphanage. He and Ulysses, a forebear of Houdini, were bound for Cabrini that night.

"Must have been at least fifteen, maybe twenty years ago," Mud Flap mused. "Only one of them was alive and that was just barely."

Houdini bleated mournfully.

"Don't care how many times you've heard the story," Mud Flap retorted. Houdini snorted and butted Mud Flap's flank. The old man ignored him, continuing to place empty baskets into the cart for the trip back to his small farm.

"They were so tiny. Couldn't have been more than a week or even a few days old. Pitiful sight," said Mud Flap, who had buried the tiny corpses under a lilac in a nearby yard.

He briefly considered keeping the surviving child. Instead he left him in the care of the Dominican sisters at Cabrini. "I used to visit the kids, bring 'em toys. That one, I gave a Teddy bear."

Mud Flap wiped a tear from his cheek, then picked up

another basket, removed a bunch of wilted onions and offered them to the goat.

"Heh-heh-heh," Houdini bleated.

"You're welcome," Mud Flap said.

# CHAPTER 9.

CAPALDINI AND GROSS were behind schedule when Chase arrived to pick up a lung. Before Chase had a chance to consider the organ's condition, Capaldini hugged Chase to his bosom and clapped his back with a meaty paw. When Capaldini let go, Chase gulped for air.

"As always, it's a pleasure to see you, my beamish boy. Have a seat won't you?" Capaldini plopped down behind his desk.

"Thanks, but I'll take my lung and be on my way," said Chase, who could see Gross poking about among the body bags.

"He'll only be a minute," Capaldini assured Chase. "That's right isn't it, Leon?"

Gross mumbled something and continued his search.

"Right," Chase said.

"I swear on my mother's grave," Capaldini said.

"Your mother isn't dead," Chase said.

"It was a figurative oath."

Chase walked toward the door. "I'll wait in the garden. The exotic one with the snakes."

Chase lounged on the edge of a man-made pond. Tiny, bright blue frogs hid beneath the foliage, salamanders slithered in the mulch and a bumblebee flew dangerously close to the mouth of a Venus Flytrap. Luckily for the bee, Venus was savoring a horse fly. Poor thing had flown into the garden, having mistaken the fertilizer for a delectable pile of shit.

Chase tapped a cigarette from a pack of cigarettes imprinted with a skull and crossbones. He lit up, inhaled appreciatively and blew a chain of smoke rings skyward. Though he was hardly a poseur, he naturally projected a hunky nonchalance that drew the chicks like a warm body draws mosquitoes. Even his thrice broken nose didn't turn off the ladies. It matched his crooked smile.

The bee alighted on a water lily, changed its mind and took an interest in Chase, who was waving the determined critter away when the side door opened and Margaret sauntered into the garden. Her hair spilled from a disheveled ponytail and like many of the nurses he knew, she was

wearing clogs. She was a drop dead gorgeous mess. Chase couldn't stop staring.

She must have been used to this kind of reaction because she smiled as she walked toward the pond. "Hey," she said.

"Hey," he said. "Nice day."

"Unhuh," she said, opening a small container.

He continued to stare.

"It's sashimi for the flytrap – a nice piece of fresh eel," Margaret said, offering the tidbit to Venus.

"She's not hungry," Chase said. "She just scarfed major horsefly."

"Usually her tastes are more sophisticated," observed Margaret, who sat down beside Chase and popped the sashimi into her mouth.

"You like it raw? Fish, I mean," he asked.

"Sometimes."

Chase felt his face flush.

Margaret laughed.

Chase didn't know what to say, so he pulled his near-empty pack of cigarettes from his pocket and offered her one.

"That stuff will kill you," she said.

"Yeah, lots of things will, including beautiful women. So how about it, are you a risk-taker?" *Now that was a smooth transition.*

Margaret smiled bewitchingly, took the cigarette,

looked into his eyes and allowed him to light the smoke for her. She took a long, ecstatic drag.

"Thanks. You're my hero."

"What if I gave you the whole pack? Would that–"

"That would be very generous of you."

Margaret took another drag, seemed ready to stay awhile, but jumped up and stubbed out the rest of her cigarette.

"Hey, those don't come cheap," Chase protested.

"I know. I'm sorry. I just remembered I'm late… so late," Margaret said, heading back inside.

"Hey, wait up," he pleaded.

Margaret turned around and winked, then placed her palm on the Instantaneous Biological Identification Device (IBID) to access the corridor beyond the solid steel door.

"You got a name? Phone number? Anything?" he yelled as the door closed behind her. "Damn."

Chase rescued the butt, put it back in the pack, and considered taking the sensible course of action of returning to Capaldini and Gross.' Instead he walked toward the garden door. "What the hell," he muttered, placing his palm on the security device.

Although his prints were on record, he didn't know whether he had access to departments other than Reclamation. Surprise. The door opened and he found himself in a corridor as white and gleaming as a near-death hallucination. A security camera pivoted in his direction. Chase mugged and waved into the lens, but instantly

regretted his actions. In hopes nobody noticed his antics, he tried a subtler approach, pretending that he knew exactly where he was going and that he had something awfully important to do. Perhaps the watchdogs in the control room would think he belonged here.

They were not fooled. One of them, balding and shaped like a loaf of bread, stood up and looked hard at a bank of monitors. He said something to his partner, put the lid on his koffey cup and headed for the exit. "I'll be back," said Officer DeRosa to his partner.


Chase tried even harder to look like an old hand when he saw the guard coming toward him. "What can I do for you…" He squinted at the nametag. "…Officer DeRosa?"

DeRosa ordered Chase to stand against the wall with his arms outstretched and frisked him with a metal detector, waving the wand under his pits, up and down each leg and over Chase's behind.

"What, do I walk like I have a bomb up my butt? You think I'd blow up something this pretty?"

"I'm not gonna give you the satisfaction of answering. Now take off the skates."

"Can't do that, man."

DeRosa whacked the wand against his palm and stared Chase down.

"Awright already," Chase said, "but I need someplace to sit down."

"Floor good enough for you?"

Chase plopped down on the cold concrete and began to take off his skates.

"Aero 220s… retro-blaster… very nice." DeRosa said. "You're a grinder. I should have known. Didn't know they allowed your kind outside Reclamation. Got any ID, champ?"

Chase produced his grinder's license along with his center pass. The guard scrutinized the ID papers, sniffed them even and handed them back.

"I used to grind when I was your age. Gave it up when I got shot."

Chase nodded sympathetically.

"How'd you get in here anyway?" DeRosa asked.

"I followed this gorgeous nurse – red hair, curves, legs out to… know her?"

"I know if she works here, she's out of your league," DeRosa said.

"I'm pretty sure she wants me."

DeRosa handed Chase his skates. "Put 'em on and get the hell out of here. Don't make me arrest you."

"Yes, sir. Whatever you say," Chase said.

"I'll even show you to the door."

"Can you at least tell me her name?"

"Go before I change my mind!"

# CHAPTER 10.

MARGARET WAS OLD-FASHIONED, preferring to check out the pre-transfers for herself. In this case, it meant dealing with nurse Nanny Broom. Nanny replenished the candy jars, was generous with her compliments and when colleagues had problems, was always a ready ear. She put holiday decorations on the bulletin boards, wore Christmas sweaters until February and spread good cheer like a hyper-mutating virus.

It was silly, Margaret knew, but she didn't trust overtly nice people, especially if like Nanny, they were elderly, slightly stooped and their knees creaked. By all rights, Nanny ought to be cranky at least some of the time.

Ultimately it didn't matter what Margaret thought.

Nanny was great at a job that most of her colleagues either feared or reviled: She babysat the vessels, hundreds of which awaited their respective fates in vast "hives" of oblong, holding tanks. A monitor on each displayed its inhabitant, floating naked and comatose in its "chrysalis," which was filled with a warm, gently moving liquid the consistency of amniotic fluid.

The vessels' vital signs were monitored religiously: EEGs, EKGs, MRIs, urinalyses, blood tests were run repeatedly. The results were fed into the central computer. If one so much as burped, the emergency response team would be notified and a taskforce deployed.

Each chrysalis expanded to accommodate its vessel as it grew from fetus to young adulthood. Every vessel was tethered to the lining by an "umbilicord," a fleshy tube through which pasty brown nutrients were inserted and pasty brown waste was excreted. Every fourth week, a depilatory was administered causing the vessel to slough off body hair.

Sur-techs – always specially abled individuals – were responsible for filling and emptying the tubes as well as cleaning the filters that collected skin shed by the vessels. Margaret and her godfather Wu had tried to come up with a more appealing solution, but all these years later, this was still as good as it got.

"Note to self: Clone Nanny," Margaret muttered as she entered the airlock of C-Bank, where an automated voice reminded her to exchange her shoes for a pair of heavy

white socks. When the lock opened on the other side, she could hear only the gentle murmur of the life-sustaining machinery. Staff spoke in whispers although the vessels were on Diazedrenal drips and couldn't hear, see, smell or feel anything.

Margaret walked past several rows before she found Nanny, who was overseeing the transfer of an eight-month old fetus from a synthetic womb into its chrysalis. "Careful not to splash," Nanny whispered to the neo-natal nurse.

After the fetus was safely stowed and the tube sealed, Nanny turned to Margaret with a bright smile. "Isn't it the sweetest thing?" she said of the fetus sucking its thumb on the monitor.

"Yeah, sweet as pie," Margaret said.

"What can I do for you today, Dr. Hughes?" Nanny inquired softly.

"I buzzed earlier about taking a look at C-921?"

"Certainly, Doctor," said Nanny, who dutifully led the way to the chrysalis housing Zoë's vessel. Margaret peeped inside, saw the changes had been made, then swiped her diagnostic N3RD across the monitor and read the results. All systems were go.

"Looks ripe to me, Nanny. What do you think?"

Nanny peered inside the chrysalis. "I think she looks like Sleeping Beauty. Is there a prince?"

"No, a lawyer."

# CHAPTER 11.

MARGARET, IN SCRUBS and booties, exited the airlock into the OR where it was so quiet you could have heard the clock tick if it weren't digital. She silently greeted her handpicked neural-transfer team. Even though both vessel and candidate were dead to this world, the rule of silence was inviolable and they only communicated via American Sign Language.

Zoë, in a body stocking of transparent syn-skin, lay on an operating table alongside her similarly clad, younger, bustier doppelganger. Sensors within the stockings synchronized their pulses, heart rates and other vital signs. Fred Neiman, Margaret's nurse-technician, also diligently moni-

tored the flux of their hormones, amino acids and neurotransmitters.

It was rare, thank God, but sometimes as they downloaded a donor's lower functions into the vessel's limbic system, the biochemical levels seesawed wildly. A sudden, rapid rise in a biochemical like serotonin could be mind-blowing for both donor and vessel. If the fluctuations became too violent, it was Fred's job to break the circuit and wait till levels returned to normal before resuming the download.

Margaret peered over her mask at Fred. A young man when she hired him, he was almost eligible for retirement. She'd duplicate him, but then everybody who worked for the center would expect to live forever.

Fred looked up at Margaret and signed. "Ready and steady, two times over."

Padma, the team anesthetist, worked in tandem with Fred. Margaret sensed that Fred was developing a crush on the younger woman. *As long as it didn't distract him.* She turned to Padma for a go-ahead. Two thumbs up meant both Zoë and her vessel would be able to sleep through multiple orgasms.

Cyan, the surgical nurse, was fussing over the surgical instruments as well as ensuring that every team member had the necessary implements. Margaret liked having the sure-handed Cyan at her elbow, supplying her every need.

Josiah, the team's computer tech, was in Margaret's opinion a bit strange. But her dad wanted him on board and

Josiah had been put through all the psych tests so there was no reason to think he was unstable. What bothered Margaret was that he seemed unable to look anybody in the eye, except when they were sedated like the client and her vessel were at that moment.

As he bent toward Zoë's face, he came so close to her lips that for a moment, Margaret was afraid he was going to kiss her. She was about to grab the little perv by the ears when he stood up and began to fiddle with the frame that held Zoë's head in position. He had replaced the late Sergei Petrov, the acknowledged king of the brain drain. Margaret considered him even better than Petrov. Otherwise she'd have fired his weird ass by now.

Josiah had already done a nuclear scan of Zoë's brain and downloaded the resulting 4D images into the central computer. On Margaret's signal, he inserted a disc imprinted with Zoë's DNA into a projector, tapped a series of neuron codes into the computer and a holographic map of Zoë's brain materialized on the OR's transparent holoscreen.

Like nations on a globe, the structures were distinguishable by their hues of purple, pink, orange and green. Nerves ran like rivers through the intracranial landscape; flashes of phosphorescence jumped the gaps between the cells.

"Looks like she's got all her marbles," Margaret signed.

"Marbles?" Josiah asked.

"An old expression… way before your time."

Margaret pulled the holoscreen down for a closer look

at Zoë's temporal lobe. She maneuvered the screen until the exact image was reflected on Zoë's shiny scalp. Josiah automatically zoomed in on the hippocampus, the seahorse-shaped structure that determines which memories and the emotions they stir will be tucked in which neural file.

Her eyes distorted behind magnifying glasses, Margaret warily drilled a minuscule hole through Zoë's cranium into the limbic region, then inserted the first of a hundred seventy-two bionic antennae into Zoë's prefrontal cortex. When Margaret hit the sweet spot, she gently released the wire, retracted its catheter and moved onto the next location. In time, Zoë's bald pate bristled with wires.

Her vessel's skull, prepped before Zoë was wheeled in, was covered in what appeared to be an aluminum hairnet. Underneath the net, the head was studded with magnetic receptors. When the antennae were inserted into the receptors, Zoë's emotions, memories, some flotsam and jetsam – whatever it was that made Zoë, Zoë – would be routed to the vessel's brain.

While Margaret prepared to complete the connection, Josiah broadcast a map of the vessel's brain on a second screen. All the structures were intact, the autonomic systems were functioning perfectly, but there were no fireworks, only a faint glimmer or activity.

"I am reminded of Tinker Bell in her death throes," Margaret signed. "Clap if you believe in fairies."

The team exchanged quizzical glances.

Margaret's staff was accustomed to what they believed

were their boss's eccentricities. So they pretended not to notice when she seemed to be speaking in tongues. She figured her obscure references gave her mystery. It gave them something to bitch and gossip about over post-op drinks at the local watering hole.

"Are we ready?" Margaret signed, eyeballing her staff. Everybody gave a thumbs-up. "Okay, then. I'm plugging in." She removed the aluminum net. The antennae were sucked straight into the receptors with an audible harmonic swoosh. The vessel's hologram grew brighter and busier as the download progressed and Zoë's hologram began to fade.

"Josiah, what are your readings?" Margaret signed.

"A little fast, but acceptable."

Margaret nodded. "Fred, how are her orexin levels?"

Fred signed okay.

"Padma, bring her up a little."

Padma complied.

Margaret's eyes darted between the two holoscreens.

"A little more now."

The vessel's eyelids fluttered almost imperceptibly.

"Again," Margaret ordered.

The vessel's eyes popped open. Chalky white and shivering violently, she looked up at the bright overhead lights and began to cry and hiccup. Margaret nodded to Fred, who injected a sedative. The woman relaxed. He was grateful this one wasn't a screamer.

"Zoë?" Margaret spoke aloud for the first time since entering the OR.

"I had the strangest dream," she said to Margaret, who took her hand and squeezed it.

"I know. It's okay. There's nothing to worry about."

"My head…"

Like all transfers, Zoë was suffering from a severe migraine.

"Give her 100 ccs of neutralizer and a bucket of aspirin," Margaret said.

Two orderlies appeared at the door. One carried a folder filled with paperwork. "We've come for the… uh, donation."

Zoë looked over at her old self. It was still breathing. "What will happen to her?"

"Padma will give her a shot and she'll drift off like she was going to sleep. And later, many lives will be saved, all because of you."

Margaret motioned to one of the orderlies, who prepared to wheel Zoë to recovery. The other stayed behind to bag and cart the donation to the Department of Reclamation. He took his time.

It took longer than you'd think for them to stop breathing.

# CHAPTER 12.

THE NIGHT WAS old and the floor was sticky by the time Chase and his buddies Homes and Heysoos finished their shifts and arrived at Potholes for a couple of beers. They managed to squeeze through the jam of warm bodies, a maneuver roughly equivalent to returning to the womb, especially on the weekends.

Women pressed against the friends, planted sloppy kisses, groped their butt cheeks as the trio pushed past sweaty groupies dancing on the tops of the few tables that weren't occupied. Their hardcore moves drew brays and whistles from the appreciative crowd, as Chase, Heysoos and Homes pushed further into the smoke-filled room.

When they reached the bar, Spider, the skinny, albino

bartender, didn't give them a chance to order. "Welcome back to Potholes," he said, plunking a cool one down in front of each of them. Chase pressed the bottle against his forehead and then his cheeks.

Homes took a long, satisfying swallow. "Job sucks. But I do gotta admit there are perks."

"To what do we owe this unexpected, yet much deserved reward?" Chase asked the barman.

"It ain't on the house if that's what you're thinking," Spider said.

Chase looked around for his benefactor. "Who then?"

"The cha-cha at end of the bar."

"Lots a cha-chas at the end of the bar. Big damn bar. Which one?"

"Infra-redhead. Dangerous type. Hard to miss," added Spider.

Heysoos, who had already spotted her, whistled under his breath. "You fucking blind, amigo? Six o'clock, Uptown pony, spilling out."

Chase followed Heysoos's stare.

"Fuck me. It's her," Chase said.

"Her who?" asked Homes.

"The hottie from HRC."

She looked up and raised her glass to the three men. They returned the gesture, mouthed their thanks and continued to stare. She nodded, smiled and turned away.

"Don't wait up for me," Chase said as he turned and headed for the redhead.

"I don't know, man. She could be messin' with your brain," Homes warned.

"Only thing gonna get messed up, chico, are my sheets."

"You got sheets?"

Chase turned his back on his bros and made his way toward the girl. Damn, she was chatting with the guy next to her.

How in hell did she get into those jeans, he wondered as he came up behind her.

"Haven't we met somewhere before?" Chance flashed a wicked smile.

She turned toward him. "Are you always this fascinating?" she asked.

"So they tell me."

"For you." Spider placed a scotch in front of her. Homes and Heysoos, goofy smiles spreading across their faces, waved from the other end of the bar.

She pulled out her cigarette case, flipped it open, took out a smoke for herself and offered one to Chance.

"I owe you."

"Thanks," he said.

"My pleasure." She pulled out a matching lighter and fired up both cigarettes.

"You take my breath away," Chase said, moving closer.

"You smoke too much." She laughed, flung her hair over her shoulder, loosing a burnished cascade down her arms and back.

"Are we square now?" she asked.

"No, not really. Now I owe you a drink." He motioned to Spider.

"Thanks, but I've got an early call. I have to be in the OR at six a.m. sharp. Oh, and there's my ride now."

A bulky bruiser lumbered toward them.

"Sorry. I really do have to get going," she said.

Chase put a hand on her shoulder. "Not before you tell me how I can find you again?"

"I wouldn't do that," she said, as the big man slipped up behind Chase.

"What?"

"Touch me."

She looked over Chase's shoulder.

Bruno reached around Chase, grabbed both arms and wrenched them behind the grinder's back.

"You wanna keep those? Don't put 'em where they don't belong," he growled.

"What the fuck is your problem, ape man?"

The big man increased the pressure. Chase felt like his arms were about to pop out of their sockets.

"Bruno, stop it," Margaret yelled over the music. "Let him go. It's okay."

Bruno reluctantly released Chase.

"Just doing my job," said Bruno, clearly wounded by the exchange.

"I know. I know. You're always looking after me. And

I appreciate it. But I am all grown up and I can take care of myself."

Bruno rolled his eyes.

"Oh, the hell with it. Since you're here anyway, let's go home."

She turned to Chase and blew a kiss. "See you around."

"Wait. How about I walk you to the door and you tell me how I can find you again?"

Bruno gave Margaret a disapproving look as she took Chase's arm. Chase could smell Bruno's after shave and feel the bodyguard's breath on the back of his neck as they pushed their way outside.

Bruno opened the door of a limo, but to Chase's delight, the girl didn't get in. "Give me a minute," she said to Bruno before turning back to Chase.

"Want a ride?" she asked.

Chase shook his head and laughed. "No way my street would hold up under that dinosaur."

"Fact is she's light on her feet. She's been outfitted with a titanium chassis," Bruno protested.

"I guess it's goodnight," she said.

"Right after this," he said drawing her away from Bruno and into his arms for a kiss so electric he wondered if this was what it felt like to be struck by lightning. He was surprised to find that his skates hadn't blown off with the surge that swept through his body.

"God," he gasped.

"Yeah," she gasped. "Your place?"

"My place."

He looked over his shoulder warily at Bruno, who demonstrated how he would gladly slit Chase's throat.

"How about we walk?" Chase asked.

"How about we roll?" she suggested, bending down to release the wheels from her chic red booties.

"It's not an easy skate." Chase doubted she would remain upright in her girly blades for long.

"I'm no rookie, if that's what you're thinking," she said, launching into a expertly executed moon walk.

"A dance move? That's all you've got?"

She tilted her head, flashed him a wicked smile.

"Awright. Follow me," Chase said, reaching for Margaret's hand.

To his surprise, she ignored the gesture, pumped her arms and sped past.

"You're going the wrong way. Like I told you, follow me if you can." He raced toward a cluster of tenements, caught air, and waited, arms akimbo, for the girl to catch up. He held out his hand again and this time she took it, allowing him to guide her.

Chase stopped at the end of a cobbled alley, fished a rusty grappling iron from its hiding place in a patch of cricket weed growing beside the brick wall. With practiced ease, he hooked a rung of the fire escape and hauled the stairs down.

They didn't meet the ground, so Chase hoist himself up first, then reached down and drew her alongside him.

Jingle bells rang and strings of spoons rattled as they made their way up. Overhead, Chase's pigeons cooed from their coop. In the alley below, a man and a woman argued, then came a round of gunfire, then a scream.

"Ambience," Chase whispered.

"Is that what you call it?" said Margaret, wrinkling her nose as they climbed past the pigeons' pungent rookery to Chase's apartment one flight above. They entered through a low window, which had been shuttered and locked – not that Chase had anything worth stealing, unless the thief was in the market for a bag of dirty laundry.

"Sorry about the mess." He straightened the cover over the mattress.

She shrugged.

"Sit down," he said. "Get comfortable. I'll get us a beer."

The apartment – one large room with a galley kitchen and a bath – was furnished in vintage bachelor. Next to the mattress on the floor, there was a cardboard box that served as a bedside table. An old leather recliner was all but covered in duct-tape. Margaret dropped down on the bed, shucked her booties and looked around while he located a couple of brown long necks from the water remaining in his Styrofoam cooler. "I like what you've done with the place," she said.

Chase laughed and handed her a beer.

"Thanks," she said. "So what's wrong with using the front door?"

"I don't have one. I tore out the stairwell and bricked

over the doorway. Believe it or not, this neighborhood isn't safe."

She smiled at him, took another swallow of her beer and stretched out on the bed.

"Can I get you anything?" he asked idiotically.

She patted the bed beside her. "What've you got?"

"Why don't I show you?"

Chase put down his beer, leaned over her and began to unzip her sweater. She pulled him into her arms and kissed him so hard and so long he almost passed out. But he gave as good as he got and she too came up gasping for air.

"Is that all you've got?"

"Is that all *you've* got?"

Chase pulled his T-shirt over his head, unzipped Margaret's jeans and then slid out of his own. He wasn't sure who ripped what off whom or in what order after that, but they both ended up naked and that was a plus as far as he was concerned.

Sex with Margaret was like wrestling down a tornado. She sucked you into her vortex, rattled your bones bloody, then blew your ass into a world where you had never been before. Afterwards, Chase was too dizzy to sit up, definitely incapable of cuddling, not that this girl seemed the type to nuzzle and share her soul.

"Where's the john?" she asked.

He nodded toward a curtained doorway. He heard her splashing off in the basin of rusty water that served as a

sink and when she returned, happily watched her smooth back her hair and squirm into her jeans.

"You're not a nurse are you?" Chase asked.

"What am I not caring enough for you?"

"Nurses don't have limos, do they?"

"If I had to guess, I'd say, probably not."

Chase lifted himself on his elbow, "No, really. I'm serious."

"Okay if we're going to get serious, we really ought to know a little something about each other. Like names. Mine's Elle."

"Mine's Charles, but everybody calls me Chase."

"Nice to meet you, Chase," she said, shaking his hand. "Now I've really got to go."

She stepped out the window and was scrambling down the fire escape, when Chase remembered he forgot to get her number and climbed down after her.

"Elle, wait up."

But she had already vanished.

# CHAPTER 13.

MORGAN HAD BEEN feeling listless and his new mistress had been bugging him about his flagging libido. He had been through a series of life crises, including the death of his first child, the disappearance of his wife and the bankruptcy of his business, but he had never ever lacked the drive to bend the world to his will, not even after Adolf and the subsequent Inundations.

Consequently, he found himself sitting on a tissue paper-covered table in a blue gown that opened behind and was too small for his thickening frame. Dr. Robert Mahmoud, his stethoscope on Morgan's chest, listened intently to Morgan's heart and lungs.

"You'd think they'd come up with something new," Morgan commented.

Mahmoud picked up another instrument, peered into Morgan's ears and nose and grunted in satisfaction. He reached for a tongue depressor.

"Say 'Ahh.' "

"Ahhh…"

"Wider," Mahmoud said, peering down Morgan's throat.

The exam completed, Mahmoud immersed the tongue depressor into a small vial of clear gel, which immediately began to clabber.

"So what does it say, Bobby? Am I going to die?" Morgan joked.

"Yes, I'm afraid so."

"Come on, I was kidding!"

"Alas, I wasn't."

"Your bedside manner leaves something to be desired."

"This is not a bedroom. And I'm not kidding."

"Bullshit, you aren't."

"Really, you are dying. See the bilious yellow strings spreading through the jelly?"

Morgan squinted at the rapidly evolving contents of the vial.

"That's camel pox. Incurable."

"Nothing's incurable."

"For you, it's incurable. I could give you vaccine, but

your immune system is too worn down to fight off even a weakened form of the virus. And the symptoms–"

"I don't want to know because I am not going to get the disease."

One of my patients vomited up her own intestines," Mahmoud continued.

"Come off it. There must be something for Christ's sake."

"The only option for you, my friend, is an immediate transfer. You've got a few weeks, maybe a month in this body before the symptoms become severe. Muscle aches, shortness of breath, stuffy nose, an itchy rash around your nipples, swollen testicles."

Morgan shook his head in disbelief.

"Now, Morgan, you know your immune system gets weaker with every renewal. If you had been younger and your telomeres hadn't already shortened, if the first transfer hadn't been so rudimentary, if you'd had a vaccination, you wouldn't be in this pickle jar."

Morgan hung his head and stared at the floor.

Mahmoud patted him on the shoulder. "It's time you had a transfer anyhow? You're going gray. You need reading glasses. You're growing a paunch. And you may not have noticed but your squash game has been suffering. I've been kicking your ass."

"Thanks, Bobby. I feel so much better now."

# CHAPTER 14.

TINY LIGHTS TWINKLED in the potted palms on Hughes' spacious penthouse rooftop, which was currently decorated to resemble a Hawaiian grotto with arching orchids, rock outcroppings and a faux waterfall-fed pool. Painted carp swam in the dancing jets of water. Parrots, their wings clipped, jabbered in the trees. Birds and water, however, couldn't match either the babble of the guests or the strains of the enthusiastic orchestra.

Margaret waltzed into the hubbub, her shoulders porcelain against the electric-blue of her strapless, sequined Galliano. She took a flute of champagne from an elder retainer's silver tray and smiled widely as she made her way

through the tipsy throng. Smile, one-two, hug, one-two, air kiss, one-two… Repeat.

"Same old, same old," said Margaret, noticing not for the first time that she knew absolutely everybody. Even the nouveau riche desalinization repairmen. Lately she had been aching for an unfamiliar face. What the hell. She'd settle for a fresh perspective, not that she expected to find that at her father's birthday party either.

She did, however, find it a bit odd that Morgan was feting his nativity. The candles required would burn down the center, she told him. It was an excuse to schmooze their clients, he countered.

"Why bother?" she had asked. "We're the only game in town."

"That's a terrible attitude, Mags. It's almost Thanksgiving, for crying out loud. Give thanks we're the only game in town."

She'd warned him everybody would be busy with the winter holidays approaching. Man, was she ever a bad judge of how people spend their time. The place was as packed as a subway car during rush hour used to be. Not that anybody here would have need of public transportation. (A good thing because the subways had been flooded for decades.)

Her father's guests weren't starving either, though they flocked around the buffet tables like ravenous gulls at a garbage dump. They loaded their plates with such scavenged delicacies as caviar, Vienna sausages, dolmades, Goya's frijoles negroes or Del Monte fruit cocktail. Margaret

nabbed a skewer of pan-braised squab from a silver platter and started across the dance floor in search of her dad.

Stepper Goodwin, a drink in one hand, cut her off with the other and looked her up and down. "Margaret, sweetheart, that is some sweet getup for a sawbones."

Margaret managed a tight smile and tried to side-step him. "How's Zoë?" she asked.

"Never better…"

"Any problems adjusting?"

"The tits are exactly the way I like them."

"I meant her, not you. Now if you'll excuse me…"

"Ah, come on. Lemme buy you a drink?"

"Thanks. I've got one."

"A dance?"

Stepper grabbed her hand and started pulling her onto the dance floor.

"May I cut in? You don't mind do you, Stepper?" Morgan smiled at the other man.

Stepper started to protest.

"Come on, Step. Zoë's over there waiting for you."

Morgan motioned to one of the younger waiters. "You know where his wife is sitting?"

"Yes, Mr. Hughes."

"Take him to her and give him a cup of koffey."

The waiter nodded, took Stepper around the waist and lead him away.

"Caffeine doesn't sober up a drunk, Dad."

"It always works for me. Come on, let's go join Pella."

Morgan took Margaret by the hand and waltzed her into the grotto, where a cappuccino blonde sat dangling her feet in the fountain. She giggled as the koi nibbled her perfectly pedicured toes.

"You must be Dad's new assistant," said Margaret, clasping the other woman's hand. *Why do they all look alike?*

"Margaret," Morgan said proudly, "Meet Pella Bovay."

"Pleased to make your acquaintance," the young woman said.

"Likewise." Margaret sat down on the wall beside Pella and kicked off her stilettos.

"I won't be outdone," said Morgan, who not only removed his shoes, but also his tuxedo jacket followed by his black tie.

Margaret took a cigarette from her evening bag, then looked to her father for a light.

"I'm not encouraging bad habits," he said.

Margaret pouted.

"Oh, all right." He got up and removed a tiny tiki torch from a nearby centerpiece and lit her cigarette.

"Cute," Margaret said. "Maybe I should have worn a grass skirt! Will there be hula dancing?"

"Yes," Morgan said, "but it will be way past your bedtime."

"We'll see about that," Margaret said.

"But I thought we were going to bed early," Pella said.

Margaret raised her eyebrows. "I can see that I'm a third wheel."

"Oh, it's not that," Pella said, cheeks flushing. "Morgan… your dad I mean, hasn't been feeling so good."

"What's wrong?" Margaret asked.

"Nothing," Morgan said.

"His muscles are all achy and his nipples itch," Pella answered.

"Your nipples itch?" Margaret asked.

He nodded.

"Have you got a stuffy nose?"

He nodded.

"Any swelling?"

"Yes, but I'd rather not discuss it."

"Understood," Margaret said.

"Poor baby," Pella cooed.

"It's weird," Margaret said. "If it hadn't been eliminated decades ago, I'd think you had camel pox, which is a misnomer as the pathogen's first known host was the llama."

"As a matter of fact, I do."

"Do what?"

"Have camel pox," said Morgan, turning to Pella. "Could you give us a minute, love?"

"Sure, hon." Pella kissed him on the lips and hurried off.

Morgan cleared his throat.

"It seems I'm dying?"

"That's impossible. Camel pox is easily cured."

"Not in my case. I've got a few weeks, a month maybe."

"A few weeks?"

"To live."

"That's insane. Who told you that?" Her lips formed a taut line and her nails cut into her palms.

"Bobby Mahmoud. I went for my physical like you wanted."

Margaret was stunned.

"I'm running low on immune cells. You know all about that." He put his arm around her. "It's going to be okay, sweetheart. All I have to do is transfer in the next couple of weeks."

She nodded and gulped down the lump in her throat.

"You can stick the pins in me yourself."

She shook her head emphatically. "How long have you known?"

"Not that long? It's nothing really."

"I can't believe you didn't tell me. That sucks, Daddy. It's really, really sucks."

"I'm sorry, sweetheart. I didn't want to worry you. We have plenty of time."

Margaret put her head in her hands.

"So am I forgiven?" he asked.

She didn't respond.

"Well, am I?"

Margaret shoved her feet back into her high heels and got up to go. "I'll talk to Mahmoud. Let's leave it at that."

# CHAPTER 15.

IRV CAPALDINI, LEON Gross and many others in the transplant community labored beyond the dinner hour on Thanksgiving. An unstable skyscraper had collapsed and thirteen pedestrians – along with three would-be rescuers – were injured or dead. The survivors needed hearts, lungs, skin, bones and teeth. Gross was up to his armpits in viscera, stripping organs from cadaver after cadaver.

Every available messenger was lined up at the door, waiting for whatever Gross could deliver, then blasting back to Mercy. The kids were grinding for free. And while it was a sellers' market, the partners decided to dispense with the customary handling fee. It was a holiday and Capaldini was feeling generous.

Gross, who had been invited to join the Capaldinis for Thanksgiving dinner, persuaded his partner to go on without him. He promised to stay behind and lock up once all the parts had been dispensed, the grinders were gone and the interns had been sent home. It was long past dinner time when Gross, with Mr. Pebbles in his pocket, set out for his late mother's house on Hillside Avenue.

Exhausted by the events of the day, Gross was glad he wasn't joining Capaldini and his wife, Sherry, for a traditional feast at Shay du Mare. "Thanksgiving without family is as empty as a roast squab without Mama's bread stuffing," he said to the uncomprehending Mr. Pebbles.

Gross had never found a girl exactly like the girl who married dear old dad. And after several tepid love affairs – invariably sabotaged by Ma Gross – he had abandoned the search for a soul mate. Capaldini's wife had tried playing Cupid after Gross's mother passed. The only relationship that took, however, was that between Gross and Mr. Pebbles. The smart-rat had followed Gross home one evening, then stood at the doorway waiting to be invited in. He had been Gross's closest companion ever since.

Mr. Pebbles couldn't say much. He didn't have a large vocabulary or a vocal apparatus adapted for speech. Mostly he squeaked and nodded and sometimes whistled to make a point. On the other hand, the smart-rat was a sympathetic listener, which was a comfort to Gross after days like this one.

As soon as they entered the Hillside house, Mr.

Pebbles headed straight for the kitchen, leapt to the table and began inspecting the kitchen counter for crumbs. Leaving him happily engaged, Gross went into his bedroom to change into his robe and slippers. When he returned, he made himself a cup of tea and put a snakehead patty on to fry.

"Sszzz…" said Mr. Pebbles, attempting to imitate the sound of the patty spattering in the hot oil.

"Very close. It's Sizz-el," Gross said and scratched the smart-rat behind the ears. Mr. Pebbles readily picked up onomatopoeic words.

Like all the other smart rats, this one was descended from a few laboratory animals that had escaped from their cages after researchers left them to drown in the Jersey floods. Yet, they bore humans no ill will. Perhaps it was because the smart-rats carried a bit of human DNA. Someday, when Mr. Pebbles had a larger vocabulary, Gross would have to ask him about that.

Mr. Pebbles was preoccupied with the fish patty, which Gross transferred to an antique china platter along with his tea and a leftover macaroni casserole. He placed the meal on the table between two plates – one with silverware and one without. He spooned a portion of the casserole along with a bit of fish onto the latter for Mr. Pebbles.

After dinner, Gross was too tense to sleep so he poured himself a glass of warm milk and set to work on a sweater he was knitting. Perhaps he could complete the garment by morning, he thought, only to nod off in his

favorite armchair. It was a brief respite, for he was awakened within the hour by the irksome buzz of his pinkie phone.

"Dr. Gross," he answered.

"Doc. It's Chiliwitz. The boys are on their way down with six donations."

"But no transfers were scheduled for today. There must be some mistake."

"All I know is what I saw, Doc."

"Be right there."

Damn, he was tired. But given the surety of a post-crash shortage of donor parts, he couldn't risk the spoilage of a single corpse. He got out of his chair, dressed and tiptoed out of his bedroom so as not to wake Mr. Pebbles. The little fellow had fallen asleep perusing a vintage copy of the children's novel, "Mrs. Frisby and the Rats of NIMH."

# CHAPTER 16.

BROTHER MATTHEW, HIDDEN inside a body bag en route to the morgue, hadn't expected it to be so cold. He was supposed to lie perfectly still, but he was beginning to shiver and his teeth were chattering. Playing dead wasn't as easy as it looked. He prayed to go unnoticed as the orderlies propelled him and his five accomplices toward the netherworld of Capaldini and Gross.

Matthew also regretted his second helping of heavenly turnip stew. His bloated stomach pressed against the waist of the snug orderly's uniform he wore and his gassy bowels threatened his sphincter with a mutinous overthrow.

"Thank you, Lord," he prayed when the carts stopped, the orderlies left and the door slammed shut. He thought

about letting go then, but the events of the day had thrown off the team's careful timing. It was far wiser, he knew, to keep the squeeze on until Brother John gave them the okay to de-bag.

"Give me the strength, dear Jesus," Matthew prayed as he clenched his cheeks even tighter.

In twenty-four years as night watchman, Bill had never had to work late because nothing ever happened. Maybe someone would forget to turn off a lamp, lock his desk or alarm a door. Otherwise, Bill did nothing more than baby-sit the dead. No job was more peaceful.

As Bill came to the end of his rounds, he imagined the delicious Thanksgiving meal his wife had prepared. The centerpiece was his favorite dish, long eel pie. He felt his mouth fill with saliva as he inspected the cold room door. It was sealed shut and he saw no signs of anything amiss.

Pie was nigh and there was no reason to bother, but Bill, not one to neglect his duties, entered the chilly space and slowly swept the ceilings, walls and floor with his flashlight. Catching nothing in its beam, Bill turned to leave when he thought he heard a muffled "phbbbt-phbbbt-phbbt-phbbt."

He stopped, put his hand to his ear and waited, but heard nothing more. "Was that a flooper? Don't be ridiculous. You must be hearing things," Bill muttered as he left and locked the door. "The dead do not fart."

As the door closed, Matthew's quivering sphincter again capitulated and a cruciferous-powered flatus trumpeted its arrival with enough vibrato to tumble the walls of Jericho. Brother Enoch, in the bag beneath Matthew, couldn't help himself. He laughed so hard he wet himself, drawing a swift reprimand from the team's leader, Brother John: "If I hear another sound from any of you, I will cut out your gizzards and sacrifice them to our dear Lord Jesus before your bleeding eyes."

Absolute silence ensued.

But for the solo of a winter cicada, it was peaceful outside Gross's home. The sedentary sixty-three-year-old would have enjoyed sitting on the stoop instead of racing back up the hill. At the top, he was gasping for air and stopped to chat with the guard on duty when Gross glimpsed a light flash inside the morgue.

"Nothing to worry about, sir," the guard assured him. "That's the night watchman finishing up his rounds."

Gross thanked the guard, crossed the yard and placed his palm on the IBID. When the doors slid open, he noticed the place still stank of Capaldini's cigar, the butt of which rested precariously on the edge of his desk. Sometimes he left it smoldering.

"We're lucky he hasn't burned the place down," Gross muttered, putting the cigar in an ashtray.

He glanced at the carts lined up in his workspace.

Somebody certainly had screwed up. Ideally, he'd have a pair of interns to assist him with a harvest of this size. Perhaps he should buzz one of them. No, they had been asleep on their feet when he had dismissed them earlier.

"Which reminds me." Gross walked to the sink, rinsed the dregs from the koffeymaker and went about preparing a fresh pot. While it brewed, he drew on his rubber apron and began to enter the cadavers' tag numbers into his N3RD.

They all appeared to be men – unusual but not unheard of – Gross concluded as he sized up the last bag. The odd thing was that even one transfer, let alone so many, had taken place on a holiday. That never happened. Maybe he didn't get the memo. He shrugged and began to unzip a bag when he was distracted by the gurgle of the koffeymaker.

"Excuse me for a moment," he said to the bag and returned to the sink to pour and gulp his brew.

"Would you look at that!" he exclaimed upon realizing he had forgotten to put on gloves before handling a cadaver. That goes to show how tired I am, he told himself, as he found and slipped on a sterile pair of gloves as well as a scrub cap.

"Sorry for the delay." Gross grasped the zipper and tugged. The zipper resisted. He yanked harder and the black bag fell wide open. Gross was engulfed in a ghastly cloud of stinking gas. He gagged, hastily covered his face and mouth and staggered backward.

"Sorry about that," said Brother Matthew, poking his

head out of the bag. "Imagine what it's been like for me in here."

Gross was so astonished, he didn't hear Brother John slip up behind him, nor did he feel pain as John slit his throat with a bone knife.

Matthew fanned the air as he climbed out of the bag. Brother John glared at the younger man. "Find something to cover him," he said, making the sign of the cross over Gross's body and pressing his eyelids closed. "I hate the hell out of that," he muttered, then raised his voice: "Okay, everybody out."

The stack of "corpses" came to life, as each of the Brethren sliced open his bag and emerged disguised as an orderly in brown scrubs. Before anybody started asking questions and thanking God, John put a finger to his lips. After they had a moment to orient themselves, he hurried them toward the elevator used exclusively for hauling corpses.

Because outsiders never rode the slow-moving lift, the car wasn't configured to impress clientele with the invulnerability of the center's security systems. It was equipped with only one surveillance camera, not the clusters hidden in the walls and ceilings of the main elevators. Although the car was fitted with motion sensors, orderlies had dismantled the array, which would have emitted a scrotum-shriveling screech whenever anyone boarded with a load.

Brother John was on camera for an instant, but as soon as he was out of range, he reached up and misaligned the

lens. On his signal, the others gathered inside. The old crate crept upward, creaking ominously as it rose. The ride was otherwise without incident and despite all the delays, the brethren arrived at the chrysalis banks precisely as the shift changed.

Brother John exited the elevator and pretended to collide with a nurse about to go on duty. He had planned to drag her into the elevator and knock her out with chloroform. Alas, her enormous, overstuffed purse popped open and its contents spilled on the floor. She knelt to gather them up.

"I'm so sorry." John looked at her plastic nametag, "Betty, let me help you gather your things."

He picked up a lipstick and hoped to disarm her with his most ingratiating smile. "You don't need this." He handed her the tube. "You're a natural beauty."

She looked at him suspiciously. "Do I know you?"

"I don't think so."

"I know all the orderlies. How come I haven't seen you before?"

"I'm new. I started a couple of weeks ago."

She looked him in the eye. "You're a liar."

"I'm sorry you think so," John said.

"I'm calling security." Betty stuck her pert nose in the air and started to walk away. Brother John grabbed her arm and pulled her toward him.

"Sorry, Betty, I'm going to have to stop you."

She wrenched away, whacked him in the face with

her purse and attempted to run. He grabbed her from behind. She snarled and bit into his forearm. Brother John yawped and let her go. She fell back against Brother Matthew, who was holding his bone knife in his hand. He didn't hesitate to cut her throat.

"Brother Matthew."

"Yes, Brother."

"Why did you kill her?"

"The Lord spoke to me."

"What the Lord didn't tell you is we needed her alive."

Brother Matthew turned white. "I've wrecked the mission."

"Unless you can resurrect Betty."

Brother John turned to the rest of the men and motioned them to go ahead. "Brother Enoch, you too. Matthew, help me drag her into the elevator."

"Aren't you going to chastise me?"

"I'll leave that to God. I'll get her feet, you take the other end."

When Matthew bent down to take the body by the shoulders, Brother John took his head in both hands and snapped Matthew's neck. Then he cut off Betty's hand, placed it in her purse and after offering a quick prayer for both, sent the elevator back to the basement.

"Where's Brother Matthew?" Enoch asked when John rejoined him and the others at the door of Chrysalis Bank B.

"He's looking after Betty," John said.

"What's in there?" Enoch pointed at Betty's purse.

John removed the nurse's bloody purse from his shoulder, reached inside and fished out her hand. He placed the palm against the IBID. The door didn't budge. He tried again. The door held fast.

"Maybe the scanner knows she's croakers," suggested Brother Leo, a safecracker turned prelate of technology.

"Maybe. But how?"

"Is it stiff?" Leo asked.

John shook his head.

Leo scratched his goatee. "Cold then."

"Could be." John put the hand under his armpit.

They waited in silence till he pulled it from its snuggery and placed it back on the IBID.

"She had a nice manicure," said Brother Simon wistfully. A reluctant terrorist, Simon had been "volunteered" despite his large girth because he resembled one of the center's orderlies. He had barely been able to fit inside the body bag.

"What about the nurse on duty?" Enoch asked.

"She won't be a problem," John said as the steel door opened into an air lock arrayed with levers, buttons and blinking lights. A female robo-voice warned them to remove their shoes, put on fresh booties and remain silent at all times upon entering the nursery.

While the others ignored the warning, Leo tapped a series of codes into one of three panels. The lights stopped flashing, a germicidal spray was released and when the air had cleared, the door stood ajar. Beyond the threshold lock

waited a vast hive of chrysalises, each equipped with a monitor that displayed its brain-dead inhabitant.

The Brethren crossed themselves as they walked among the tanks, absorbing the eerie images. Although they had enthusiastically damned the dupes to hell, none of them had ever seen one. They had known the vessels would look human, yet expected to find some demonic confirmation of their inhumanity. A cloven hoof, a vestigial tail, budding horns, a third nipple.

John could see the men were having second thoughts. Even Brother Paul, once a knee-breaker for a Jack syndicate, had tears in his eyes, for Christ's sake. John cleared his throat. "They look like us, don't they?"

The others nodded.

"But they aren't like us. Are they?"

The brothers looked confused.

"We were born of the sacred union between man and woman, assigned souls by God in our mothers' wombs. We are children of Heaven."

"That's right," one said.

"They are envelopes made of flesh, empty shells created by man."

Brother John gauged the group's reaction. Only a couple of men seemed to be listening. More hokum then. John gestured broadly. "Soulless abominations, anathema to the Lord. They breathe not by His leave, but by the unholy machinations of the antichrist."

Brother Paul had stopped crying. That's a good sign,

thought John, observing the rest were more or less focusing on his words.

"It will not be easy, or pretty, or spiritually uplifting. But it must be done. We have sworn to teach these heretics a lesson. We have been chosen, my brothers, as soldiers of the Lord."

"Amen," Enoch said.

"Amen," echoed another.

"His will be done," said a third as Brother John gathered the team around the nearest chrysalis.

"Before we begin." He reached into the front of his smock and removed a drawing of a white male in his late twenties.

"Take a good long look." Brother John handed the picture to Brother Enoch. "Pass it around."

"You see it, shout out. Don't even think about harming it. Are we clear?"

"Yes, brother," they chorused.

"Excellent," said John, directing Leo to unlock and open the first chrysalis.

When Leo finished, John reached inside the tank, removed a four-year-old female and cradled her dripping body in his arms. "I know you've practiced on dolls and dummies. This thing is just like a doll. It has no soul. It has no mind. It doesn't feel a thing," said John, who then snapped the vessel's neck and dropped it on the floor.

Simon gasped.

"It gets easier," John said. "Now get moving. We've wasted too much time."

Simon slipped away from the others, who surprised themselves with how quickly they took to butchery. The brother was weeping when he reached the aisle between the last row of tanks and the back wall. He could still hear the sounds of the carnage: the men grunting, the glass shattering and most sickening of all, the thuds the bodies made when they hit the floor.

He couldn't go any further, so he braced himself against the back wall and slowly eased to the floor. He had put his fingers in his ears and decided to hide here for as long as necessary, when he felt the wall give way and fell backwards into a hidden chamber. It held a single chrysalis.

Simon struggled to his feet and crept toward the tank. Could it be the one? He said a little prayer before he looked into the monitor. "Oh, my God," he whispered. He was a hero and he didn't have to harm anything or anyone to earn that status.

"I've found it," Simon shouted once and then again before Brother John, his face and body splashed with gore, rounded the corner and beheld the chrysalis.

"What have you found, Brother Simon?"

"Uh, it looks kind of like the guy in the drawing."

Brother John looked into the monitor. "Thank you, Jesus," he crowed. "We've found our dupe."

John looked at Leo.

"Want me to do the honors?" Leo asked.

John nodded.

Leo wiped his blood-spattered spectacles on his shirt and began a careful examination of the chrysalis latch. "Got a little hitch here," he said. "I'll have to dismantle the locking mechanism. It's wired directly into the alarm system."

"You've got eight minutes before the shift changes," John warned. "I don't want to have to whack another nurse. The rest of you, place the explosives."

Brother Leo took a pair of snips and a screwdriver from his tool pouch, said a quick prayer and proceeded to clip wires and block relays with reckless speed. When he tried the latch, there was a click-click, whir, click and it released.

"What do you see?" Brother John asked.

"Uh, looks like a holo."

"It's hollow?"

"It's a hologram," Leo said.

# CHAPTER 17.

SERGEANT DEROSA STARED at the clock on the security console. He watched his future vanish as the seconds ticked away. He bit into his current solace, an onion hoagie with extra goat cheese. No, he wasn't as fit as he had been as an officer with the Peace Patrol. What did it matter? All he and his partner, Petersen, did was flatten their butts as they eyeballed the many monitors, dusted the equipment and oversaw the sentries on their rounds.

The last security guard to sign out had turned in his report and hurried off home for his Thanksgiving feast. Petersen was beginning to read the report when an indicator light began blinking. The sprinkler system activated in Chrysalis Bank B, but the holoscreen showed nothing

amiss, the dupes were nestled all snug in their tanks. Probably another false alarm.

"Yours, mine or ours?" Petersen asked.

"I'll take it. Guard my sandwich."

"No problem, amigo."

DeRosa shined his badge with his shirtsleeve, hoisted his gun belt over his belly and trotted into the elevator for the chrysalis banks. As soon as he entered the car, he smelled the smoke, which had begun filling the shaft. This is not a drill, he told himself.

"Holy shit and salvation." He pressed the button again and again in a silly effort to force the elevator into rocket mode. When the doors sluggishly slid open, DeRosa was pushed back by staff trying to escape. He didn't bother to announce that he had locked the car in place as he fought his way into the corridor.

The sergeant's eyes were stinging and he began to cough as he ran into the floating ash and the thickening smoke. He remembered a handkerchief in his pocket, which he wrapped around his mouth and nose. Up ahead he could see the flames shooting from the open bank despite the sprinklers.

He put his thumb to his ear and spoke into his pinkie. "Petersen, I need you. Fast as you can. It's no drill, man."

"On my way, sir," Petersen replied. "Oh, uh, what do you want me to do with your sandwich?"

"Forget the sandwich. Get your ass up here."

DeRosa squinted through the haze at the devastation. Chemical fires stank of sulfur and burnt rubber. Shards of glass cut through his thin-soled shoes. From what DeRosa could tell, every piece of equipment had been either been damaged or destroyed. Replacement costs: astronomical.

DeRosa walked farther into the room, toward the tanks, before he noticed he was up to his knees in blood, waste and flotation gel. Vessels, some twitching like beheaded chickens, some trailing umbilicords, some hacked in pieces lay all around. He called Gabe, then vomited till he couldn't anymore.

# CHAPTER 18.

MARGARET, HER FACE sooty around the edges of her surgical mask, aimed her fire extinguisher at a burning corpse and when that was smothered doggedly moved on to the next. It hadn't been enough to merely kill them. This wasn't a massacre; it was a snuff party. The bastards had been having fun.

The center's fire and safety squad struggled with the stubborn chemical fires, while DeRosa led the search for survivors. Gabe's men photographed the scene from every angle; cordoned off the bodies from which they took DNA samples; collected metal fragments, bits of cloth, fingerprints and glass shards as they made their way toward the rear of the bank.

DeRosa offered Margaret his condolences and predicted, "Whoever did this, Gabe is gonna saw off their 'nads with a rusty nail file. Then he's gonna make them watch while he feeds their nuts to the gators."

The floor had been sealed off and the center staff told that a fire, now contained, had flared in the vicinity of the freight elevator. Consequently the cafeteria would be closed on that level until further notice. All calls were jammed and nobody was allowed to leave the center.

The chaos was more or less under control by the time Morgan, who had been at a Giants-Jets game, burst through the doors. He staggered and Gabe reached out to steady him. Brushing Gabe away, Morgan squared his shoulders and gave every indication, in case anybody doubted him, that he was in charge of his emotions, his gut and the situation.

"Welcome to motherfucking Dante's motherfucking Inferno."

Margaret ran to her father's side, pressed a surgical mask into his hand. "It'll help with the smell."

Morgan gave her a quick hug and pulled the mask over his nose and mouth before turning to Gabe. "Any survivors?"

Gabe shook his head. "None that I know of. Let me check in with DeRosa and see if the boys have anything to report."

"Yeah, go on," Morgan said.

Margaret watched as Gabe rolled up his pants cuffs and gingerly stepped into the shallow lake of blood. "What a clothes whore," she muttered as she watched him tiptoe toward DeRosa, who was kneeling by a body bag laid along the far wall.

"Come on, Dad, let's see what's up," she said, motioning toward DeRosa, whose ear was pressed to the body bag.

"I think I hear something," DeRosa said.

Margaret put on her stethoscope, but before she could bend down to listen, Gabe poked the bag with the point of his boot. Someone whimpered. They all heard it this time.

The burly sergeant looked at Gabe, who pulled out his gun and nodded his okay. DeRosa carefully unzipped the bag.

"Oh, my God," he shouted. "It's Nanny, everybody. Nanny, are you okay?"

The nurse began to wail.

"Come on, let's get you out of there," DeRosa said as he freed her from the bag.

The nurse looked around in bewilderment, followed by shock, then began to weep uncontrollably.

"It's gonna be okay, Nanny," DeRosa said.

As Nanny shuffled with him toward the exit, her thick socks soaking up the gore, she stepped on something soft and giving. DeRosa urged her on, but she knelt, picked up an infant and cradled it in her arms.

"Who could do such a thing?" she asked.

DeRosa took the small body from her, handed it to an underling and sent Nanny off with a nurse, who whispered words of consolation and promises of a nice warm cup of tea.

DeRosa rejoined Gabe and the Hughes. "Poor old dear," he said.

"Poor dear, my ass. She's the only witness," Gabe said.

"Yes, sir, she is, but–"

"But nothing. Put her under house arrest," Gabe snapped. "I want somebody with her at all times. Every time she takes a shit, I want to know about it."

"You got it," DeRosa said, deciding on the spot to ignore the part about monitoring the suspect's BMs.

"No police. Absolutely no press," Morgan warned. "If word gets out we can't protect our clients' property... If one of your people talks, I'll rip out his larynx."

Gabe nodded. "I'll do my best, only the thing is, there's always somebody got a grudge and loose lips."

"Wrong answer."

"Understood," Gabe said. "All lips will be sealed if I have to staple each and every pair together myself."

"That's better," Morgan said on his way out.

Gabe looked down at his soiled trousers in sorrow. "I fucking loved these pants."

"May they rest in peace." Margaret turned and followed her father's tracks across the gluey floor and into the hallway.

# CHAPTER 19.

MARGARET, HER HAIR in a loose chignon, smoothed the wrinkles from her navy blue sheath, and allowed Bruno to walk her into the Little Chapel of the Vexed. Founded early in the previous century, the Vexed sect railed against the irritants of the era: telemarketers, junk mail, spam, reality TV, poor cell-phone reception, humiture, discontinued lipsticks, gridlock, feral cats, invasive species, Crocs and fat people.

The memorial service for Leon Gross was about to get underway. A harpist plucked a mournful refrain as new arrivals slipped into the simple, wooden pews. Field lilies, powerfully fragrant, were piled against an empty bier at the front of the chapel.

Margaret asked Bruno to take a seat while she went down front to offer her condolences to Irv Capaldini and his wife, Sherry. Bruno looked doubtful.

"Oh, come on. You're being overprotective. I'm perfectly safe here. We're among friends."

"You don't have any friends."

"Longtime acquaintances then. I introduced Leon to Irv like twenty years ago. I went to Columbia with Leo's grandmother," said Margaret.

The hire had been genius on her part. Leon had graduated from med school with high marks, but he suffered from Asperger's Spectrum Disorder and wasn't socially adept. The morgue was the perfect fit for a doctor who wasn't good with patients.

"It was my way of paying it forward – or would it be backward?" she asked.

Bruno shrugged. "Does it matter?"

Bruno wished the Little Chapel still had a functioning soundproof screaming chamber. He could use one about now. Margaret had never listened to reason, which was all the more galling now, after the terrorist attack on the chrysalis bank. And although Bruno recognized some of Gabe's men among the mourners, he searched the crowd for fundie knuckle-draggers. An assassination attempt was not out of the question now that END had become so brazen.

He watched Margaret settle in the pew alongside the Capaldinis. She shook hands with Sherry, whom she barely

knew, then hugged Irv. She tendered her sympathy and asked if there was anything she could do for them.

"Leon was such a brave man for trying to stop the bastards," she whispered to Irv, among the few who knew that Gross had not died of a massive heart attack as had been reported. "By the way, where *is* Leon?" asked Margaret, who had looked in vain for a coffin.

Capaldini pointed toward a small ivory container on the bier. "There wasn't a lot left of him to bury."

Gross had literally donated himself to the poor, explained Capaldini, who had gathered up all that was left of his partner – a spleen, a sphincter, both knee caps – and placed them in a jewelry box that had belonged to Gross' mother. He hoped his friend would approve. Margaret assured him that he surely would.

"The man was a saint, I tell you. He'd give you the skin off his back," he said to Margaret.

"Yzessh." A small rodent peered at her from Capaldini's breast pocket.

"Mr. Pebbles," explained Capaldini. "I promised Leon I'd look after the little guy if anything ever happened. Poor thing has been inconsolable. I hope the service isn't too much for him."

"I'm sure he'll be fine," said Margaret, who had no knowledge whatsoever of a smart-rat's emotional makeup. She patted Capaldini's pocket.

Mr. Pebbles hissed at Margaret.

Capaldini smiled apologetically.

The harpist began to play "And the Blind Shall See," causing Capaldini to cry some more. Sherry hurried over and pressed her hankie into his hand. Margaret took the opportunity to excuse herself and rejoined Bruno.

"Do you want to stay for the service?" he asked.

She shook her head. "I'm not good at funerals."

"Who is?" Bruno, still on high alert, walked her outside.

"Maybe if I went to them more often? Only, you know, there aren't many opportunities."

"Maybe," Bruno said, continuing to guide her toward the sedan.

"Yo, Elle." Chase, wearing his best jeans and a borrowed suit jacket, walked toward them, followed by a woman wearing too much lipstick and a shiny purple cocktail dress.

"Who's your friend?" Margaret asked.

"This is Fran, my dispatcher. Fran, meet Elle."

"Nice to make your acquaintance," Fran said.

"Likewise." Margaret smiled and shook Fran's hand.

"Elle's the nurse I was telling you about," said Chase, his eyes aglow.

"Come on, *Elle,*" Bruno said. "We're late for your doctor's appointment."

"Are you okay?" Chase asked Margaret.

"It's nothing really."

Fran took Chase by the hand and tried to pull him away. "Come on. We'll be late," she protested.

"Give me a break," Chase said to Fran, who let go and walked toward the chapel door.

"So what are you doing here?" Margaret asked.

"I'm a pallbearer."

"Well, good luck with that."

"Let's go in!" Fran again.

"Meet me later? I'll be at Potholes," Chase pleaded.

"Maybe."

"*Elle*, we really must be going now." Bruno helped her into the back of the car and took his place behind the wheel.

"You're not, are you?" Bruno asked.

"Not what?"

"Meeting him?"

"Who?"

After all these years, Bruno knew when to give up. "Think about it is all I ask," he said.

"Should I or shouldn't I? Hmmm. Okay, I've thought about it."

Bruno rolled his eyes.

Margaret was enjoying the fling. And that's all it was. Experience had taught her that her life was too complicated for serious relationships. When they learned her true identity, lovers were as apt to propose blackmail as marriage. Then there were those who feared their dicks would fall off from spelunking vessel poon.

What she wanted, needed desperately, was a diversion. Over the years, she tried distracting herself from

her woes with drugs, makeup, massage, expensive choco-lates, meditation, French lessons, aromatherapy, wine tasting, scrap-booking, piano lessons, knitting (honestly) and skydiving (after Wu's death). None was as effective as a drink and a fuck or a really long run. Sometimes she just didn't feel like running.

# CHAPTER 20.

TO MAKE ROOM for the Renewal Center, Morgan Hughes had razed all but one of a cluster of half-timbered, Tudor-revival manors. The surviving building he gave to his daughter. Margaret was seldom enchanted anymore, but she had fallen in love with the house's fairy-tale architecture: the turrets, leaded glass windows, balconies and chimney pots. Totally Mary Poppins.

The house, which Bruno occupied full time, was Margaret's only retreat. From her bedroom balcony, she could see Madison Hill, Harlem Meer and even Mount Morris – a few of the other islands formed by the Inundations – as well as the top floors of those skyscrapers yet to collapse into the bay. Boats, most equipped with winches, were moored

among the buildings, awaiting the return of the scrabbers off diving among the ruins.

The skyscrapers' upper stories had long since been looted. The scrabbers brought up submerged treasures: imported wines, liquors, jars filled with capers and pimentos, bottles of Balsamic vinegar, silver, china and crystal, sculptures of plastic, stone and metal. Without the scavengers, the upper crust would have nothing on which to spend its money.

After leaving the funeral, Margaret and Bruno sat on the mansion's patio, companionably sipping a rare, single malt Scotch distilled in the Orkney Islands. She had paid a fortune for the recently recovered fifth, but didn't skimp when pouring their drinks. Bruno stuck his big nose into his tumbler and inhaled the peaty aroma, then took a dainty nip.

"It smells like smoke and it tastes like fire," he said happily.

"To Orkney." Margaret held up her tumbler.

"To the Orknians." Bruno touched his glass to hers. "May they rest in peace."

"Here, here." She threw back the amber liquor and immediately refilled her tumbler. "Glass was half-empty. Can't have that."

"You might want to pace yourself," Bruno cautioned.

"Yeah, yeah." Margaret leaned back in her wicker chair and made a show of sipping her scotch. Bruno rolled his eyes, but said nothing.

As the sun faded, a new array of floodlights illuminated the property. Morgan had ratcheted up security since the break-in. Guards, armed with dogs, 80-gauge repeaters and MX60s, swarmed over the grounds, eventually encroaching on the screened patio where Margaret and Bruno had planned to spend the evening.

"Fuck this." Margaret was reminded of everything she was trying not to think about. "Bruno, come on. Let's get out of here."

"Negative. It's too dangerous. And I have my orders."

"Then I'll drive myself." She got up, swayed slightly. "Wanna come? Last chance."

Bruno knew he wouldn't be able to stop her unless he tied her up and shoved her into a closet. Maybe not even then. He sighed. "All right. I'm driving though. Where do you want to go?"

She raised an eyebrow, smiled slyly.

"I don't know why I bothered to ask."

# CHAPTER 21.

OUTSIDE CHASE'S APARTMENT, Margaret had second thoughts about popping in on him. Maybe he was plowing that senior cha-cha, Fran. What if he didn't want company; more specifically, what if he didn't want her company? Not possible, she decided and hurled a stone at the string of spoons that served as his burglar alarm.

In a matter of seconds, Chase threw open the window and demanded to know what the fuck was going on.

"Is this a bad time?" Margaret called.

"It depends on who's asking."

Chase stepped out onto the fire-escape, wiped the sleep from his eyes and looked down at her through the steel grating.

"It's me, Elle. You invited me. At least, I thought that's what you meant by later."

"Give me a minute." He ducked inside, pulled on some jeans and clambered down the fire escape to help her up.

"It'll be easier if you lose the heels," he suggested.

When they reached the top level, he stopped and removed the clasp from her hair - not that she needed any help letting her hair down - and kissed her gently.

"You're gorgeous. But before I demonstrate my adoration, that dress has got to go." Chase found the zipper of the dark blue sheath she was still wearing.

"Can I at least come in first?" she asked.

He pulled away. "Be my guest," he said, taking her hand as she stepped over the windowsill. "You wanna sit down or something?"

Margaret plopped down on his bed.

"I feel like killing somebody," she announced.

"Hope it's not me."

She stood up, then sat back down. "Actually I'm in danger of exploding with rage."

Chase rubbed his chin thoughtfully. "So you want me to light your fuse?"

"Something like that, yeah."

"You want some conversation - maybe a glass of water, first? Or do you just want a free ride?"

"It's not like you're not going to get anything out of it."

Pout, pout. She could play the coquette as well as the next centenarian.

He leaned over and kissed her and she didn't really know why exactly, but she began to cry.

"What is it?"

She wiped her nose and gulped.

Oh, yeah. Of course, she had been a friend of Leon Gross, too. He'd never forget trying to carry that jewelry box with five other pallbearers. They ended up burying him in his own back yard. Capaldini dug a hole with a garden trowel. Man.

He wiped her eyes with the corner of a T-shirt he had worn earlier that day. "I know how much you must miss Leon. I miss him too, but you must have been really close. So go on, let it out."

She buried her face in his chest and began to sob. He held her till she quieted. "Why don't you lie down for a while?" He plumped up the pillow. "C'mon."

"I didn't come here to sleep." Still she put her head on the pillow and closed her eyes. Chase smoothed her hair from her face, a gesture she remembered from her childhood all those lifetimes ago. Together they drifted off.

When Chase awoke, he began to ease out of bed so as not to wake her. He made it to the edge of the mattress before she rolled over and grabbed him from behind. "Don't even think about it," she growled.

Then she pounced.

Chase felt like a catnip toy in a tiger's playpen. She

pulled his hair, clawed his chest, chewed his ears, and, he could swear, purred the entire time. Bruising kisses begat a wrestling match that ended on the floor. He held her down. This time, she didn't try to escape.

"This is all there is, you know," she said, as he pinned her arms behind her head and bit her neck.

"Whatever you say, darling," he said, entering her with ever more insistent strokes which she welcomed with thrusts of increasing desire. It felt as if they melted into one and that is how they fell asleep again.

Margaret, now dozing alongside him, woke when he got up to pee. The sound of his running water followed her as she padded into the kitchen and took two beers from the cooler. She wondered if it was the same one he used to carry donations.

Chase still hadn't reappeared, so she took a tour of his bookcase. It held extra skates, a Teddy bear of a certain age and a homemade frame with a photograph of a doughty nun. She traced the name Elle in the dust of the top shelf. When Chase came back into the room, she handed him a beer. He kissed her on the cheek and took a long pull from the bottle.

She picked up the picture. "Who's the chica in the nun suit?"

"That's my mother... was, I mean. She died of the flux."

Margaret looked baffled. "Your mother was a nun?"

"She wasn't my real mother. But she raised me from the time I was a baby."

"What happened to your birth parents?"

Chase shrugged. "Hell, if I know."

"She never told you?" She nodded at the picture.

"Sister Beatrice is dead now and anyway she didn't have a clue. She found me and my Teddy on a pew at St. John's Cathedral. And that was all there was."

"You could do a DNA trace," she suggested.

"What for?"

"Aren't you curious? Don't you want to know who you are, where you came from? Meet the folks?"

"I know who I am. And my parents had nothing to do with the brilliant outcome. In my opinion, you are what you've done and who you've known and where you've been. Stuff like that."

"That's one theory."

"Besides I hear relatives are overrated. Come on, bring your beer. You can tell me all about your loving family."

"I don't have a lot to tell. Nothing extraordinary." She stepped over the window ledge and onto the fire escape.

"Tell me anyway."

"Well, you already know my dad."

"I do?"

"Yeah. Only you don't know you do."

She smiled enigmatically.

"Elle."

"Yes."

"Why did you come here? Why bring your troubles to me?"

"Because you're the only person I know who doesn't know me."

She tried to kiss him. He brushed her away.

"What's wrong?"

"I don't know what the fuck you mean by that. I was hoping for something along the lines of 'because I like you' or 'I trust you' or 'you seem like a nice guy.'"

"I thought I just showed you how I felt about you."

He turned away from her and climbed over the windowsill. She followed him inside.

"You're right. I'm sorry. You do seem like a nice guy. I mean you are a nice guy."

He waited.

"Make that a great guy," she said.

"You forgot good-looking."

Margaret grabbed him by the ears and planted a kiss on his forehead. "And sooo good-looking. And I do like you." She hesitated. "I like you a lot. I guess I'm a little scared by it is all."

# CHAPTER 22.

GABE HAD THE gumshoe juju – like the movie dicks who amble onto a crime scene, look under the bed and immediately spot the clue the city's sharpest sleuths have repeatedly overlooked. If anybody could figure out what happened to the boss's dupe, it would be the indefatigable security chief. Of this, he was certain.

Chrysalis Bank B had housed a hundred and seventy-five vessels including those of a movie producer, a fashion designer, a golf pro, a talk show host, three businessmen and a slew of lawyers. Some had been so badly burned or mutilated that only scraps of flesh or bits of bone remained, yet the DNA experts had accounted for all but one vessel. And that one belonged to Morgan Hughes.

Gabe and his men had scoured the crime scene so painstakingly that he was more apt to give birth to a litter of puppies than find a fresh clue. Still he had the feeling he was missing something and wanted to give his juju another chance. A return to the scene of the crime was in order.

The putrid stench had lessened since the noxious gases had dissipated and the remains had been removed. Gabe was glad to be rid of his gas mask, though he still needed a handkerchief to cover his nose. He stepped carefully around the edge of what had been the ocean of blood. Now blackened and hardened, it formed a checkerboard of parched and misshapen polygons across the floor.

Gabe had never doubted that END was behind the destruction. The bastards made little effort to cover their tracks: their bloody sandal prints, crude explosives, even a shred of a hair shirt caught on a sharp edge. It was enough evidence to turn the case over to the "authorities," but the media would glom onto the story and the reputation of the Hughes operation would be compromised.

He had assigned undercover personnel to monitor the Reverend's activities and to infiltrate END rallies, church services, and bingo games. And because he continued to believe someone on the inside had been involved, he oversaw a search of the HRC's personnel files. All they revealed was how well the company's strict hiring practices had worked. Aside from reprimands for tardiness, frequent absences or inappropriate wardrobe choices, he found

bupkis. As for nurse Nanny, whom he personally interrogated well, he had never dealt with such a ninny.

Every crime has a motive. Hast's motive continued to elude Gabe. Maybe God told the prick to have a little fun fucking with the heretics. Petty, yeah, but a first-class detective sniffs all the hydrants. Gabe reminded himself of this as he walked around the place where Hughes' chrysalis had once rested. There was no gel, no guts, only the scorch marks from the chemical fire.

Gabe stared down at the floor and then beyond. The unstained circle was a deserted island in the vast ocean of dried blood. Could the absence of evidence be evidence in and of itself? He closed his eyes and squeezed his brain muscles. The whacks had gone out of their way to trash the chrysalis bank. Tissue had been discovered throughout the space except in this location.

So all of a sudden, the fucks morph into neat freaks. Gabe shook his head. Those douches weren't that sophisticated. Nobody was capable of obliterating all vestiges of DNA. There were always traces, even if they were only subatomic.

Gabe circled the chrysalis' footprint. Once, twice, three times. He stopped. There was another possibility. The tank might have been empty. It happened. Vessels were moved to pre-op prior to transfer or in rare cases, terminated when a client died or could no longer afford the monthly payments.

Even if a staff member had become distracted and

failed to make an entry, which had never happened in HRC history, the boss had not requested a transfer. Neither had his daughter. He didn't need his juju. He had logic and it told him that the chrysalis had been occupied – although it too had been clean of DNA – and Hughes' vessel was surely in the possession of the Reverend Orville Hast.

This was a vessel napping, plain and simple. All the carnage was merely camouflage. Those ass-wipes were smarter than he'd figured.

# CHAPTER 23.

SOME OF THE HRC's more prudent and prosperous clientele maintained spare vessels in the facility. None of them – except for one of Hughes own – were stored in the bank destroyed by END. The corporation had done its utmost to make amends. Morgan had personally showered the injured parties with cash, his sincerest apologies and other freebies. Lawsuits were never the less filed and damage claims made. Ultimately, however, there was a limit to what the corporation could do.

Young patrons would reach middle age before their new vessels' brains were developed enough to survive transference. In the interim, all medical care including cosmetic surgery was on the house. Older clients – body age

of thirty-seven and above – were given the choice of taking their chances and waiting or accepting a suitable spare until their replacements had matured sufficiently.

Morgan was relieved when what he hoped was the last of the lawyers packed up his briefs and left him a little less wealthy, but alone in his opulent penthouse suite. He was much weaker lately and his cushy club chair beckoned. Before he could collapse into its dark leather embrace, Pella cracked open the door to announce Gabe's arrival.

"Show him in," Morgan said, taking a seat at his conference table. "Oh, and get us some java."

"Take a load off," he said to Gabe, who lowered into the chair opposite him. Papers littered the table's surface.

"Looks like you've been busy," Gabe said.

"Margaret tells me you have, too." Morgan moved a pile of briefs out of the way to make room for the mugs Pella placed before them. Hughes stirred goat's milk into his koffey, then offered the pitcher to Gabe.

"All the vessels have been accounted for," Morgan said.

"Except…" Gabe began.

"Except for mine. Yeah, I know. But I've got spares. Two of them."

"Yes, sir. But you may want this one back anyway once I tell you who got a hold of it," Gabe said before launching into a summary of his suspicions.

"Then why hasn't Hast gone to the press? Or demanded a ransom? Or crucified the damn thing?" Morgan wondered.

"I'm thinking he wants to make you squirm some before he makes his next move."

"You see me squirming?" Morgan's pale face had taken on color and his eyes were glittering.

"No, sir, I do not." Gabe was glad to see his news had energized his boss.

"We can't let him get away with this. God damn it."

"We won't," Gabe assured him, getting up to leave as Margaret, her eyes red and puffy, burst into the room.

"You look terrible," Morgan said.

"I feel worse," she said.

"I have news that might cheer you up."

She blew her nose.

"Hast kidnapped my spare."

She looked doubtful. "How do you know?"

"Gabe figured it out." Morgan beamed at his top cop.

"You're sure?" she asked Gabe.

"Mostly," he said.

Tears spilled down Margaret's cheeks.

Gabe watched Morgan put an arm around her. "No worries, hon. Even if Gabe's wrong, which he never is, I've got two more."

Margaret shook her head and sobbed. "No, Daddy. They're gone, too. Both chrysalises are empty. I opened them myself."

# CHAPTER 24.

SCORES OF FUNDIES clad in their robes and Jesus sandals hurled bottle rockets over the hedge of the Hughes Renewal Center. A few exploded on the other side, but Gabe and his men shot most of them down in mid-air. It was almost festive, observed the Reverend Hast, who stood atop a stepladder hollering words of encouragement to his followers.

Hast congratulated himself on the power of his rhetoric, which had inspired several followers to throw themselves against the electric fence. Puffs of smoke rose from the clothes of those who were fried, as did the stink of burning hair. Police fired tear-gas into the crowd, then chased the coughing, crying protesters through the haze.

Those who stood their ground were cuffed and dragged into paddy wagons as news teams eagerly captured the action.

The Reverend Hast climbed down from his step-ladder, turned his best side toward the cameras and volunteered his wrists for cuffing. A young policeman approached, followed by a news anchor and all the cameras were focused on Hast when Brother John jumped between the Reverend and the rest.

"This better be good," Hast barked as John took him by the elbow and tried to guide him away from the melee.

"It's way better than good, Reverend. Way better. But we do need to hurry. I don't want to risk a disconnect."

Hast hesitated until he realized the cameras were turned on other subjects and followed John to the battered Volkswagen Beetle that was the Reverend's designated personal conveyance. The car was outfitted with bald tires, a hand-me-down holophone and a hood ornament in the shape of a crucifix. When the sun hit Jesus's face just right, He seemed to be winking.

"There's a call for you, Reverend. On the holo, sir." Brother John's eyes gleamed. "It's Hughes. Morgan Hughes."

"You can't be serious." The Reverend almost peed his cassock.

"I'm dead serious."

"Give me a minute." The Reverend took a sip of water from John's canteen and straightened his collar. John brushed the dust from Hast's shoulders, opened the door

for him and ran to the other side to climb in beside the cleric.

"Ready, sir?" John asked Hast, who nodded and cleared his throat. John turned on the holophone and Hughes' blurry face appeared on its small, dusty screen.

"Well, well, Mister Hughes. Seeking salvation at long last are we?"

"Were that the case, I would have contacted a superior being. You are the furthest thing from–"

"I don't wish to trade insults. If you have a point, I suggest you get to it," Hast huffed. "I've got a rally to lead."

"And I've got a corporation to run. So let's get down to business."

"What business is that?"

Hughes smirked. "Spare me the act, Hast. Tell me how much you want."

"How much do I want for what?" Hast glanced at John for a reaction.

Hughes cursed under his breath. "We both know you have something that belongs to me. Harm it and you will see God much sooner than expected."

"Like I said, I have no clue what you're talking–"

Brother John squeezed Hast's knee before he could say more.

"Uh, give me a minute," Hast said and put Morgan on hold.

"He thinks we have his vessel," John whispered excitedly, "which means he doesn't have it either."

Hast was briefly baffled, then realization dawned. Back on the holophone with Hughes, he practically purred, "Perhaps I can be of help after all."

"What's this going to cost me?"

"I don't believe you can afford it," Hast vamped.

"There's nothing I can't afford. Name your price."

"My price? How about your immortal soul? Yes, perfect. That's my price."

"According to you, I don't have a soul. How about something more tangible? Say a large donation from an anonymous supporter? I'll make the check out in your name. Think about it," Hughes said as the screen faded to black.

# CHAPTER 25.

FRAN MANAGED FLEET'S dingy storefront office from behind a plastic barrier so scarred it was arguably opaque. The walls were yellowed and the floor, well, don't get her started. All those damn skates scuffing up the wood. Every time she threatened to quit, the boss swore he'd fix up the place. A raise, alas, was out of the question. Speaking of which, it was payday and the space was beginning to fill with grinders waiting for their cash.

Chase, who had come straight from a run, stuck his head over Fran's barrier and puckered up his lips.

"Gargh." She rolled her chair back. "You stink and you are – yuck – sweating on my desk."

"Come on, give us kiss. Make life worth living," Chase begged.

"Go wash your face – and wash your pits while you're at it," she ordered, pointing toward the break room.

He stared at her with pleading puppy-dog eyes.

"I mean it," Fran said, unable to suppress a smile.


Chase found Heysoos propped against a heavily scuffed wall watching a cheap holovision. Homes napped on a funky sofa that also accommodated two cute grinder chicks. One had her wrist in a cast that everyone had signed; the other's shin bore a long scar that she had integrated into a snake tattoo.

"Pretty ladies." Chase flashed them a sexy smile.

"We ain't interested," said the tattooed girl. "Put them teeth away."

Chase laughed and gripped, bumped, pumped and slapped Heysoos's hand. Homes opened one eye, closed it again.

"Money's late again?" Chase asked.

"Does a pigeon shit on a statue?" Heysoos replied.

Chase pulled out the remainders of a McSnake 'n' Cheese, offering Heysoos a bite, which his friend declined. Chase finished off the sandwich and washed it down with a swallow of water from his canteen. He handed the container to Heysoos, who took a swig.

"Warm and stale," he said.

"You're welcome," Chase responded.

The girls swore at the screen when it briefly lost the signal.

"What are we missing?" Chase asked.

"Larry King's jawing some cross-hugger," Heysoos said.

Chase got up and fiddled with the gadget till he relocated the signal. The grinder recognized the Reverend Hast.

"Larry's been sucking the Rev's dick," one of the girls said.

"Setting him up for a question he don't wanna answer," said Homes, presaging the silver-tongued interviewer's next query on the violent activities of the Right-to-Death movement.

The Reverend asked if Larry was referring to a recent incident during which a few overzealous participants had run amok. One disciple, Hast recalled sadly, had thrown himself on an electric fence around the HRC and was summarily fried. The Reverend looked directly into the camera and begged others not to follow the martyr's example.

"Yeah, yeah," King said dismissively. "Throwing bottles and toasting zealots, that comes with the turf. I'm talking about persistent rumors of terrorist activities and increasingly divisive rhetoric."

Hast denied the accusations in a reasoned, temperate manner. He silently cursed the booker who had sworn the show would be about the role of religion in a bifurcated society.

"All this tsuris!" King shook his head, his dark locks fell

and he pushed them from his eyes. "For what, Reverend? For what?"

"Saving souls, Larry. What could be more important?" Hast countered. "That is not to say that I advocate violence to achieve our goal."

"Which is to outlaw human cloning?"

"Yes."

"Because man shouldn't play God?"

"That's right."

"Let me play devil's advocate for a minute," King said, adjusting his suspenders meaningfully. "Why not play God, Reverend? After all, you claim He created us in His own image. If that is so, it follows that mankind's invention is divinely inspired, no?"

The Reverend responded with the patience one accords a small child. "This may be argued, yes, Larry. A man may be divinely motivated, for truly all inspiration comes from our Heavenly Father. The operative word, of course, is 'Father,' for it is He who assigns a soul to each of us while we wax in the womb."

"In the womb, eh?"

The Reverend nodded sagely. "If you are not begot of woman, you are unknown to God and therefore, you have no soul. And without a soul, you simply are not human."

"So you're telling me I don't have a soul?"

"That's what the Good Book tells us."

"You believe that shit?" Heysoos asked.

"What?"

"That vessels got no souls."

Chase shrugged. "I slept through that class."

He took a sip from his canteen, offered it to his friend.

"Would you do it?" Heysoos asked.

"What?"

"Get duped."

Chase picked up his fanny pack and shook it. "You hear any jingle?"

"Hypothetically," Heysoos said.

"Sure, why not?"

"Like the Rev said, man. Dupes aren't human. They got no souls."

"Old Man Mud Flap says everything's got a soul. Even rocks." Chase said. "And you know what else? Jesus was a dupe. Hell, he was resurrected. That's like being trans-ferred."

"That's wack, tio."

"No, it's not," Chase persisted. "The Father, the Son and the Holy Ghost. I mean, what's that shit about?"

"You're going to hell, amigo."

# CHAPTER 26.

CHASE'S MIND WAS wrapped around Elle like she was refried beans and he was a tortilla. Try as he might to focus on his mission, his mind wandered back to her. But not thinking about Elle was still thinking about Elle, so why deprive himself of his X-rated fantasies?

Because he told himself he had already done a dangerous and stupid thing by forgetting his helmet, which he realized when he saw a swarm of gnats ahead and went to pull down his visor. *Elle, it's all your fault, but I forgive you, sweetheart.* Or would she prefer darling? Or maybe *mi amor?*

Dang, he was whipped and he had only reached the middle of the hill. He was paying for his extracurricular

activities, practically idling even, which made Chase easy prey for the strung-out jack addict who jumped into his path. The kid's hands were shaking, his nose was running and he was dripping pee-colored sweat. Jack was one nasty drug.

Chase had decided to run through him when the junkie raised and pointed a sawed-off shotgun at him, ordered him to stop and "hand over the jingle or you're dead meat."

"I got no fucking jingle and if I did, I wouldn't give it to no punk-ass junkie," Chase hissed.

"I'm not fooling wid youse," the junkie warned.

"Me neither," said Chase, lunging at the kid, who freaked and ran back into the weeds. Chase went after him, but the grinder didn't get far. He caught a blade in a pothole, wrenched his ankle and smashed his skull against the curb.

There he would have remained if Fred Neiman hadn't been fantasizing about Padma Singh, his colleague on Dr. Hughes' transfer team. He was content with his wife, whom he called the missus, and certainly would never act on his passionate urges. But he could dream and that was exactly what he was doing when he tripped over Chase on his way to the Hughes Center.

"What the heck?"

Fred slowly pushed himself off the body, which had

broken his fall, and got on his knees. Mistaking Chase for a drunk, he tried shaking him awake. When that didn't work, he yelled into his ear until Chase stirred and moaned.

"Hey, buddy, time to get up," he repeated.

Chase moved his head and Fred noticed the fresh blood and using a clean handkerchief, began to apply pressure to Chase's head wound. With the other hand, he pinky-phoned Dr. Hughes to tell her that he'd be a little late for surgery... and by the way, could she send an ambulance?

"What's happened? Are you okay?" Margaret asked.

"Me, I'm fine. But I found this grinder unconscious on the side of the road. He needs an ambulance."

"A grinder? What does look like?"

"Like he needs an ambulance!"

Fred stayed with Chase till his identification was confirmed and he was admitted to the center's small emergency clinic. By the time Fred joined his colleagues, the transfer patient, an opera singer, had been rolled into the operating room. The Italian tenor's love affair with his fork was shown off to obscene effect by the skimpy syn-skin. Every bulge and gully, glob and sag was exposed. Alongside the singer, his perfect vessel waited, as empty-headed and as skinny as a scarecrow.

Not one to seek the spotlight, Fred hoped he might creep into the OR unnoticed by the team. Dr. Margaret Hughes, however, would have none of it.

"Fred has been playing Good Samaritan," Margaret

signed. "Aside from sudden death, there's no better excuse for tardiness."

His colleagues stifled smiles and mouthed their good mornings to Fred, who waved sheepishly, then hurriedly linked his monitors to the sensors in the syn-skins of both patient and vessel. When he had finished his calibrations, he glanced at Dr. Hughes. She wore an expression that surprised him. She looked worried.

# CHAPTER 27.

UGLY PEOPLE, OH, how Dr. Miles English missed them. Old people, too. The cosmetic surgeon was idle more often than he liked now that genetic engineering and life extension technologies had robbed him of patients. He couldn't remember the last time he had sculpted, let alone lifted a face. Why he hadn't employed his considerable talents since he had enhanced Zoë Goodwin's breasts.

On a scale of one to ten, Dr. English was a five although when he looked in the mirror, he saw an eight. In his opinion, men could be too pretty – straight men anyway – but that wasn't a problem for Charles Lyman, the young man under his care. His nose had been broken and badly

set, if it had been set at all, and his brow had been gouged open in a bad fall.

"That's going to leave a nasty scar," observed nurse Nanny, who had requested and received a new assignment following the destruction of the chrysalis bank.

"I don't leave nasty scars. I don't leave scars of any kind," huffed English, bending close to Chase's face to trim away the ragged flesh.

"Sorry, Doctor."

"These are single-thread sutures, very delicate," he said as he began to neatly close the wound.

"Yes, Doctor."

English stepped back to admire his effort. "I don't like to pat myself on the back, but that's fine work... He'd be a good-looking kid if he had his nose fixed," he said, manipulating the crooked proboscis. "It appears to have been broken more than once."

"He's a grinder, poor thing," Nanny said. "They break every bone in their bodies eventually."

"I'm going to straighten it out," English declared.

"But that calls for more anesthetic and he has a head injury," Nanny protested.

"I'll make it quick," said English, who ordered the anesthetist to "shoot the boy up."

"Maybe we should call a neurologist for a consult or at least an ENT," she suggested.

"Nonsense," said English. "I have seen his CAT scan.

His bell was rung, that's all. His vitals are normal. He'll be fine."

Nanny believed the doctor's choice was reckless and toyed with the idea of yelling for the doctor on duty. Instead she decided it would be safer for the patient if she stayed put. And as the operation progressed, she did become less apprehensive. English was working quickly, with precision and surprising passion. He whistled while he worked and although his mask covered his mouth, she was certain he was smiling.

"He's going to be a handsome devil. Hard to tell with his nose starting to swell though."

"Yes, doctor," Nanny replied as English continued to admire his work.

"Too bad about the teeth. Whatever happened to braces? Hmmm. Perhaps a chin implant would distract attention from that overbite."

"I don't think there's time. The ER is booked," Nanny said.

"Too bad," English said with a sigh.

Without waiting to be told, Nanny piloted Chase's gurney down the hall and transferred him to a bed in a private room.

The quiet, the clean sheets, the antiseptic aroma: Chase knew he was in a hospital and that hospital sure wasn't Lawd Hav' Mercy. He had no idea how or when he got

here and he was too dopey and in too much pain for a coherent examination of his situation. His head was throbbing, his mouth was dry and he couldn't breathe. It felt like somebody had shoved a pair of sweat socks up his nose.

When he tried to raise his arm, he felt the tug of the intravenous tube inserted into his wrist. It was only a duct of soft plastic, yet he was so weak it might as well have been a sack of anchors. The blue plastic bracelet around his wrist identified him as Charles Lyman, which sounded right. He squinted at it through swollen eyes. It was real stylish.

At Lawd Hav' Mercy, they tore up old linens, wrote your name on a strip and tied it around your big toe. If you died, there was no need either to remove the strip or to waste more cloth. No, this wasn't Mercy. But where then? He tried to get up again when a blurry someone – a woman judging by the floral scent – appeared at his bedside.

"What happened?" he asked.

"You took a nasty spill, but you're going to be right as rain. The doctor has patched you up good as new."

"Where am I?"

"You're in a clinic at the Hughes Renewal Center," she said. "You couldn't be in a better place."

Nanny offered him a glass of water and a straw and helped him slurp up some liquid. "Your poor head… Oh, and your nose." Soothed by her clucking, Chase drifted off.

After the opera singer's transfer was completed, Margaret shucked her gloves, removed her visor and exchanged her booties for a pair of sandals. She wanted to make a mad dash for the clinic. Instead she forced herself to return to her office and began to search the files for new admissions.

She found only a few entries and none of them was named Chase. There was a Charles Lyman. Described as a male in his early twenties, he had been admitted that morning with a head injury. That had to be Chase. No question about it, she thought, as she hurriedly scrolled through the file for details: His skull hadn't been fractured – good – but there had been considerable swelling of the frontal lobe – not so good. He'd been unconscious for… unknown.

Margaret got up from her desk, pulled on her white coat and set out for the emergency clinic, taking the path through the garden where she and Chase met. It dawned on her that she was acting like a lovesick teenage girl in a movie about hot vampires. Well, she did have a crush on a grinder, for fuck's sake. Fuck being the operative word.

*Get a grip, doctor. You're a grown-up and grown-ups do not give in to hormonal urges. They are aware of the possible consequences. So believe me when I tell you that you do not want to risk your reputation for a booty call.*

Except she not only lusted after Chase, but she liked him. He reminded her of the extinct, mythic American cowboy: decent, hardworking and dashing in his weathered way. Not that it mattered anymore. She had already decided

to end the affair before Chase had his accident. It was best to avoid attachments to people, pets or anything else that might die on her.

But as a gifted neurosurgeon, she was practically obligated to have a look at Chase's head injury. She would check in on any other similarly afflicted patient – at least, that's what she told herself – as she crossed the smooth macadam of Morgan Hughes Drive. Figuring it best if she went unnoticed, she ducked behind a water tank and waited for the nurse on duty to take her break before slipping into the clinic.

Once inside, she raced up the stairs to the right and quickly located Chase asleep in one of the clinic's few private rooms. "Poor baby," she whispered, tiptoeing closer to his bed.

He looked like a club boxer who'd gone up against the world champ. His face was bruised, his nose splinted and his eyes swollen and purple as plums. A visual assessment told her these injuries weren't life threatening, but she was obliged to unwrap his bandages to inspect the damage to his skull. She was impressed. The wound had been expertly cleaned and sutured.

"Fine work, isn't it?" asked Dr. English, popping into the room to catch the chief of neurosurgery eyeballing his handiwork.

Margaret jumped and whirled around.

"Oops, did I startle you? Sorry about that," English said.

"No problem, Doctor. I was admiring your needle-point."

"Ah, so that explains your sudden interest in the center's emergency facilities."

"Don't be ridiculous." She hugged her old college friend. "And don't expect me to shower you with compliments."

"Well, then what are you doing down here?"

"Fred Neiman, one of my people. I don't know if you know him."

"Fred. Oh, sure. Nice fellow."

"Just as I thought. You've never heard of him."

Dr. English grinned. "Anyway…"

"Anyway, he found this young man on his way to work and asked me to check in on him."

"This Fred must be something special." Dr. English lifted an eyebrow with Machiavellian innuendo.

Margaret smiled in spite of everything. "Stop it. You'll wake the patient."

Chase opened his eyes on cue. He looked up at the two of them. "I know you," he said softly.

"Yes, son. I'm the man who patched you up," said Dr. English. "And you are going to be one handsome fellow. I promise you that."

"Not you, her," Chase responded.

Margaret shrugged her shoulders. "He's hallucinating."

"I'll go and get his nurse," English said.

He didn't have to go far. Nanny magically materialized

in the doorway, carrying a glass of water and a tiny paper cup filled with pain pills. Although she must have been eavesdropping, Nanny begged their pardon. She hadn't meant to interrupt their conference. And oh, what a surprise it was to see Dr. Hughes so far from her usual haunts.

"You must be a very important young man," Nanny said to Chase. "Dr. English *and* Dr. Hughes! Oh my."

Dr. English, ignoring Nanny, threw an arm around Margaret's shoulders and gave her a sloppy kiss on the cheek. "Come on, Maggie, my love. You can buy me dinner."

Margaret pulled away from English's grasp, wiped the spit from her cheek. "I think I'll take a rain check."

"Oh, no, you don't. I insist on catching up," said English as he took her arm and started toward the door.

Margaret looked over her shoulder at Chase. He looked so confused, she was tempted to run back, put her arms around him and tell him the truth. But Dr. English hurried her away before she could give into the urge.

"Elle," Chase murmured a few minutes later.

"Yes, dear. Are you talking to me?" Nanny asked.

"No, the nurse."

"I'm your nurse, dear."

"So be-au-ti-ful…"

Nanny was flattered for she had always perceived herself as handsome for her age. Beautiful, on the other hand,

was more than charitable. Nanny patted Chase's hand. "You've had a very bad fall, dear. Perhaps it's worse than we thought."

# CHAPTER 28.

SERGEANT DEROSA'S EYEBALLS were raw from reviewing hundreds of surveillance discs recorded in the six months prior to the break-in. Employees entered and exited with tedious conformity. They passed in the halls, rode the elevators, climbed the stairs and used the toilets without incident. The work was pointless.

Nobody had access to the facility without the proper ID. Not even a fruit fly. The IBID was foolproof. It read fingerprints, scanned retinas and compared the DNA traces on its surface with those on file. Oh, and it could recognize your scent. If your stuff wasn't on file or your credentials weren't kosher, a siren would sound. You'd never get past the threshold, you might even end up dead.

DeRosa blushed at the memory of the extensive examination he endured as a new employee of the Hughes Corporation. He had been scraped, probed, measured and mapped by scores of fastidious, squinty-eyed lab techs. Nothing was sacred, no portal unexplored. He'd taken to asking, "See anything you like in there?" Nobody laughed.

After three days of analyzing the visual records, DeRosa gave in to temptation and began to fast forward the discs. He would have zoomed right past the incident if Chase hadn't stared into the camera and acted the fool.

"Cocky, little schmuck. I remember you." DeRosa hit reverse, switched to play and watched himself roust the kid and heard himself ask: "How'd you get in here anyway?"

"I followed this gorgeous nurse – red hair, curves, legs out to… Know her?" the kid replied.

DeRosa rewound the disc, then played the frames that showed Margaret entering and the door closing behind her. A millisecond later, the door reopened and Chase entered the corridor.

DeRosa got up, stretched and poured himself a cup of day-old brew. When he returned to his chair, he watched the segment over and over till he was sure of what he had seen. Without a doubt, the grinder had somehow breached the center's sophisticated security system.

That still doesn't prove he was in on the chrysalis bank job, DeRosa reasoned. For all he knew, the kid could have an alibi. They'd have to check. But it was one hell of a discovery. Worth a fat bonus, he congratulated himself, as

he journeyed from his cubicle on the first floor to Gabe's more commodious digs on the next.

DeRosa knocked before barging into the security chief's windowless, yet pleasantly appointed office. Gabe, in the act of shaping his nails, was about to curse the intruder, but quickly grasped that DeRosa was bursting with excitement.

"What's up?" he asked as he returned an emery board to his manicure kit.

"You're not gonna believe this." DeRosa handed the disc to Gabe, who popped it into the viewer. He watched the door close behind Margaret and open again as Chase entered. He watched it once more. Then he got up and slapped DeRosa's broad back. "You're a fucking genius. This is bigger than big."

DeRosa beamed. Gabe offered him a glass of tepid recycled water. DeRosa took a reluctant sip.

"How'd he say he got in?" asked Gabe.

"Said he slipped in behind Dr. Hughes."

"Ha. We know that's bullshit. Let's run his prints, do the usual crosschecks. I'm going to pay a call on Dr. Hughes. Could be she rigged the door to stay open. Maybe she had an assignation with our boy."

Margaret was rushing toward her office when Gabe tried to corner her for a quick conversation. He ran along beside her

till he was huffing. "Dr. Hughes, this is important. It'll only take a second. Please… it's about the attack."

"Okay, spill." She continued to walk briskly until they were a few feet from her door. She looked at her watch.

"We've got a suspect. We got pictures of him entering the building through the garden door. He said he was following you."

Gabe held out an image copied from the disc. "This is the guy."

Margaret took the picture from his hand and looked it over carefully.

"Recognize him?"

"Yeah. That's the organ guy. Pretty hot, huh?"

"Not my type," Gabe replied.

"I bummed a smoke off him. That's about it."

"Did you get his name?"

She shook her head. "Sorry."

"Did you know he followed you inside?"

"No. Is that a crime?"

Gabe grimaced. "It's suspicious."

"How so?"

"He doesn't have a universal clearance. Yet he walks right into the center without tripping an alarm."

"The sensors didn't pick up anything out of the ordinary?" she asked.

"His body language, blink rate, pulse, everything was consistent with those of a young man in pursuit of a sexually desirable mate."

Margaret guffawed. "So you've discovered that I am sexually desirable. Am I under arrest?" Margaret batted her lashes.

Gabe snorted. "I thought you might have noticed something unusual."

"Sorry, Gabe. I've got nothing. If I remember anything significant–"

"Or insignificant. Somebody let those bastards in and I'm looking for anything out of the ordinary."

"Where's the disc? It might jog my memory."

He put his hand in his coat pocket, pulled out the disc and handed it to her. "Enjoy. It's action-packed."


Margaret hurried into her office to have a look at it. Gabe was right. With Chase's lowly clearance rating, he shouldn't have been able to get inside. She called up copies of the prints and patterns recorded by the IBID as well as those of Chase's on file. They were identical. Phew. So he's kosher. No big deal.

# CHAPTER 29.

WHEN GABE RAN Chase's retinal and palm prints, the central computer found two matches: The first was Morgan Hughes. The second was Charles Lyman, a grinder with head wounds recently admitted to the ER. A computer error, decided Gabe, who asked the techies to investigate. When they found no system malfunction, Gabe ordered the tests repeated at both the center and at an independent lab. The results were the same.

He turned next to the biotechnicians. Could the samples taken from either of the men have been contaminated?

They were not, the biotechs assured him.

Could someone be playing a practical joke?

Negative.

By any stretch of the imagination, could it have been an act of God?

The biotechs stopped taking Gabe's calls.

With the hope of finding even the tiniest of glitches, Gabe went through the results one more time. When he finished, his desk was covered with koffey-stained spreadsheets, colored pencils and handwritten notes. If he accepted the findings – and he didn't seem to have a choice – there was only one conclusion consistent with the facts: The grinder with the busted head was one of Morgan's missing vessels.

Gabe smoothed his hair into place, pushed his feet into his cushy goatskin loafers and made his way through the same door Chase had entered without the necessary credentials. In the garden, he knocked over a bag of leaves, earning a testy tirade from a groundskeeper.

"Go fuck yourself," Gabe yelled over his shoulder.

He was panting and sweaty by the time he charged through the clinic doors and into the lobby. Sadly there was nobody at the front desk to bully. A sign instructed, "For service, please ring." Gabe walloped the bell repeatedly, but received no response. He was about to ring again when he heard a toilet flushing and a woman call out, "I'm coming. I'm coming. I've got to wash my hands first."

A door opened, closed and a moment later, Nanny turned the corner and pretending to be happy to see the

security chief, opened her arms wide and walked toward him.

"Don't even think about hugging me," he warned.

Nanny's smile faded. "I take it this is a business call."

"Of course, it's a business call. We're not friends are we?"

"We're colleagues."

Strictly speaking, they weren't, but Gabe didn't have time to argue the point. "I'm here about a patient. Name is Charles Lyman."

"Such a sweet young man," Nanny cooed.

"I don't need a character reference. Only his room number."

"He doesn't have one any more," said Nanny, now as starchy as her uniform.

"You're fucking kidding me."

Nanny gritted her teeth. "He was transferred to Mercy after his Medi-Pal ran out."

"What? That rat hole? He'll probably be dead before I get there."

"You have no reason to yell at me. I had nothing to do with it." Nanny began to sniffle, took a hankie from her apron pocket and daubed the corner of her eyes.

"Then who did?"

"How should I know," said Nanny, beginning to whimper.

Gabe swore some more and stormed off to commandeer a chopper.

When she was sure Gabe wouldn't return, Nanny locked the clinic doors and called her contact. Charles Lyman was no ordinary grinder. Dr. Hughes' visit had alerted her to his special status. Now the security chief comes looking for him. She didn't know how long Gabe would believe her lie. Lyman would have to be moved to a secure location as soon as humanly possible.

# CHAPTER 30.

BROTHERS SIMON AND Enoch, masquerading as Mercy paramedics, hadn't stop praying since they first beheld the municipal hospital's dilapidated ambulance. It was an emergency vehicle, Simon observed, in that one courted an emergency simply by climbing aboard the godforsaken rattletrap.

At least, they weren't able to go fast, he consoled himself, as they crept up the hill toward the Hughes complex. They had been told to pick-up a "package" from Sister Nanny. Alas, hours seemed to pass before the sister stepped from the mists and waved them to the side of the boulevard.

Enoch pulled over, but left the engine idling as he and

Simon followed the sister behind a tall hedge. A heavily bandaged patient rested on a gurney.

"Is this the package?" Simon seemed dubious.

"Were you expecting me to wrap it in tissue paper and put a bow on top?" Nanny was rarely sarcastic, but she sometime found the brethren vexing.

Enoch continued to wait for an answer.

"Yes, Brother, that's the package. Be very careful with it," she instructed before returning to the clinic.

"We will," they promised, then pushed the gurney beyond the hedge and proceeded to descend an uneven embankment. Enoch, in the rear, struggled to hold the gurney back. "Simon, guide the front!" he cried as the cart gained speed and nearly toppled into the drainage ditch at the bottom of the slope.

Simon grabbed a side rail and kept the conveyance from overturning, but not before the patient was jolted out of his sedated state. "What the fuck?" came the muffled demand from inside the bandages.

"Nothing to worry about, friend. Hit a little bump's all," Enoch said, righting the gurney with Simon's help. They then rolled it to the rear of the ambulance and with considerable difficulty lifted it inside.

The plus-sized Simon, gulping for air, climbed in behind the gurney and shut the double doors. At least, he tried. The doors fell open when the latch failed to engage. Simon tried to close them again and then again without success.

"What's the problem?" asked Enoch from behind the wheel.

"The doors won't lock," Simon grumbled.

"Hold on." Enoch got out and shambled to the back of the vehicle. After slamming the doors shut, he leaned against them for good measure. As he stepped away, they creaked open. Enoch, who didn't enjoy being mocked, even by inanimate objects, kicked the bumper, then the defiant doors themselves.

"I've got an idea," he said after calming himself. "Tear me off a piece of one of those sheets. I'm going to tie these suckers together."

"I don't think that'll hold," Simon objected when Enoch finished.

"It'll do fine."

"Shouldn't we test the knot?"

"Nah," Enoch said, climbing back into the driver's seat.

During the back and forth, Chase pulled the bandages from his eyes and began to reconnoiter his surroundings. "Lawd hav' mercy," he mumbled when he realized he was traveling in a municipal meat mobile. He had hitched many a ride on a Mercy wagon and sometimes helped the EMTs move or stow the gurneys.

"What's going on?" Chase asked the hefty EMT seated on a bench beside him.

"You're going for a nice ride," the man said.

Now that his vision had cleared, Chase noticed that Simon's belly had burst through the buttons of his too snug uniform. And despite the hospital's hygiene rules, he was wearing Jesus sandals. Mercy didn't hesitate to hire disciples of Hast. Chase had known some. But filthy, open-toed shoes on the feet of an EMT! Like the hospital's environment wasn't toxic enough already. Something smelled and it wasn't just Simon's funky footwear.

"Where are we headed?" Chase asked.

"Mercy Municipal Hospital," Simon answered.

Nobody affiliated with the hospital ever referred to it as Mercy Municipal. It was always Lawd Hav' Mercy. Besides that he knew everybody who worked at Mercy and he had never seen either of these dudes. Despite his pain and the drugs, Chase figured he was being lied to by a pair of fundies for reasons unknown.

"You've been transferred," Simon told him.

"Somebody must have made a mistake," Chase said. "So if you'll drop me off at the bottom of the hill, I'll be on my way."

"Mercy's okay. It's got a bad rap is all."

"Yeah, right. But if it's all the same to you, I'll be getting out now."

"Sorry, but we can't let you go," Simon said.

"Driver!" Chase shouted. "Stop, I'm getting out."

Enoch kept driving.

"I'm warning you." Chase yelled.

Enoch snickered.

Chase, whose adrenalin had now kicked in, was not only more alert, but also more alarmed. What the hell did the fundies want with him? He didn't think they were into human sacrifices, so maybe this is how they recruited followers. Chase decided he didn't want to find out.

He was weak, yes, and woozified. But with a weapon – the needle from the IV in his wrist would do nicely – and the element of surprise, he might as well attempt to escape.

"Where are we *really* going?" Chase asked Simon.

"To Mercy Municipal, like I said."

"Then you're going the wrong way."

"No, we're not."

"Yes, you are."

Chase could see he hadn't quite convinced Simon, but the brother did slide into the front seat to confer with Enoch.

"Geez, Simon," Enoch yawped. "He's been in a coma. He doesn't know whether he's coming or going. Christ Almighty."

"But he sounds perfectly rational," Simon insisted.

Enoch harrumphed.

Chase hurriedly released the restraints holding him to the stretcher and unfastened the clasp that held the gurney in place during transport. The wheels creaked and Enoch was all ears. "What was that?"

Simon turned. Chase opened his eyes with what he hoped was convincing innocence.

"Did you hear anything, kid?"

Chase shook his head.

"Must have hit a bump or something. I better check out the back," Simon said to Enoch.

Chase asked for water and Simon poured some into a cup and offered it to him. Chase, the IV needle hidden in his palm, wasn't close enough to make his move. "Could you lift me up so I don't spill it all over me?" he asked sweetly.

When Simon obligingly leaned toward him, Chase thrust the needle into the brother's neck and tore open the flesh. Simon gasped like a gutted fish and grabbed his throat. He looked at Chase in disbelief as his blood spilled down the front of his dingy uniform and into his lap.

Chase, whose face and hospital gown was also splattered, tried to shove Simon away. But the brother was failing fast. When Enoch twisted around to see what was going on, Simon fell across Chase's chest and the gurney began to roll. Enoch tried to hang onto it and the steering wheel at the same time, but Chase rocked forward and with the extra momentum provided by Simon's weight, rammed through the back doors and bounced onto the roadway.

The gurney plummeted downhill, veered across the road and crashed against a guardrail. Chase, eyes squeezed closed, was catapulted into the air and into the field beyond. His landing was softer than he had imagined. The late, doughy Simon had broken his fall as effectively as a mattress.

Chase was shaking, his temples were pounding and his

bloody gown stuck to his skin. Simon, his head cocked at a strange angle, stared into his eyes. Chase closed them, apologized for the inconvenience and crawled down the hillside. He collapsed in the high weeds, but knew he should get moving right away. If Enoch survived the rest of the ride, the paramedic was sure to come back for him.

*All I need is a moment to catch my breath*, Chase told himself, unaware that he was already sound asleep and dreaming. Elle was trying to tell him something, only she was so far away he couldn't hear what she was saying.

# CHAPTER 31.

OLD MAN MUD FLAP had left Houdini in the corral with the other goats to finish his feed. When Houdini had eaten all of his mash and hay, he decided he was in the mood for dessert: perhaps a mouthful of milkweed or a bouquet of late flowering kudzu.

His mouth watering, the goat squeezed between an ailanthus tree and a rickety fencepost and wandered toward the greensward that once separated the north from the south lanes of the elevated highway. The strip was overgrown with kudzu, but the deer had finished off the blooms.

Houdini found a wad of paper to his liking and chewed it as he meandered toward a favorite field behind the

abandoned row houses on Lower Gravel Road. The lot was a veritable smorgasbord of edible weeds: Cat's whiskers, cheater onions, knap vine, knot plant and wolf berries. In summer, a paradise for butterflies.

As Houdini waded into the high weeds, he nibbled at the knap vine, sniffed at the wolfberries – too vexing – and gradually worked his way toward a stand of ripe milkweed, beneath which Chase dozed. The goat, either recognizing him or mistaking him for food, stuck its warm, wet muzzle into the grinder's face and licked his cheeks, nose and chin.

Chase, who had dreamed of nuzzling Elle, awoke with a smile to discover the goat staring down at him, its lustrous lop-ears framing its long face. Chase's face was wet with… yuck… was it goat spit? Something about the animal was familiar. Chase worried his brain for a clue, almost retrieved it, but at the last second, it skittered away. Trying to capture a memory was like trying to swat a no-see-um. He gave up and closed his eyes.

"Heh, heh, heh," the goat nickered.

Chase looked up at him. "Houdini?" he whispered, triggering a swift-moving montage of recent events: the jack freak, the emergency clinic, the old nurse, Elle's visit, the phony EMTs. Had he killed one of them? He was hoping that was only a bad dream, when he heard Enoch cry out from the roadway. The brother must have discovered Simon's hefty corpse.

Houdini began to bleat.

"Shhh. You are determined to get me killed," Chase whispered.

"Baaaaaa."

Enoch must have seen Houdini's movement in the weeds because someone, undoubtedly Enoch, was swishing toward them through the tall grass. Chase, still in his hospital gown, got down on all fours, bare butt to the sky. He crawled till he ran out of cover alongside a gravel roadway at the field's edge. He hunkered down and silenced his breathing. It felt like he had been like that forever. Maybe he had eluded Enoch.

Rustling in nearby foliage scotched that theory. The brother was closing in. Perhaps he should give himself up. Chase peeked through the weeds, expecting to see Enoch. Instead he spied Houdini ambling toward a row of townhouses. Any one of them would make a sweet hideout.

Praying the goat would do nothing to attract Enoch's attention, the grinder pulled himself to his feet and ran staggering for the nearest house, a brick structure with a sagging roof. He broke the lock on a basement window and climbed inside. After a quick search of the premises, he collapsed on an old blanket found in a storage bin and tried not to think about how thirsty he was.

It was so quiet he could hear his heart thumping and a high-pitched buzzing. Could a mosquito get inside your skull? Chase squeezed his eyes closed, the better to wring information from his battered brain. The sound got louder,

almost derailing his train of thought. Then it came to him. *A pinkie phone.* He had a freaking pinkie phone.

He placed his thumb to his ear and his pinkie to his lips. "Fran?" he gasped.

The response was a shrill, garbled electrical noise that made his head hurt more. He pulled his hand away and folded it into a fist. The static was gone. He tilted his head this way and that, but the silence was absolute. He could no longer pick up a signal. He gave up, wrapped himself in the blanket and fell asleep.

A storm of Wagnerian ferocity blew over the island that night, but Chase slept through its fury. He was awaked by the granddaddy of all skull-knockers, which was compounded by an alarming supposition: What if the suspicious paramedics really were new on the job? And what if in his head injury-induced paranoia, he had committed murder? Chase could turn himself in, plead insanity… or he could go on the lam.

In either case, he'd need food and water, clothes and most of all, his skates. He climbed the rickety stairs and began to explore the kitchen. Finding nothing but mouse turds and fallen plaster, he headed into the dining room to continue his search. A rasp stopped him in his tracks. The front door knob turned.

Panicked, he scrambled back to the basement and was about to shimmy out the window, when he saw a man, the ambulance driver, lurking outside. He crept across the dusty floor back toward the stairs, jumped at the sound of a crash

followed by heavy footsteps overhead. Somebody must have kicked the door off the hinges. He was trapped. He did the only thing he could - wedged into the darkest corner and hid under the blanket.

Brother John ordered Brother Enoch to search the rest of the house while he followed the footprints leading to the basement. Gun drawn, John sidled down the stairs. He almost laughed when he saw a body-shaped lump under a blanket.

"Come on out, kid. I know you're under there." Brother John crouched and picked up the covering.

Chase took one look at the gun and raised his hands.

"Don't worry I'm not going to shoot you," said the cleric, lowering his revolver.

Chase dropped his arms. John pulled out his handcuffs and placed them around Chase's wrists. "Sorry, friend, I can't take any chances."

"What do you want with me?" Chase asked with what he hoped sounded like righteous indignation.

"We're trying to save your life."

"I don't know who you think I am, but you've got the wrong guy. I don't need saving."

"That is entirely possible," Brother John said. "However, until we find out otherwise, you're in our care. We're going to feed you, clean you up and give you a home with us."

"Thanks, but I've been taking care of myself since forever. So if it's all the same to you, I'll be going."

"I can't let you go outside like that." Brother John picked up the blanket and wrapped it around Chase, barely covered in his flimsy hospital gown.

"Don't stand too close," Brother Enoch warned from the top of the stairs. "He's more dangerous than he looks."

John waved his gun under Chase's nose. "As am I, Brother. As am I."

Houdini was meandering toward home by the time Old Man Mud Flap reached Lower Gravel Road. The goat bleated a greeting, picked up its pace and when it got close enough, bumped its owner's thigh. Burrs had attached themselves to Houdini's ears and berry juice stained its chin whiskers.

"You're a pretty sight. I hope you didn't pick up any ticks," Mud Flap said while fastening the goat's lead to his collar.

Houdini shook his head and snorted.

The goatherd made a cursory examination of the animal's coat. "I'll do a thorough check later."

As Mud Flap turned for home, he glimpsed two brothers. One held a gun while the other handcuffed a third man into a canopied golf cart. One of the brothers caught Mud Flap watching them and started toward the goatherd, but apparently changed his mind and climbed into the golf

cart. The driver released the brake and the vehicle began to roll toward Mud Flap.

He got a good look at the captive as they passed. Though his face was badly bruised and his head was bandaged, he seemed familiar to the old man, who stood there wracking his brain. "Half-heimers," he groaned.

Houdini's patience had run out and he bleated in frustration.

"Of course," Mud Flap exclaimed. "It's that nice young man who wanted to start a goat farm. He looks awful. Something is amiss, Houdini. A grinder without his skates? Something must be terribly wrong."

They walked a while in silence. Mud Flap pondered what he had seen. "They were religious fellows. I'm sure of that," he said. "Zealots of some kind. Pigheaded lot."

Houdini grunted.

"Ever wonder what their God has against goats?"

Houdini didn't respond. Perhaps he was anxious to get home.

"A goat can't be easily manipulated," Mud Flap explained. "A sheep on the other hand does what it is told. Abides with the flock. Hmm. Maybe I should have become a shepherd."

# CHAPTER 32.

THE SABRE TX-40 hovered over an expanse of crumbled asphalt that served as the Mercy Municipal Hospital parking lot. The blades were still turning when Gabe climbed from the aircraft and with a calculated swagger, waded through the ankle-high litter toward the entrance of the emergency room.

Gabe pulled out his corporate ID, shoved it under Big Beulah's nose and tried to brush past the admitting nurse.

"Where you think you're going?" Beulah asked as she stepped between him and the doorway.

"Maybe you don't realize who I am," said Gabe.

"I don't care who you are. You ain't getting past me

without the proper credentials. This is a municipal facility. You got no authority here."

Gabe let her see the gun in his shoulder holster. "I'm ordering you to get out of my way."

Beulah didn't budge.

"Come on, boys. We're going in," said Gabe to the two men accompanying him.

"I don't think so, short stuff. You wanna shoot me, be my guest." Beulah folded her mighty arms. "I got no burdens on my soul."

The bitch also had backup. The pack of grinders he had seen lounging on the stoop arranged themselves around the nurse.

"You gonna shoot us all?" the leader asked.

Gabe considered it, but decided he didn't want to be on the nightly news. He knew he had been outmaneuvered. He turned his back on the opposition and with his men, headed back to the Sabre.

"Lawd have mercy on youse," the nurse called after them.

"Fucking cow," Gabe said to his men. "We'll land on the roof and take 'em by surprise."

# CHAPTER 33.

MORGAN HAD VIEWED the scan of Margaret and Chase in the garden and struggled with the sight of his overtly flirtatious daughter and his vessel. Didn't she realize? Even with the broken nose and the scarred, weathered skin – even if the grinder was physiologically twenty-five years younger. Wouldn't you think she would recognize her own father? Not that the so-called Charles Lyman was in actual fact her father. Not yet anyway.

And then to learn that she had visited Lyman at the clinic… What was that about? He hadn't been able to learn more because she wasn't at home or at the office and she wasn't answering her pinkie phone either. It was the same

with Bruno, whom she doubtless enlisted in whatever cockamamie scheme she had cooked up involving Lyman.

"AHEMMM!" Stepper Goodwin cleared his throat, rousing Morgan from his reverie.

"What? Sorry, Stepper. You were saying?"

The attorney steepled his fingers and leaned back in his chair. The good old boy did his best impression of a British barrister. "While strictly speaking, there is no precedent in this matter, the law is clear. You cannot own a person. For that is most assuredly slavery."

"But he is not strictly speaking, a person," Morgan argued. "I not only own him, Stepper, hell, I am him… it."

"Of course, you can own a vessel that has been grown from your own cells."

"Exactly!" Morgan exclaimed, slamming his fist on the desk for emphasis.

"The question here, however, is more complex," Stepper continued. "To wit: If a vessel experiences independent consciousness, does that fact, in and of itself, qualify said vessel as a quote-unquote person?" he leaned in conspiratorially. "I think we can argue persuasively it does not."

Morgan nodded.

"Then again," Stepper added, "it could be argued as persuasively, that it does."

"Here's the thing, Stepper. Between you and me, I don't intend to ask permission."

"I don't think the courts would look kindly on that," Stepper said. "But what the fuck do I know."

As Morgan helped himself to a third Scotch and offered to top off Stepper's drink, Gabe called with the news that Morgan's vessel had been transferred from the Hughes emergency clinic to Mercy hospital.

"What?" Morgan yelped. "This is a catastrophe? How'd it happen? Who gave the order? What the fuck am I paying you for?"

"I don't know who gave the order. I know it's fucked up, but I swear on my mother's grave that I will have Lyman back safe and sound within the hour."

"For fuck's sake, keep an eye out for Margaret. I don't want her consorting with it," Morgan added.

"I'll do my best, boss," Gabe yelled over the noise of the helo.

"She has to be told as soon as possible."

"Begging your pardon, sir, I think maybe that information ought to come from you. You are her father and that's kind of the issue."

"Whoever gets to her first – me, you, Bruno. We've got to warn her. It might try to turn her against me, maybe take her as hostage."

"Will do, boss," Gabe shouted. "Only I don't think we need to worry about that. Lyman does not appear to have a clue about his, I mean *its*, identity. And no way it knows Margaret's your kid. She'd never give her real name to a booty call."

Gabe glanced out the window. "Gotta sign off. We're landing."

The pilot set the helo down gently on the soundest section of Mercy's rotting roof. Gabe and his men made their way across the tar surface to a broken skylight, through which they entered the hospital's guano-splattered attic and proceeded into the stairwell.

Gabe assigned his men to search every room on every floor. "Thorough, boys. Don't just look under the beds, look under the bedpans."

# CHAPTER 34.

"ON WHOSE SAY SO?" Margaret demanded of nurse Nanny when she learned of Chase's transfer to Mercy Municipal. Nanny ducked her head and shrugged.

"You don't know," Margaret snapped. "You are telling me you would allow just anybody to walk in here and remove a patient without trying to stop them. I don't believe it. You're too professional for that."

"They said they were from Mercy, so I assumed..." Nanny began to sniffle.

"For Christ's sake, stand up and take it like a woman," Margaret growled as she got Bruno on her pinkie phone.

"This isn't over," she said as Bruno pulled into the circular drive.

Margaret's rage had turned to anxiety by the time Bruno dropped her off out of sight of Mercy's main entrance. Now she was scurrying, her white coat fluttering behind her, toward the heavy oak doors. How, she worried, was she going to talk her way past security?

She was amazed when a guard tipped his hat, held the door open and wished her a merciful day. While she hadn't expected to encounter security on a par with the HRC's, she didn't think they would let a stranger walk in off the street. "Guess there's a lot of that going around lately. Not that I'm complaining," Margaret muttered.

Searching for a sign pointing the way to the ICU, she flagged down a harried, young nurse hustling through the lobby. "Excuse me, nurse," Margaret began.

"Oh, thank God, Doctor." She looked at Margaret's nametag. "Doctor Hughes."

"Yes, that's me. Only I don't work here. I'm not affiliated."

"Doesn't matter. So long as you're a doctor. You are aren't you?" The nurse grinned at her little joke.

"In a manner of speaking."

The nurse continued to race ahead of Margaret. "This way, Doctor. Please, hurry."

What could she do? Margaret followed the nurse down a corridor. Its walls – maybe once a sunny yellow- were stained and jaundiced. Patients who weren't critical paced the halls, their friends or relatives in tow. Those too

sick or weary to stand sat on the floor, wrapped in blankets, their backs against the wall.

Whores with split lips, kids with broken arms, crazies with wind-milling eyeballs, reached for her hand or pulled at her white coat. The nurse grabbed Margaret's hand and dragged her along as she shoved her way down the corridor. The doctor was a little green. The smell of bloody bandages, soiled diapers and body odor was overwhelming.

"You've never volunteered here before?"

Margaret shook her head.

"It's always like this. Clogged as a fat man's artery."

"I need to get out of here," Margaret gulped.

"Here, suck on this lemon drop," said the nurse. "It'll help with the nausea."

Margaret unwrapped the candy, popped it into her mouth and savored the mouth-puckering sensation.

"Better?" asked the nurse.

"For the time being," said Margaret, hesitating as they approached a small, seemingly angry crowd.

"It's okay," said the nurse, who took Margaret by the elbow and led her into the middle of the group. A pregnant pre-adolescent lay hemorrhaging on a makeshift bed of blankets. An elderly man, his clothes saturated with blood, wept at her side. Heysoos, who had accompanied the pair to the hospital, held a canteen to the girl's lips.

"Here we are, doctor," the nurse said.

"What do you mean 'here we are?' This kid belongs in the OR."

"The ORs are full. This is the best we can do," the nurse explained.

"You can't expect me to deliver this baby. I'm a brain surgeon."

The pregnant girl screamed. The old man wailed.

Margaret kneeled beside the girl and automatically began examining her swollen belly. "She isn't even in her third trimester," muttered Margaret, unexpectedly thankful for her stint in the maternity ward while interning at Columbia Hospital Center.

The rotation had been uneventful – if screaming women giving birth could be described as uneventful. Under the best of circumstances, it was like a horror movie down there.

"Too bad babies don't come from cabbages," she said.

Heysoos looked up at Margaret. "Don't I know you?"

Margaret shook her head, even though she recognized him as Chase's friend. The crowd pressed closer.

"I guess I'm stuck," she said.

"Looks like it," the grinder said.

Margaret caught the eye of an elderly woman hovering nearby. "Granny... Yeah, you. Put a pillow behind her head and another under her back. And get more blankets to keep her warm."

The senior complied and Margaret covered the girl's knees with one of the blankets, then poked her head between them to examine her. The girl screamed at her touch. As Margaret had feared, there were no signs a birth

was imminent. This was a disaster in the making. The placenta was torn and the baby would suffocate unless she performed an immediate C-section.

"I need a scalpel, gloves, antiseptic, anesthetic…"

"I'll try," said the nurse. "It'll be a while."

"She doesn't have a while."

Margaret turned to the crowd once again. "Anybody got a knife, anything sharp?"

"I have a bone knife," said a brother, "if that would help."

"I guess it'll have to," said Margaret, taking the knife from his hand.

"The Great Physician will steady your hand, Doctor."

"You don't suppose He can supply anesthetic?"

"How about this, Doc? I took a little nip is all," slurred a man as he offered her a bottle of vodka.

Margaret poured some in the girl's mouth, some over her own hands and the bone knife and the rest over the patient's belly. She asked the grinder to hold her still. The priest prayed. Margaret took a deep breath, pressed the blade into the girl's belly and swiftly made a vertical cut from her navel to her pubic area.

The girl passed out, the grinder turned green and the priest became silent. Margaret reached into the womb, pulled out a baby girl and cut the umbilical cord. She wiped the mucus from the infant's mouth and the baby let out a wail. The crowd oohed. The old woman took the baby, wrapped her in a blanket and presented her to the old man.

"Where's the father?" Margaret asked Heysoos.

Heysoos pointed to the old man.

"Lord have mercy," she said.

Heysoos grinned. "Now you're catching on."

"Would you stand by," she said, "while I close her up?"

"Sure thing," he said.

"It would be a whole lot easier if I had a needle and thread."

"Will a box of sutures do?" asked the returning nurse, who also handed her a bottle of antiseptic.

Margaret took the supplies, turned back to her patient and flung her long hair over her shoulder and out of her way.

The gesture reminded Heysoos of somebody. The doctor looked familiar and now he knew why. She was the chica from Potholes, Chase's new girlfriend, the nurse.

"You're not a doctor," he said.

Margaret continued to stitch up the girl's abdomen.

"If you say so."

"You're a nurse." He held her eyes. "You could have killed that girl."

"She didn't need my help for that. She would have bled to death and the baby would have drowned in her mother's blood. And for your information, I am more than a doctor, I'm a surgeon, a fucking great one. See how neat that cut is?"

Heysoos nodded. "Uh, I apologize, Doctor –um?"

She pointed to her nametag.

"Dr. M. Hughes,'" Heysoos read the tag aloud. "The M is for…"

"Margaret."

"As in Dr. Margaret Hughes."

"That would be me."

"I'm Heysoos, pleased to meet you."

Margaret laughed.

"Wow. I can't wait to see the look on Chase's face. He thought you were a nurse. Wow."

"You've seen him?"

Heysoos shook his head. "Nobody has. No offense, but we figured he was, um, with you."

Margaret ignored the insinuation. "He's had a serious accident."

"Is he okay?"

"He's had a concussion, his scans were so-so. The thing is, you never know with brain trauma."

"He's not dying?"

"I don't think so. I hope not. I haven't seen him since he was transferred here."

"When?"

"Early this morning. I came here to find him."

Heysoos nodded. "Everybody knows Chase. Docs, nurses, techs. If he's here, we'll find him."


Gabe and his boys heard cheers and applause as they scrambled down the stairs to the first floor. They ran toward the

sounds. Gabe was stunned to see Margaret standing in the center of the crowd with blood on her hands, in her hair and on her clothing.

What had these maniacs done to her? Gabe whipped out his revolver and warned the crowd to fall back. The old man, thinking that Gabe meant Margaret harm, stood up with the bone knife in his hand and started to step in front of the doctor. Gabe shot him in the kneecap and the man buckled to the floor.

"Are you insane?" Margaret screamed. "Put the gun down."

"You," Gabe pointed his gun at Heysoos. "Move away from the lady. Hands in the air."

Heysoos did as he was told.

"Margaret, are you all right?" asked the unusually solicitous Gabe.

"I'm fine. Couldn't you ask first and shoot later? For Christ's sake." She knelt down to examine the injured man.

"Sorry about that, but no. From where I'm standing, it looks like a mob scene. They're shouting; you're surrounded; you're bleeding. The way I see it, you are in mortal danger. That's your classic shoot-first scenario."

She tore up some leftover sheets to stanch the flow of blood from the old man's knee.

"What are you doing here?" Gabe challenged.

"That's my business. Why are you here? That's also my business."

"I'll explain later. Most important thing now is putting you in touch with your dad."

"Okay, I'll give him a buzz after I fix this guy up."

"Sorry, Doctor. It can't wait."

"It'll have to."

Gabe put his hand under her elbow. "I've got a Sabre on the roof. One of the boys will escort you up and Pete will fly you to the center."

"Get your hands off me. I'm not going anywhere till I get this man some help."

"I'll shoot him again. I don't want to, but I will if you don't come with me now."

Margaret glared at him. "What's so important?"

Gabe smiled enigmatically, cleared his throat and bent down to whisper in her ear. "What I have to tell you isn't the sort of thing you'd want to share with the world. At least, I don't think it is."

"Go ahead then," she said, feeling his breath on her neck as he began to tell the tale. She felt faint and her knees buckled, but Gabe caught her around the waist. She righted herself and stood on her own.

"Somebody get her some water," Gabe ordered.

Heysoos came forward with his canteen. She shooed him away. "No, take me home," she said to Gabe.

# CHAPTER 35.

HEYSOOS AND HOMES began the search for their friend by questioning Big Beulah. According to her records, Chase had never been admitted to Lawd Hav' Mercy nor had an ambulance been dispatched to the Hughes Center in, well, Beulah couldn't recollect that far back.

The friends also enlisted the help of staff in searching the hospital for any trace of Chase from the janitors' closets to the intensive care unit. The other grinders agreed to keep an eye out for any sign of him during their runs. What they feared most was finding his body or maybe only a piece of it. So far, nobody had come up with anything.

When Fran didn't hear from Chase, she told them she had asked an old flame on the police force to do some

checking around. Chase hadn't been found dead nor had he been thrown in jail. There were no warrants out for his arrest and nobody had reported him missing.

Subsequently Heysoos and Homes searched Chase's apartment for a message of some kind or perhaps evidence of foul play. Finding nothing, they took a couple of beers out of the not-so-cooler, fed the pigeons before they left and wondered where to look next. They tried Capaldini, who was clueless, as was the nurse who had cared for their friend in the clinic.

Chase hadn't befriended his neighbors, except for two little kids who idolized him. The pair were teasing a hissing cockroach on the stoop of a moldering brownstone when the two grinders rounded the corner.

"Wanna see me eat him for a quarter?" asked the boy.

Heysoos and Homes shook their heads.

"It's real entertaining, worth lots more," the girl cajoled.

"I don't approve of children eating bugs. How about I give you a quarter for some information?" Homes proposed. "Me and my friend are looking for a guy who lives around here."

"A grinder," Heysoos added, "Long hair, funny nose, about this tall…"

"Chase," the kids chorused.

"Have you seen him today?"

"Nuhuh."

"Yesterday?"

They shook their heads.

"This week?"

They shook their heads again.

"Does this mean we don't get the quarter?" the girl asked.

Homes pulled a couple of coins from his fanny pack and gave one to each. Joyous, they clapped their hands and scampered off to put their prize to use.

"Were we ever like that?" Homes wondered aloud.

"Like…"

"Happy little kids?"

"I don't think orphans do happy," Heysoos said.

Homes shrugged and the two continued walking, questioning the fans as they poured into the old "UDWEIS STA." Homes looked up at the letters over the entrance of the arena and asked, as he always did, "What do you suppose it means?"

"Why do you keep asking?" Heysoos demanded.

"I got an inquiring mind."

"Good, we've got more inquiring to do if we're gonna find Chase."

They queried gang lords and consulted street people, urging them to keep their eyes open. They went back to the orphanage where the two of them and Chase had grown up together. The place had been taken over by fundies.

"Now what?" Homes asked.

"We keep looking."

"Where?"

Heysoos shrugged.

"We could try Old Man Mud Flap," Homes said. "He hears things."

"Might as well."

The friends pulled on their helmets and skated toward the produce stand on Water Street. Mud Flap, who had packed up and harnessed Houdini to the wagon, smiled broadly at the grinders. "I'm so glad I found you," he said.

"It's the other way around," Homes protested. "We found you."

Mud Flap ignored him. "I have seen curious events of a troubling nature."

"Yeah, like what?" Heysoos asked.

"Your friend…" Mud Flap began.

"Chase? You've seen him?"

"The grinder, yes," Mud Flap responded.

"Where, man?"

"When?" Homes added.

"A couple of days hence, Houdini and I were strolling down Lower Gravel Road where we were passed by three men in a golf cart. Two were wearing cassocks."

"Must have been fundies," Homes said.

"The third was wearing a blanket and had been hand-cuffed to the cart. His head was bandaged, but Houdini and I recognized him anyway."

"It was Chase," Heysoos guessed.

Mud Flap nodded.

"It doesn't make any sense," said Heysoos. "Chase

hates those fuckers. What would he be doing with brethren?"

"Maybe they're going to drink his blood," Homes said. "I've heard stories…"

"They are probably mythical, though we cannot dismiss the possibility," Mud Flap said. "We must mount an immediate rescue mission. We will take the cart and I will hide you both under a load of pole beans."

Heysoos shook his head. "I'm allergic to pole beans."

"And I'm allergic to carts," Homes added.

"It'll be faster if we skate. And first we've got to get word to Chase's girl."

"How we gonna do that? You got her phone number?" Homes snorted.

Heysoos glared at his buddy. "Shut up and let me think."

Mud Flap was about to offer a suggestion when Heysoos snapped his fingers. "I've got it," he said and set off for Irv Capaldini's with Homes on his tail.

# CHAPTER 36.

MARGARET STARED AT her father in disbelief. Should she cry? Laugh hysterically? Kill herself, kill him, poke out her eyes? Had she wanted to have sex with her father these hundred years? What was wrong with her? Why hadn't she seen the resemblance?

By contrast, Morgan was almost blasé. "I've had time to get used to the idea," he said. "Really, when you think about it logically, your attraction is perfectly understandable."

"You do realize that I was sleeping with him?"

"I wasn't sure. I appreciate the confirmation. And it's not a him. Take that into consideration, as I have, and it isn't really such a big deal," Morgan said, hoping to reassure her.

"It's incest, Dad. Don't you get it? I've been fucking my

own father. Does Electra ring a bell? Or did you forget everything you learned at Yale?"

"No, sweetheart, you diddled my vessel. It was a mix-up. It could have happened to anybody."

"Are you insane?"

"When Gabe first told me, I went a little crazy, too. But I've had more time to mull this over than you have. Technically you didn't do anything wrong. You need a little time to think all this over. That's all."

Morgan smiled at Margaret, held his arms open wide. "Now, come over here and give me a hug."

Margaret pulled back.

"You're my daughter and I love you more than anything in this world. It's over now so let's put this um, unfortunate development behind us. What do you say, sweetheart?"

Margaret's unshed tears blurred her father's features, but his declining health showed in his halting gait and stooped shoulders. She was still thinking about punching his face in when Morgan crumpled to the floor. A luxurious oriental carpet cushioned the blow.

"Oh, my God!" Margaret screamed.

Pella ran into the room, saw Morgan lying on the Persian Isfanhan and immediately rang Dr. Mahmoud.

Margaret knelt beside her father, then put her ear to his chest to confirm that his heart was still beating.

"I'm okay," he whispered. "A little weak."

Mahmoud, who had an office one floor down, arrived

moments later, a vintage medical bag in hand. Morgan protested, but Mahmoud crouched down to do his own check of Morgan's vital signs. He cluck-clucked as he poked and prodded.

"The muscles have begun to atrophy. Nothing can be done to slow the process, but I would recommend bed-rest," said Mahmoud, helping Morgan to stand.

Pella took his hand and drew him toward the leather sofa, while the doctors huddled. "It's imperative," said Mahmoud to Margaret, "that Morgan beg, borrow or buy a spare vessel and transfer without delay."

Margaret had already located the perfect replacement. It had belonged to an author of legal thrillers who had died under mysterious circumstances. It was a bit young at seventeen, but came from the same northern European gene pool. The coloring was a good match, as were the contours of its body and face. And she had consulted with Dr. English, who guaranteed that he could easily augment the resemblance.

"I know it's not ideal, Dad. But it is our only ethical option," Margaret said.

"No, no fucking way," Morgan growled. "I'm giving Gabe a little time to find my vessel. He's got new intelligence from one of his operatives."

Margaret's heart leapt, but she feigned no interest in this welcome news. Chase was still alive. She had to change her father's mind. "There is something you might want to consider before you make a final decision."

"And what might that be?"

"Chase's injury. We don't know the extent of the brain damage and we may not know for six months, maybe longer. He might develop severe headaches, vertigo, depression, insomnia, concentration problems, slurred speech…"

She looked at her father for a reaction.

"Go on," he said.

"Some patients become suicidal, some become violent, some suffer memory loss… The bottom line, the irony, if you decide to do this, is you may never be the same again."

Morgan smiled. "I am hardly the same now. My testicles are like blimps. They are so fucking huge, I need clown pants. In comparison, brain damage doesn't sound so bad."

Margaret gave him a sad little smile. "Dad, don't do this. You're sick and you're not thinking straight. Please, please, reconsider."

She headed for the door.

He called after her. "I'd rather wear a used condom than transfer into another man's vessel."

"Well, then you're being an ass," she said, slamming the door behind her.

By the time Margaret got back to her office, she was calm enough to call Gabe for the latest word on Chase's whereabouts. Although an undercover operative reported strange goings on at END HQ, the security chief denied receiving

new information. He nevertheless assured her that she would be the first to know the minute he had anything relevant.

# CHAPTER 37.

CANDLELIGHT DANCED ON the limestone walls of the monastic room where Chase had been held since he was snatched by the brethren. So much light from a single candle, he marveled, as he lay on his cot and watched the flickering shadows. There was little else to do.

He had tried to escape straight away by throwing his weight against the wooden door. As he expected, it was heavy and soundly bolted. His search for air vents, trap doors or secret panels was also futile. Escape was impossible without an accomplice. If nobody was hunting for him – not that they would think to look here – he might never get out at all. He might fucking rot here. He'd never see Elle again.

The slap of sandals on the path outside interrupted his morose ruminations. Then came a perfunctory knock, followed by the turning of a bolt. When the door creaked open, Brother John entered in a blaze of sunshine. Briefly blinded by the light, Chase squinted and shaded his aching eyes. Although he couldn't make out the face, he recognized the garb of a fundie brother and backed away.

"It's okay. I haven't come here to hurt you," Brother John said, placing a cassock, sandals and some skivvies on the cot.

Chase's eyes hadn't adjusted, but he recognized the voice. "You're the asshole who kidnapped me and locked me up in here."

"I know it must seem that way to you, but I did not kidnap you. My brothers and I removed you from harm in accordance with God's wishes. You have many enemies."

"Far as I know, I don't have any enemies other than you and your wacko pals. And if I am not mistaken, you are holding me against my will and that's not what I call friendly." He looked at the clothes. "What have you people got against pants?"

Brother John gritted his teeth. "Once you learn why we saved you, I believe you will not only come to respect us, but to understand that we are holding you for your own safety."

Chase groaned, pulled on the robe and started toward the door. He was surprised when the brother made no attempt to stop him and went outside. He was in what must

once have been a formal garden. A dry fountain, its basins clogged with leaves, twigs and seeds, stood at its center. And statuary angels with broken wings watched over small plots of vegetables.

Famished, Chase picked a handful of beans from one of the rows and stuffed them in his mouth. John promised to treat the grinder to a hearty breakfast as soon as he had been introduced to and spoken with their glorious leader. Chase assured John that he didn't give a shit.

"I believe you'll change your mind once you meet him," John said.

Chase grunted, but said nothing more as they walked along a tiled arcade leading to an elaborately carved oaken doorway. Beyond its threshold was a Gothic chapel, lighted by candles and the sun glinting through the broken panes of the stained glass windows.

"Once upon a time, this was a French monastery," John announced proudly. "It was overrun with squatters and jack fiends until the Reverend reclaimed the property."

"You mean he took it."

"In the name of God."

"In the name of bullshit."

Brother John scowled, pushed the imposing door open and ushered Chase inside. "Please, watch your language and keep your sacrilegious opinions to yourself while in the Reverend's presence."

Chase snorted, but was awed in spite of himself as he took in the vaulted ceiling and the carved stone columns.

Though he wanted to stop and stare, John hurried him past the wooden pews on either side of the central aisle. At the end, Reverend Hast knelt before a simple altar. They would wait till he finished his prayers, whispered John, guiding the grinder into a pew. Chase complained of feeling dizzy and lay down beside him, then closed his eyes and pretended to sleep.

The Reverend rose stiffly, adjusted his prayer shawl and acknowledged Brother John who apologized effusively for interrupting the Reverend at prayer. Hast waved him off as he walked toward the pew and looked down at Chase, an arm flung over his eyes to disguise his wakefulness

"So this is the abomination. It looks so real."

John nodded.

"Does it know from whence it came?"

"Not in a million years," John replied. "The poor sap."

"Perhaps we should reveal the truth," Hast said. "It should have a chance to repent, if that's possible considering that it has no soul."

Chase snored softly.

Hast removed his prayer shawl and handed it to John, then straightened his toupee. "How do I look?"

"Very distinguished," John said.

"I've promised to speak at the Righteous Youth's Awards Dinner. I must scurry."

"But I thought you wanted to speak with it."

"I fear it will have to wait," Hast said, waving over his shoulder.

John looked down at Chase, who appeared to be sleeping quietly, and covered him with Hast's shawl. The kid needs sleep, thought John, slipping out quietly. He would ask Brother Enoch to keep an eye on Chase while he tended to more pressing matters.

As soon as the door closed behind the brother, Chase got up and searched for another way out. Discounting the door, the stained glass casement high above the altar was the only exit. There was no easy way up and it would be a shame to shatter something so beautiful.

It would also be pointless to duck under the pew. The only result – an idiot's game of hide and seek that he was sure to lose. It was too late now anyway. Someone was at the door. Chase hurriedly draped the prayer shawl over his head and shoulders and knelt before the altar as Hast had done. A pair of silver candlesticks sat on either side of a crucifix, facing a bronze bowl of weak wine. Light crept up the across the stone floor as the door opened behind him.

He could hear the scuff of sandals as somebody, probably a brother, slowly approached the altar. Chase didn't dare look back at him, but then he spoke. "Reverend, I didn't realize you were still here."

It was Enoch.

"Brother John has assigned me to guard the abomination."

"Come and join me, brother," Chase said imitating to

the best of his ability, the Reverend's euphonious baritone. To the grinder's relief, Enoch approached, knelt beside him and bowed his head. Chase muttered under his breath for a few moments more, then rose to go.

"Nature calls," he intoned.

Enoch wasn't fooled this time. He looked up and Chase caught the recognition in Enoch's eyes. "Why I ought to kill—"

Chase grabbed a candlestick and clobbered him over the head.

"Sorry, man." Chase slipped out the door and looked for a way out or someplace promising to hide. The best option seemed to be a flight of stone stairs leading to a grassy terrace supported by a high retaining wall. When he reached the top, Chase ran to the edge of the wall and looked down. He could see the river and a ribbon of the old road that ran beside it far below.

He was about to go back the way he had come when Brother John burst into view and started yelling. "Don't do it. Stay where you are, Charles. You'll die from the fall. At the very least, you'll never skate again. Let me help you."

The rest of his words were drowned out by the thunderous "thup-thup-thup" of an oncoming helo's rotors. A Sabre, observed Chase, who took advantage of the diversion and ran to the far end of the terrace.

"There, right there on the edge," Gabe yelled at Lunt, the pilot. "Can you get any closer? I wanna see his face."

Lunt nodded and flew as close to the cliff as he dared.

"Gotta be the boss's dupe," Gabe said.

"A good guess," Lunt agreed.

Gabe pulled out a bullhorn, directed it toward Chase and shouted: "Charles Lyman, are you Charles Lyman?"

Nobody ever called him Charles, so Chase didn't realize the guy was yelling at him. He looked up, but didn't know Gabe. He did recognize the Hughes logo printed on the chopper's side.

Gabe tried again. "Hey kid!" he shouted. "Are… you… Charles… Lyman?"

Chase heard him this time, only he wasn't sure whether or not to answer.

"You must have the wrong guy," Lunt said.

"Don't think so. Maybe it's the wrong question." Gabe put the bullhorn back to his mouth and shouted, "You want to get out of here?"

"Affirmative," Chase hollered, vigorously nodding.

"Hold on. We're coming down."

"Oh, no you're not!" Brother John pulled his revolver from his cassock, took aim at the Sabre's rudder, shot, missed and shot again.

"What the fuck!" Gabe swore.

"I think the brother is firing on us," Lunt said.

"Motherfucking hypocrite." Gabe drew a semi-automatic with his initials carved into the handle and aimed

at Brother John's shaved head. The Sabre bucked and the bullet hit a tree instead.

Brother John rolled behind a statue of the Pieta and returned fire. Once again he tried to bring down the aircraft, only this time, he aimed for the windshield in hopes of hitting the pilot. Gabe got off a shot. It missed the monk, exploding the Madonna's head.

While they exchanged rounds, Chase jogged for the stairs leading back to the chapel. His head began to pound.

"Dupe's on the run," Lunt shouted.

"Go after him," Gabe yelled.

"Will do."

On the ground, Brother John ran toward the stairs, turned toward the Sabre and fired again. This time he hit the fuel tank. Gabe, furious now, pulled the trigger and Brother John lurched backward and grabbed his bleeding bicep. Before Gabe could get off another round, Brother John made it up the stairs and vanished from view.

Even though he could no longer see Chase, Gabe got back on the bullhorn: "Charles, we aren't going to hurt you. We're friends."

*Wow. He'd never been so popular.* Chase knew bullshit when it was shoveled. He could practically smell it when it was this deep. Friends? His friends didn't fly Sabres, his friends didn't own guns. *Thanks, but no thanks.* For now, he'd take his chances with the devil he knew. When he looked back though, Brother John was no longer right on his tail.

Chase trotted from chapel to chapter house, from Romanesque architecture to Gothic. John was still nowhere to be seen. Unfortunately several armed brethren were perusing the grounds dead ahead. Chase ducked into the nearest doorway and gasped for breath. The brethren stopped outside. Chase tiptoed away from the door and down a long corridor and began to clamber up the steep and narrow stairway at its end.

He stopped to catch his breath. When he heard the door open, he resumed his climb. By the time he reached the fourth flight, Chase could hear footfalls behind him and he heard a man calling his name. It was Brother John. He was almost on top of him.

"I'm here to help you," John called out. "I'm a friend."

"Bullshit," yelled Chase upon reaching the head of the stairs. He spied a ladder leading to what he imagined must be an attic.

"If you knew the truth." The cleric gulped for air. "If you knew who you really are."

"I'm not listening," yelled Chase, continuing to climb.

Chase stepped on the bottom rung of the ladder, found it was sturdy and moments later stood in a small square room with a huge bell in the center.

What was this place? Chase thought to pull up the ladder just as John reached the landing below.

"You're in the belfry, Charles. There's no way out," John called.

The belfry was less a room than a platform for the bell-

ringer. Four vertical windows, glassless, not only let in light, for which Chase was thankful, but let out the clanging of the bell. Three openings overlooked the grounds seven stories below; but a fourth offered a view of a rooftop covered in Spanish tiles. Chase spied the rope that hung from the bell's yoke. He doubted it was strong enough to hold his weight if he were to rappel from the tower to the roof – unlikely given his current condition. Even if he made it safely, he'd have to figure out how to escape from there.

"Charles, please come down before you hurt yourself?" John begged.

"Shut up or I will fucking jump," Chase shouted.

Staring out the west window, he could see the Sabre still circling the compound. Chase had nothing to lose. He would help the helo find him. That bell had to be one hell of a noisemaker. He took a deep breath, reached for the rope and pulled as hard as he could. The bell swung, though not enough to waken the clapper. Chase tugged twice more. On the third attempt, the bell finally tolled.

He crawled onto the window ledge, willing the crew of the Sabre to hear the bell over the chop of the blades against the sky. But to Chase's dismay, the Sabre was moving away from the tower. He ripped the hood from his cassock and waved it at the departing aircraft. He hollered at the top of his lungs and still it continued toward the river.

"Did you hear that?" Gabe asked Lunt.

"The church bells?"

"No, the ringing in my ears."

"I love church bells. When I was a boy, they rang every hour on the hour."

"Then how come it's nineteen minutes after four?"

Gabe's juju was talking to him. His teeth were itching, a sure sign he had better follow his intuition.

"Turn around. I want to take one more look."

"We're gonna splash soon if I don't juice up this bird," Lunt warned.

"I said turn the fuck around."

"Roger that." Lunt turned back to the compound.

Gabe spotted a cluster of brethren staring up at the bell tower. "Over there," he hollered. Lunt flew toward the crowd. Gabe followed the brethren's eyes. Chase screamed and waved from the window ledge.

"In the window," he yelled.

"Yeah, I see him."

"Get as close as possible."

Lunt maneuvering into a position opposite the window.

Chase stood on the ledge.

"Don't jump," Gabe screamed.

Chase cupped his hand behind his ear. The chop of the helo rattled the bell clapper. Gabe grabbed a rope and mimed throwing it to Chase.

Chase leaned out precariously, but the rope swept past him and slapped against the tower wall.

"That's not gonna work," Gabe yelled.

"Hang on, I've got an idea." Lunt swung away from the tower and climbed into a hover directly above the tower window.

Chase, craning his neck to follow the helo, was unaware of another danger. Like Rasputin from the frigid Neva River, Brother John was emerging from the floor below the belfry. Relentless and bloody, he crept toward Chase and seized his robe seconds before a rope ladder slammed into the window. John yanked Chase backward. The grinder lost his balance and fell on top of John.

Chase had knocked the wind out of John, but not the fight. The brother tired to rise to the occasion one more time.

"I don't think so," Chase said not unkindly and punched him in the face. It felt good, but there was no time for a respite. Chase regained the window ledge and looked up at Gabe.

"Come on," Gabe shouted. "We're running out of fuel."

Chase hesitated, looked behind him and saw another brother climbing into the belfry. The brother was almost on top of him when to his amazement, Chase stepped out the window.

Chase, his arms wrapped around one rung and his feet on another, felt the rope snap taut as the ladder rebounded.

The orange tile roof of the chapel fell away as the helo rose and turned toward the river. So this was flying. Chase had never ridden in an aircraft before, much less dangled from one like a giant tea bag. Swinging to and fro. It was fucking scary. And that was before the Sabre dropped over the bluff and started skimming along the road. They were so low now, Chase could almost touch the roadbed.

"Pull up, pull up," he screamed.

"Relax," Gabe shouted.

Chase shook his head.

Gabe brandished a Bowie knife. "Drop and roll when I cut the rope," he yelled.

"Are you crazy!" Chase shouted.

"Ready?" Gabe took a whack at rope.

"No!"

"Good," Gabe yelled as the strands gave way. "I'll be back for you."

Chase released the ruined ladder, doubled into a ball and landed on his side. He checked himself for injuries. Nothing new was broken, although he had welts in new places and rope burns on his hands. He could hear, but no longer see the Sabre, and that was fine by him.

River Road, or the Old Road, had been a beautiful parkway, rebuilt weeks before Adolf broke through the Bridgewater Dikes. Now covered with decades of silt and

sewage, it was crowded by a forest of junk trees and riotous with prickle grape and poison ivy vines.

Lunt was an experienced helo jockey, but he nixed landing on the mucky ground. Gabe responded with a fusillade of motherfuckety-fucks, spat rat-a-tat-tat from his pie hole.

Lunt was used to Gabe's mouth and waited till the other man finished his tirade before making his suggestion: "We should go back and pick up a few men. We're running low on fuel anyway."

"No time for that," Gabe snapped. "Turn back and drop me off. We can't see anything from up here anyhow. I'll hail if I need back-up."

Lunt promised to return at warp speed.

# CHAPTER 38.

THE SABRE PASSED directly over him, but Chase doubted he could be seen through the cloud of mosquitoes for which he had become an all-you-can-suck buffet. His head wound was throbbing like the object of a romance heroine's desire. He was also hot, hungry and needed a beer followed by a bucket of water. He figured he couldn't get any more miserable. That was before he reached the tidal marsh where every step was a struggle between man and the incredible sucking sludge.

Redwing blackbirds scolded from thickets of reeds and crows from the skeletons of trees that had died in the salty water. Chase caught and ate handfuls of the small crabs that skittered around him. They were tinged green and soft-

shelled and if cooked properly might be delicious. Straight from the bog, though, they tasted of mud. He had eaten worse and they helped with his thirst. Still, he dreamed of a cold one and of sharing it with Elle.

He hadn't heard the Sabre in a while. That didn't mean his alleged friends wouldn't come back for him. He sure wasn't hanging around to find out. He didn't trust those guys even though there was a chance Elle had sent them. Since when did medics come to the rescue bearing arms. Cops, yeah.

Chase had had minor scrapes, but he had never been in big trouble with the law. But with a cracked skull, he reminded himself, he might have forgotten whatever it was he had or hadn't done and to whom. Better to stay on his own, he decided, slogging toward a line of trees edging the Old Road. He would follow it into Scrabber Town, where he could hideout till he learned why he was suddenly so in-demand.

After hiking several more miles, he felt he had put sufficient distance between himself and whoever might come after him and began to look for someplace to rest. He left the road, found a shady spot and stretched out on a log beneath. It was as comfortable as any bed he had ever known and he slept like a stone.

Gabe followed Chase's footprints into the marsh. Standing at the edge of the quagmire, the unhappy, middle-aged

security chief questioned his career choice. He had been infatuated with the by-gone glamour of gumshoe-noir: rain-slick streets, spluttering neon nights, lazy ceiling fans. He could see himself in a fedora and a trench coat. Of course, it was too fucking hot for a trench coat even if he could find one.

"I should have gone into waste removal," he muttered, bending down to take off his tasseled loafers followed by his shirt and trousers. He then placed his gun in the trousers and wound them around his head like a turban. This he secured with a favorite leather belt.

Naked except for his skivvies, Gabe picked up his shoes and socks, intent on holding them above the mud and carefully tested the muck with his toe. It seemed firm enough so he took a step and then another and several more. So far so good, he thought, unaware that with the very next step, he would be up to his nipples in glop.

Gabe thanked God that he was tall as well as dark-haired and handsome. He liked to think positively. Then he cursed the fates, the motherfucking dupe and Margaret Hughes whom he suspected of arranging Charles's escape.

"Worse than a man, always thinking with her dick."

When he stopped spluttering and calmed down, he spotted a stand of trampled cattails. Good. The dupe had passed this way. Gabe tried to follow the trail, but he was no match for the sucking mud.

"I could die here. And I still have so much to give," he wailed.

Reluctantly he put down his shoes and began searching for roots, reeds, anything he could use to pull himself gradually closer to the cattails. By the time he reached them, he knew he couldn't go any further. He would wait for Lunt's return in the skimpy shade provided by the grasses.

To protect himself from sun burn and mosquitoes, he rubbed mud on his face and shoulders. He tried to relax. But his leg muscles quivered from the exertion, his mouth felt dry and his underwear was wedged in his butt crack. There was nothing worse, Gabe decided right before the charley horse, a wild stallion of a muscle spasm, bit into his right calf.

Gabe howled at the pain, startling a vulture, which croaked in disgust as it launched itself from a dirty globe atop a rusted light pole. Gabe, startled in turn, tensed up. His muscle clenched again and this time he shoved his fist in his mouth to keep from crying out and alerting his quarry. *As soon as I close this case, I'm going to get back into shape.*

He wiggled his toes, stretched as best he could. Try to relax, he told himself. Quiet the mind, deep breaths, benumbing mantra… ummhhhmmm… ahhhhmmm… ohmm… Fuck it. What he needed was a massage. But to reach the cramp site, he would have to stick his head in the mud and keep it there while he kneaded the stricken muscle. At best, he'd wind up with mud-stuffed orifices. At worst, he'd smother. Then again, he might drown. The tide was waxing and the marsh was filling with water. A family

of northern snakeheads swam by. Gabe hated mother-fucking snakeheads. They were air-breathing fish with feet. Where the fuck was that motherfucker Lunt?

At least the cramp had eased. Perhaps if he wrapped his arms around the clump of cattails, he would gain enough leverage to pull himself forward. It was a long shot, but long shots were a dick's stock-in-trade. It also beat drowning. Having pinpointed his motivation, Gabe launched himself upward to reach the reeds. This time the calf muscle bunched itself into the knot of all knots and Gabe shrieked like a preteen at a pajama party.

The scream jolted Chase from his log nap. Probably Fran. He automatically felt around the ground for his blades. Only there were no aero-Dynes and this wasn't his rack. Oh, and Fran didn't scream like a freak, and now his body ached as much as his head. Damn. He was sorry to realize he wasn't having a nightmare. At least, he didn't think he was.

Chase stood, stretched and saw the light was fading. In another hour, he could leave the cover of the trees without fear of being spotted from above. Meanwhile, he decided to stick to the tree line. Perhaps he'd score some wolfberries, provided the birds hadn't finished them off. It was late in the season after all.

"EEEIIIAAIEE!!"

The blood-curdling screech drove any further musings

from his mind. It had come from the marsh and sounded like a vixen's scream… or was it more like a terrified child? Damn. Chase turned back to investigate, cautiously picking his way along the matted grass at the edge of the muck. He'd lost weight, but felt the stuff give a little with every step. Not that it mattered. If some kid was in danger, he had to keep going.

He had crept more than half way around the marsh when he begin to doubt himself. What would a kid be doing out here anyway? Why didn't he hear a third scream and a fourth? For all he knew he had been hallucinating. He squeezed his eyes shut, opened them again. Nothing had changed.

The last, pale pink streaks faded from the sky and he could no longer distinguish reeds from water. Camouflaged by his covering of mud, Gabe clung unseen to the reeds only a rowboat's length away. He tried to scream, but he had lost his voice. He held on with one arm and waved with the other. Chase peered into the distance, shrugged and turned toward the sparse woods.

Gabe opened his mouth and forced out a croak.

Chase stopped, listened.

"Elp!" Gabe rasped.

"Anybody there?"

"Ur left."

Chase squinted. Gabe waved. Chase located him and waved back.

"Yo," Chase yelled. "Need some help?"

Despite his dire straits, it was all Gabe could do to stifle a snippy retort. Better not to cut off his nose while he still needed it. A simple yes would do.

"I'm stuck."

"Got it," Chase called. "Hang in there. I'll be right back."

"Urry," he said hoarsely. "Tide's coming in."

Chase headed into the trees and searched for a branch long enough to reach the screamer and light enough to drag without much difficulty. He settled on an ailanthus sapling, which was thin and slippery, but with a little effort, he readily wrested it from the humus. He wrinkled his nose at the odor of cat piss released by the bruised ailanthus leaves and retraced his steps as quickly as the fragile soil would allow.

By the time he returned with the stinky sapling, the water was already lapping Gabe's chin. The last vestiges of the security chief's dignity had been washed away and he was bathing in the warmth of his own pee. "Hurry, please. Oh, please," Gabe wheezed.

Buoyed by adrenalin and acting on instinct, Chase had given no thought to the identity of the screamer. While considering the mechanics of the rescue attempt, however, his cerebral cortex was roused by the input and promptly initiated contact with the would-be rescuer: *Brain to Chase. Brain to Chase. Do you read?*

Chase cocked his head to the side, then looked behind and above him.

"What are you waiting for?" Gabe croaked. "Throw me the branch."

Chase nodded and inched closer to the marsh's edge.

*Hold up.*

"Huh?"

*Who the hell is this guy? And why is he here? Is he like on a nature walk? I don't think so.*

"Good point," Chase whispered.

"What's the hold up?" Gabe demanded.

"I have a few questions," Chase said aloud.

"There's no time. I'm drowning!"

Chase pretended to be leaving.

"Okay, what do you wanna know?"

"What are you doing here?"

"Fishing. I'm a fucking fisherman," Gabe growled.

*Recognize that voice?*

"Huh?" Chase asked his cortex.

*It's the guy from the helo.*

"Yeah, you're right."

Chase returned to Gabe. "You were in the helo. Don't lie to me or I'll let you drown. Who are you?"

"Name's Gabe."

"Why are you following me?"

"Supposed to bring you back to the clinic."

"Who sent you?"

"Hughes."

"What does Hughes want with me?"

"Get me out of here and I'll explain." Gabe swallowed a mouthful of the rising water, gasped. "No more time."

"Damn it," growled Chase, who had never been prepared to let the man drown. He might be a lapsed bead-counter, but the sisters had insisted on daily Catholistenics. As a youth, he sat, signed, stood, knelt and choked his beads until resistance was futile. Thence he was inculcated with an absolute sense of right and wrong as well as the guilt to ensure his adherence to the church's teachings.

Chase leaned over the water and with a loud grunt, cast the ailanthus within Gabe's reach, while still holding on to the rooted end. Gabe grabbed the sapling with both muddy hands. Chase tried to drag him to shore, lost his footing and fell backwards. As he righted himself, he saw that Gabe's shoulders were now above the water.

"One more time," he shouted.

Gabe grunted an assent and renewed his grip on the sapling. Chase redoubled his efforts. Nothing happened at first, but Gabe gradually wriggled free of the muck. Chase's muscles were quivering by the time he hauled the gasping Gabe ashore. Exhausted, both men fell back onto the matted grass. Gabe never thanked him. Chase didn't notice.


As soon as he was able, Gabe sat up and began to squeegee the muck from his chest and legs. He washed his hands and face in the brackish swamp water and was about to pull off

his muck-filled underwear when he noticed Chase watching him.

"Would you mind?" he asked.

"Not at all." Chase was more than glad to turn his back while the dude stripped.

Gabe removed his briefs and examined them. *Ugh.* He tossed them aside, then unbuckled the belt that had held the bundled clothing atop his head. He removed and inspected his gun. Relieved to see it wasn't wet, he then pulled on his trousers and slipped his gun under his waistband.

"What's taking so long?" Chase asked.

"Bout done." Gabe put on the shirt, but left it unbuttoned. "Okay, I'm decent."

When Chase turned around, he almost laughed. Gabe was way over-dressed for the swamp. Then he glimpsed the handle of the gun peeking above Gabe's trousers.

"What's with the piece?" he asked.

"I feel naked without it."

"So were you gonna kill me if I didn't come willingly?"

"Nobody's killing anybody," Gabe said. "I'm under orders to bring you back alive. You're no good to us dead. You must know that."

"Right, okay then." Chase stood up and eased away from Gabe. "In that case, I guess I'll be going."

"I didn't say I wouldn't shoot you in the kneecaps." Gabe pulled the gun from his waistband. "Sit back down,

will you? I don't want any trouble. And I'm betting you don't want any more either."

"I should have let you drown," said Chase as he eased back to the ground.

Gabe agreed. "Looking at you now, I don't know where you got the energy to drag me out of there. Kudos."

"Fuck you."

Now that the dupe's face wasn't as swollen, Gabe thought maybe he could see some resemblance to the boss man.

"What are you looking at?" Chase asked.

Gabe chuckled. "You really haven't figured it out, have you? A smart kid like you."

"If I was smart, would I be here?"

"Good point," Gabe agreed.

"What haven't I figured out?"

Gabe knew he should shut his yap, but he did owe the dupe a little something, a clue maybe. "Have you ever been inside the center?" he asked.

"Yeah, just about every day."

"I'm talking about the main building."

Chase thought about it and shook his head.

"You're sure?" Gabe asked.

"I'm not sure about a damned thing. I could be hallucinating and you could be a figment. Or possibly a frog."

"I'm no motherfucking figment."

"Sorry," Chase said. "It's the hole in my head talking. Go ahead."

Gabe cleared his throat and spat out a gobbet of mud. "Okay, here it is one more time. Have you ever stuck so much as a toe inside the HRC?"

"Yeah, the clinic."

Gabe shook his head.

"The organ depot."

Gabe shook his head again.

"Well, I've kind of been inside. Not far though. Security stopped me in the corridor."

"How did you get in?"

"I don't know."

"What did ya do, yell abra-fucking-cadabra?"

Chase looked bewildered.

"For fuck's sake. There's only one way inside. You have to get past the IBID."

"No, a nurse... I followed a nurse inside," Chase insisted.

"Think, kid. How do those fucking IBIDs work?"

Chase shrugged.

"DNA fingerprinting," Gabe said.

"So?"

Gabe shook his head wearily.

Chase pondered the new information, but came to no conclusions. He was out of practice when it came to logic – all his recent decisions had been instinctual – and his rusty synapses protested the sudden intrusion. His thoughts

skittered away even as he was about to catch them and he was so tired of trying. He probably shouldn't sleep. He was aware of that, but was soon dreaming of Elle, her silky skin, her lips, the way her hips swayed... as the security door closed behind her.

*The door closed behind her. Repeat after me. The door closed behind her.*

Chase opened his eyes. He remembered now. He had brushed the IBID on his way in and had been granted access to the center's most secure building. His genetic code must closely match another staffer's. Or maybe he had a twin brother. The notion filled him with joy. That had to be it. Didn't it?

On the other hand, that was no plausible reason for all the fuss. They sent Gabe to rescue him from Hast because they discovered he had a twin brother? Had they planned a surprise reunion and become afraid he'd couldn't make it? That sure didn't explain the fundies' involvement. This is nuts. *I'm nuts.*

Gabe was slumped over and snoring softly. *Time to make a run for it.*

Chase had barely begun to inch away when Gabe sat up and ordered him to stay put.

"Or what?"

"Remember the bit about the kneecaps?"

Chase nodded.

"Sit."

Chase sat.

Gabe looked up. "Where in motherfucking hell is Lunt?"

He tried to raise the pilot via his pinkie phone to no avail. The transmitter must have shorted out when his ear canal filled with swamp water.

# CHAPTER 39.

MORGAN'S NO LONGER handsome face was splotchy and drawn, his tongue was raw and his balls were so inflated that he had to lie on his back with his legs propped on a tower of pillows. Obliged to assume temporary control of the company, Margaret kept her dad involved in decision making as long as she could. But the more painkillers he took, the more agitated and delusional he became. He had begun to suspect his daughter of wanting total control of the family business and had ordered Stepper Goodwin to sue her "doubling-crossing ass."

Stepper pretended to file the papers and Margaret stayed away from her father unless he was sleeping. Given the demands of her new position, she had little time to

spare anyway. Pella, to whom Margaret would be forever grateful, seemed never to leave his side. She read to Morgan, fed him mashed potatoes and fabricated upbeat progress reports on Gabe's quest to retrieve his vessel.

Pella might have changed his diapers, too. Margaret preferred not to know. As long as it wasn't her wiping her father's junk, she was a happy camper. That didn't mean she spent any the less time agonizing over Morgan's rapid deterioration or his irrational demand that he take over Chase's body. Stubborn prick.

She knew it was pointless to try to change his mind now. He would probably accuse her of betraying him for her lover. But once he got used to his healthy new body, surely he would forgive her. It didn't matter anymore. She was determined to do what she believed was the right thing. And soon. Robert Mahmoud had given Morgan no more than two – three days tops – to live in his pox-riddled body.

Margaret agreed with Mahmoud and ordered her staff to prep the vessel she had selected as an ideal genetic match for Morgan. Unlike Chase, the vessel was without scars, scrapes or potentially serious mental defects. She had pointed all this out to Mahmoud, who nevertheless rejected her "moral quibbles."

"My patient's wellbeing comes before everything else," he spat. "You're a doctor. You ought to know that."

"And everybody else can go fuck themselves. Is that right, Bobby?"

Margaret stormed back to her office, poured herself a koffey and took a cigarette from a yellowed ivory case and lit up. If the smoke alarms went off, so fucking be it. She leaned back in her worn leather chair, took a drag and exhaled some of her rage along with the smoke. Bobby Mahmoud's worthless, fucking opinion was irrelevant as long as Chase evaded Gabe's dragnet.

The security chief claimed to have eyeballs all over the archipelago. A man with a bandaged head and banged up face ought to attract attention. Yet Chase had not only eluded Gabe's finest but his closest friends. She felt certain Heysoos would have contacted her otherwise.

Maybe he escaped… maybe he was dead… maybe she should get a grip. She sat up, put her cup aside and checked her schedule. Aside from calls to place and records to review, she had nothing for a couple of hours. She fished a peppermint candy from a jar her assistant had given her. It was probably meant to remind her that Christmas was around the corner.

"Leslie," she yelled.

"What boss?" came the response from the outer office.

"If anybody needs me, I'm going shopping."

Margaret changed into jeans and a sweatshirt, then threw a pair of baggy scrubs over the ensemble. She took a wad of cash from the safe and stuffed it in her backpack along with her rollerblades and an HRC baseball cap.

In the elevator, she gathered her hair into a ponytail and pulled the bill of the cap over her eyes. Upon reaching

the basement, she stopped briefly to pull off her scrubs and put on her blades. She caught a glimpse of herself in a window – Yeah, she could pass for a grinder – and pushed off.

Rolling incognito, she felt stronger than she had since this debacle began. Although as she cruised toward the 177th Street exit, she had the oddest feeling someone was spying on her.

# CHAPTER 40.

THE HEATHENS HAD snatched the vessel and killed Brother John. Now everything depended on Nanny. When the Reverend suggested they replace Chase with the dying mogul's daughter, the devoted disciple accepted the assignment. She didn't know how she would deliver the doctor to the Reverend, but the Lord would show her the way. Praise His name.

She was beseeching Him as she cut across the Hughes' precious lawn on her way to Margaret Hughes' office. Her prayer was interrupted when a wary groundskeeper shooed her back onto the roadway. "God forbid, the grass should bend," she hissed, stepping off the curve and into the path of a golf cart, whose driver cursed as he sped around her.

"Tsk. Tsk." Nanny chided, then was nearly mown over again. This time by a shapely young woman – probably a grinder.

"Wow." She sure wished she had a body like that. She did once. And the long red hair. Well, it was never red, but... "Lord Jesus on toast," she whispered. "That's Dr. Hughes. Oh, dear. Oh, dear. What on earth is that filly up to?"

The nurse quickly dismissed the idea of calling out to Margaret. What the heck would she say if she did get the doctor's attention? She would follow her instead. First, she needed a pair of wheels. One of the orderlies always parked a scooter outside the clinic. Alas, scooting required both stamina and balance. But Nanny suffered from exercise-induced asthma as well as inner ear problems. For her, standing on a curb was precarious.

The Lord Jesus would not have chosen her if He had lacked faith in her steadfastness. She prayed for guidance, pointing out that said guidance was needed pronto. And glory be, before she got to amen, a vision of a wheelchair popped into her head. A deus ex machina indeed.

Without hesitation, she ran back into the clinic, commandeered the first vacant chair she could find and pushed it toward the 177th Street exit. She stopped at the overgrown passageway, peeked around the stone column and spotted Dr. Hughes gliding north and west before she vanished over the hill. Nanny wheeled herself to the spot

and looked down at the twisted, rock-strewn ribbon of road. No shoulders, no railings, no curbs.

"Sweet baby cheeses!" Nanny exclaimed. "If the devil had a driveway…"

Her legs quivered and her heart galloped. She took a deep breath and crossed herself several times. "Lord, give me strength," she prayed and pushed off.

Although she went from zero to what she guesstimated was ninety mph in seconds, the old nurse safely negotiated a slight curve by leaning into it as she had seen grinders do. But as she came out of the turn, the wheelchair hurtled forward. If the thing had wings, it would have lifted off. At least, it felt that way to Nanny whose cotton skirt was billowing like a mainsail. She fumbled for the hand brake, found it and squeezed,

The chair slowed, but she smelled burnt rubber and saw smoke rising from the tires. Uh-oh. For fear they'd blow, she released the brake and the chair barreled toward a sharp turn. Her cap flew off and her gray hair spilled free as she veered around the corner on two wheels before toppling over the edge.

Nanny landed hard, but a nest of kudzu cushioned her fall. Nothing was broken, but everything hurt. She shook off the grogginess and moaning piteously, picked herself up and righted the wheelchair. What she saw lifted her spirits as surely as a Sunday sermon: A road that seemed almost level by comparison to the one she just escaped. While the route was not as direct as the one the doctor chose, Nanny

reminded herself that the race is not to the swiftest, and off she spun.

Landing Road had tested Margaret's skills on wheels, which she had wildly overestimated. She was a good skater, damn it. It only felt like she had traveled further on her buttocks than on her blades. As she picked herself up one more time, she vowed to stay upright all the way to Scrabber Town. Fortunately she didn't have far to go and the road surface was smoother the closer she got to the bayside neighborhood.

Most of the city's salvaging operations were headquartered on Landing Road, which bisected a thin slice of land wedged between the wharves on one side and the marketplace on the other. The ragtag community, with its roomy tents, campfires and goat-drawn carts, resembled a Gypsy encampment. Residents who didn't live on shore, dwelled in the brightly colored boats and barges nudged against the battered wharves.

Able scrabbers embarked on daily or sometimes longer missions to reclaim sunken treasures: china, gold, silver, coins, gemstones, mirrors, medicines, booze, eyeglasses, bathtubs, cook pots and so forth. Seniors roamed the shoreline in search of tampon holders, Styrofoam peanuts, bottles, bags and condoms. The bottles and cans went to the dairymen and the brewers. The rest they crafted into potholders, picture frames and children's toys.

Margaret liked to support the craftsmen, but her assistant had broadly hinted that she wanted a pair of flip-flops from Santa. She stopped at a vendor whose shelves were usually stacked high with casual footwear, much of it made of rubber or plastic. Today all that remained was a pile of mismatched Crocs and one pair of black vinyl galoshes.

The vendor was able-bodied. Most were missing at least one limb and had given up scrabbing because they could no longer dive, dig or man a winch. Hooks, peg legs and eye patches were as prevalent today as in the age of discovery. Maybe this man's brains were addled. He offered to sell her two pink Crocs – both for the right foot. She declined and pressed through the crowds. Maybe she'd find something for Pella. Jewelry perhaps.

Scrabber Town was a popular destination year round, but at Christmastime when strings of lights, wreaths and displays of plastic trees decked the stalls, the marketplace swarmed with shoppers. Rent-a-cops, disguised as elves and gingerbread men, watched for shoplifters and pickpockets and sometimes intervened in fights between customers over mutually coveted items. Bruno had once had a sparring match over a quartet of chrome-plated hubcaps.

She couldn't forget Bruno. Something, anything for the car would do. She remembered an auto parts dealer north of the market and turned toward the wharves, picking up her pace as the crowds thinned and fewer pedes-trians stepped into her path. She hadn't counted on the little

girl who was caught up in a game with her playmates and scampered into her path.

Nanny's hands were numb and her biceps were spent by the time she intersected Landing Road. She would need help if she was going to catch up with Dr. Hughes and soon found an enterprising urchin willing to push her for a price. She pulled several warm bills from her bra and they proceeded to the marketplace.

"Give it all you've got, little man," she instructed.

The boy quickened his pace.

"I'm late for a date with my granddaughter. I don't want to miss her."

With every block, the street became more congested and the boy was forced to slow down. Nanny became increasingly antsy as they trudged toward the periphery of the marketplace. The boy suggested they would make better time if they headed for the wharves. He slipped through a small opening in the crowd and Nanny spotted a red ponytail.

"Oh, my God! Faster, faster. That's her," Nanny yelled.

The boy raced toward Margaret. He didn't see the little girl run into her path and was at ramming speed when Margaret stopped dead, lost her balance and fell into the wheelchair. Nanny gasped. The little girl began to bawl. The terrified boy ran away.

"What in the-?" Margaret shouted.

"It's okay, Doctor. I've got you," Nanny reassured her startled passenger.

"Nanny?" Margaret swiveled around to make sure she was truly sitting on the nurse's lap.

"In the flesh."

When the wheelchair rolled to a stop, Margaret slid off the nurse's lap and took a moment to get her bearings. An abandoned seafood shack, its weathered shutters aslant, marked the end of Scrabber Town and any semblance of road maintenance.

"Welcome to the boonies," Margaret muttered, reaching down to retract the wheels on her skates.

"Fancy meeting you here, Dr. Hughes."

Margaret, who was still trying to absorb the uncanny coincidence, nodded blankly.

"Well, I best be going." Nanny gave herself a little push, which brought the doctor back to the moment.

"What's with the wheelchair?" she asked.

"My arthritis is acting up."

"Part of getting old," Margaret said.

Nanny sighed.

"I'll give you a push." Margaret stepped behind the chair and turned it back toward Scrabber Town.

"Thank you, Dr. Hughes, but I'm not going back to town."

"Where are you going?"

"To see a patient."

"I didn't know nurses made house calls."

"This is a special case."

Nanny attempted to rotate the wheelchair on her own.

"Let me do that." Margaret did an about face toward a stand of scraggly locusts, populated by a flock of roosting grackle. A couple in a nearby clearing, nestled beside a campfire and roasted eel on a spit. Otherwise the area appeared uninhabited and with daylight fading, the woods augured menace.

"Are you sure you're headed in the right direction?" Margaret asked.

"Absolutely, positively without a doubt," Nanny assured her.

"Exactly where is this patient of yours?"

"Not far."

Nanny gripped the wheels and with a mighty grunt, trundled ahead a few inches.

"The road gets a lot steeper. You're not going to make it in that chair," Margaret warned.

Nanny rolled forward.

"Have it your way," said Margaret, turning back toward Scrabber Town.

"You might remember him," Nanny blurted. "You came to visit him at the clinic."

Margaret stopped.

"Charles, the grinder with the head injury," Nanny added.

Margaret didn't move.

"He's under the protection of the church now. Reverend Hast has asked me to have a look at him as a precaution."

With studied nonchalance, Margaret closed the gap between them. "Why don't I have a look at him instead? I'll call Bruno. He'll take you home."

"I wouldn't think of neglecting my duties, Doctor."

"I insist." Margaret walked a few yards up the road.

"You'll won't get past security," Nanny called after her.

"I'll manage," Margaret said saucily.

Nanny snorted. "Oh, no you won't. Brethren shoot first and ask for an ID second. But the guards are expecting me. I'll say you're my assistant."

Margaret looked at her dubiously. "You're willing to do this for what reason?"

Nanny lowered her head and when she looked up again, her eyes were glistening. "My patient's welfare means everything to me."

Maybe Nanny was lying. Maybe fate had intervened. Either way Margaret had a chance to rescue Chase and to save Morgan from himself.

"Well, then we best get moving." She stepped behind the chair, ignored Nanny's perfunctory protest and headed for the Reverend Hast's hilltop headquarters.

The road grew narrower the higher they climbed. Nanny was heavier than Margaret had figured and as it grew darker, the chair fell into rut after rut. After wrestling it

free yet again, Margaret needed a breather. She stopped, pulled a canteen from her backpack and took a long swallow. Offered the canteen, Nanny gratefully accepted, breaking the silence with her noisy gulps.

"Nanny, something's bothering me."

"What's that, Doctor?"

"Why this route? It's insane. I mean, why not go to the front door?"

"That's a good question and I intend to answer it, but first I need the little girl's room."

Nanny stood up and looked for a likely spot in the woods. "Why don't you sit down and rest until I get back?"

"Watch out for poison ivy," Margaret cautioned.

"You can count on it," Nanny promised and limped off into the underbrush.

When Margaret could no longer see the nurse, she eased herself into the chair. It was not only a welcome respite from schlepping Nanny, but also longer than expected. And that's after taking the decreased urinary flow and diminished urethral pressure of Nanny's aging bladder into the equation. Where was the old gal?

Margaret pushed the chair off the road and began to trace the nurse's path into the woods when she heard the rustling of weeds.

"It's about time," Margaret said, looking up to face Nanny. Only it wasn't just Nanny. An elderly brother held a basket of berries in one hand and a Saturday night special in

the other. He seemed to be pointing it at her, so Margaret raised her hands.

"Look who I ran into! Brother Eli," Nanny announced merrily. "He was picking wolfberries. Isn't that lovely?"

"You can put your hands down," the brother said to Margaret. "Just don't go running off."

"Put the gun away, before you drop it," Nanny ordered. "Dr. Hughes isn't going anywhere. She has a vested interest in our cause."

Margaret lowered her hands. "What's a brother doing with a gun?" she asked.

"Berry thieves. You can't be too careful," said Nanny, taking the frail brother by the elbow. "It gets worse at the end of the season." Nanny scanned their surroundings for lurking scoundrels. "We best be going, Doctor."

As she walked toward the wheelchair, Margaret wondered if she should trust the pair. Were they in cahoots or was their meeting a coincidence? Nanny didn't seem surprised to find him holding a gun on her. (Although thanks to the nurse, he had tucked the weapon into his sash.) Of more concern, was the nurse's swift and sudden metamorphosis from lame to game. Margaret didn't believe in miracles.

"All aboard," Margaret said, taking her place behind the wheelchair. Nanny's large book bag, which hung on the back, swung against her legs.

"I can walk from now on," said Nanny, striding toward Margaret.

"Don't you want your stuff?" Margaret detached the bag and held it out to the nurse.

When Nanny reached for it, Margaret shoved the chair into the nurse. She fell backwards and Margaret high-tailed it into the woods.

Brother Eli ordered her to stop.

Margaret didn't and a shot rang out.

Nanny yelled something about trusting her.

Margaret kept running.

They kept calling. But their voices were becoming indistinct. She felt something trickling down her leg. It was blood. Brother Eli's bullet had grazed her calf. She took off her backpack, found a kerchief inside and sat down to bandage the wound. Now how was she going to get past the security guards and rescue Chase?

# CHAPTER 41.

THE BUTTONS OF Irv Capaldini's shirt no longer strained against his belly. He had lost his appetite for food, sex, or even making a hard sell after Leon Gross's murder. Capaldini missed his partner more than he could have imagined and he hated inflicting his blue mood on his wife. Sherry must have hated it too, because she bought him a car, a stripped-down, red Camaro ragtop, to distract him from his grief.

According to its provenance, the Camaro was recovered from a cargo ship and had been rehabbed by one of the finest conservators of pre-Delugian artifacts. In any event, the headlights were failing and Capaldini was bound for an auto parts dealer in Scrabber Town. If he was lucky, he

might locate a pair of bulbs and surprise Sherry with a bushel of zebra clams.

Capaldini relished the quiet and the riffle of wind in his thinning hair as he cautiously motored down the hill toward Landing Road. Moments after making the turn, he slowed to a crawl as shoppers crowded around to touch and ogle his vintage wheels. The next thing you know he was waving and smiling like a politician running for office.

He quite enjoyed the fuss, if not the pace, as he inched toward Al's Chop Shop & Oyster House. Candles glowed in welcome from the windows of Al's place, but fearing for his car's safety, Capaldini decided not to stop. With a blast of his horn, he scattered on-lookers and picking up speed, drove till he couldn't see them anymore.

He was well past the convergence of Landing and River roads when the Camaro's engine, running on a mixture of pigeon fat and grain alcohol, began to hiccup. Capaldini eased up on the accelerator and searched for a place to pull over. With his weak headlights and the fog wafting inland, it wasn't going to be easy.

He stopped, put the car in reverse and was about to back up when a shout rang out and he slammed on his brakes. Had he hit somebody? His heart hammering, he climbed out of the car and made out a woman sitting on the side of the road.

"Are you okay?" he asked.

"In a manner of speaking," she replied.

"Oh, thank God. I was afraid I'd hit you."

"At that speed, the worse you could have done was dent me."

She took off her baseball cap and the Camaro's racing lights caught her face.

"Dr. Hughes? What on earth are you doing here?" He reached down and helped her up.

"I'm searching for a friend."

"A friend of yours, out here?"

"More of a patient. Actually, you might know him. He's a grinder."

"A grinder. Hmmm."

"Chase Lyman."

"Yeah, sure. Good kid."

Margaret nodded.

"Damn." Capaldini slapped himself in the forehead.

"What?"

"I knew I had forgotten something. I was supposed to get a message to you. Only the thing is I've been swamped without Leon."

"What's the message?"

"The fundies have him."

She nodded.

"Please accept my sincerest apologies."

"Done," she said.

Capaldini was no longer listening. He was staring over her shoulder. He looked as if he was seeing ghosts. Margaret swung around to see Nanny and Brother Eli emerge from the mists.

"Stay where you are or I'll shoot," the brother said, wheezing and waving his gun unsteadily in one hand while clutching his basket of berries in the other.

Capaldini showed no fear. He seemed amused by the situation. "I'm guessing you folks are missionaries," he said. "And if you're this desperate for converts, what with the gun and all, I'm thinking you must have a monthly quota and you haven't met it. Am I right?"

"We have no need of missionaries. Everyday our flocks grow fuller. We are beloved by the Lord," Brother Eli declared.

"A good man to have on your side, the Lord, or so I hear," Capaldini said. "I'm of a different persuasion. Businessman first, last and foremost. I figure the Lord has got better things to do than help me sell uvulas."

"No need to talk dirty," the brother chided.

"I believe you are thinking of the vulva, Brother Eli," Nanny said. "You're celibate. Your confusion is understandable."

"Sister, please," the blushing brother pleaded.

Capaldini rushed the flustered gunman, slapped the weapon from his hand and retrieved it before the aging brother quite realized the gun was gone. Eli's primary interest was saving his berries.

"Now, you stick em up," Capaldini said.

Nanny and Brother Eli, who didn't seem to notice the tables had been turned, exchanged baffled looks.

"What do you want to do with them?" Capaldini asked Margaret.

"Tie them up. Have you got something?"

"Keep an eye of them." He handed the gun to Margaret, then opened the trunk of the Camaro and pulled out a pair of jumper cables. "These ought to do the trick. We can put a bow around 'em and leave them for the night prowlers."

"Tie them up, but bring them along."

"Why? Where are we going?" he asked.

"To rescue Chase. Nanny knows the way and we'll need her sooner or later."


After binding their hands behind their backs, Capaldini ordered Eli into a bucket seat and nudged Nanny onto his lap. He then looped the unused portion of the cable around their waists and tied it securely.

"My apologies, Brother Eli, for this unfortunate intimacy," Nanny demurred.

"Please keep wiggling," he responded, a grin spreading across his face.

Capaldini fought to keep the vehicle on the narrow road. The Camaro lurched over another pothole and Eli voiced a small, satisfied peep.

"How much further?" Margaret asked.

"There's an entrance around the bend," Nanny replied.

"Any guards?"

"Hardly anybody ever comes in this way."

"Yeah, but are there guards?"

"I don't remember seeing any."

Margaret leaned forward, pressed the gun to the brother's cheek. "How's your memory, friend? Any better?"

"You won't shoot," he said.

"Sure I will." Margaret cocked the gun.

"Three. There are three guards."

Margaret put the gun into the waist of her jeans.

Capaldini saw light glinting through the trees. "There it is."

"Pull over," Margaret said.

"I've got no room to pull over."

"Okay. We'll leave the car here. You stay with it. Nanny, you're coming with me."

"I'm coming, too," Capaldini insisted.

"No, you don't have a disguise. You'll give us away."

"Neither do you," he said.

"I hadn't thought of that."

"Look in my bag," Nanny volunteered. "There's a cassock."

"A bomb is more like it," Capaldini said.

"I wouldn't hurt the doctor," Nanny sniveled.

Margaret snorted.

"Untie me and I'll open it," the nurse bargained.

"No, I'll open it," Margaret insisted. "Everybody out of the Camaro."

After Capaldini freed Nanny and Eli, Margaret retriev-

ed the bag from the back seat. She reached inside and pulled out a cassock and a pair of Jesus sandals. She gasped at the stench of feet, musk and dung that clung to the gear. Breathing through her mouth, she pulled the robe over her head and tied a rope sash around her middle. After she removed and stowed her blades in her backpack, however, she balked at sticking her feet into the sandals.

"Eeyuh. There's manure all over the soles," she said

"That's *Holy* Shit!" Brother Eli corrected her. "It brings good luck, like a crow pooping on your head."

She rolled her eyes. "Untie him, Irv, will you?"

Capaldini released Eli.

The brother massaged the red indentations around his wrists.

"Take off your clothes and get in the trunk," Margaret instructed Eli.

When he refused to move, Margaret sighed, pulled the gun from her waist and waggled it at him.

"To strip before a sinner is a sin," he said.

Margaret opened the trunk. "So get inside, get undressed and when you've finished, hand me your stuff."

The brother grudgingly climbed into the trunk, waited till Margaret turned her back, then did as he had been told. First came the cassock, then the sandals and last of all, the brother's sacred underpants. Margaret handed the robe and shoes to Capaldini, then picked the last up with a stick and looked inquiringly at her friend.

"Not for love nor money."

Margaret laughed.

"You can have these back," she said to Eli.

Capaldini draped his jacket around the brother, gagged him and left him on the floor of the small trunk.

"Don't worry, Brother Eli. I'll be back for you," Nanny vowed.

Her promise elicited a muffled grunt from inside the trunk.

"I don't know why you have to be so mean," she said to Margaret.

"Oh, puhleeze. The man took a shot at me. If you think that's mean, wait and see what I do if you try anything funny."

The fog provided cover as Margaret, Nanny and Irv, carrying Eli's berry basket, stole around the corner and caught sight of END's security guards. Three men, armed with assault rifles, stood watch over a pair of eight-foot-tall wrought iron gates strung with garlands of berries and twigs. An oil lamp in the window of the blockhouse provided enough light for Margaret to make out the guards' stoic demeanor.

She and Capaldini were not only out-manned and out-armed, but when it came to the grounds, geographically challenged. They would have to trust the navigation to Nanny.

"Is there any way around these guys?" Margaret asked.

Nanny didn't answer.

"If you don't tell me the truth this time and we come under fire, I'll need something to hide behind and you will be it."

Nanny nodded. "This is the only way in."

"What about the fence?"

"Electric, set on cremate."

"Okay, then. We walk in as if we own the place. Nanny will do the talking. Won't you, Nanny?"

Capaldini twisted her arm just enough to elicit an answer.

"Ouch. You don't have to be so mean."

"You made me."

"Shhh," Margaret warned. "Remember we're all friends. Let's act like it."

"Sorry," Capaldini said.

"After you," Margaret instructed.

Nanny led the way as they walked into the middle of the road in full view of the guards. Within moments, one of the guards pointed his flashlight in their direction.

"Who goes there?" he called.

"It's Nanny. I've come at the Reverend's request."

The guard walked toward them, shined his light in their faces. "Nanny, of course. Forgive me. We've been on high alert."

"High alert!?" she gasped. "Whatever for?"

"The antichrist's men attacked. They killed Brother

John. The Reverend has vowed to shoot them out of the sky if they have the guts to return."

Nanny began to sniffle. "Poor dear Brother John. I can't believe he's g-g-gone…"

"He is sweeping the heavenly hearth," the guard consoled her.

"Praise Jesus," Nanny said.

"Praise His name," Margaret said.

"Like she said," Capaldini added.

The guard eyed Nanny's companions. "Who are these two?"

"My assistants. If others are wounded, they may be of help."

"Only a few minor injuries."

"Praise Jesus," Margaret said.

"Praise His name," the guard said.

"Praises be unto Him," Nanny said.

The guard ushered them through the ornate gates. "The Lord be with you," he said, making the sign of the cross.

"And with you," Nanny said.

"And with you," Margaret said.

"You also," Capaldini murmured.


The splendid ruins of five medieval monasteries, now Hast headquarters, loomed before them. As a gentle rain began to fall on the gardens, they sought shelter under the chapel's

tiled arcade. The brethren murmured prayers inside their cells.

"Where's Chase?" Margaret whispered to Nanny.

She led them around the chapel and down a flight of stairs to what had been the curator's office of this once famed New York museum. Light leaked from beneath a nondescript single panel door.

"He's in there," Nanny said.

"They left him unguarded?" Margaret was dubious.

"There's a med-tech with him. He's still too weak to run away."

Margaret looked at Capaldini. "I don't trust her, Irv."

Nanny squealed before Margaret could clamp a hand over the nurse's mouth. "Stuff something in her face and shove her in a closet," Margaret said. "We'll come back for her if we need her."

"All I have are my socks," Capaldini said. "I wouldn't feel right."

Margaret reached under her robe, shucked off her bra. "Here. It's sweaty, but…"

"Very attractive," Capaldini said. "Open wide," he ordered Nanny.

Margaret ensured the nurse's silence by pressing the gun under her chin. Capaldini opened a door to find a closet stacked with prayer books. Shoving Nanny inside, he closed the door and pressed a chair under the knob.

Margaret suggested they take the med-tech by surprise. Capaldini would slam through the door, while she pro-

vided cover. Capaldini was ready to hurl himself forward when the beefy brother Amos, a rehabbed Kalashnikov at his side, opened the door and invited them inside.

The room, which might have been cozy under different circumstances, was monopolized by a gigantic wooden desk. The Reverend Hast posed behind it on a barber's chair. But as Margaret quickly determined, Chase was nowhere to be seen.

"Oh, dear, you look so disappointed," Hast said. "You were expecting someone else?"

In no mood for taking crap, especially from him, Margaret eyed the Reverend with cold-blooded contempt. When she started toward him, Hast could hardly keep himself from crawling under his desk.

Brother Amos reached for Margaret's arm, but Capaldini knocked the other man's hand away. Amos made a second grab, Capaldini pushed him back and Amos threw a punch, which Capaldini ducked with surprising agility.

"That's enough, Brother Amos," Hast said.

Amos hesitated.

Capaldini remained wary.

"He's on edge," Hast said. "We were recently attacked. I believe your father's security forces were involved."

He turned back to Amos. "I don't believe the doctor wishes me any harm."

"Not for the time being," Margaret said.

"Brother Amos, why don't you shake hands with the doctor's companion?"

"The name's Irv." Capaldini half-heartedly accepted the brother's hand.

"Give Irv a tour of the grounds while the doctor and I have a tete a tete."

"Thanks, but I'll stay," Capaldini said.

"I'd prefer speaking privately with Dr. Hughes," Hast said.

"Go on, have a smoke or something," Margaret urged. "I'll be okay."

After the two men reluctantly departed, Hast invited Margaret to sit down. She pulled a chair from the corner and placed it across from the Reverend.

"Would you care for lemon water?" He reached for a pitcher, poured a glass and placed it in front of her. "So refreshing," said the Reverend, helping himself to a sip from his sweating tumbler.

"You know what would be refreshing?" Margaret asked. "If we could skip the bull plop."

"As you wish."

"You orchestrated this charade?" Margaret asked.

"Obviously."

"Used Nanny to trick me into coming here?"

"Yes. I felt it was wiser to speak face-to-face."

"Where's Charles?"

"The abomination? He's in good hands."

"I'm making no deals until you produce him."

"Yes, yes, I know. But please allow me to outline my proposal."

Margaret waited.

"What I am going to tell you will come as a shock," warned Hast, sweetening his tone so as to spare her the coming jolt.

"Not to worry. I've always been a grounded individual."

Hast raised his eyes to the ceiling panels, painted in a rough approximation of the Sistine Chapel. "Lord, give me strength," he pled.

"Should I hold my applause? Or will there be a second act?"

"Please, this is extremely painful for me."

Margaret looked at her watch.

"I hope you can put aside your cynicism for a moment and open your mind to what I have to say."

"Well, say it!"

"First, a bit of a set up. Ahem. I had done Larry King's show – one of my best appearances ever. I went back to the green room to get my cape and finding the room empty, I knelt to thank God for my triumph. And lo, He appeared to me over a bowl of fruit. And verily, He spoke unto me."

"What does He/She sound like? High, squeaky voice? Booming? Majestic? Tabernacular?"

"He speaks to each of us in His own way. In my case, He was firm, as would be a parent instructing a beloved son."

"So it was sort of like, you were Jesus."

Hast grimaced. "I was speaking metaphorically. We are all His children."

"Good to know," Margaret said.

"He called me by my given name, Orville Righteous Hast the Third, then charged me with a mission so incredible that I can hardly believe it myself. So I know you might find it hard to accept."

Hast cleared his throat. "He hath commanded me to shepherd His church into the 23rd century."

Margaret smelled a fish.

" 'But Lord, I am a middle-aged man,' I replied. 'I have no access to the Fountain of Youth.' "

He glanced at Margaret for a reaction. She wore a faint smile.

"When I heard His command, I felt as Abraham must have when God bade him kill Isaac. 'Dearest Father,' I begged, 'ask anything of me, except this.' He answered me not. I realized that even if it meant the loss of my eternal soul, I must obey His command without question."

Hast bowed his head.

"Let me guess," said Margaret, "God wants you to order yourself a vessel."

Hast nodded without lifting his head.

"In return for which, you will produce Charles."

"Yes, but I would expect other concessions."

Margaret laughed. "If there are any concessions, you'll be making them."

"For now, I have the advantage," Hast countered. "All

I ask in return for the so-called Charles Lyman, aside from absolute secrecy, is that the fetus be carried to term by a surrogate mother and delivered from her womb. That will give God a chance to transfer my soul from this earthly body to that which I will assume."

"You want your own Virgin Mary?" Margaret asked.

"I don't think of it that way," he said.

"How do you think of it?"

He didn't answer.

"You know, there is no guarantee a vessel will be viable unless it is reared in a chrysalis," Margaret said, "And there is the matter of a surrogate mother who would keep her mouth shut. But you probably plan to kill the chick after the bun is out of the oven. Who is the lucky lady by the way?"

"Among others, Sister Nanny has volunteered."

Margaret rolled her eyes.

"We'd have to jump start her womb," she said, transitioning to her doctor mode. "It can be done, although I'd recommend a younger candidate. No older than twenty-seven."

"So you'll do it?" asked Hast.

"Produce Charles Lyman. Then we'll talk. I don't have time to waste so do it now."

"You didn't think we'd be foolish enough to keep him here?

"Where is he?"

"We have a safe house in Scrabber Town. You can have him once we sign a contract for the procedure."

"Charles first, paperwork second," Margaret growled.

Hast shook his head. "I believe I have the upper hand at the moment." He pushed a contract across the desktop.

Margaret picked up a pen and signed the paper. "Satisfied?"

Hast smiled and pressed the contract against his chest.

Margaret put her pinky to her lips. "I'll call for a Dragonfly."

# CHAPTER 42.

GABE HUSTLED CHASE into the cockpit, then climbed aboard the Sabre, now hovering several feet above the sliver of land that had been their refuge during high tide. "What took you so fucking long?" Gabe shouted at Lunt, who started to explain. "Never mind," Gabe interrupted. "Just give me the motherfucking earmuffs."

Lunt handed Gabe an extra comset, noticed Chase wasn't wearing his seat belt and sternly ordered him to buckle up. Chase twisted to show Lunt his bound hands. Lunt untied the belt and Chase reluctantly strapped himself in.

"Who is this?" shouted Gabe into the comset microphone.

"HQ Operator Densai speaking" came the response.

"This is Gabe Munro. Put me through to Morgan Hughes ASAP."

"Yes sir. Right away," said Densai, who then hurriedly made the connection to Hughes' office.

An affable, canned message explained that the call would be redirected to Dr. Margaret Hughes' office, where-upon the caller's every want would be satisfied in a timely and felicitous manner. Gabe's call was transferred to Margaret's voicemail which invited him to call back during regular office hours – weekdays between… unless this was an emergency… or he could leave a message… blah, blah, blah."

"Are you shitting me?"

"What's that?" Lunt yelled over the clamor of the rotor.

"The boss's daughter. She's not fucking available right now…"

"Maybe she's with a patient," Lunt suggested.

"Maybe she's taking a crap," Gabe snapped. "I don't give a shit. The fact remains, I can't fucking get through to her."

Gabe was left with one choice. "Operator, you there?"

"Yes, sir."

"Get me that motherfucking quack, Dr. Mahmoud."

To Gabe's relief, Mahmoud answered immediately.

"Doctor, Gabe Munro here. I've got good news. You can start prepping your patient."

# CHAPTER 43.

NURSE-TECH FRED Neiman and his wife were playing double fantucci with their neighbors, the Eickhorns, when Bruno screeched to a halt in front of their house, ran up the steps and pounded on the door.

"What in heaven's name?" asked Mrs. Neiman, putting down her cards. "Don't peek at my hand," she joked as she stood.

Fred excused himself and followed his wife, who had her hand on the knob.

"Let me, dear," insisted Fred. "You never know who might be on the other side, especially during the holidays. All those break-ins."

Mrs. Neiman gave her husband that "don't be such a

big silly" look and turned the knob to discover the imposing driver on the other side.

"Why it's Dr. Hughes' chauffeur," Fred announced.

"Are you Fred Neiman?" Bruno asked.

Fred nodded.

"And I'm Mrs. Neiman," his wife said. "Would you care to come in? We're playing double fantucci. Are you a card player Mr… Mr? I'm afraid I didn't get your name. Introductions, please, Fred."

"Sorry, ma'am. Another time," said Bruno, who took Fred by the arm and hustled him into the car. Fred rolled down the window to wave goodbye to his wife.

"What's this about?" Mrs. Neiman yelled.

"An emergency," Fred shouted as Bruno sped toward the renewal center.

Bruno said nothing more, but Fred knew of the bodyguard's devotion to Dr. Hughes. For whatever reason, she needed her team and Fred was ready to serve. He also disliked the Eickhorns almost as much as double fantucci and, holiday or no, he was happy to escape.

# CHAPTER 44.

MACY HAD REMOVED the doors of her Dragonfly to lighten the rotorcraft's weight and increase air speed. According to the flight chief, this would be the most important run of her life (code: TLC ASAP VIP). She climbed into the cockpit, lifted off the helipad and set a course for END headquarters.

"Are you sure about that location, chief?" Macy asked.

"Is there a crack in my ass?"

"Haven't had the privilege of... I wouldn't know, sir. But I take your point. Cloisters it is."

"Macy."

"Yeah."

"Don't do anything crazy. Or you're grounded. Hear me?"

"Not to worry," Macy promised, although she did divert every so slightly from her flight path to save time. Faster was better in her humble opinion and sure enough, she reached her destination in record time. A good thing because visibility was intermittent. Damn. She was playing peek-a-boo with the church towers – now visible, now wreathed in mist.

Sure, she had flown in thicker soup, dodged higher obstacles, but ASAP was ASAP and it was going to be a bitch to land. Macy circled the complex in search of a clearing – usually it didn't have to be much bigger than a bathtub – but it was dark. A barren field would be ideal.

Macy chanced dropping closer to the ground. The bird was noisy, but she thought she heard shouts and descended a little further. There they were standing in a circle of light spilling from a ring of lanterns. Four people. All of them looked to be brethren. Weird. Macy was expecting two passengers, neither of them fundies. Though they called and waved to her, she was hesitant to land.

Then one of them, a woman, drew off her hood and shook out her hair. The long, iridescent locks blazed in the firelight. It had to be Dr. Hughes, figured Macy, who had taxied the doc around the islands on previous occasions. VIPS didn't come any VIPer. This must be the place.

Macy went with her assumption and brought the Dragonfly down inside the illumined circle. The ensuing

downdraft snuffed out the lanterns, fluttered the cassocks and tested the staying power of the Reverend's ebony toupee.

"I can only take two," Macy yelled over the chatter of the blades.

"But there are three of us," said Margaret, brushing her disheveled hair from her face.

"That's okay," Irv said, gesturing with his thumb. "I've got my car."

"You're sure?" Margaret asked.

"Absolutely."

"Brother Enoch, please see Dr. Hughes' companion to the gate," Hast said.

Irv gave Margaret a hug and followed the brother.

The Reverend struggled to board the Dragonfly, so Margaret gave him a boost and Macy hauled him in. Margaret climbed into the seat behind him. Macy gasped and pinched her nose as the reek from the two cassocks engulfed the tiny cabin.

Margaret laughed, looked down at her robe. "I converted, didn't you hear?"

"Well, Doc, you do stink to high heaven."

Macy began her ascent. "Sorry for saying so."

"Apology accepted."

Macy revved the engine and lifted off

"Question," Macy said, staring at Hast.

"Yeah."

"Is that who I think it is?"

Margaret nodded. "Macy, meet the Reverend. Reverend meet Macy."

Hast acknowledged the introduction, then gazed out the open doorway.

Margaret's pinkie phone buzzed. "Hughes here."

It was Mahmoud. As she listened, she stared daggers at the Reverend. "On my way," she said and hung up.

"A safe house in Scrabber Town?" she said accusingly.

"Yes, we have a safe house in Scrabber Town."

"But you don't have Charles Lyman."

"Um, I never said he was there." He slipped a bone knife from his robe and pressed the blade against Macy's throat.

"There's no need for theatrics," Margaret chided. "Put the knife down. You'll get what you wanted." There was no way she was going to miss the chance to out the man's hypocrisy to his congregation.

Hast didn't budge.

"Don't be stupid. Macy is the only one who knows how to fly this thing."

The Reverend hesitated, withdrew the knife. "I will not hand over my weapon. I don't trust you."

"Fine. Whatever."

"Hard to kill two people with one knife," Macy added, as she picked up airspeed and swung toward HQ.

"Any chance we can catch up with a Sabre?" Margaret asked.

"We'll got a better shot if we unload some weight," Macy said.

They both turned to Hast.

"You wouldn't," he said.

Both women shrugged.

# CHAPTER 45.

THE DRAGONFLY TRAILED the Sabre by a quarter-click, but Macy knew her bird was faster and more maneuverable than the armored copper chopper. She'd catch up.

Margaret was biting her fingernails at the prospect of Gabe getting the jump on her. Then too, she wondered if the young pilot was as skilled as she was cocky. When Margaret voiced her concern about the poor visibility, Macy urged her not to worry. "I know where all the tall trees are. Ha ha. Buildings, too."

Not exactly comforting, thought Margaret as they skimmed over crumbling chimney pots and rusting air

conditioners, coming so close to the rooftops that feral roof cats hissed and fluffed up their tails.

This, however, was merely a preview of Macy's derring-do. She would outstrip herself when they caught up with the Sabre within blocks of the HRC. Warning Hast and Margaret to hang on, she sped up in an attempt to overtake the heavier aircraft. From her passengers' perspective, they were suddenly within inches of slamming into the other aircraft's rudder.

"We're going to die!" the Reverend screamed.

"Nah," said Macy, who quickly dropped down and with the daring of the young and insanely confident, flew under the bigger bird and aimed for the HRC's helipad ahead.

The proximity sensor on the Sabre blared.

"What's that?" Chase yelled.

"My ex-wife," Lunt answered. "Hold on."

He jammed the stick left and down, causing the Sabre to dip and roll, and in the process, lightly clipped the Dragonfly's blades.

"Motherfucking shit-for-brains. You fucking trying to kill us?" Gabe shouted.

Lunt smiled, kicked in the afterburners and raced ahead.

"Damn!" Macy yelled, now struggling for control. "That's just plain rude."

The Dragonfly bucked and pitched. It took everything Macy had to gain any measure of control as they lost altitude at an alarming rate.

"We're going down," she yelled.

The Reverend utilized all decibels in pleading for heavenly intercession. "Father, help us… Lift up your children, oh Lord… Your faithful servant beseeches Thee."

"Pray to Macy, she's holding the stick," Margaret snapped.

"Jesus Christ in a pancake!" Hast screamed as they met the ground.

# CHAPTER 46.

AS THE SABRE lowered onto the helipad, Chase surveyed the Renewal Center rooftop for an escape route. It didn't look promising. The building's ledge with its frieze of scruffy pigeons was separated from the landing site by channels of broken glass and was surrounded by a chain-length fence crowned with a skein of razor wire.

At the far end, desalinization and cooling plants gurgled and roared under the care of an elderly, sun-leathered mechanic and a couple of pilots hung outside the flight chief's shack while waiting for assignments. Chase didn't think they'd give him any trouble.

On the other hand, the roof was teeming with security personnel. Most were packing semi-automatics, although

some held shoulder-mounted missile launchers. Probably in the event of an air strike. Two stood at the entrance to an elevator shaft, which appeared to be the only sane way off the roof.

Gabe beamed at the martial display. He nudged Chase's shoulder. "Impressive, eh?"

"More like excessive," Chase replied.

Even if it meant jumping off the roof, he resolved to escape. The fall might kill him, true, but he had survived his encounter with the curb and his leap from the Cloisters tower. If his luck didn't hold… well, anything was better than surrendering to these bastards. He still didn't know what they had planned for him.

Lunt landed the Sabre so ably that Chase didn't realize they were down until Gabe tapped him on the shoulder and told him it was time to go. Once they were out of the cabin, Gabe took Chase by the arm and ushered him toward the elevator shaft door. He was almost casual about it.

*Now's our chance.*

It was his cerebral cortex again.

*Go, now.*

Chase jerked free of Gabe's grasp and sprinted toward the fence.

Gabe cursed himself. He shouldn't have been surprised by the grinder's bravado. Not that his gutsy move would

change anything – unless the crazy motherfucker was thinking of jumping.

"Damn fool. Stop him," Gabe shouted though his men had already encircled the runaway and were trying to herd him toward their boss.

"Get out of my way," Chase barked at a guard who had drawn his gun and was pointing it at the fugitive.

"Or are you going to shoot me?" Chase could see the guard debate the question in his head. Shit. He sure hoped Gabe had been serious about keeping him alive.

"Nobody is going to shoot anybody." Gabe stepped into the circle and started toward Chase.

"Don't come any closer," Chase warned.

Gabe stopped. "I don't want to hurt you, but I can't waste any more time. If I have to, I won't hesitate to use other measures."

Chase pretended to consider Gabe's words.

"All you're doing is putting off the inevitable," Gabe added.

Chase ducked his head as if resigned to his fate and Gabe started toward him. Chase retreated and a la Houdini rammed the nearest guard in the gut. A foolish mistake given his head wound. The big man didn't go down, which enabled him to catch Chase before the grinder fell.

"He knocked himself out," the puzzled guard said as he lowered Chase to the rooftop.

Gabe stooped down and felt for Chase's pulse without

luck. "This is a hospital for fuck sake. Get me a doctor," he ordered.

The guard ran for the elevator, but an elderly nurse with a black bag in hand was already hurrying toward Chase and Gabe.

"I'll take it from here," said the woman, nudging Gabe aside.

"Do you know who I am?" he huffed.

"Can't say as I do. Can't say as I care."

She left Gabe to stew while she checked Chase's neck for a pulse, listened to his heart and lifted his eyelids to assess the dilation of his pupils. "He's alive," she said, "but there's no telling how much more damage he's done to his brain."

"You do realize who *he* is?"

"Of course, I do. Dr. Mahmoud is waiting for us in pre-op."

"You could have said something."

"Didn't see any need to bother," she said, then motioned to a pair of orderlies who had been standing by. "Come on, let's get him into pre-op."

# CHAPTER 47.

MACY WRESTLED THE controls as the Dragonfly wobbled and dropped precipitously. Margaret braced for contact. Hast covered his eyes.

Macy engaged the landing foils, which were designed to minimize any impact, and managed to pull up the nose seconds before the craft collided with the roadway.

The foils did their job, crumpling and absorbing much of the shock, but the right strut buckled and the cabin lurched, coming to an uneven, shaky rest on the cracked and pitted pavement.

Two toothless stoop-dwellers whooped and broke into applause, this being the most entertainment they'd enjoyed in years. Hast fumbled with his seatbelt, managed

to free himself, then rolled out onto the concrete. There he found solace by curling up in a large pothole. Margaret eased out behind him, followed by Macy who made a quick assessment of their predicament.

"I suggest we start walking," Macy said.

"Any idea where we are?" asked Margaret, who had yet to regain her bearings.

Macy nodded. "Center's back that way, about two blocks to the left."

Margaret kicked off her holy shits, pulled her blades from her backpack and hauled ass.

"What should I do with him?" Macy shouted, but Margaret was already out of earshot.

# CHAPTER 48.

FRED JOINED HIS colleagues on Dr. Hughes' surgical team in the staff lounge for a pre-operative rundown. The chief neurosurgeon was usually first to report, but was nowhere to be seen. Dr. Mahmoud, who arrived last, seemed to fancy himself in charge. "Over her dead body," Fred muttered to Padma, who nodded and smiled.

Mahmoud closed the door behind him and apologized for asking them to give up their holiday. The situation was extraordinary, however, and no other team was ever considered for the job. Fred shared a knowing look with Padma.

"Can't believe he's lasted this long," Fred said under his breath, as Mahmoud announced that Morgan Hughes

would be undergoing an emergency transfer. Both Hughes and his vessel, he informed them, were prepped and waiting in the operating room. Dr. Margaret Hughes had been delayed, but was on her way.

This confirmed the rumors that had been circulating since Dr. Hughes took over the administration of the HRC. The final proof awaited in the OR, where Morgan Hughes lay skeletal and sedated on a heated operating table. Fred doubted he had the stamina to survive the transfer and signed the same to Padma, who signaled her wholehearted agreement with his assessment.

Josiah seemed distracted, maybe even sleep-walking, but that was Josiah's way. Unable to catch his eye, Fred bent to his monitors though he had little to do till Dr. Hughes arrived. Fred looked for her, but glimpsed only the scrub nurse through the ready room window. It was strange – just how strange Fred discovered when an orderly wheeled another body into the OR.

"What's this?" Fred signed.

"Somebody goofed. Sent you the wrong dupe." The orderly unlocked the brakes of the gurney bearing the healthy vessel Margaret had selected. He rolled that gurney toward the exit and replaced it with the new arrival.

"This is unheard of," Padma signed.

Fred nodded and tapped the orderly on the shoulder. "Maybe you better show us some proof."

"Not a problem." The orderly pulled a crumpled paper from his pocket and handed it to Fred.

Sure enough Dr. Mahmoud had authorized the exchange. Fred shared the information with the others as the orderly shifted the newcomer onto an operating table.

Dr. Hughes isn't going to like this.

Padma checked the clock. She was Hindu, but everybody celebrated Christmas. She hoped her kids wouldn't mind if Santa was late this year. "Where is Dr. Hughes? It's very late."

Fred shook his head.

"Maybe we should hook him up. We can begin as soon as she arrives," signed Padma, removing the warm blanket covering the vessel.

"Oh, my God," she whispered.

The vessel looked like it had been in last month's skyscraper collapse. Cuts and bruises showed through the skimpy body suit. The gash on its head had scabbed over, but the area was inflamed and probably also infected.

Fred couldn't quite place the puffy and discolored face, but he had a feeling he had seen it somewhere before. "This has to be a mistake," he signed.

"There's no mistake," signed Dr. Mahmoud, who must have slipped in while they were distracted. "That is Morgan Hughes' vessel."

"But he looks nothing like Mr. Hughes," Fred signed.

"Mr. Hughes looks nothing like Mr. Hughes."

"Even if you're right, it's been hurt," Padma signed as she looked down at the battered vessel.

"The wounds are superficial," Mahmoud responded. "I

have examined it and I can assure you that I found no reason to postpone the procedure."

Fred couldn't believe his ears. "It would be a miracle if there was no damage to the frontal lobe."

Mahmoud smiled at Fred as if he were a small child and not a particularly bright one. "Do you have a medical degree, Fred?"

Fred's eyes narrowed.

"Well, I do." Mahmoud looked from Fred to Padma, who ducked her head to her chest.

"Anybody else have anything to say?"

Cyan, the surgical nurse, shook her head no. Josiah remained oblivious.

"No? Then let's get this show on the road."

Nobody moved.

"I assume you'd all like to keep your jobs," Mahmoud signed.

Padma hesitated, then began to place suckers on the vessel's chest. Fred made adjustments to his monitors. It couldn't hurt to check the vessel's vital signs.

"That's the ticket," Mahmoud signed.

"Where is Dr. Hughes?" Fred asked.

"I'm going to check on her now."

As soon as he left, Fred began signing frantically. He was worried. This was too weird. If anything went wrong, they would be blamed. He didn't want to continue without Dr. Hughes' approval. He didn't trust Mahmoud. Perhaps they ought to at least try to call Dr. Hughes.

The others agreed. Fred put his pinkie to his lips, spoke the doctor's number only to receive a message that internal communications were temporarily interrupted. He went to the exit, intent on getting through to Dr. Hughes somehow. But the door was locked. Fred squinted through a peephole and to his alarm, spotted a security guard looking back at him. He banged on the door. The guard ignored him.

"Come on. Come on. Come on." Margaret fretted as she waited seconds for the elevator to arrive. As soon as the doors opened a crack, she shoved through and plowed directly into Mahmoud.

"Dr. Hughes, Margaret. Thank goodness. Your father is failing fast," said Mahmoud, regaining his composure.

"I can't do anything without my staff."

"All present and accounted for," Mamoud said.

The doors were closing when Gabe stuck his hand between them and stepped into the compartment. He had cleaned up and was feeling more self-assured in a crisp cotton shirt and light wool blazer. He smiled at Margaret. "I'm glad you could make it."

"I'll bet you are," Margaret said, ignoring both men until the elevator stopped and she pushed into the hallway.

Gabe was practically glued to her ass. He was lap-dance close.

She whipped around and pushed Gabe back toward the elevator. "What do you think you're doing?"

"I'm coming with you. I want to watch."

"Not on your life," she said.

Mahmoud stepped between them. "There's no time for this nonsense," he said to Margaret. "He can watch with me from the ready room."

"As long as he stays out of my OR."

Margaret continued down the hall, made a sharp right turn and barged into the OR's locker room. She quickly shucked off her clothes and threw them in a pile against the wall. "Well?" She looked at Mahmoud, who began to disrobe.

"You, too," she said to Gabe.

"But I changed right before coming here."

"Go on," Mahmoud ordered.

"I don't suppose you have a hanger."

Margaret harrumphed. Gabe settled for folding his garments and placing them in a neat stack.

He stopped at his skivvies.

"Those, too," said Margaret. She and Mahmoud had already removed their undergarments. Once Gabe had complied, she palmed the IBID, releasing the latch of a small sterilizing chamber. The three crammed inside. While a recording informed them of ready room dos and don'ts, they were engulfed by a disinfectant cloud. On the other side, nurse Xian waited with a set of fresh scrubs for Margaret.

"What about me?" Gabe asked.

Margaret ignored him as she pulled her shirt over her head. Mahmoud opened a metal cabinet, took a set of greenish brown scrubs for himself and handed another to Gabe.

"Now these are some ugly motherfucking jimjams." Gabe held them at arms-length. "Whadaya call this shade? Cirrhosis?"

Margaret finished scrubbing her hands and wriggled her fingers into snug, sterile gloves as Xian helped fit a surgical cap over her hair and placed the straps of a mask over her ears. Margaret mumbled her thanks and started for the airlock between the ready and operating rooms.

"Hold on. I'm coming with you," Gabe said, pulling booties over his bare feet.

"No, you're not. We had an agreement," Margaret reminded him. "You'll have to watch from there." She pointed to the picture window that opened on the OR. "You might be carrying some undiagnosed disease. I can't risk it."

# CHAPTER 49.

AS MARGARET STEPPED into the airlock, a red light began to blink in the OR. Although everything looked copasetic through the porthole, Fred practically assaulted her when she stepped into the room.

"What is it? What's going on?"

"Thank God, you're here," he signed. "We tried to get help, but…"

"Help?"

"There's been a huge mix-up. An exchange…"

She waited for him to go on.

"The vessel. It's badly damaged."

"Damaged?"

"Like it's been in an accident. Cuts and contusions all over."

"And a blow to the skull," Padma added.

Margaret's heartbeat kicked into overdrive.

"There's one more thing," Fred signed.

"Yes."

"I don't think this one's a vessel *and* I think I recognize him. Remember the grinder I rescued?"

Margaret nodded, now virtually certain she would find Chase in place of the designated replacement. She followed Fred across the OR and waited for Cyan to lift the blanket. What she hadn't anticipated was the overwhelming anguish she felt on seeing Chase prepped for transfer.

"Who authorized the exchange?" she asked

"Dr. Mahmoud."

"God damn, son of a bitch."

Margaret stormed to the ready room window and began signing vehemently to Mahmoud. He couldn't look her in the eye. "My hands are tied. It's not my decision," he signed.

"What's she saying?" Gabe asked.

"In short, it's no go unless we agree to her demands."

"Which are?"

"The vessel known as Chase goes free and we return the replacement."

"Tell her okay. Wait for her to walk away, then open the airlock. I'm going in."

Gabe burst into the OR. "Everybody back to work," he shouted at the startled personnel.

Nobody moved.

"I'm giving the orders from now on. Is that understood?"

Padma shook her head. Cyan stared at him in bewilderment.

"I'll explain it to you the simplest way I know how." Gabe drew his pistol from his waistband and waved it overhead. "Now do you understand?"

The team members nodded.

"Good. Everybody get to work."

They looked questioningly at Margaret.

"Go back to what you were doing," she signed as she closed in on Gabe.

"You're not in charge here. I am," she hissed. "And I'm ordering you to put the gun away and shut your mouth. You want action. You know my demands."

Gabe spoke quietly, but with menace. "I can't believe you would betray your own father. That is his vessel, plain and simple."

"No. It's far from simple."

"Oh, but I forgot, you have other uses for it, don't you?"

Margaret slapped Gabe so hard he staggered backward.

"Damn," he said, gingerly touching the red handprint on his cheek.

"Now that I have your attention – I do have it, don't I?" Margaret asked.

Stunned, Gabe slowly nodded.

"I love my father, no matter what you think. But my father is not of sound mind and he's not in charge. Fortunately, I am both sane and the acting CEO. That means you work for me. And I do not believe he has the right to appropriate the body of a sentient human being."

"I don't care what you believe," Gabe said. "I care about your father's wishes. And I am asking you, insisting really, that you honor them… not to mention all the fucking work I put into fixing this mess."

"Thanks for everything. A check is in the mail."

"The boss wanted his vessel. I got him his vessel. And that's where you're putting him. Sorry, but I don't get paid to make moral judgments. Anyway I'm done talking."

Gabe backed away from Margaret and walked around the operating table and looked at Fred. "Sorry, pal," he said before pressing the barrel of his gun into Fred's temple.

"You get the picture or do I have to explain it to you?" he asked Margaret.

"You'll kill Fred if I don't start the procedure," she said stonily. "I know you think you're doing what my dad would have wanted. Instead, you're putting him in grave danger. He may not survive."

"Just get on with it."

"I'll need Fred."

Gabe took the gun from the technician's temple and stood aside.

"Now what?" Fred signed.

"We proceed as usual," she signed. "At least, we pretend to."

Fred furrowed his brow. "Say again."

"We fake it. Put on a show for that asshole. It's not much of a plan. It's all I've got for now. Tell the others."

Fred nodded and passed the word to Padma and Cyan, but Josiah was fixated on his finicky 4-D scanner. Margaret turned back to her patient with the hope that one of them would get through to the obsessive tomographer. Moments later, she began the round of "good-to-goes."

Padma gave a thumbs up, followed by a recitation of pre-surgical readings: "BT, BP, CP, PC, ECG, HTTP, PCP, DILF, all systems protracted."

"Fred?"

He responded with an okay sign, as well as a laundry list of levels. "GABA consistent, CB1 moderate, glutamate skewing delta…"

Since Margaret had no idea how long Chase had been out before he arrived in the OR, she was worried about continuing the anesthetic at high levels. Padma more than agreed with the doctor's concerns. She was, in fact, fearful of keeping him under any longer at all.

"It might help," Fred signed, "if I slow its metabolic rates. That should reduce the dosage necessary to keep it under."

"Should?" Margaret signed.

"Yeah. I'm afraid that's my best guesstimate."

"Okay, do it." Margaret turned to Josiah. "How about it, Josie?"

Josiah bowed slightly and on her signal, fed Morgan and Chase's respective neuron codes into the SPECT/PET 2000. Once that was done to his satisfaction, Josiah scanned the two brains. The next step, aligning their holograms, didn't appear to be going well.

Margaret wasn't surprised.

"I have a misalignment." Josiah signed. "There's a slight variation between the two holos."

"Let's see." Margaret bent over his monitor. "Age-related shrinkage. Can't be helped. You'll have to do the best you can."

Josiah nodded and while she looked over his shoulder, he fitted the outline of the smaller image into the larger. "That's about as good as it gets," Margaret signed.

But Josiah didn't respond. He continued to stare into his monitor. Chase's hologram was a riot of cerebral activity. Josiah unexpectedly shot up from his seat and began signing frantically. "Oh, my God. Oh, my God. This is unbelievable! We can't go on. Oh, my God!"

Margaret, still assuming he was in on their ruse, was puzzled by the theatricality of his reaction. His gestures were sweeping and Margaret feared, wild enough to draw Gabe's suspicions.

"It's okay," she said in hopes of tempering his performance, but he only became more agitated.

"It's not okay. See for yourself," he signed, projecting the two holograms, side by side on the overhead clear screen.

Sparks flew as thoughts skipped from synapse to synapse in a giddy array that should have been limited to Morgan's holo. The vessel's ought to have glimmered fitfully, like a lovelorn, female firefly signaling in the grass. But instead it was as active as, if not more active than that of the elder Hughes.

"Do you see it? Do you?" Josiah demanded of his colleagues.

They all nodded, but he was troubled by their lack of emotion.

"This vessel has developed higher brain functions," he signed. "Technically it's alive."

"Yes, we know," Margaret said.

"YOU KNOW?"

"Please, Josiah, calm down. You're going to make matters worse," Margaret signed. But her warning came too late. The Rubicon had been crossed, the glove had been smelt, the chicken had been plucked and once again Gabe was brandishing his piece.

"Don't fucking move," he yelled. "Shut your yaps and put up your hands."

"You," he said to Josiah. "Step away from Dr. Hughes

and walk toward me. Hands up. Anything funny, you're vulture *foie gras*."

"Who is this absurd little person?" Josiah demanded.

"You're calling me little, you fucking, freakazoid ass-pixie."

"Holster that thing before you kill somebody," Margaret shouted.


Margaret's voice reached Chase through the fuzz induced by Propofol IV. He was waking up.

"Padma," Fred signed, "his eyelids are fluttering."

"I'm increasing the drip," she responded. "It'll take a minute to work."

"Too late," Fred signed.

Chase opened his eyes and quickly squeezed them shut against the light. "Where am I?" he mumbled.

"Shhh. Don't talk," Fred whispered.

Gabe, who was equipped with dog ears, stopped arguing. "It's awake," Gabe said, pointing at Chase. "What are you people trying to pull?"

Nobody answered. They were all staring at Chase. Especially Josiah.

"I'm thirsty," Chase said.

"Get him some water," Margaret said to Cyan, who filled a cup and held it to his lips.

"What happened?" he asked after taking a sip.

"You fell and hurt your head." Margaret bent over to hear him better.

He touched his head, puzzled when he felt the syn-skin cap studded with magnets. "My hair feels lumpy."

He studied Margaret's face. She smiled. Chase caressed her cheek. "I don't remember much, but I remember you," he said groggily. Margaret reached for his hand.

Gabe grimaced. "I knew it. You were fucking him."

"No need for that kind of talk," Fred said.

Padma, who had one eye on her cardiac monitor, cried out. "Doctor, your father's ECG ST is elevated in two leads."

Margaret pulled away from Chase to look at Padma's monitor. The neon squiggle representing her father's heart rate seesawed wildly.

"What's going on?" Gabe asked. "Is he okay? He fucking better be okay."

"He's fibrillating. Damn it, Dad."

"Is that good?"

"He's having a heart attack." She turned to Cyan. "I need atropine."

The nurse readied a hypodermic and a vial of the stimulant. Margaret took the needle and jabbed it into her father's withered chest. The cardiac monitor registered a weak response, then nothing.

"Not on my watch, you don't!" Margaret took the paddles, zapped her father once, twice and again. The dial remained motionless.

"I need another 150ccs atropine and a vasopressin chaser."

She stabbed the second hypo into his heart and this time was rewarded with a palsied beat. He was alive. That alone was not a reason to party.

"Josiah, any damage?" Margaret asked.

"Take a look." Josiah projected a revised image of Morgan's brain on the clear screen.

Margaret sighed. "There's significant deterioration."

"That's it," Gabe said. "Start the transfer."

Margaret looked down at her father. Tears welled up in her eyes. She looked at her team, studying one anxious face after another. "He saved my life – my sister's life really. Long story," she said.

"We can't wait any longer, Doctor," Josiah said.

"You hear that?" Gabe asked.

"I'm not going to let my father die." Margaret wiped away a tear and leveled her gaze at Gabe. "I'm not letting anybody die in my OR, not even you."

Gabe waggled his gun at her.

"Either shoot me or put that gun away and go get Mahmoud."

Gabe hesitated, then to Margaret's relief, he grunted his acquiescence and left to find Mahmoud. She had a lot of work to complete before he returned, beginning with Chase.

"Fred," she said, "please remove my friend's restraints."

Still in a fog, Chase sat upright on the table and tried to

take it all in. Margaret put her arms around him, kissed his forehead, the tip of his nose and last of all his lips. "I love you," she whispered. "Be well."

# CHAPTER 50.

THERE WERE HICCUPS, but the procedure was going amazingly well in Fred's opinion. Although faced with unknown variables, he and Padma reacted swiftly to maintain correct levels. And for all his nay saying, Josiah aligned the holograms of donor and replacement within the acceptable range. They were, after all, remarkably close.

This didn't mean the operation would be successful. For all anybody knew, Morgan might wind up with the IQ of a squash. Regardless of the outcome, however, they were pioneers. Stored synaptic data had never been transferred into an adult who only minutes earlier was totally alert and functioning independently.

Behind the ready room glass, Gabe was rapt as he observed the last moments of the procedure. Mahmoud stood over the corpse of what had been Morgan Hughes. He nodded to an orderly who approached the operating table and with dignity befitting the occasion, removed the carcass.

"Padma, please wake our patient."

Padma nodded.

Mahmoud, now poised over the recipient, removed the syn-skin skullcap. "That's more comfortable, I'm sure," he whispered tenderly into the pink ear.

Seemingly in response, the eyelids flickered.

Mahmoud leaned closer. "Mr. Hughes… Morgan? Is that you?"

Margaret blinked and gazed up into Mahmoud's muddy brown orbs. "Uh… yes, sort of," she said, her eyes traveling to the faces of the medical personnel hovering around her. "Are we finished?" she asked.

Fred gave her a thumbs up.

"Damn. This hurts more than I remembered," she said. "Padma, would you get me a painkiller?"

Padma prepared a syringe as Fred helped Margaret sit upright. She turned to him. "How were my GABA levels? I feel a little lightheaded."

"Scary high, but within parameters," Fred said.

"We'll have to adjust our protocols somewhat. I think my glutamates were more in the gamma range." She scooted to the edge of the table and swung her legs over the side.

Fred and Padma stopped her from standing. "It's too early, Doctor."

Mahmoud stared. "I... I don't think it took," he stammered.

"Nonsense," Margaret said. "What did you think would happen? I would forget everything I knew? Quit gaping."

She spied Chase behind the ready room window.

"He was a nervous wreck," Fred told her.

"Poor baby." She smiled broadly and waved.

Chase waved back.

They gazed into each other's eyes.

"Padma, please help me get dressed. I'm weeks behind on my work," she grumbled. "Bobby, would you ask Pella to prioritize my task list?"

"You mean Leslie, don't you?" Fred corrected. Margaret looked puzzled. "Your assistant?" he continued. "Her name is Leslie."

"No... I..." She stared at Chase. "I mean..." She touched her face pensively.

*Oh jeez...* she thought. *What am I going to do about Pella?*

# ACKNOWLEDGEMENTS

I would like to thank each of the following friends and colleagues who contributed to this book in some significant way: Rose Jacobius, Pamela DuMond, Lloyd Rose, Grant Jerkins, Ben Mufti, Susannah Costello, Sekita Ekrek, Zobeyda Monaco and J.T. Roy.

And I would like to thank my husband, Ed Schneider, for his support, encouragement and suggestions (though not always well taken), and for sometimes cooking dinner.

# ABOUT THE AUTHOR

www.johnnelsonphoto.com

**Rita Kempley**, writer, journalist and editor, spent nearly 25 years in the dark as a film critic for The Washington Post. Thousands of screenings later she swears she can review a movie without seeing it. In addition to covering the Cannes and Sundance film festivals, she profiled scores of film personalities.

Rita was awarded an Alicia Patterson Fellowship to explore sexual myth in American cinema and is the author of the futuristic thriller, THE VESSEL, in addition to five screenplays. She lives with her husband, Ed, in Washington DC.

Made in the USA
Charleston, SC
30 September 2012